Victory : RUN

The Story of Victory Payne

Book 1

Devon Hartford

COPYRIGHT NOTICE

Cover Model: Myles Leask

Cover Photo by Alex Wightman

POD Paperback ISBN: 978-0-9897697-9-2

POD v1.1.2

DEDICATION

This book is also dedicated to the amazing women of shred guitar who were all inspirations for this novel: Nita Strauss, Courtney Cox of The Iron Maidens, Juliette Valduriez, Orianthi Panagaris, Ruyter Suys, Nori Bucci, and so many others.

You gals rock!!!

The Rules of Rock & Roll

There's only one rule in Rock & Roll:

DON'T SLEEP WITH ANYONE IN THE BAND.

Period.

RUN 1

Chapter 1

VICTORY

The world famous rock club, The Cobra Lounge, is located at the heart of the Sunset Strip in Hollywood, California. It rumbles around me as the opening band quakes the building with their hard rock sonic assault.

I put on the finishing touches of my makeup in the green room mirror backstage.

The green room walls are dotted with photos of all the famous bands who have played here. My bandmates surround me in the small no-frills room, waiting impatiently to go on stage.

The throb of booming bass guitar and kick drums pound the walls. The bass is so intense that my bottle of mascara does a buzzing dance across the makeup table in time with the beat.

Bzzz. Bzzz. Bzzz. Bzzz.

There's a quick knock on the green room door before it swings open. The music from the stage is suddenly twice as loud.

The club's stage manager leans inside the room. He's an older guy with longish hair and gold pirate earrings. Vintage rocker. He barks at us over the sonic storm, "YOU GUYS ARE ON IN FIFTEEN MINUTES! GET READY TO ROCK!"

My bandmates and I nod at him. We're all smiles. This is our first time playing at "The Cobra." It's a really big deal to be here. Over the last forty years, most of the biggest bands in rock have played here.

Bobby, my drummer, hollers at the stage manager, "WE'RE GONNA KNOCK THE FUCKIN' WALLS DOWN, MAN!"

Rex, my bass player, shouts, "HELLS YEAH!"

The stage manager puts his hand to the headset mic in his ear, listens intently to whoever's on the other end, then chatters a reply, "Copy that." He turns back to me and says, "THE HOUSE IS PACKED WITH PEOPLE HERE TO SEE YOU GUYS! GET READY TO BLOW THEIR MINDS!" He pulls the door closed, muting the sound of the band on stage, and he's gone.

My band, Skin Trade, has built up quite a fan base in the L.A. music scene over the last two years. We have a growing following on Facebook, YouTube, and Twitter. We're positioned to break big. We have so much momentum, it's gonna happen soon. I know it.

Rumor has it that a bunch of record producers and music execs are in the audience tonight. This is our chance to show them we can bring the house down. We've worked so hard to get here, I'm not even nervous thinking about it.

I'm so ready for this.

I return my focus to the old school makeup mirror in front of me. Big globe lightbulbs surround the glass. I put the final artful touches on my smokey eyes and glimmering black lipstick.

When I finish, I slide my chair back and spin in front of the mirror. A leather clad rock & roll assassin smiles back at me.

Long hair: primped.

Dangerous dark makeup: perfect.

Killer leather outfit: sexy as hell.

I wear a short midriff golden studded black leather biker jacket, skin tight low-ride lace-up and studded black leather pants, black stripper heels covered in golden spikes, and a gold studded black leather bra.

I did my best to put together an outfit that looks like it came from that girl genius who runs Toxic Vision clothing and makes all her outfits by hand. She and I have the exact same sense of heavy metal style.

Deadly sexy.

Rex grins at me, "Your male groupies are gonna break their dicks off in their jeans when they see you walk on stage tonight."

The pouty curl of Rex's lips and his fitness model body have gotten him laid more times than I can count. If he owns a shirt, I've never seen him wear one. His stage attire is shirtless with tight pants and motorcycle boots. With all his ink, the girls drool over Rex's delicious bad boy bassist looks at every show.

Bobby, our drummer, eyes me up and down and winks at me. He has the most gorgeous mane of long hair I've ever seen, male or female. With his stage makeup on, he's the perfect blend of handsome and beautiful. He's a total rock and roll lion. He blurts, "I'd fuck you."

My voice drips with sarcasm as I say, "Thanks, Bobby. But, do I have to take a number and wait for you to finish screwing your pride of four girlfriends first?"

Bobby really does have four girlfriends. Amazingly, none of them know about each other. I don't know how he does it. My guess would be his groupie girlfriends all suffer from starry eyed denial. The ladies always seem to have a thing for the wild drummer types.

"For you," Bobby grins, "I'll make an exception. You can *come* to the front of the line."

I ignore his innuendo and chuckle, "Wow, that makes me feel special."

Rex snickers, "Want me to leave you guys alone for two minutes?"

"Two minutes!" Bobby laughs. "I need two hours, bro. You know how horny I am before a show."

"I know, dude," Rex frowns. "You're always trying to fuck my leg like a dog," he chuckles.

Bobby makes a hound dog sound, "Aaah-ROOO!!!!"

They bump fists and laugh.

Men. I roll my eyes. I'd be surprised if Bobby could even get it up for me, considering how often he has sex.

"Just give me a blowjob, Victory," Bobby begs while drooling over my skin tight outfit.

I smirk, "Ask Rex for one. I still need to warm up my hands."

Bobby grabs his crotch lustily, "You can warm your hands up on my shit."

I shake my head, "I need to play my scales on my guitar, dumbass."

"My shit's as big as a guitar neck," Bobby says confidently. "Got the big headstock and everything."

"You wish," Rex chuckles.

I pat Bobby on the shoulder affectionately, "I'm sure you'll find yet another ignorant slut to hook up with tonight."

Bobby grins, "The ignorant ones are the best kind."

Boys will be boys.

I'm used to the constant sexual tension of being the only girl in the band. And this is rock and roll, so it's all about the sexual tension. It helps that Rex and Bobby are like my brothers. They would never cross that line. Besides, I already have a boyfriend, and I'm a one man kind of woman.

From outside the green room, the opening band goes quiet and the crowd cheers. A minute later, the club P.A. starts playing canned music to keep the energy up. The tune is Back In Black by AC/DC. It's mandatory tuneage at every hard rock show between bands, but the song still makes me smile. Angus Young makes his guitar growl like no one else.

The energy and history of The Cobra buzzes around me. I can't wait to become a part of it. I take a deep breath and let it out slowly. It'll only be a few minutes while the stage hands shift the band gear around.

Then we take to the stage.

I step past Bobby and grab my guitar case from where it leans against the wall. I unlatch it, pull out my white cream colored 1987 Fender Stratocaster, sling it over my shoulder, and plug into my Line 6 amp. My Strat is the same axe the late Jimi Hendrix played at Woodstock, and the same one played by the great Yngwie Malmsteen. Those guys are my top two guitar heroes.

As my fingers fly up the strings, a spray of melodic notes flow out of my small Line 6 practice amp like rainbow raindrops. Not a light drizzle, but a downpour. I've been playing guitar for so long, I don't really need to warm up anymore. But I do, because more than anything, I love playing electric guitar.

It's my addiction.

My name is Victory Payne, and I'm 100% rocker chick.

Rex watches me play and nods approvingly at my improvised soloing. His face eases into a hot sultry smile. "Shred that shit up, Victory." He slings his bass over his muscled shoulder and lazily fingers the strings. He isn't plugged into an amp, but I can hear the click and rattle of his bass strings join time with mine.

I do a series of quick trills on my strings with my left hand, then start tapping the fretboard with my right, just like Eddie Van Halen, the godfather of two hand tapping.

My high-pitched notes dribble out of the Line 6 speakers like liquid candy.

"Play it!" Bobby grunts as he machine guns a staccato rhythm on the countertop in front of him with his drumsticks. He taps his boots on the green room floor like his feet are on the kick drums, keeping perfect time with my impromptu solo. A thick mane of hair swirls around him as he bangs his head energetically. Pantene totally needs to give him a contract. Even in the dim light of the green room, his hair shines like spun silk.

The three of us continue improvising a series of rocking riffs in perfect time.

A gleeful smile creeps onto my face as we play. I have the best bandmates in the world. We've played together on and off for the better part of five years. The last two, we've been dedicated 24/7 to our band, Skin Trade. Of all the musicians I've ever played with, the connection Rex and Bobby share with me is the closest thing I've ever found to a telepathic link. We anticipate each other's every move. Countless fans have told us we're the tightest live band they've ever heard.

I don't know what I'd do without them. I can't imagine being in any other band.

Our impromptu jam ends on a crescendo and we're all smiling from ear to ear at our shared creation.

"Did someone tape that shit?" Bobby asks.

"I'll remember it," I say, meaning it.

Rex glances around at the photos on the green room walls and marvels, "Can you believe The Doors played here?"

"And Guns N Roses," Bobby adds.

"Don't forget Led Zeppelin," I say.

"And Avenged Sevenfold," Rex grins.

"And Metallica and Wild Child," Bobby says.

"I think King Diamond even played here," Rex says. "Now *we're* playing here. A year from now we're gonna be headlining arenas across the country."

"You know it," I smile proudly at both of them.

We've worked our asses off getting this far. This is our night to shine in the spotlight. I can only imagine what's going to happen when we hit the stage. It's gonna be insane.

The door to the green room opens and Scott Walker struts in. He is the lead singer and leader of our band.

He's also my boyfriend.

Scott is the walking incarnation of rock & roll. Tall, lean, angelically handsome yet devilish and dangerous. Silver pants hug his slender legs and hang low on his hips, revealing the V of his flat stomach beneath the hem of his tight black T-shirt, which is emblazoned with bold white letters that say "FUCK.". Tattered black combat boots complete the outfit. His short blond hair is spiked, and mirrored sunglasses cover his eyes.

Scott is everything all fathers with daughters worry about. Scott was born with the natural ability to seduce all females. I know from experience. He doesn't even try, and women gravitate to him. When he opens his mouth and sings, all female legs within earshot part willingly.

On most nights, mine still do.

But, after being Scott's girlfriend for two years, I know there's more to him than first impressions. With all that beauty and talent comes a mountain of heartbreaking work. Scott can be higher maintenance than a walking toddler with sticky fingers. But he's worth it. At least, that's what I've always told myself.

"Damn, Vic," Scott says, "you look fine as hell tonight, babe."

I hate it when he calls me Vic. It sounds like a guy's name. Telling him it bothers me never works. Scott does what Scott wants. I've learned to pick my battles with him.

Scott squeezes my ass possessively, staking his territory. I'm nobody's property, but I can pretend to be if it keeps the peace this close to show time. Yet another battle I've let Scott win. He can be very insecure.

Scott turns to Rex and Bobby and says, "I bet you guys want a piece of this, don't you?"

He's referring to me like I'm a half pound of ground beef. He's not always like this. I swear.

"She looks great," Bobby says politely, staring at the floor.

"Totally," Rex says blandly, pretending to tune his bass.

Scott has a temper and he likes to bait people to see if they'll challenge him. Rex and Bobby know not to ruffle Scott's feathers. When he's around, they never say anything about my looks, good or bad.

We've all learned to handle Scott. Considering Scott writes all the music and lyrics, and sings our songs, we don't have much choice.

Scott does what Scott wants.

Scott slaps my ass and digs his fingers in hard. "You putting on weight, Vic?" He arches an eyebrow at me.

That eyebrow makes other women melt.

At the moment, I'm over it.

I frown at him, "No." I say it more defensively than I want to. There's no way I'm gaining weight. I count calories like I count time in my head. It's so automatic, I don't even think about it anymore. Image is as much a part of making it in music as the music is, but it's a necessary evil. I moved to Hollywood to make it big, not get a big ass.

Changing subjects, I say, "We should head to the stage." I step toward the door. "We're on in five minutes." I glance at Rex and Bobby, "Come on, guys."

They stroll toward the green room door.

"I'll catch up with you guys," Scott says, "I need five minutes alone."

Bobby chuckles, "Like the Pantera song? You gonna kick someone's ass?"

"Naw," Scott says, "just need to get my head together."

With Rex and Bobby standing behind me in the door frame, I shoot Scott a glare they don't catch. I know what 'getting his head together' usually means. I told him to quit snorting blow months ago. He promised me a hundred times he'd quit. He's probably nervous about tonight's show. I get it. But cocaine is never your friend in the long run. It's wrecked more of my friends than I care to count. Scott thinks he's different from everyone else. He thinks he's special. In some ways, he is. Too bad the blow doesn't see it that way. But I'm not going to call Scott out in front of the band and give him a "Say No To Drugs" lecture five minutes before stage time at the biggest show of our careers.

"You sure?" I ask Scott, tilting my head and widening my eyes accusingly at him. It's my last ditch plea for him to stay straight for the night.

Scott lowers his mirrored shades so I can see his ice blue eyes. They're as mirrored as his sunglasses. Inscrutable. "Promise," he says softly. "Just need to focus for a few minutes."

I can't tell if he's lying. Then again, I never could.

The stage manager pops his head through the open doorway. "Four minutes and counting, people. Get to the stage."

"After you," Rex says to me.

"Ladies first," Bobby grins at me.

"Don't sweat it, Vic," Scott says, "I'll see you on stage."

Rex and Bobby herd me out of the room.

"Don't be late," I warn Scott as I walk out the door.

"This is rock and roll," Scott chuckles. "Shit never goes as planned."

Chapter 2

KELLAN

I goose the throttle of my black on black Honda CBR1000RR. I wait at yet another traffic clogged stoplight on Sunset Boulevard in the heart of the Hollywood Hills.

The weather is pleasantly warm.

It's after ten o'clock, but you'd think it was rush hour with all the energized club goers in their cars cruising the Sunset Strip on a Friday night.

My bike looks like a stealth fighter that can hit Mach 2 easily, which it pretty much can. But all I've been doing the last half hour is crawling on it from red to red.

The sidewalks are as packed as the street and littered with faces I recognize from the covers of Us Magazine, People, The National Enquirer, TMZ, Gawker, and every other gossip mag and website you can think of.

All of the people flash tanned skin, showing off their new clothes from the trendy shops on Melrose, revealing tight muscled bodies and flawless skin. It's a big fucking high school "look at me" spectacle that makes me want to laugh. I ignore the dudes with their personal trainer cross-fit bodies, but not the long legged half-naked babes.

They're always a bonus.

The restaurants and bars on both sides of the winding street glow bright with neon and a million different colored lights. The colors ricochet off the polished chrome, glass, and steel of the cars, and dozens of office buildings squeezed between some of the hottest nightclubs in the world: The Whiskey a Go-Go, The Roxy, The Viper Room. Business and entertainment go hand in hand in Hollywood. This town is like Adult Disneyland.

I still can't decide if I love it or hate it.

Like I said, the babes help.

Speaking of which, there's a custom silver Porsche 911 Carrera convertible next to me with its top down. The two knockout blondes inside wearing painted on dresses are eyeing me like I'm candy, which I am.

I lean back in the saddle of my CBR with my gloved hands on my hips. My ink covered arms popping out of my black t-shirt flex impressively. My helmet visor is already up because I haven't gone faster than twenty since I got onto Sunset. So I flash my baby browns at the blonde hotties so they can see my trademark smolder.

"What's your name," the passenger side blonde says.

"God," I chuckle.

The two blondes giggle like schoolgirls.

Yeah, it's always been this easy for me. Girls started throwing themselves at me when I was eleven. I'm not making this shit up.

"You sure are cocky," the blonde driver says.

"The cockiest," I say smugly, "in every way you can imagine." It's like a game to me. I try to come up with the cheesiest lines I can possibly think up and see if the girls still fall for my shit.

They always do.

The passenger blonde shifts in her leather bucket seat to give me a show. Her knees part slowly. Her skirt creeps up her toned tan thighs inch by inch. I can almost see home plate.

With a sultry smile, she says, "How do we know you're not exaggerating?"

My dick stirs in my pants. Business as usual. "I don't have to exaggerate," I say. "I just state the facts."

The stoplight turns green, but the dumbfucks turning onto Sunset have gridlocked the road. There's nothing for me to do but wait and play more games with the foxes in the convertible.

Passenger Blonde turns to her girlfriend, who is smiling from ear to ear, and says, "Should we take him home?"

Driver Blonde is blushing, but she tries to play it down. She acts all confident when she says, "Why not?" Her lips are trembling with anticipation.

Passenger Blonde giggles again. She turns back to me with sudden arrogance and says, "He's probably a troll beneath his helmet."

It's a challenge I'm happy to meet.

I glance at the gridlock still blocking the road. Traffic isn't going to move for another two minutes at least. I indulge the girls and take my helmet off. I unveil my cocky grin.

Both their eyes widen as their mouths drop open.

I almost blurt laughter in their faces as I think of several jokes about blow jobs. But, even I have limits.

"Oh my god," Driver Blonde gasps.

"That's me," I interject cockily.

"You're gorgeous," Passenger Blonde says. "Are you a model?"

"Sure," I say. It's not true, but they'll never know. I may as well be. I've been scouted enough times. But I turned all of them down. The last thing I want is some lame fuck modeling career derailing my music.

I chuckle at how ridiculous this situation is with the blondes. It's real, but it's unreal. I know plenty of dudes who don't live a life anywhere close to mine. Whenever I tell my buddies stories, they never believe me. Oh well. I know it's true.

"Okay," Passenger Blonde says, "We're totally taking you home."

Driver Blonde leans across her friend, flashing me her cleavage, which I can tell is fake, but expensive. I'd like to get my hands on them later, but I've got shit to do. Driver Blonde's eyes are sultry with desire when she says, "Follow us, okay?"

I strap my helmet back on. The gridlock in front of us has cleared and the light turns green again.

"Sorry, ladies," I say. "I'm late to see a band play at The Cobra Lounge."

I rev my Honda and my bike bolts across the intersection. I bullet between rows of cars that are going two miles an hour. I'm tired of waiting for traffic.

I smile to myself as I glance in my side mirror at the blondes stuck in their Porsche a block behind me. There's a thousand more like them on the streets of Hollywood tonight. I'll find some other ones later.

It's good to be me.

Chapter 3

VICTORY

The eyes of everyone in the backstage hallways are all over me and my skin tight rock & roll assassin outfit. The stage hands, the opening band members leaving the stage, random hangers-on, and the backstage groupies.

All of them act mesmerized.

I want to scream at them, "It's just a stupid costume!" But I tune them out instead. My mind is on a more pressing issue. Because me, Rex, and Bobby are making our way to the stage without Scott.

When we get to the stairs leading up to the stage, I say to Rex and Bobby, "I've gotta hit the ladies room."

"You're not nervous, are you?" Rex asks.

"Hell no! I gotta pee," I lie.

Rex grins at Bobby, "She's nervous."

"Want me to hold your guitar?" Bobby asks.

"Oh, uh, sure." I lift it over my head and hand it to him. "Back in a sec," I singsong.

My smile goes grim the second I strut around the corner of the narrow hallway in my hooker heels. I ignore the guys gawking at my cleavage as I shoulder past them.

I need to check on Scott.

I hope I'm not too late.

The green room door is closed and locked when I reach it. I wiggle the knob. Damn, he's probably two or three lines in by now.

"Scott?" I rattle the door knob. "You in there? Scott?"

The door whips open and a guy in a gray suit walks out holding a slim leather briefcase.

Surprised, I snap at him, "Who the hell are you?"

Suit Guy doesn't even blink as he walks past me and down the hallway.

Scott stands in the green room, his arms folded across his "FUCK." t-shirt. His mirrored shades rest on top of his head. He glares at me with his equally mirrored eyes.

Hands on hips, I glance over my shoulder in the direction suit guy went then say to Scott, "Is that your new dealer?"

Scott chuckles. "You could say that."

"What's that supposed to mean?" I growl.

"Where's your guitar, Vic? We have a show to play."

"Quit calling me Vic, and quit changing the subject, Scott. Was that guy selling you dope?"

"Why, you want your own eight ball?"

"You know I don't do coke. Who was that, Scott?"

"There you are!" the breathless stage manager says from the green room doorway. "You guys are on in one minute! Let's go!" He spins his hand in a circle, motioning for us to get moving.

Scott struts past me, "Come on, Vic. We have a show to play."

What could Scott possibly be up to? I can only guess. But knowing Scott, I know I'll guess wrong.

Chapter 4

KELLAN

The line outside The Cobra Lounge coils around the building. The people waiting are animated and excited to get inside. The bouncers are checking everyone for contraband: drugs, alcohol, weapons, the usual shit.

I walk straight to the front of the line. I know the head bouncer. "What up, Tony!" I clap him on the shoulder while he shines his flashlight in some babe's handbag.

Tony is a brawny retired Marine who loves to smash heads when people get out of line and flirt with the female "talent" who come through the doors every night. His body builder arms and broad shoulders stretch his black t-shirt with its blood red Cobra Lounge logo across his barrel chest. When Tony's not working here, he's at the beach working on his tan and staring at bikinis. He looks up at me and smiles, "Kellan! What up, dog!"

We fist bump, pop fingers like our fists just exploded, then grip hands and do a man hug.

"Good to see you, bro," I smile. I come to The Cobra all the time, and have helped Tony sling sloppy drunk customers out the front door out of boredom when the bands suck. I'm always joking he needs to put me on the payroll.

"You here for Skin Trade like everybody else?" he asks.

"Yup," I say as I whip my ticket out.

"Paying customer and everything," Tony chuckles. He would probably comp me if I didn't have a ticket, but I wasn't going to risk missing the show. The buzz about Skin Trade has been off the hook.

I say, "People keep telling me I need to check out their axeman."

Tony nods. He doesn't follow the bands. He just knows the names on the big marquee over his head on any given night.

I glance down the line of people and notice a bunch of girls wearing Skin Trade t-shirts. From what I've heard, the lead singer is some kind of heartthrob, maybe even the next Jim Morrison. A real rockstar poet. There's plenty of dudes wearing Skin Trade shirts in line too. That means the music doesn't suck. The guys also come to scam on the chicks, but you never see this many dudes for a band that sucks, no matter how many hotties turn out.

I lift my arms out for Tony's benefit and say, "You need to pat me down?"

"You carrying?"

I grab my crotch with one hand, "Just my gun."

Tony smirks at me, "Toy guns don't count."

"What can I say? All the ladies like to play with it," I grin.

Tony shakes his head, "Get inside before I make you wait in line with everyone else."

"Thanks, man," I slap him on the shoulder.

"Hey!" some hothead rocker chic in line yells from behind me. "No cutting! Wait like the rest of us!"

I turn around and turn on the heat. "What's your name?" I ask, gazing into her eyes.

She melts when she looks up at me. "Ariel," she mutters softly, suddenly bashful, like she just met her favorite rockstar.

She's cute in her scoop neck Mötley Crüe t-shirt and tight black jeans. I graze my thumb softly across her cheek. She nuzzles into it unconsciously.

"See you inside, Ariel," I say warmly, letting my fingers linger on her cheek.

Tony shakes his head at me. "You should be a controlled substance, kid."

I hike my eyebrows at him, grinning like a teenager.

"Move it, pretty boy," he smiles, "I've got work to do."

I swagger into the crowded Cobra Lounge like I own the place.

One of these days, I'm going to be the big band on stage everyone's lining up to see.

Until then, I'm going to enjoy myself any way I know how.

Chapter 5

VICTORY

I make my way through darkness, unafraid because my Fender Strat hangs from my shoulder like a weapon. Glow-in-the-dark tape on the black stage floor guides me to my position, stage right.

The audience shouts a chanting war cry.

"SKIN TRADE!!"

"SKIN TRADE!!"

"SKIN TRADE!!"

Frenzied female voices desperately scream, "SCOTT!!!!" like a bunch of dying cats. The shrill sound stabs my ears like icepicks.

I'm used to it.

My earplugs blot up the high end, otherwise I think those screams would drive me insane.

A dim red light over the drum kit illuminates Bobby as he climbs in.

Rex waits expectantly in near darkness stage left.

Bobby shouts out at the top of his lungs, *"One! Two! Three!—"*

I spin the volume knob on my Fender to ten with the edge of my hand. My guitar instantly feeds back with a ringing squeal.

"—Four!"

A split second later I bang out power chords in time with Rex and Bobby.

We play our most popular fast tempo tune, Slave To You. It's aggressive and gets the crowd moving. I can feel the pounding bottom end of my Marshall 4x12 speaker cabinet hammering into the backs of my legs. The sound is so loud, it creates a breeze of air across the bare skin of my ankles.

The perfect volume.

I'm smiling like crazy when the stage lights come up to full and I can see the audience moshing and banging heads in time to the daggered Slave To You riff. Half the guys at the foot of the stage in front of me are pumping devil horn fists in the air.

I make eye contact with one of them and flash him a smile.

He shouts at the top of his lungs, "Victory!!! Fucking play it!!!"

This isn't the first time someone has shouted my name at a show. I swear, it gets better every time it happens. The adrenalin rush is incredible. There's literally nothing on the planet like people screaming for your music. It's overwhelming. Shivers run up and down my arms and legs and my chest tightens with the thrill.

Fuuuuck meeee.

It's better than sex.

It sounds impossible, but it's true. In the infamous words of the one and only Joan Jett, I love rock n roll.

Scott runs on stage in his silver pants, black "FUCK." t-shirt, and mirrored sunglasses. He holds his mic stand in front of his hips two-handed like a spear. His legs are spread wide and his body whips and spins in sync with the band.

The screeching girls go nuts when they see Scott, their high octave wails cutting above the blaring music of the band by another ten decibels.

Scott nods and smirks at them with pursed lips like he expects no less. He leans down at the front of the stage to briefly caress several of their reaching fingers with his. The women he touches clutch their hands to their breasts like they're holding onto a piece of Scott. Many of them wear t-shirts that say "I Am A Skin Slave."

We started seeing these shirts on more and more girls at our gigs over the past year. It turned out that Scott's groupies were making the shirts themselves.

Scott loved it.

Me, not nearly as much.

I still feel a pinch of jealousy when I think about the hordes of women who lust after Scott. But I've trained myself to mostly ignore it for two years straight. What used to be a stabbing assault of jealousy is now merely a prickly pinch. It's not like I had a choice. What was I going to do? Tell our female fans to stop liking our singer so much? Not a chance.

Someone in the crowd flings a black lace bra on stage and Scott catches it one-handed. He knots it around the top of his mic stand and flashes his tongue hungrily at whoever threw it.

I roll my eyes.

Sure, there's always a nagging piece of me that can't stand watching Scott lap up the female adulation, but I tell that part of me to ride it out while Scott pulls in the fans and builds up our band.

It's all part of being up and coming rockstars.

I have my own share of male groupies lusting after me at the moment. The guys grouped at the base of my side of the stage are trying to stare up the crotch of my skin tight leather pants.

My guitar blocks their view because I wear it low.

Sorry, boys.

They love the tease.

But I have no real interest in my male fans. As long as Scott never crosses any lines with his groupies, I'm cool.

The Vari-Lites hanging over our heads flash through a sequence of hot red patterns that cascade across the stage while a hot spotlight follows Scott. He cockily holds the mic stand near the base with one hand like a really long sword, and chants out the first verse of Slave To You:

"Take me on
Get me off
You'll always be
the problem that I got

Pull me in
Let it out
Scream my name
Every time you shout"

The whole time he's singing, he's rubbing his free hand across his flat stomach. The girls in the audience are starry eyed and slack jawed. I resist the urge to kick their mouths closed with my stripper shoes. With them down on the floor and me up on the stage, it would be way too easy.

But I can't kill our fans.

We need them.

After the verse riff, my fingers blaze up and down the neck as I play a quick fill of trills before the chorus.

A cute guy at the foot of the stage yells, "Play it for me, Victory! WOO HOO!!!"

It's nice to have fans who actually appreciate my musical skills and not just my tight outfit.

"Show us your tits!" some other guy shouts.

Had to go and ruin it for me, didn't he?

I smirk at him. At least they're shouting for me and not Scott. It could be worse and the house could be empty.

"Scott!" a girl screams from where she sits on top of some guy's shoulders. She lifts up her Skin Slave t-shirt and shows Scott her tits.

Grinning, I shake my head.

It's only Rock & Roll.

I hope the guy who wanted to see my tits is getting an eyeful of the braless groupie, cuz he's not going to see mine.

Scott is of course loving it and pointing at tit girl as he sings the pre-chorus:

"I need you
I breath you
I only want to please you

Take me
Break me
I am the slave to you"

Tit Girl screeches, "Make me your slave, Scott!"

Scott sings the first line of the chorus directly to Tit Girl, "Slave to yooouuu!"

Tit Girl looks ready to faint from Scott's attention, like his voice is beaming pure orgasmic love into her heart. It's a common reaction, no matter how misguided it may be.

Rex also sings into his own mic on stage left, harmonizing with Scott as they repeat the chorus together.

Scott arches his back and holds his mic stand out to the audience like it's his cock jutting from his pelvis.

Every woman in the audience shouts out the next line of the chorus in time with the music, "I AM A SLAVE TO YOU!"

Scott is so in love with being adored by his fans.

But now it's my turn to shine. It's time for my guitar solo.

My fingers machine gun up the neck of my guitar and all the guys swarming in front of me shout my name like they want to eat me alive. They eye me hungrily with their lusty gazes.

In this moment, they all want me.

I give it to them.

I yank on my Fender's whammy bar and high harmonic squeals sing from my Marshall amp like a primal scream.

I'm having the time of my life playing for this huge crowd of adoring fans.

Chapter 6

KELLAN

The Cobra Lounge is so packed with people, Skin Trade starts before I'm inside the main room. I can't see the stage, but I can hear the band blaring through the house sound system. The intense volume rumbles the whole building.

The tune sounds promising.

Judging by the crowd's response, the fans love them.

I've been waiting to see Skin Trade play for months. Everyone's been saying, "Dude, you gotta see Skin Trade play live. Their guitar player is unreal."

I've heard that before.

But then I'm always disappointed.

With all the anticipation I've built up, the only way Skin Trade's guitar player is going to impress me tonight is if he's Jimi Hendrix back from the grave.

When I finally squeeze through the doors into the jam packed main room, it's a broiling mosh pit maelstrom. Black-clad bodies swirl and bob on waves of pure testosterone.

I consider diving in, but I've moshed my ass off hundreds of times at shows. Tonight I want to watch the band.

From where I stand, the P.A. speakers block my view of the left side of the stage. I can't see the guitar player. The quickest route to a better view is straight through the mosh pit.

I scan the chaos, looking for an opening.

Concert shirts of every hard rock and metal band imaginable flash past me. Iron Maiden, Judas Priest, Sepultura, Alice in Chains, Godsmack, Mastodon, Slipknot, Lamb of God, Scorpion Child, Five Finger Death Punch, Dragonforce. Best of all, several people wear Wild Child shirts, my favorite metal band of all time.

Awesome.

I'm totally in my element right now.

When I'm about to take a step into the pit, a big raging bull locomotives past me. He's a beefy guy with a short mohawk, handle bar mustache, a ratty Slayer t-shirt, and lace up combat boots. He's taller than everyone in the pit by a few inches, and wider by at least two feet. By the look of him, he only has sex with women who are unconscious. Whether he knocks them out himself or looks for the ones passed out under pool tables at biker bars is anybody's guess.

A second later, Bull Locomotive mows down a little guy two feet to my left. The kid seems too small and gangly for the intensity of this pit. He's down on all fours and he's gonna get trampled. I lift him by the arm pits, pulling him to his feet and out of the pit.

When I get a good look at him, he's way too young for a 21 and over club. Not that I care. I used to sneak into clubs like this all the time to see shows when I was young. But I looked over 21 by the time I had a driver's license. I wonder how this kid snuck in tonight?

I shout over the music, "YOU OKAY, KID?"

"YEAH," he shouts, "THANKS, MAN," he smiles sheepishly and rubs his forearm, which is bright red and glistening where the flesh is freshly abraded. He wears a classic "Metal Up Your Ass" Metallica t-shirt that has a fist thrusting a dagger out of a toilet bowl.

"MAYBE YOU OUGHTA SIT THIS ONE OUT?" I suggest. "TAKE CARE OF YOUR ARM?"

"FUCK NO!" he smiles. "IT'S A BATTLE SCAR!"

I offer him my fist, which he bumps, and say, "YOU'RE HARDCORE, KID."

He grins and charges back into the mayhem.

I shake my head, smiling. I was the same way just a few years back. I'm sure he'll be fine. But I'll keep an eye out for Bull Locomotive in case the guy decides to be a dick all night.

I weave through the pit, dodging whirling bodies. Several bounce off me, but I ignore them.

I'm about to squeeze back into the crowd on the edge of the pit when I see Bull Locomotive barreling toward me from the corner of my eye. His elbows are flailing like he's some kind of human demolition machine. I think he plans on chopping me to pieces with his elbows.

I turn to face him.

An image of a traditional bullfighter flashes through my head, the kind who wear those fancy embroidered outfits that all the Latin ladies love. Those guys are rockstars in Spain and Mexico.

Bull Locomotive's eyes gleam when he sees me. His lips peel back over his teeth as he chugs toward me, elbows flailing double time.

I widen my eyes with mock fear as he closes the distance. At the last second, I spin out of his way. He stumbles past, completely off balance, his intended target not where it was supposed to be.

I'd make a pretty good matador.

I don't even need a red cape.

I find a gap in the crowd and ease up to a group of five girls wearing t-shirts that say "I Am A Skin Slave." Their attention is riveted on the lead singer of the band. Based on their fine backsides, two of the girls look hot enough to take home. I dig their tight rocker chick jeans. If I'm going to get a better view of the band's guitar player, I'll have to squeeze through them and their tight jeans.

I kind of like how that sounds.

Time to work my magic. "'SCUSE ME, LADIES," I holler, making sure to flash my smile back at all of them as I push through their ranks.

When they realize I'm not a low browed mouth breather busting up their good time, their faces go from annoyance to hypnotized in a heartbeat. They unconsciously circle around me, forgetting about the band playing on stage entirely.

All five of them undress me with their eyes. One of them boldly touches my chest. I suspect if I stood here long enough and smiled at them dumbly, they would literally start undressing me and get down to business.

Lucky for me, it turns out all five of them are reasonably cute from the front. Maybe I'll take them all home after the show and have a menage-a-six or whatever you call it.

The one touching me fawns and rests her warm hand on my chest. She asks, "What's your name?"

Just because I'm here to see this guitar player everyone is talking about doesn't mean I have to be rude. I gently lift fawning girl's fingers from my chest and kiss the back of her hand gently. "Kellan Burns," I say. "You guys staying here for the whole show?"

All five of them nod in unison.

I look each one in the eye thoughtfully and say, "Then I'll catch up with you guys after."

All five are still nodding hypnotically.

I turn back to the stage and continue knitting between the people crushing against each other desperately in an attempt to be closer to the band.

On stage, the spotlight shines on the lead singer as he sings into the mic. His stage presence is flamboyant and captivating. I'm not surprised he's the local heartthrob. I smile when I notice his "FUCK." t-shirt. I like the guy already. Then I notice the handsome shirtless bass player with an eight pack on display. No wonder there are so many chicks here tonight.

If I joined the band, we'd rule the world.

I've heard enough of the music since I walked in the door to know the band is pretty damned good. They're super tight. I'm betting they rehearse five days a week at least. These guys are pros.

But I haven't heard any guitar solos yet. That's what I wanna hear most. If the guy sucks, maybe I'll talk to the band about replacing their crappy guitar player with me because I don't suck. If the dude is awesome but ugly, I'll still talk to the band. I've got the chops *and* the looks.

I bob my head around some girl sitting on her boyfriend's shoulders. I finally catch a glimpse of a guitar player, but shoulders girl is flailing her arms, so all I really see of the guitar player is really long hair.

Could still be some ugly dude with a wig.

I shift right and finally see the guitar player full on.

It's a girl.

A really hot girl with a tight body.

Is *she* the lead guitar player everyone has been telling me about? Her rhythm playing is solid, but the real test is the solos.

I continue working my way toward the stage to get a better view of her.

She looks incredibly sexy in her tight leather outfit, but I still haven't seen her face. She's banging her head too much and her hair's flailing all over the place. Under all that hair, she could easily be a butter face, a.k.a. "everything is hot but her face."

The song transitions riffs and she rips into a shredding guitar solo.

Holy fuck.

She's incredible.

I'm instantly mesmerized.

My eyes glue to her left hand as it dances across the fretboard. Her fingers butterfly up and down the neck. Her right hand rapid-fires notes like a machine gun. Only guy I know who plays like that is the legendary Yngwie Malmsteen.

But this ain't him.

It's this chick.

Now I *know* she's a butter face. That's the only explanation for how good she is on guitar.

A hot babe isn't going to sit inside practicing scales day after day with a metronome when every guy on the planet buys them free shit the second they walk out the house. Yeah, this girl's gotta be heinous under the long hair. She's gotta be snaggle tooth *dogged* to be this good.

I can picture her: bucked out teeth, cross eyed, huge witch moles on her nose and shit. Probably has a voice like a ferret on crank or a warthog with indigestion.

But damn, can she fuckin' play.

I can't believe what I'm hearing. And I've heard a lot of amazing girl shredders in my time. I've watched Nita Strauss and Courtney Cox of The Iron Maidens play live at Paladino's out in the valley. They're amazing shredders and they're both hot. Too bad they both had boyfriends when I asked them out. But they're not the only hot shredders out there. There's Orianthi Panagaris, Ruyter Suys, Nori Bucci, and tons more all over the world.

But none of them are as good as this Skin Trade babe on stage. She takes the cake.

That's why she *has* to be fucking grotesque.

She's too damn good.

Mystery girl slips her guitar pick between her hidden lips to free up her right hand. Then both her hands work eight fingers on the fretboard like spider legs. The sound is a neo-classical melody at warp speed, but fluid, hypnotic, incredible, like Yngwie and Jennifer Batten had a love child.

Without realizing it, I've wedged all the way through the crowd. I'm at the foot of the stage, trying to get a better look at this mystery guitar goddess hidden under her pile of hair.

Her left hand slides up the neck of her Fender to the 22nd fret and she wails on the whammy bar with her right. Her Strat screams in her hands. She flips her head back and her hair hangs in the air for eternity, framing her face.

Her incredible face.

She's as beautiful as her playing.

This babe is too good to be true. I blink my eyes, thinking I'm dreaming.

But I'm not dreaming.

I'm in awe.

Next thing I know, I'm adjusting my dick in my pants. It's jammed down the leg of my jeans like a tree trunk. I'm so turned on watching her play, I'm having an auditory orgasm. I wonder if I'm gonna shoot my load right where I stand.

Her final high note continues to sing out and her right hand flies up in a victorious fist.

The crowd erupts with roars and cheers of approval.

I shake my head and smirk to myself.

She's fucking amazing.

My dick is harder than steel.

I need to meet this girl bad.

Then her eyes lock on mine and I'm done.

Chapter 7

VICTORY

A random guy at the foot of the stage reaches up and grabs at my ankle where I've got the toe of my platform heel planted on the speaker monitor at the front of the stage. Another guy does the same thing a moment later. They're just trying to touch me because I'm on stage, but if I'm not careful, one of them is going to accidentally trip me.

I'm working the whammy bar on my Fender, coaxing screaming feedback out of my Marshall half-stack.

Every guitar solo has to have a big finish.

I've always wanted to set my guitar on fire at the end of the show like Jimi Hendrix, but I've only got one guitar. Maybe I need to set myself on fire instead. Nikki Sixx used to do it at Mötley Crüe shows all the time.

I look at the guys in the crowd below and spot this big hot handsome guy standing head and shoulders above everyone else.

And like that, I *am* on fire.

I'm up in flames like I've never been in my entire life.

Not only is the hot handsome guy taller than all the others, he's so beautiful, it hurts. Standing amongst the other metal heads in the crowd, he's like a giant diamond shining from a pile of grimy coal. I have the sudden image of me grabbing that diamond and shouting "My precious!" like I'm that weird bald Gollum dude in the Lord Of The Rings movies.

On top of that, he stares at me with his priceless brown eyes like he's discovered the secrets of the universe. Maybe he wants to yell "My precious!" too?

Crazy nervousness suddenly tickles through my entire body, which is odd, because I never get nervous on stage. I think Brown Eyes is causing it. His awestruck baby browns have this unguarded wonder that slips beneath my defenses and ignites my being with pure lust.

The heat that sweeps through me makes the audience induced

adrenalin rush I was riding seem like a light breeze. This new fire is a hurricane of heat, exploding out from my heart and cascading down my stomach to splash against the base of my pelvis, right at the root.

My core heats up and I'm suddenly broiling inside my stage costume.

Heat.

I want to fan my face, but my hands are busy on my guitar working the strings.

I have to keep playing, but I can't stop looking at this guy. Every cell in my body explodes like bombs. Inside me it's World War Four.

My subconscious tugs at my frazzled awareness and reminds me I need to keep playing!

Rex and Bobby start the final verse riff of the song without me!

Shit!

The sound of my fuck up is noticeable.

Scott shoots me a frown like I'm losing my mind. Maybe I did. Maybe Brown Eyes knocked it right out of my head and it's spinning on the stage floor like a dropped quarter.

Fortunately, I know our songs so well, it only takes half a second for me to fall back into sync with the band.

Scott shakes his head and sings the third verse of the song.

While I play, all I can think about is Brown Eyes. And the overwhelming sense of guilt washing over me. I haven't been this attracted to a guy. Ever. Sure, Scott is handsome and hot, and in the past, he had that same mystic pull on me that he has over his groupies tonight.

But Brown Eyes makes me feel something entirely different. Something profound and extremely rare. This is a big deal. Like tectonic plates are shifting inside me for the first time. Like some ancient sealed doorway to my heart that I never knew was there has been cracked open and the light of truth is pouring out of me for the first time.

I struggle to hold myself together and keep playing as the band winds up the song.

Bobby hammers on the drums like he does at the end of most of our songs.

Rex plants one boot on the drum riser. His back arches and he stares up at the colored stage lights overhead, aiming his bass guitar at the ceiling while his fingers rattle the strings.

Usually when we're getting ready to hit the final note of a song, Rex and I both hold our guitars up high beforehand and wait to swing them downward in time with Bobby's last smash on the drums. Right now, my guitar hangs from my shoulder in its usual relaxed position because I'm in la-la land thinking about Brown Eyes.

I'm going to miss my cue.

Scott bumps his shoulder into mine, "What the fuck are you doing, Vic?!"

I look at him, my eyes deer in headlights wide, convinced he's reading my mind. Although Scott is the jealous type, he usually forgets I exist when a crowd full of women are screaming at him and begging him to make them his Skin Slaves. But the rest of the time, you'd think his jealous nature was the frontman of the Jealousy Band.

That Scott is noticing me right now tells me I've gone too far. The worried look distorting his face is proof that he's reading my mind.

I guiltily twirl around so I'm facing the drum riser like Rex, and manage to lift my guitar up and swing it down in time with him and Bobby.

When the band goes silent, the crowd explodes with applause and cheers.

Normally, Scott greets the crowd at this point and flirts with the audience. Instead, he wraps an arm around my waist and clutches at my bare stomach with hooked fingers. In a hissing voice, he snarls, "Don't fuck the show up tonight, Vic! There are a bunch of record people in the audience."

"Ow!" I shout, "Scott, you're hurting me!" The crowd is so loud, no one in the audience can hear us, but Bobby and Rex notice. They're both surprised and not sure what to do.

Scott relaxes his hand, but yanks me into his side again. He hisses into my ear, "What's gotten into you, Vic?"

"Stop calling me Vic!" I pull away and glare at him wide eyed. I can feel where his fingers dug into my exposed stomach. I bet he left red marks. Jerk. But if I say anything now, I'm going to incriminate myself by sounding guilty and probably piss Scott off even more.

I take a deep breath to calm myself while Scott drills me with his silver eyes over the top of his mirrored shades.

Scott and I haven't exactly been the picture of perfection in the relationship department lately. We haven't had sex in over a month, which is the longest we've ever gone without. Not because I haven't wanted to. But Scott has become increasingly distant. In the beginning he was the one initiating sex multiple times a day. Lately I've been the one doing it, but he always shuts me down. Yeah, I've started wondering what happened to our passion. Is it the drugs? Or the groupies? Is he seeing one of them? Or four like Bobby? Or forty? Who knows. It's not a ridiculous assumption. Newsflash: *Rock singer sleeps around!* That's such a cliché it's not even interesting.

"We love you, Scott!!!" several girls in Skin Slave shirts scream from the foot of the stage.

Like I was saying.

Scott releases his hold on my waist and turns to engage his adoring fans.

He shouts into the mic. *"Hello, my Hollywood Skin Slaves!"* Then he goes to work flirting with every single one of them. The girls hang from his words like he's speaking directly to them and only them. They're all glassy eyed zombies starving for a bite of man candy.

Then again, so am I, because Brown Eyes is staring at me again like he's witnessing a miracle.

Or my undoing.

Chapter 8

VICTORY

For the next two songs, it takes all of my concentration to ignore Brown Eyes.

In the middle of our fourth song, Bullet Proof, I'm about to start my guitar solo after the second chorus when Scott suddenly repeats the chorus, singing right over my solo. I'm instantly pissed.

I have no choice but to switch gears and play the riff for the chorus.

Scott bumps me with his hip and jams his mic in my face. What's he doing now?

In my ear, he shouts, "SING IT, VIC!"

I've heard Scott sing the lyrics in rehearsal so many times I know them by heart. That doesn't change the fact I'm not going to sing them.

Scott looks at me expectantly, jabbing the mic at my mouth. It may as well be a flaming torch based on how I flinch away from it.

I'm not going to sing.

(*don't sing*)

It's not that I *can't* sing.

(*never ever sing*)

I *don't* sing.

(*never ever ever sing*)

I *won't* sing.

(*sing*)

Not ever.

(*singsingsing*)

Not after what happened

(*Stop!!!*)

when...WHAM! I slam the mental doors shut before I start thinking about it. Otherwise I'm going to crumple into a puddle of blubbering rubber and flood the stage with tears.

I'm never going to sing again.

And that's that.

"COME ON, VIC!" Scott shouts.

My lips are clamped closed. I shake my head.

Scott drapes his arm around my shoulders and sings the first stanza himself, his face and mic an inch from mine,

"Bullet proof heart of stone
Make you need me to the bone"

Then he jabs the mic in my face again.

I wince.

(*never ever sing*)

Having Scott so close, trying to make me sing when he *knows* I don't sing, on stage no less, makes me physically nauseous. He knows better. Why is he tormenting me like this?

I shoot him a harsh look, but it bounces off his mirrored sunglasses, which are once again covering his mirrored eyes. Not that there's much difference.

Scott sings the second stanza, his arm still holding onto my shoulders,

"Cock my hammer, pull my trigger
Let it go, let me go"

I take a deep breath, trying to relax.

I remind myself that Scott doesn't *know*. Sure, I've told him I don't sing many times. But he doesn't know *why*.

(*Stop!!!*)

Maybe Scott is just trying to push me out of my comfort zone? I huff a silent derisive laugh. He certainly managed that.

Then, as if for the first time, I take note of the content of Scott's lyrics for Bullet Proof. How had I not noticed the innuendo before? Maybe I was unconsciously blocking it out. Scott is basically telling all his Skin Slaves that he wants to fuck them with his love gun. No wonder he has so many groupies. And he wants me to sing it with him? He's lost his mind.

But none of that is nearly as painful as the fact that I'm never going to sing.

(*never ever ever sing*)

Scott will always have the spotlight. My only time to really shine is during my guitar solos. And now Scott is preempting my solos like he did a minute ago? What's his problem?

I feel so flustered right now, all I can do is stare at my feet.

Don't think about singing Don't think about singing Don't think about singing

That's not helping.

I wish Scott would let go of my shoulders. He's making me uncomfortable.

My eyes are hot. I'm going to start crying. I need a good distraction or else I'm going to take my guitar off and throw it neck first through the nearest amplifier like a spear. Or wield it like a battle axe and chop Scott's head off.

Scott.

Yuck.

I shake my head and smirk to myself and glance at the crowd. Oh yeah, I'm supposed to be playing a show. For them. Not indulging in an onstage pity party. Luckily I know Bullet Proof so well, I haven't missed a beat.

Scott releases his hold on my shoulders and leaps on top of the two center monitors at the front of the stage. He sings the final lines of the chorus balanced with one leg on each monitor, thrusting his crotch at the audience,

"Baby, I'm your bullet proof
I lean into your groove
Between your legs, baby
I'm your bullet proof"

Now that Scott isn't hanging all over me, I can snicker as I listen to his lyrics. I roll my eyes and shake my head.

Scott, Scott, Scott.

He's so rock and roll.

I strut to the front of stage right and plant one platform heel on top of my own monitor. I can be rock and roll too.

Good thing I'm wearing pants and not a skirt because I suddenly notice Brown Eyes staring up at me from between my legs. He's grinning and pointing a finger gun at me and pretends to shoot my crotch. I get the impression he's mocking Scott's lyrics. Ha! I break into a fit of little giggles.

The giggles get bigger as I saunter a few steps backward, breaking eye contact with Brown Eyes. If I don't, I'm going to laugh so hard I won't be able to play. I shake off the laughter as best I can, concentrating on my hands.

I take a deep cleansing breath and feel better immediately. I needed that.

Thank you, Brown Eyes.

I'm not sure if I'm supposed to play my guitar solo now, or if we're going to skip it? I make eye contact with Bobby and Rex. They transition straight into the final verse, and Scott sings the lyrics. I guess we're skipping my solo.

Again.

I wish they'd given me the memo before the show.

The more I think about it, the more it irks me.

Whatever, boys. I'll bring it up backstage.

I've never been afraid to call my bandmates out on their bullshit. In private, anyway. Never on stage. Scott really should've given me some warning.

I bury my irritation by focusing on my playing.

The verse riff is pretty basic, so my hands are totally on auto pilot. Next thing I know, I'm analyzing Scott's Bullet Proof lyrics again.

What's up with the bit about the heart of stone, and making you need him? My chest tightens and I suddenly wonder if that's how Scott sees me? Does he view me as an adversary? That's no way to build a relationship. Is it possible Scott is way more fucked up than I realized? Lead singer of a hard rock band?

Gee whiz, you think?

And what about the line, "Let it go, let me go?" Is Scott trying to tell me something through his lyrics he doesn't have the balls to tell me to my face?

I shake my head and glance at the crowd, not liking where my mind is going. I need another distraction or I really will chop Scott's head off with my guitar. In front of our biggest crowd ever. While that might generate a lot of buzz for the band, I won't be able to reap the rewards if I'm stuck in prison for murder.

I notice Brown Eyes pointing his finger gun at me again. He's smiling a mile wide.

I smile back at him.

This time, he squints one eye like he's taking careful aim at my crotch. After he fires his finger gun, he blows pretend smoke from his index finger.

I throw my head back and outright laugh.

I laugh the entire time Scott sings the final chorus about how he's bullet proof.

I laugh at Scott.

I laugh at his lyrics.

And I laugh because if I don't, I'm going to cry over the fact I'm not singing on stage.

(*never ever ever sing*)

I'm *never* going to sing on stage.

(*sing*)

All I can do is laugh at my pain.

(*singsingsing*)

Chapter 9

KELLAN

The crowd on the rail batters my back, but I don't care.

I'm 100% focused on this hot chick guitar goddess. I'm totally amused that I made her laugh at my stupid finger guns while she's on stage.

For some reason, I feel like I'm in a movie scene and I'm playing the lone astronaut trapped on a desolate planet with no other people for twenty years. When the rescue rocket finally lands, the person who comes out of the rocket is the hottest, coolest babe in the history of hot babes. The fact that the astronaut hasn't seen a single woman in twenty years makes the rocket babe a million times hotter. Right now, despite all the choice babes I've had in my life up to this point, I feel like that astronaut.

None of the women I've hooked up with have had a tenth of what the guitar goddess has in looks and talent. Even if she's mute and can't talk, we can spend the rest of our lives playing guitar together and never get bored. I can tell. The way she plays, she has substance and depth. She's not just technically good. She plays with heart and guts. Her guitar is an extension of her voice and you can hear every emotion in the notes she plays.

Incredible.

And right now, I'm soaring like that stranded astronaut because me and this guitar goddess are connecting like crazy. Which is weird, because I can tell there's a weird tension between her and her bandmates as they play through their set. She keeps frowning at them because things aren't going as planned. But they shrug it off like it's no big deal. It could just be regular band drama. Or something more serious?

Who knows.

All I really care about is my guitar goddess. Now that she's seen me, she can't keep her eyes off me. Every time we trade a look, she blushes and hides her face in her hair.

I still have a rager in my pants.

If I can find her outside the club after the show, I'm totally going to hook up with her. If she skates out of here, I'll track her down and hook up with her later.

But I *have* to talk to this guitar goddess.

She starts her next solo. I air guitar along with her, mimicking her moves. I make sure to waggle my tongue a lot and cross my eyes. She giggles when I do. I don't know why I'm acting so smitten. I never act goofy around girls. I don't have to. I just nod and smile and that's about all it takes.

But I'm entranced by Guitar Goddess' virtuosity.

Am I turning into a fanboy at her feet?

Could be.

She doesn't know it, but I can tell where she gets most of her licks. Jimi Hendrix, Ritchie Blackmore, tons of Yngwie, legato George Lynch moves, even some ultra melodic Vito Bratta and Joe Satriani. But she ties everything together with her own original approach.

Maybe me and her will stroll down to The Viper Room for drinks after the show and talk guitar until we close out the bar. Then we can go back to her place and hook up. Because she is incredibly hot. Her liquid leather pants leave nothing to the imagination. If her Strat wasn't hanging between her legs, I'd be staring at her crotch half the time.

While the lead singer is singing to his adoring female fans, Guitar Goddess saunters right over to me for like the tenth time.

I shout up at her, "IS YOUR NAME JAMIE HENDRIX?"

She frowns and smiles. "WHAT?"

It's so loud, she probably can't hear me. "I SAID, IS YOUR NAME JAMIE HENDRIX!!!"

She shakes her head and points at her ears.

If I was anybody else, this would be the point where Guitar Goddess politely ignored me and went back to playing her set.

Lucky for me, nothing ever goes normally in my world.

I wave my hand at her, signaling for her to come closer. I'm slightly surprised when she leans down toward me.

Undeterred, I say, "IS YOUR NAME JAMIE HENDRIX?"

It takes her a moment, then a second later she expertly drops the melody riff from Purple Haze right into the middle of her band's song, then continues like everything was normal.

We'll definitely have to talk guitar over drinks now. Based on how she made a joke with the Purple Haze lick, this chick is fucking cool. I smile from ear to ear thinking about it.

Her bass player frowns at her because he noticed the Purple Haze lick. I'm sure no one in the audience noticed, but her band did. Whatever. I'm having a blast.

When the goddess plays her next guitar solo, I'm air guitaring along with her and cheering with the guys around me, making twice as much noise as any of them. I get so into it, I slap time with both my hands on the monitor speaker where she's resting one of her spiked heels like we're playing together.

She smiles at me and I'm in heaven.

The lead singer struts over to her side of the stage with his mic stand in both hands, swaying to the groove. Out of nowhere he hip checks her and she stumbles back, taking her foot off the monitor to maintain her balance.

She almost trips on her platform heels, but manages to recover.

What a dick move.

The singer points a finger gun at me and shoots it.

Then he flips me off.

Whoops.

Is he the boyfriend of the guitar goddess?

If he is, she needs a new boyfriend.

Me.

Chapter 10

VICTORY

I nearly break my ankle when Scott bumps me off the front monitor. "WHAT THE HELL!" I shout at him while still playing my guitar.

His sunglasses hang from the collar of his "FUCK." t-shirt, so I can clearly see the edge in his eyes. This is Scott's "I'm pissed" look.

Fabulous. Just what I needed.

Guilt pours over me, washing away my indignation. I shouldn't have been flirting with Brown Eyes. During a show no less, and right in front of my boyfriend! I'm an idiot. I never flirt with guys. I have boundaries. I guess I got carried away. Oh well. Nobody's perfect.

I smile at myself. I lay all blame on Brown Eyes. He's quite handsome, and that joke he made about me being named Jamie Hendrix was pretty funny. I love that he caught when I played the Purple Haze riff during our song Stick Shift. It's hard to notice things like that during a live performance of music you've never heard before, everything whizzes by so fast. I bet Brown Eyes is a musician, or at least super into music.

The only thing I know for sure is he's a stranger and he's going to stay that way. I have a boyfriend. Best to put Brown Eyes out of my mind.

Only I can't.

For the rest of our set, all I can think about is Brown Eyes. He stays right where he's been at the edge of my side of the stage the whole show. I try to spend as much time as I can on the other side of the stage, switching places with Rex. But Rex inevitably works back to stage left, and I'm forced right back in front of Brown Eyes.

I do my best to ignore his grins and goofy air guitar. I hang back by Bobby's drums and pretend Brown Eyes isn't there.

But Scott doesn't. He seems to have taken a sudden heated interest in Brown Eyes.

For the fourth time, I switch sides with Rex, and suddenly I notice Suit Guy standing against the wall. He's the same guy I thought was selling coke to Scott in the green room before we went on stage. I never would've noticed him if I hadn't been avoiding Brown Eyes.

Suit Guy stands with his arms folded across his chest, intently watching the stage. Surrounded by headbangers in denim and band t-shirts, Suit Guy looks totally out of place. His eyes are on Scott, but he also scans the audience shrewdly. He's not here to enjoy the show. He's here on some kind of business.

Now that I'm getting a long look at Suit Guy, he seems way too straight to be Scott's dealer. Scott only buys from guys we know, always in small quantities. We don't know this guy, and if he's a dealer, he's the high volume kind.

Is Scott getting involved in something I don't want to know about? Was Suit Guy's briefcase hiding a kilo sized block of ice? It didn't look big enough to me, but what do I know?

I shudder as I stare at Suit Guy.

I don't want to think about it.

I make my way back to my side of the stage.

During the next song, I notice Brown Eyes resting his muscled arms on my monitor, bobbing his head with the music. I find myself suddenly mesmerized by the sight of his arms. They're like body builder arms and covered in tattoos. I'm suddenly aware of the fact that Scott's arms are toothpicks by comparison. What would it be like to have Brown Eyes powerful arms wrapped around me?

What the hell am I thinking?

I shake myself out of my onstage daydream. How long was I staring at those ink covered arms? I have no idea, but I'm punched with sudden dread when I see Scott strut up to the monitor Brown Eyes leans against.

Scott stomps his boot down hard, aiming for Brown Eyes' hands.

I gasp but Brown Eyes is quick to react, and all Scott stomps is the edge of the monitor.

A second later I'm at Scott's side and I growl into his ear, "What are you doing? Those are our fans!"

This is all my fault.

Scott glares at me while I continue to play guitar, "What are *you* doing, Vic?"

Before I can respond, he's back at the front of the stage, ignoring me. I really wish he'd stop calling me Vic. It drives me nuts. He usually only does it when something is wrong. But he's been calling me Vic since before I saw Brown Eyes.

Am I missing something?

I shake my head. I can't worry about it now. I'm on stage. I should be concentrating on the show, not Scott's issues.

And not Brown Eyes.

For the next three songs, I pretend Brown Eyes doesn't exist. It's a good thing, because on our last two songs, Scott repeats the choruses over my guitar solo once again. Rex and Bobby play along like we always do it this way, but we don't.

Rather than look stupid, I skip my solo and play the chorus riffs. We need to present a united front to our audience, so I suck it up. Rex and Bobby seem not to notice when I shoot them questioning looks.

Are they ignoring me? This is really strange behavior for them. Scott, not so much. But Rex and Bobby? We *never* fall out of sync. What the hell is going on? The band really should've said something to me about changing things up so much before the show.

I'm suddenly nervous but don't know why.

A few minutes later, we're wrapping up our final song.

Bobby hammers every single drum and cymbal in his kit, all four limbs flailing to make maximum noise.

Rex is at the front of the stage, strumming his bass above a group of girls reaching for his legs.

Scott is balancing on the front monitors above the reaching hands, wailing into his mic with a long drawn out gravelly scream:

"Yeeeeaaaaahhhhhh!!!"

I stand at the front of stage right and Brown Eyes is back, smiling up at me. He's clapping his hands over his head. Then he sticks his thumb and index finger in his mouth and blows a shrill whistle.

"We're Skin Trade!" Scott shouts into the mic. *"See you next time!"*

The band makes noise for another ten seconds. Then we all watch Scott jump back off the monitors and onto the stage. When his feet touch down, Rex, Bobby and me hit our final notes and the stage lights go dark.

The crowd roars.

Despite all the strangeness I felt on stage, we rocked the house.

Chapter 11

VICTORY

We make our way down the stairs backstage.

The stage manager is right there, clapping, "Awesome show, you guys. Unbelievable." His smile is genuine and ecstatic.

The band files down the hallway that leads to our green room. All the stage hands and backstage fans are cheering and patting us on the backs and shoulders. The women are practically fainting at the sight of Scott, Rex, and Bobby.

Plenty of the men paw at me. I'm used to it. People always want to touch you when you've given a great performance. They want to be a part of it somehow, closer than everyone else. That's when you know you've made a lasting impression.

Everyone chatters at us:

"You guys rocked!"

"That set killed!"

"Fucking incredible!"

"Skin Trade is the best fucking band ever!"

"No one has ever rocked The Cobra like you guys just did!"

I take it all with a grain of salt. They might forget our names by tomorrow or throw shit at us the next time we play. You never know.

Scott, on the other hand, seems confident. He sucks up the praise like it's a given, like his superstardom is now secured.

Two girls wearing Skin Slave t-shirts suddenly rush us in the crowded hallway, bumping past people to get to Scott. One of them holds out a Sharpie pen and gushes, "Sign my boobs!" She lifts her t-shirt, exposing bulging cleavage practically popping out of a black satin bra.

Scott signs with obvious enjoyment.

The other Skin Slave holds out her wrist and squeals, "I'm going straight to a tattoo parlor so I can ink it into my skin permanently!"

Scott is loving it.

Eventually, the four of us arrive at the green room door. We're all sweaty and amped, and the boys are raucous. But I'm not.

Because I see Suit Guy leaning against the door.

Scott stops short.

I'm not liking this.

Scott turns to Rex, Bobby, and me, and says, "Can you guys give me a minute?"

Bobby and Rex both nod, "Yeah, sure."

I blurt, "What's going on?"

"This'll just take a second," Scott says firmly. He opens the door and follows Suit Guy inside the green room.

I'm confused when I say to Rex and Bobby, "Do you know that guy?"

Rex raises his eyebrows, his face slack, "Never seen him before."

"Me neither," Bobby says.

I step toward the door, about to knock on it forcefully, but stop my knuckles an inch from the wood. I turn back to Bobby and Rex, "He's not one of Scott's dealers, is he?"

"I don't think so," Bobby reiterates.

It's not like Bobby is watching Scott around the clock. He's too busy with his head between the legs of his four girlfriends. Scott could've changed dealers at any point.

We wait for several more minutes in silence. I'm about to knock again when the door whips open.

Scott holds the doorknob firmly, like he expects me to try to push past him. He asks, "Can you guys give us five more minutes?"

"What's going on, Scott," I demand.

"Five more minutes," he says.

I search his eyes, but they mirror everything back at me.

"Five minutes," he repeats, then pulls the door shut.

It latches with an ominous click.

Bobby and Rex shrug, as lost as I am.

Scott and odd behavior are besties, so all we can do is wait. While we do, more people pass by and compliment us on our show.

The good energy is catching and I'm swept away by everyone's enthusiasm.

At one point, the stage manager walks up and says, "Got word from the owner. He wants you guys back in two weeks."

"What!" I smile big.

"Hells yeah!" Rex grins.

"We're on our way, guys!" Bobby cheers.

The stage manager smiles back at us, "See you then!" He walks off, talking into his headset.

"Can you believe it?" I say to Rex and Bobby.

Rex, as confident as ever, rubs his palm across his shirtless abs and says, "Of course. We're Skin Trade."

Bobby nods agreement.

Joking, I say, "Bobby, does this mean you need to add more ladies to your stable?"

Bobby holds up a pair of black lace panties.

"Where'd you get those?" I ask.

"An ignorant slut threw them at me."

Rex grabs at the panties, "She meant them for me!"

Bobby yanks them out of his reach, "She's my ignorant slut, dude!"

Rex grabs again but misses.

I laugh, "You guys are the ignorant sluts. Don't you two have enough girls already?"

They both chuckle, "No!"

All the weirdness I felt onstage between me and Rex and Bobby is now completely gone. For a second I consider mentioning it. But it obviously doesn't matter anymore. We had a great show. I don't know why I got all worried.

Scott opens the door and says, "Hey, guys, uh, can I talk to you for a second?"

Suddenly miffed again, I ask, "Aren't you done with whatever you're doing that's so secret, Scott?"

"Not really," he says. "Guys? Come on in."

Rex and Bobby walk through the green room door and I follow. Scott stops me with a halting palm, "Just Bobby and Rex."

I'm instantly furious, "What's going on Scott? If this is a band meeting, I'm part of it."

He arches his eyebrows and his face screws up in a weird way I've never seen before, but he doesn't say anything.

I go on the offensive, "And what was that shit onstage with you singing over my solos? Did it ever occur to you to tell me and the band before the show that you were going to cut my solos?"

The only answer I get from Scott is his weird bent look.

He pushes the door closed in my face.

"Scott!" I shout.

The door latches before I have time to react. I can't believe he closed the door in my face. When I grab the doorknob, it's locked.

What the hell is happening?

I suddenly go cold.

Something has gone way wrong.

Chapter 12

KELLAN

The calm sea of bodies surrounding me is sweaty and lethargic. Everyone spent their energy on the band. It's like a post sex drowsiness now that Skin Trade is off the stage. I plow through the noisy crowd as quickly and politely as possible. Since I was on the rail the whole show, I'll be the last to leave if I don't make headway, which I need to do. I've got a date with Destiny, or whatever the hell Guitar Goddess' name is.

I'm going to find her and introduce myself before she leaves the club.

I squeeze past the five Skin Slave babes who I flirted with earlier. They look like they're waiting for someone. The lead singer of Skin Trade?

Two of them call out, "Hey, Kellan!"

Nope. I smile to myself. They were waiting for me.

I don't care.

I'm wound up to find the guitar goddess.

Unfortunately, the sluggish crowd is bottle necking at the front doors. All I can do is be patient.

Normally, I'm a laid back dude. I've learned all I have to do in life is lie back and wait for stuff to come to me. The good stuff always does. Especially women.

My whole life, women come to *me*.

But tonight, I'm in a hurry.

Me, Kellan Burns. In a hurry.

What the fuck is happening to me?

It's all the fault of the Guitar Goddess. First, she's smoking hot. I mean, seventy foot billboard, swimsuit issue hot. Choice meat, triple A, triple X, triple whatever the fuck. She's all of those things. But I've been with loads of top shelf tail. Only thing is, top shelf tail doesn't know how to play guitar like Jimi Hendrix or George Lynch.

That's why I'm desperate to talk to this Guitar Goddess. *Talk* to her. About guitar. It'll be a marathon twenty hour rap session about the instrument we both know better than the backs of our hands.

Talk about verbal foreplay.

It's freaking me out.

In a good way.

"I've been looking all over for you," a gravelly voice whispers in my ear, blowing hot rank breath across my face.

It's not the Guitar Goddess.

It's that Bull Locomotive dickhead from the mosh pit.

I'd forgotten all about him.

He growls in my ear, "You and me need to have a little talk."

Chapter 13

VICTORY

I feel like an idiot standing outside the green room with my guitar over my shoulder while my band is inside with some strange guy in a gray suit.

Cold chills still tingle across my skin.

I tell myself it's because I'm cooling down now that I'm off stage and my adrenalin has run out. Plus, they have the A/C on backstage, and there's not hundreds of thrashing bodies heating up the hallway like in the main room.

The random people around me are a welcome distraction from my unease. They stop to compliment me, recount their favorite parts of our show, tell me how awesome I am. Several ask for my number. Some are dudes who are obviously trying to get into my pants. They get fake phone numbers or the brush off, whichever is faster. Others, some of whom are women, ask if I give guitar lessons. I tell them to look me up on Facebook. The serious ones will get back to me.

Eventually, I take my guitar off and rest it on the floor, balancing it on its butt. I hold the headstock with one hand like I'm posing for a photo shoot. I tell myself it looks less dumb if I pose while I wait outside the green room, but I don't quite believe me.

Whatever.

Twenty minutes later, I remember that my band is sitting behind a locked door with Suit Guy and I'm not invited to the party.

I picture them holding huge bags of blow and swinging them at each other like they're having a huge cocaine pillow fight. The air is filled with a misty white haze, bringing new meaning to the concept of contact high, which I can say from experience is bullshit. You can sit in a hot box with a bunch of stoners smoking cigar sized spliffs and not get high.

But I've never been in the middle of a cocaine pillow fight, so maybe I'm wrong. I snicker to myself. When Skin Trade sells a million albums and we're huge rockstars, we can have one, just to find out.

I slump against the green room door and examine my nails like I'm waiting for the bus, still holding my guitar with one hand.

I'm tired of waiting. I consider knocking on the door. Screw them. They can come find me when they're ready.

I walk outside for some fresh air, holding my guitar, still in my sweaty stage costume. I need to change out of it and take a shower.

This is lame.

Chapter 14

KELLAN

Lucky for me, Bull Locomotive, who I'm now thinking of as Bull Breath because he smells like shit, isn't stupid enough to start up with me while we're boxed in with the rest of the slowly departing ticket holders. At the very least, he'd never make it past the bouncers without getting nabbed.

Not that I'm worried.

I do my best to ignore him, but he keeps jabbing elbows into my kidneys or stepping on my steel toed boots. I don't think he's figured out they're steel toed, and he grinds away with his combat boots like it's hurting me.

"Dude, would you knock it off?" I ask, irritated. I would do something more aggressive, but half the people around us are women, and I'd like to avoid throwing Bull Breath into one of them or having him swing at me and inevitably miss, but end up breaking some poor girl's nose instead. I've seen it happen. Fighting in close quarters like this is not the way to go.

"I'll knock it off," he sneers, "Soon as we get outside."

I shake my head and sigh, "Have you not noticed I'm bigger than you, bro?"

"You're taller, but I'm solid muscle. I've knocked out guys twice as tall as you."

"But you haven't knocked me out," I chuckle.

"Yet," he grunts.

I sigh. The truth is, I don't want to get all banged up teaching this guy a lesson. I want to meet that Guitar Goddess. I know most chicks usually love a guy who can fight, but there's too many cops outside on Sunset this time of night. I don't want to get cuffed and stuffed and miss a chance to chat up the guitar goddess.

So I ignore Bull Locomotive and continue waddling behind a few hundred people as we inch toward the door.

What seems like an hour later, I'm finally passing through the front doors. Tony is there with two other bouncers, keeping an eye out for bad behavior.

I wonder if Bull Breath is going to follow me around the corner or start shit in front of the bouncers. If he starts up in front of Tony and the boys, he's stupider than I thought. Or he's having second thoughts about fighting me and he's hoping the bouncers will jump in before he gets hurt.

Who knows.

When I say goodnight to Tony, Bull Breath doesn't do anything.

I know if I hang with Tony for awhile, he will be happy to chat, and Bull Breath might get the message and wander off. But then I might miss the Guitar Goddess. For all I know, she's climbing into some limo right now. Or the band's van. It's not like they're The Rolling Stones.

Fuck it. I keep walking and head around the side of the building for the back doors.

And Bull Breath follows.

Fine. But we'll have to make it quick.

Chapter 15

KELLAN

"Kick his ass!" someone yells from the crowd of Skin Trade fans circled around me in the alley behind The Cobra Lounge as I dance out of range of Bull Breath's flying fists.

The gloomy alley glows orange from all the city lights bouncing off the moisture hanging in the air. One thing about L.A., the only time you ever see stars is when they're walking the Red Carpet.

Bull Breath swings on me about twenty times, but every blow misses because I'm dodging with sidewinder steps or deflecting the guy's meaty hands with carefully timed open-hand blocks.

No matter what he does, he can't lay a finger on me.

I haven't swung on him once. After half a dozen misdemeanor lock ups for brawling when I was younger, I avoid fights at all costs. My music career is way more important. If the cops show up now, I won't have a single offensive wound on my hands.

Bull Breath tries to rush me, but I pivot my hips and squat down, jamming my knee into the bundle of nerves that runs behind the head of Bull Breath's fibula, just below the outside of his knee. I don't even take my foot off the ground. It just looks like I'm squatting down and turning my hips.

Bull Breath's knee buckles when I hit it with mine, and he stumbles forward, nearly face-planting on the cement before his hands go down to break his fall. He still has forward momentum, so he looks like he's running on all fours.

Finally, he has to stop and rest at the far side of the ring of bystanders. He pants heavily in front of two random guys wearing Wild Child concert shirts.

Bull Breath bends over at the waist and rests his elbows on his knees while he catches his breath.

He's getting tired.

If I wear him out completely, everyone walks away happy.

Someone yells, "Kill him!"

I turn and see the yeller is the Metal Up Your Ass kid who got trampled by Bull Breath inside the mosh pit an hour ago. The kid's eyes gleam with excitement as he shouts, "Kick his ASS!!!"

That boy wants blood.

I chuckle to myself. Although it would be nice to teach Bull Breath a lesson about picking on people his own size, I think Metal Up Your Ass can go home and get plenty of blood on his xBox or PS3 and no one'll be the worse for wear.

I notice the five Skin Slave babes I talked to inside are part of the circle watching the spectacle.

One of them shouts, "Hit him, Kellan!"

Not gonna happen.

I need to end this quickly and peacefully, not make things worse. I want to go find that Guitar Goddess before she leaves.

Bull Breath finally stands upright and flexes his fists. He wants more.

Where are the zookeepers when I need them? I could totally use one of those tranquilizer guns right about now.

Bull Breath charges and I do the matador dance again, spinning away. I give Bull Breath a boot in the ass for good measure because I'm getting impatient.

The crowd suddenly parts and Bull Breath stumbles headlong into a telephone pole beside the building. He doesn't hit with his head, but his shoulder connects with a loud CRACK!

He sags against the pole and slides down, his neck grinding along the coarse wood. He's gonna have neck slivers. Serves him right. He gets up slowly, shaking it off. Then his face shrinks down to a pinhole of pain and he grunts. His shoulder that hit the pole looks weird. He touches it gingerly with his other hand.

I think he broke his collarbone, that's why it looks wrong. He's not moving the injured arm at all.

"Fuck," he hisses.

Excellent.

My work is done.

Oh, wait. Not quite.

Bull Breath glares at me with his pinhole eyes. His heavy browed face is dark with anger, "I'm gonna fuck your shit up, motherfucker."

I gotta give the guy credit, he's got a lot of heart. Not much in the way of brains. But plenty of heart.

I smile at him, "Any time you're ready." This should be easy. He's already out of commission, but he's too stupid to realize it.

He charges me, pumping his arms, but as soon as the injured arm goes up, he drops to his knees in agony. The whole shoulder on that side dangles six inches lower than it should. I think he tore some cartilage. A lot of cartilage. That's gonna take forever to heal. I hope he has good insurance.

Not my problem.

Do I play Good Samaritan and call 911?

Naw, he can find someone else to help him. I've wasted enough of my time on him already.

At that moment, good fortune smiles upon me, which it usually does, and one of the back doors of The Cobra Lounge opens up.

Destiny walks right out, in all her tight leather heavy metal glory.

Chapter 16

VICTORY

I open the back door of The Cobra Lounge and walk right into Brown Eyes. More precisely, the headstock of my Fender hits him in the stomach.

"Oof!" he laugh grunts. "I knew you were dangerous with that thing!"

"Sorry!" I blurt. "Are you okay?"

"Yeah," he grins.

We stand there staring at each other like dumb teenagers.

Wow, he's really hot now that I'm standing toe to toe with him. Tall, athletic, rugged, and leading man handsome. His muscled arms are covered in sexy tattoos.

He runs a hand through his hair, his biceps and triceps flexing like he's posing for a photo shoot for "Sexiest Man Alive" only he's not. He sounds bashful when he says, "You were awesome back there."

"Back where?" I'm suddenly flustered. I don't know what he's talking about.

"Onstage?" he says uncertainly. "With your band?" He raises his eyebrows "Playing guitar?"

"Oh," I smile. Wow, I sound like an idiot. I feel my cheeks heat. I know I'm blushing. What's wrong with me? I have a boyfriend. He's inside the green room of The Cobra Lounge, twenty feet behind me. An image of Suit Guy flashes in my head and my flush fades as I go cold. Something is wrong with Scott, I know it.

"Love the Strat," Brown Eyes says.

"What?" I'm totally confused.

He flicks his eyes at my guitar, "Your Strat?"

"Oh, uh, thanks."

"I take it you're a Hendrix fan? You dropped that Purple Haze lick into your song onstage."

"You caught that?" I say skeptically.

"Totally," he smiles. He has really nice teeth.

A voice in my head says, Hello! You have a boyfriend!

I grin stupidly at Brown Eyes. I'm going to get into trouble if I keep talking to him.

He says, "You're a big fan of Yngwie, aren't you?"

He sure asks a lot of questions. Usually guys as hot as him are dumber than doorknobs. He's way too cute to know who Yngwie is.

"Yeah," I say nervously. I need to get away from him. Now. I look around for the best escape route. Down the alley behind The Cobra, or out to the side street? I'll be alone in the alley with Brown Eyes if I go that way. Not a good idea. Bad things might happen. The kind of bad things I like.

To the side street!

My heels click-clack across the bumpy asphalt in the alley.

Brown Eyes falls into step beside me and says, "Your Marshall sounds awesome. Did you have it modified, or is it a stock head?"

He's talking about my amplifier, the one I use on stage. I say, "It's stock, but I use a DOD Overdrive pedal for my leads, sometimes a Tube Screamer, just like—"

"—Yngwie," he finishes.

I smile at him. How did he know that?

My head shouts at me, What are you thinking, girl! B-O-Y-F-R-I-E-N-D! His name is Scott? Remember him!!!! Back in the green room? Wake up, Wendy Wandering Eyes!

I start walking again, willing Brown Eyes to leave me alone. Not that I want him to. But he needs to go before I do something as stupid as I'm feeling right now.

To distract myself, I examine the black stains dotting the cement beneath my feet. I believe the stains are old bubble gum. They're everywhere in L.A. I wonder idly how many billions of pieces of gum have been spit out of people's mouths all over L.A. in the past thirty years. Doesn't anybody use the trash? Heathens.

I nervously notice Brown Eyes hasn't disappeared. We're walking down the sloped sidewalk toward Sunset Boulevard, through a crowd of people who've obviously just come out of The Cobra from seeing my show.

"That's her!" someone shouts and points at me.

"Victory!" another guy hollers.

I might have gone unnoticed walking amongst this rock and roll crowd in my black leather stage costume, but the creamy white Fender Strat in my hands is a dead giveaway I'm with the band. Now everyone is circling around me like I'm famous, which I'm totally not. This is too weird. I turn on my heel and head back up the sidewalk, trying to escape.

"You've got fans," Brown Eyes chuckles beside me.

"Don't you have some place to be?" He's totally creeping me out. But every time I look at him, I don't want him to go anywhere. He's too beautiful to be creepy.

I need to get back inside the Cobra and hide from him and everybody else.

"Kellan!" a group of girls in Skin Slave t-shirts squeal as they surround Brown Eyes.

Talk about fans. The five rocker girls are fawning all over Brown Eyes like he's a movie star. Maybe he is. This is Hollywood. I don't really care either way. I'm just happy they've intercepted him and I don't have to worry about him following me.

He grins at the girls like it's Christmas and Santa left a bunch of slutty women under the tree for him.

I roll my eyes.

Men.

I turn the corner and walk behind The Cobra Lounge and head toward the back door.

When I reach it, I discover it has no knob. I didn't think to check for one on my way out five minutes ago because doors usually have knobs on both sides. Duh. Oh well, last time I make that mistake. I pound on the steel door with the bottom of my fist.

"Hey! Wait up!" Brown Eyes hollers as he trots around the corner of the building.

Someone needs to open the back door and let me in. But nobody does. I glance at Brown Eyes and say, "Don't you have your fangirls to attend to?"

"Huh?"

"Those Skin Slaves back there? The ones worshipping you?"

He frowns, then a cocky grin settles onto his luscious lips. "Jealous?"

My eyes flick between his lips and his smoldering eyes. Lips, eyes, lips, eyes, lips, eyes...Snap out of it!

He nods confidently, "You're jealous, aren't you?"

I shake my head and give him my best standoffish look. "No," I say dismissively.

He's not buying it.

"What?" I scoff. "You need to check your ego, buddy." Pretending like I'm bored of him, I pound on the door again and tap my foot impatiently. Nobody answers.

Brown Eyes asks, "Want me to hold your guitar?"

"Huh?" I shake my head. "I can hold my own guitar."

"Just offering," he shrugs.

The back door is not opening. I'd kick it, but I don't want to scuff my spiked platforms. I paid good money for them.

"So, uh..." Brown Eyes stammers into silence. He sounds slightly nervous. He doesn't seem like the type, not when he has all those ladies chasing him.

"Don't you have some place to be?" I ask a second time.

"Nope."

Sigh. He's not making this easy on me. I glance at him from the corner of my eye. Even in my peripheral vision, he's a sight to behold. Pretending I don't want to ogle him is becoming increasingly difficult.

He suddenly leans against the steel door of the Cobra with his elbow, causing his arm muscles to bulge impressively and his torso to curve languorously. His t-shirt lifts above his jeans, revealing a row of chiseled abs.

Mmmm, muscles. Scott doesn't have muscles like this. Most men don't have muscles like this.

Stop looking!, my head shouts.

I clear my throat, which is now filled with frogs, and I start coughing.

"You okay?" he asks.

"Yuh-yes," I hack, trying to smile my way through the frogs.

He grins.

I melt.

This is bad. I pound on the steel door. There's a reason it doesn't have a knob on the outside. Because it wants to make a fool of me. It's working. Stupid door.

I realize the cold fear that had chilled me when Scott practically shoved me out of the green room minutes ago is now completely gone. I'm on the verge of a hot flash, and not because of the warm L.A. weather. It's the hot heap of man meat standing next to me.

"Can I play your guitar?" Brown Eyes asks suddenly.

"No! You can't play my guitar!" Nobody plays my guitar, except me. Or my dad, who owned it for years before officially giving it to me one Christmas when I was a kid.

Brown Eyes wraps his fingers around the neck like he's going to take it.

I tighten my grip.

He says, "I want to see what the action is like."

I growl defensively, "Excuse me?" Then I remember that "action" refers to how high the strings float above the fretboard. I thought he meant something else. Silly me.

My fingers relax against my will and he takes the guitar from my hands. This is a momentous event. I can't believe I'm letting him hold my guitar.

He slings the strap over his shoulder and the guitar hangs just below his neck, comically too high.

I giggle, "You look like a dork!"

"I look like a jazz player," he laughs.

"Same thing," I laugh.

"Pretty much," he chuckles.

"Do you even know how to play?"

He gives me that cocksure grin again and says, "Of course I know how to play."

"Smoke On The Water, maybe," I say derisively. It's probably the easiest rock song ever written.

He plucks out the opening chords from the Deep Purple classic with his fingers: G, B-flat, C.

"Ooh," I coo, "he can play! You're a regular virtuoso!" With the guitar up around his neck, I can't help but laugh at him.

He doesn't seem to care, he's all smiles. It's a good look for him. Who am I kidding? Every look is a good look on him.

He lifts the guitar off his shoulders and lowers it to his side.

That's what I thought. He's a total poser. A crappy guitar serenade might get other women to take their pants off for him, but it's not going to work on me. I make a pouty face, "That all you got?"

"You got a pick?" he asks.

"Huh?"

He points at my hand, which still grasps the yellow Tortex guitar pick I used during the show. I forgot it was there. I'm always holding guitar picks without realizing it. It's a habit.

I hold it up, "You mean this?"

He takes it from my fingers, squats down on the ground and squeezes the guitar between his legs, so it's held at a comfortable playing position for him.

I'd like to squeeze *him* between my legs.

SHUT UP!

I'm such a bad girl.

My guitar isn't plugged into an amp, but in the relative quiet of the alley behind The Cobra, I can hear just fine as he picks out a pearl necklace of juicy notes from my Fender in the form of an E minor arpeggio. The strings sing and I nod appreciatively.

Then he starts sweep picking again, his fingers flying across all six strings in an elegant dance as his left hand works up and down the neck.

Wow, he's really good.

He looks up and gives me a smarmy smile.

"Showboater," I say.

"Yup," he grins, stands, and offers me my guitar.

"Aren't you gonna serenade me some more?"

"Only if you pay extra," he says with an insinuating grin.

I actually want to see what all he knows after that display. I bet we could trade licks and teach each other a thing or two. "My purse is inside. I don't have any cash on me."

"There's other ways to pay…" he says suggestively.

My head shouts at me, STOP! YOU HAVE A BOYFRIEND!

I clamp my teeth shut in a wide smile, keeping the objection to myself.

The next thing I know, Brown Eyes is leaning toward me, leading with his lusciously lickable lips. His glimmering eyes burn into mine.

I press back against the steel door behind me, willing myself to pass through it like a ghost, but it's solid metal. I'm stuck! No escape!

Who am I kidding? I don't want to go anywhere. But I don't want Brown Eyes knowing that!

My own tongue betrays me and slips between my lips, gliding across the top of my loosened mouth.

WHAT AM I DOING!!!

I suck my tongue back into my mouth like a frog and clamp my lips shut. That should send Brown Eyes a hint.

But he keeps leaning toward me.

WHAT IS HE DOING!!!

I blurt, "What are you doing?!"

His cocky face stops an inch from mine and he murmurs, "Giving you back your guitar."

The headstock of my Fender slowly grows, rising into my field of vision as Brown Eyes thrusts it upward. My awareness of the phallic quality of a guitar neck is complete and total in this moment.

Brown Eyes is a professional tease. He holds the guitar between us, his hot eyes boring into me.

I'm boiling now. My heart races. My thighs are literally quivering.

The big phallic Fender guitar neck hangs in the air between us.

"Aren't you going to grab it?" Brown Eyes suggests salaciously.

Is he talking about the erect guitar neck?

I need a cigarette. Or anything phallic I can stick between my lips. And suck on.

STOP!!!

I'm trapped between a stiff steel door and Mr. Mandsome. The only thing standing between him and my decency is a rock hard guitar.

Oh, Jesus, where is my head at?

Did I say head?

I'm about to break down into tears of frustration and insane laughter when the door behind me pushes open.

Saved!

I slide inside the back door of The Cobra Lounge. That's not a sexual pun about anal sex. I'm a girl, and I don't make puns about penises and sex.

Chapter 17

VICTORY

I stumble down the hallway toward the green room.

I take my time, because I'm still heaving and sighing from whatever that was between me and Brown Eyes. I need to calm down before I confront Scott and the boys.

For a second, I can't even remember why I'm not in the green room with them. My head is...elsewhere.

Oh yeah. Scott, Rex, and Bobby are inside talking to Suit Guy. In private. Without me.

I stop short in front of the locked green room door. It's blankness taunts me. Screw you, door. I rattle the knob and knock repeatedly. I'm suddenly wondering if the boys have left the club without me. They better not have, or I'm going to use a rusty bear trap to tear them all new assholes.

The stage manager walks by and says, "Did you get locked out?"

"Oh!" I gasp, surprised by his arrival. "Yeah." I give him a girlish damsel in distress smile out of habit. When in trouble, flirt. Err, wait, that's what almost got me in trouble with Brown Eyes a minute ago. I flatten my damsel smile into a more respectably 'nun in trouble' smile.

The stage manager lifts a huge key ring which is attached to his belt by a chain and sorts through keys until he finds the right one and slips it into the lock and twists the knob. "There you go," He smiles.

And there I go, right into the mouth of madness.

Chapter 18

VICTORY

"You can't kick me out!" I shout, on the verge of hot tears. I hold them back. I'm not crying in front of my band. I never have, and I'm not about to start now.

Scott, Rex, Bobby, and Suit Guy, whose name I have learned is Brent Ransom, stand together on the far side of the green room, a united front. Scott has just spent five minutes explaining to me why things aren't working out with the band. Well, not *explaining*. More like dismissing me with way too many words.

"You can't do this, Scott," I plead.

"I'm not kicking you out, Vic," Scott says flatly, "I'm leaving the band. And I'm taking the name Skin Trade and my songs with me."

"Wait, what?" I say, totally confused. "How is that any different?" I demand. If he takes the name and the music, the fans are going with him. The fans I've worked hard to help cultivate. Sadly, hard work doesn't count. Song ownership does, and the fact that Scott is the voice of Skin Trade. I have nothing to bargain with here except loyalty. I hope Scott can appreciate that.

I say, "We started Skin Trade together, Scott. This is *our* band. You and me and Rex and Bobby."

Scott shrugs his shoulders.

I say bluntly, "Scott, you can't quit. We've built up a following. I've put my heart and everything I have into this band." I'm begging now, but it's all I have.

My eyes dart between Rex, Bobby, and Scott. I don't even look at Brent

Ransom.

A minute ago, Scott explained that Brent works for Tantalus Records, the biggest hard rock label there is. Brent looks like he knows as much about hard rock as Josh Groban. He's also the devil incarnate as far as I'm concerned. Scott revealed that Brent came out to watch the show tonight. To see Scott. Not Skin Trade. Scott. Now he's offering *Scott* a record deal. Not the members of Skin Trade as a band.

Scott.

My head is on spin cycle trying to make sense of this. My chaotic thoughts bang and thump around inside my skull like a wash load of knotted wet bed spreads spinning out of control.

From what I've gathered, Scott knows Brent Ransom quite well. I don't think to ask how damn long they have been besties behind my back.

I say to Rex and Bobby, "You guys are okay with this?"

"It's up to them," Scott says.

"What?" I blurt, "You mean Rex and Bobby can vote me in or out?" If that's the case, I'm not worried. They'll totally vote me in.

"No," Scott says. "They can stay with me. If they want."

I can't imagine why Rex and Bobby would, not after this show of loyalty from Scott. I'm sure me and Rex and Bobby can replace Scott in no time. We'll write our own songs. Fuck Scott and his "Fuck." t-shirt.

Gnawing at my gut is the very real fear that finding a vocalist with star potential is nearly impossible. Even in Hollywood. Think of all those amazing vocalists on all the talent TV shows you never hear from again because they fade into obscurity after one or two albums. The reality is that I need to keep this band together, or I run the risk of fading into obscurity myself.

I glare at Rex and Bobby and blurt, "Well?"

They both look embarrassed. I've never seen them look embarrassed. They avoid eye contact like they'll explode if our eyes meet. Maybe they will. If I can manage to channel the overloading rage inside me, I'm going to slice everyone in the room in half with the lasers I plan to shoot from my eyes.

I can't believe Rex and Bobby are abandoning me too.

Sheepishly, Bobby says, "It's good money, Vic. How can I say no?"

Now he's calling me Vic too. I shake my head at him, "By saying no, dumbass." I'm so pissed right now I wonder if I'm going to explode. I wasn't able to shoot lasers out of my eyes at Bobby just now like I'd hoped, thereby releasing the pressure pounding in my head. I'm going to have a wicked migraine in about three minutes. I can feel it.

Bobby whines, "You know I'm practically broke, Vic."

"Don't call me Vic," I growl.

"Sorry. Victory, you know I'm tired of eating Ramen noodles and Pabst for dinner every night."

I snarl, "So quit buying the Pabst, and spend the extra cash you save on mac and cheese. I'll throw in a carton of orange juice for you every week so you get your vitamin C." I'd offer to cook him gourmet four course dinners on a nightly basis, but I don't have any extra cash to spare. He's not the only one on a Ramen diet. I can't even afford OJ for myself.

Bobby looks away.

"It's just business," Rex says meekly. "I need money. I'm tired of hiding my truck every night from the repo guys."

There's no way I can make truck payments for him. I know he's at least two thousand in the hole. I say forcefully, "Get rid of your truck. I'll drive you wherever you need to go." I'll totally be Rex's chauffeur if it means keeping the band together. "All you have to cover is gas money."

Rex glances at Scott for guidance.

Even with his mirrored shades hanging from the collar of his black "Fuck." t-shirt, Scott's entire face is a mirror. He's as stone faced as a statue. Not the handsome Greek ones. One of those evil statues of a demon or a gargoyle in a graveyard.

"I thought we were a band!" I shout. "I thought we made a pact to stay together no matter what! I've promoted this band like my life depended on it! How can you guys throw me away like this?!" I'm nearly hysterical.

I can't believe my entire world is coming apart before my eyes. Bobby and Rex are like my brothers.

But Bobby and Rex are silent.

Correction, *were* like my brothers. They're kissing me goodbye as they plunge the knife into my back.

"Sorry, Vic," Scott sighs, bored by my tirade. "Things change."

I snort a laugh and scoff, "I guess they do."

After an infinite moment of utter disbelief, I can see that the three of them are going to go through with this. Rage rockets up my throat. I'm about to slice Scott to bits with my tongue when I'm stopped short. If Scott has so little loyalty that he can go behind my back and force me out of the band, what does that say about our relationship as boyfriend and girlfriend? Can I assume Scott and I are no longer an item?

What the fuck?

I don't even want to ask. I'm so done with Scott. I shoulder past him to grab my guitar case. Scott's eyes suddenly widen like he thinks I'm going to smack him. I totally should. But it wouldn't change anything.

I suddenly realize I don't even have my guitar. I left it outside in the hands of Brown Eyes. He has really thrown me off balance tonight. I would never hand my guitar to a stranger in an alley and walk away. But I did. I need to get my head examined.

First, I need my guitar case. I grab it and strut toward the door of the green room, my heels clacking pistol shots on the concrete floor. After I rip the door open, I turn and shout, "Good luck finding a replacement guitar player, you fucking pricks!"

Scott smirks at me, "There's as many guitar players in Hollywood as there are aspiring actresses. I bet every guy at our show tonight plays guitar."

At that exact moment, Brown Eyes leans his head into the doorframe, holding my Fender Strat in his hand.

"See?" Scott smirks. "Here's a guitar player now."

A barrage of fresh guilt assaults me as I lock eyes with Brown Eyes. It surges over me in a big nauseous wave. I suddenly wonder if Scott is pissed at me because he saw me flirting with Brown Eyes during our show? Is that why he's pushing me out of the band? I wouldn't put it past him. Talk about passive aggressive. Good thing Scott didn't see me out back with Brown Eyes a minute ago. I feel ashamed of my behavior.

Scott studies Brown Eyes with an amused look. "Shit, Vic, I bet this guy plays guitar better than you do. Hey, buddy, you play guitar?"

Wow. Scott's not even waiting until my ashes are cold to start dancing on them.

Brown Eyes says to Scott, "Sure. Why?"

"I'm auditioning guitar players next week," Scott replies. "You've got a good look. How good are you?"

Brown Eyes looks into mine and smirks, "I can give her a run for the money."

I'm suddenly hot all over, once again.

Brown Eyes' sultry gaze has cooked my brain and burnt out my entire nervous system. My legs shake and my fingers quiver. Heat blooms in my armpits. I swallow with a dry click. I couldn't speak if I tried. I'm going to collapse if I don't relax and take a deep breath. But I can't. Brown Eyes is so ridiculously handsome, my lungs won't work. Flashing through my mind are the words, "He stole my breath away," which is totally stupid, but a fact in this instance.

Get a grip! I shout at myself. Quit acting like a gushing little girl!

I blink my eyes forcefully and break eye contact with Brown Eyes. Nagging at the back of my mind is that image of his eyes burning into mine while my cock shaped Fender headstock is poking up between us.

I inhale to clear my head, but instead of a smooth expansion of my ribs, my breath comes in a series of skipping hitches. I probably look like I'm in the middle of a spasming orgasm to anyone watching the loose lipped slack jawed look on my face as my eyes are magnetically drawn back to

Brown Eyes against my will. I can't help myself.

I don't want to stop looking at him.

Scott says quizzically, "Hey, isn't that your guitar, Vic?"

I tear my gaze away from Brown Eyes and watch Scott's eyes narrow suspiciously.

I hazily realize that I'm totally incriminating myself acting so gaga in front of Scott. My attraction to Brown Eyes has to be the most obvious thing in the room. If Scott didn't pick up on it before, he will now. Any second Scott is going to level a stiff finger at me like we're at a witch trial and shout, "She's the guilty one! Adulteress!" I'll be wearing a big scarlet A sewn to my outfits until my dying day.

I laugh nervously and yank my guitar out of Brown Eyes' hands. Panicked, I say to him, "Thanks! You can go now!"

Brown Eyes is confused.

So am I.

Looking for distraction, I hastily stuff my Fender inside its case and latch it shut.

Then I watch the wheels turning in Scott's head. He stares at Brown Eyes for several seconds before saying, "You were the guy doing all the air guitar in front of the stage during our show, weren't you?"

"Yeah," Brown Eyes grins innocently. "But I play for real. When are auditions?"

Does Brown Eyes not realize I've been kicked out of my band? Then my heart stops short. Is it possible that Scott might replace me with Brown Eyes? The idea makes me want to vomit.

I've got to get out of here before I crumble in front of everyone.

This is not my lucky day.

Chapter 19

KELLAN

Wow, today is my lucky day.

I guess the guys in Skin Trade decided they needed a second guitar player? I have no doubt I'll nail the audition. I have a feeling me and the Guitar Goddess will make a great team.

My mind is alive with possibilities as I gaze at her gorgeous face.

Over the years, rock has seen many legendary guitar duos: Rudolf Schenker and Matthias Jabs of the Scorpions, Dave Murray and Adrian

Smith of Iron Maiden, James Hetfield and Kirk Hammett of Metallica, Zacky Vengeance and Synyster Gates of Avenged Sevenfold, Danny Daggers and Chainsaw of Wild Child.

But never a notable guy-girl duo.

Maybe me and the guitar goddess will be the first. It'll take a ton of work. We'll be joined at the hip 24/7. It doesn't hurt that she's smoking hot. I will gladly lock hips with her. Front to front, front to back, back to front, back to back, whatever works. The positions are endless.

I throw some smolder at the Guitar Goddess, gazing into her eyes. I notice her killer cleavage popping out of her studded leather bra in the bottom of my vision. It takes everything I have not to stare at her chest when she's standing only a foot away.

I tear my eyes away from hers and say to the lead singer, "Name the time and place, and I'll be the first and last guy you audition."

Nobody says anything.

Am I missing something? I glance at all the faces in the room. Everyone looks uncomfortable.

Yeah, I'm missing something.

Band drama?

"Hey, buddy," the lead singer growls at me, "you done drooling over my girlfriend?"

Girlfriend?

Shit.

I was right all along.

She needs a new boyfriend.

Good thing I showed up when I did.

Chapter 20

VICTORY

Scott scowls at Brown Eyes, then says to me, "You know what, Vic? Why don't you go home with this guy. You couldn't stop looking at him during our entire set."

My jaw drops. "Shit, Scott. Is that what this is about? Are you kicking me out because some random guy was checking me out at one of our shows?" I say it with utter disbelief.

Scott arches a self-satisfied eyebrow, "Random? What the fuck is he doing carrying your guitar around for you? Is he your roadie?"

"What? No! I was outside waiting for you to tell me you're *kicking me out of our band!* This guy asked me about my guitar." That's when the bomb in my brain goes off. "And like it fucking matters?" I'm furious. "You kicked me out. Were we going to keep dating while you replaced me with another guitar player? Or have you already picked out the choicest of your Skin Slaves to be your new girlfriend?"

Scott's inscrutable face breaks into a grin.

"I knew it!" I shout. "You're seeing someone!"

He doesn't deny it.

Now I'm as mad as a hand grenade. If I had one, I'd pull the pin, toss it in the green room with Scott, Bobby and Rex, and pull the door shut. Too bad I don't have a grenade. But I do have…Brown Eyes.

I look up at him. I'm so angry, I probably look like a rabid hyena, but I don't care. "Hey, you," I say to him.

Brown Eyes is confused.

"Come here," I say as I reach up and grab the back of his neck and pull his face down to mine.

He doesn't resist.

Suddenly I'm kissing Brown Eyes to make Scott jealous.

And the room disappears.

I'm floating in the clouds and expect at any moment for angels to start strumming harps while singing church music.

His lips are so soft. I wasn't expecting that. He looks so hard, I'd thought maybe his lips were made of steel, or something equally masculine. He has a hint of beard stubble and it tickles the inside of my upper lip. I giggle girlishly, spiraling away into the moment.

His tongue slips into my mouth and I taste him. Sweet, tangy, yummy. I inhale deeply and smell this mandsome guy. His scent slides down my spine, tumbles around in my stomach until I'm glowing, then flutters up my chest. Whoa.

This is kissing.

All other kisses before this one were clumsy fumbling and sloppy puppy dog tongues. I'm talking about every guy I've ever been with. Including Scott. They were puppies. Now I'm kissing a man.

Finally.

It rocks.

Who knew?

Am I still breathing? I don't know for sure.

His hot tongue plunges into my mouth with savage desire. I'm vaguely aware of him pulling me closer. His muscled chest pushes into me, forcing me against the doorframe. I barely notice it, my head is still floating in bright white clouds of pure ecstasy. But I notice his chest. It's massive, muscled, manly and pressing into me with hot need.

Yes, I'm wet.

Damn, where am I again?

I feel Brown Eyes caressing my cheek with his hand. A hand that plays guitar like a master. He also seems to be playing me like a master as his hand glides down the curve of my jaw to my neck. I quiver and shiver in his hands as more raindrops of pure pleasure drizzle down my cheek, my neck, between my breasts, and finally settle in my belly like a jelly bean spell. I'm candy all over and I want this amazing man to lick every inch of my body until he gets to my soft center.

Sweet revenge.

"Ahem," a voice coughs.

Where am I again? Am I in public? I'm not entirely sure if I'm wearing clothes or completely naked. What's going on?

I open my eyes.

Brown Eyes' face is inches from mine. He looks…melted. It's the only word I can think of to describe his dark chocolate eyes.

Melts in your mouth, not in your hands. No, that's wrong. I melted in his mouth *and* in his hands. And I want more!

"Ahem!" Scott coughs again.

As my senses return, I take stock of myself. Back on planet Earth? Check. Clothes? Check. Super hot guy two inches from my face? Check. If only I could figure out what was bothering me so much a minute ago. Everything seems perfect now. What was the problem again?

"I guess that settles that," Scott says.

What is he yammering on about? I don't know.

Then I notice I'm holding my Fender in one hand and the case in the other.

I forgot.

Scott kicked me out of our band.

I glare at him.

Scott glares back and grumbles, "How about I leave your stuff outside the apartment and you can pick it up in the morning? After you spend the night with your new boyfriend."

What?

Chapter 21

VICTORY

I hold back my tears until I'm outside The Cobra Lounge, strutting up the side street that runs north off Sunset, heading to where my car is parked. Tears river down my cheeks and drip from my chin.

I can't believe they betrayed me like that. Two years of work on the band! Two years! Thrown away in two seconds!

Getting kicked out of Skin Trade feels like getting kicked out of my family. I love my family. I can't imagine the shock I'd feel if they told me to hit the road. Wait, I can. It would feel like what I'm feeling right now. Total annihilation. Nuclear destruction.

I falter and stumble in my heels, catching the toe of my platform on a crack in the sidewalk. I catch myself before I fall.

I'm not going down.

Yeah, it's symbolic.

I'm not letting those assholes back in the green room break me.

No fucking way.

And my relationship with Scott? Two wasted years. He is an absolute snake, a jerk, a joke, and a lie. Did I ignore the signs? Probably. Either that, or I'm the dumbest girl who ever dated a guy in the history of dating.

I'm so mad at myself, I don't think I'm the least bit sad. Disappointed, frustrated, and hurt. But I'm not sad. I have to start over at square one. Find a new band and work hard to build it up. It's going to take a lot of work. This time, I'm writing all of the music. Too bad I have to find a singer to…

(*singsingsing*)

…sing them. I don't even want to think about it right now.

As for a new boyfriend? Forget it. Who needs men?

Not me, sister.

I pause for a moment. Where the hell did I park my car? Oh, who cares. The walk will do me good.

"Hey!" someone shouts behind me, "Destiny!"

Whoever it is can bite me. I need to go home and regroup. Home. I don't even want to think about home. Home is the studio apartment I share with Scott.

Fuck, fuck, fuckity fuck. I can't stay there.

"Destiny!" the voice shouts again. I hear boots clomping up behind me.

I whip around and shout, "I'm not your Destiny, or whoever the fuck you're looking for—"

It's Brown Eyes.

Damn

His dark deep-set chocolatey eyes search mine. This guy is gourmet man candy. The kind with a creamy middle I'd like to suck on. I stifle a giggle. What has gotten into me? I just got kicked out of my band and broke up with my boyfriend. I should be miserable. But I'm not.

I smile at Brown Eyes and shake my head. In a friendly voice I say, "What do you want?"

"Uh, I'm not really sure what happened back there…"

I roll my eyes, "Me neither." Is he talking about the scene between me and Scott, or the fact that I kissed him?

"Well, uh, can I walk you to your car?"

I'm baffled by his boyish charm. He doesn't strike me as the type. He has Player Bad Boy written all over every inch of his gorgeous self. But I feel like we're school kids and he's asking permission to walk me home. Maybe he'll pluck a flower from some random garden and ask if I'll go steady with him. This is so weird.

"What?" he asks earnestly.

"Nothing," I grin.

"Which way to your car? Up the hill?"

I look around and realize the street we're on dead ends two houses up. "I, no. It's down on Sunset."

He motions down the street toward Sunset with this courtly, gentlemanly gesture, and offers me his hand. "After you?"

"Sure," I smile, curling my fingers into his.

"Can I carry your guitar for you?"

At this point, he's held it so many times, I'm not worried about it. "Yes, please," I grin, handing it to him.

The school girl, school boy image is now complete. Perhaps cookies and Kool Aid will be waiting for us when we get to my parents' house. We can watch cartoons and music videos on YouTube together.

A second later, we're walking along the house lined street that could be any street in America, except for the fact that Sunset Boulevard is two blocks away. And we're holding hands.

It seems so natural.

I like how it feels.

It feels peaceful.

The last thing on my mind is getting kicked out of Skin Trade and breaking up with Scott. I wince at the thought, suddenly afraid Brown Eyes will bring it up.

He doesn't.

We say nothing.

In our silence, everything is said.

I'm in candy wonderland again.

Sweet heaven.

Chapter 22

VICTORY

"There's my car," I say, pointing toward my eleven-year-old white Nissan Altima. I like that it matches my guitar.

I pop the trunk and put my guitar inside.

"Thanks again," I say to Brown Eyes as I climb into the driver's seat.

"You gonna be okay getting home and whatnot?"

"Sure," I smile as I buckle my seat belt.

He's leaning against my open door when I realize that a rose colored fuzziness has been dampening my sanity whenever I'm around Brown Eyes. I realize I don't even know his name.

"Hey," I grin, "what's your name, anyway?"

"I think I've seen God," a helium shrill female voice says from behind Brown Eyes.

He stands up and turns to face an expensive silver Porsche convertible. Two plastic blondes sit inside, plump lips strained over crystalline teeth as they drip all over themselves with desire for Brown Eyes.

"You two stalking me?" Brown Eyes asks them with a cocky smile. He sounds like an entirely different person than the man I hastily kissed inside The Cobra Lounge ten minutes ago.

"Yes, we're stalking you," the driver says. She's as soulless as a photograph. The kind that has been Photoshopped to death. There's nothing real about her.

"Where's your bike?" the passenger asks with an implied giggle in her voice. She is the mirror image of the driver, and equally flat and dimensionless.

"Parked," Brown Eyes tells them.

Does he know them?

Suddenly my opinion of him dissipates in a gust of distaste. That rosey haze pillowing around us earlier is replaced by granite walls. I don't think I want anything to do with a guy who is friends with two blonde dumbshells like this.

I pull my door closed with a bang.

My instinct is to drive off and let them get friendly, but I'm parallel parked between an old Oldsmobile and an SUV that are both too big for their spaces. It'll take a ten point turn to get out of this space, and I'll look like an idiot as I go forward, reverse, forward, reverse an inch at a time. I don't want the blonde audience. Not that it matters. With their Porsche in the way, I can't go anywhere.

I can address that.

I crank down my window and tug on the back of Brown Eyes' shirt. "Hey! Can you ask your girlfriends to move? I'm stuck."

I half expect him to be so entranced with the Tinsel Twins that he ignores me completely, but he surprises me and spins around to lean on my doorframe.

"What's up?" he smiles.

Damn, he's too handsome for his own good. The Tinsel Twins are living proof. But that doesn't change my heated response to his hotness. I momentarily forget that I wanted to forget about him. "Um, I'm stuck here until that Porsche moves."

"Got it," he winks at me smarmily.

Based on his smarmy smile, I imagine he's wondering how he can take all three of us home with him.

He leans back against the doorframe of the Porsche and I notice his arms flexing. I want to simultaneously stroke his arms and slice up the blondes with the nearest piece of broken glass I can find.

The line of cars backed up behind the silver Porsche start to honk impatiently.

Brown Eyes points down the street, explaining something to the blondes that I can't hear, then stands up. The blondes pull ahead slowly in their Porsche and turn into the open space in front of a fire hydrant two cars in front of me with hazard lights blinking, obviously waiting for Brown Eyes to join them.

He turns and leans back into my window.

He smiles.

Am I supposed to melt?

I smirk sarcastically, "Do you need to go?"

Am I disappointed that a guy this good looking is as interested in me as he is in the two hobags of artificial sweetener inside that silver Porsche? No. I think his sincerity earlier was as artificial as he is. The sooner he gets out of my way, the better. I should've guessed he was too good to be true.

He frowns gently. I think he's confused.

I turn the ignition on my Altima and sneer, "You can move now."

"Hey, uhhh..." he stammers softly, now sounding like the man who held my hand earlier, "I know you had some pretty heavy shit go down with your band members tonight. Do you need any help or anything?"

I arch an eyebrow, "Don't you need to tend to your flock of admirers?"

He cocks his head in the direction of the Porsche, "Who, them?"

My other eyebrow raises up to join it's sister.

He shakes his head and smiles, "I don't know them."

"That's funny, because they acted like they know you."

His grin dimples, "They *want* to know me. But do I want to know them?"

"Wow, you're worse than my boyfrie—" I stop myself. Yes, Scott is also this cocky. But he sure as hell isn't my boyfriend anymore.

Brown Eyes' face softens. "How long were you guys together?"

"Two years." Do I really want to talk about this with a total stranger? A hot sultry muscled stranger who can play guitar? I'm torn.

He says firmly, "You're better off without him."

I nod. If I talk, I'm going to start bawling in front of Brown Eyes. I still love Scott. The hate hasn't erased it. Yet. It will, in time. But not tonight.

Brown Eyes smiles, "Are you sure you don't need any help tonight? Or just someone to talk to?"

Craziness takes my wheel and I say, "Wanna help me move? I'll buy you pizza. Isn't that the usual price?"

He smiles and shakes his head, "What, out of your boyfriend's place? Tonight?"

"Yeah." I'm not going to sit around and hope Scott changes his mind about us. I'm done.

"I'll follow you on my bike. It's parked in front of The Cobra."

"Want me to drive you to it?" I don't want him getting sidetracked by the plastics in their Porsche. Does this mean I'm a tad jealous and possessive already? Maybe it does.

So what if this turns into a rebound fling?

I deserve it after what I've been through tonight.

Tonight, Brown Eyes is all mine.

The blonde dumbshells in the silver Porsche can suck it.

After he climbs into my car, I drive past the Porsche and I notice Brown Eyes wave at them.

One of them shouts, "Where are you going?!!"

I pretend to ignore them, but a sly smile spreads across my lips and in my head I'm flipping them both off.

He's mine, bitches!

Chapter 23

VICTORY

Brown Eyes follows on his black motorcycle as I drive my Altima up the windy road in Silver Lake that leads to Scott's apartment. The streets are narrow and crowded with cars. Most of the people living around here work in the film business or are musicians. I like my neighbors.

I'll be sad to say goodbye. Not that I'm going to have some formal goodbye party. I'm stealing out of here like a gypsy in the night.

Speaking of stealing, I should steal something of Scott's that'll really piss him off.

It's the least I can do.

I park my car in the first available space. Since we live in a studio apartment, we don't even get a space. It's not like a big apartment complex anyway. It's a hundred year old house divided into several different units. The owner lives on the top floor. Scott and I share a little room you enter from the back of the house. It has a bathroom with a shower, but no kitchen. We cook on a hot plate and do dishes in the bathroom sink. It's cheap. That's what counts. For me and Scott, music always came first.

I feel a pinch of grief as I lock my car door and march up the old stone steps to the house. Who am I kidding. It's no pinch. My grief is crushing. But I don't want to deal with it right now. Right now, it doesn't exist.

I push it down.

But it isn't cooperating. I waver on the steps and lean a hand against the stone railing to steady myself. I squeeze my eyes shut, holding in the tears. I can't believe Scott dumped me like this. I'm going to sit down and cry.

"Hey," Brown Eyes says, jogging up the steps behind me.

"That was quick," I sniff.

"It's easy to park a bike. Even in L.A. You should get one. You've already got the right outfit." His eyes rove up and down my body.

I'm reminded that I'm still wearing my stage costume. Yes, I look like a rock and roll hooker, or assassin, depending on how you look at it. But I'm dressed in leather from top to bottom.

"Thanks," I say. Time to get this over with.

I trudge up the rest of the steps and we walk around back. The light on the side of the house is out again. I keep telling the owner I'm going to get raped one night. He doesn't seem to care.

I open the flimsy door, which is a hollow interior door. It doesn't even have a deadbolt. Just a lock in the knob. Fort Knox it is not.

The door swings open. "Welcome to my palace," I say.

I flip on the lone overhead light and it paints everything in a bland glow. The single room contains an unmade queen sized mattress, a wardrobe style moving box where my and Scott's clothes hang, stacked plastic drawers I bought at Target for the rest of our clothes, a pile of shoes, one of those half-size refrigerators, a hotplate, paper plates and plastic utensils, a few glossy band posters and photocopied show fliers of local bands on the walls, and little else.

"Nice poster," Brown Eyes says, nodding at my Jimi Hendrix poster.

"Oh, thanks," I smile.

"You gonna fit all this in your car?" Brown Eyes asks. It's a joke but I don't laugh.

I want to laugh, but I can't. If I try, I think I'll cry instead.

I tear a black plastic garbage bag off the roll in the bathroom and start stuffing my clothes inside. Brown Eyes gets a second bag without me asking and starts helping.

He asks, "Anyone ever told you ya live like a stripper?"

I frown, "Anyone ever told you that you act like an ass?"

"Frequently," he chuckles and opens a drawer full of my underwear.

"Not those," I bark.

"Why, are they your boyfriend's?" he quips.

"No," I chuckle and smile genuinely. "They're mine, silly." I start grabbing handfuls and stuffing them into my bag.

"In that case, I should totally help."

Before I can stop him, he lifts up a pair, twists his fingers into the waistband, and pretends like he's flossing his teeth with them.

"What are you doing?" I gawk.

"Something stuck in my teeth," he grins.

I roll my eyes. "Into the bag," I command.

He smiles and tosses them into my garbage bag.

"If you see any bras," I grin, "don't touch them."

"Why, are they all sweaty and gross?"

I shake my head and grimace, "No, I just don't want you trying to put them on like an athletic cup or whatever."

"For my giant balls? I never thought of that. If they're good for boobs, they're good for balls, no doubt."

I roll my eyes, "Just don't touch them."

It takes all of fifteen minutes to pack everything up. He jokes with me the entire time. It keeps me from thinking about Scott, and I'm thankful for that.

We end up using three garbage bags which sit hunched together on the edge of the bed. The third bag holds my shoes and haircare paraphernalia: dryers, curlers, brushes, product, scrunchies, etc. And the paper plates and plastic utensils. Scott can buy his own. Jerk.

"Crap," I say.

"What?"

"My makeup bag is still at The Cobra. My amps are still there too."

"We can go get them," he offers. "I'll totally help."

"Uh, no, I can do it." I pick up one of the garbage bags with both hands. It weighs a ton, but I can manage.

Before I can say anything, he winds his hand around the tops of the other two bags and lifts them with one arm like they're weightless. "Here," he says, motioning to the one in my hands.

"I've got it," I say and head out the door.

"Suit yourself." He slings the two bags over his shoulder. "After you." He follows me outside. "Oh wait, you forgot your Hendrix poster."

Before I say anything, he sets his bags down, walks inside, and peels the poster off the wall.

I wasn't going to worry about a five dollar poster. Not that I have five dollars to spare on another one.

While rolling the poster in his hands, he says, "Can't leave this behind."

I smile, "I guess not."

He walks outside, hands me the poster, and pulls the door shut. "Want me to lock it?"

"No," I say. "I'm hoping someone will steal Scott's stuff."

"Dirty laundry and an old mattress?" he asks skeptically, picking up the garbage bags.

"Well, maybe some hoodlums will trash the place and use up all of Scott's security deposit."

He rolls his eyes. "Not gonna happen."

"We could trash the place?" I suggest. "Write 'Helter Skelter' in red spray paint all over the walls? Maybe Scott will think I've been murdered and he'll feel bad." I doubt it.

"I like the way you think," he grins. "Total Hollywood Babylon. But no. Let's get your amps."

I don't look back as we walk down the stone steps. The sooner I forget about it, the better. We stuff the loaded trash bags in the trunk of my car and I slam it shut. It feels like an ending.

"I'll meet you at The Cobra," Brown Eyes says.

"Okay," I say. I can feel my nose twinkling. I'm surprised I have any smiles left at this point.

Chapter 24

VICTORY

I park my Altima behind The Cobra.

Brown Eyes swings his leg over his jet black motorcycle like he's done it ten thousand times. He takes off his helmet and swaggers toward my car.

I'm acutely aware of the swing of his hips, which are a narrow platform for his muscled chest and broad shoulders. No wonder so many women have eyes for this young man. I can't pull mine away.

"Doing all right?" he asks with obvious compassion.

"Yeah, fine," I smile as I climb out of my car. I get the sense he thinks I'm distraught about Scott and the band, which I am, but I was also half hypnotized watching him walk. I'll keep that bit of information to myself.

We walk to the back door of The Cobra together. I wish I'd changed out of my stage costume. I don't feel like a rock and roll assassin at this point. Yoga pants and a comfy baby tee sounds perfect right now. It'll have to wait.

I'm about to rap on the steel back door with my knuckles when I pause. "What if Scott's still here?"

"They're your amps, right?" Brown Eyes asks.

"Yeah."

"So fuck 'em. We're getting your amps." He knocks on the door for me.

We wait. No one opens the door.

"Should we try the front?" I suggest.

"Sounds like a plan."

The crowd outside is totally gone. I guess my trip to and from Silver Lake to get my stuff was long enough for everyone to clear out. I hope Scott and the boys didn't take my amps so they could sell them. At this point, anything is possible.

We walk down to the entrance on Sunset. There's a beefy bouncer standing out front looking bored.

"Tony!" Brown Eyes says to him.

"Kellan!" Tony smiles. "Whatchoo doing back at the club?"

They hug like best buds.

Brown Eyes tips his head toward me, "Came to get her stuff."

"Who's your friend," Tony asks, smiling at me.

I finally realize that I don't even know Brown Eyes' name. I guess it's Kellan? But he doesn't know mine, yet he has seen my underwear drawer, helped me move, and kissed me. Well, I suppose I kissed him, but same difference. I can't decide if it's totally bizarre that neither of us ever asked names, or some kind of strange twist of fate that spending time with a total stranger seems totally normal. Not that names matter. I know Scott's name, and look where that got me with him.

I shake hands with Tony, "My name is Victory. I played the show tonight. With Skin Trade." I glance up at the marquee. Seeing Skin Trade up there in big letters makes me nauseous. Three hours ago, it made me proud. What a sad turn of events.

"Oh!" Tony grins sheepishly. "Sorry. I never get inside to see the acts. Makes sense though, Kellan hooking up with the hottest female in the joint, and the star of the show no less."

I start to blush at the compliment, then notice Kellan run a hand through his hair. I think he's blushing too. He seems to swing between boyishly cute and overly cocky every other minute. I can't seem to pin him down.

Tony grins at both of us, "What can I do you for?"

"I need to get my amps," I say.

Tony looks confused. He sure doesn't know much about music for a guy who works at a music club.

I say, "The ones I used during the show. They should be backstage? And my makeup bag is in the green room."

Tony finally nods, "Gotcha. You know where everything is?"

"Yeah," I answer.

"Have at it." He slaps a heavy hand on Kellan's shoulder. "Watch out for this character. He's nuthin' but trouble."

I arch an eyebrow, "Oh?"

Tony's face softens into a broad smile. "I'm kiddin'. Kellan is a good kid." He slaps Kellan's shoulders a few more times.

Kellan rolls his eyes.

"G'wan," Tony motions inside. "I gotta lock up anyway. You guys can go out the back. Make sure you close the door good and tight."

"Will do," Kellan says.

We walk into the nearly empty night club.

Inside the main room a couple of janitors have big trashcans on wheels with different colored spray bottles hanging from the rims, and they're picking up trash and sweeping. The house lights are up and the place doesn't seem nearly as romantic and exciting as it did when I was on stage.

As we walk across the wide open floor, I say, "Your name is Kellan, right?"

He nods.

"Interesting name," I say. I wait for him to ask about mine. People usually do.

He doesn't.

I frown, "Aren't you going to ask about mine?"

"Ask what? It's Victory. What am I supposed to ask?"

"I don't know," I say, frustrated. "People usually ask me about it because it's different."

He stops in the middle of the main room, "Do you want me to ask," he grins cockily, "or do you just want to talk about your name?"

I open my mouth to object, then close it. "You're annoying." I try to hide my smile, but I don't do a good job.

He grins at me, "So?"

"Is this how you always act with the ladies?"

"No."

"Fine, I won't talk about it," I smirk and start walking.

He follows, "Okay, tell me about your name."

I say nothing. Two can play this game.

"Aren't you going to tell me?" he asks.

I glare at him, "See how it feels?"

He grins and shakes his head, "I don't need to know. You brought it up."

I stop in my tracks and spin around, my fists clenched at my sides. "You are infuriating! You know that?"

He chuckles, "So?"

I narrow my eyes, "You're one of those one date guys, aren't you? The kind who women are dying to go out with because of your—" I wiggle my hand at him and wrinkle my nose, "because of your *hot body,*" I say like it disgusts me, "but as soon as they spend any time with you, they never want to see you again, do they?"

With cocky confidence, he says, "I only need one date."

I roll my eyes, "Has anyone ever told you that you're a pig?"

His eyes gleam with humor, "Oink."

I scowl at him and jab my finger at him repeatedly like I'm going to say more, but all that comes out is, "Uuuugh!" I spin again and march across the room without him.

He hollers at my back, "Has anybody ever told you that your ass is as hot as your head?"

I smile from ear to ear, but I refuse to turn around and let him see it. I keep marching. I notice that the two janitors have stopped sweeping and are leaning on their brooms, watching the fireworks display.

"The way you're walking right now," Kellan says, "makes your ass wiggle in a way that makes me want to bite it."

I stop and spin, my fists on hips and I glare at him with all the glare I can muster.

He smirks, "The front's as good as the back. But I think I prefer the back."

My eyes goggle.

The nearer janitor laughs.

The other janitor nods agreement.

I shake my head, "All of you are pigs!"

Kellan and the two janitors erupt into laughter.

I flip them off.

They laugh harder.

I turn around, and start walking, but with less march, so my ass isn't putting on a show for Kellan and the janitors.

"Walk however you want," Kellan hollers, "your ass still makes me want to bite it."

I can't win.

"She's a keeper," one of the janitors says behind me. "Go get her, son."

I secretly savor the comment.

"Too much work," Kellan says.

I almost falter but keep it together. I remind myself I'm here to get my amps.

"If you don't want her," the other janitor says, "I'll take her."

Now I feel like a piece of meat.

"I got her handled," Kellan says.

I whip around again, stopping in my tracks. I shoot a look at all three of them that is so dirty, a hundred janitors couldn't clean it. Then I set my sights on Kellan, "Handled? Are you serious?"

"You're gonna need to hogtie her," the older janitor says. "I think I've got rope in the back."

The younger janitor chuckles.

Kellan drawls, "Rope won't work on a fox like this. You gotta outsmart 'em."

I can't decide if that's a compliment or not. Based on the way he's grinning, I'm leaning toward compliment.

He strolls up to me. It takes all day. As soon as he's close enough, I punch him in the arm as hard as I can, which is rock solid. I don't let him know my hand now hurts.

The older janitor says, "She's got spunk, that one."

"Careful," I threaten Kellan in a low voice, "I've got spunk."

He's now standing inches away from me. "I've got spunk too," Kellan grins. "Loads and loads of it."

I narrow my eyes. I'm not going to acknowledge the innuendo. I stare him down.

His eyes drop toward… his crotch. He arches an eyebrow, like he's daring me to look.

I don't. I just keep staring at his eyes. His smoldering eyes.

He stares back. Yeah, he really is too damn handsome for his own good.

Against my will, my lips loosen into a big smile. "I need to get my amps."

I turn and survey the stage, hoping to put this fire out, and wondering if my amp is still onstage where I left it. It's not. A nervous snake unwinds in my belly, and snuffs out the fire that was there a second ago.

I can't afford to buy a new amp right now. I really hope it's in the back. The door leading backstage off the main floor is wide open. I walk toward it, confident that Scott and the boys are gone. I hope my amp didn't go with them.

Kellan follows and we pass the vintage rocker stage manager in the hallway backstage. He says, "You still here? I thought you'd gone home."

"I came back for my amp. Have you seen it?"

"I put it in the green room with your other stuff. Your bandmates said you'd pick it up. Door's open."

"Thanks," I smile.

The stage manager gives me a friendly wink while walking past us and turns down another hallway.

Kellan and I walk to the green room. I heave a sigh of relief when I see my Marshall head on top of my 4x12 speaker cabinet in the corner, next to my Line 6 practice amp. The cables and chords are neatly wound and resting on top. I doubt Scott or the band did that. Probably the stage manager. I'll have to thank him again on the way out.

I pick up my Line 6, which is small enough for me to carry by the handle bolted to the top. It's awkward, and I have to lean to one side and use both hands, but I can manage. "Can you push my Marshall?" The amp head and speaker cabinet are more than half my height and weigh a ton, but it has wheels on the bottom.

Kellan walks over and picks it up with the big handles on both side of the speaker cabinet. I've never seen one guy carry the amp like that. Usually it takes two guys because it's so bulky.

I smile, "It rolls, you know."

"And now it floats," Kellan says.

"You don't get a trophy for carrying it," I quip.

"Any prize will do."

I can't decide if his boldness scares me or thrills me. I don't dwell on it. I walk out the door, lugging my amp, and stop. "I forgot my makeup. We'll have to make two trips."

"You can put it on top of the Marshall."

"Will you be able to see? We can make two trips."

"Just put it on top of the amp."

I do, and he's right, he can easily see over it. "How tall are you?"

"Tall enough," he grins.

We walk the amps outside together and I make sure the back door is locked tight.

Kellan sets the amp down next to my car. "Unlock your car and I'll put it in."

I have a hot flash as I mull over the various meanings of "put it in."

I unlock one of the back doors and Kellan slides the cabinet in like it's weightless. Usually two people have to wrestle it in the back seat because it barely fits. Kellan makes quick work of it, but not without a lot of muscle flexing, all of which I watch with quiet excitement.

He puts the Marshall head in the front passenger footwell and the little Line 6 practice amp in the seat, then walks back around and runs his hand through his hair, smoothing it out of his face. "All loaded," he smiles.

I hold up my makeup bag and grin, "You forgot this."

He shakes his head and cocks a grin, "Now you really have to tip me." He walks it around to the front seat with the amps.

"I should go," I say more despondently than I want to.

"You have a place to go? A friend's or something?"

"Yeah," I lie. I haven't thought my escape plan through that far ahead. I open the driver side door. I can feel myself lingering, not wanting to leave. But it's for the best. I need to get some headspace. I have a lot to process right now. As nice as it would be to curl up in the muscled arms of this amazingly talented and equally mysterious man who I know next to nothing about, I really don't want to do any rebounding. Not this soon, anyway.

Time to cut this short. I wince smile, "You've been totally helpful, Kellan. I can't thank you enough."

"My pleasure." He's so tall, he's resting his elbow on the roof of my car. His abs are poking out between his shirt and jeans again. He has to be doing this on purpose.

"You should go," I say, and run my car key down the center of his chest. I'm flirting, and I can't help it.

"I should," he grins.

I'm getting hot, and he can tell.

"Okay," I say, "I need to go." I start to slide into the driver's seat.

"You shredded the shit out of your axe on stage tonight." He grins, "I've never seen a girl play guitar like that."

I smirk at him. Surprise. He's a sexist pig. Oh wait, we determined he was a pig earlier. This is just further proof. I narrow my eyes into harsh slits.

"Shit," he continues, ignorant of his piggishness, "I've never seen a dude play like you."

I can't tell if he's back pedaling. But the way his eyes are roaming over my low cut top, tonguing my cleavage with his rapacious gaze, I suspect all this guitar talk is just a way to get into my pants. Not that I'm entirely opposed to the idea.

I sigh and smile, "What do you want?"

He ignores my question, "You stole that eight finger lick in that solo near the end of your set tonight from Jennifer Batten, didn't you?"

Now I'm intrigued. I frown, "How the hell do you know about Jennifer Batten?" Only old dude guitar players and girl guitar players know who Jennifer Batten is.

"I went to a guitar clinic she did in my hometown when I was like fourteen. I totally crushed on her after that for the longest time."

"She's old enough to be your mom!" I'm not sure how old Kellan is, probably not more than twenty-five or maybe twenty-eight. Either way, Jennifer Batten is at least twice his age.

"So?" he shrugs. "You've heard her play guitar."

I'm not exactly sure what he means by that. I can't imagine a guy like Kellan ever looking at a woman over the age of twenty-five for the rest of his life because he won't have to. He's going to have his pick of nubile young women until his dying day, I would bet.

Which begs the question of why he's hanging out with me? Sure, at twenty-two, I'm in his age bracket, but I'm hardly a pick. I'm a newly dumped rocker chick with no money, no place to live, and garbage bags for luggage.

It doesn't make any sense.

Nothing about tonight makes any sense.

Which is why I need to be alone right now. I don't want to make things worse by doing something stupid with Kellan. I know I'll regret it. I'm going to have more emotional baggage than all my possessions put together after my tornado break up with Scott and Skin Trade. I might be fun company tonight, but the hurt and heartbreak are going to knock me down tomorrow. I won't be any fun then. Kellan is not going to want to stick around.

Who would?

I drop my head as memories of Scott's betrayal flood my mind, chilling me from head to toe. My long hair curtains my face as the pain seizes me. My entire body prickles like an infected wound. I don't want Kellan watching me as war rages in my guts. I feel physically sick, like I'm coming down with the flu. I can't decide if my chills are from the night air, which has noticeably cooled, or the sadness I told myself I wasn't going to have to deal with.

With great effort, I mumble, "You…should go."

"You okay?" Kellan asks gently, brushing hair away from my eyes so he can see my face.

I accidentally glance at his eyes, those smoldering eyes that pinned my heart to the stage over an hour ago. They have the burning ember look of a flame top '56 Sunburst Strat. Everything about this guy seems to be on fire, and it's catching.

I'm getting hot again.

His heat is burning away my sadness.

He leans toward me and I feel his warmth.

I welcome it.

A second ago, my heart had frozen into a dark broken thing, smashed into cold black chunks by Scott's betrayal. But Kellan's burning eyes staring into mine ignite a flame in my chest that I secretly feared might be dormant for years to come. Warmth flows from this smoldering man into me.

Adrenalin rush.

I want him.

I want Kellan.

The next thing I know, he's feathering kisses across my lips and I'm desperately clutching his t-shirt, pulling him into me. His passion burns away all of the frigid pain in my bones. Kellan's fire fills me, warms me, consumes me.

I don't want to be cold tonight.

Not tonight.

I fall into his arms.

His hands slide down my back and grip my ass. He pulls me into his hips and grinds against me.

His tongue invades me and heat pours down my throat. I drink him in. His fire fills my belly. I'm lost in his arms, and never want to be found.

I moan into his mouth and he swallows my desire.

A hand wedges between my legs, and forces its way up to the crotch of my leather pants.

"I want this," he seethes between his teeth, hissing into my ear. "I want to take you home."

I'm stopped short by his sudden rugged behavior.

I can't remember the last time I had sex with Scott. But I know one thing.

I haven't been turned on like this…ever.

My eyes narrow as Kellan's fiery gaze burns into me. Heat rushes up from between my legs and broils up around my neck. My abdomen is suddenly a furnace as I feel desire ignite me.

Need.

I'm ready to combust in the arms of this perfectly handsome man.

I shake my head.

No.

This is all a lie. How could I feel what I'm feeling for Kellan less than two hours after Scott betrayed me and broke my heart? No, this will never be more than a rebound fling, a cruel hoax. It can't fix my heartbreak.

Only time will.

If I let things with Kellan go any further, I'm going to get hurt twice as bad as I already am.

That's the last thing I need.

I mean, I don't even know the first thing about Kellan. I don't even know his last name.

His strong hand squeezes the wet softness between my legs, the fire that burns beneath my leather pants. I moan. It feels *sooo* good. Maybe just for tonight…

Just tonight.

"I'm gonna make you mine…" he growls into my ear, his voice low in his throat. "…all mine."

The warm glow inside my belly goes from hot buttered rum to needles and glass in a split second. I freeze at those words. Scott's words. He was like this in the beginning. Hot, passionate, dominating. When the heat and passion faded, his dominating nature didn't.

I'm not going to fall for it twice.

I push Kellan away from me. In a strong voice, I say, "Stop. Now."

He pulls back from me slowly. "You okay, Vic?"

No he didn't. "Don't call me Vic," I glare at him. "Ever."

The icicles return in my chest and I know this has all been a lie. A cold, hard lie.

He backs away and says in a vaguely confused voice, "Sorry, hey, what —?"

I slide into the driver's seat of my Altima. "I need to go."

He's resting one hand on the open door and I can't pull it closed.

"Hey," he says softly, "I'm sorry. I kinda thought Victory was your stage name or something. I wasn't sure what to call you."

I scowl, "Then maybe you should've asked?" I pull my car door closed hard, expecting him to resist. Controlling guys always fight you on everything.

Surprisingly, he doesn't resist and my door slams shut loudly. I jam my key in the ignition and start the car.

He knocks gently on my window. He's now kneeling beside my car. The look on his face is different. Not Mr. Hot & Dominant any longer. It's that same look he had earlier, an innocent bashful kid who wants to pick me flowers on the way home from school.

I roll my eyes as I roll my window down. "What?" I say, exasperated.

He leans his forearms on my doorframe, and rests his chin on them.

Why does he have to be so cute? I hate cute. I feel the ice melting again. Thankfully, the door is between us. I buckle my seat belt for safety. I don't want to get in an accident with Kellan.

He smiles, "What about that pizza you promised for helping you move?"

"Some other time?" I try to smile, but I know I'm grimacing.

His eyes search mine for awhile.

I really hope he lets this go. At least for tonight.

"Okay," he says softly. He stands and pats the roof of my car. "Drive safe."

I watch longingly as he strolls to his motorcycle. I'm pretty sure there's an all night pizza place somewhere in L.A. Maybe I should at least buy him a slice?

No, I need to be alone. I better go.

I drive off into the darkness.

Alone.

It's for the best.

Chapter 25

VICTORY

The Hollywood sign shines down on the twisty neighborhood street where I park my Altima. I know the secret trail that leads up to the sign high on the hillside is only a block away. I consider hiking up to it in the darkness because it has a great view of all of Los Angeles and it seems like the perfect place to ponder my future. But at this point, I'm too tired to move.

Expensive houses surround me and there's little to no traffic up here. I don't like the idea of spending the night in my car in the middle of Hollywood, but I can't afford to waste gas driving to someplace safer like Pasadena or the Pacific Palisades.

This will have to do.

A glimmer of city lights flicker through the screen of neighborhood trees circling my car. It seems so peaceful this far away from Sunset

Boulevard, which has traffic on it 24/7, like most streets in L.A.

I'd love to own a mansion in the Hollywood Hills someday. I smile to myself. I already have one. It's a bit cramped and doesn't have a bathroom, but it does have a great view and bucket seats.

After I left Kellan at The Cobra Lounge earlier, I parked on a side street six blocks away and started calling all my L.A. friends. I called everyone I could think of to ask for a couch to crash on.

Nobody answered.

Considering that my closest friends (Rex, Bobby, and Scott) are now my worst enemies, I'm not surprised. Unfortunately for me, I let my friendships outside the band fade over the last two years as I focused everything on my relationship with Scott and building up Skin Trade. The consequence is that my forgotten friends have most likely demoted my phone calls from "Oh, it's Victory. I should answer this," to "Oh, it's Victory. I don't have to answer this. I can call her back later. Much later."

I can't blame my old friends. I was the one who drifted away. Of course, when I woke up this morning, I would've sworn that Rex, Bobby, and Scott would always have my back, and you can't be friends with everybody.

I guess I chose wrong.

Time to start working on my old L.A. friendships again. The idea lifts my spirits. I'll start first thing in the morning.

I recline my seat back as far as it will go, which is nowhere because of the Marshall 4x12 speaker cabinet in the backseat. And my Line 6 and Marshall head take up the passenger seat. I guess I'll be sleeping sitting up.

This blows.

Looking for distraction, I turn on my Altima's radio. The first thing I hear is the middle of Sex Type Thing by Stone Temple Pilots. A sex type thing is

(*Kellan*)

the last thing I want to think about right now.

The next song I hear is Young In Love, the hit ballad by pop diva Layce. Poor timing, girl. I've got a ways to go until I'm young in love again. If it ever happens. I have a whole lotta heartbreak to work through first.

I twist the dial again.

It lands on Gangnam Style by Psy. I'm instantly grinning. That wacky tune always puts me in a good mood.

Maybe I need to call Lucas and Logan Summer. I know they haven't forgotten me. They'd totally let me crash at their place, but it's two hours away in San Diego. I'd have to drive back and forth for work. Not an option I can even remotely afford.

Man, I'm too close to broke for comfort.

That's when it hits me. All those people after the show at The Cobra Lounge who asked me about guitar lessons. I should've been taking down phone numbers. They're all potential paying students. I could be calling them all up tomorrow about giving them lessons instead of hoping they'll look me up online and get back to me. But I blew them all off thinking I didn't have time for them.

Hindsight is always perfect.

Oh well.

Maybe I need to take a few days off work, drive to Bakersfield, and stay with my dad while I get my head together and figure out where to live and what to do next. I know Dad would love to see me and have me hang around the shop and work on cars with him. But that's almost as far as San Diego and Dad will try to force gas or rent money on me, which I know he can't afford. It'll also feel like running away from L.A. when what I should be doing is putting a new band together.

On the radio, Gangnam Style transitions into Roar by Katy Perry. I crank up the volume. I've loved this song since the first time I heard it, no matter how jealous I am of

(*sing*)

Katy for getting to sing it.

(*singsingsing*)

I get shivers when she sings the first verse. It's like she's singing about Scott, or someone in her own life who was just like Scott, someone who pushed her around and told her what to do until it nearly broke her spirit. But she didn't give up, didn't let that person break her. She got angry, she learned to believe in herself, and she showed everyone how strong she was.

The chorus of Roar unfolds and I feel my body tingle.

Sing it, sister.

(*don't sing*)

I can roar too. Whenever I plug my guitar into an amp and crank it up, I'm *way* fucking louder than a lion.

(*never ever ever sing*)

A wicked grin spreads across my face. I'm not letting Scott the Bastard get me down. First thing tomorrow I'm going to show my claws to the world and roar my ass off with my Fender and my Marshall.

(*sing*)

I refuse to give up on my dreams of being a big time

(*singsingsing*)

guitar hero.

Katy Perry repeats the chorus of Roar, and I can imagine the way I'd play her vocal melody on my guitar if I was on stage with her in front of a hundred thousand screaming fans while my guitar wails out the notes at a million decibels.

(*SIIINNNNGGG!!!!*)

I'm not giving up on my dream. It all starts tomorrow.

Tonight, I'm staying right here.

I punch the power button on the radio, shutting it off.

I fold my arms across my chest, determined to go to sleep. It doesn't take long to realize it's cold in my car. I can't run the engine all night to keep the heater going.

I groan and pop the trunk with the inside latch. I stomp around to the back of the car and fish through my garbage bags.

Yeah, I'm a bag lady.

So what.

Pillows! Why didn't I think to take the pillows from our bed? I mean, Scott's bed. The "our" part of it is ancient history. I should've taken the blankets too. Let Scott sleep on a bare mattress. I consider going back to the apartment. Scott will probably be there. I don't ever want to see his face again.

Scratch that idea.

I remember Kellan saying he wanted to take me home. *So* not what I need right now. I sigh audibly and smile to myself. Maybe…no. It would be the stupidest thing I could possibly do right now. Lucky for me, I don't have his number, he doesn't have mine, and I never have to worry about him again, thank goodness. He's way too confusing anyway. I don't care how hot he is.

And he called me Vic.

Some stupid voice in my head says, He didn't know. It was an honest mistake.

I don't want to think about it.

I bet his bed is really warm, the voice giggles coquettishly.

I don't want to think about it.

Really warm…

I DON'T WANT TO THINK ABOUT IT!!!

I yank a hoodie and a pair of baggy sweats out of the garbage bag in my trunk and slam it shut. Damn it, I'm still wearing my stage costume. I'm not going to sleep in a studded leather bra and leather jacket. And skin tight lace up leather pants which are sticky from sweating in them dancing around onstage. If I spend the night in them, I worry they won't come off in the morning without glue remover.

This is lame.

I growl as I walk back to the driver's door and reach down to pop the trunk latch again. Then I sift through my garbage bags until I find a baby tee and my yoga pants. Why didn't I change at the apartment when I had the chance? Because stupid Scott might have shown up at any second.

Stupid, stupid Scott.

Now I have to figure out where to change my clothes. I could change in the street, but there's too many streetlights, and the ever present orange L.A. glow. And rapists hiding in every bush.

I'll have to change in the car.

Peeling off a pair of lace up leather pants in the driver's seat when you can't recline the seat is something best left to experts, or a contortionist. I fumble my way through it, hoping no one is filming this, because if anybody's watching, they're getting a free show. All I ask is they cut me in on the deal when they sell the footage to TMZ. Who am I kidding? Nobody gives a shit about seeing my sorry ass in underwear.

Kellan does…

SHUT UP!!!!

When I'm in my yoga pants, extra sweat pants, baby tee, and hoodie, I slide on the pair of fake Ugg boots I bought at DSW. Now I'm hot from all the exertion. But it won't take long to get cold, so I pull my leather jacket over me like a blanket. I remember I'm still wearing my make up.

I don't even want to deal with it.

I reach into my purse and pull out my twelve dollar Tac Force rape knife. The rainbow blade pops open when you press a button on the back. Yes, the blade is rainbow colored and cost me an extra three dollars, but I'm a girl, and I'm worth it. I fold the blade closed and clutch it to my chest. So far, I've never used it on a rapist, but you never know.

I close my eyes and attempt to sleep.

In the silence, thoughts of warm Kellan keep teasing me. I'm never getting to sleep if I keep thinking about him.

I turn the radio on again. This time for moral support. Music has always been there for me when nothing else was.

Tonight is no exception.

Wrecking Ball by Miley Cyrus drifts out of the radio speakers. Whoever runs the universe couldn't have picked a better song to play for me right at this moment.

I remember watching the Wrecking Ball video with the camera right on Miley's face while she opened her broken heart to the world and cried out those lyrics. It really affected me when I saw it the first time. When I watched the director's cut, which doesn't have the cheesy footage of a naked Miley straddling a swinging wrecking ball but instead holds the camera on her tear stained face for the entire song, I was so touched by her vulnerability, I too was crying by the end of the video. There are a couple points in it where she is so overcome by emotion, she can't even sing the lyrics to the song. I remember wondering what prick douche bag had done that to her, and when was he going to be executed for being such a total ass.

As Wrecking Ball plays, I'm smacked in the face by the line about wanting to open up your boyfriend's heart and he pays you back by breaking yours. That describes Scott to a tee.

Images of him and his ugly mirrored face at The Cobra Lounge tonight assault me. Memories of all the times we fought because Scott said I was trying to get too close or was being too needy flood my brain. So many fights. For what? For nothing. Tonight he smashed everything we had all to pieces. As quick as Miley's wrecking ball.

I feel you, girlfriend.

All men are wrecking balls. Show me one who isn't.

I laugh cry as an image suddenly pops into my brain. Scott standing in front of a brick wall as a wrecking ball falls right at his face. Splat goes his tomato head.

Yeah, that's what Scott deserves.

I can feel tears sliding down my cheeks. Good. I won't have any makeup left to wash off by morning.

Stupid Scott.

Stupid fucking Scott.

I can't believe he did this.

I start sobbing a few seconds later.

There's nothing funny about how I feel.

Every muscle in my body tenses at the same time as agony spikes into me. My stomach clenches and I try to fold into myself. I want to disappear. Sadness and hurt fight it out inside me. Confusion crashes into me. My world is now upside down.

This is going to be a long night.

The only thing I have to help me through it is my music.

I hope my car battery doesn't run out before morning.

RUN 2

Chapter 26

KELLAN

WHAM!

I take a hard shot to the ribs, but block most of it with the side of my elbow. A stiff right hand bullets toward my chin, but we're in such close quarters, my left fist deflects it when I launch my arm to the heavens. It connects with the edge of his jaw.

He staggers back in the sand and shakes his head.

"Want more of that shit?" I grin around my mouth guard.

My good buddy Dubs Moses spits out his mouth piece and holds it in his gloved fingers, "Damn, Kellan. You got lead in your glove?"

Anybody else would've been out cold if I hit them that hard. Dubs isn't anybody.

I chide, "Dude, don't be a pussy. You're still on your feet." I don't mention that my ribs are pounding where he connected a second ago.

For the past hour, we've been sparring on the soft sand of Venice Beach. We're both sweaty and tired. It's early morning, the sun is barely awake, and we're both wearing bright red pads on our fists, feet, and heads.

If we didn't wear the pads, the lifeguards would've called the beach cops and had us hauled off for fighting. The pads make it obvious we're just practicing. Plus, we know the lifeguards on duty this morning. They let us stay. If the beach was actually crowded, they'd ask us to stop sparring or do it someplace else. Since it's empty, we got in plenty of punching.

After I catch my breath, I say, "Ready for more punishment?"

Dubs grins, "Careful, son. You get all cocky and your shit gonna get knocked out."

"You wish."

Dubs is a good buddy of mine. He wears his hair in inch long Afro twists, which at the moment sprout from the top of his red head gear. He likes to tell people his ebony skin is Africa black. I'm not quite sure what he means, but his skin is super dark and he says it makes him more mysterious, which always makes me laugh. He plays bass in a Reggae band and I like to give him shit because he doesn't have dreads. I call him a Reggae poser but he always tells me you don't have to be Rasta to be Reggae.

Dubs also freelances as a personal trainer. His impressive muscled physique is his calling card and draws in plenty of clients. Most of them are bored rich women who live in Santa Monica or Venice and love his dangerously flirty personality. I'm always telling him he should charge ten times what he does and fuck them instead.

Like the brothers in the band Bad Brains, Dubs has a deep interest in a wide range of music, from jazz to funk to hard rock and metal. And he's damn good on bass in all those styles. Me and him have jammed tons of times but it never pans out into us forming a long-term band. I can't blame him. His Reggae band actually gets paid for playing shows, unlike most metal bands we know.

Aside from music, the thing Dubs and I talk about the most is women.

Still holding his mouth piece in hand, he smudges sweat from his face with the side of his elbow and asks, "You bang anybody last night?"

I chuckle, "You stalling? Too tired to fight more?" I put my mouth piece back in and dance in the sand while circling my fists Rocky Balboa style.

He laughs, "What I tell you about gettin' cocky, Rocky?"

I jeer, "Throw something, bitch."

He puts in his mouth piece and we hammer away at each other for another five minutes. We're both exhausted and our punches are getting slower. At one point, I throw a wide right. He dodges it and I stumble into the sand, rolling smoothly onto my back.

I could get up, but I don't feel like it. I grunt, "I'm done."

He drops his ass into the sand next to me and leans back on his hands, his legs outstretched. He asks, "Call it?"

"Yup."

We smack hands and I sit up.

I ask, "*You* bang anybody last night?"

"Band practice."

"I thought you guys had groupies at all your rehearsals waiting to suck your dicks afterwards."

"Naw, man. They suck dick while we playin'."

I laugh heartily. "Now I know why all you Reggae bass players wear your guitars so high. I always thought it looked fucking lame."

"Easy access, son," Dubs chuckles.

"Dude, the only women at your rehearsals are your moms."

He frowns, "You talkin' shit 'bout my momma?"

I laugh. "You know I love your mom."

"All right then."

"Cuz she loves my dick," I blurt lewdly, "especially when I give it to her hard and fast."

"You did *not* just say you is fuckin' my momma!"

"I think I did," I grin and spring to my feet. I sprint as fast as I can down the beach, heading toward the hard sand touching the water.

Dubs is after me like lightning. We pound sand for about fifty yards, shoulder to shoulder, trying to outpace each other. It's an even race until we both run out of gas.

We slow to a stop and we're both huffing and puffing, bent over, hands on our knees, for at least a minute.

"I smoked your ass, son!" Dubs shouts as he straightens up, clenching a fist in my face.

"Ha!" I blurt. "The only thing you can smoke is herb, my man."

"True that," Dubs chuckles. "You hungry?"

"Yeah. Let's get some food on the boardwalk."

We walk back to our pile of stuff and shove our pads into duffle bags. I drink the last half of my big water bottle in five long swallows.

Before drinking from his own water bottle, Dubs asks, "Who you nailin' tonight?"

"Probably that chick Savannah who gave me her number last night."

We walk across the sand toward the buildings on the boardwalk.

Dubs asks, "She the one you saw play at The Cobra?"

"Naw, that was Victory."

"Shit, playah, does every girl you ball have a stripper name?"

"Usually," I grin.

"When you nailin' Victory?"

"I don't know, man. I don't have her number."

"Yeah, but you know what band she in, right? Track her down that way."

I shake my head, "She got kicked out. And I don't know her last name."

Dubs laughs, "You *never* know their last names."

I snicker, "True that."

"Did you Facebook her?"

I nod, "I couldn't find shit."

"You think Victory her real name?"

I laugh, "Do you?"

He chuckles, "Naw. Probably Sally or Mavis or some shit."

We walk to a Mexican taqueria on the Venice boardwalk and buy breakfast burritos. We eat them sitting on top of a cement picnic table facing the beach, watching the surfers slide along the waves as the rising sun warms our backs.

I chew a bite of my burrito silently.

Dubs asks, "You thinkin' about that stripper girl, ain't you?"

"Victory?" I huff, "Yeah."

"Forget about her. There's a hundred other Hollywood hotties waiting to climb your stripper pole tonight, dawg."

I snicker, "Yeah."

But I can't stop thinking about Victory.

I wonder if I'll ever see her again.

Chapter 27

VICTORY

I scream for my life.

"OOOWWW!!!"

Someone stabs an icepick into the side of my neck, jolting me awake.

Pure terror floods my veins.

I'm being attacked in my car.

I never should've slept here.

FUCKING SCOTT!!!

A second icepick stabs the other side of my neck and I'm wide awake behind the wheel of my Altima. My arms flail at my attacker as I sit bolt upright in my seat and scream again.

"OOOOWWWW!!!!"

Where's my rainbow rape knife?! I must've dropped it when I was asleep!! I need to find it so I can start stabbing my attacker before I'm dead!!

Wait.

Clarity sinks in now that I'm fully awake.

It's not icepicks. It's my neck. It's locked up like a bank vault. I must have slept on it all wrong.

I drop into my seat and jolts shoot from my shoulders to my scalp. My neck throbs like crazy. I never knew you could get cramps in your scalp.

Fucking Scott.

Wow, I can't move without more shooting pain. I do my best to take in my surroundings only using my eyes.

The blue sky is bright overhead and the sun is up, but this part of the Hollywood Hills is still in cool blue shadows. Wake Me Up Before You Go-Go by Wham! plays quietly on the radio.

Ha, ha, DJ Universe.

Good thing George Michael didn't drain my car battery.

I don't know what time I finally conked out last night. I cried over my breakup with Scott and the band for hours while listening to sappy lovesick pop songs. Thoughts of Kellan constantly got in the way of my grieving. I don't know if that made things worse or better. Either way, I was torn between the north and south poles of pop: Boys Boys Boys on the top of the world (thank you, Lady Gaga and Kellan) and Heartbreak Hotel on the bottom (thank you, Elvis Presley, but no thanks to you, Scott).

Anyway, none of that matters now. Scott and Kellan are both behind me for good. I'm starting a new chapter in my life.

My name isn't Victory Payne for nothing.

I remember that I never washed my makeup off last night. I need to check my mascara. I must be a raccoon at this point.

When I reach up to adjust the rearview mirror, my neck sings with exquisite pain as the icepicks go crazy.

I drop my arm and sit frozen in place once again. I'm afraid to move and start the icepicks stabbing again.

But I need to move. It'll loosen things up. A walk will help. I carefully reach over and open the car door. More stabbing pain, but I get the door open and step gingerly onto the street in my fake Uggs and PJ's.

I remove my leather jacket with infinite care and drop it into the car.

Today is going to be hot. The morning is already warm.

I nearly lock myself out of my car when I remember my keys are still in the ignition. Do I leave them and risk having someone come along and steal my car? After the way my Altima treated my neck last night, I don't know that I care.

Screw my keys.

I hope some joy rider wrecks my car.

I slam the door shut, which is a mistake. The icepicks go to work on my right shoulder.

I wince as the pain bites into me.

The only solution is to start walking.

I take a few tentative steps away from my car when I remember my Fender is in the trunk with all my clothes. And my amps are in the seats. Shit. Everything I own is in my car.

I go back and carefully open the door. My first instinct is to lean inside and take the keys out, but I'm afraid if I do the glassy muscles in my neck will shatter into a thousand pieces, causing my head to fall off. Not that that sounds like a bad thing at the moment. Sudden death seems preferable to the pain I'm feeling. My entire back, neck, and shoulders are slabs of hard clay leaking acid into my body. If I don't start moving, I'm going to lock up on the spot like a statue. Birds will roost on my head and poop in my hair.

Time to move.

I lean into the car reaching for my keys and my shoulder threatens to lock. That's not gonna work. I have to sit down like I'm getting in. When my butt drops into the seat, lightning bolts shoot from the base of my spine to the crown of my head.

What a way to start my day.

I twist my keys free and carefully climb out of my car. After locking it, I walk old lady slow down the street.

The houses are all expensive looking. So are the SUVs and cars in the driveways.

Luckily it's Saturday morning, or else people would be on their way to work, walking out to their cars and looking at me funny. I'm so glad I changed out of my black leather rock & roll assassin costume last night. Otherwise, I'm sure someone would think I was a hooker and call the cops. I'd be picked up for pandering and likely spend the day downtown. Even if that didn't happen, I never would've been able to walk in my hooker heels with all the icepicks in my back. The fake Uggs are way better. So what if I'm strolling through a strange neighborhood in my pajamas?

Two kids in red and blue soccer uniforms come running out of one of the houses, followed by a mom in a tight fitting pastel pink velvet jogging suit and platinum blonde hair. The mom is a Hollywood cliche. I can't decide if she dresses this way to be ironic or if she takes herself seriously.

"Hey, mom," the little girl says, "That lady is wearing pajamas outside! Doesn't she know pajamas are only for inside?"

The little girl isn't helping my mood any. I flash a fake smile at her and think to myself, Your mom is wearing pajamas too, you little weasel!

The boy asks, "Mom, why is she walking like a zombie?"

"Don't say that, Tyler," the mom chastises. She glances at me like I might be a kidnapper.

Tyler asks, "Should I get Dad's gun and shoot her, in case she's a zombie?"

I'm never having kids.

"Tyler!" the mom shouts. "That's not nice! She's not a zombie. Now, get in the car. We're going to be late for your game."

"Mom, why is she wearing clown makeup?" the girl asks.

"I'm with the circus!" I shout angrily.

Tyler frowns, "What circus? Is there a circus in town? Mom, can we go?"

The mom hustles Tyler and his sister into the back of their SUV. She gives me a concerned look, "Are you okay, honey?"

I grimace, "Slept in my car."

She frowns like she's skeptical.

"My neck cramped up," I hiss through clenched teeth.

She walks toward me and stops a few feet away. "Do you need anything? Are you in trouble?"

Her obvious concern belies her plastic looks and catches me off guard. It all comes pouring out when I say, "My boyfriend dumped me last night and kicked me out of our apartment and our band. I don't have any place to go."

"Mom!" Tyler leans out of the backseat window. "We're going to be late!"

"Hold on a second, Tyler," she barks, then turns to me. "Do you need help?"

I smear tears from my cheeks and cough when my neck muscles slice together painfully. "I'm okay. I'll be fine."

"You don't look fine. Are you sure you don't need anything?"

She's so genuinely concerned, I can't help myself. I say, "I really need to pee."

"Do you want to come inside and use the bathroom?"

"Are you sure?" I say nervously. I'll pee in someone's bushes if I have to.

"Yes, I'm sure."

"Mom!" Tyler shouts. "We're going to be late!"

"Hush up, Tyler! Your game can wait!"

"No it can't! If we're late, I don't get to play!"

"Tyler!" the mom shouts, ending all argument.

Tyler sighs loudly and his head sinks back into the SUV.

The mom looks at me, "My name is Stephanie. You can call me Steph." She extends her hand, tentatively at first, like maybe I have the plague. "Oh, what am I doing. You're fine." She practically grabs my hand from my side and shakes it.

"Ow!" I wince.

She grimaces. "Are you sure you're okay?"

Embarrassed, I say, "Like I said, I slept in my car. My neck is cramped up really bad."

Steph nods, "That's the worst. I hate sleeping in the car. I haven't done that since I was a teenager. What's your name again?"

"It's Victory. My name is Victory."

"That's a nice name," she smiles. "Let's get you inside."

"Mom!" Tyler shouts, "I'm going to miss the game!"

"Hush up, Tyler! You and your sister wait in the car."

Steph leads me into the house, one arm around my shoulders like I'm a decrepit old hag. At the moment, I feel like one.

The two story house is professionally decorated. Although everything looks expensive, it's also inviting. Wow, when can I move in? I hope those kids realize how good they have it. Maybe Steph can adopt me and I can be their big sister. I'll teach them music in exchange for room and board.

Steph leads me to a guest bathroom. The sink is marble and rests on top of a curly spiral of iron. Fancy golden decorative candles sit on the window sill above the sink. There's a bidet next to the toilet. A flat screen TV mounted on the wall faces them both. I've never seen a TV in a bathroom before.

There's a knock on the door. Through the door, Steph says, "I brought you a clean towel to wash up."

I open the door and smile at her.

She's holding a fluffy towel thicker than a down comforter. "Will this work?"

I take it from her, "Yeah. It's perfect."

"I have facial cleanser in the cabinet next to the sink. It'll be gentle on your skin." She examines my face carefully, "I wish I had skin like yours, Victory." She shakes her head. "You can't be more than eighteen," she smiles.

I do my best to grin, "I'm twenty-two, but thanks."

"Well, get busy. Otherwise I think Tyler might go looking for his dad's gun so he can protect me from zombies." She chuckles and is about to pull the door closed.

I ask, "Do you need to take your kids to their game? I can totally just pee quick and get out of your hair. I don't have to wash up."

Steph waves a dismissive hand, "You go ahead and wash up. Tyler can wait. Aubrey's game doesn't start for two hours, so she's fine. But if Tyler is late, he's late. Technically, he should be sitting out today anyway because he thought it would be fun to use his father's golf clubs to behead my rose bushes. His father insisted the boy is merely showing an interest in golf. Yeah, right," Steph chuckles. "Can I get you anything to eat? A sandwich or something?"

I'm going to cry, but I don't.

"You know what?" Steph says, "I'm going to veto my husband on this one. Tyler needs to learn not to be a rose murderer. Go ahead and take a shower. Get cleaned up. We have time. I'll get the kids out of the car and make you something to eat."

A lone tear dribbles down my cheek. I can't help it. Steph is too nice for words. All I can do is nod silently.

"There's body wash and shampoo and conditioner in the cupboard with the face wash." She wrinkles her nose. "None of it's the cheap stuff. It'll feel good on your skin. And you'll feel better under that hot water. We have a big tank, so you won't run out. Stay in as long as you want. I'll get you when the food is ready."

Steph smiles at me and gently pulls the bathroom door shut. "Enjoy."

The latch clicks softly and I'm sobbing on my knees on the soft bathroom rug.

It's amazing how a random act of extreme kindness can do that to you.

Chapter 28

VICTORY

"Mommy, is Victory our new babysitter?" Aubrey asks, staring at me while I eat the turkey sandwich Steph made for me.

Aubry sits beside me at the sun drenched island bar in the middle of Steph's gigantic kitchen. The sun has crested the hills.

Aubry is six and a half. I know because she's told me three times since I came out of the shower. She's super cute and asks a million questions.

"No, honey," Steph says before taking a sip of her iced tea. "You already have a babysitter."

Steph glances out the windows at the sun bright day and says, "It's going to be a hot one today."

"Mmm-hmm," I mumble while chewing on my sandwich. I'm used to the heat. I grew up in the desert, in Bakersfield, which is hotter than L.A.

The bar where I sit is easily four times the size of the studio apartment I shared with Scott until last night. The semi circle countertop is polished stone, I'm not sure what kind, but it looks expensive and it seats eight. Six light fixtures dangle from the ceiling above the counter, and each one has a fancy glass shade that looks hand made. The cabinets in the kitchen are all cream colored wood. I can't figure out where the refrigerator is until Steph opens one of the big cabinets in the wall, which turns out to be the fridge. I thought all refrigerators were white metal and people stuck bills and stuff to them with magnets.

Steph asks, "Victory, would you like a glass of almond milk?"

"I do!" Aubrey pleads.

"I was asking Victory," Steph chastises gently. "You had yours at breakfast."

"Oooh!" Aubrey pouts.

Steph ignores her and looks at me, holding up a carton.

"I've never had almond milk."

"It's good," Steph smiles, "I'll pour you a glass. You look like you need it."

The almond milk tastes like vanilla and I like it. I finish my sandwich and blot my lips with the cloth napkin Steph gave me. The only place I ever see cloth napkins is at restaurants. Steph is way classier than any mom I've ever known. She's way richer too.

"Would you look at the time?" Steph says after glancing at the fancy clock on the far wall. It's made from a piece of rock that matches the countertop and has dimensional metal numbers attached all the way around, almost like a name badge on a car.

I've never seen a clock that matches the counters.

Steph smiles and takes my empty plate and puts it in the dishwasher. "I really need to get Aubry to her game."

"Oh, cool," I say. "I should be going anyway."

"Tyler!" Steph hollers, "Let's go!"

Tyler is sitting on the gigantic leather couch in the room connected to the kitchen, playing video games on a movie theater sized flat screen TV. "I missed my game, remember! It's already over," he complains.

"You're going to watch your sister's game," Steph commands.

"I don't want to watch Aubrey play!" he moans. Explosions boom from the TV as Tyler blows up spaceships and kills aliens.

"You're going whether you want to or not!" Steph says in a strong voice. "Turn off your Playstation."

"Fine!" Tyler grumbles, drops his game controller on the couch, and lumbers around toward the kitchen, looking suspiciously zombie-like.

"Put your controller away," Steph orders. "I don't want to sit on it again. The last time I did, I had a bruise on my butt for a week!"

Tyler does as ordered but sighs heavily as if his mom just asked him to re-roof the house.

Steph smiles at me like everything is normal and sighs herself, "Ready?"

I stand up and push my barstool under the counter. I would do more to show my gratitude, but Steph does everything before I have a chance.

Aubry slides off her stool and runs out of the kitchen.

"Aubry!" Steph barks at her back, "Did you go to the bathroom?"

"Noooo!" Aubry calls out from the other room.

"Then go to the bathroom!"

I hear what I think is the guest bathroom door close a second later.

I say to Steph, "You make motherhood look so easy."

She chuckles, "It's all an act. Besides, I've had practice. Tyler, go wait in the car."

He trudges out of the room and moans, "I don't want to go. I missed my game!"

Steph rolls her eyes then smiles at me, "Is there anything else I can get you, Victory? A banana for the road?" Before I can object, she peels one from the bunch in the fruit bowl on the counter top and hands it to me.

"Thanks. I can't tell you how much I appreciate all this."

"Don't worry about it," she smiles and glances around. In a low voice she says, "I didn't want to talk with the kids in the room, but are you okay?" She's got this compassionate look on her face that makes me want to unload my life story on her.

I'm so grateful for her genuine interest. But I'm afraid if I start talking, I won't stop. And she has to take her kids to soccer. "I'm fine, really," I say way more confidently than I feel. "I can take care of myself."

"You're not in any kind of trouble, are you?"

I shake my head, "No. Nothing serious. I just need to find a new apartment. I can manage."

She levels a serious motherly look at me similar to the one I saw her use with Tyler and Aubrey many times this morning, "Are you sure?"

I grin, "I'm fine. Really."

"I went to the bathroom," Aubrey says, standing at the hallway entrance to the kitchen.

"And we're off!" Steph smiles at me.

We walk out to her driveway together.

Steph asks, "Where is your car parked, Victory?"

"Oh, a couple blocks from here."

Steph eyes me suspiciously, "I'll drive you. Hop in." When Steph opens her door, she starts yelling, "Tyler! No more Angry Birds on my iPhone! In my purse, now!" She holds out an expectant hand.

Tyler hands it over with a scowl, "But I had fifty thousand points!"

Steph ignores him and grins at me, "He's a goblin. I don't know where he came from."

I giggle and climb into the front passenger seat.

Steph starts the car.

From the back seat, Aubry says, "Can you play my Kidz Bop CD, Mommy?"

"Sure, honey," Steph says and pushes a disc into the player. The Kidz Bop version of One Direction's Best Song Ever plays as Steph backs the car out of the driveway.

When the chorus starts, Aubry sings along quietly to herself, but changes the lyrics to, "You are the best mom ever!"

I glance back at Aubry and see that she's looking out the window, singing simply because she feels like it. It's obvious she's not doing it to get anyone's attention.

Steph turns to me, her eyes damp, and mumbles, "That's why I'm a mom."

I get choked up too. Maybe my die hard music career dream is a waste of time and happiness is as close as your family. All I need to do first is find myself a good man like Steph did and get started. Except when I consider what I went through with Scott, maybe that's harder than building a successful music career.

Who knows?

I certainly don't.

Steph drives us up the street toward my car.

"There it is!" I point.

Steph stops the SUV beside my Altima.

I smile, "Thanks again, Steph. I wish there was some way I could repay you."

"There is," Steph says while she searches through her purse. "Here, take this."

I hold out my hand and she slips a twenty dollar bill into it. "Oh," I say, "I can't take this."

"You will, and that's final," she grins. It's a gentle smile. She's not mothering me, but she's clearly insisting. "Use it for lunch and dinner, okay?"

"Okay," I nod.

"Now, I have to get Aubrey to her game. You take care of yourself, Victory."

"I will," I giggle.

They drive off and I'm feeling a million times better than I was an hour ago. The shower at Steph's house has done wonders for my cramped neck. The icepicks are gone and the clay slabs have softened into pliable leather. I'm hoping all the cramping will be gone by the end of the day. I don't have to pee, which is good, and I have a belly full of lunch and love.

I stick my key in the lock of my Altima and turn it. It doesn't click like it usually does. It's already unlocked. I could've sworn I locked it.

Oh well.

I notice my speaker cabinet in the back and…my Marshall head is not in the front seat. Neither is my Line 6 practice amp.

Wait.

That can't be right.

I watched Kellan put them in the front seat myself last night. My speaker cabinet is in the back seat where he put it. So where did my Marshall head and Line 6 go? I don't get it.

I sit down in my car and close the door and look around thoughtfully.

I remember when I changed in the car last night, my Marshall and Line 6 were in the passenger seat, so it was super cramped changing. I remember.

I remember! They were right here!

No!

NO!

Someone broke into my car!

Someone stole my amps!

This can't be.

Fear seizes my chest.

I jump out of the car and check the trunk. It's not even latched. It's open about an inch. Rocks drop down my throat. I can't breath as I yank the garbage bags out of the trunk and drop them on the street.

I choke.

I stop breathing.

My guitar is gone.

My precious white Fender Strat.

My *baby*.

Stolen.

Panic coils around me like a big jungle snake and crushes the wind out of me.

My only guitar is gone.

My dad gave me that guitar. He bought it new when he was 18 and played it until he gave it to me for Christmas when I was seven. It's the best guitar I've ever played. Nothing can replace it.

What am I gonna do?

My first thought is to run down the street after Steph and beg for help, not that she could or would do anything. But it doesn't matter anyway.

She's long gone.

Now I am in serious trouble. I don't have enough money in the bank to replace my amps and my guitar. Not even close.

I'm screwed.

"SCOOOOTTTTT!!!" I scream at the top of my lungs.

This is totally his fault. HIS FAULT!

Fuck, fuck, FUCK!!!

What am I going to do?

I slump against the side of my car, throw my head back, and scream at the top of my lungs again.

"SCOOOOTTTT!!! YOU FUCKING PRIIIICCKKKK!!!"

Chapter 29

VICTORY

Fucking L.A.

It took less than an hour for someone to find my car in a rich neighborhood and break into it. Are there roaming packs of car thieves looking for any opportunity to make a quick score, no matter how much it hurts the victim?

Yes.

Why did I ever move here?

No!

I can't think like that.

I won't let this setback stop me. I'll find another guitar. Maybe I can borrow one. I just have to find someone who can lend me one that isn't a piece of crap. I'll make some calls later today.

Right now, I have to get to work.

Before leaving Steph's neighborhood, I change into a sleeveless Whitesnake t-shirt and tight jeans in the seat of my car. I accessorize with a selection of cheap bracelets and necklaces I have in the trunk. The fact that my jewelry wasn't stolen is proof of its value.

I apply eyeliner in my rearview mirror and run a brush through my air dried hair. It's messy, not matted. Good enough. I pull on my thrift store motorcycle boots and I'm ready to go.

Hollywood traffic on Saturday morning is as bad as any other day in L.A. I hammer my steering wheel with my hands while I wait at a stoplight on Sunset Boulevard.

"Shouldn't you people be relaxing in bed!" I shout to no one. "I have to get to work!"

Nobody cares.

Welcome to L.A.

Everyone who moves to Los Angeles learns quickly that life in L.A. is hot, expensive, grid-locked around the clock, and there is no parking. Unless you're rich, in which case, it's hot, expensive, grid-locked around the clock, and there is no parking.

There's no escaping it.

L.A. is an equal opportunity aggravator.

I finally reach guitar alley on Sunset Boulevard. It's a two block stretch in Hollywood that has about twenty guitar and music stores on both sides of the street. I don't know how they all stay in business being so close together.

The biggest store, Guitar Central, is the size of your average department store. I can get lost in that place for hours on end. On any given day, you're likely to cross paths with one or more famous musicians shopping to pick up another guitar to add to their collection.

Despite all the cars already driving the streets, it takes forever to find parking because there really are fewer people going to work on a Saturday morning, which means no free spaces in the neighborhoods.

Not long after I moved to L.A., I realized there are twice as many cars in the city as parking spaces. If people didn't drive around at all hours, there would be constant rioting over the lack of parking.

Eventually some guy in gym clothes climbs into a Jeep at the end of the street and drives off. I floor it to get to the open space before someone else swoops in to steal it.

I parallel park in the space, which is between one of nine apartment buildings on one side of the street, and old bungalows and an Elementary school on the other.

Earlier I discovered that whoever broke into my car punched out the lock on my front passenger door with a screwdriver. I can lock it from the inside, but anyone walking along with their own Craftsman brand skeleton key can easily get in.

I hope my stuff is safe out here. Not that I have any options. Or much left worth stealing. I tell myself my stuff will be fine and walk toward Sunset.

The day is heating up to a broil.

The concrete sidewalk bounces the heat back at me while the black asphalt sucks it up and saves it for later, when the sun goes down. The asphalt will hold the heat long into the night like a brick oven.

Good thing my t-shirt is sleeveless. I need to practice not sweating because my access to showers is now limited, unless I go down to Venice or Santa Monica and use the outdoor beach showers.

At least I have a swimsuit.

I may be living in it for awhile.

Despite my predicament, I still have a job that I love.

Once on Sunset, I open the door to Big Momma's Guitars. The sleigh bells hanging from a leather thong inside the door jingle my arrival. The interior is A/C cooled.

What a relief.

The walls are lined with real wood paneling that gives the shop a pleasant cedar scent. Vintage acoustic and electric guitars and basses hang from the walls, all of them recognizable to any serious collector.

Big Momma's is owned by Karen Boone and Johnny Stokes. They're both old hippies. I think they're married, but I'm not entirely sure. Neither wear rings. They're the happiest couple I've ever known, beyond perfect for each other. Lightning in a bottle.

Everyone should be so lucky.

Framed black and white photographs hang on the walls as proof of their timeless love. Each photo shows Johnny and Karen in the 1960s and 70s partying with every famous rock musician you can name from that era. Mick Jagger, Robert Plant, Joni Mitchell, David Bowie, Elton John. There's too many to list. But in every photo, Karen and Johnny ignore the superstars surrounding them. They're more interested in each other and are always pictured smiling while holding hands, or kissing each other affectionately on the cheek or romantically on the mouth, or draping their arms around each other like best friends.

"Morning, Victory," Johnny smiles at me. He's a handsome aging hippie with a trim silver goatee. Most days, like today, he wears a fringe leather vest over a variety of tie-dyed t-shirts, and often bell bottoms.

Johnny is at work behind one of the glass counters that holds a collection of guitar strings, slides, capos, and picks. A red Gibson ES-335 hollow body electric is cradled in a plush purple-furred guitar block laying on the counter. The guitar is the same one still used by Chuck Berry, and the one Marty McFly uses when he plays Johnny B. Goode in that old 80s movie Back To The Future.

Johnny B. Hippie is changing the Gibson's strings and works with the same easy patience he always exudes. Johnny is never in a hurry.

"Hey, Johnny," I smile. "Is Big Momma here?"

"Not yet," Johnny says casually. "She went to the farmer's market to buy fruits and vegetables."

I walk behind the counter and slide the bottom panel on one of the glass cases aside, stash my purse inside, and slide it shut.

Ready for work.

I work here part time. The pay isn't great, but it beats working at a coffee shop or waiting tables, and I'm closer to the music business. I cherish the homey, family atmosphere. It's low stress.

"How was your show last night?" Johnny asks.

My stomach swims with eels. I really don't want to get into it. I force a smile, "Good."

"Just good?" he chuckles. "You played at the world famous Cobra Lounge and it was just good? Man, when Karen and I played there in the sixties we thought we'd arrived."

I've heard demo records of their music from back then, like actual vinyl records. Karen and Johnny sounded amazing together. I'm surprised they didn't become more famous.

Johnny shakes his head while he tightens the tuning peg for the B string with a plastic string winder crank. "When are you gonna slow down and smell the flowers?"

"I tried. They stank," I grin.

He chuckles and looks up from the guitar, "You guys have a bad show?"

"You could say that." May as well tell him. "Scott kicked me out of the band," I sigh.

"What? You're kidding."

I shake my head.

He frowns, "That's a drag."

I nod.

Johnny's palpable sympathy gives me some perspective, like it's all a big joke that I can share with friends. It's almost funny, when I think about it.

I say, "Scott kicked me out right after the show. Show was awesome, by the way." An image of Kellan watching me from the audience playing dorky air guitar at my feet springs into memory. "Yeah, the show was all kinds of awesome. Afterward, not so much," I smirk.

Big Momma pushes aside the beads leading to the back room, which has a door to the parking lot behind the shop. Canvas bags exploding with greens hang from her arms. She chuckles, "I knew Scott wasn't worth a piss in a windstorm."

There is nothing big about Karen Boone except her heart and her personality, and maybe her boobs. She's a small, slender, curvaceous woman with dark olive skin and long curly dark gray hair she refuses to color. At my grandmother's age, Karen is still beautiful and exotic. She's Middle Eastern, but she's not entirely sure what kind. I like to think she's some kind of old world hippie Gypsy.

She walks up to Johnny and smiles, "I got Swiss Chard like you asked."

"Thank you, sweetheart," he leans down and kisses her affectionately on the mouth. He's at least a foot and a half taller than her.

Karen lingers in the kiss for a long time, her hooded eyes gazing up into Johnny's. He grins from ear to ear like a lovestruck teenager. She withdraws from him reluctantly and says, "I'll finish the rest of that later," meaning the kiss.

Johnny blushes. He's sixty something and he's blushing.

I can't believe those two have been together for decades. They give me hope that love is eternal.

If you find the right person.

Karen unloads the bag of groceries into a full sized refrigerator in the back corner behind the counters. She hums melodically the entire time.

She has an amazing voice. On the old records, she sounds like a cross between Janis Joplin and Ann Wilson from Heart. Total badass ballsy babe stuff, but with a very feminine quality.

Johnny starts to hum, harmonizing with her.

I recognize the melody. It's one of their old tunes, Always Be.

When the last of the groceries are put away, Karen glides toward Johnny, her long skirt flowing behind her. They're now singing together in perfect union, their voices filling the quiet guitar shop with warmth and love:

"To the stars above
and the earth below
The angels sing
Forever free"

I'm overwhelmed with emotion listening to them. The way they sing *together* melts my heart. I yearn to sing

(*singsingsing*)

as freely as they do. But I can't. I can't even sing alone in the shower. Because...

(*don't sing*)

Because...

(*never ever sing*)

The memory strains inside my brain, trying to knock down the walls of mental cement I built around it. I refuse to crumble.

(*Stop!!!*)

I'll never sing.

And that's that.

Normally, I'm never jealous of people who sing, especially with hard rock. I'm more than happy to focus on the guitar playing. That's why I was content

(*singsingsingsingsingsing*)

being on stage with Skin Trade and having Scott handle all the vocals. I had my guitar in my hands. My guitar sang for me.

(*never ever ever sing*)

I grit my teeth.

My Fender.

My baby.

My *voice*.

It's gone.

Forever.

I inhale sharply, about to sob, but trap the sudden emotion in my chest.

I've become an expert at trapping my emotions. I always hold them inside until I have my guitar in my hands.

Then it all comes out.

Like thunder.

I shake my head imperceptibly, my lips tight with anger. I can't believe my guitar is gone.

(*sing)*

I need to stab something.

(*Stop!!!*)

Johnny and Karen are still singing. They draw closer together as they harmonize the last lines of the song, Johnny pulling Karen into his arms. She rests her hands softly on his chest and gazes into his eyes as they sing:

"In your eyes
I find my peace
You and me
Will always be

Forever
Forever free"

My chest softens and the pain in my heart eases. Johnny and Karen weave real magic when they sing together. It's intoxicating and irresistible. A piece of what they share has permeated my skin and blossomed in my heart. For a moment, the hole in my heart left by Scott and my stolen

(*singsingsing*)

guitar is filled by the love flowing out of Johnny and Karen.

Although the beauty of their song is undeniable, I've never entirely understood the lyrics. Does it mean they'll always be together, or always free? Maybe it means they are together forever and free at the same time? Is that even possible? I don't know, but Johnny and Karen sure make it seem like the connection they share is the greatest thing ever.

Karen rests her cheek against Johnny's chest and he kisses the top of her head gently, lovingly.

I'm ready to start blubbering. They are so happy together I can't stand it. In a voice near tears, I laugh, "I hate you guys."

Johnny is blushing again. He grins at me.

"My goddess," Karen says, waving her hands in her face. "I need to sit for a moment." She's clearly overcome by her own emotions.

Entranced, I mutter, "I'll never understand why you guys weren't more famous."

Karen smiles warmly at me, "We never cared about any of that."

"We only care about each other," Johnny smiles. "Since the day we met, we've had everything we needed. We have each other." He pulls Karen back into his arms and kisses her softly on the lips.

More than ever, I envy what these two have. I thought maybe I had found it with Scott, but that turned out to be a lie. After our first year, I knew Scott and I didn't have what Johnny and Karen have. But at least we had our band. I shake my head. *His* band. Skin Trade was never ours.

That much is now obvious.

"So," Karen asks after taking a moment to collect herself and smooth her colorful skirt, "what happened with Scott?"

"Scott's a used up douche," I sniff.

"I could've told you that," Karen smirks. "What did he do?"

I chuckle and shake my head, "He signed a record deal behind my back. Without me. Rex and Bobby decided to go with Scott. Which left me out of the band."

"What a drag," Johnny shakes his head, "So much for loyalty. Another reason me and the old lady never worried too much about the fame or the money. Both will mess with a person's mind in the worst way."

"I know, right?" I muse.

Karen walks up and hugs me, "You're better off without Scott. That cat's energy was all wrong for you."

I laugh, "You could've told me sooner!"

Karen holds me at arms length, lifts her delicate brows, and smiles, "It wasn't my place to order your heart around. I'm not a prophet."

Johnny encourages, "Everything in its time, Sunshine." He rests a loving hand on my shoulder, "When one door closes, another always opens."

I frown, "Too bad Scott's door slammed in my face. I think it broke my ego's nose." I rub my nose like it hurts.

Karen laughs at my comment.

Johnny grins, "Follow your bliss and the universe will open doors where there were only walls." Johnny says stuff like this all the time.

I say sarcastically, "Where do you get all your Yoda bullshit?"

Unfazed, Johnny smiles, "From Joseph Campbell. That cat knew a thing or two about love. He was also a big influence on George Lucas and the old Star Wars movies. That was before your time, but Lucas put a lot of Campbell's ideas into those movies."

I grin, "So that *was* Yoda bullshit?"

Johnny laughs, "Don't you know, Victory? It's *all* bullshit. And that's George Carlin, not Yoda."

"Who?"

Karen laughs, "Look him up. George Carlin will teach you all about bullshit."

I giggle, "What's to know about bullshit? It's cow poop."

Karen tsk tsk tsks, "So young."

Despite how much the memory of last night's disaster still stings, I always feel better after talking to Johnny and Karen. They're like my adopted L.A. parents.

Once everyone is settled in, Johnny goes back to work re-stringing the Gibson. I neaten things up behind the counter, not that there's much to do. I end up back watching Johnny work on the guitar. It's such a beautiful instrument.

Karen leans against the counter on both arms, standing between Johnny and me. Her fingernails tick-tick-tick on the glass. She sighs and looks morose. Something is on her mind.

I ask, "Something wrong?"

She sighs again heavily. "Victory, we need to talk."

Worry seizes me, like I messed up somehow and she's going to lecture me. I glance over at Johnny.

He sets down the new A string he was about to put on the red Gibson and gives me a heavy look.

"What?" I say nervously, glancing between them.

Karen is obviously uncomfortable. This isn't like her. She says sadly, "There's no easy way to say this, Victory. Johnny and I have been talking."

Why does this suddenly feel like a break up? Are they going to fire me? Please, no. I can't lose all my L.A. friends inside of twelve hours. I feel my bottom lip quivering. Please, I plead in my mind, don't do this, please don't.

Karen continues, "Business has been very slow at the shop for several months. I'm sure you're aware of that."

I nod hopefully, as if merely knowing there's a problem will somehow turn this ship around before it hits an iceberg.

Karen says, "What you don't know is that our landlord has decided not to renew our lease. But even if he did, I don't know that we could afford it."

My eyes goggle. "You guys are gonna move the shop someplace cheaper, right?"

Karen shakes her head, her eyes dark and mournful, "Johnny and I aren't kids anymore. We don't want to go through the hassle of searching for someplace affordable." She looks at me, her face sad, "Victory, Johnny and I have decided to close the shop."

"You can't do that!" I plead. "You guys have been here forever!"

"Thirty four years," Johnny nods heavily.

Karen sighs, "We can't compete with the corporate guitar chains anymore. And the online?" She rolls her eyes and waves her hands dismissively, "Forget about the online."

"Not our bag, baby," Johnny jokes half-heartedly.

"Johnny and I are ready to retire, honey."

"But I love it here," I sniffle. "I love you guys. This place is like home to me..." After last night, it's the only home I have left in L.A.

Karen places her palms gently on my cheeks, "You're such a sweet girl, Victory." Her eyes are wet.

"When are you guys going to close?"

"Not for a couple months," Johnny says.

Phew. At least I still have a job that long. Maybe I can change their minds? Bring a bunch of new business into the shop?

Karen takes a deep breath before saying, "In the mean time, because business has been so slow, we need to ask if we can cut back your hours?"

I'm touched that she's "asking."

I get it.

I've been over to Johnny and Karen's apartment for dinner several times. It's a small one bedroom place in a building four blocks from here. It's warm and inviting, but it's obvious that they don't have a lot of money. I know they share a car and usually walk to work. I bet they've kept the store open the last few years out of love more than anything else.

I nod my head solemnly, "I understand."

"We can still use you on the weekends," Johnny says optimistically.

Two days a week?

I don't make that much as it is. But cutting my wages by more than half? I'm screwed. I barely made ends meet living with Scott in that craphole. I'm gonna have to get roommates. I hope they don't mind living with a musician. Or I could always move into the YWCA. Because nobody ever steals things from people who live at the YWCA. And I hear the management *loves* having a musician practicing electric guitar at all hours.

Maybe I need to get chummy with some of the rehearsal spaces in town? I bet I could crash in one of the rooms at night and shower at the beach like I planned.

Man, I hate being homeless.

Sigh.

I'll figure it out.

Somehow.

Suggestions, anybody?

Chapter 30

VICTORY

The front door jingles. A young guy with long rocker hair wearing a Wild Child shirt leans inside, "Hey, you guys mind if I hang a flier on the door?"

"What's it for?" Johnny asks.

"Guitar Central is hosting L.A. Gunslingers next month. First prize is $5,000."

I forgot all about it. Guitar Central hosts the contest every year. It's a Battle Of The Bands style thing with a focus on guitar based rock. They've been doing it for years. I totally need to enter. I could use the prize money. Too bad I don't have a band. Fucking Scott.

"Right on, man," Johnny says, "go ahead and hang it up."

The rocker guy tapes the flier on the inside of the door. "Thanks, bro," he says before walking out.

Johnny says to me, "You should sign up for that."

"I kind of need a band," I remind him.

"No you don't. Just get up and play guitar. They'll love you," he smiles

"Thanks, Johnny. The only problem is I don't have a guitar."

"What about your Fender?"

My gut clenches at the mention. I don't want to make more problems for Johnny.

He frowns, "Something happen to your Fender?" He's probably reading the misery on my face like it's a giant flashing sign.

I nod, "Someone broke into my car and heisted it."

"What? Someone took it?" He looks like I told him someone kidnapped my kid. "Your old man gave you that guitar, right?"

I nod.

"Man, that's heavy." he shakes his head. "It makes me sad that some people get that desperate." He sighs, "What're you gonna do for a guitar? You can't get ready for the Gunslingers contest without a guitar."

I know where this is going. "I can't..." My eyes are already hot.

"I don't want to hear it," Johnny insists. "Which one do you want?" He motions toward the wall of expensive vintage guitars with his chin.

"Oh, I couldn't..."

He shakes his head. "Can't nothing. You're taking a guitar. I don't want to hear any argument." He's serious.

"Ahh...can I just borrow one? I'll pick one out later, at the end of my shift?"

He nods, "Fine. But you're not walking out of here without a guitar."

My eyes are damp, but I hold back the tears. Johnny's generosity makes me giddy with joy and appreciation. It also freaks me out because the cheapest guitar in the shop costs $3,500. Borrowing a guitar that expensive makes me nervous.

I'll have to make some calls to see if I can borrow a cheaper guitar from someone else. But it's nice knowing I have access to one of Johnny and Karen's if it comes down to that.

$3,500.

It makes me nervous just thinking about it.

So I won't.

The rest of the morning passes slowly.

Few serious customers come into the store. Karen wasn't kidding about how bad business has been.

On a Saturday, we always have lots of walk ins because the shop is on Sunset, which draws plenty of tourists. But few of them are in the market for pricey vintage guitars. I totally get it. I could never afford any of the guitars hanging from the walls of our store.

I don't want to think about guitars right now. Because, yay, I need to find a place to live.

The shop has an old computer that barely works. I scour Craigslist for something affordable. Sadly, everything cheap looks suspicious. I love the ads that say, "Free rent. Female roommate for mutually beneficial living arrangement. Please send recent photos of yourself."

Gee, I wonder what that's about?

I wonder how many desperate girls in my situation are willing to suck up something like that? It makes me sad. I would never trade sex for free rent. Not in a million years. How desperate do you have to be to do that?

I hope I never have to find out.

Needing a break from my housing search, I walk over to the L.A. Gunslingers flier taped to the front door and take a closer look. I really wanted Skin Trade to play at Gunslingers this year because it's not just prize money, it's also great exposure.

I guess Skin Trade doesn't need any exposure now. Scott took care of that with the record contract he signed.

Fucking Scott.

But I need all the exposure I can get because I'm a nobody without Skin Trade. If for some reason Scott, Rex, and Bobby play Gunslingers without me, I will literally walk on stage and stab them while they play. That will get me all kinds of exposure.

Just not the kind I need.

Back to square one.

Around one o'clock, while Johnny and Karen are out for a walk during their lunch break, the jingle bells ring as the front door opens.

A new customer is silhouetted by the harsh Los Angeles sunlight. I'm happy for the distraction. Maybe he'll buy something, unlike all the Looky-Loo's we've had today.

The tall slender figure walks inside like he's stepping from the pages of an expensive fashion magazine. He's tan, clean cut with thick swept back blond hair, and handsome in a way that can only be called dashing and debonair.

His off white double breasted suit is impeccably cut. His high white collared shirt is pin-striped blue and white and goes perfectly with his patterned emerald tie and breast pocket handkerchief. The vibrant brown buttons on his jacket match his shimmering brown leather loafers. He's the full color modernized version of an old time black and white movie star.

While fiddling with one of his fancy gold cufflinks, he casually glances around at all the guitars.

Yeah, he's too sophisticated to be called a guy. He's a man. Not like the men I grew up around. They all rode Harleys, got in bar fights, and thought the height of fashion was a tattered leather jacket with a motorcycle club patch on the back. This man is elegant and self assured. Confidence gleams from his eyes like he's considering buying everything in the store.

In short, he looks too rich and handsome for his own good.

He's the blond, upscale, classy version of Kellan, but with less muscles.

I've been running into a lot of hot guys lately. Maybe Johnny was right about doors closing and opening.

I ask from behind the counter, "Can I help you?"

"Yes," he smiles a $400,000 smile. "I need to buy a guitar." He hasn't looked at me yet, he's busy analyzing the stock on the walls like he knows what he's looking for. "There it is!" he grins. "A gold top Les Paul. Is that a '57 or a '58? I can't tell from the pickups." His eyes are riveted on the guitar like a hunter who has spotted his prey.

He sure knows his guitars, which surprises me. He doesn't look like the kind of guy who knows the first thing about guitars. Business and money, yes. Music? Not even. He looks like he wouldn't know a quarter note from a bank note.

I say casually, "It's a '58."

"Is it for sale?"

"Yup."

His eyes are still glued to the guitar, "How much?"

"I'll have to check, but I think it's $30,000." I pull out the three ring binder beneath the cash register that has all the prices in it, written in pencil or ink by either Johnny or Karen. They avoid using computers whenever possible. I flip through the binder until I find the price. I grin, "$29,995. I just saved you five bucks."

"Very generous of you," he chuckles, still not looking at me. His teeth flash brightly and he's got an amazing profile. He jokes, "I don't think I could've afforded thirty thousand." Finally, he turns to look at me. Everything on his face changes. "Hello," he says softly, his eyes gleaming.

I'm taken off guard. Seeing him front on I realize he's more incredibly handsome than my earlier quick looks had promised. Flawless comes to mind. Oddly, I don't like feeling attracted to him. Not one bit.

He asks, "Do *you* work here?" He says it like it's an impossibility.

I smirk, "I'm behind the counter, aren't I?"

His smile softens, "Of course." He seems slightly embarrassed. "That was rude of me."

"I would have to agree," I say cockily, trying to hide my nervousness. Why is he making me nervous? Guys never make me nervous. Oh yeah. This isn't a guy. This is a dashing man who obviously has money. And he's at least thirty. I don't know how to act around men like him. I feel like I'm going to use the wrong fork at the dinner table or not curtsey or whatever the fuck rich girls do.

"It's just that—" he stops himself. "I don't want this to sound presumptuous, but shouldn't you be on a catwalk in Paris? Or perhaps Milan?"

"Where's Milan?" I sound stupid, but all I ever did in Geography class was listen to remembered songs in my head. I've been doing that since I was little, whenever I get bored.

"Italy," he says with no judgement.

I half expected him to give me shit for not knowing.

He asks, "Have you never been?"

I chortle like a dummy, "I've never even been to San Francisco." Why am I spouting everything that comes to mind all of a sudden? I never show my hand so quickly. I make them work for it. Not that I'm on the market twelve hours after Scott dumped me. But a girl can window shop.

He arches an eyebrow, "Would you like to go?"

"To San Francisco?" I frown.

"No, to Milan."

Is he serious?

"I know this fabulous restaurant in the heart of *Milan* called *Cracco*. *Carlo*, the owner, serves the finest *Italian Nouveau* cuisine you could ever hope to find. You will think you've died and gone to heaven. And their *sommelier* is one of the best in the world." His accent changes when he says the Italian words and names. I realize that there is a flow to his speech, a distinct sense of melody and rhythm. His voice is resonant and I imagine his words appearing in the air as notes on sheet music. I wonder if he sings? He must, the way he talks.

I ask, "What's a sommel yay?"

He smiles indulgently, "*Sommelier* is French for wine steward."

"What's that?" Wow, I sound dumber by the sentence. But something about this guy pulls it out of me and I can't stop myself.

"The task of the *sommelier* is to procure, properly store, and serve wine. He assists the chef in making decisions about which wines to serve with which dishes."

"Isn't it just like, red with steaks and white with fish, or something like that?" I'm not totally ignorant.

He smiles, "Something like that. Perhaps I can take you to *Milan* tomorrow and give you a thorough demonstration of all the possibilities?"

Tomorrow? Show off. Yeah, he's not just talking about wine and food. I'm sure he'd like to demonstrate my pants off and explore my possibilities. I need to steer the conversation back to business. "No, thanks. Do you want to see the '58?"

"I would."

I have to get the ladder from the back room to bring down the guitar. I predict Mr. Goldenblond Milan will stare at my ass while I'm on the ladder. I walk into the back and lug the ladder out front. I open it into an A and climb up to grab the Les Paul. To my surprise, Goldenblond is not standing in a position that allows him a view of my butt. He might have a view up my t-shirt, I can't say for sure, but I'm wearing a bra.

When I glance down, his eyes are locked on the Les Paul.

I climb down the ladder carefully, holding the guitar in one hand. I've had practice, so I make it look easy. My first day on the job, I almost dropped a '62 Telecaster, but I've improved since then.

I hand Goldenblond the guitar.

He takes it carefully in both hands like he's inspecting it but doesn't know what to do with it beyond look.

I ask, "Do you play?" I half expect him to shred on it like Kellan did last night. But that's unlikely.

"Guitar?" he says thoughtfully. "Not really. I can pick a few notes, but I prefer to leave the playing to the experts."

"So why are you buying it?" I've learned to talk like the sale is a done deal. Karen taught me that.

"It's a gift. For a friend. A very special friend."

"A girl?" I ask. Maybe he's married and it's for his mistress.

He shakes his head and smiles, "No."

Aaaahhhh. That explains everything. He's gay. The guitar is for his secret mastress, or whatever you call a man mistress. But I notice he isn't wearing a wedding ring. And he was hitting on me super hard. Maybe he's bi? Yeah, he's one of those rich as shit thrill seeker types who needs everything in life to be dangerous and adventurous every minute of the day.

He examines the guitar some more. "Should I assume everything works?"

"What, the guitar?" I ask, confused and slightly offended. We don't sell guitars that don't work. Johnny checks everything before he buys anything for the store, and if something doesn't work, he fixes things himself before the guitar goes on the wall.

Goldenblond smiles with tons of indulgent innuendo, "Yes…the *guitar*." He stares at me like I'm lunch. His eyes caress my neck. How is he doing that? I can literally feel my neck getting hotter.

"Yeah, it works," I say sarcastically. Unlike your moves, buddy. I break his eye contact and my neck cools instantly. I'm not falling for his Slick Rickery.

"Can you show me?" Goldenblond asks.

"You mean the authentication papers?" Collectors always ask for them before anything else. The store keeps them all in a filing cabinet behind the counter.

"No…" he purrs, "…the instrument. I would like to hear it *played*."

I can tell he's lumping me into the same category as the guitar from the way he says "instrument" and "played."

Yes, he's undeniably charming. But no, he's not going to play me.

No way.

I tell myself it's just Goldenblond's handsome looks, which I refuse to fall for. It's obvious he likes trophies from the way he dresses and from his interest in expensive guitars. My price is more than he can afford. I like a man with a wallet full of sincerity, which this guy has none of. Scott acted super charming in the beginning. Oh, how that changed.

Back to business.

My job is to sell guitars, not a piece of my ass. I'm going to play Goldenblond's game because I'm not going to fall for it. I know better. If a little flirtation is good for business, I'll turn on the charm.

It's just a game, right?

Besides, I'd love to tell Karen & Johnny I sold the gold top Gibson for a bucket o' cash while they were at lunch. Maybe the shop can stay open an extra month.

I say, "I thought you said you didn't *play*?" I say the word "play" like I'm saying blowjob. "How are you going to know if the *guitar* is any good or not?" When I say "guitar" I stare at the Gibson, which he's holding in front of his crotch. I giggle. I've done this before. Girls, don't try this at home. Unless you've dated enough hot guys who are pricks to know better. It usually takes only one before you figure it out.

Fucking Scott.

Goldenblond smirks, "I know what I like." His eyes beam into mine, priceless green jewels that match his tie and handkerchief.

This guy is as subtle as an earthquake. No way he's gonna shake me up. I'm wise to his game.

He holds the guitar out to me, hand around the neck of the guitar, expecting me to take it from him. "Indulge me," he says. I notice his cologne now that his hand is literally four inches from my face.

I have to admit, I like it. It smells classy, like limousines and lear jets to me. Not that I would know. But it's not oil changes and muscle cars, that's for sure. Variety is the spice of life, right?

I arch an eyebrow, briefly glance at the guitar like there's no way I'm touching it. I spin my back to him, leaving him holding nothing but his *guitar* in his hands.

I sashay over to the counter then bend over, pretending to search for an instrument cable behind it.

Now I know he's checking out my ass. I can feel it, but I'm wearing tight jeans, so it's only PG-13. I roll my eyes out of his line of sight while my ass is in the air, waiting for him to take the bait. I'm gonna hook this fish. It's just business. I'm a saleswoman.

Once I know he's squirming on the line, and in his pants, I say, "Found it!" like I didn't know where the instrument cable was all along.

When I turn around, I giggle once and make eye contact while strutting toward him. I brush my shoulder against his when I plug the cord into an old Fender Tone Master.

Once the vacuum tube amp has warmed up, I sit down on top of another one of the store's amps and rest the guitar on my knee. I turn up the volume to a modest level, and strum a few gentle chords on the Les Paul. I let the last chord ring out and flip the pickup selector switch back and forth so he can see that both pickups work properly, then twist the volume and tone knobs on and off to show they work too.

"See?" I smirk. "Everything works."

"I said I would like to hear the instrument *played*."

"Would you now?" I flirt.

"I suspect you can do a better *job* than that."

I scrutinize his face, "What kind of *job* would you like?"

His luscious mouth widens into a smile and he chuckles, "Whatever kind you prefer."

He really is dashingly handsome. My face is heating up against my will. I ease my lips into a controlled smile. "If you insist," I tease.

He has this look on his face like he's sizing my head for a plaque to fit on his wall between the heads of the other women he's mounted, both in bed and on his trophy wall.

I'm willing to bet Goldenblond is one of *those* guys.

Time to give him a show and bag the sale. He's not the only hunter in this lodge.

No one else is in the store, so I turn the amp up to a decent volume. I caress the neck of the Les Paul and coax notes from it like I'm dipping Goldenblond's honey wand in the honey pot and I'm drizzling golden goodness all over it. Too bad I only use my honey on unsuspecting fly brained fools like Goldenblond.

I almost break into laughter. I never act like this with customers. I have too much self respect. But he's totally asking for it.

I continue to play a seductive melody on the Les Paul. Before I realize it, I'm caught up in the sensuous solo that I'm spinning from the strings of the guitar.

I can't fake it when I play. If I'm playing something sensuous, I have to feel the sensuality, or else it sounds fake. In good music, your truth always comes out. So what if Goldenblond is totally hot and I'm a little bit turned on right now and it's totally obvious to him.

When I finish my improvised guitar solo, I'm burning up beneath my sleeveless Whitesnake t-shirt.

He grins at me, his face relaxed into a sultry smile. "Mmmm, that was fantastic."

I can't decide if he's talking about my playing, the guitar, or me. From the look in his eyes, probably all three.

"I'll take it," he grins, staring me down.

Wow, sales for $30,000 guitars usually take a bit more work than this. I'm not complaining. "I'll go get the case from the back."

"Is it the original case? I know that's important."

I nod, "Yeah. Be right back." I take the guitar with me since I'm the only one in the store. I pause half way to the back room when I realize the ladder is still out there. He could easily climb up and snatch any one of the guitars off the wall and run out the front door while I'm in the back. Just because he's wearing a suit doesn't mean squat. After my Fender was stolen from my car in a rich neighborhood this morning, I'm gun shy.

I say, "You know what? I have to wait for the owner to get back from lunch. I'm thinking they moved the case for this one." It sounds like a lame excuse, but I can't think of a better one.

I'm torn because I don't want to lose this sale. It means a lot of money for the shop. For Johnny and Karen's retirement. If I make this guy wait, he might change his mind and walk out of here.

"I'm in somewhat of a hurry," Goldenblond says.

Shit.

He asks, "Can I have it delivered?"

"We don't usually do that," I stammer. We've never done that.

"How about I throw in an extra thousand and pay right now?"

I can't say no to that. "Okay." I glance around for a place to put the guitar. The plush purple guitar block is empty. Johnny finished restringing the hollow body ES-335 before he and Karen left for lunch, so I set the Gold Top Les Paul on the block.

I pretend to smooth my shirt down but really I'm wiping the sweat off them because I'm going to sell a $30,000 guitar! Johnny usually handles the really big sales.

I ask, "How did you want to pay?"

"Cash."

I'm suddenly nervous. Who carries that much cash? I bet it's counterfeit. Too bad we don't have one of those magic pens you see at the post office to check if the money is fake. I guess I can hold the bills up to the light and check for that tiny strip inside the paper that says which bill it is. But even if he pays with hundred dollar bills, that's 300 bills I have to scrutinize in the light! That'll take an hour or more! I never imagined cash could be such a pain in the ass.

Goldenblond says, "I can see you're nervous about the cash. How about I pay by cashier's check. I can run to the bank and get one right now."

The last thing I want is for him to walk out that door without paying. He might never come back. "Ahhh..."

"Credit card then?" he asks. "You take them, don't you?"

"Yeah, but..." there's a 3% service charge from the banks, which in this case is nine hundred bucks.

He says, "You don't want to lose money on the service charge, do you?"

I shake my head.

"All right," he smiles. "You drive a hard bargain."

He's being nice. At this point, I'm not driving any bargain. He's got the wheel.

What can I say? This is the first time I've sold a guitar this expensive. Goldenblond is now totally in control of this deal. I suspect that's his usual state of being.

He says, "Let's make it thirty-two. How does that sound? And I'll pay by credit card. Right now."

"Perfect!"

He pulls a wallet out from inside his suit jacket and hands me a black card with only gold numbers and the VISA symbol.

I say, "I should probably see your driver's license?"

"Of course," he hands it to me.

The photo looks like him and the name matches the one on the card: JULIAN WHITTAKER.

Of course, when I swipe his card, I have to call the bank and put Goldenblond Julian on the phone to confirm his identity.

Even with the bank on the line and his driver's license, the idea of letting a $30,000 guitar go out the door makes me way nervous. To my relief, Johnny and Karen return from lunch before Goldenblond gets off the phone.

Johnny says, "You're selling the Gold Top?"

I nod enthusiastically, "For $32,000!"

"Far out," he chuckles.

Karen arches an eyebrow and smiles, "Victory, maybe we need to let you run the shop full time. You have a knack for this."

"Thanks," I grin before running in the back to get the case for the Les Paul, which is exactly where I knew it was.

When I come back out, Goldenblond Julian is chatting with Karen and Johnny.

He's saying, "... and your salesgirl made me an offer I couldn't refuse."

"Oh?" Karen asks.

"She promised to deliver the guitar directly to my house."

"She did?" Karen smiles at me.

"I did?" I say, confused.

Goldenblond arches an eyebrow at me and extends his hand, "I'm usually not this rude, but I never asked your name?"

I shake his hand firmly, "Victory Payne."

"Victory? That's a fascinating name. Is it short for Victoria?"

I giggle against my will, "Sometimes people ask me that—"

(*rude Kellan never asked me about my name*)

"—but no, it's simply Victory."

He nods thoughtfully, "Victory Payne," he smiles eloquently, "That is a fascinatingly poetic name. I sense it suits you well, I think."

I nod dumbly.

We're still shaking hands ten minutes later, or it seems like ten minutes. I tug my hand from his and he releases it.

Goldenblond nods to Johnny and Karen, "And now, I must bid you all *arrivederci*. I have to run." He pulls a business card out of his wallet and hands it to Karen. "Call this number and speak to my assistant. She will make an appointment for your lovely salesgirl," he winks at me, "to drop off the guitar. Sometime next week?" He glances between me and Karen.

Karen looks to me for approval.

"Yeah," I smile, "Next week!"

Goldenblond winks at me, "I'll make it worth your while." Then he strides out the door.

"Worth your while?" Karen chuckles when Julian is gone. She glances at Johnny, "Victory has a new admirer." She flutters to the door to spy on Goldenblond Julian. "His car is even nicer than his suit," she says. "He looks a bit square to me, but you could do worse. He's quite handsome," Karen says girlishly.

Her excitement is catching and I patter up behind her. I can see Goldenblond merging into traffic on Sunset in a black Ferrari. The motor revs to a high dangerous whine then drops into second gear. It reminds me of the sound of dive bombing the whammy bar on a loud distorted electric guitar. The Ferrari makes its own kind of automotive music. I guess you could say Goldenblond has good taste in noisemakers.

I'm not sure about the rest of him.

Karen hands me Julian's business card.

All it has printed on it is his name and a single 323 area code phone number. If I hadn't seen his Ferrari and watched him drop $32,000 on a guitar, I'd think it was a fake business card.

My life gets more interesting by the hour.

At this rate, I'm going to win the lottery and fly a spaceship to the moon before dinner.

Chapter 31

VICTORY

A small boy dances to my left. He can't be more than six years old. He's got moves that put the late great Michael Jackson to shame. I've been calling him Junior Jackson in my head all evening because he's that good.

He's also my nemesis.

For the past two hours, I've been busking at the Third Street Promenade in Santa Monica with all the other performers who come out to make money off the crowds, trying to score some extra cash which I desperately need.

Junior Jackson is stealing my thunder.

Apparently, the spectators prefer his dancing over my guitar playing.

I should've brought a battery powered amp. Too bad I don't have one.

The unamplified classical guitar I'm playing is the one Johnny let me borrow for the night. I wanted something no frills, but the closest thing the shop has is this Contrares. Sure, it's no frills in the sense that it doesn't have a whammy bar or any of the fancy stuff you find on an electric. It's just wood and nylon strings. It's also worth $6,000. Yes, it's the cheapest acoustic in the store. Johnny insisted I borrow it when I told him I was going busking. I just hope it doesn't get damaged out here. The slightest nick will lower the value of the guitar.

Nothing to stress about.

So here I sit, on the drum throne I had to also borrow from the shop. It's really just an adjustable stool, but no one likes the word stool since it also means poop. Of course, throne means toilet, so what's the difference?

Anyway, I'm doing my very best to charm people into donating to the Get Victory Payne Off The Streets fund with my too quiet guitar playing.

So far, I've made all of $7.72 since I started playing at sundown.

Junior Jackson is to blame. I want to hate him, but I can't. He's too damn cute.

I've heard it said that in movies or TV, a performer never wants to share the stage with an animal or a kid because animals and kids always steal the show.

They were right.

Junior Jackson is living proof.

Junior showed up shortly after I did and has been charming everyone's pants off all night. Even mine. Nobody wants to hear some chick play classical guitar. Everyone wants to watch Junior Jackson dance.

$7.72.

What a fortune.

At least I'll have lunch money for tomorrow.

At the moment, Junior Jackson is busting moves to Stayin' Alive by the Bee Gees. The entire crowd can see that Junior Jackson, based on the way he walks, is totally a ladies man of few words. Which isn't a surprise, because I don't think he's finished kindergarten.

Junior Jackson doesn't let that stop him from being a total charmer.

His parents run a large boom box and applaud between every song. Junior Jackson's money hat sitting on the sidewalk is crammed full of cash, and the crowd drops more bills on the green mountain by the minute. I'm sure his parents have quit their day jobs and live entirely off the money Junior makes, or they soon will.

But hey, I've made $7.72.

I glance around at my surroundings.

Maybe this was the wrong choice of venue?

No, the Promenade is the perfect place for performers. It's an outdoor shopping mall three blocks from the beach. Wall to wall shops, restaurants, and movie theaters line both sides of the permanently closed off streets. The roadway between the buildings has been converted to contain topiary shrubbery, fountains, vendor carts, newsstands, outdoor seating at most of the restaurants, and plenty of bench seating for everyone else. Every night of the week, the Promenade draws big crowds of locals and tourists with money to burn.

Unfortunately for me, I'm not the only street performer who has figured this out. They take up every bit of available space in sight.

To make matters worse, Junior Jackson is not the only child prodigy stealing my thunder.

To my right is a teenaged girl behind a keyboard wearing too much makeup and a fancy hairdo. She can't be older than fifteen. She plays nothing but covers of Kelly Clarkson hits. For some songs, she accompanies herself on the keyboard, on others she stands up, sings to a karaoke track, and works the crowd like the Promenade is a 10,000 seat arena.

Everyone "Oohs" and "Aahs" at how good she is.

The man who wheeled in her P.A. earlier in the evening and is probably her dad cheers and claps loudly between every song. Sometimes he throws money into her keyboard case like he's just another spectator.

The girl's keyboard case is wide open and looks like an overturned Brinks truck. I'm surprised she doesn't have her own security with all that cash spilling out. Her stack of professionally produced CDs for sale are going like hotcakes. All she needs to really ruin my money mojo is a dancing poodle in a pink tutu. Or she could team up with Junior Jackson. They'd be unstoppable.

Whatever.

My only complaint is that

(*don't sing*)

her P.A. is turned up way too loud and I don't have an amp. Nobody can hear my Contrares over her.

(*never ever sing*)

I'm sure Little Miss Clarkson is hoping to be discovered by some music executive, big time producer, or a power player from one of the big talent agencies nearby, just like everybody else. I can't blame her. I just wish she'd be a little more courteous to the people who don't

(*never ever ever sing*)

have as much money as she does. If someone hadn't stolen my Fender and my Marshall, I could play so loud it would blow the makeup right off her face and knock her hairdo over. But I don't

(*sing*)

have my amp anymore.

So I make do and try to tough it out.

I continue to play a variety of fingerstyle J.S. Bach pieces transcribed for the guitar by Andrés Segovia. They would sound great someplace quiet.

I heave a sigh of frustration. I set up in my spot before Little Miss Clarkson by at least an hour. I probably should've moved when I saw her wheeling in her P.A. with the help of her dad.

Too bad I'm not

(*singsingsing*)

some proud parent's cute little show stealing pumpkin munchkin like Junior Jackson or Little Miss Clarkson.

At least I have a bunch of creeper stalker types who've made donations to my cause. So what if it was only an excuse to look down my shirt? Their money is as good as anyone's.

All $7.72 of it.

Yeah, time for me to

(*singsingsingsingsingsing*)

move.

I latch up my guitar case and look for a quieter section of the Promenade. I should've done this sooner. Now the place is wall to wall people. I can barely find standing room anywhere, let alone a quiet place to set up.

The last thing I want to do is interfere with the other performers who set up early like I did. I pass them by with a sigh.

The magicians with their nearly naked assistants.

The comedy jugglers with their eggs and chainsaws and flaming swords.

The human statue guys with their golden tuxedos (there's always more than one of them on the Promenade), and their matching top hats and sunglasses and metallic makeup. I love how they hold still until someone gets too close, then suddenly whir their hidden mouth whistles and robotically remove their top hats, holding their hats out for a donation like mute out-of-work C-3POs.

It's a living.

The only place left for me to set up is near the Barnes & Noble at the corner of 3rd Street and Wilshire Boulevard. Not as much foot traffic as the middle of the outdoor mall, but better than nothing.

Too bad this end is where all the homeless street kids come to loiter, and they don't tip for shit. They're too busy begging the nicely dressed Promenade clientele for change so they can get drunk or high later.

Worse, I'm wearing an unzipped gray hoodie over my cutoff Whitesnake t-shirt and jeans. The nicely dressed Promenade clientele who do all the tipping look at me suspiciously, like I'm another vagrant teenager. Or should I say not looking, because they're totally ignoring me.

Whatever.

I sigh.

I'm not going to give up just because I'm getting a snooty attitude. I may be broke and living out of my car, but I'm on a mission to make it in this town as a musician. That hasn't wavered one bit.

So I keep playing.

Nickels and dimes dribble into my guitar case over the next hour. Even a few dollar bills. Too bad I'm not singing a sad mournful tune.

(*Stop!!!*)

That would really bring out the sympathy dollars. Oh well.

(*never ever ever sing*)

I don't sing.

End of story.

I've almost finished playing my way through Segovia's transcription of Bach's Cello Suite in C. It's soothing and I always enjoy playing it. When I finally finish, my hair is hanging in my face. I was so into it, I didn't look up from my guitar for half an hour.

A few people clap and squat down to put money in my guitar case. I've got a nice little pile forming. Yay! Looks like at least fifty bucks! The night hasn't been a total waste.

As my little crowd clears out, someone in the back is still clapping.

"Well, well, well," Kellan says as he emerges from the crowd, "if it isn't Viki Hendrix, in the flesh. Or should I say Sharon Isbin?"

Sharon Isbin is a badass babe who is world renowned for her classical guitar skills. I'm no Sharon Isbin on the classical guitar. I know Kellan's just pulling my leg, but I can't help but smile up at him, "What are you doing here?"

He's as hot as the last time I saw him.

Unfortunately, the last thing I need in my life right now is more hot guys. Seriously. It's been less then 24 hours since Scott betrayed me. Hot guys don't fix broken hearts. They're just bandaids.

But...Kellan is yummilicious. What's the harm in chatting with him for a few minutes? We're in a public place? What's the worst he can do?

Then I see his fake-o date.

I smirk to myself.

I think he pulled her off the shelf in the doll aisle at Toys "R" Us and also bought the Dumb Slut clothing set to dress her up in. I mean, I'm sure she's smart. Why would she be dumb? No, she's not an idiot, not with her fake-o facial expression. She probably has a Ph.D in Slut-ology.

I was totally right about Kellan. He goes through women like I go through guitar strings. A new one every night.

Then I realize this action figure girl looks vaguely familiar.

Was she one of the Femme Flakes in the silver Porsche last night when Kellan walked me to my car? Ahh, who can tell, they're all the same: short skirt, high heels, long legs, plastic boobs, plastic hair. Everything about her is expensive and designer.

She takes one look at me and chucks a look at me like I'm a garbage dumpster that smells. She radiates impatience.

Kellan doesn't seem to notice her irritation. He asks me, "That was the Segovia transcription you were playing, wasn't it?"

"You know it?" I'm shocked. He knows way too much about guitar. I repress the sudden urge to bash my Contrares over Femme Flakes' head and ask Kellan if he wants to get coffee someplace and talk guitar. I don't because: one, I don't want to hurt Johnny's guitar and two, I'm never that forward with guys. But something about Kellan always has me doing strange things. What is it about him? I mean, besides how hot he is?

Kellan pulls out his wallet and drops a twenty into my guitar case. "I haven't heard someone play Bach like that since Christopher Parkening."

Femme Flakes glares at Kellan like he should be spending that twenty on her. He doesn't seem to notice.

I, on the other hand, am blushing like crazy because comparing me to Christopher Parkening is a huge compliment. Parkening is a legend on the classical guitar and he still teaches master classes at Pepperdine University up the coast in Malibu.

Considering Kellan knows a thing or two about guitar, his compliment is huge. I search his face for any trace of bullshit. None.

Yeah, I'm blushing like crazy.

Kellan asks, "How late are you gonna play tonight?"

"Till they kick me out," I grin.

"You're hardcore, Victory."

I'm secretly pleased he uses my name.

Femme Flakes notices my smile and is none too happy. She whines, "Let's go, Kellan. I want something to drink."

What a brat.

Kellan arches an eyebrow at me, "Catch you around?"

Femme Flakes snarls at me, but Kellan doesn't notice.

I shrug my shoulders at Kellan, not wanting to start a cat fight, "Sure." I'm vaguely pained knowing that Kellan and I don't have each other's numbers. It's not every day you bump into someone randomly in L.A. It's a huge city.

Femme Flakes and Kellan are already fading into the crowd, her arms wrapped possessively around his elbow. She snuggles against him.

I hope you're comfortable, bitch.

Whoa, where did that voice come from?

I'm not into Kellan.

And why am I glaring daggers at Femme Flakes' back?

I'm not going to think about it.

I need to keep playing and make some more cash before the crowd fades away to nothing.

Chapter 32

KELLAN

My brain has officially melted.

It's dripping out my ears onto my shoulders.

My eyes have glazed over.

I sit across from Savannah at one of the tall bar tables inside Monsoon Cafe having drinks, nodding a lot and pretending to listen to her ramble.

Picture one of those hand crank meat grinders, and Savannah is cranking it gleefully around and around and around. A steady stream of hamburger meat falls into a bowl in wormy wet red chunks, only it's not hamburger, it's my brains.

"...and I told Kylie she should totally get a boob job, it's a career decision, an investment, I got mine when I was eighteen, it's so much easier to shop for dresses when you have boobs," she giggles, "everything just, I don't know," she crinkles her nose, "fits better, you know..."

I nod. Well, it's more like I'm nodding off. I suddenly snap my head upright so it doesn't loll against my chest with my mouth hanging open. If you time it right, it looks like you're paying attention instead of sleeping with your eyes open.

Savannah the Brain Grinder has been going on and on like this for over an hour.

I'm slowly dying inside.

Something about her voice reminds me of TV commercials. Not in a good way, like when you hear a good voice-over artist who knows how to modulate their delivery for maximum effect. I mean like when you're watching a TV movie and toward the end, the commercial breaks are like eight minutes long, and you get that constant stream of useless advertising bullshit you don't wanna hear because it's ruining the movie.

I realize that's exactly what Savannah is doing. She's ruining my movie. Everything coming out of her head sounds like it was put there by TV commercials or whatever she reads in fashion magazines. *If* she can read, which I'm leaning toward she can't.

That means everything coming out of her mouth is fed into her head by a satellite dish. She probably has a little DIRECTV receiver dish mounted inside her empty skull.

That's my conclusion, anyway.

"...and we walked into the Tropicana, you know, the bar in that hotel behind the Roosevelt, on Hollywood Boulevard, anyway, Paris Hilton was having drinks at the bar and we had drinks with her, she bought drinks for everyone, she's so much nicer in person..."

I notice at this point that Savannah doesn't end her sentences. Life is just one long monologue for her with nothing but commas.

I'm kicking myself for talking Savannah into getting drinks here at the Monsoon. I should've suggested punctuation lessons instead. I'm pretty sure she was held back in kindergarten thirteen times before the educational system gave up on her and sent her out into the world to bore people with her comma talk.

Instead of taking Savannah back to grammar school like I should've, I told her that Monsoon's has a great bar, which is true. But the real reason I wanted to drink here is because the restaurant is right across from Barnes & Noble where Victory is playing outside on the Promenade.

I kind of want to keep an eye on Victory. I still don't have her number. Now that she's out of her band, I don't know when I'll bump into her again. I need to score her digits before she takes off tonight.

I'm pretty sure if I put a life size cardboard cutout of me in my barstool and walk outside long enough to get Victory's number, Savannah won't notice I'm gone.

"...told her I can't decide if I should move to West Hollywood so I can be near the Beverly Center and the shopping on Melrose, or stay in Beverly Hills in my parents' three bedroom guest house," She gets a faraway, thoughtful look, which on her is more thoughtless than thoughtful. "I don't know, it's so much easier when my dad takes care of everything, if I buy a house, then I have to clean it myself," She laughs between commas and touches my forearm while rubbing her knee against mine under the table, "I mean, you know, hire the maids and everything, I *hate* doing that..."

Maybe I should go home with this airhead.

Maybe not.

I'm stuck because she drove us here in her Porsche. My bike is parked on her parents' gigantic driveway in Beverly Hills. Most chicks love riding on the back of my bike. But when I told Savannah she had to wear a helmet, she said there was no way she was messing up her hair.

That should've been my cue to cancel the date. Because, when we got to the Promenade earlier, Savannah turned this into a shopping date. We've walked into every shoe and clothing store here. I could tell she's probably worthless in bed four shoe stores ago, because everything is about her, her, her.

Funny thing is, if I hadn't sucked it all up, I wouldn't have bumped into Victory tonight.

Turns out Savannah isn't completely worthless.

Now I just have to figure out how to get rid of her.

Chapter 33

VICTORY

It's another couple hours before the crowds are so thin there's no point in staying.

When I pack up my guitar, I see one of the same gangs of teenagers passing by who've been coming and going all night. I'm surprised security hasn't kicked them out of the Promenade based on their behavior. Two of them have skateboards, and skateboarding isn't allowed inside the Promenade.

Most of the other groups of teens I've seen all night are a mix of guys and girls. This group is all dudes. I can tell they're wound up tight.

One of them drops his skateboard near where I'm sitting and starts practicing his kickflips. His buddies cheer him on.

I wouldn't mind except Kickflips sucks, no matter how much his grungy black Vans shoes, giant t-shirt, and the backwards ball cap on his head scream California skater. He keeps tripping all over his board. On one attempt, his board gets trapped between his legs, standing straight up. He almost lands balls first on the nose of the board. I stifle a chuckle.

A couple of his buddies join him, doing ollies or rail slides off nearby benches.

It doesn't take long for me to realize they're showing off. I can tell because they keep stealing glances at me between tricks.

In my head, I hear lyrics for Avril Lavigne's song Sk8er Boi, but these probably aren't the guys Avril was singing about. These particular sk8ers are total spazzes and not at all cute.

Time for me to go.

My guitar case has more money in it than I expected to make tonight. A lot of it's change, so I have to pull it all out before I put the Contrares in the case. I don't want to scratch the guitar on the coins. It would be easier to get the money out if I set the guitar down, but the top of the drum throne isn't perfectly flat, and I'm paranoid the guitar will fall off, and I'm not going to put it on the cement, so I hold it in one hand. I wad up all the bills with my free hand and stuff them in my purse.

I forget what I'm doing for a second, and the guitar is sticking out behind me as I'm bending over for the bills when one of the skaters blows by behind me, nearly hitting the bottom of my guitar.

"Hey!" I shout, "Watch it!"

The skaters laugh. I know they're playing with me.

"Why don't you guys go down to Venice and skate at the skatepark where you're supposed to?"

"It's too far," Kickflips whines.

"It's two miles," I counter. "And you're actually allowed to skate there. They've even got pools."

"You can't skate there after dark," one of the skaters says.

These guys are idiots. "You can't skate here ever. Why don't you go break the rules at an actual skatepark? Then you're only half breaking the rules."

None of them respond. They just skate near me, circling like skate sharks. I should ignore them.

Still holding the Contrares in one hand, I tip my guitar case so all the change pools in the bottom corner. Then I toss it by the handful into my purse. I don't know how much I made, but it's at least a hundred bucks. I'm sure Junior Jackson and Little Miss Clarkson made ten times as much, but whatever.

Once I get all my money in my purse, I lean over to put the guitar in the case.

"WATCH OUT!!" one of the skaters shouts as he bombs past me.

I stand up suddenly, looking around for what the problem is.

A half second later, one of them slams into my back and I fall face first onto the concrete.

Luckily, the Contrares breaks my fall.

CRUNCH!!

I'm right on top of it and one of the skaters is on my back. "Get off of me!" I shout. I twist and roll him off of onto the concrete like a sack of sk8er garbage.

"Oh shit!" one of the other skaters gasps.

The one who was on top of me groans, "Fuck, my wrist..."

"Fuck your wrist!" I scream. "You broke my guitar!" I stand up and shake the broken guitar over him. The spruce top has been caved in near the bottom. The bridge has popped clean off and the springy strings spray out in every direction. "It's ruined!"

It turns out, the guy on the ground is Kickflips.

What a surprise.

He doesn't even notice my guitar. He's busy rolling around on his back and moaning while he holds his forearm to his chest protectively. "I think it's broken..."

"I'm going to break your other wrist, dumbass! Look what you did!"

He's in too much pain to care.

The other skaters circle around us, rolling slowly on their skateboards, gawking it all in.

Don't they ever get off their skateboards?

"Dude, are you okay?" one asks while circling.

"That was a nasty fall, bro," another says.

"Fuck," Kickflips moans, "I can't move my fingers." He holds up his hand to show everyone. The hand is bent at a weird angle from his wrist.

I say, "You guys need to take your buddy to the hospital."

"We don't have any money," one of the other kids says.

I can relate. But I say, "He still needs to go to the Emergency Room."

Kickflips groans, "I don't have insurance."

Why does this suddenly feel like it's becoming my problem? I glance at the Contrares. It's ready for firewood. What am I gonna do?

"Five-oh!" one of the skaters blurts. "Cops!"

His buddies skate off toward Wilshire Boulevard and turn the corner, gone.

"Nice friends," I grumble to Kickflips.

Two cops on foot jog up to us.

This is lame. I was all ready to go home and count my money while kicking my feet up and sipping on a hot cup of...shit. I don't have anyplace to go. Oh well. May as well spend my night here with Disaster Dan, a.k.a. Kickflips.

Man, this totally blows.

It takes only about two minutes to explain to the cops what happened. They can see I'm a performer.

"Do I have to hang around?" I ask one of the cops.

He's really tall but has a boyish face and one of those military haircuts. "No. Paramedics are on the way. You're free to leave whenever you want, miss."

It's funny him calling me "miss." He can't be more than fifteen based on his baby face. "Thanks," I smile, shaking my head.

Free to go where? To the bubble bath waiting for me at my mansion? Actually, that sounds nice. I convince myself that's exactly where I'm going.

I'll deal with the disappointing reality of my cold car later.

Babyface smiles, "Sorry about your guitar. I wish there was something we could do."

"Me too," I smirk.

"You could try taking him to small claims court."

"He told me he's broke."

"Sorry," Babyface shakes his head and gives me one of those thin smiles that says, "I feel bad, but I'm not actually going to help you out."

I roll my eyes, "Thanks." I pick up my drum throne, and the guitar, which is now in its case. What am I going to tell Johnny? That he can take the money out of my paychecks? Which I will no longer be receiving when the shop closes, which will be long before I payoff the guitar?

I'm cursed. That's the only possible explanation I can think of.

Fucking Scott.

Is he some kind of silver eyed Voodoo King who put a hex on me? He needs to be stabbed.

Man, I need a drink. Despite the cash in my purse, I really can't afford one.

I laugh quietly to myself as I trudge to my car. Someone will probably jump out of the darkness and snatch my purse before I get to my car, which I parked in one of the garages on 4th street. I spent twelve bucks on the garage because I told myself my car would be less likely to be broken into. Not that I have much left to steal.

I walk to Wilshire and go half a block to the alley that runs between the parking garages and the shops. I scan the shadows for purse snatchers.

Seeing none, I proceed.

Twenty feet into the alley, I hear the scrape of boot heels behind me.

I spoke too soon. I glance over my shoulder and see a huge hulking figure in the shadows behind me. I can't make him out because he's passing through a dark area between lights, and there's not many in the alley to begin with. My heart seizes.

Yeah, I'm totally cursed.

This is too lame for words.

I quicken my pace, put the drum throne under my arm holding the guitar case, and reach into my purse for my rainbow rape knife. I pop the blade open before withdrawing it slowly. I let it dangle casually at my side.

If Boot Heels tries anything, I'll drop the drum throne to free up my arm holding the guitar case. Now that I'm not worried about the Contrares, I'll gladly use the case to bash with one arm while stabbing with the other.

I'm not going down without a fight.

This is your unlucky day, Boot Heels.

Scrape, scrape, scrape.

Everything slows down as I hear the pace of the boot heels accelerate behind me. I will bash the bones in those boots into powder if they get too close. My heart hammers in my ears and time turns into syrup.

I'm all ready for the stab and bash, if it comes to that. But I'll try running first. It often works.

I put my head down and sprint like crazy. I imagine I'm a cheetah going for broke. Not a gazelle. I'm never the stupid gazelle. But everyone knows that a big ugly hyena can kill a cheetah, so speed is of the essence.

I drop the drum throne and it clatters against the asphalt in the alley. It's worth maybe fifty bucks. I'm worth way more.

"Hey!" Boot Heels shouts. "Wait!"

Is he kidding? I'm not waiting around to chat.

The stairwell to the parking garage is fifty feet in front of me. I can get there before Boot Heels catches up to me and run up to the fourth floor where my car is parked, but not without dropping the broken Contrares. Considering it's totaled, it's not worth dying for. Johnny will understand.

Sorry, guitar, it's you or me, buddy.

"Hey, Victory! Wait up!"

I stop in my tracks and whip around, "Kellan?"

"Who did you think I was?" he chuckles.

"Holy shit!" I set the guitar case down and fold into a squat, clutching my arms to my stomach. I'm ready to puke, I'm so scared. "You almost gave me a heart attack!" Adrenalin mainlines in my veins. "Fuck! You scared the shit out of me!"

"Sorry," he grins as he bends to pick up my drum throne.

I'm beyond surprised as I look up at him, "What are you doing here?"

"Looking for you," he smiles.

"More like stalking! I thought you were a rapist!"

"Not my style," he grins. "Although I've had a few women try and rape me in the past."

"You wish," I spit.

He shrugs, "I'm not asking you to believe me. I was there. I know what happened." He gets a wistful, faraway look. "I always have to remind them no means no. But drunk chicks can get pretty insistent. What can I say? I'm always in high demand."

Why do I believe him? I shake my head and suddenly picture Kellan's head inflating to the size of a hot air balloon because of all the hot air that comes out of his mouth, and he floats away into the sky, never to be heard from again.

I blurt out a laugh.

Kellan grins, "What?"

"I'll tell you later," I shake my head. "What are you doing here anyway?"

"I came to collect my debts."

"Debts? What debts?"

Kellan acts hurt, "You forgot already? You still owe me a pizza."

"Still hung up on that?" I joke.

"I'm a hungry guy. I eat a lot. I'll take free pizza anyplace I can get it. I mean, pizza I *earned*. You're not going back on your word, are you?"

"No," I sigh, standing up slowly. Now that my adrenalin is fading, the nausea has kicked in. My guts are in knots. I drop my knife to my side, hoping he doesn't notice. I feel sort of stupid having it out, but I don't want to call attention to it. I'd slip it into my purse all ninja like, but my hands are shaking too much. I'd probably slice a hole in my bag, which I can't afford to replace. I'm not about to use trash bags or paper grocery sacks for a handbag. That's going too far.

"What's with the knife," he motions with his hand.

That didn't work. I smirk, "You."

"You gonna cut my shit?"

"If necessary. Keep your distance." I raise the knife half heartedly then drop it to my side. "I'm exhausted."

"You probably should eat something—"

"I couldn't eat a bite. My stomach is totally—"

"—in need of pizza," he interrupts, "I bet you haven't eaten since you got to the Promenade.

He's right, but I roll my eyes, "You don't quit, do you?"

He shakes his head, grinning. "Nope. You need to eat."

Changing the subject, I say, "Hey, what happened to your date?"

"Her?" he chuckles, "I took her home and put her away in her display case."

I frown, "That sounds like a creepy serial killer comment."

"I meant the one she has in her own apartment. You know, like she's a doll and shit, all fake and whatnot? Her batteries ran out. How's that?"

"That makes her sound like a sex toy." I shake my head and smirk, "Are you sure you've had sex with an actual woman? I mean, with lines like that, you're not getting into anyone's underwear."

"It's never been a problem," he says cockily.

Now that he's standing in the light, his brown eyes beaming at me and that stupid smile of his stretching across his even teeth, I know he's not exaggerating. I have no doubt drunk women have thrown themselves at him to the point of embarrassment at some point in his lifetime. Probably several points in his life.

I shake my head and roll my eyes. "Walk me to my car? I need to uh... get home." Home is where the car is, I always say. But I'm not telling him.

We start walking.

He says, "Did you find an apartment already? Since last night?" He's quick.

"I meant, to my friend's place."

His eyes narrow, "Which friend?"

"Uh, Bob?"

He nods, eyes still narrowed, "Bob who?"

"You know, Bob. Bob Smith." I don't sound convincing.

"Uh huh. You're going to sleep in your car again, aren't you?"

"No!" I lie. "I'm sleeping at Bob's! He has a huge guest room. Big soft bed. Lots of pillows and a fluffy comforter. It's luxurious." I wish.

"Wanna crash at my place?" he smiles.

Yes! No! Close your face before your tongue falls out! Because I'm drooling, I can tell.

"Ahh..." I stammer, "I shouldn't. Bob would be, ah...worried. He's expecting me."

"Look, N.Y. and C.'s is just up Wilshire, near eleventh. They serve New York *and* Chicago style pizza. And they're open till 3:30. We'll buy a pie, get it to go, and eat it at my place. You can crash on my couch."

The offer is tempting, but probably not a good idea.

He says, "You can stretch your legs out, lie flat. I'll even give you your own pillow and a blanket."

I don't tell him that I had no pillows last night and my neck was killing me this morning.

"In the morning," he smiles his captivating smile, "You can have full access to the bathroom. I've got a shower and everything..."

I'm having a hard time saying no.

"...but you have to scrub it first, if you want to use it," he finishes.

"Your shower?" I frown. "No deal. I'm not cleaning your shower. It's probably got black mold and two inches of guy grime glued to the walls."

"What is guy grime?" He sounds confused.

"If you have to ask, I'm not cleaning it off."

He chuckles, "It's spotless. I don't live in a dump."

I scoff, "We'll see about that."

Chapter 34

VICTORY

N.Y.& C. Pizza is packed with people.

It wasn't crowded when Kellan and I got here shortly after midnight. But the after hours bar hoppers slowly trickled in and filled every table.

The small one-room restaurant buzzes with youthful late night energy.

Me and Kellan sit against the wall in one of the black and white vinyl booths that look like car seats facing each other. I decided it was less complicated to eat here rather than get the pizza to go and eat at Kellan's.

The walls of N.Y.& C. are painted red. On one hangs framed photos of the Statue of Liberty, the Brooklyn Bridge, Yankee Stadium, and Yankees jerseys. On the other hangs photos of the Chicago skyline, Wrigley field, and Cubs jerseys.

We ended up with a thin crust New York pie at my insistence. Kellan wanted a thick crust Chicago style, which I argued against. He asked me if I was counting carbs, which I heatedly denied. The compromise was to order an Empire State, which has sausage, pepperoni, meatballs, salami, and extra cheese.

Despite the fact I owed Kellan a pizza for helping me move, he wouldn't let me pay for it.

While he chews on a slice of pizza, I say, "I told you I'd buy you a pizza. Let me pay you back."

He shakes his head, smiling and chewing. After swallowing, he says, "There's no way I'm making a girl living in her car buy me dinner. You can make up for it when you get back on your feet."

"I don't like owing people," I huff.

He smiles, "Deal with it." He gulps down the last swallow of his pint of draft Guinness.

"How do you drink that stuff?" I grimace. "It looks like tar."

He smacks his lips, "Mmmmm, tar. I hear that Guinness strains old wet cigarettes into the bottles to fill them. It's not even beer. And I'm gonna get another glass. You want one?"

"I'm good. I get enough tar breathing L.A. air."

"True that," he grins. "They've got Bud Light if you're worried about carbs."

"I'm not worried about carbs," I deny. "I'm not much into beer."

"You want another soda? And don't say Diet anything," he smirks.

"Get your beer," I say dismissively and wave him off.

He walks up to the counter in the back of the room.

I can't help but check out his butt in his skinny jeans, which he fills out to perfection. Despite all the interesting "people-watching" I could be doing in the crowded room, I can't take my eyes off Kellan. He's friendly with the guy behind the counter, and the people sitting at the counter. It takes all of thirty seconds for him to start chatting with the two hipster guys sitting at the back counter where Kellan is standing. They're laughing, Kellan's laughing, you'd think they were best buds, but I'm pretty sure he's never met them before.

I really like that about Kellan. He seems so easy going all the time. Considering I lost my closest L.A. friends when Scott kicked me out of Skin Trade, and Rex and Bobby jumped ship and went with him, maybe Kellan is the perfect person to befriend first.

Friends? A voice in my head laughs heartily. Are you nuts? You can't be friends with a hottie like Kellan. It will NEVER work. You have been warned.

I ignore the voice. It doesn't know what it's talking about.

Kellan and I can totally be friends.

He returns with his Guinness and a bottle of tea a few minutes later. He offers me the bottle, "Here. Unsweetened tea. It isn't diet and it doesn't have any carbs."

"I told you, I'm not counting carbs!"

"Uh huh," he grins.

I'm not going to reveal that I count calories all the time. But never carbs. "What do I owe you for the tea?" I pull some busking money from the wad of bills in my purse.

"Put your money away," he frown-smiles, "you're not paying for anything."

"Fine," I sulk, putting my money back in my purse.

He holds his beer up for a toast.

I ask, "What are we toasting?" I twist the top off the bottle of calorie free tea. For all I know, it could have a *million* carbs. But it doesn't have any calories. That's all I care about.

He says, "To you getting back on your feet."

"I can drink to that!" I clink my tea bottle against his glass then sip it.

The 20 inch pizza on the table between us is nearly gone. I had one slice.

"Mind if I finish this off?" Kellan asks, reaching for the second to last slice.

"You paid for it," I smile.

"I did," he grins and chomps on it greedily.

I marvel, "How can you still be hungry this late?"

He shrugs and chews, "I run a lot."

"So," I ask, "what's with the Gibson shirt?"

He's wearing a black t-shirt with a Gibson USA logo on the breast. Only guitar players wear guitar brand shirts.

"My main axe is a Les Paul," he says around a mouthful of food.

I groan, "Les Pauls weigh a ton."

He chuckles and wipes his fingers and lips on a napkin.

I really enjoy watching his lips.

His lips say, "Katy Perry plays a Les Paul. What's your excuse?"

I scowl, "Do you always talk like a sexist pig?" Emphasis on the sexy part. Damn, his eyes sparkle in this light. They're like topaz gemstones or something.

"How does comparing you to Katy Perry make me a sexist pig?"

"Because you're *comparing*," I growl.

"I'm comparing you to a woman." He cocks an eyebrow, "That's sexist?"

"No, but the way you cocked your eyebrow just now *is*," I snicker.

He shrugs and grins.

A fresh wave of people come in the front door of the restaurant. The small room suddenly feels overcrowded with all of them waiting in line to order.

"We should go," Kellan says. "We've been hogging this table for two hours."

That long? Wow, I've had so much fun talking with Kellan, I didn't even notice. I think I'm also dreading what happens next. I could sleep another night in my car, or risk crashing at Kellan's. I'm afraid of what might happen. My crazy side wants to throw caution to the wind and to Kellan. My sane side reminds me my two year relationship with Scott ended abruptly last night.

"Ready to go?" Kellan asks as he stands up and downs the last of his Guinness.

Looking for an excuse to stay, I say, "Are you okay to ride your motorcycle? Maybe we should stay awhile longer."

"What, after two beers in two hours on top of almost an entire twenty inch pizza? I think I'm good to ride. The beer is all trapped in my stomach with the grease. I'll be fine."

He's probably right. I remind myself I don't have to make any decisions until I get to my car.

We squeeze through the crowd inside and walked outside to the sidewalk on Wilshire. It's almost 2:00am and the night air is still warm.

Gotta love it.

L.A. does have a few perks.

Kellan's black Honda is parked right in front of N.Y. & C.'s. Parking is never a problem for motorcyclists. Maybe I need to get a bike. I know how to ride. My dad taught me on dirt bikes when I was little. And if I got a bike, parking it next to my Altima every night and sleeping in my car would seem almost normal.

I shake my head. One, that's stupid, and two, I can't afford a bike anyway.

Kellan already has his helmet on, "You ready?"

Now or never. "Ahhh…" I glance across the street at my Altima. I scored good parking because we got here late at night but before the after hours rush. Had it been the middle of the day or now, I would've been stuck parking three blocks away from N.Y. & C.'s.

"Hop in your car," Kellan says. "Let's go."

Wow, I need an excuse. I can't do this.

Going back to Kellan's place is a bad idea. It doesn't take a genius to figure that out. I'm fragile right now. Not that I let it show. Kellan is hot. It would be way too easy to let him comfort me. I don't know that I have the strength to resist his advances, which we both know are waiting in the wings. I don't know that I *want* to resist them.

Which is why I need to sleep in my car.

Again.

"My place is like a mile from here," he says. "Let's go."

I glance at my car. I glance at Kellan. Fuck it. I can't help myself. "Okay." I jog across the street between passing cars and climb into my Altima.

I'm going to regret this.

Somehow.

Maybe not tonight, maybe not tomorrow.

But way too soon.

In the mean time, I'm going to enjoy myself.

Chapter 35

KELLAN

I keep an eye on Victory's Altima in my side mirror as we cruise down Wilshire. Even this late, there's still traffic. Not as bad as during the day. But L.A. never sleeps.

A bunch of pedestrians start to cross one of the many big striped crosswalks spanning Wilshire in this part of Santa Monica. There's no lights at these crosswalks, so you have to keep your eyes open for people. Pedestrians almost get hit all the time. Sometimes they do get hit, and it's never pretty.

As it is, I'm surprised there's not more rear enders between cars because inevitably someone isn't paying attention and has to slam on the brakes to avoid hitting the pedestrians. The cars behind are never ready for it, and every time it happens, it's a close call for everyone involved.

I know better.

I ease up behind the SUV that is already stopped for the people crossing. The lane to my left is open and the BMW driving in it slams on the brakes when the idiot driver finally notices the pedestrians at the last second, laying down twenty feet of rubber. Of course, it was hard for the BMW to see the pedestrians because the SUV in front of me was blocking the BMW's view. Perhaps if the BMW had been paying attention…

Like I said.

Idiots.

I turn in the seat on my Honda and nod at Victory while I smirk and cock my thumb at the BMW.

She smiles back and waves from her Altima.

I instantly forget all about the idiots in the BMW.

Damn, Victory really is fucking hot. Triple XXX and girl next door all at the same time.

I can't get over how she doesn't act like 99% of the hotties I've dated in L.A.

Most L.A. babes are well aware of the value of their looks and use them at every opportunity. It gets old. That's why I'm always using stupid lines on them, seeing if I can fuck things up, because I don't care one way or the other who goes home with me.

They're all lame anyway.

But Victory is something different. Sure, I totally want to bang her. Who wouldn't? Any guy breathing would beg to be with Victory. But she doesn't know that. Or if she does, she doesn't act like it. Either she's innocent, and all I want to do is protect her, or she's wise to it and doesn't obsess about it, in which case I totally respect her.

The people crossing in the crosswalk have made it safely to the far side of Wilshire. The SUV in front of me pulls forward.

I toe the shifter on my bike and gradually accelerate up to the speed limit. Victory follows.

And, oh yeah, Victory shreds on guitar like Yngwie Fucking Malmsteen. You don't run into a girl like that every day.

Or any day.
Yeah, Victory is fuckin' awesome.
I totally want to bang her.
Does that make me a pig?
I guess it does.
I smirk to myself as we turn onto my street in West L.A.

Chapter 36

VICTORY

Kellan flips up his helmet visor and says, "This is it."

He straddles his bike, his boots on the ground. He leans his weight on the handlebars and his arms flex in a sexy dance of tight taut flesh.

I nod dumbly, keeping my lips pressed together so I don't lean out and lick his arms until the tattoos come off.

Muscles.

He says, "Follow me. I'll find the closest space we can, then walk you back to the apartment."

I nod dumbly.

More muscles.

He accelerates slowly down the street.

I stare at his ass.

Mmmm. It looks so good on the motorcycle.

He stops at the end of the block and looks back at me.

Oh! I'm supposed to follow.

I drive toward him, cautious not to rear end him because all I can think about is his rear.

Two blocks later, Kellan stops his bike, waving and pointing at an open space beneath a glowing streetlight. I like that the space is well lit. My car is less likely to be broken into.

I sigh to myself. I was never paranoid about parking in L.A. before this morning. Stupid car thieves.

I park, get out, and lock my car. Hopefully no one will notice that the passenger door lock is mostly useless.

"Ready," I smile.

Kellan circles his bike slowly in the middle of the street until he stops beside me. "You know, you're the only girl I've seen who wears a Whitesnake 'Slide It In' concert shirt. Did you find that at the bottom of some thrift shop somewhere?"

I shake my head, smiling, "It's my dad's shirt. He got it at the show, way before I was born. He gave it to me forever ago."

"Really?"

I nod proudly. My dad rocks.

Kellan grins, "Nice. Most women don't want to wear a t-shirt that has a cheesy white rattlesnake with tits. But I think it's awesome." He glances at my chest, presumably to look at the graphic and not my boobs.

The Whitesnake graphic is literally a white rattlesnake that is coiled to strike and has scaly human breasts, which it thrusts forward provocatively.

Kellan motions toward the back seat of his bike. "Hop on babe, you and me are going places," he chuckles.

I shake my head, "Okay, but only because you like Whitesnake."

He laughs, "All women like the white snake," he says suggestively.

I roll my eyes, "Keep talking like that, and I'm filing a restraining order."

He chuckles again and glances into my car at the big Marshall speaker cabinet in the back seat. "Oh shit. I forgot about your stuff. You probably want to bring your Fender and that classical inside. Don't want to leave a couple nice guitars like that in your car all night. Or your amps." Still straddling his bike, he leans down so he can see into my passenger seat. "Hey, what happened to your amps?"

I wince.

"What?" he asks uncertainly.

"Someone broke into my car this morning and took everything."

His eyes goggle. "That sweet white Strat you played last night at The Cobra?"

"My dad gave me that guitar."

"No shit?" he commiserates. "That fucking blows. I'm sorry, Vic—"

I scowl the instant he says Vic.

"I mean, Victory. Sorry. I forgot. Victory."

I like that he remembered.

"Anyway," he says, "I'm really sorry about your guitar. At least they didn't take your classical."

"You mean the Contrares?"

He nods.

"It's not mine. I had to borrow it for tonight." My guts knot thinking about it. How am I going to explain the broken guitar to Johnny and Karen tomorrow?

"What?" Kellan asks, concerned.

I don't know if I want to talk about it. I already feel bad enough. But I look at Kellan's eyes beaming out of his helmet. They glint back the streetlight overhead like smokey jewels. Against my will, I say, "Some skater punk knocked me over onto my classical and totaled it."

"No fucking way!" he gasps, taking his helmet off.

I nod.

"You have the worst luck, Victory," he chuckles.

"Not helping," I hiss, hunching my shoulders. I'm so pissed about the Contrares I want to bite someone's face off.

"Wow, you look like that snake on your shirt!" he snickers. "With tits and everything!"

The smile on Kellan's face is so big and genuine and friendly, I know he's trying to make me feel better. I punch him in the arm. "Jerk!"

"Ow!" He rubs his muscled arm.

Not only did my dad teach me how to ride dirt bikes and play guitar, he also taught me how to make a fist and not punch like a girl.

I shake my head, "Don't be a baby. I didn't hit you that hard."

"I don't know, Vic—I mean Victory, I think you might have broken something." He winces like he's dying.

He's not really hurt. I really appreciate that he's working hard to get my name right.

He says, "Well, do you want to grab some sweats, or whatever you sleep in, and go inside?"

"Ahh..." I consider the Contrares in my mind. I don't know how to repair a broken acoustic, but luthiers can do amazing work. "I should probably bring the guitar inside."

"That's not gonna fit on the bike. Hop on. I'll park my bike, then we'll come back for your stuff."

"I can walk." I'm somewhat worried about snuggling up to that ass of his on the back of his black Honda.

"I'll go slow."

And make me have to snuggle up against him that much longer? I don't think so. "I'll walk. Or I can wait right here."

"I'm not leaving you here."

I like that he's protective. "I've got a knife."

"Is that a threat or are you telling me you'll be safe at your car?"

"Both," I grin.

"Quit being a girl, and hop on the bike."

My eyes goggle. "A girl! Now I'm totally gonna stab you in your sleep. No, wait! I'll cut your balls off! Don't think I won't!"

"As long as my dick still works, I'll get by."

"I'll cut your dick off too!"

"You'll need a chainsaw. It's like a fucking tree trunk." He grabs his crotch and makes a growly face. Then he shakes his head and laughs, "You're crazy, you know that? Hop on the bike."

I give him a shrewd look before slowly climbing on behind his... behind. I put my hands on his shoulders. "If you feel anything sharp against the side of your neck, that's my knife."

"Duly noted." He puts his helmet on without strapping it and rides us back to his apartment complex. He parks the bike inside the courtyard and locks it to a post with a big steel cable lock.

We walk back to my Altima through his neighborhood. It's quiet here compared to Wilshire Boulevard. Our stroll reminds me of walking in my neighborhood in Bakersfield when I was growing up. Me and my high school buddies would wander aimlessly, sharing a single six pack of PBR, trying to get drunk but not, and totally content having nothing to do but stroll. Walking with Kellan feels the same way and I like it. It's a nice break from the go, go, go attitude I've had since hitting the streets of Los Angeles when I left Bakersfield and my buddies behind.

At my car, I pull one of my black plastic garbage bags out of the trunk, and the Contrares, before slamming the trunk shut. "Ready," I say.

"You wanna bring your Marshall cab inside? I've got room."

"After the last twenty four hours? Yes. I'm not taking any chances." That applies to my speaker cabinet *and* Kellan.

Kellan pulls the Marshall out of my car like it weighs an ounce. I'm staring at his flexing muscles the whole time.

Who am I kidding? I don't stand a chance.

What am I getting myself into?

I'll worry about it tomorrow.

Chapter 37

VICTORY

I'm on the couch with Kellan.

Oh. My. God.

I never thought it could be like this.

With him.

This *good.*

My head is spinning.

The chemistry, the passion. The heat. It's incredible.

It's primal.

Like he's invading my *soul*...

We are two people working in perfect harmony, making beautiful music together. I've never felt a connection like this. I thought Scott and I had an intense connection in the beginning. But it wasn't like this.

Not even close.

This is paradise.

How could I have doubted it?

A strand of hair hangs in Kellan's face as he eyes me with his baby browns. "Wanna do that again?" he grins.

"Totally," I sigh, nearly breathless. "I can't believe we didn't wake your neighbors."

"We totally need to record it this time," he says, standing up from the couch.

"Okay," I smile. "That trill you added in the middle was amazing."

He smirks, "Thanks. But you totally set it up with that D major arpeggio. It always amazes me that a major chord can sound so dark. I always thought they were the happy chords."

"Not at all," I smile. I turn up the volume knob on the Ibanez RG550 that Kellan is letting me play. The Ibanez is plugged into one of his little practice amps.

Kellan's got a bunch of amps around his apartment living room and several different guitars on guitar stands or hanging from the wall. There's a big table across from the couch that has a computer, mixing board, and monitor speakers. He has several different mics and mic stands, and sound baffles on his walls to absorb echoes. It's a mini recording studio in his living room.

I play a series of major arpeggios in response to Kellan's comment, moving them up a half tone at a time.

He nods, "That's wicked. It sounds like pure evil. I love it!" He's standing in front of the table with the computer on top. There's a condenser mic on a small stand in front of it. "This should catch the sound of both guitars pretty good."

"You must have thick walls. I could never play my guitar this late in Scott's place. The landlord always shut me down."

"As long as I don't crank it at night, nobody complains."

"That's awesome," I say.

He suddenly looks excited, "You know what? We should film this too. Put a video on YouTube."

I frown, "Can we just record the audio? I don't want to fix my makeup."

He chuckles, "You look hot. You're makeup's fine."

I roll my eyes, "How about my hair?"

He grins, "You're such a girl."

"Kellan! You know women are judged on their looks. It's like, no matter how awesome you are at what you do, the men on the planet are going to deduct points from your accomplishments for not having your hair and makeup perfect."

"The women too," he chuckles. "They're worse. Women are women's worst enemy."

"See?" I frown. "I haven't looked in a mirror all day. I worked eight hours then went to the Promenade to busk for six. Please, let's just do audio, or hide our faces like every other guitar player does on YouTube."

He grins, "Come here."

"What?"

He motions with his hand, "Come here."

I arch an eyebrow.

He rolls his eyes, walks to the couch, and grabs my hand. I put the Ibanez on the couch and he pulls me into the hallway. My chest locks when I suspect he's pulling me into his bedroom. He pulls me into the bathroom instead, and stands me in front of the mirror.

He stands behind me and pulls my long hair out of my face and behind my shoulders. I automatically look away.

"Look," he commands.

"What?" I whine.

"Look in the mirror."

I do. "What?"

"You're perfect. After working fourteen hours, you're perfect."

I realize I should be exhausted, but I'm not. I think the excitement of hanging out with Kellan has pushed my tiredness away. Looking in the mirror, I'm surprised I don't have huge black plastic garbage bags under my eyes.

"I'd totally fuck you," Kellan snickers.

"You'd fuck a knothole, you knothead."

He frowns, "Hardly. I have high standards. You look fine."

"Fine?"

He grins and winks, "I said I have high standards. Anyway, 99% of guys would think you look smokin' right now. We're filming it."

"At least let me touch up my eyes first."

He rolls his. "Make it quick."

I grab my purse and spend two minutes on my makeup before returning to the couch and picking up his Ibanez.

He's leaning over the computer. "Camera's all set up. You ready to rock?"

I nod.

He hits record on the computer and sits back next to me on the couch, picking up his royal blue skyburst Les Paul.

The metronome on the recording software clicks off: one, two, three, four, and then the drum track starts…and we're playing the harmonized riff together again.

It's magical.

The riff is extremely complex, and we just made it up over the last hour or so. We play through it like we've rehearsed it a thousand times. I thought I had a tight connection with Bobby and Rex, but this is the next level.

Kellan and I play together like we've got wires running between our heads or like a four armed being that plays two guitars at the same time. It's uncanny.

Few musicians ever connect with someone who is their total equal, both technically and stylistically. It's almost like he's my brother, or we're identical twins or something.

It's epic.

We finish the riff, which is almost an entire instrumental song at this point. I end by wiggling the whammy bar on the Ibanez and Kellan bends a high screaming note on his Les Paul.

He holds has hand up for a high five and I slap it.

"That was awesome," he says, standing up to stop the recording. "Let's listen to it." He grins like a little kid on the playground who has just discovered that tag is the most fun game ever invented.

He hits play and sits on the table, listening intently.

At first, I'm barely paying attention to the video. All I can do is watch Kellan watching the video. He sits on top of the table, one boot on the ground, the other half-bent leg dangling a boot in the air while he rests his elbow on the jeans of his bent thigh.

I drool over the casual way Kellan relaxes into everything. I can't decide if he looks like he's posing or if this is how hot men have conducted themselves since the beginning of time, and fashion photographers have merely learned which moments to capture that best magnetize a woman's attention. Whatever it is, Kellan has it. That fabled "it" factor you always hear about in Hollywood, whether it's hot bands or A-list actors.

Kellan has *it*.

But what sets him apart from the average superstar is that Kellan has depth.

As the rough recording of our mini song plays out, Kellan is absolutely focused on the part I played. Not his own amazing playing. Every time I hear my guitar stand out in the playback, where I did some particularly awesome riffs (if I do say so myself), Kellan is air guitaring along to them like it's the most awesome guitar playing he's ever heard.

"Yes!" he cheers. "I need to hear that again."

He backs up the recording with the computer mouse and plays my solo again, air guitaring along with it. "That's fucking shredding right there, Victory," he grins and holds his hand up for a high five.

I slap it and he lets the recording play through to the end.

"Damn, Victory, you're incredible." He shakes his head, awed, "I can't believe you came up with those riffs off the cuff."

I shrug, but I'm smiling from ear to ear. Who doesn't like being acknowledged for a lifetime of hard work? Scott never gushed over my guitar playing like this. Not once.

Kellan smiles, "You're incredible. Truly talented."

"You're not so bad yourself," I say, trying to diffuse his enthusiasm. It's so much, I'm almost uncomfortable. If it wasn't for the fact that he's an equally amazing player, I'd think he was bullshitting me.

He drops back into the couch next to me. His t-shirt slides up an inch, revealing his hard abs. He says, "I'll post that shit online tomorrow."

I don't register his words, but I feel his heat. It pours off of him. It's alluring and I realize I'm chewing on my lip, eyeing him up and down. I would love to rip his shirt off and play him like a guitar. My eyes pop ever so slightly at the thought. I hope he doesn't notice.

"Damn, Victory, we could turn this into a complete song. We need to find a drummer yesterday and lay that shit down on tape."

All I register is the word "lay."

He beams at me, "Don't you think?"

I stare at him, "What?"

"Earth to Victory, you there?"

I shake my head and massage between my eyebrows. "Oh," I sigh, "I must be more tired than I realized. I didn't sleep well in my car last night. It's super late."

"Wanna hit the sheets?"

YES!!

NOOO!!!!!

I stammer, "Ahh…"

"You can sleep in my bed if you want."

My eyes goggle. "Slow down, Casanova!"

"I meant, I'll sleep on the couch," he grins. "Give you the comfy bed to make up for sleeping in your car."

"That's sweet, Kellan." But his bed will smell like him and I will be unable to sleep a wink. Or, I'll dream about him all night long, tossing and turning, thinking about his hot self. Either way, I will wake up tomorrow a frustrated mess. As it is, I don't know how I'm going to sleep on the couch without going nuts.

He arches an expectant eyebrow.

I open my mouth, struggling to find some kind of response that makes sense and doesn't incriminate me. "Couch," I say, my head circling dramatically as it nods and shakes at the same time because I can't make up my own mind. "Yes, the couch! Definitely the couch!"

"All right, I'll grab you some pillows and blankets."

Not from your bed!!!

I heave a sigh of relief when he pulls clean sheets, bedding, and a pillow from a linen closet built into the apartment's short L-shaped hallway that leads to the bathroom and bedroom.

"You can clean up in the bathroom while I make up the couch," he says.

"Okay."

I close the door to the little bathroom and brush my teeth and wash my face. His towels match the shower curtain, which I peel back so I can check the tub. He wasn't kidding. No guy grime in the whole bathroom. He doesn't even leave his toothpaste uncapped. It's put away in the medicine cabinet. And no porn magazines on the toilet tank like some guys I know. Instead, he has the latest four issues of Guitar World magazine stashed in a nice woven magazine rack beside the toilet. Maybe he watches his porn on his smart phone? Nah, something about Kellan tells me he doesn't need porn. He has plenty of floozies for that.

Which is why I need to refrain from becoming one of them.

After I change into my yoga pants, I walk out of the bathroom.

He stands proudly beside the couch, "Will this work?"

Wow. The couch is all made up. It's not a fold out, but he tucked the sheets around the cushions, and he even folded the top sheet back. I wonder if he put a mint under my pillow too.

"Uh," I laugh, "yeah."

"Well, I'm off to bed," he smiles. "I'll leave my door open. In case you want to have sex in the middle of the night."

My eyes bulge, "Kellan!"

"What? You know you're thinking about it."

"No I'm not!"

He smirks confidently, "That was the weakest denial I've ever heard."

So what if he's right? "Do I need to sleep with my rape knife?" I threaten, even though I'm basically bluffing.

"Why, so you can rape me at knife point?" He grins, "I can totally do kink."

"That's not what I meant! I meant you, you jackass!"

"I wouldn't be worried about me..." He lifts his Gibson t-shirt over his head and his dancing abs are liquid rock cocaine. They beg to be licked. He takes about an hour to pull the shirt off entirely, flexing every muscle known to man in the process. "...I would be worried about you," he drawls seductively as he slaps his t-shirt over one incredibly well-muscled shoulder. "You're not going to be able to resist."

I jab my finger toward his bedroom, "Out!"

He chuckles and leans against the opening of the L-shaped hallway. His jeans ride low on his hips. Intricate tattoos cover his muscled arms. He's got more abs than I can count, he's got the V, and he knows how to use both. He totally practices posing in the mirror. It's the only rational explanation for how damn sexy he is at every single moment.

I reach down into my purse. "This—" I pull out my rape knife and the rainbow blade pops open with a swift click, "—will be under my pillow. If you want to wake up in the morning with your nut sack intact, you'll keep that in mind."

Kellan chuckles, "You're too bad ass for your own good, *Vic*." He's clearly calling me Vic to irritate.

I wave my knife menacingly at him, "I mean it *Smellan*. Unless you want to go ball-less, you'll stay in your room."

"Easy, Lizzie Borden," he soothes. "You better put that shit away before you cut your own balls off."

"I don't have balls!"

He chuckles, "You act like you do." He grins, undeterred, "Anyway, I can see you're serious about raping me. I'll make sure to lock my door."

"Go to bed!" I huff.

"Night, Victory," he winks and turns.

Oh my god. He has those little dimples above his butt. The tops of the cheeks rise above his jeans and flex sexually when he struts around the corner to his bedroom.

Good thing I've got my rape knife.

I'm going to use it to cut his jeans off and have my way with him.

Chapter 38

VICTORY

I totally can't sleep.

I flip and flop around on the couch. I've laid here for two hours since

Kellan walked into his bedroom. Sleep is nowhere in sight.

Gee, I wonder why.

All I can think about is Kellan's butt and the way his jeans hugged it. It was the last image I saw before turning out the lights.

His butt is burned into my brain.

He wasn't kidding about locking the door.

When I heard him latch it and click the lock over, he said through the bedroom door, "I've got a padlock on the inside. You're never getting in."

Not that I tried. But, boy, I considered knocking about a hundred times. Not that I would ever do such a thing. But I would give it serious consideration. Take it before the committee of opinions in my head. Let them vote on it. If the decision was unanimously in favor of knocking, I would have no choice but to knock.

Ladies? I ask the committee in my head. How do you vote? Knock or no knock?

I don't even have to ask.

We all know the answer is yes.

But I can be a vicious dictator.

I will not knock!

I sigh heavily and stare at the dark ceiling.

The faint glow from streetlights and the apartment building lights outside glint off the sparkly flecks embedded in the popcorn pattern of the ceiling. Hoping to summon sleep, I try counting the artificial ceiling stars. It's not sheep, but it will have to do.

Sadly, every time I close my eyes, I don't see sheep or stars.

I see the top of Kellan's perfect bottom.

The truth is, if I'm being honest with myself, Kellan is amazing. In every way. He makes me feel good, and I barely know the guy. And the way we play guitar together? When you set everything else aside, our guitar chemistry is unbelievable.

But the last thing I want to do is trash our musical connection with a frivolous rebound fling that can only end badly. Kellan is not a one woman type of guy. We'll never be right for each other as boyfriend girlfriend.

But we can be friends for sure.

Besides, considering Scott dumped me and kicked me out of Skin Trade last night, there's no way I'm getting involved with any men for months. Maybe years.

I need to grieve first.

But I can make decisions about friends. Everyone needs friends. And I need to put together a band. Kellan is perfect for both.

We can be friends and bandmates.

Nothing more.

And, ladies? Yeah, you guys? The panel in my head? The ones who keep telling me to go knock on Kellan's door? We all know what happened the last time I slept with someone in the band.

Did you forget already?

Fucking Scott Walker?

Yeah, him.

Good riddance.

I'm not sleeping with Kellan.

End of story.

Go knock!!!!

SHUT!!!! UP!!!!!

Chapter 39

KELLAN

I'm wired.

Like I snorted a bag full of crank and I'm not coming down for another ten hours.

All because of Victory.

I want to jump out of bed and finish that song we started earlier. I know it's good music. It won't take much to work up the whole thing. I'm gonna find us a drummer. Maybe Joaquin, if he's not busy.

Me and Victory need to start recording tracks A.S.A.P. We spun musical gold tonight. Or should I say platinum, because we're going to sell a million fucking records of what we come up with.

Between me and Victory, it's an endless stream of ideas. I've never worked with another guitar player as good as her or as easy to work with. She's totally creative. Good ideas pour out of her.

I'm in heaven working with her.

It doesn't hurt that she's so fucking hot.

Man, I'm a little surprised I didn't fuck her the second we walked into my apartment.

I chuckle softly to myself.

If she was any other girl, she would've begged me to bang her in the alley behind N.Y. & C.'s after we had pizza. But I have to actually turn up the heat with a girl for that shit to happen. It always works. But with Victory, I guess I just, I don't know, didn't think about it. We were too busy talking guitar and everything else except sex.

If Dubs could see me now, he'd rail on me for turning into a chick. He would totally flip.

I grin.

Whatever.

I don't need to prove anything.

I flop onto my back and lace my fingers behind my head. My Jimi Hendrix poster on the wall between my Wild Child poster and my mirrored closet doors catches my eye.

I've had my Jimi poster for as long as I can remember. It's the exact same one Victory had on the wall at her old apartment last night. No way I was letting her leave hers behind, which she almost did. I bet she'll say something about mine when she finally sees it. But she seems to be avoiding my bedroom like it's some kind of hot zone.

I smirk to myself. Any place where I'm at is definitely a hot zone.

She probably thinks I bring tons of chicks home all the time, which I never do. I always go to their houses so I can leave whenever I want. It's easier that way.

If I ever get Victory in here, it'll be a fucking inferno. Strangely, it's turning out to be more work than I expected. I can handle it. I didn't learn how to play guitar overnight. It's taken years to get this good.

Given the proper motivation, I'm not afraid to work hard for what I want.

Funny thing is, I don't think I've ever wanted anything as bad as I want Victory in my entire life. Except maybe the first time my mom played Hendrix's Voodoo Chile for me. I went nuts and begged her for a guitar. She said we didn't have the money. Man, I worked hard then. I got a paper route, mowed lawns, raked leaves. Whatever it took. I wanted a guitar and nothing was going to stop me from getting it.

Me and guitar have been inseparable ever since.

I feel the same way about Victory.

I want her.

Like the first guitar I ever bought, I'm going to do whatever it takes to make Victory mine.

Whatever it takes.

Even if I have to mow Victory's lawn or plow her furrow or plant my seeds or rake her leaves.

I grin.

I don't even know what raking her leaves means. But when it comes to Victory, I'll do it.

I cackle quietly to myself and try to sleep.

Chapter 40

VICTORY

A thin sunbeam slicing through a gap in the window blinds wakes me up, spearing right into my closed eyes. The inside of my eyelids glow bright red. I squinch my lids and roll over, burying my face into the couch cushions.

The apartment is silent. I don't know what time it is. I'm guessing from the angle of the sun and the relative quiet outside, it's still early. Too early. But at least I slept for a few hours. I don't know how I did it.

I need to get ready for work at Big Momma's.

I grimace.

The Contrares.

What are Johnny and Karen gonna say when they see it?

The case sits on the floor to the side of the couch. I *so* don't want to deal with it. Everything in its time, or whatever Johnny said.

I hope their usual hippie mellowness is in effect when I show them the guitar. Maybe I can say I forgot it? Leave it here and deal with it next weekend? I will take that into serious consideration.

But now I have to go to the bathroom.

I slide the covers back and tiptoe to the bathroom.

Kellan's bedroom door, which is four feet from the door to the bathroom, is wide open. Kellan is sprawled out on the queen sized bed.

Naked.

He lies on his back, one muscled arm folded behind his head. The corner of his sheet covers his privates and part of his thigh, but he's pretty much naked.

I make a strangled gasping noise that is way louder than necessary. I slap my hand over my mouth, holding it in.

His body is truly incredible. Lying down, he's as hot as he was standing up. He is flawless masculine muscled perfection.

I'm hypnotized.

He stirs in bed, not quite awake, and the sheet moves, seemingly under its own power, or else there's special effects guys off camera pulling it with a fishing line so I look like an idiot staring at Kellan's hidden junk like a traffic accident about to happen. In a good way, of course.

A second ago, the sheet was rumpled over his jumblies. But now, so little is left covering him, it drapes neatly over his magnificent morning wood, leaving little to the imagination. Big Sur has never seen Redwoods so big.

My hand is still clamped over my mouth. I'm openly ogling. Kellan's going to wake up any second and catch me peeping.

To the bathroom!

I spin in the hallway and slam my shoulder into the sheetrock. Doesn't hurt my shoulder, but it makes a nice hollow thump loud enough to wake a dead redwood.

Oh, wait. The redwood is already awake.

I stumble through the bathroom door and lock it behind me before Kellan sees me.

Disaster averted.

I heave a sigh of relief while I sit on the toilet.

Now, if I can only get out of the bathroom and grab my garbage bag of stuff and get out of here before he wakes up, I'm in the clear. But if Kellan wakes up before I'm gone, I'm gone. If I know what I mean. And I do know what I mean.

Redwoods…

Between Kellan's guitar playing, and a body equally as good as his guitar playing, he's the most criminally sexy man ever invented. And with him lying around naked and hot, how am I supposed to keep my hands off him? I don't stand a chance.

Geez! How long does it take to pee!

I finish up five seconds or five hours later. I quietly open the door an inch, peeking out to make sure Kellan hasn't woken.

I nearly jump out of my skin when he's standing right in front of the crack in the door.

I blurt, "Kellan!" and slam the door in his face.

He laughs.

My heart races and I'm breathing like a steam engine at top speed. There's no way I'm leaving this bathroom. He could be completely naked. The door was only open a split second before I closed it, so I didn't have time to survey between his legs for record breaking redwoods.

There's a soft knock at the door.

I singsong, "I'm not in here!"

He chuckles.

"Go away!" I say.

"I need to take a leak."

"I'm not coming out!"

"It's my apartment. I need to pee. Show mercy," he snickers.

"No!"

"Don't make me go in the kitchen sink."

I grimace, "You'd pee in your own sink?"

He sighs, "It's that or the rose bushes outside. My neighbors hate that."

"That's their problem!"

"Come on, Gigi."

"Gigi?" I bark, "Who's Gigi? One of your countless girlfriends?"

"No, I said, Gee Gee. For Guitar Goddess. Since you don't want me calling you Vic, I needed to come up with a new nick name for you."

In that case, I kind of like Gigi.

"I really need to go," he says through the door.

"Fine. Are you dressed?"

"No," he says casually.

"Put some pants on! I'm not walking out of here until you do!" Yes, saying that was physically painful for me, but it had to be said.

"Hold on," he groans, his voice muffled as he pads into his bedroom. "Okay. Pants are on. Can I piss now?"

I snicker, "Say please."

"I can't believe you're making me beg in my own apartment."

"It's just one little word," I coo, "a magical little word, and fewer syllables than abracadabra or open sesame."

"You're such a pain in the ass," he grumbles.

"But I bet I'm nothing like the pain in your bladder."

"Fuck it. I'm using the kitchen sink," he grunts and I hear thudding feet.

I open the door, "Okay! You can use the bathroom," I giggle.

He's half way across the living room, on his way to the kitchen. He's wearing boxer briefs. Holy shit, he's totally sexy. Sex perfection. The briefs hug his butt. Ohhhh gawd. I'm melting all over again.

When he turns, and I see his abs, I whimper. I hope he didn't hear me. I'm paralyzed in place, standing in the doorframe of the bathroom.

"May I?" he asks, standing right in front of me.

I'm blocking the doorway. I can't actually walk, but I manage to collapse against the doorframe.

He squeezes past me, his chest brushing up against…mine.

He suddenly stops.

He's not moving a muscle.

I *can't* move a muscle.

He gazes down at me, cocky as hell.

My heart whirs like a blender in my chest. My insides spin out of alignment. My nipples go rigid. Heat explodes between my legs. I'm only wearing my panties and the Whitesnake t-shirt I slept in. My nipples poke against the soft cotton. At least the shirt is black so it's hard to notice. But I feel entirely naked with nothing to shield me from his heat.

His eyes are on fire.

I can only imagine what his redwood sized white snake is doing right now…

But I can't look down to find out.

My eyes are locked on Kellan's.

He leans toward me.

He's going to kiss me.

If it ends up being anywhere near as good as when I kissed him in front of Scott, I'm going to have sex with him. I won't be able to stop myself.

His mouth is half an inch from mine.

I feel his heat.

This is it. I'm so ready.

His lips peel into a grin. "You're lucky I have to pee," he smirks and pushes past me.

I stumble into the hallway and the bathroom door slams in my face.

That was way too close for comfort.

I have zero willpower when he's nearly naked.

There's no way I'm getting out of this apartment without having sex with him.

Unless I leave before he finishes peeing.

Good thing I don't have much stuff.

Living in your car has certain advantages.

Chapter 41

VICTORY

"Are you leaving?" Kellan asks, standing in the bathroom doorway.

I gasp and nearly jump out of my boots. I've got my jeans on, my garbage bag of stuff is on top of my big Marshall speaker cabinet, as is the Contrares in its case, and I'm pushing everything out the front door.

I'm afraid if I turn around and see him in his boxer briefs, I won't leave. Over my shoulder, I say, "I've got to get to work."

"Don't you want to shower and eat something before you go?"

Do I detect a note of concern in his voice? Or perhaps disappointment? I think I do. My heart warms at the thought, mostly against my will.

One of the various committees in my head starts a shouting match. Don't fall for Kellan! You're rebounding! Get out while you still can! He's a total male slut! Run away!

"Uh..." I stammer over my shoulder, "I don't want to be late for work."

"What time is work?"

"The shop opens at eleven." I still can't look at him. I hang my head over my Marshall.

"You realize it's only seven thirty?"

"There might be traffic."

"On a Sunday?"

"It's L.A."

"Not three hours worth."

"You never know," I wince. I don't even believe it myself.

"Take a shower. We'll go get breakfast around the corner."

I finally turn to face him. Abs. Chest. Shoulders. Tats. That was a mistake. I examine my fingernails, considering. "I really could use a shower. But you have to put on a shirt and pants if you want me to stay."

He laughs, "I *told* you, you totally want to have sex with me."

I roll my goggling eyes, then command, "Pants, shirt. Now."

He chuckles but doesn't move.

I push my Marshall toward the front door and say, "Bye!"

The little caster wheels catch on the metal threshold plate and the Contrares case rockets off the top of the Marshall. It bangs on the ground. "Fuck!" I blurt.

"Ooh!" Kellan grunts. "I hope you didn't break it again," he says sarcastically.

I whip around, fuming, and glare at him.

"What? You said it was totaled."

I shake my head, "You…are a complete *ass*."

His face softens sympathetically. "Relax. Take a shower. Get some food in you before you go to work." He takes a step toward me.

My palm shoots up like a stop sign. "Pants. Shirt. Now!"

"All right," he sighs and walks into the bedroom. He returns a minute later in shorts and a Lynch Mob t-shirt.

"I said pants!"

He shakes his head, "No deal. It's too hot for pants."

I reluctantly break into a smile. "Nice shirt, by the way."

"George Lynch rocks."

"You know he's almost sixty and he's still a total hottie?" I almost tell Kellan he'll probably age just as well as George, but don't. His ego is already too big. I shouldn't have mentioned it.

"I wouldn't know," Kellan says. "Get cleaned up, and let's go eat. I'm starving."

"You ate a 20 inch pizza right before bed and you're hungry?"

"Good point. I'll go for a run while you shower. Don't lock me out," he grins.

Before he leaves, Kellan pulls the Marshall inside and puts the Contrares back by the couch. He gets clean towels out of the linen closet in the hall and hands them to me.

He says, "I've only got guy soap and shampoo. But I should have some moisturizer under the sink. Do you need anything? Like razors or whatever? I can get them at Rite-Aid on my run."

"Oh, uh, sure."

"Be right back."

He closes the door before I ask if he needs money.

I have no idea how long he'll be gone. I turn the water on in the shower. When it's warm, I climb in and let the water fall all over me. Wow, I'm tired. I'm running on fumes at this point. It's going to be a long work day, but I'm too wired from Kellan and everything else to sleep. I'll have to have a gallon of espresso every hour on the hour, or I'm never going to make it through the day.

For now, I'm going to relax in the shower. I make do with Kellan's manpoo. Err, somehow, that's not a good name for man shampoo. Maybe I'll skip my hair. I washed it yesterday. I think I'll just relax under the hot water for awhile…

…and fall into a steamy daydream. Kellan is the leading man. Everything is misty. We're outside in a jungle somewhere. He's shirtless, but not wearing those stupid running shorts. He's got jeans on and his thick hair is swept back, a lone lock dangling above his manly brow and burning brown eyes…He looks really good. He lays me down on a bed of rose petals. My arms are over my head and I luxuriate under his warm caress as he squeezes my breasts in his manly hands and his tongue slides down my tummy. He lingers on my navel, his tongue probing, slick and demanding, tickling and teasing, then he slides down the rest of the way, to my heat, to my wetness, to my—

Knock! Knock! Knock!

"Yo, Gigi!"

My eyes snap open. I realize my fingers are between my legs. I guiltily flail my arms up in the air like somebody just shouted "Stick 'em up!" and almost slip in the tub and crack my head wide open.

"Hey, Victory!"

"What!" I scream.

"I bought you a razor and lady's shampoo. And some antiperspirant. Unlock the door and I'll set them on the counter."

"I thought you went for a run!"

"I did."

"Didn't you just leave?"

"I left a half hour ago. Have you been in the shower the whole time?"

Oh, wow. How long was I in that steamy jungle with Kellan? "No!" I lie. "I just started."

"Oh good. Then you can use the razor. Unlock the door and I'll leave everything on the counter."

What am I going to do? I look around and realize the door opens toward the shower, so he can't see me. But, despite the pattern on the shower curtain, it's mostly transparent. If he sticks his head around the door, he'll have a clear view of me.

I lean out of the shower and unlock the door. "No peeking!"

He opens the door and I see his hand reaching in, holding a bulging Rite Aid bag.

"No peeking!" I warn again. I can't see his face in the mirror, which means he can't see me, but I'm not taking any chances.

He sets the bag down and closes the door.

I step out of the shower with one foot, dripping water all over the floor, grab the bag, and pull it back into the shower. I stand away from the shower head and look into the bag. It's filled with different razors, two shampoos and three conditioners, antiperspirant and deodorant, and several types of lotion. He bought half the store.

"Thanks!" I shout.

"I wasn't sure what you wanted," he says through the door, "so I bought different stuff. Hopefully something in there will work."

I'm touched. Scott never bought me anything. I always blamed it on us not having any money. But a bottle of shampoo or a deodorant isn't exactly expensive. Scott knew what brands I used, or at least I assumed he did, but he never bothered to buy me any.

This Kellan character is turning into a regular Prince Charming. Who needs glass slippers or diamond rings when you have your choice of body lotions?

Chapter 42

VICTORY

There's already three people waiting outside the Blue Daisy Cafe on Wilshire when Kellan and I walk up to the front door ten minutes before eight, but we manage to snag a table outside under the awning.

I order an Eggs Florentine crepe that includes a mixed organic greens salad with walnuts and a tangy dressing that reminds me of spiced oak and nutmeg, in a good way.

Kellan gets smoked salmon Eggs Benedict and apple bacon with zucchini hash browns.

We both order the Turkish lattes, which are smooth and creamy, and I'm pretty sure laced with speed. I won't be needing a caffeine refill for at least six hours.

While I slice up my crepe with my knife and fork, I ask Kellan, "So, how'd you get rid of Femme Flakes last night?"

Kellan frowns, pausing his coffee cup half way to his mouth, "What's a femme flakes?"

I giggle, "Your date at the Promenade? How'd you get rid of her?" I slide a bite of crepe into my mouth.

"Told her I had the squirts."

I hastily grab my napkin and hold it over my mouth while I laugh really, really hard. I don't know why that sounds so funny, but it is. "You did not!" I say behind my napkin, my mouth half full of food.

He sets his coffee down. "I did," he grins. "I made about ten trips to the bathroom while we were inside Monsoon's having drinks. When she finally asked what I was doing, I told her I had the shits real bad." Kellan sips his Turkish coffee and smiles cockily, "Chick like her denies that shit even exists. After I told her, she bolted."

I laugh again. Normally, diarrhea is never my favorite meal topic, but for some reason, Kellan's story is hilarious. "She *left* you there?" I gasp

He chuckles and shakes his head, "No. She was decent enough to drive me to her place where my bike was parked. I moaned the whole way there like I was going to let go in my pants any second. She kept asking if she needed to pull over and let me out. Didn't want me soiling her leather seats. Every time she asked, I grunted, 'Keep driving! I can hold it! I can hold it!'" Kellan winces and wraps his arms around his stomach like he's in pain. "She was all over the road, totally panicking, ran at least three red lights."

I'm laughing so hard, tears are brimming in my eyes.

He continues, "When we pulled into her driveway, she pretty much ran inside her house and never came out. Didn't even ask if I needed to use the bathroom. Poor thing. I think I traumatized her talking about pooh. Broke her brain. She's the kind of girl, if she ever has babies, will never change a diaper in her life. She'll pay someone to do it for her."

I shake my head, "I know the type."

"Throw a rock in L.A., and you'll hit two or three of them," he chuckles. "Anyway, what the fuck is a Femme Flake?" He takes a bite of his zucchini hash browns.

I shrug, "I don't know. Just what I was calling her in my head. She seemed like she had about as much personality as a female corn flake."

He chuckles, "A *female* corn flake? I didn't realize corn flakes had genders."

I throw a leaf from my salad at him.

"What?" he laughs.

I roll my eyes, "You were the one who went out with her."

He shrugs, "Yeah, but who'd I spend the night with?" He winks.

"That doesn't count." I realize I'm feeling vaguely jealous of Femme Flakes, which I shouldn't, because I'm not going to date Kellan. We're going to be friends. So it shouldn't matter who he goes out with. So I can ask all the questions I want and not worry about what his answers are. "How'd you end up going out with her anyway?"

"I gave her my number when you and I were outside The Cobra. She called me up yesterday."

"You gave her *your* number? And *she* called? Isn't it supposed to be the other way around?" I really can't believe him.

He shrugs, "For most people."

"You're such a cocky bastard!"

He smiles his squirts-eating-grin and says, "Does it bother you?"

I roll my eyes, "You love it, don't you?"

"Who wouldn't?"

"Kellan, you are so self satisfied it makes me sick."

He cocks a thumb behind him, toward the front door of the Blue Daisy. "Bathroom's inside. Make sure they have toilet paper before you unload."

I shake my head and snicker, "Kellan, what am I going to do with you?"

He grins at me. That stupid, cocky, sexy grin that makes his burning brown eyes sizzle, "Anything you want. That's why I left the door to my bedroom open last night. I was hoping you'd put the moves on me."

"I thought you locked it?"

"Naw, I just wiggled the knob around like I was. It was open. All night *long*..." he says suggestively.

When he says long, I think of redwoods.

Hot. I'm suddenly hot.

Kellan is too much.

I reach for my ice water and gulp down two big swallows. I can't fan my face because he'll notice.

Our waiter walks up right then and sets the check on the corner of the table. He smiles, "You can get that whenever you're ready. No rush."

"Thanks," I smile at him before he walks away.

Before I even notice, Kellan's wallet is out and he's sticking money inside the black vinyl check holder.

"Hey!" I holler, "You can't pay for breakfast! You paid for pizza last night."

"So?" He closes the check holder like it's the end of the argument. "Pay me back when you have money. You ready?"

I nod.

We stand up and walk back toward his place together.

When we reach the street leading to his apartment, and we have to cross at the light, his hand brushes mine. Is he trying to hold my hand? He doesn't seem like the type. Or is he just twisting to check out the woman with the low cut top, inflated boobs, puffed up lips, gold plated hair, and aviator sunglasses waiting at the stoplight in her Audi convertible?

I'm sure to guys who frequent strip joints, she's gorgeous. To me, she looks like a clown. I mean, not like I care. Kellan can look at any woman he wants.

Even the clowny ones.

Kellan and I are just friends.

We cross in front of Sausage Lips. I call her that because to me her lips look like Kielbasa sausages covered in thick lipstick. She lowers her aviators and smiles at Kellan as we approach her car. It's impossible not to notice the way she flirts with Kellan with her eyes. Then she nibbles on the tip of her pinky fingernail like some kind of pin up poster girl. I notice she has a bejeweled French manicure. Very classy.

"Is that Angelina Jolie?" Kellan whispers to me.

"I have no idea," I huff. "Do you know her?"

"Who, Angelina Jolie?" he asks.

Geez, I suddenly wonder if he does know Angelina. She's probably cheating on Brad because Brad really doesn't hold a candle to Kellan.

"No," I scowl, "the woman in the car."

Kellan shakes his head, "No, I don't know her."

"You're acting like you do," I hiss. Why am I hissing?

"Hey," Sausage Lips smiles as we pass right in front of her car.

Kellan says, "What up."

Sausage lips says, "Three one oh, seven nine seven…"

I hiss, "She is *not* giving you her phone number."

Kellan chuckles, "I think she just did."

I half try to stomp on his foot while walking, but it's a lot harder to do when you're dealing with a moving target. Plus, he's wearing boots, so what would be the point, plus, we're just friends. So it really isn't necessary.

As we reach the other side of the street, I'm as cool as can be.

Kellan and I. Are. Just. Friends.

A voice in my head laughs, Ha ha ha.

Bitch.

Chapter 43

VICTORY

When we walk inside Kellan's apartment, his cell phone rings. It couldn't possibly be Sausage Lips, Kellan didn't give her his number. Unless he somehow managed to dial her number while his phone was in his pocket and now she's calling him back?

I'm going crazy.

I've never been jealous in my entire life.

What the hell is happening to me? I just broke up with Scott. I mean, he dumped me. But it was totally like I broke up with him one second before he dumped me, like I knew in my mind, like ESP, he was going to do it, and I beat him to the punch.

Kellan puts his hand over the phone, covering the mic, and says, "I have to take this call."

I grimace and say dismissively, "Go right ahead." I walk into the bathroom. It's the only private place I can go.

I hear him talking through the bathroom door. I don't even have to pee. But I turn on the faucet and run the water.

I can still hear him.

"Hey, Chloe! What up, girl?" He pauses, then laughs, "Yeah, it's been awhile…"

Geez, how many women does Kellan have waiting for him? Never mind. I don't want to know. I flush the toilet to make more noise.

"…Three o'clock? That works…Yeah…" He chuckles. "Did you work on the exercises I showed you?"

I pick up a copy of Guitar World from the rack by the toilet. The guitar players from the Black Veil Brides are on the cover. I try to read while leaning against the sink. It doesn't help.

I can still hear Kellan.

Based on his side of the conversation, it sounds a lot like he's talking about gymnastics routines that involve blow jobs.

"Remember, Chloe," he admonishes, "I don't want you hurting

yourself like last time. So make sure you're warmed up before I get there..."

Now he sounds like he's parenting, which is really gross. But I'm sure all his women have the brains of a breakfast sausage, so he needs to tell them what to do all the time.

"...Yeah, I want you to be loose and relaxed..." His voice has that smarmy quality I've heard several times since I met him.

I grimace.

Disgusting.

Warmed up? Loose and relaxed? Is it possible Kellan has naked women waiting for him all over town, lounging on their beds in nightgowns, and he shows up at the appointed time for a pump and dump?

Do I even want to know?

"...and don't forget the stretches I showed you last time...Yeah. Wouldn't want you pulling a muscle," he chuckles.

That deserves an O.M.G. He's the biggest manwhore I've ever met. And I was right about the gymnastics thing.

What a slut.

"...Yeah, I'll be ready," Kellan finishes, "See you at three."

I can't help myself, I have to say something. I rip open the bathroom door and march into the living room. "How many floozies do you have waiting for you any given day of the week?"

"Floozies?" He's confused.

I jab my fists against my hips, "Yeah. How many?"

He cracks a slow grin, "Usually just three or four, depending on the day."

"Three or four! I'm surprised your dick still works!" Why am I so mad? I don't know, but I'm pissed!

"She's one of my students," he smiles.

"Students?! What, do you *teach* them?"

He nods.

I can't believe what I'm hearing. "Women come to you for *sex* lessons? Do they pay?"

For a second, he looks thoughtful, then his grin is back, "Every time," he says confidently.

I shake my head slowly. I'm going to be sick. "You're a gigolo, aren't you?"

His eyebrows raise slowly. He grins wider. Then he breaks into laughter.

"You're horrible!" And I mean it. "You're a prostitute! How could I not have figured this out before? That's why Femme Flakes asked for your number! How much did she pay you?"

"You should see your face right now," he laughs again.

"You're disgusting! You're a man hooker, Kellan!"

He folds at the waist and laughs even harder.

"It's not funny!" I shout. "And you're going to see another one of your Janes at three!"

"Janes?" He stands upright, his face red, laughing heartily.

I wiggle my hands, irritated, "Janes, you know, like female Johns? Hooker regulars?"

"Hooker regulars?" he laughs harder.

I fold my arms across my chest, "You are the grossest man I've ever met in my life, Kellan. You're a prostitute, and you're *proud* of it!"

He laughs and laughs and laughs, near tears.

I march toward the front door, intent on leaving. He grabs my elbow. I yank it out of his hand.

He chuckles, "Wait."

"What?!" I bark.

Slowly his laughter subsides into snickers. He shakes his head. "Savannah, my date last night, did not pay me. Chloe, the girl on the phone, is one of my guitar students."

"What?"

"Guitar?"

I'm shaking my head, not believing him.

He strums an air guitar several times, "You know, the instrument we both play?"

"Wait, that was a guitar student?"

He nods, "Yeah."

"You give lessons?"

"Don't you?"

That stops me short. I shake my head, "Not lately." I really need to round up some students and bring in some extra cash.

"You should get back into it. All these west side Brentwood parents pay a ton for their kids to get lessons from the best in the business. And you're as good as anyone I can think of."

"Thanks. I mean, wait," I wobble my head, "don't change the subject and try to distract me with flattery. Are you telling me you're really not a manwhore?" I'm still doubtful.

He shakes his head.

I narrow my eyes, "How do I know you're not lying?"

He breaks into more laughter. When it subsides, he says, "I think you *like* the idea of me being a male hooker. I think it turns you on."

I'm not going to answer that on the grounds that any response will convict me. "I need some air." I walk out the front door and pace in the courtyard outside until I calm down.

When I walk back inside I say, "You're really a guitar teacher?"

He nods calmly, "Yeah. I have anywhere from five to fifteen students on any given week. And before you get any ideas, Chloe is twelve. You'd like her. She's a lot like you. Totally driven to master guitar. But she's only into rockabilly. Has thick black plastic hipster glasses. She fingerpicks on a huge Gretsch hollow body that's twice as big as she is. Cutest thing I've ever seen," he grins.

I can picture it. "Really?"

"Yup."

I hate that it matters to me what women Kellan involves himself with.

"Anyway," Kellan says, "Those tracks we laid down last night were incredible."

I nod, still dwelling on my confused and likely disastrous attraction to Kellan. Is it going to be a problem?

Kellan continues, "If we can round up a solid drummer and bass player, we could flesh out a complete song in no time."

I gaze at Kellan, amazed by how quickly he shifts from talking about sex at the restaurant ten minutes ago to talking seriously about music. He's not some simple minded hottie who does nothing but chase girls. He has ambition. I totally respect that. I also like the fact he wants to form a band with me. That means he's thinking long term. Maybe he sees me as more than just a throw away distraction. At least, that's what I'm telling myself. Bands form and break up all the time. This may just be a passing phase for him.

He's certainly fly by night with women.

Who knows.

Kellan says, "I've got a drummer buddy who might be a good fit. He's wicked on the double bass. I can email him the rough track we did last night and see what he thinks, have him record some rough drums over our guitars. I also know a guy who kicks ass on bass. Unless you know some people?"

I'm somewhat surprised he's asking. Scott was always telling me and Rex and Bobby how things were going to be. Scott didn't ask for input. He issued orders.

"Uhh," I say, "I can think of a few people. Actually, I know a couple guys, Lucas and Logan Summer. They're brothers. They play bass and drums and they're really good. And totally cool. I think you'd like them."

Kellan smiles, "Blood brother rhythm section?" He chuckles, "Sounds like a band name."

"What?" I ask.

"Blood Brother Rhythm Section."

I grin. "How about Blood Brother Syndicate?"

"Love it. You wanna call them and set up a time for us all to jam? Maybe tonight?"

Wow, Kellan doesn't waste any time. I say, "I'll have to check with them. There's only one problem."

"What's that?" he asks.

"They live in San Diego."

"That's like two hours away, right?"

I nod.

Kellan says thoughtfully. "Do you think they'd be willing to move to L.A.? I mean, if things work out?"

"Oh, I don't know. They're total surfers and might miss the waves in San Diego."

"Tell them to move to Venice. They'll fit right in. So, who do we get to sing?"

The mention of singers makes me want to hurl. All I can think of

(*don't sing*)

is Scott. Scott had L.S.D. in a bad way. Lead Singer's Disease. If I never have to deal with another lead singer, it will be too soon.

Kellan muses, "Maybe we can do the singing ourselves. I've sung backing vocals in a bunch of bands. What about you?"

Stab.

(*never ever sing*)

I do my best to hide my horror.

Kellan may as well have asked me if I liked to torture small animals or stab myself repeatedly in the stomach with a pitchfork. All I can manage is a crazy head shake.

Kellan looks at me quizzically, "You must've sung back up once or twice?"

I shake my head more fervently.

(*never ever ever sing*)

Kellan frowns, "Did I say something wrong?"

"Ahh, no, it's just that, I, uh..." I look around for the closest distraction or hole to hide in. Now would be a good time for the Big One, the fabled earthquake that's supposed to level Los Angeles someday, to hit. Earthquakes are always a good subject changer. At the moment, I would welcome one because

(*Stop!!!*)

the fault line in the middle of my heart is cracking open and the raw emotional pain I keep buried inside is going to rip me open and scatter my guts to the four winds.

(*never ever ever ever sing*)

"Fine," Kellan grins, "you don't have to sing. That's cool. Maybe I'll be the singer. I've done it before in some of my old bands."

My heart is crushed underneath the wheels of a cement truck. I can't do this. I can't

(*sing*)

be in a band with Kellan, who I'm obviously extremely attracted to, and have him be the lead

(*singsingsing*)

singer. Heck, I probably shouldn't even consider being in a band with him at all. But if he's the lead singer? Forget it. It's Scott all over again.

I tried to tell myself Kellan and I can just be friends, but who am I kidding? Being in a band together will be walking into a minefield. One wrong step and BOOM!, it all blows up in my face.

I can't.

I just can't.

I'm not going to make the same mistake twice.

Black resolve rushes through my veins. When I leave for work a few minutes from now, I'm going to pack all my stuff in my car, and never look back. I'm moving forward with my life, not making the same mistakes over and over again.

Kellan chuckles, "Or we could just find a singer. Playing guitar and lead singing is a ton of extra work."

White relief waterfalls out of my heart and peace returns. Maybe we could make it work? If he's not the singer?

(*singsingsing*)

Maybe.

Kellan smiles, "We can be old school. Me and you can be like Eddie and Michael in Van Halen and sing three part harmony with our lead singer. I've always wanted to do that. It'll be awesome. We'll be co lead guitar and co backing vocals." Happiness beams from him like a kid opening Christmas presents and finding everything he ever wanted.

(*don't sing don't sing don't sing*)

My throat clamps shut. It's not gonna happen. And there's no way I can tell Kellan why I won't ever sing. Besides, he seems so enthusiastic, so innocent, I don't want to disappoint him by telling him this Christmas he gets socks or rocks.

I nod half-heartedly.

That white waterfall in my heart goes gray and murky.

"Well," Kellan says, "call your buddies Lucas and Logan and let's set something up. If we can get shit together quick enough, we might even have some tunes ready for L.A. Gunslingers over at Guitar Central."

"You know about that?" I ask.

"Of course." A huge smile widens across his face, "With you and me writing songs, we could totally take first place. And that's just the beginning. Sky's the limit." He gives me a long, amused look as he mulls over the possibilities. "Now I'm all excited about forming a band," he grins. "If your pals are cool, we might just be in business."

I can't escape the feeling I've blundered right into that minefield I was so worried about.

I wonder how long it'll take for one of us to trigger something explosive

(*Stop!!!*)

and everything blows up in our faces?

Maybe I need to tell Kellan a band isn't going to happen and stop things before we *both* walk into a bomb lawn.

Chapter 44

VICTORY

The drive to work is a slow death march.

I dread the looks I will see on Johnny and Karen's faces when I show them the busted Contrares. Will they fire me on the spot? I don't know how I can possibly pay them back in a reasonable amount of time. I've never *had* much money, never *made* much money, and $6,000 is a number that makes me nauseous thinking about it.

I turn on the radio. Hopefully some good tunes will ease my worries. The first song I hear is the boppy pop hit Your Love Is My Drug by Ke$ha.

While I drive along Sunset through the windy part where all the mansions are, between UCLA and the Strip, I think about how Ke$ha uses a dollar sign for the S in her name. I'm thinking I need to use the cent sign for the C in mine, like so:

Vi¢tory

And put a zero in for the O, to show how much money I have. That's me. Broke ass Vi¢t0ry.

Not a single cent to my name.

Trying to get my mind off of money, I listen to the lyrics of Your Love Is My Drug.

Sure, I stop thinking about money, but only because now I'm picturing Kellan lying in bed nearly naked and I can't stop. Abs, abs, arms, tats, abs, eyes, chest, hair, abs, shoulders, tats, abs, abs, abs...

Kellan is totally drug worthy, although, from the way I find myself obsessing about that crazy body of his, a more appropriate title for the song would be Your Abs Are My Drug.

I'm thinking Ke$ha must have written the song about Kellan. Considering that Kellan and Ke$ha both live in L.A., it's the only rational explanation for where she got the idea of comparing a guy's love to a drug, because no other guy on the planet is as hot as Kellan.

I totally need to ask him if he ever dated Ke$ha.

Anyway.

The song on the radio changes to Boy Toy Ploy by Layce. It's an uptempo dance anthem about a girl who dreams and schemes about how to finally catch the hot guy she always wanted but could never get. When she finally attracts his attention and he decides to hook up with her, she quickly realizes that her hot guy is a hot mess and she's better off without him.

Hmmm.

Sounds like Kellan to me.

I believe Layce lives in L.A. too. I snicker to myself, imagining she met Kellan at some point and wrote Boy Toy Ploy about him. It's totally possible. Based on her lyrics, it makes sense.

Anyway, I bet if I were to hook up with Kellan, it wouldn't be long until I was listening to Boy Toy Ploy repeatedly and wondering how Layce was able to perfectly predict my disastrous path with Kellan.

I decide I need to take Layce's lyrics to heart.

Kellan is obviously a hot mess and I'd be smart to avoid stepping right into his hot mess. And I'm not talking about the yummy kind of mess. I'm talking about the brown kind.

I snicker to myself.

It's glaringly obvious that all female pop singers don't write songs about Kellan. I'm just imagining they do.

What does that say about my feelings toward Kellan?

It doesn't say brown, that's what.

When I reach Big Momma's Guitars, luck shines on me and I find a parking space around the corner. Parking meters are free on Sundays in Hollywood. But that means I'll have to face Johnny and Karen sooner.

And tell them about the Contrares.

Where is Ke$ha and her dollar signs when I need her? She probably has six grand to spare. But I've never been one to shy away from trouble. I steel myself and walk to the shop with the Contrares in hand.

I notice the L.A. Gunslingers flier taped to the front door when I open it.

I could really use the $5,000 first prize.

Maybe I can do like Johnny said and get up on stage by myself and just play. If I win, every cent will go straight to Johnny and Karen. For that to happen, I totally need to start practicing.

But I still don't have a guitar.

I can't ask Johnny and Karen to borrow another one now.

Hmmm. Maybe Kellan would lend me one? He has a ton. I'm sure he'd let me use his Ibanez from last night. I liked it quite a bit. But that will tie me down to him more than I'd like. I heave a sigh. I'll worry about it later.

Moment of truth.

I open the front door of the store.

Johnny is behind the counter with Karen.

"Morning, Victory," Johnny smiles. "How did the Promenade go last night?"

I can't hide my worry. It's probably shining from my face like searchlights.

"Did something happen?" Karen asks, concerned. She can always tell.

"Kind of?" I wince. I set the guitar case on the counter in front of her and Johnny. Best to get it out of the way. I wince, "There was a bit of an accident. When I was putting away my guitar at the end of the night a bunch of skaters were messing around. One of them bumped into me."

Johnny frowns, "Did he scratch the guitar with his skateboard or something?"

I smile thinly, "You could say that…" I can't bear to open the case.

"Let's take a look," Johnny says, unlatching it.

He lifts the lid.

I squint my eyes shut in preparation for atomic detonation.

"Far out, man," Johnny says.

Karen's eyes bulge like I've never seen them bulge, "That's quite a scratch," she chuckles throatily.

I had expected a bigger reaction from them. If someone busted *my* $6,000 guitar, I'd go on a stabbing spree. "Can you fix it?" I ask, fully aware of how stupid a question it is.

"Far out," Johnny mumbles, picking the guitar up by the neck.

"No, don't!" I blurt.

The bottom of the guitar clatters onto the glass counter top.

We all wince in unison.

"It'll make for some good kindling," Johnny chuckles. "Too bad we never use the fireplace in L.A. anymore."

Karen rolls her eyes, "We never had a fireplace."

Johnny nods and smiles at her, "That's right."

Karen whispers conspiratorially to me, "He took the brown acid at Woodstock."

Brown.

Tee hee.

Johnny snickers, "I heard that. And no, I didn't."

Wait, did he hear my mental laughter?

Or was he talking to Karen?

Karen shakes her head and smiles, "You did, Johnny. I remember. You took the brown acid and—"

Tee hee. She said brown again.

"—you freaked out and had the worst acid trip of your life. I had to constantly reassure you that you didn't have a cannibalistic tentacle growing from your third eye chakra, and Captain Kirk had not beamed you up to the Enterprise."

Johnny chuckles, "I don't remember that."

"Imagine that, Victory," Karen chuckles sarcastically, "Johnny doesn't remember the brown acid!"

I laugh.

Smiling, Johnny sets the guitar neck in the case, and the six strings still attached to the bridge slide around like a slippery sextopus or whatever you call a cannibalistic six armed monster.

"Watch out, Johnny," Karen jokes sarcastically, "it bites."

Johnny shakes his head, "I'm not having any flashbacks now." He kisses Karen on the cheek.

I glance between them.

They're both smiling.

So, I guess the broken guitar isn't a big deal? Maybe I'm hallucinating their mellow reaction? I mean, to me, $6,000 is a *huge* deal. I've never had that much money at one time in my entire life. It'll take me years to pay them back.

Johnny looks at me and says, "I think the Contrares needs a proper burial."

They don't seem to be mentioning anything about the money.

I may as well take the initiative. I say, "I can totally pay you guys back for it when—"

Johnny interjects, "No worries."

"—I get the money. I'll work here for free until you guys close the shop, and—"

Karen smiles, "Relax, honey, it's no big deal."

"—I'm going to look for a second job first thing tomorrow—"

Johnny sighs, "Look how mixed up she is about owing us."

"—so I can pay you back with that money too. If I have to eat nothing but cold Ramen and walk everywhere to save gas, I'll do it," I finish, nearly out of breath.

I usually never get this worked up about things. But I've never owed anyone six grand before.

Johnny says to Karen, "You thought that Woodstock acid was bad? Look what money can do to a groovy girl like Victory. Her head is all inside out about paying us like it's more important than breathing."

"Her head isn't inside out," Karen says, "it's her root chakra. It's knotted."

"My what?" I blink.

"Your root chakra," Karen smiles, "at the base of your spine, near your tailbone. It's attached to survival issues and money.

Johnny laughs, "I always knew money and assholes were close brethren."

"Victory," Karen smiles, "Take a deep breath, honey. And put your whole body into it."

"Huh?"

"Take a deep breath," she says soothingly, "and let it out slowly. Try to feel it in your toes."

I inhale deeply and imagine little mouths on the tips of my toes inhaling too, which makes me grin.

"Doesn't that feel better?" she asks.

"It does."

Johnny says to me, "Pay us back when you can, Sunshine."

Karen admonishes me, "And don't you start eating junk food to save money. It's counter productive. Your body needs nutritious whole foods from Mother Nature, not a bunch of chemicals in shiny plastic wrappers."

"Okay," I say, "but I'm totally paying you guys back as fast as possible."

Johnny smiles, "If that will make you feel better, then that's what you should do."

Wow, I'm having a hard time believing him. "But it's six thousand dollars."

Johnny lifts his brows, "And?"

"Are you serious?" I ask, still in disbelief.

Karen smiles at Johnny, "I think we blew her mind."

I guess they're serious. I throw my arms around them both and hug them tightly, "You guys are awesome."

Johnny says, "What you see in us is merely a reflection of what's inside you."

I giggle, "More Yoda bullshit?" My eyes are wet.

They both laugh at the same time, but are interrupted by the ringing of the shop phone.

"I'll get that," Karen answers. "Big Momma's Guitars?" She listens, then looks over at me. "Yes, she is...Uh huh...Yes, she can. Let me grab a pencil." Karen pulls an old pencil out of the cup of pens and pencils by the phone, and jots something down on a scrap of paper.

I have no idea who Karen is talking to, but I can tell they're talking about me.

Karen continues, "No problem at all. I'll send her right over with the guitar. My pleasure. And it's been a pleasure doing business with you." Karen hangs up.

I ask, "Who was that?"

Karen arches a suggestive eyebrow, "That was Julian Whittaker. The handsome blond suit who bought the gold top Gibson Les Paul yesterday. He wants you to deliver his guitar. Today. He sounded impatient to see you."

Excitement flutters through me. I'd almost forgotten about Julian.

But it seems he didn't forget about me.

Chapter 45

VICTORY

My Altima spirals up the winding road into the Hollywood Hills. The sun is high overhead as I crest another hill along the road.

I catch a glimpse of the Pacific Ocean ten miles to the west. Too bad L.A. has so much traffic, otherwise I'd probably make it to the beach way more than I do.

Julian Whittaker's house is only a few miles from the shop. I looked up the address online and drew a map for myself before I left, but the roads around here are so squiggly, I hope I don't get lost.

The radio plays.

I tap the wheel with my fingers in time to the bouncy reggae beat of Jessie J's hit single Price Tag, featuring B.o.B.

It's the perfect music for this perfect weather.

When the song ends, it slides right into a tune I haven't heard before. It sounds like Layce, but I don't know this one. Maybe it's a new single? It doesn't take long before I'm dancing in my seat, weaving my shoulders to the beat.

It's a bittersweet song about a girl who thinks guys don't dig her, so she's trying to talk herself up to be more confident and believe in herself.

The chorus is super hooky, and by the third time I hear it, I'm singing along.

"I'm
So
Irresistible
Boyz
Want me
Cuz I got the flow"

I smile from ear to ear, alone in my car, the windows down, the breeze in my hair.

"I'm
So
Irresistible
istible

Irre
sista
sista
bah-bah-bah-bah
buuuull"

My voice is light, smooth, and airy. I haven't had this much fun since

(*Stop!!!*)

My throat chokes and knots into a handful of gravel. I cough several times, unable to sing as the song finishes the final repeat of the chorus.

Tears dribble down my face and I wipe my cheeks. Good thing I'm not wearing mascara.

The song ends and the D.J. on the radio says, "That was the new single 'So Irresistible' by Layce from her upcoming album 'I Rise' produced by those star making whiz kids Mad Max and Lord Jah—"

I pull my car over at the first parking space I find on the winding road and put the shifter in park.

I'm panicking, on the verge of total meltdown.

The D.J. continues, "…you can meet Layce in person at Amoeba Music in the heart of Hollywood this afternoon…"

My chest spasms and I try to lock it down, but there's no stopping it this time.

(*don't sing*)

"…people were already lined up half way around the building when I drove by Amoeba on my way to work this morning…"

I cough out a hoarse shout, a rebellious "NO!" but it breaks up into useless shards of broken conviction.

(*don't sing*)

I sob so hard I start wheezing.

(*never ever sing*)

I don't know how long it lasts.

At some point a gardener's truck drives toward me on the narrow road. Garden tools sprout from it like metallic porcupine quills. Rakes, brooms, edgers, lawnmower handles, and leaf blowers. The driver looks at me as he passes on my left.

I hide my face in my long loose hair until he's gone.

(*never ever ever sing*)

I check myself in the rearview mirror and smear my cheeks clean.

I'm tempted to turn my car around and go home. Then I remember I don't have a home. I'm already sitting in it. I consider finding the nearest cliff and driving my miniature mobile home over the edge.

I sigh heavily.

Giving up has never been my style.

I just need to get my shit together and deliver the guitar to Julian Whittaker.

After a few minutes of deep breathing, I put my car in drive and continue toward Julian Whittaker's house. The houses get bigger and fancier the higher I go. I make a wrong turn and have to back track. I'm happy for the delay. It gives me more time to collect myself.

When I reach the address, I'm back to my old self again.

All I find is a long curving wall of green bushes interrupted by a nondescript black gate. Beside the gate is a brick column with fancy brushed metal numbers mounted on the front. On the side of the column is a speaker box with a button.

I press the button.

A second later, a female voice says, "Yes?"

"I'm here for—" I cough and clear my throat, "I'm here with the guitar for Julian Whittaker?"

There's no response. A few seconds later the gate rolls open silently.

So mysterious. Like, whatever goes on behind these gates is illegal and super exciting.

Who knows, maybe it is.

The road to the house is maybe 200 feet long. It curves up to a driveway with a six car garage burrowed into the hillside beneath the house. A bunch of expensive cars are parked in front of it.

I recognize the black Ferrari Julian drove yesterday. It's a 458 Spider with red interior. The top is off. It reminds me of the old Batmobile, except way sexier.

There's also a high end black Range Rover with silver trim. I know a little bit about fancy super cars like Ferraris and Lambos, but not much about high-end SUVs.

The third car I totally know. It's a 1970 Dodge Super Bee. The whole car has been lowered but the rear end is a couple inches higher than the front, giving it that sloped dragster look. The custom rims are oversized with low profile tires. The car is metallic apple green with a black stripe around the trunk. The intake paths on the twin hood scoop are also painted black. It's got rear quarter panel side scoops and running lights beneath the quad headlights, none of which is stock, but looks like it should be. Someone spent a bundle on this mod. I wish my dad was here to see it. He'd love it.

If the Dodge is Julian's car, he has way better taste than I gave him credit for. It's one thing to throw a bunch of money at a Ferrari. It's another to take a classic muscle car and make it better. That takes art.

Maybe Julian isn't as Metrosexual as he seemed yesterday.

The house above the garage is all white and straight lines. It has lots of windows and a 1960s modern minimalist feel to it.

I like it.

I park my Altima to the side, so I'm not blocking any of the cars, and pull the gold top Les Paul out of my back seat where I stowed it on the floor. I didn't want to make the Les Paul slum it with my two garbage bags of stuff still in the trunk. Les Paul deserves better.

I carry the guitar up the square stone stairs that lead to the front door of the house.

I ring the bell and wait.

The sound of a garage door moving below drifts up to where I'm standing. I glance down toward the driveway.

Someone walks out between the cars.

My first thought is that Julian has come to meet me at my car. Very thoughtful. I should walk down to meet him.

Then I notice the guy has a big leather top hat with silver buckles around it and a huge pile of curly black hair sprouting from beneath the brim. He's wearing a leather jacket, torn jeans, and boots. When he opens the door of the Dodge Super Bee, I see he's wearing mirrored sunglasses.

He's so far away, I can't be sure, but I think that is…

"Victory!" Julian says after whipping open one of the front doors.

I almost jump out of my rocker boots, "Jesus!"

Julian chuckles, "Sorry. I didn't mean to frighten you."

My heart pounds in my chest, but I look back down at the driveway at the guy in the Dodge. The engine has that 4 rpm idle speed I love on a Mopar.

Chug. Chug. Chug.

Rugged poetry.

The car backs up and does a three point turn in the driveway.

"Is that—" I turn to Julian, "is that Slash?"

Julian nods, "Yes."

"Like, Guns N' Roses Slash?"

"The same," Julian grins pleasantly.

I can't help myself. I'm star struck. Part of me wants to run down the square stone steps to the driveway and ask for Slash's autograph before he leaves. But I keep it together and pretend like it's no big deal.

Not.

SLASH!!!

I gush, "What's Slash doing here?" I never figured Julian for the kind of guy to have Slash at his house. Maybe some Wall Street guys or Bill Gates or whoever. But freakin' Slash?

"I'm talking to him about doing some work on an upcoming project of mine."

"You *work* with Slash?" I'm losing my mind.

Julian grins, "Not yet. But I might. Let me get you a drink inside."

"Oh, okay."

Julian wears a tailored button down shirt over chinos and Adidas tennis shoes. A huge change from the suit and tie look he wore when I met him. Now he's almost hipster preppy. The top two buttons of his shirt are undone, revealing the hint of a lithely muscled chest. He's quite tan and I notice his arms are defined and criss crossed with veins, but he's not overly muscly. He has more of a swimmer's body with broad shoulders and long legs. Not bad. I wonder if he did modeling at some point? He's more than good looking enough. It would explain his practiced casual body language.

Inside the house are more clean lines and minimal decor. The furniture is low profile white rectangles and the floor is light colored wood. I can't decide if it's sterile or peaceful. Maybe that's the same thing? I wouldn't know. But it's definitely impressively expensive without being obvious.

Julian smiles, "You can set the guitar down over there." He points to a round elevated side area connected to the living room. Two steps lead into it. Glass windows go all the way around, from the floor to the super high ceiling, almost like a giant glass test tube. In the middle of it is a black grand piano surrounded by cellos, those big violins I think are called violas, and regular violins, all resting on elegant wood stands. There's also a bunch of hand carved sheet music stands.

I walk up the two steps.

"Wow," I say, "Do you play all these?"

"What, the instruments?"

"Yeah."

"Frequently," he smiles. "You can set the guitar in the corner. Let me get you a refreshment."

I put the guitar down beside the cello and follow Julian into the naturally lit kitchen.

A very attractive classy looking woman in a cross front keyhole blouse stands at a long counter doing something on an iPad. Her blouse tucks into pleated wide leg pants cinched with a thin belt. The pants cover her peep toe pumps. Her hair is fancy and up, like she's going out for the evening, but it's just past lunch time. Standard issue rich housewife.

I can only guess this woman is Julian's girlfriend or wife. It's Sunday, after all. Why else would she be here if she wasn't with Julian?

Compared to her, I look like a slob in my ripped jeans and boots. For once, I'm not wearing a black concert t-shirt. Instead, my shirt is white and form fitting and I bought it new, but it still has a random black print on it.

Anyway, I was right about Julian. He's a scammer, hitting on me when he has a glamorous wife waiting at home.

"Victory," Julian smiles, "this is my assistant, Colette."

Colette looks up from her iPad and walks over to shake my hand. Her shoes clack on the cold tile floor. We shake, and she says, "Can I get you something to drink?"

I smile, "Uh, sure. Water?"

Colette grins, "Flavored, filtered, smart, or gassed?"

"Gassed?" I giggle. Gassed sounds like farts. Doesn't sound very smart to me.

"I'm sorry," Colette smiles indulgently, "Americans use the word sparkling. What would you prefer?"

I think she has some kind of European accent, but I can't tell for sure.

I stammer, "Oh, uh, regular, I guess?"

Colette gets a squarish glass from a cupboard, puts some ice chunks from the fridge into it, and fills it from a special little spout on the sink. She hands me the glass with a smile.

"Thanks," I nod. I probably could've done that myself, but whatever. I'm not used to being served, but I guess I'm the guest.

Colette turns to Julian, "Do you need anything else?"

"Not right now, thank you, Colette," Julian nods and he casually slides his hands into his pockets. He's more laid back than yesterday, but still seems posey to me. I wonder if he's one of those guys who never relaxes all the way. Too soon to tell.

Colette walks out of the room.

I sip my water. Julian isn't saying anything, just staring at me with a vaguely creepy look on his very handsome face, which makes me uncomfortable, so I say, "So, you're a musician?"

He nods, smiles, and his face relaxes noticeably, "I am."

"What do you play?"

"Primarily the violin, cello and viola. But I also dabble on the piano and a few different wind instruments."

"But you don't play the guitar?"

"Not like you," he grins, his face finally relaxing and losing the last of his creepy look. "That's why I asked you to play the Les Paul at the store yesterday. I suspected you might know your way around a guitar better than I do. Apparently, I was right."

I shrug and sip my water.

"Speaking of which," he grins, "I wonder if I could ask a favor of you?"

"Sure."

"Can you put that gold top Les Paul to work for me?"

I frown, "I thought you said it was a gift."

"It is, but before I send it along, I'd like to make a recording with it."

"I'm not sure what you mean…"

"Follow me," he says and walks out of the kitchen.

I shrug and set my water down on the counter with a soft clink.

Over his shoulder he says, "Bring your water with you. This may take awhile."

Yes, master.

Yeah, right.

Julian's weird.

I leave the water behind and walk back to the big living room. If I didn't know Colette was in the house, I might have made an excuse to leave. Oh well. I've got my rape knife in my crappy leather purse. Julian can try anything he wants if he doesn't mind getting stabbed.

When I turn the corner into the living room, he's holding the gold top guitar case in hand. He glances at my empty hands and smiles, "Not thirsty?"

"Nope," I grin confidently.

"This way," he says, striding casually past me with the guitar.

I follow him down a long hallway and we descend a long staircase. Are we going to the sex dungeon?

There's several closed doors in the downstairs hallway. Probably has girls chained up with ball gags and their tits hanging out, all covered with whip welts.

Julian seems like the type.

He opens one of the doors, "After you."

No murder victims. But I've just died and gone to heaven.

Chapter 46

VICTORY

Julian's secret room is a huge high-end recording studio.

In his freakin' house.

He and I are standing in the control room, which has racks and racks of recording gear along the back wall. Their front panels blink a rainbow of colored lights.

The front wall has high-end monitor speakers sitting on top of a huge multi channel mixing console with about a thousand buttons, knobs, and sliders. Through the control room window over the console, I can see the wood paneled recording room which currently has a bunch of chairs, music stands, microphones, and various musical instruments scattered around.

"Holy shit," I blurt.

Julian smiles, "You like?"

I nod, "Yeah." I've been in some pretty fancy studios around Hollywood, but nothing this nice. And not in someone's freakin' *house*. I'm so jealous of Julian. Lucky bastard. "What do you use this for?"

He chuckles sarcastically, "Recording?"

I roll my eyes, "You know what I mean. What kind of recording?"

His flashing green eyes take on a new glow as he speaks, "It ranges across the entire spectrum. I produce everything from albums to rough demos. I compose music for film and television, as well as commercial advertising. Sometimes I produce a video game soundtrack or two. I even did a few audio books while going through a minimalist phase. I wanted to focus entirely on the rhythm and melody of the solo voice using only the spoken word, and to see how the process was done. An incredible amount of work goes into an audio book, but it was a fascinating learning experience."

He clearly loves his work.

I gaze at everything in the control room and drool over all the recording equipment I could never afford but dreamed of having.

This place is paradise. I could live here and never come out. Well, not until I recorded an entire album first, then I'd come out and tour like crazy. Wow, the possibilities.

Too bad it's not mine.

Underneath all of my excitement at seeing this amazing recording studio is the constant awareness of Julian. He's really not as weird as I first thought. Maybe a bit formal for my tastes, but he seems as thoughtful as he is handsome.

Julian sets the Gibson case on the floor and opens it up. He holds out the golden guitar, "Take this."

He's so insistent.

But from what little I know about him, I bet it's part of how he got where he is now. He has a gigantic recording studio in his house. He can't be all bad. Plus he's got those emerald eyes that are beaming heat directly into me. I grab the guitar and roll my eyes, "What do you want me to do with it?"

"Play it," he smirks. At least he has a sense of humor.

Duh. I fish a yellow Tortex guitar pick out of my purse. I always keep a few handy. Never know when you're gonna end up in a fully equipped recording studio!

Julian picks up a phone mounted to the wall beside the console and punches one button. "Colette? Please send Max to the studio. Thank you." He punches a few buttons on the control console and turns to the computer keyboard to the side. "Have a seat," he says, motioning to the couch behind the console.

I feel like ignoring him, but what the heck. I was going to sit down anyway.

"Listen to this," he says and clicks the mouse on the computer.

It's some kind of clichéd twelve bar blues lick over bass and drums. It's the kind of thing you would expect a robot to write if you asked it to play the blues. Without vocals, it's boring. It's over before I know it, maybe one minute long, a fraction of a complete song.

The control room door opens.

A young guy with shaggy dyed black hair walks in. Probably Max. He has a choker necklace of silver beads. Silver rings dangle from his ears. He's dressed in black from head to toe. His black t-shirt says Sex Pistols in white print, and his fingernails are painted black. He has a smattering of tattoos on his forearms. He looks my age and is very cute. Do I detect a vague family resemblance between Max and Julian? I'm not sure. Max seems way too rocker goth to be related to Julian.

Max smiles at me and mutters, "Hey."

"Hey," I smile back.

"Max, meet Victory," Julian says.

Max and I shake hands. He has nice hands. They're warm but not sweaty.

He plops down on the couch near me and stretches his arms out on the back of the couch. He seems totally comfortable.

Julian says to me, "Give it another listen." He plays the short blues song again.

Yeah, it's lame.

When it finishes, Julian says to me, "What do you think?" He's smiling like he's proud of it.

I'm not sure what to say. I don't want to be rude. Did he write this? It sounds amateurish to me. "Well, uh, it's nice?"

Julian prods, "And?"

I frown for a second, because he's ordering me again. I pause to be rebellious before I say, "Sounds like the blues?" Like robot blues. I don't know what else to say.

"Be honest," Julian encourages.

"You really want to know?" I ask.

Julian nods. "Don't pull any punches."

"Uh, it sounds stiff—" Max snickers when I say stiff "—Like a machine played it. The chords are interesting, but it doesn't have any heart."

Julian nods like that was the right answer, "Exactly."

"What is this for, anyway?" I ask.

"It's a commercial for an erectile dysfunction drug."

"What?" I chuckle.

Max says sarcastically, "It's for dudes with floppy dicks."

Julian rolls his eyes at Max's comment.

I can tell Max and I are going to get along fine.

I ask, "Are you guys serious?"

Max nods.

Julian chuckles, "Very much so."

"Did you record this?" I ask.

"No," Julian says. "Someone else did. The advertising agency handling the account asked me to deliver something with more pizazz. Listen to this version." Julian cues up another track on his computer. "This is my version," Julian said. "Max did the guitar and bass work."

Oh great, I hope it's better than the last one. I don't want to sweat it out trying to tap dance if it sucks.

Julian plays it.

Fortunately, this version is much better. It's snappy, has different chords, and a nice little hook right at the beginning.

I'm relieved it doesn't suck. I say, "That's pretty good."

"But it could be better," Julian says, "right?"

I glance at Max. What am I supposed to say? Of course it could be better, but I don't want to hurt Max's feelings.

Max holds up a hand, "Don't worry about me. I'm not a blues player.

But Julian told me to take a stab at it."

"It's actually pretty good," I smile.

"But?" Julian prompts.

"Um..." I stammer.

Julian smiles, "Why don't you give it a shot. With the gold top."

Confused, I say, "You want me to play it? On the Les Paul?"

"Yes. Max, can you set up an amp for Victory?"

"No problem," Max stands up and glances at me, "You want to pick an amp?"

I go with the flow. "Sure."

Max motions to a rack of guitar amplifiers in the corner. Bogners, MESA-Boogies, Marshalls, on old Soldano, every high end amp you could want. "Pick one," Max smiles.

"If we're going for blues," I say, "I'll take the Soldano." I've never played one, but I can name ten different albums recorded with one.

Max pulls a coiled guitar cable off the wall and unwinds it, plugging it into the amp. "Do you want a strap for the Paul? Or you can sit. Up to you."

I like how casual Max is compared to Julian. "Oh, uh, I'll take a strap."

Max grabs a black leather strap and hands it to me. I fit it to the guitar and sling it over my shoulder. It weighs a ton. I remember Kellan's comment about girls playing Fenders because they're lighter than Les Pauls.

Kellan can suck it.

Max connects me to the Soldano and flips the switches on the front.

I turn up the volume knob on the guitar and no sound comes out. "Where's the speakers?"

"In the isolation booth," Max says. He steps over to the control console and twists some knobs.

Now I can hear the guitar coming through the studio monitor speakers. I start twisting dials on the front of the Soldano until I get a tone I like.

I glance at Julian. He's just watching. Does he do anything? Or just order people around? Who knows.

Julian says, "I'm going to play back the song without Max's guitar track."

"What key is it?" I ask.

"The song is in A," Julian says.

It plays through one time. Mostly I listen, but I add some stuff at the end when I have a feel for it.

I ask, "Can you loop it?"

Julian clicks on the computer and starts the short song again. It plays through several times and I jam the entire time.

I start by throwing in chords and fills to punch up what I'm hearing. Then my playing evolves into a funky blues riff with spunk, which seems fitting for a dick hardener commercial. After the tenth time, I'm totally into it. My body sways and my head bounces along with the music. Eventually, I get my idea nailed, and now I'm just going for it, putting everything into it, moving my body like I'm on stage. At the end of probably the twentieth take, I stretch my final note out, finished.

I totally owned that song.

Julian and Max both clap.

"Yeah!" Max shouts.

"Not bad," Julian says.

I smile, "Play back that last take."

Julian does. I sound awesome. I'm totally proud of myself. Without thinking, I reach out to Max for a high five, which he returns, as happy as I am.

"Now," Julian says abruptly, "let's see how it plays."

"Huh? I thought we just played it," I say.

"With the commercial footage," Julian clicks around on the computer and brings up video editing software on another monitor.

It takes only a few seconds for me to see the problem. I played too many notes for the slow vibe of the footage.

The commercial features a good looking older guy with salt and pepper hair. He's behind the wheel of a convertible Ford Mustang, looks like a '64, somewhere on the open road. A woman sits in the front seat beside him. She's beautiful, but probably too young for him. It's a montage and they go from place to place like they're on a driving vacation somewhere. Lots of long shots showing the Mustang cruising through scenic locations.

My playing needs to be more laid back. Maybe relax the funk. A little slow hand will do the trick. I say, "Okay, I know what to do."

"Wait," Julian commands, "you need to hear the voice over first. That'll change everything."

"Okay, play it," I order.

Julian tosses me a surprised look.

I arch an eyebrow. Julian's not the only one who can tell people what to do. He needs to know nobody bosses me around, unless they want to be bossed back.

Julian's lips slip into a faint smile and he plays the commercial once again, now with the voice over.

A male narrator with a smooth macho voice drops in at various points in the footage. "...It's about having the freedom to do what you want..." The actor on screen kisses the woman on the cheek while driving the

Mustang. Wind whips through their hair. "...*When* you want, because you're a man who has worked *hard*..." The actor slaps the woman's skirt covered butt as they walk across a motel parking lot. "...And you know how to play *hard*..." The actors sit in a jacuzzi and clink wine glasses (which doesn't seem like hard play to me). "...And you're not going to let all that *hard* work go unrewarded..." Laughing, the actors fall onto a king sized bed with a great view of the sunset behind them. They kiss romantically and the sun blows out the frame to gold then white.

Julian looks at me.

I blurt "That guy is cheating on his wife with that woman!"

Max laughs, "That's what I said!"

Julian smiles, "I don't judge. I get paid."

I'm not sure what to make of that comment.

"So," Julian says, "Do you want to give it another shot now that you've seen the footage?"

"Sure," I say. "Can you loop it with the video?

"Yes," Julian starts recording again.

This time, I scale back what I play. I'm really liking the Les Paul. Not surprising for a $30,000 guitar. I just hope no skaters come along and smash into me. After a few takes, I stop, satisfied with my playing.

Julian stops the recording and frowns, "I'm not feeling it."

I'm disappointed. I thought I played fine.

He asks, "What happened to that soulful stuff you played at the guitar shop yesterday? That was perfect for this. Can you recreate that?"

"I don't know. I have to feel it. I'm not feeling it with this commercial."

"Why?"

"I guess I think the commercial is lame? The guy is obviously cheating on his wife. Or he divorced her for a younger woman. Look how young she is compared to him. The advertisers are saying, 'Buy our dick pill, and you'll bang young babes.'"

Max snickers.

Julian asks, "What were you feeling yesterday when you played for me at the shop?"

I'm totally not going to answer that because I'm not telling Julian I was flirting with him like crazy when I plugged in the gold top and my attraction to him all came out in my playing. He doesn't need to know I got carried away yesterday because I'm not letting it happen here today.

"Look," Julian says, "Try to think about the perspective of the target customer. Imagine you're some older guy, and for whatever reason..." he shakes his head and gestures with his hands like he's covering up a dirty lie, which he is, "...and now you're going on a road trip with a young woman who is going to rock your world."

"But he's cheating on his wife!" I protest.

Julian rolls his gleaming green eyes. At the moment, his handsomeness makes him smarmy. He says, "Victory, this is advertising. It's all about telling people, 'Buy our product and your life will be better.' Our place is not to judge what they do with the product. Maybe the guy in the commercial lost his wife of twenty or thirty years in a car accident, went through a normal grieving process, then met a younger woman who is going to make everything better."

I shake my head, "That's ridiculous. That's a fantasy."

"Exactly. Sell the fantasy. Ready to record?" Julian's hand hovers over the keyboard.

I don't have a choice. The recording starts. My first few attempts are laughably bad. I'm not buying any of Julian's bullshit. But I try to focus on his rosy story, like the old dude in the Mustang lost his wife and his two adult kids are now out of the house. He's all alone until this young woman comes along and she sees how the guy is still a loving dad and provider, but he needs a woman to give him back that love he lost…and all of a sudden, I'm totally into it. I play a fun, flirty, hopeful riff with some funky trills and hooky bends. I throw in some humorous accents at the right moments.

Julian stops the recording after I finish and says, "That's perfect. See how easy that was?"

Actually, it was. "Can you play it back?"

He does. After, he says, "What do you think?"

I smile, "I like it. It's sappy, commercial, and clichéd. But I like it."

"Good. I do too. And now you get paid. Handsomely. Because that's how advertising works."

"Huh? Paid?"

He nods and pulls his wallet out of his pocket. He counts out ten hundred dollar bills and hands them to me.

"What's this for?"

"For your expert guitar playing."

I shake my head, "I can't take your money."

"Why not? I want to use your track in the final mix. I have to run it by the ad agency for approval, but I think they'll like your approach."

"Uhhh…"

"We're talking about a truckload of money from the agency for doing this," Julian says seductively.

I frown, "Wait. How much is a truckload?" I'm not going to be one of those musicians who gets ripped off.

Julian arches an eyebrow, "Enough."

I smirk, "Then maybe I should get more than a thousand?"

He looks at his watch, which is fancy and gold like everything about Goldenblond Julian and his expensive house. He says, "It took you, what, an hour to play through all the takes? I'm giving you a thousand dollars for an hour's work. Sounds like good money to me. That's two million a year if you worked full time. Does that sound fair?"

"Take the money," Max says, "Julian doesn't pay me nearly that much."

Julian says sarcastically, "Poor lad, living hand to mouth, wondering where his next hot meal is going to come from at the orphanage."

Max shakes his head dismissively, but he's smiling.

I get the sense Max isn't complaining about however much money Julian pays him.

Max says, "Seriously, Victory, a grand an hour is way better than most studio musicians make. Take it."

Julian says to me, "You'll have to sign a standard consent waiver that transfers ownership of your playing to the pharmaceutical company. Do that, and the money is yours."

The stack of bills sits on the edge of the console mixing board, begging me to take it.

I could really use that thousand dollars.

So what if the dick pill commercial is lame?

Like a starving animal, I reach out for the money cautiously, barely aware of the gold plated bear trap waiting to snap shut around my wrist.

Ah, what am I worried about? Nothing is going to hurt me. This is win-win all the way around.

What's the worst that could happen?

Nothing I can think of.

I snap up the money.

That gold plated bear trap wasn't quick enough to catch Victory Payne.

Julian arches an eyebrow, "Excellent. Then we have a deal?"

"Yup," I grin.

See?

No golden bear traps.

Chapter 47

VICTORY

We walk upstairs to Julian's big living room. I glance at the attached test tube room with the piano and cellos. Why do I keep thinking of it as a test tube? Like it's in a science lab?

Whatever.

Julian says, "I'll have the ad agency email you a consent waiver tomorrow. You're not in the AFM, are you?"

"What's that?" I ask.

"The American Federation of Musicians. The musician's union."

"Do I have to be in the union or something?"

"No."

"Oh," I smile, "that's awesome."

"Regardless, the ad people may or may not choose to use your track. We won't know until I hear back from them. In either case, I want to have things free and clear, legally speaking, before I send them your track."

I ask, "If they don't like it, do I have to give the money back?"

He smiles, "No, it's yours to keep. You did the work."

"Are you sure?" I say with obvious doubt.

"Very much so. And I believe they're going to like your work best of all the takes I send them."

A random thought suddenly occurs to me, "Wait, don't tell me Slash was playing for the commercial before I got here?"

Julian smiles, "Oh, no. Slash was here to talk about a record I'm working on."

"The gold top Gibson isn't for him, is it?" I ask excitedly.

Julian grins and arches an eyebrow.

"It is! I played the guitar you're giving to Slash!"

He nods.

"Wow, that's awesome! I mean, it's like the reverse of getting to play Slash's guitar, but it's still awesome!" I sound like a teenager, but we're talking about *the* Slash.

"Think of it this way. Slash will be playing the guitar *you* played."

I don't see how that's special. Oh, I get it, Julian is complimenting me. I do my best not to blush.

"By the way," Julian says, pulling out his wallet. He removes another stack of bills.

Geez, how much money does this guy keep in his wallet? Maybe he really did have thirty grand cash on him yesterday at the shop.

He counts out several bills and says, "I owe you this for delivering the guitar. A thousand dollars, like I promised. Remember, this is for you. For delivery. Not the shop."

"That's very generous of you, but I really can't."

"Victory, you need to learn to negotiate. You're going to get taken advantage of in the music business if you don't. I wouldn't have all this," he motions around at the house, "if I told everyone I can't accept their money."

That makes sense. I don't know why it bothers me so much. I guess I wasn't raised that way. I'm used to paychecks and clocking in and out for my shift.

Julian lifts my hand from my side and squeezes the bills into it. "This is yours, okay?"

I don't tell him I'm going to give it to Johnny and Karen when I get back to the shop because I owe them for the Contrares. "Oh shit! I need to get back to work! I've been gone almost two hours!"

"I'm sure they'll understand. Before you go, I need your email address, for the consent waiver."

"Oh, uh..." how do I tell him I'm not checking email much while I'm living in my car and I can't afford a smart phone?

"Or you can come by my house later in the week, sign a copy of the waiver, and leave it with me. I'll take you to dinner after."

"What?" I blurt, surprised.

"I would really like to see you again, Victory. You're a fascinating young woman."

"Are you asking me out on a date?" I say with minimal coyness.

He lifts my other hand, the one not clutching a thousand in cash (the first thousand is buried at the bottom of my purse), and kisses the back of it. I notice again how smooth and tan his skin is.

"Yes," his green eyes flicker as he gazes into mine.

His lips feel soft and warm on my hand.

Jolts sizzle up my arm and dive into my belly, where they bounce around pleasantly, leaving me tingling. He looks double dashing while kissing my hand. His eyes sparkle up at me with obvious interest.

Yeah, he's totally hot. And not some lame banker or stock broker.

"Okay," I say.

"Good. Then we can discuss the possibility of having you do some more session work for me. I suspect I've just scratched the surface of your musical potential."

"More?"

"More work, and more money. I predict you and I will be spending a lot of time together in the recording studio in the very near future."

After we say goodbye, I float down the square stone steps outside to my Altima while my head spins.

I vaguely remember Johnny saying something about doors opening and closing.

I'm still tingling when I park near Big Momma's Guitars.

Chapter 48

VICTORY

"You didn't tell us you're living in your car!!" Karen gawks.

I lean against the glass counter top in Big Momma's Guitars, "I guess I forgot to mention it?" Too embarrassed is more like it. But it slipped out when I told Johnny and Karen I was going to use the two grand Julian paid me to pay back part of the Contrares.

"Don't tell me Scott kicked you out," Karen growls. "I have half a mind to put a hex on him."

I grin. I wish she would. But instead of requesting a hex, I say, "No. I moved all my stuff out on Friday night after our show."

"And you slept in your car?" Karen gasps.

"Only one night," I say defensively. I don't know why I feel bad, but I do.

"Why didn't you call us?" Johnny asks, obviously hurt. "You could've crashed at our apartment."

"It was late?" I say lamely.

Karen shakes her head, "That's no excuse. You're staying with us until you find your own place."

Their apartment is really small. I feel bad.

"We insist," Johnny says.

"In that case," I say, "I should totally give you the money I made to pay for the Contrares."

Johnny shakes his head, "That money is yours, Sunshine. Like I said, pay us back when you can afford it."

"But the shop is closing," I argue.

He scoffs, "It's not because of you or that busted Contrares. Me and the old lady want to retire. We're fixed up good when it comes to money."

"You're sure?"

Karen rests her hand on my wrist, "Use the money you earned to find a place to live or buy a new guitar. Whichever you choose, Victory. Johnny and I will be fine." She pats my wrist several times.

I say, "You guys are totally sure?"

Karen and Johnny nod in unison.

Johnny says, "And you're welcome to stay with us until you get situated. Right, Momma?"

Karen nods, "It'll be nice to have someone keeping us company at the dinner table for a change."

"Wow, you guys," I feel my eyes heating up, "Thank you so much."

They both hug me at the same time. Johnny and Karen are all about the free hugs.

I feel loved.

Then I tense when I remember that all my stuff is at Kellan's.

All the distractions of the day have noticeably cleared my head on the topic of Kellan.

Jumping into a band with Kellan and crashing at his apartment is craziness. An image of him lying naked in bed flashes through my mind. I shiver pleasurably, which is bad. I can't think clearly around him. He makes my head spin way too much. One night of jamming with him and sleeping on his couch was fine. I managed to resist his charms. But two nights and starting a band will lead to trouble. Those abs and arms of his will wear me down. And his cute butt?

I don't stand a chance.

What I need right now is my own space to get grounded after my break up with Scott and Skin Trade.

Tonight, I'm going to crash at Johnny and Karen's. First thing tomorrow, I'll start looking for a cheap room somewhere. Then I'll do a job search and talk to Julian about that session work he mentioned. That's the sensible thing to do.

Not sleep in an apartment with hot naked Kellan and start a band with him.

I'll just have to break the news to Kellan gently.

My stomach knots at the thought.

Chapter 49

KELLAN

The YouTube upload status bar crawls slowly to the right while I sit in front of the computer in my living room.

I type in a title: "Ms. Yngwie Malmsteen - Hot girl guitar shredder." This video, the one I recorded with Victory last night, will get more views with a title like that.

In the description, I put, "Victory, the former lead guitar player of Skin Trade, shreds on guitar like she's Yngwie Malmsteen. Accompanied by Kellan Burns."

Too bad I don't know her last name. Oh well, most people probably don't either. I bet her stage name is just Victory anyway.

I add as many tags as I can think of, typing in the names of all the guitar shredders I can, both male and female, plus a bunch of music terminology. I want to get the guitar nerds watching her video. Most of them are guys and they'll come in their jeans when they take one look at Victory. But when they hear her play, they're going to shit themselves or their brains will explode. Afterwards, probably half of them will give up playing guitar out of jealousy.

I already know this video is going to blow up big.

Juliette Valduriez already has 3.5 million views for her "Girl Shreds on Guitar" video, but I think Victory is gonna get more.

It's only a matter of time.

I grab my skyburst Les Paul and sit down on the couch. I strum it, unplugged.

Now we just need to round up a good drummer and bass player so me and Victory can start writing tunes.

When the video finishes loading, I set it to public so the whole world can see it.

Then I load up my recording software and start recording various riff fragments I come up with, or jot down lyric ideas.

Man, I wish Victory was here right now so we could write together. No worries. I'll see her tonight when she finishes work.

We can write songs together until we fall asleep.

I'm grinning like crazy thinking about it.

I should hit up Ralph's and stock up my refrigerator so we can work without interruption. I'm kind of in the mood for sub sandwiches and I'm out of French bread and prosciutto.

I can't wait to see Victory.

I hope she likes sub sandwiches.

Chapter 50

VICTORY

"Hello? Anybody home?" I say as I lean my head inside the front door of Kellan's apartment. I unlocked it with the spare key he gave me before I left for work this morning.

No answer.

I step inside. The apartment is hot and stuffy. Kellan must've had it closed up all day and it cooked in the L.A. heat.

I carefully lean my head around the corner of the short hallway leading to his bedroom to make sure he's not taking a naked nap or something.

Nope. I'm all alone.

Time to get my stuff and get out of here.

It doesn't take long to throw everything into my black garbage bag. I wheel my Marshall cabinet out the front door with the garbage bag on top.

I'm about to lock the door when I realize I still have his key. I don't want it. I walk inside and leave it on his computer table in the living room where he'll see it, then lock the front door on my way out.

Made it.

Now I just have to wheel my Marshall and my garbage bag to my Altima down the block, and I'm outta here.

Why does it feel like sneaking out of here before Kellan returns is so important?

My intuition tells me so, that's why.

When I get to the street, I lower my Marshall from the sidewalk to the asphalt easily. Getting it into my Altima by myself is going to be a bit more work. Kellan made it look like nothing. But I'm not big and buff like him.

I roll the cabinet up to my car and open the back door. I stand with hands on hips. What's the best way to do this? Besides hiring a day laborer or two from outside Home Depot to load it up?

I don't have the money or the time to spare. I need to get out of here.

I'll figure it out.

I lift one end of the Marshall, which weighs a ton, but I manage to hook the front casters on the edge of the Altima's door frame. Of course, there's another foot to go before the front end of the cabinet actually rests on the back seat cushion. Damn, why can't this thing fit in the trunk? Not like I could lift it, and there's no sense wondering.

Maybe if I lift up the back end and push toward the passenger door? That's ridiculous. What I need is a ramp or an engine hoist.

I do my best to muscle the bottom front edge of the speaker cabinet onto the back seat. Made it. Now I just have to push the whole thing all the way up onto the seat.

Let the heavy lifting begin.

I squat beneath the back end and push with everything I have. Wow, this thing is really heavy! I strain with all my muscles and feel like I'm going to pop a vein in my neck or give myself a stroke. Not gonna work. I set the back end down on the street.

"Need some help?" Kellan says, straddling his black Honda.

"Oh!" I jump. "Where'd you come from?!" I hope I don't sound surprised or guilty, because that's how I feel. I must've been so focused on getting my Marshall into the car, I didn't notice him ride up.

He puts the kickstand down on his bike.

"I've got it," I insist.

He smirks at me, "You sure?"

I pick up the back end handle, but it's quickly obvious this won't work because I'm not tall enough. I set the cabinet down on it's rear casters with a huff. I have to shove the thing in. If I can.

Kellan swings his leg over the bike, takes his helmet off, and sets it on the gas tank. He's also wearing a backpack, which he takes off and sets on the seat. "I'll do it."

"I told you," I sigh, "I've got it."

He shoulders past me, picks my Marshall up like it's weightless, and slides it in the backseat.

"Thanks," I say flatly.

"You're welcome. Taking off?"

"Uh, yeah." I was really hoping to avoid this discussion, but my stealth retreat was delayed by lack of man power.

"Got someplace safe to stay?" he asks coldly, his charm and humor all gone.

Did I do that? Make him mad? I feel bad. "Yeah," I nod, "at my friends' place. They said I could stay there as long as I need to."

"Awesome," he says like it's the least awesome thing ever invented.

I feel like I owe him an explanation or something, but he doesn't seem to be asking for one. I search his darkened eyes, but he quickly breaks eye contact.

He says sourly, "I should park my bike and get inside."

I notice a baguette of French bread poking out the top of his backpack on the motorcycle seat. I ask, "What's with the French bread? Making sandwiches?"

"Got a date tonight," he says absently.

I gasp, "You have a date?" Why am I not shocked? But why am I slightly jealous?

"Yup." He flashes a hard humorless smile and stares into my eyes, "Don't you know I have a date every night?" All of his light-hearted cocky confidence is gone. "Different chick every time."

Now he's trying to hurt my feelings. He's pissed, but he's hiding it.

Is he mad because I left without telling him? It's the only reason I can think of. "Kellan, I'm sorry. But I just broke up with Scott and the band. I need some time to, you know, get over it? Sort things out? It's probably best I do it on neutral ground."

"Neutral ground?" he asks with a tinge of sarcasm.

How to answer that diplomatically? "Um, not at a guy's place who I just met?" Why do I feel like I'm making weak excuses? I'm not. It makes sense, right? Kellan would be a rebound, and we both know it.

Right?

The committee in my head is silent.

"Whatever works," he sighs.

Is he *not* angry? I can't really tell. Now he seems disinterested. Maybe this is proof I was no more than a fling for him all along? That our connection was just due to the late hour and the beer he drank and my exhaustion and all the pizza? Yeah, that has to be it. I'm sure Kellan jams with other guitar players like me all the time. They're all over L.A.

Just like Scott said.

I'm just one among Kellan's many.

Kellan says, "I need to go get ready." He hops on his bike, puts his helmet and backpack on, and rides up the driveway into his apartment complex.

I watch him go while I stand in the middle of the empty street.

Should I go talk to him?

Yes?

No?

Yes? No?

Yes? NO! Yes? No!! Yes? NO!!!!

YEEEESSSS!!!!

Now my committee has an opinion.

Stupid committee.

I sigh harshly and stalk across the street.

His bike is locked up like before and I step onto the stoop of his front door. I raise my hand to knock. My knuckles pause an inch from the door when I hear him chattering away on his phone through an open window in the kitchen.

He chuckles, "She was lame, man...Yeah...Total waste of time." Kellan doesn't sound angry now. He sounds relieved.

Is he talking about me?

I'm not lame.

He says to his phone call, "I need to focus more on music anyway, not waste my time on some stupid chick."

I'm not stupid! And I'm not a waste!

Kellan's officially an ass.

Most manwhores usually are.

I should've known better.

Kellan is as bad as Scott.

What was I thinking last night when I decided to crash at Kellan's apartment? I wasn't, that's what. I should've sucked up another stiff neck and slept in my car.

I turn on my heel and march to my car.

I need to find a guitar and put a band together.

Without stupid Kellan.

Chapter 51

KELLAN

I dribble the ball a few times on the outdoor court, fake left, then shoot right around my buddy Dubs. He tries to hip check me off balance, but I twist and slide by. Two steps and I spring upward, floating toward the basket. I dunk the ball one handed through the rim.

Dubs grins, "You the only white man I know can jump like that." His hands rest casually on his hips.

I go after the bouncing ball, then dribble slowly back to him.

We're at one of the Venice Beach ball courts, near the handball walls. The sun is pink and hangs inches above the ocean to the west. Dubs and I are both wearing shorts and are shirtless. It's a tough call to say who has better abs. Plenty of ladies have stopped to gawk. We pretend to ignore them, but both of us keep tabs out the corner of our eyes.

Dubs waits at the back of the free throw circle.

I bounce pass him the ball, scrub sweat off my forehead with the back of my arm, and square up in front of him on the balls of my feet.

Dubs dribbles slowly then suddenly explodes and tries to power by on my right. I go after him, right in his face, but he zags left at the last second and drills upward, spiraling the ball unexpectedly.

My fingertips brush leather, but he powers it through the hoop.

Dubs laughs, "Too bad you ain't the only one who can jump. Eighteen fourteen." He walks slowly toward the ball, which rolls lazily past the baseline.

I put my hand to my ear like I can't hear, "What was the score again?"

He grins as he picks up the ball, "Eighteen fourteen."

I nod like I'm stupid. "Who has eighteen? I can't remember, is it me or you?"

He chuckles, not answering.

"That's what I thought, LeBron," I grin.

Dubs dribbles slowly back to the free throw circle. "What'd you say earlier on the phone about that shorty Savannah?"

"I said she was lame. A total waste of time."

"When we sparred Saturday morning, you said she was tight. Had a rockin' body and shit." He bounces the ball for emphasis. "Said you couldn't wait to bang her Saturday night."

"Yeah, but when I took her out, I found out she had rocks in her head. You could hear them banging together like a bowling alley when she walked."

He chuckles, "But you ain't fuckin' her head."

"Dude, when was the last time you got a blowjob? I'm not putting my dick anywhere near a bowling alley."

He cackles, "That don't make no sense, dawg."

"But you're laughing," I smile.

"You know what I mean, playah."

"What can I say," I shrug, "Savannah was twelve strikes short of a perfect game."

"Yo, ain't a perfect game twelve strikes?"

I nod.

Dubs chuckles, "I get it. She dumb." He bounces the ball once, "What about that honey you met Friday? The stripper?"

I laugh, "She's not a stripper. I told you this morning she just has a stripper name. Victory."

"Shit, son, every girl you date is a stripper. Or looks like one." He bounces the ball, "Victory got rocks for brains?"

"Naw, she's pretty damn smart. Amazing guitarist."

"She hot?"

"Smokin'."

"You ever find her online?"

"I bumped into her last night when I was out with Savannah."

He gasps, "No shit! They fight?!"

I smirk, "Yeah, bro, cat claws and everything."

"Now I *know* you shittin' me."

"They didn't fight," I grin.

"You get Shorty's number this time?"

"I took her home."

His eyes goggle, "Say WHAT?! You banged Savannah *and* Victory? The same night? Shit, playah, that some serious Don Juan shit right there."

I shake my head, "I didn't bang either one. I cut it short with Savannah and hooked up with Victory after. We had pizza and chilled at my pad all night."

"And you didn't ball her? I thought you said she was hot. She have some stank ass pussy or some shit? Crabs and lobsters crawlin' out like a horror movie and shit?" He laughs hard.

"No, man," I chuckle. "She didn't have crabs or a stinky pussy. I didn't even see her pussy."

Dubs suddenly looks very confused and worried.

He says, "Do I know you? Is your name Kellan Burns?" He weaves and bobs in front of me while clutching the basketball in both hands and scrutinizing my face. "You look like Kellan Burns. You *act* like Kellan Burns. You *smell* like Kellan Burns," he wrinkles his nose comically. "But the Kellan Burns I know don't take home no hotties without fuckin' 'em."

I chuckle, "I'm the real Kellan Burns."

"You must be sick then. That's it." He puts a palm on my forehead like he's checking my temperature. "But you don't have a fever…" He suddenly snaps his fingers in my face. "I know! You done lost your mind, son!"

"I'm not losing my mind," I grin.

His eyes goggle even wider. "Oh shit! You like her! You *like* her! You in love or some shit?!"

I shake my head, "Not even close. She's just a cool girl. I didn't feel like fuckin' is all."

Dubs gives me a shrewd look and nods doubtfully several times. "When you seein' her again?"

Sudden anger tenses every muscle in my body. In two seconds I'm going to explode into shards of rage that will impale everyone in a hundred foot radius, including Dubs. I growl, "I'm not."

"You sure?" He bounces the ball once.

"Yup," I grunt. My jaw grinds. I can feel the muscles bunching. I need to punch something.

(*Giselle*)

Dubs bounces the ball again and narrows his eyes, inspecting my face. His voice is suddenly calm and compassionate, "You sure you not into her? Cuz you actin' like you sprung, dawg."

I shake my head, "I'm not falling for Victory, man."

"You ain't foolin' me, dawg. You actin' like you was when you met Giselle, yo."

I stop dead in my tracks. Every muscle in my body freezes to ice.

(*Giselle*)

Dubs holds the basketball against his hip and rests a comforting hand on my shoulder. "Don't let some stripper bitch named Victory under your skin, dawg. She gonna fuck your shit up good. You know what I'm sayin'?"

I give Dubs a cold threatening stare, "Back off, man." I'm a second away from going off on

(*Giselle*)

Dubs.

He ignores my warning. "No way I'm lettin' you fall for some new bitch gonna do you wrong like Giselle did, Kellan. Feel me?"

I hiss through my clenched teeth. I can't look Dubs in the eyes because I feel like mine will burn a hole through whatever I look at right now, including him. I pin my eyes on the asphalt basketball court.

"Giselle a bitch, dawg," Dubs says quietly. "A low class ho, yo. And she still under your skin. You gotta forget about her. Sooner the better."

I growl, "She wasn't a bitch."

"Yeah, whatever. I was there, son. I saw what she did. That was some low class shit, yo. *Low* class."

I don't want to talk about Giselle. I don't want to think about Giselle. I want to put

(*Victory*)

Giselle completely out of my mind.

I grunt, "Pass me the fucking leather."

"All right, playah," Dubs says cautiously and steps away from me. He bounce passes the ball.

I take it to the net.

Nobody gets the best of me.

(*Giselle*)

I'm not going through the same shit twice.

Fuck Victory.

I don't need her.

RUN 3

Chapter 52

VICTORY

"Victory, I'm going to take you someplace special," Julian Whittaker says, "It's something of a secret..." he arches an eyebrow, "...but you have to sign the consent waiver first..."

I snicker, "You make it sound like we're going to do something illegal, like go to a sex club."

"Oh," he warns, "it *will* be illegal. If you don't sign first..."

"Is it dangerous?" I ask suggestively.

Julian cocks his head thoughtfully and his lips ease into a wicked grin, "It could be dangerous, but only to your taste buds. Now sign," he says insistently.

I grin, "Are you going to hold my dinner hostage tonight if I don't sign?"

"Yes." He holds out an expensive golden fountain pen, waiting for me to take it. "And I'll hold *you* hostage after dinner if you don't sign the contract," he smirks.

I say flirtatiously, "Will you hold me against my will until I beg for *release*...?"

He grins and arches an eyebrow, "If I don't get my release form, you won't be getting any *release* from me..."

I giggle.

The contract sits on the edge of the long marble island in the kitchen of Julian's modernist mansion in the Hollywood Hills. Late afternoon light pours through a wall of windows that reveal the lush green backyard garden surrounding a rectangular pool.

"Sign it," Julian orders. His commanding presence only makes him slightly more sexy than he already is. Then Goldenblond slowly thrusts his fountain pen in my face. Julian's pen is rigid, golden, and proud. Just like Goldenblond himself.

Because the day is so warm, I'm wearing a V neck t-shirt which is a tan heather, not a concert shirt (for once), frayed denim cutoffs that are way too short for prime time (Daisy Duke would be shocked, Bo & Luke Duke would be drooling, but Julian is way too cool to drool), and ankle strap flat sandals. Leather bracelets adorn my wrists and a pewter feather pendant dangles below my boobs on a necklace. Auburn tinted aviator sunglasses rest on top of my head, holding my long hair out of my face.

I totally don't look like a rocker chick.

Okay, I vaguely look like a rocker chick.

But more like a 1970's hippie rocker instead of my usual hair metal vibe.

I can't help it.

I'm a rocker chick no matter what I wear.

"Well?" Goldenblond says expectantly. He still holds his golden fountain pen inches from my lips. Not a golden showers fountain pen, that would be gross, but a rigid golden-barreled pen. I wonder if the ink cartridge is filled with fancy pearlescent gel ink or just regular old writing ink? The only way to find out is to see what squirts out the tip.

When I sign my name with it.

Because it's just a pen.

Right?

We all know I'm only talking about Julian's writing implement. Right, ladies? You all totally know what I mean. I'm talking about the kind of writing implement used to seal the deal.

A golden barreled pen.

It's just a pen.

Seriously.

I grin and chew my lip while my eyes dart between the pen and Julian's emerald orbs. Not the orbs between his legs, beneath his own golden fountain pen. I'm sure those orbs are made of the same gold as his pen, not emeralds. I'm talking about the exquisite emerald orbs set deeply in his finely structured brow, the orbs glimmering with intensity as his gaze glides languorously between my eyes and my lips.

Julian chuckles, "Sign the consent form. I already emailed my rough mix of the erectile dysfunction commercial track over to the ad agency." He pauses and frowns, "What did you call it the day we recorded it?"

I giggle, "A dick hardener pill?"

He nods and grins, "Yes, the *dick hardener* commercial. I sent off the music. The account manager overseeing the *dick hardener* project is excited about our new version, which includes your guitar work, so I really need you to sign the waiver. Otherwise, the agency can't pitch it to the pharmaceutical company."

Now we're definitely not talking about pens!

"Why not?" I ask innocently.

"Because, if the people at the pharmaceutical company hear your version and like it, they're going to assume they can use it. But if you don't sign the waiver, they can't use it. Then they'll be pissed. *Hard dick* pissed," Julian quips.

Nope, not talking about pens!

I snicker, "You sure like to talk about hard dicks."

"What can I say?" Julian chuckles, "I'm a hard dick kind of guy. No soft dicks allowed in *my* house."

Until now, I wasn't sure if Julian had much of a sense of humor, but apparently he does. I say, "You know, with all those dick hardener pills guys are taking by the handful these days, they must have dicks made of granite."

Julian quips, "Then they are welcome in my home any time. Now sign the waiver," he says insistently, "Or I'm going to show you why you never want to incur the wrath of a hard dick."

"Oh?" I gasp coquettishly. "Why?"

His emerald eyes shine, green glints that flick sunlight into mine as he narrows his lids and grins, "Don't make me show you," he threatens. "Respect the dick."

I'm leaning both arms against the long cool marble countertop island when he slides his hand down my forearm, which sends shivers up to my shoulder. He lifts my hand off the countertop and slides his hot golden fountain pen into my waiting fingers.

The pen is hot because he's been holding it in his hands, but it was already hard before he handed it to me.

This time, I'm not talking about a hard dick.

It's just a pen.

I promise.

For, ahem, signing contracts.

"Sign," he smiles.

I notice that Julian's hand is very warm as it grips mine and I'm getting very hot. This was not how I imagined the signing of the consent waiver would go. But I guess I should've known better. When you start off a relationship working on dick hardener music together, dicks tend to get hard.

Heck, *everything* gets hard.

Even fountain pens.

The kind with pearlescent ink.

I squeeze Julian's golden pen in the sheath of my fingers while his thumb caresses the taut bud forming in the crease of flesh where my curled index finger grips the shaft of his golden pen. His thumb turns slow circles, going around and around and around my knuckle's fleshy bud of folded skin, and it's not erotic at all.

Because we're still talking about pens and hands, people. They're used for signing contracts, which is purely a business arrangement. And we all know not to mix business with pleasure.

This is strictly business.

Seriously.

"Ooh..." I purr and lower my lashes seductively, still gazing at Julian's emerald orbs. Yeah, I'm not getting into this at *all*. I crinkle my nose, "Your pen is so *hard*..."

I'm such a tease.

Julian shakes his head like he's half-drugged, unlocking our gaze, but he's smiling. He reluctantly releases my hand at last, breaking the spell.

"Sign," he orders. He slides his hands into his pockets like that's the only safe place for them at the moment.

I sigh and shrug my shoulders, reluctantly turning off the flirt.

I glance at the contract.

I mull over what Julian said earlier about what happens if the ad agency sends my guitar track to the pharmaceutical company. Honestly, when you consider the distraction of Julian's golden pennilingus, I'm surprised I remember any of what he told me in the last five minutes. I guess I was multi-tasking.

Anyway, if I refuse to sign this consent waiver, I could mess up Julian's entire project with the ad agency. I suddenly feel powerful. Without my agreement, it's back to the recording studio for Julian. Although I barely know him, I already have the strong sense that Julian is used to getting his way.

Ms. Mischievous, one of the more vocal voices in my internal committee, is curious to see what poor wittle Juwian will do if he doesn't get his way. Yes, I want to see him squirm. Or throw a tantrum. On him, it might be very sexy. I also think it might do Julian some good to have things go off the rails once in awhile. I swear by it. What did Johnny say to me at the shop the other day? When one door closes, another opens?

Look at all the fun I've had since Scott kicked me out of Skin Trade.

Then Ms. Sensible, one of the presiding members of my mental committee, reminds me that Julian has already paid me a thousand bucks for my guitar work, and I don't want to go back on my word.

Ms. Sensible is not the fun one.

Sigh.

But she's good at reading contracts.

I pick up the consent waiver from the countertop and glance over it.

Yesterday, I went into Big Momma's to use their computer to read up about session musician waivers. I have a vague idea of what to look for on this one.

Julian's Session Musician Agreement doesn't say anything about future royalties for me. It just mentions the $1,000 he already paid me. That's okay. Because it's not like the commercial jingle for a dick hardener pill is going to suddenly shoot to the top of the iTunes download charts and I'm going to miss out on royalties.

I take the pen from Julian, which really is nothing but a pen, and scribble my name on the contract.

Sealing the deal.

With a pen.

Okay, okay. It's stiff and golden, just like Goldenblond Julian, but it's only a pen.

"Thank you," Julian smiles. "I'll have Colette email a copy to the agency today. Now you're officially a session musician, Victory." He holds out his hand for me to shake. "How do you feel?"

I almost say, "Spent," but instead I shake his hand and grin, "Like a working musician!" It's pretty damn awesome.

"I assure you, Victory *Payne*..." his beautifully sculpted lips spread to reveal his pristine white teeth, "this is only the beginning..."

His smile is genuine and pleasingly suggestive but there is something vaguely ominous about his words.

I'm not going to dwell on it.

I say innocently, "Let's go get that dinner you promised me."

He smiles devilishly, "It would be my pleasure..."

Who doesn't like pleasure?

Ms. Sensible, who likes to think she runs my internal committee 24/7 (but doesn't) frowns like the spinster she is, and raises her hand so she can be counted amongst the pleasure haters.

I ignore her.

Pleasure, here I come!

Chapter 53

VICTORY

Outside, we walk down Julian's square stone steps to the driveway beneath his house. His black Ferrari 458 Spider is parked under the hot sun. Julian jogs around to the passenger side and opens the door for me, "Madam," he grins.

"I'm nobody's madam," I laugh.

"Would you rather I call you m'lady?"

"That makes me sound old," I grin.

Julian mocks a British accent, "I rather thought it made you sound like the queen."

I chuckle and slide into the leather bucket seat of the Ferrari. If Julian wasn't so damn dashingly handsome, I'd give him shit about his accent. But I'd rather just look at him.

He closes the door gently and walks around to the driver's side. "I think this is top down weather, don't you?"

It's definitely warm enough. "Sure."

Julian presses a button and the Ferrari's roof folds inside the back of the car like a Transformer robot. "Ready?"

"Tally ho!" I joke.

Julian starts the Ferrari and it purrs. It's not American Muscle like I grew up around with my dad, but it'll do.

The Ferrari creeps down the curved driveway until we're on the street and the front gate rolls shut behind us.

Then Julian fires up the Ferrari's afterburners and I'm pushed into the leather seat back as the car rockets down the winding road. The surrounding greenery and the houses in the Hollywood Hills are a multi-colored blur.

I learned a thing or two from my dad about how to drive fast cars. I can tell immediately that Julian is an accomplished driver. He handles the corners expertly, breaking before he enters the turn, feathering the gas lightly through each curve to keep the car level and compensate for any unevenness in the pavement, and accelerating out into the straightaways. Not that there are many straights up in the Hills.

I'm whipped from side to side in my seat as Julian takes turn after turn with total confidence. It's like being on a roller coaster at Magic Mountain. It feels more dangerous than it actually is because Julian knows the road and the limits of his car. If he didn't, I'd tell him to slow the fuck down or let me drive. But there's no need.

I enjoy the hard acceleration of the Ferrari's deceptively smooth power, and the g-forces of the turns.

I love every second of it.

I'm kind of surprised, actually. I expected Julian to be a more sedate driver. But I think his generally restrained mannerisms camouflage the beast beneath. I guess he's kind of like the Ferrari that he drives. Very expensive looking with clean seductive lines and everything perfectly maintained. There's nothing rough around the edges or brutish about an expensive Ferrari, but it's undeniably a high performance race car.

Julian is the same way.

He wears an expensive polo shirt and cargo shorts with leather boat shoes that reveal his tan muscled legs. His defined legs flex as his feet work the gas and brake. I'm somewhat surprised to see him in shorts. Maybe he's not conservative at all, just upscale, like everything he owns.

His fingernails are neatly manicured and have the sheen of clear matte polish. His golden blond hair is perfect, as always. Just a hint of disarray, but too styled to be called messy.

His face is hard and focused as he drives, eyes narrowed, a slight tension and menace around his mouth as he handles the corners of the road. His profile looks hand carved by angels or the god of beauty or something. If Aphrodite had a brother, he'd look like Julian.

Yeah, Julian is a total Ferrari.

Which is why I'm having a difficult time not thinking about orgasms sitting inside his Ferrari. All the acceleration and high intensity turns are mixing around my tummy and all the muscles in my pelvis pleasantly. Having a hot guy like Julian sitting next to me is the icing on the cake. I'll keep that information to myself for now.

Ms. Sensible reminds me that as hot as Julian is, I'd rather explore a business relationship with him. If he can get me more session work as a guitarist for a thousand bucks an hour, my money problems will be solved. I need to keep things between us strictly professional.

The fingered muscles of Julian's forearms dance as he works the steering wheel around a particularly tight corner.

I feel the rear end of the Ferrari slip loose at the apex of the turn. Julian power-slides the car out to the edge of the pavement. We pass within inches of rolling over the side of a steep drop off into someone's immense backyard garden. Despite the loss of traction, Julian steers confidently into the skid and maintains control throughout the turn, narrowly avoiding disaster. We whip out the end of the curve and accelerate down the road.

The thrill of it tightens all the muscles in my pelvis with electrified excitement.

Business.

It's all about business.

I will act totally professional with Julian at all times.

But I can think all the dirty thoughts I want.

At the bottom of the road, the Ferrari levels out and we turn onto Sunset Boulevard. Julian's driving relaxes. There's too much traffic and too many stoplights for a car like a Ferrari. Once again, the car and Julian are caged animals biding their time before the next chase.

I ask, "Where are we going?"

"It's a surprise," he says mischievously.

"Let me guess. There's going to be waiters with thin mustaches wearing penguin suits and the maitre'd is snooty and French and you're going to slip him a Benjamin so we get a good seat."

"Something like that," Julian chuckles.

We drive for awhile down Highland, until we're in the Melrose area.

Julian stops and signals left. We're about to turn into a parking lot for either a Yum Yum Donuts in a strip mall or the 76 gas station across from it.

We can't be having doughnuts for dinner. I ask, "Do you need to get gas?"

"No," he says.

I ask skeptically, "Are we having doughnuts for dinner?"

Julian arches an eyebrow at me. "Is that a problem?"

"No! I just didn't peg you as the doughnuts for dinner type."

Julian laughs. When there's an opening in traffic he turns into the strip mall parking lot. We drive slowly past Yum Yum.

"No doughnuts?" I whine comically. "I was all set to have a maple bar for dinner!"

Julian grins, "If you're still hungry after, we'll get maple bars."

"Yay!" I clap like a little girl.

We drive past a dry cleaners, then Tasty Thai. I can do Thai. I bet I could even buy dinner. Tasty Thai looks like the kind of place where we can both eat for less then twelve bucks including tip.

Instead, we park in front of Raffallo's Pizza.

The sign for Raffallo's is red letters on a yellow field, surrounded by light bulbs. The sign has a cheesy 1970s Vegas quality I like and also says, "ITALIAN FOODS. EAT HERE OR TO GO. BEER & WINE." There's a big yellow arrow shaped sign hanging from the overhang that says OPEN and it points at the front door. This is totally my kind of place.

I hop out of the car before Julian can get the door for me.

He stands beside me, already around the car, and says, "I was going to get your door for you." He looks disappointed, almost like a junior high school kid on his first date ever.

"Oh! Sorry. Do you want me to get back in the car?"

He smiles warmly. "No, but promise me you'll let me get the door to the restaurant."

"Promise," I grin.

We walk to the front door and I stop so he can open it for me.

"After you," he opens the door and motions inside.

"Thank you, sir." I walk into the pizza joint and it's nothing like what I was expecting. No red and white checked table cloths or neon beer signs or old arcade games in the corner. In fact, it's not even a pizza joint. It's a trendy restaurant. Marble floors, designer decor, strangely shaped squarish barstools, all manner of pots and pans hanging over the bar and the open kitchen area behind it. A bunch of chefs busily prepare food.

When they see us, the cooks in the kitchen all yell out, "*Bonsoir!*"

I'm not quite sure what to do, so I wave bashfully at them.

Julian smiles, "Welcome to Trois Mec. I had to call in a favor to get tickets only two days in advance."

"Tickets?" I blurt. "What kind of restaurant sells tickets?"

"This one," he grins.

The atmosphere is raucous and casual. The sound system pumps out French hip hop. I can't understand the lyrics, but I like the strange style of the music. None of the customers are dressed up.

A handsome guy behind the bar with a thick French accent and lots of tattoos chats with one of the customers sitting on a barstool.

Julian says, "That's Ludo Lefebvre behind the counter. He owns the place. If you watch any cooking shows, you've probably seen him on TV."

I don't, but I nod, then realize that Ludo is chatting with Jake Gyllenhaal. I almost say something, but I learned awhile ago that it's not cool to gawk at celebrities if you live in L.A. It's not like I see celebrities every day, so it's kind of a big deal, but I play it down with a shrug. But it's Jake frickin' Gyllenhaal! I say nothing.

Ludo notices us and waves at Julian. In a thick French accent, he hollers, "Julian! Good to see you!"

Julian cocks a smile at Ludo and salutes him with two fingers.

One of the waiters seats us at a corner table. My menu has no prices on it. I ask Julian, "Does yours have prices?"

"No. It's a set menu for everyone."

"I don't get to pick?"

"Nope. But we get everything listed on the menu."

"Everything? I'm gonna be stuffed! You're going to have to rent a truck to drive me home!"

"Don't worry," he grins, "the portions are reasonably sized. This isn't a pig trough."

I read over the menu. The starter snacks include tangy buckwheat popcorn, sushi rice with salt cod cream (whatever that is, but I know I like cream) and fennel fronds, and cubed garlic bread. For appetizers, it looks like we get raw beef with grilled yogurt, fermented black walnut, and caramelized eggplant. I look up from my menu and grin, "I haven't eaten anything and already my mouth is watering! I've never heard of half the stuff on here. It all sounds delicious."

"It is," Julian smiles.

We'll also be served a second appetizer of grilled cabbage with creamy miso flan and fennel pollen. Pollen? Isn't that for bees? Well, I guess if bees like it, it must be good, because they make honey with it. For the first main course, we get potato pulp, brown butter, bonito flakes, onion soubise, and salers.

"Hey, Julian," I say, "what's potato pulp? It's not like what you get in

O.J., is it?"

"No," he smiles. "It's puréed. Like a blended mashed potato, but creamy and quite delicious."

"And salers?"

"A kind of French cheese. You'll like it."

I nod. Cheese is good. The other course is duck with endive, pear, wild juniper berries, and candied oranges. Mmmm, fruit with meat. And for dessert, two courses. You can never have too much dessert. The first is apple butter, creme de brie, and toasted barley. The second is roasted sunchoke ice cream choux and fermented black garlic caramels.

I ask, "What's sunchoke ice cream choux?" I pronounce it "chooks."

Julian arches an eyebrow.

I frown, "Sorry, I don't know how to say shit in French. Well, I've heard it's *merde*, but that's as far as my French goes." I wink and stick my tongue out at him.

He smiles and says, "A sunchoke is a variety of artichoke. They're quite good. *Choux—*" he says it like the word chew, "—is a dessert pastry. Have you ever had *profiteroles* or *croquembouches*?" His French accent is way better than mine.

"No," I shake my head.

"How about an *éclair*?"

"Nope." I'm feeling a bit too white trash at the moment. Not that I *am* white trash. My neighbors growing up were white trash, but they were just my neighbors. I don't think that makes me white trash. Besides, now I live in L.A., which means I'm a starving musician, but not a white trash starving musician. There's a difference. Anyway, I don't think L.A. has white trash. They can't afford to live here.

Julian asks, "Have you ever had a cruller?"

"Oh yeah. Totally. I was thinking about getting one at Yum Yum. The chocolate ones are my favorite. I don't know French, but I know doughnuts," I wink.

"*Touché*," he grins. "That's French for touch, by the way." He reaches across the little table and picks up my hand in both of his. He strokes the backs of my fingers gently with his thumbs.

I'm thinking about stiff golden barreled pens all over again!

Woo! Heat! Where's my glass of ice water? I *so* need one right now. I think my face is broiling and my toes are definitely tingling.

Julian aims his blazing green eyes at me, "Ice cream *choux* is a full scoop of *creamy… delicious…* sunchoke ice cream," he draws out the words creamy and delicious seductively, "*squeezed… between…* two layers of *plump* pastry…"

Gosh, I don't know why, but the way he talks about ice cream sounds a lot like sex talk to me. He makes plump pastry sound like either my legs or my boobs, and we all know what the creamy part refers to. I need to fan my face, but won't because it'll probably encourage Julian to continue with his sexy food talk. It sounds corny, I know, but Julian is so handsome and so sincere and his eyes so damn sparkling, I'm totally falling for his hot buttered corn cob. I mean bull shit.

Julian did say when he first asked me out that this was a date, so I can't blame him for trying. But I was hoping to keep things more on a friends level, despite my flirting earlier when he waved his stiff golden fountain pen in my face.

I shouldn't have opened that door, I guess.

Ms. Sensible reminds me to be careful I don't open too many doors too quickly. Johnny should've warned me that opening doors can be dangerous.

Luckily for me, the waiter arrives with the first course, "*Monsieur*?" the waiter prompts. There's no place for the food with Julian holding my hands across the table.

Julian casually releases my fingers from his warm hands. I withdraw reluctantly, making room for the food. The waiter sets our appetizers down.

Everything looks and smells delicious. My mouth waters, wet with anticipation. I'm already having a foodgasm.

By the way, only my mouth is wet, because it's only anticipating food, and my gasm is strictly related to eating. But I can't wait to taste everything. And I'm totally not talking about eating or tasting anything stiff and golden.

Just the food.

Me and Julian dig in to the tangy buckwheat popcorn, popping morsels into our mouths.

Needless to say, the food is every bit as delicious as it sounded on the menu. So many plates come to the table, my entire dinner conversation with Julian seems to revolve around what we're eating and how yummy everything tastes. Julian says something interesting about all of it. He really knows his food. The portions are just the right size so I don't feel bloated by the time I pop my fermented black garlic caramel into my mouth at the end of the meal.

"Wow!" I beam while chewing, "that was all incredible." I giggle and hold my fingers in front of my mouth, realizing I was chewing while talking. Manners aren't usually my thing, but I'm doing my best.

Julian smiles, "I thought you'd like it."

Still chewing on my caramel, I grin, "Totally."

"If you still want," he grins, "we can always get crullers and maple bars from Yum Yum."

I shake my head, giggling, "I'm way too stuffed! But thank you, Julian. You totally know how to treat a lady."

"Dinner and doughnuts," he chuckles and winks, "works every time."

Chapter 54

KELLAN

"Anybody else waiting outside?" I ask Dubs.

Dubs sits on a chair in the corner of his hot garage, which doubles as a rehearsal space for his Reggae band, The Revelers.

We've been auditioning guitar and bass players all day. They've all sucked for one reason or another.

"Hold up," Dubs stands, "I'll check the front." He wears a skin tight light blue t-shirt with a peace symbol on it and a floppy knit reggae cap with a brim. The cap is black and trimmed with green, gold, and red.

"Dude," I chuckle, "aren't you hot in that fucking cap? Your garage is an oven."

"Ain't you heard, K-dawg? No amount of heat gonna make me lose *my* cool."

I roll my eyes.

He smirks and struts past me, pimp style, "That's right."

"That's *wrong*, bro," I holler as he climbs the two steps into the house.

My buddy Joaquin Delacruz is filling in on drums. He sits behind the drum kit normally used by Dubs' Reggae drummer. It's only a five piece kit, but Joaquin plays it like it's eleven. The kit doesn't even have a double bass pedal, but Joaquin has been machine gunning the kick drum with one foot all afternoon.

Soft light from the fading day drifts through a single window. The garage is dim and hot from baking under the L.A. sun all afternoon. The walls are covered with hanging oriental rugs for sound baffling, Bob Marley posters, a pot poster featuring a big black marijuana leaf superimposed over green, gold, and red stripes, and a six-foot cloth Jamaican flag. The grill of Dubs' gigantic vintage 2x15 bass speaker cabinet in the corner is painted green, gold and red. Several bongs of various sizes sit atop the amplifiers. Two lava lamps undulate and glow in opposing corners.

I turn to Joaquin, who is shirtless, brown skinned, wears ratty skater shorts, and glistens with sweat. He's covered in tattoos that go all the way up his neck. He also has zero percent body fat because even when he's not playing drums, he's constantly fidgeting.

Joaquin grew up in East L.A, which he calls East Los. He's easily the most amazing drummer I've ever played with. He's the 25 year-old Mexican skate punk version of Neal Peart from RUSH. He pays his rent doing session work for studios all over L.A. It keeps him super busy. But we're always talking about forming our own band. *If* we can find the right mix of people. In all the time I've known him, we never have. Good band chemistry is hard to find.

I ask, "Joa, what'd you think of the last guy?"

Joaquin smears a white towel across his face then drapes it over the drum rack pipe. He says in his thick East Los accent, "You mean that chingada Dave Mustaine wannabe with the Dimebag purple beard, homes?"

"Yeah."

"I think he wannabe hittin' the woodshed and practicing more before he goes on any more auditions. You shoulda offered him guitar lessons, ése."

Sarcastically, I say, "Did he look like he could afford guitar lessons?"

"Vato couldn't afford new strings. He was missing the high E on his V." Joaquin is referring to the Jackson Flying V the guy was playing.

I huff a big sigh, "How many people have auditioned so far?"

"Six."

"Shit, is that all? It feels like sixty, they've all been so bad. I can't believe the people I found online are the same ones who played today. None of them are nearly as good as their demos."

"Probably stole them from other musicians, homes," Joaquin offers.

"No doubt."

Dubs walks into the garage followed by a beautiful punk rocker girl with long neon pink hair. She carries a beat up ESP guitar case in one hand and a small Crate practice amp in the other. She can't be more than nineteen. She has a nose ring, an eyebrow ring, and a stud poking out below her lower lip. Her ripped up Wild Child T-shirt strains over an amazing rack. The shirt is only a half shirt and it reveals a flat stomach. Her belt is made of bullets, she wears skin tight red plaid pants, and her boots are Doc Martens. She's pretty damn hot.

She asks, "Where can I put my guitar?"

Dubs points, "Over there is good."

She sets the case down, giving us all a view of her red plaid ass, which is heart shaped and leads to her narrow waist.

While her back is turned, there's an unspoken conversation that happens between me, Dubs, and Joaquin. None of us utters a single word, it all happens with our eyes, but we may as well be communicating telepathically. The conversation goes like this:

Joaquin: *Ay, mamacita…*

Me: *Fuck me, are those tits real? They're too perfect not to be.*

Joaquin: *Ay, mamacita…*

Dubs: *You see that ass? Mmmm-MMMM!*

Joaquin: *Ay, mamacita…*

Me: *Which one of us gets to fuck her?*

Dubs: *None of you all. I saw Shorty first.*

Joaquin: *Ay, mamacita…*

(Joaquin doesn't get laid much because of his work schedule)

Me: *How about we let her decide.*

Joaquin: *Ay, mamacita…*

Dubs: *I let you know if she any good.*

Me: *In your dreams, bro—*

"You guys ready?" Neon Pink Hair asks, her guitar already slung over her shoulder.

Picture me, Dubs, and Joaquin stumbling all over each other like a bunch of left footed gorillas, only we do it entirely with our eyes.

Neon Pink Hair looks at me expectantly.

"I'm sorry," I say apologetically, "who are you again?"

She smirks, "I'm Switchblade. Who the fuck are you?"

I chuckle, "I'm Kellan. I sent you the email? You don't have a picture on your website. With a name like Switchblade, I guess I wasn't expecting —"

"A girl?" she says defensively.

"No," I chuckle, "it's not that…"

Her eyes dart between me, Dubs, and Joaquin like she's a cornered wolverine. She says sarcastically, "Considering how you three dicks are sizing me up right now like I'm dinner, I'll give you zero guesses why I don't put my picture on my website. So put your dicks in your pants and let's jam, or I'm the fuck out of here, you cock knockers."

"Oh!" Dubs guffaws, "No she didn't!"

Joaquin cackles loudly.

I chuckle and grin, and Switchblade's feral face relaxes into a smile.

Dubs says, "Her guitar playin' as smart as her mouth, I vote you go with the shorty."

"All right," I say, "let's see what you can do with that George Lynch Kamikaze of yours."

Her ESP guitar has graphics like a World War II fighter plane, which is the perfect look for Switchblade. She plugs the guitar into her practice amp, cranks it up, then fires off a slick high speed riff like a pro. Me and Joaquin recognize it immediately. Eruption by Eddie Van Halen, the classic solo guitar players play to say, "I shred." She does it note for note.

"Órale, ésa!" Joaquin cheers.

Switchblade is amazing. When she finishes, she sneers cockily, "So, what the fuck are we playing? Or are you guys gonna stand around with your dicks in your hands all day?"

"Joder, ése," Joaquin says to me, "that girl can shred."

Dubs asks her, "You play Reggae? Maybe you can join my band instead of his," Dubs chuckles, nodding toward me.

"Fuck Reggae," Switchblade says dismissively. "I'm here to play fucking metal."

"She got a mouth on her," Dubs laughs.

Switchblade is such an awesome guitar player, all I can think is, *Victory who?*

I forgot all about her.

And I'm digging the pink haired punk look. It doesn't hurt she's wearing a Wild Child shirt. They're my favorite fucking band.

And that ass of hers?

Damn!

Chapter 55

VICTORY

Julian drives us up Highland in his Ferrari with the top down. The sun is done for the day and the city lights go to work, twinkling dots and dashes of color against the black night sky. The temperature is perfect for a slow evening drive.

I say, "Thank you so much for dinner, Julian. It was totally awesome."

"My pleasure," he smiles.

I ease comfortably down in my leather bucket seat, "I can't get over how you paid for dinner in advance when you bought tickets. That's so weird. I've never been to a restaurant that sells tickets."

"Now you have," he grins. "I wonder what other interesting things I might expose you to?" he says suggestively.

"Well, just don't expose yourself. You can get a ticket for that," I grin.

He chuckles and shakes his head, "That wasn't what I had in mind."

"Well, you've already exposed me to being a session musician for TV commercials. That was awesome." I want to say that I'd be happy to record more guitar parts for whatever dick commercials, cat litter commercials, or toilet bowl cleaner commercials he's working on next because I need the money. I can't live out of Johnny and Karen's apartment forever. But I don't want to sound presumptuous or shallow, like all I care about is Julian's money, so I don't mention it. If he has more work, I'm sure he'll tell me.

He says, "Now we need to have you record guitar parts for something more interesting. Perhaps an album—"

"Are you reading my mind?" I blurt.

"No. Why?"

"Nothing. Continue."

He nods, "I was going to say, I have several album projects right now that could use some of your magical fretboard expertise."

Concerned, I ask, "I wouldn't be taking work away from Max, would I?"

"You mean because we used your guitar track instead of his on the *dick hardener* commercial?" he grins.

"Yeah."

He shakes his head and smiles, "No. Max and I are producing partners. We both do whatever needs to be done, so you won't be taking any work away from him. In fact, you'll be helping him. Having you present to handle all the guitar parts means Max can focus on any of a thousand other things that we need to accomplish on any given project."

"Really?"

He nods. "Speaking of which, you don't sing, do you?"

My stomach seizes and threatens to squeeze all of the fancy dinner I just ate back up my throat. Why did Julian have to go and ask that?

(*never ever sing*)

Couldn't he have asked something less personal, like whether or not I'm on my period? Regardless, I can't answer. I'm speechless, in a bad way.

He frowns and glances over at me when I don't answer, "Did I say something wrong?"

"Uh, no, it's just—"

(*never ever ever sing*)

"—I, um…" I stammer into horrified silence.

A concerned look settles onto Julian's face. A moment later, he flips on the Ferrari's turn signal and pulls over to park in a free space along Highland. He puts the car into neutral and looks right at me.

I avoid his eyes.

Out of nowhere, he boldly asks, "Do you want to talk about it?"

Two things strike me like hammers to my heart at the exact same moment: the sensitivity, sincerity, and concern in Julian's voice like he genuinely cares, and, the fact that I absolutely cannot talk about this with him. Or anybody. I don't even like talking to myself about

(*Stop!!!*)

why I don't sing.

I do my best to pretend Julian isn't peering into my soul as my shields crack around the edges.

I can't let him in.

Nobody gets in this far.

(*Victory!!!*)

In two years, Scott never got in this far.

(*never ever ever sing*)

I do what the possums do and play dead.

After a moment, Julian says apologetically, "I'm sorry, that was very forward of me. But I can tell it bothers you. I don't like it when people are hurting. It makes me want to help them." He sighs, "I'm sorry. You barely know me, and that was rude of me. I shouldn't have asked."

Who is this guy? Some kind of self help guru? Guys don't talk like this. Guys hate talking about feelings. I'm totally weirded out right now. Plus, he sounds all formal again, like when I first met him.

Julian puts the car into gear and eases the Ferrari back into the flow of traffic. He drops the subject completely and we drive in silence for several blocks.

At the next red light, we roll to a stop.

A BMW convertible pulls up next to us. It's filled with giggling girls with puffy lips and teenage facelifts. None of them are over thirty, but they all look like they've had work done. They immediately take notice of Julian's Ferrari, then Julian.

Hands off, ladies, one of my committee members barks in my head.

"Hey-ey!" the girls in the BMW singsong with identical voices. They sound like they were all manufactured in the same blow up doll factory in the Valley where they also make novelty dildos and shoot How-To porn.

Julian nods politely and says, "Ladies."

Suddenly, I'm totally jealous.

Nearly everyone in my entire internal committee is shouting at the tops of their lungs for me to grab the nearest rock or tree branch and bash in the heads of these blow-up dolls. Ms. Sensible, who resides in the only remaining sane part of my brain, warns that the vacuum between the Blowbags' ears will suck the brains right out of Julian's head if he keeps talking to them, and I should probably do what the rest of my committee says and start popping Blowbags with the nearest sharp object.

One of the Blowbags asks Julian in a shrill voice, "Where are you going, sweetie?"

"Forward," Julian says.

I hope he isn't interested in girls like this. If he is, it will seriously lower my respect for him, music producer or not.

"Where?" the Blowbag asks.

"Forward," Julian points straight ahead.

The Blowbag looks confused, like she did the first day she learned multiplication tables in school, which for her was probably junior year. "Where?" she frowns.

Julian shakes his head imperceptibly and mutters to me, "Which do you think is larger, her chest measurements, or her IQ?"

I chuckle, "Do you even have to ask?"

"I'll wager that the cup size of her bra is the same letter of the alphabet as the overall letter grade average she received upon graduation."

I snicker, "I don't think they give out G's or H's in high school. Anyway, I doubt she made it to graduation."

"I think you might be right."

Luckily, when the light turns green, Julian turns onto a side street, leaving the Blowbags in the BMW behind.

Julian asks, "Would you like to get a drink someplace? Or go back to mine?"

Considering my car is parked in his driveway, I can't tell if that's his way of propositioning me or offering to take me home. So there's no confusion, I say, "I should get home."

Julian's cell phone rings in his pocket. "Bear with me a moment. That's Colette. She never calls this late unless it's important." He pops a Bluetooth earpiece in his ear and answers the phone, "Yes?"

Chapter 56

KELLAN

"Say WHAT?!" Dubs blurts in surprise.

"I'm serious," Switchblade says.

I frown and say to her, "Dude, there's no way a girl as hot as you is gay!"

"Dude!" she says sarcastically, "There's no way a guy as pretty as you has a dick!"

Dubs and Joaquin both cackle and bump fists with Switchblade.

We all hit it off so well back at Dubs' garage that we spent two hours jamming. We even wrote a song. No vocals yet, just riffs. But it's catchy, and everyone nailed their parts by the end. You'd never know it was the first time we'd all played together.

Afterward, Switchblade drove us to The Canal Club on Pacific Avenue in the heart of Venice to buy everyone sushi and beer. It turns out Switchblade is 29, but you wouldn't know it from looking at her.

The Canal Club is packed with people drinking, eating and chattering up a storm.

I haven't been able to keep my eyes off Switchblade since she walked into Dubs' garage. She's totally hot, totally shreds on guitar, totally hilarious, and I'm totally bummed she's gay.

"Wow, Kellan," Switchblade says, "it's the 21st century and you still haven't heard of a lipstick lesbian?" She plucks a piece of Volcano roll off the communal tray with her chopsticks and pops it into her mouth.

I say cockily, "The only lipstick I know anything about comes out my dick when I'm painting some chick's face."

Joaquin laughs heartily and bumps my fist, "Orále, ése!"

Dubs yammers agreement, "That's right."

Switchblade shakes her head, still chewing on her volcano roll, "Now you know why I don't fuck guys." She rolls her eyes, "You're all idiot mouth breathers."

I smile at her and sigh longingly, "Such a waste."

She grins while chewing on the crispy tempura and fried shrimp roll, "I could say the same thing about you, pretty boy."

"How?" I ask.

She winks, "It's a waste you don't have a pussy!"

Dubs and Joaquin laugh.

"Maybe I do," I say flirtatiously. "You wanna check? Inspect my premises for wall to wall carpeting?"

"Okay," she grins, "but if I find any balls, I get to punch them as hard as I can." She slams her little fist loudly on top of the high bar table between the four of us. Glasses and bottles clink hazardously toward the edge of the table.

"Don't do it, dawg!" Dubs warns with a big smile on his face, "Bitch be crazy!"

Switchblade smiles and nods at Dubs, "What he said."

Joaquin tips back his Corona to swallow some suds, then asks her, "Chica, you *sure* you don't miss gettin' dick sometimes?"

She spits out the words "Do you?" before taking a long swallow of her ultra dark Avery Mephistopheles Stout beer.

Me and Dubs guffaw.

I have to swallow my beer so I don't choke on it. I set my glass on the bar table while I continue chuckling and wipe stray beer from my lips with the back of my wrist.

Joaquin shrugs like he's disappointed and says to Switchblade, "I'm just sayin', if you change your mind and want some dick, let me know, ésa."

She smirks, "If you cook yours up and flop it in a taco with a whole lotta hot sauce, I'll take you up on it right now. I've got meat scissors I keep handy for just such an occasion," she jokes and uses her chopsticks to make a snipping motion.

"Dude," I say to her, "what the fuck are meat scissors?"

"Douche," she says it like it's my name, "quit calling me dude, or you'll find out."

Dubs bumps fists with her again.

We all munch on sushi in friendly silence.

"Hey, Joaquin," Switchblade says, "How long have you been playing drums? You're pretty fucking good."

"The bateria?" he looks up thoughtfully, "Fifteen years?"

She asks, "Is bateria the Spanish word for drums?"

Joaquin nods, "Sí."

"That's rad," she smiles. "Bateria sounds like canons."

I say, "When Joa plays them, they always do." I pronounce his nickname 'Wah'.

Joaquin grins.

I clink beer bottles with him.

"So," Switchblade says, "are we a band, or what?"

"I'm in," I say instantly. "What about you two lazy mother fuckers?"

"Who we gonna get to sing?" Dubs asks.

"I'll sing," I bark.

Dubs says, "You gonna do that cookie monster death metal shit, or actually sing?"

"I'll sing," I say.

"Then I'm in," Dubs nods.

I turn to Joaquin, "What about you? You too busy recording drums for MasterCard commercials and Kidz Bop covers, or you gonna man up and play metal?"

"I'm in, homes" Joaquin says.

"All right!" Switchblade cheers, holding up her pint of stout.

We all clink glass.

Switchblade asks, "What are we gonna call ourselves?"

I say jokingly, "How about Four Non Dongs?"

Switchblade cackles, "Love it!"

"Hell naw," Dubs frowns.

"I quit, ése," Joaquin quips.

"We'll think of something," I say.

"We can't waste too much time," Switchblade says. "L.A. Gunslingers at Guitar Central is coming up quick."

I arch an eyebrow at her, "You know about Gunslingers?"

Switchblade scoffs, "Every musician in L.A. knows about fucking Gunslingers."

"True that," Dubs nods.

Joa says, "We clean that shit up, homes!"

"Damn right," Dubs agrees.

I eye the three of them. They're all way into the idea of us playing Gunslingers. Exactly what I was hoping to find. Switchblade was the missing link. Now we've got the makings of a serious band. We just need a name and a few more tunes and we're going to kick heavy metal ass.

I raise my beer and cheer, "Let's do it!"

We all clink glass again and throw back more suds.

I clunk my empty bottle on the table and stand up off my barstool, "Now I gotta take a leak."

"You asking permission to leave the table?" Switchblade barks sarcastically.

"Fuck no," I frown. "But maybe you want to help? Takes four hands to hold my shit. It's like a fucking fire hose when I set it off," I smirk.

Switchblade rolls her eyes, "Is that supposed to impress me?" She shakes her pink hair, "You're on your own, flyboy. Or should I say fly dick?"

Dubs and Joaquin chuckle and exchange grins with Switchblade.

She's the perfect fit for us.

I weave through the crowd toward the men's room in the back.

I totally dig Switchblade's smart mouth. But the truth is, I'm relieved she's gay. The last thing I need is a bunch of girlfriend

(*Giselle*)

drama getting in the way of my band. Getting a band off the ground is hard enough as it is without any added bullshit.

I walk out of the men's room a few minutes later and work my way back toward my buds.

"Nice ink," some random girl says to me as I squeeze past her.

I'm wearing a short sleeve T, so my muscled arms and all my sharp tats are clearly visible. I turn to look at her. BAM! Hottie alert. She has a huge pile of tightly curled red hair framing her delicately sculpted porcelain face. Redheads aren't normally my thing, but when they're as hot as this babe, I make an exception.

Once Red sees my face, her blue eyes lock on mine. "Hey," she says then sips from her margarita glass. "What's your name?" She's already twirling her fingers in her hair. Game on.

I chuckle, "Kellan."

"Kellan…" Red purrs and narrows her eyes, "That's a sexy name."

I snicker internally. This is too easy. I size her up. Ample porcelain cleavage strains out of her tight low cut top. Narrow waist, nice hips, long legs hanging out of her short skirt. She's easily an 8.5, maybe even a 9. Most men would do anything to get in this girl's pants. She's the kind of babe they'd be bragging to their friends about for years and years if they could manage to bag her. I know I can.

Red says, "I really like your tats." She slides her icy margarita glass down my forearm.

"Me too," I say, not even trying. Do I let her take me home?

She obviously wants me. She hoods her eyes seductively and asks, "Can I buy you a drink?"

Yeah, chicks ask to buy me drinks all the time. It sounds ridiculous, but it's true. I suddenly blurt, "You're not a musician, are you?"

"No. Should I be?"

I shake my head, "No. You're fine the way you are."

She smiles alluringly, "How about that drink?"

I glance toward my table where Dubs sits with Switchblade and Joaquin. They're all laughing and smiling like old pals. I catch Dubs' eye. He takes a good look at Red and raises appreciative eyebrows. I see him mouth the word, "Damn!" He gives me the "Go for it, dawg," nod.

I grin in response.

I'll find my own way home tonight. I mean, tomorrow morning.

I cock a wicked grin at Red and say, "Sure. Anything you want."

Chapter 57

VICTORY

"That's not good," Julian says to Colette on his earpiece while casually steering the Ferrari with one hand. He nods several times. "I was afraid of that. They're not going to use it, are they?"

Is he talking about my guitar tracks for the dick hardener pill commercial? I hope not. I was kind of excited to think my playing would end up on TV. Oh well. At least I got paid. That's the good news.

"Okay," Julian says to Colette, "tell them we'll come up with something else… When do they need it? … Friday? … It'll be tight, but we can definitely have something rough for them by end of day Friday. Is Max in the studio right now? … No? Can you track him down? … He's probably at the Viper Room trying to pick up women…" Julian chuckles, "Yes, that's Max. I've been thinking about buying a chastity belt for him. Can you price them for me, Colette? … Where? … Try Agent Provocateur. Or try The Pleasure Chest. They're open late," Julian smiles. "Yes, have them send some samples over tomorrow. We'll find one that fits Max with minimal chaffing."

Wow, it sounds like Julian knows a lot about sex shops and chastity belts.

"What? …" Julian snickers to the phone, "No, I don't think Max needs extra large. He's most likely small or extra small." Julian turns and winks at me with a big grin, then returns his eyes to the road and continues with Colette, "Don't tell Max I said that," Julian grins and chuckles again. "In the mean time, keep texting him. Tell him to get his butt to the studio if he wants to keep his balls."

It's nice to see Julian's sense of humor coming out. It looks good on him.

"Okay," Julian says to Colette, "I'll be back at the house in twenty minutes." He hangs up and smiles at me, "Sorry about that."

"Oh, it's okay." Truthfully, I'm slightly disappointed that I don't get to choose whether or not Julian and I will share a drink, whether at a bar or at his place. But it's probably for the best. Need to keep that friends line drawn in the sand so nobody steps over it. Him or me.

Curious, I ask, "Is there something wrong with the dick pill commercial?"

"Huh?" he looks confused. "Oh, no. That call was about a different project I'm producing."

I wait for him to say more but he doesn't.

We drive back to his house, up the winding roads into the Hollywood Hills. Julian doesn't race this time, just cruises along at the speed limit. His mind is obviously elsewhere. I imagine he's thinking about whatever mysterious project Colette called about.

I have to admit, I'm disappointed.

When we arrive at the gate to his house, he stops the car while the gate wheels slowly open, then cruises up to the driveway and parks. I wait in my seat while he jogs around and opens my door.

He extends his hand, which I take, even though I really don't need help getting out of a car. Even if it's a low slung Ferrari. I have leg muscles. But it's sweet and romantic and I kind of like that Julian is such a gentleman.

"Thank you," I smile as I stand.

"My pleasure," he grins.

"I had a great time tonight," I hint.

"Me too," he says.

He's now supposed to line up another date with me.

He doesn't. He just slips his hands in his pockets like he's posing for a fashion photographer again.

"Uhhh…" I stammer.

"I should get inside," he says apologetically. "Max should be here any minute and I need to prepare things in the studio."

"Um, okay?" This wasn't how I expected this evening to end.

"Screw it," he grunts.

Huh?

He yanks his hands out of his pockets and hooks one hand around the back of my neck and the other cradles my hip. For a second, I think he's going to dip me into one of those old school black-and-white movie kisses. Instead he pushes my body against the side of the Ferrari with his.

His hot mouth devours mine greedily.

I'm so surprised, I can't even think to resist. His tongue plunges into my mouth and wrestles with mine. His hand on my neck caresses me, his thumb stroking across my ear, skimming along my jaw. His other hand reaches behind me and grabs my ass, squeezing hard and pulling me into him forcefully. Then he thrusts his pelvis into mine abruptly, pinning me back against his expensive car.

I kind of expected Julian to be the kind of guy worried about scratching the paint job.

How wrong I was.

But I was right about his beast beneath.

It's a hot iron bar pressing through his cargo shorts.

I'm instantly wet and totally ready. All I want right now is for him to push my cutoff denim shorts down around my ankles and fuck me right here against his Ferrari. Or he can throw me on the hood and fuck me there.

I don't care.

As long as he lets his beast out to fuck me.

His hand squeezes my breast through the thin material of my V neck shirt. A thousand butterflies take wing in my breast and flutter across my chest. Rose petals blossom between my legs as I come alive. I lift one leg and hook it around Julian's thighs, pulling him into me.

He pushes into me deeply and groans into my mouth.

I swallow his hot desire.

Both his hands slide down my sides, curve over my hips and coil behind me, pulling my ass even more forcefully forward into his rigid manhood. He hisses and grunts and nips at my neck with greedy teeth.

This is really not what I expected from Julian.

I'm pleasantly surprised.

His hands are hard and forceful on my ass, digging into the muscles savagely. It feels like a good hard massage, the kind that releases exquisite tension, and I want more of it.

Pleasure flickers between my legs as I feel his fingers prying me apart, pulling at my ass. I moan as staccato pleasure explodes and implodes repeatedly in my core, the muscles spasming with anticipation.

I haven't felt this way since...

(*Kellan*)

...I don't remember.

He pushes me against the Ferrari and unbuttons my denim shorts. He rips the zipper open and his fingers grab the waistband of my thong and he pulls hard upward. The material of my damp underwear pulls against my folds and I like it.

I narrow my eyes and stare at Julian, daring him to go further.

His face is contorted with angry lust, his teeth clenched and bared like an animal ready to attack. His eyes glow with green fire. He hisses through his teeth like he wants to take a bite out of me.

I bite my lower lip and grab his thick golden blond hair with both hands, curling my fists into it, and pull his mouth toward mine.

He attacks my lips again, ravaging me with his need.

I'm lost to the onslaught of passion dancing between us.

I'm barely conscious of the hot stiff finger sliding into my slickness. I moan low as it hooks up and thrusts deep inside. Every muscle in my belly clenches and quivers.

I want more.

Headlights crawl up the driveway.

Someone is driving up from the main gate.

Julian's hand leaps out of me.

I frantically button and zip my shorts.

The big black Range Rover I'd seen parked here the first day I came to the house now rounds up the driveway. Its headlights splash voyeuristically across me and Julian, pinning our shadows to the garage door behind us like guilty suspects.

Julian thrusts his hands into his pockets, pretending a casualness his crooked collar and ruffled polo shirt denies.

The Range Rover stops and Max hops out.

"Man, I'm totally sorry," Max says like he's expecting Julian to chew him out, "I was in the Viper Room, and the music was super loud. My ringer was on, but I didn't hear it till just now. I drove here as soon as I saw the fifty messages from Colette."

Julian nods at Max, "Fine. Now we have work to do. Did you talk to Colette?"

"Yeah," Max says.

"And she brought you up to speed?"

"Yeah."

I still have no idea what emergency work Julian and Max have in the studio. Honestly, it sounds exciting. I would love to be a part of it. It must be a big deal for both of them to drop everything late at night like this. And based on what I know of Julian, I bet they're going to be paid plenty for their troubles.

Yes, I'm jealous.

But I don't think I'm invited.

I shrug my shoulders uncertainly and say to Julian, "Should I go?"

Julian gives me this long look which has nothing to do with recording studios or making money from music. The green flames in his eyes say it all. He doesn't want me to go. I can see that he doesn't want to work with Max on whatever awaits them in the studio nearly as much as he'd like to keep working on me.

I'm up for either.

Both promise excitement I never dreamed possible.

Julian huffs a big sigh and says to Max, "Do you think we're going to need any guitar tracks on this?"

Max glances at me and says thoughtfully, "Probably not. I think tonight is going to be all about synthesizer samples."

Julian nods like that's not the answer he wanted.

"But…" Max says, "it's always nice to have a fresh set of ears for new ideas?" He looks at me hopefully.

Julian closes his eyes firmly and takes a deep breath. After a moment, he says, "As much as I'd like to, Victory, I think Max and I need to get into our regular groove on this one. But we may very well need those fresh ears Max mentioned tomorrow or the next day." He looks disappointed, but his Mr. Responsible side is now running the show. "You should probably go."

I stuff my hands into the back pockets of my shorts and shrug my shoulders again, "Okay." I do my best not to sound disappointed. I mean, they're about to do something that sounds really awesome and important and fun, and I'm not included.

Oh well.

"I'll call you in a day or two, Victory," Julian says. "You can come by the studio when things have calmed down and give a listen to whatever

Max and I come up with. How does that sound?"

"Sounds great."

We all say goodbye politely and I climb into my Altima and drive home.

Alone.

Hot, bothered, and alone.

Damn it.

Oh well. It's probably for the best.

I'd told myself earlier I wanted to keep things between me and Julian on a business level.

Stupid Ms. Sensible.

She doesn't know how to have any fun.

Her and Julian's Mr. Respectable can suck it.

Chapter 58

KELLAN

"Oh," Red hisses in the silent darkness. "Don't stop. No, don't stop..." She moans and her fingers knot in my hair. Her thighs quiver around my ears. "Oh my god," she gulps, her hips bucking against my face. "Oh, oh, oh... Oh, Kellan. I'm gonna, I'm gonna...oh, oh, oh! I'm gonna COME! OH! KELLAN!!!" She's screaming now. "AAAHHH!!!" She almost sounds like she's crying. "OOHH!! Ohmygod! OH!!!!"

My dick is totally soft in my jeans. I'm kneeling on the fake wood floor inside the front door of her apartment. Her back is pressed against the front door and my head is up her skirt. My hand holds her thong to the side with my disinterested fingers.

I felt like I owed her for the drink.

But I'm not even close to being into this.

I stand up and she slides down the door until her butt settles on the floor, her knees splayed wide apart, her skirt hiked up to her wet crotch.

She has a huge smile on her face. She gazes up at me and laughs, "Was that your idea of foreplay?"

I'm amused. It's always nice to make someone feel good. It's always better to give than receive, right? I smile at her and offer my hand.

She takes it and I pull her to her feet. Then she stumbles toward her kitchen, working her skirt back down her thighs. "Can I get you anything? A drink?"

"Water is fine."

"I have beer," she suggests.

"Whatever."

She grabs two bottles from the fridge and pops the caps with an opener that she leaves on the counter. She hands me a beer, and takes my free hand in hers and leads me to the couch.

"Wow," she chuckles, "that was incredible."

I smile politely.

We sit down on the couch.

How can I leave without hurting her feelings? Is one orgasm enough? Or does she need my dick to call it even? There's nothing worse than getting a chick all worked up to fuck, and then you change your mind. All of a sudden that feminist "no means no" bullshit goes out the window and you become public enemy number one because you don't feel like fucking anymore. I know. It sounds stupid. But it's happened to me before. What can I say? Sometimes even I'm not in the mood. I don't know why. Just sometimes,

(*Victory*)

I'm not.

Red drops her head back on the couch cushion, "Ohmygod, Kellan. I need to catch my breath after that." She chuckles and sighs. Then sighs again.

I still don't know Red's name. I smile dumbly and sip my beer.

She laces her fingers through mine and we're holding hands.

Great. I know where this is going.

"So, Kellan," she gives me the big eyes, "tell me more about you."

"What do you want to know?" I ask absently.

"Do you have a girlfriend?"

(*Giselle*)

I chuckle, "No."

"That's good news," she sips her beer and lifts up my hand to examine it. "You have really big hands."

And?

"What do you do with them?"

"I'll give you three guesses."

She smiles, "Ooh. I like games."

I bet she does.

"Hmmm," she purrs, "Let me see. I bet you like to build things and tear them down and get your hands dirty. Are you a mechanic?"

I shake my head, "No. But I do all my own work on my bike."

"You ride a motorcycle?"

"Yeah," I shrug and sip my beer.

She says, "Why am I not surprised?" She sets her beer down on the coffee table in front of her couch so she doesn't have to release my hand. Then she drapes her legs over mine and runs her free hand through my hair. "I like a guy who rides a motorcycle."

Most women do.

She asks, "Do you do construction work?"

I shake my head.

"I know! You're a grip or one of those hard working handymen on a movie set? They're always sexier than the actors."

I shake my head with less emphasis than before. This is a drag. But I don't want to be totally rude.

"So," she asks curiously, "What *do* you do, Kellan?"

I sigh, "I teach guitar to kids."

She smiles, "You're a music teacher?"

I nod and sip my beer. I really don't feel like beer right now.

"That is *so* precious, Kellan! I bet you're totally good with kids."

"They seem to like me well enough."

She leans back, her eyes gleaming. "How did I get so lucky tonight?"

I'm feeling the exact opposite. This is going south fast. She's already picking out wedding dresses and engagement rings in her head.

"You really teach kids?" she asks like it's impossible.

"I do." I can't help it. I always enjoy talking about my kids. I smile slightly, "This one student of mine, Chloe, she's twelve but she's so into guitar, you'd think she was twenty or thirty cuz of how hard she works." Now I'm smiling a lot. Chloe is totally cool.

Red nods and gazes into my eyes. Her pupils are dilated like black dimes, like she's trying to suck me right into her heart where she's already making a nest for the two of us.

Shit, I shouldn't have said anything about the kids. I need to lie more. I should've told her I was out of work and lived with my parents. Or was married or gay. Anything but the truth. Shit.

Her eyes narrow thoughtfully, "Is that why you asked me earlier at The Canal Club if I was a musician? Because you had a bad experience with one?"

Damn it, she figured

(*Victory*)

it out. Red is too smart for her own good. And why did she have to fucking ask that? I sigh heavily.

Excited, she says, "You did, didn't you?"

Now she's getting all Dr. Phil on my ass. She's going to pry and pry until she gets to my wounded

(*Giselle*)

heart and try to fix me. I hate that shit.

"No," I say. "It's just that a lot of musicians

(*Victory*)

are flakes."

Red combs her fingers through my hair, "Well, you don't have to worry about me, Kellan. I'm not a musician." She swings her legs off of my lap and slinks up to me, pressing her breasts against my muscled arm. She nuzzles my cheek affectionately. Then she licks my ear for awhile, which I usually enjoy, but I'm not into it at the moment. She nibbles on my earlobe then purrs softly, "Would you like to go to bed?"

No.

Moment of truth.

You know those scenes in movies when they're on a spaceship or a submarine, and someone triggers the self destruct mechanism? Everyone onboard runs around desperately, trying to get to the lifeboats or escape pods before the ship blows into a billion pieces?

That's what I'm feeling right now.

The only difference is there's no *Whoop! Whoop! Whoop!* or blaring warning klaxons going off while the lady computer voice does the countdown. Instead, Red's apartment is dark save for the street lights peeking through her blinds, and it's totally silent.

The tension builds to maximum as I stretch this out, knowing what's coming next. I'd like to enjoy the calm before the storm.

But I can't wait forever.

3…

It starts with a big sigh on my part.

2…

Red senses it instantly. She pulls back reluctantly.

1…

I lean forward. In a low voice, I say, "I have to go."

0…

I can't help but look her in the eyes. Her pupils are now pinholes, shielding her heart from further attack.

"What?" she grunts.

"I need to leave."

She frowns, her beauty warped out of true by her impending rage.

I should've walked away from

(*Giselle*)

Red at The Canal Club.

What can I say. I'm human.

I needed

(*Victory*)

a distraction.

I stand up.

Red sinks into the couch and folds her arms protectively across her chest. Not because she's afraid I'll attack her, but because she doesn't want me to see her broken heart.

Yeah, I'm a dick. But my dick isn't interested in Red.

(*Victory*)

And like most dicks, mine is dumb as fuck most of the time.

(*Giselle*)

"Go," Red hisses.

I know better than to say anything. If I say even a single word, she'll blow sky high. I can feel it.

I walk quietly to her front door and let myself out.

When her door clicks softly shut behind me, I hear her shout, "*Asshole!!*"

Whatever.

She bought me a drink. I gave her a great orgasm. What's her problem?

A better question is, what's my problem?

(*VictoryGiselleVictory*)

I trudge down the stairs that lead up to her second story apartment and walk onto the street in front of the building.

While I look around and get my bearings, I hear her yell out a window behind me, "Fucking jerk!!"

CLACK!!

A woman's shoe bounces across the sidewalk a few feet in front of me. I turn and see Red's arm cocked, another pump in hand. I bet it hurts to get hit with the pointy heel.

Guess I was right about

(*Victory*)

Red.

Whatever.

I lean my torso suddenly back as shoe number two flies past my face.

Women.

I walk home in darkness.

It's five miles from Venice to my apartment in West L.A. and takes over an hour.

I enjoy the peaceful otherworldly quality of the orange streetlights and the quiet neighborhood streets close to the ocean.

I need to clear

(*GiselleVictoryGiselle*)

the cobwebs out of my head anyway.

When I walk into my apartment, I'm clear about one thing.

I'm not making the same
(*Giselle*)
mistake
(*Victory*)
twice.
I have a band with my good friends to focus on.

Chapter 59

VICTORY

My sense of loneliness is complete when I let myself into Johnny and Karen's dark apartment.

I totally need to unwind after my crazy so-called "just friends" date with Julian and think things through. It didn't go quite like I'd planned.

I'm also a little wound up and need a little alone time to let off some steam. If you know what I mean.

A long loud feminine moan rolls out of the back bedroom.

I wince.

One thing I didn't know about Johnny and Karen until I started crashing on their couch is how much sex they have. They're like a couple of rabbits.

Loud rabbits.

I can totally hear them having sex over the Indian sitar music accompanying them in the bedroom. Twingy-twang, twingy-twang, twing, twang, moan.

"Oh!" Karen gasps.

"Yes!" Johnny grunts.

I can't believe they're both in their sixties.

"My yoni is in full bloom, Johnny," Karen hisses. "Give it to me harder."

I can't believe what I'm hearing. But I've heard it most nights since I've been staying here, so I'm getting used to it.

"Your lingam is my yew tree," Karen moans. "Oooh! Plant your seed in me! Johnny!"

I don't even know what a yoni or a lingam is. But I have a pretty good idea.

Johnny grunts louder, "Oh! Oh! Oh! Oooohhh!!!"

For most people, that sound means they're almost done having sex.

Not these two. I know from experience they can go on and on for hours.

Seriously.

The first time it happened, they woke me up.

I thought it was an earthquake.

Nope.

It took forever for them to finish. I had pillows and couch cushions squeezed over my head until the sun came up. At breakfast that morning (it was a Saturday, so we all got up at the same time to go into the shop for work) I expected an embarrassed vibe at the table while we ate, but Johnny and Karen acted like nothing weird had happened.

Hippies.

I never knew Free Love included a Free Show.

"Yes, Johnny! Yes!!"

Thud! Thud! Thud!

So much for my alone time. No way I can relax with that racket. But I still need to use the bathroom. My thong is soaked through because of Julian's explosive passion. Not soaked with *his* passion, like I'd hoped. Just my own solo passion. Anyway, I need to change my thong before I go elsewhere to kill time until Johnny and Karen finish.

WHAM! WHAM! WHAM!

I hope they don't knock the building down.

I can see those little needles at the Earthquake Research Center wiggling all over the paper. The scientists are probably going nuts right now.

So am I.

I flip on a glass shaded lamp in the tiny living room and dig through my black plastic trash bag of clothes until I find a clean pair of underwear. I'm pretty sure I can clean up in the bathroom without bothering Johnny and Karen.

Johnny gasps, "Your eyes are spiraling blue Danubes, baby. Your hair is on fire like the burning bush."

What the hell are they doing in there? Do I need to call the fire department? I tiptoe to the hall bathroom and close the door as quietly as possible.

"Ooooh, baby," Johnny groans, "I feel all six of your sanskrit arms caressing my soul with a thousand rainbow fingers. Take me to nirvana, baby. I'm ready to go. Ooohhh!!"

Karen coos, "You're having an acid flashback, baby. But I can smell your infinity..."

I repress a snicker. What?! I think they're both having a flashback.

"AAAHHH!!!" Johnny shouts, "Golden elephants! I see golden elephants!!!!"

"Go with them," she moans, "and take me with you!"

I almost blurt laughter at that point.

Johnny moans, "Your mouth tastes like the number three! It's never tasted like the number three before!"

Okay, I really have to get out of here. I don't want to interrupt their journey to Wonderland or Candyland or whatever plane of existence they've floated away to.

I finish up in the bathroom as quietly as possible and leave the apartment.

Now I have an hour to kill. Or four. Who knows with those two. I wish it wasn't so late. But there's no way I'm falling asleep while Johnny and Karen bang their way through the doors of perception.

Chapter 60

VICTORY

I drive to the 101 Cafe on Franklin Avenue.

The cafe is kitty corner to the old Hollywood Tower, an art deco apartment building which I've heard is haunted by the ghosts of movie stars. The Hollywood Tower is the inspiration for the Disneyland ride The Twilight Zone Tower of Terror. People still live in the Hollywood Tower today and I've snuck inside late at night hoping to see the ghost of Rod Serling and ask for his autograph, but he never showed up.

I park on a side street and walk into the 101 Cafe. It's busy with late night diners, but I find an empty seat at the counter. The decor here is awesome. It's got a mid 1960s vintage vibe I love. One of the walls is made of lava rocks, they've got brown vinyl wrap around booths, hanging globe lights over each fake wood table, and swiveling brown vinyl bar stools bolted to the marble riser running beneath the long fake wood counter.

I order a large hot cocoa with a fluffy head of whipped cream and a slice of cheesecake. I'm not really hungry, but they'll boot me out of here if I don't buy something.

My phone rings and I pull it out of my purse.

Kellan.

Great.

He's the last person I want to talk to right now. I need to change my phone number. I heave a heavy sigh and silence the call. Of course, I wait with anticipation for the voicemail to come in.

None does.

Neither does a text.

I'm somewhat disappointed.

But it's probably for the best. I don't need to be tempted by Kellan right now. It would be way too complicated. I don't want a repeat of Scott.

Ms. Adventurous suggests coyly that I just sleep with Kellan.

He is pretty damn delicious. I mean, me and Kellan don't need to be in a band together or anything. It can just be sex.

No, that's stupid.

Kellan totally wants to work on music together. And he wants more than just a physical fling. I don't know why I'm so sure of this, but I am. I'm somewhat surprised he does, because he's a total slut, but something about the way he acts with me is different. Almost wholesome.

Like a well behaved Boy Scout.

An image flashes through my imagination: Kellan lying asleep in his bed nearly naked, muscles galore and tattoos aplenty on display, with nothing but the corner of his bed sheet covering his junk,

Kellan? A Boy Scout?

As if.

With a grin, I slowly spear a triangle of cheesecake off my slice of pie and fork it into my mouth. My lips close around the yummy morsel and I slide the fork slowly out while quietly chuckling to myself.

Nothing about Kellan is remotely wholesome.

Which is good.

But he is trouble for me.

That much I know for sure.

I'm not even close to being ready for a relationship with him or anybody else.

Like Julian.

I shake my head. How did I wind up with awesome guys coming at me from every direction the day after Scott dumped me? And what was up with that look Max gave me?

Welcome to my own hot mess.

When it rains, it pours hot guys.

I slurp some hot chocolate through the creamy coolant of the whip cream head. Mmmm. Sugar.

The yumminess doesn't stop my heart from spiraling into a tailspin whenever I think about stupid Scott. Luckily, I think my life has been so crazy since the breakup, I haven't had time to process the fact that my two year live-in relationship with him exploded in my face less than a week ago. Which is good, because I need to focus on finding a place to live. But my heartbreak didn't go away. It's waiting in the wings to kick my ass the second I let it. And I'm not the kind of girl to sweep

(*singsingsing*)

everything under the rug.

In the mean time, I have my money troubles to deal with.

I still owe Johnny and Karen $6,000 for that busted Contrares. I still have my eye on that L.A. Gunslingers first prize of $5,000. If I won that, with the cash I have, I could pay them back. But I really need to move into my own place. Although I adore Johnny and Karen, I can't live with their nightly love-ins much longer. Which is good, because the longer I wait to move out, the less money I'll have. It's now or never. Then I have to figure out how to get a guitar.

"Oh my god! Victory! Is that you, honey?!"

I turn and see an old friend of mine, Olivia Blunt. She wears a vintage white fur coat flecked with black. It looks like what Cruella de Vil wanted to make with the pelts of the 101 Dalmatians. I hope it's fake. If it's not, knowing Olivia, she bought it at a vintage store, so I won't hold it against her. Liv never buys anything new off the rack.

Right now, she looks very 1950s. Her black hair has bangs and Bettie Page waves. Her tight black dress, circular red plastic earrings, red vinyl belt, and red pumps complete the vintage look. When I used to hang with her regularly before I got busy with Skin Trade, she was always a total vintage vixen. She hasn't changed one bit.

"Liv!" I shout gleefully and she throws her arms around me.

She squeals, "I see you finally learned how to dress! You don't look like a mullet headed hesher for once!"

"I don't have a mullet, Liv!"

"It's the clothes, girlfriend. Last time I saw you, you were way too 1980s, and not in a hip ironic Madonna way, but a post disco REO Speedwagon or striped spandex pants Iron Maiden sort of way. Not classy, No, no, no. Not even trashy. Just plain fashion lazy," she scowls.

I sneer, "I like metal bands and concert shirts. Sue me."

"I tried," Olivia grins, "but I couldn't afford a lawyer. Anyway, for once you look like you shopped at Forever 21, not Trends That Are Spun," she's holding her hands up and making finger quotes.

I glare at her for awhile then say, "How many puppies did you kill for your coat, Cruella?"

She blurts hearty laughter and smothers me with another hug. "So good to see you, Victory. It's been forever, girlfriend. I totally got your call the other day, but I've been so busy, I forgot to call you back." She makes a pouty sad face.

"No worries," I smile. "Want to help me finish my cheesecake?"

She glances at it, "Looks tempting."

Unfortunately, there's no place to sit. The barstools to my left and right are occupied.

Olivia squeezes between me and the guy sitting to my right. "There's always room for the skinny bitch."

The tall guy sitting beside Olivia is folded over a cup of black coffee. He has pompadour hair, a pencil thin mustache, a baggy Teddy Boy sport coat, and pointy leather shoes. He's reading a thick book and looks like he should be smoking a cigarette but isn't. He's the perfect man for Olivia. Style wise, anyway.

When Olivia takes a good look at him, she says, "Ooh, hello! You don't mind if I sit on your lap, do you?"

He looks up, his brows pinched, and says, "Sorry?"

"Can I share your chair?" Olivia asks.

"Ahh..."

Olivia sits her butt on the edge of the stool and hip bumps Pompadour several times, "Scootch... just... a smidge... more..."

Pompadour is too surprised to resist. He and Olivia end up with one butt cheek apiece on the chair, and one foot on the marble riser beneath the barstools.

Olivia says to him, "You can tip me for services rendered later. Twenty percent will be fine."

Pompadour chuckles, "Okay, whatever." He sips his coffee, sets the cup back in its saucer, and continues reading his thick tiny print book while sitting on one butt cheek.

I goggle my eyes at Olivia when she turns to face me. The impish grin I've missed twinkles her features.

She lowers her voice and says apologetically, "So I heard Skin Trade is looking for a new guitar player."

I roll my eyes, "Fucking Scott."

Without asking, Olivia takes the fork off my plate and helps herself to the cheesecake. She nods dramatically, "That's what I said. He's a total creepo douche tool."

"Yup," I smirk.

"Have you found a new band?" She bites carefully around her cheesecake morsel so she doesn't smear her red lipstick.

"Not yet. I've been too busy looking for a new job and a new place to live."

Olivia chews her cheesecake, her cheeks puffed around the bulging bite, and nods, "Mmmm. Mmm-hmm." She blots her lips carefully when she's done, thrusting her chest out like she's posing for a pinup poster. Olivia tries to pose like pinups as often as possible.

I totally love Olivia.

She says, "You can crash at my place any time."

"Thanks, Liv." I'm so glad she offered. It's nice to feel like you have friends watching your back, even when you don't need it. "I'm already staying with Johnny and Karen."

"You moved in with the hippies?" she grins. Olivia knows them well from visiting me at the shop in the past.

"Yup."

"Do they grow their own grass and walk around the house naked like it's a nudist colony and take you on acid trips when it's time for a vacation?"

"Pretty much," I grin.

"You can't stay there. Next thing you know, you'll stop shaving your legs and start wearing bell bottoms and hippie head bands." She grimaces at the thought. "If that ever happens, we're no longer friends," she jokes.

I chuckle, "Don't worry. I'm gonna try and find a studio apartment somewhere in Hollywood."

"You sure? If you stay with me, we could have slumber parties and bake cookies and talk about boys."

"Do you even know how to bake?" I ask skeptically.

"I can bake a pop tart. Does that count?"

I roll my eyes. "Anyway, thanks, Liv. Really. But I think I need space to decompress after Scott."

"I understand. But you let me know. Okay?"

I nod. "How's the music business treating you?"

She rolls her eyes dramatically, "It's slow going, sister. Things are way more competitive today than they were two years ago."

Olivia does odd jobs all over town for the recording industry. She's a whiz with Pro Tools, the industry standard recording software, and knows a lot about audio engineering. She's also an amazing singer and does backing vocals for all kinds of bands. With all the people she knows, I'm surprised she hasn't made it big already.

She sighs, "I need a big break soon, sister, or I swear I'm gonna hang it up and become a celebrity dog walker for the rest of my life."

"I thought you hated dogs?"

"I do. But I'm desperate. And nobody hires cat walkers. Anyway, I want a job where I don't have to sit on my ass and get fat eating bonbons."

I sneer, "Who eats bonbons anymore?"

"I eat bonbons. And I eat way too many. You should see me when I've got my head in the cans deep in the middle of a mix." She's referring to mixing music while wearing headphones.

I giggle, "I can totally picture you dripping ice cream all over the keyboard and blaming somebody else."

"Exactly. Anyway," she sighs, "I need to put a band together. One that's going to make some money finally. Wanna help?" As well as singing like a diva, Olivia also plays a mean keyboard.

"What did you have in mind?"

"I've been thinking some kind of bubblegum punk with a feminist edge."

"What, like Avril Lavigne?"

"No, sister," she frowns. "Not *that* bubblegum. I was thinking something with more attitude and less assitude."

I grin. "Hmmm, something like No Doubt?"

"Sort of. But I want to do something different. No use walking the same roads Gwen Stefani already traveled." She pulls out her iPhone and swipes the screen until she gets to her music. "Listen to this. I recorded it last week. Still working on vocals."

It's a peppy, funky disco beat that sounds retro but modern at the same time. The guitar work isn't what I usually do. But maybe I need to branch out beyond hard rock and metal for a change.

"I know what you're thinking," Olivia says, "No guitar solos and not enough distortion."

I smile, "You know me too well."

"This is just rough tracks. You can add embellishments, or we could just write stuff from scratch. I don't care. As long as it's new and it's catchy. I want to sell, sell, sell, girl! I need a hit single! Like, yesterday! I'm sure a couple of Lolitas like us can come up with something new to turn heads and blow up some skirts."

Olivia's enthusiasm is catching.

"Okay," I smile. "Why don't we get together soon and write? I'm totally up for it."

"Perfect," she grins. "We'll seduce the socks off the world with our bombshell songs."

I glance at my phone to check the time. "I should probably go. I need to get up early tomorrow and look for a job." I put money down on the counter to pay for my cheesecake and hot chocolate and stand up to leave.

Olivia slides off the barstool she's been sharing with Pompadour for the last half hour.

"Before you ladies leave," he says, "I was wondering if I might ask for your number."

"Who, me?" Olivia says brazenly. "I'm flattered but—"

"No," he smiles thinly, "I meant your friend." He gives me a long look.

I stammer, "Oh, uh, I'm not dating anyone right now. Sorry."

"Fair enough," he says. He turns to Liv, "How about you?"

"Are you serious?" Olivia gawks. "After you just asked my friend out?

What, am I leftovers? I don't think so."

"Well, I thought—" he stammers.

"You *didn't* think," she flicks her fingers at him. "Skedaddle, Daddy-O. Or Mustachio, or whatever your name is, Mister Hipster."

He smirks, "Hey, you were the one who stole half my seat."

Olivia frowns, "And you never tipped me! I said twenty percent!"

He shakes his head, "No way. You didn't render any services." He glances down at his crotch.

"How about I knee you in the balls and we call it even?"

"Liv!" I hiss.

"Let's go, Victory," she laughs and pulls my elbow while leaning into me. She mutters, "I think that guy likes my kink and is seriously considering my offer. We need to leave before I do something stupid."

I stumble along beside her, "I thought you were waiting for friends?"

"You're a friend, and you're here. Mission accomplished!" she giggles.

I laugh as Olivia pulls me outside onto the sidewalk in front of Cafe 101.

"It's so good to see you again, Liv," I smile as we hug.

"You too, sister. Call me," she waves as I walk to my car.

Chapter 61

VICTORY

Of all the job listings I found online, the one I'm most excited about is the one for the interview I'm driving to right now. I really want this job.

My old Altima cruises westward on the 10 freeway.

As always, the sky is clear, the weather is hot, and I'm in a good mood. It's past rush hour, which is even better because traffic is light, leaving my mind free to roam.

I still haven't heard from Julian since the night we kissed after our dinner date a few days ago. And what a kiss it was. I squirm in my seat just thinking about it. So why hasn't he called?

Did I weird him out somehow?

Considering Julian was the one who threw himself at me, it doesn't seem likely. And he promised to call me so I could come by his studio and listen to whatever super-important mystery recording work he and Max had to do that night.

Too bad he never did.

I was hoping Julian might be more than a handsome distraction and actually hire me to do more session guitar work, but he hasn't done that either.

Good thing I'm not the kind of girl to wait around. Hence, today's interview.

The ad I found for it online read:

GUITAR INSTRUCTOR WANTED. Stage and performance experience required. (got that) Advanced technical skills preferred. (got that too) Basic music theory knowledge required, extensive knowledge a plus. (yup) Must be able to work with kids of all ages. (I'm sure I'll manage).

The name of the company?

Rock & Roll High School.

I'm super excited about my interview. I made sure to arrive early. No way I'm gonna screw up this opportunity.

I exit the 10 freeway at Cloverfield and drive into Santa Monica. I park on the street near the Rock & Roll High School building, which is crammed between a bunch of other random businesses on Wilshire Boulevard.

Ever since my Fender and my amps were stolen out of my car, I feel nervous about leaving it unattended, even on a busy street like Wilshire. Not that I have stuff in it. Everything is tucked safely away at Johnny and Karen's apartment. But I still worry someone might try to steal my car. If that happened, I'd be done.

L.A. has a zero tolerance policy for carless musicians.

Luckily, I had enough money to buy a replacement door lock cylinder from a Nissan dealership. I borrowed Johnny's tools and installed the new cylinder myself. Dad would be proud. I really need to give him a call. But right now, I have a job interview.

The front of Rock & Roll High School resembles a glammy eighties night club, which reminds me of RATT, Mötley Crüe, and Bon Jovi. Can't go wrong with that trio of rocker bad boy bands. Works for me.

When I reach for the front door, it opens from inside. I take a quick step back to avoid getting smacked in the face.

The guy coming out the front door says, "Whoa! Sorry! I almost knocked you over." He's really tall and has short brown hair and beard stubble. He wears a short sleeve black button-down gas station attendant style shirt that has a white and red name tag patch that reads Dennis.

I look up and it's Paul Gilbert. *The* Paul Gilbert. I blurt, "Oh my god! You're Paul Gilbert!" I slap my hand over my mouth, bashfully embarrassed.

He nods and grins, "Yeah, I think so. I should probably check my I.D. Sometimes I forget," he winks.

I can feel my inner fan girl explode inside my head, hammering her way out. I can't stop her. "Oh my god! Street Lethal was the first album I ever owned! My dad gave it to me for Christmas when I was a kid. That album is a classic!"

"Wow," he chuckles, "I feel old." He looks me up and down and asks me skeptically, "You like Racer X?"

"*Like* Racer X? I love Racer X! I know every song on that album! I totally love Y.R.O.! I spent weeks figuring it out." I'm just babbling now.

He nods and smiles, "You can play Yngwie Rip Off?"

"Well, not as well as you, " I say demurely.

He frowns suddenly, "You look really familiar. Have we met before?" He sounds genuine, not like it's a pick up line.

"No. I would've totally remembered meeting you, Mr. Gilbert," I giggle nervously.

He chuckles, "Please don't call me mister. Call me Paul."

"Okay," I say bashfully. Inner Fan Girl is jumping up and down, doing cartwheels, and the happy dance, all at the same time. I'm going to faint soon.

He rubs his beard stubble, "Yeah, I've seen you online somewhere. Playing guitar." He cocks his head thoughtfully. "I think it was on YouTube."

"Really? I don't have any YouTube videos. Was it with my old band Skin Trade?"

He narrows his eyes thinking, "I'm not sure. Hey," he smiles, "I've got to run. I'm late for an appointment. It was really nice meeting you. What was your name?" He holds out his hand.

I shake it. "Victory. Victory Payne."

"Nice to meet you, Victory. See ya," he waves casually.

"Bye!" I wave frantically, my hand flapping like a frightened dove as I watch him walk down the street.

Holy crap! Paul Gilbert! I want to chase him and hug him and thank him for being one of my biggest guitar heroes of all time.

But I have a job interview.

Paul Gilbert!

I take a deep breath to calm myself down. I need to act vaguely professional during my job interview. But, but, but!

Paul Gilbert!

I take a final deep breath before I walk purposefully inside Rock & Roll High School.

Chapter 62

VICTORY

Since it's summer, I'm not surprised to see several kids sitting on chairs in the Rock & Roll High School waiting room. The kids are between the ages of maybe seven and sixteen. Most of them have guitar cases in front of them. One boy, who can't be older than eight, has drum sticks in hand and is beating out time on his denim covered knees to whatever music is pumping through the white earbuds of his iPod.

This is my kind of place.

Some of the kids have moms with them. Most of the moms have that overdone casual look of upscale west side L.A. Moms. Perfect makeup, overly tan, manicured nails, and expensive brand new workout clothes. It's a fact that almost everyone in L.A. works out at the gym or the yoga studio or takes kick boxing or runs or rock climbs or whatever.

There's an empty seat next to the mom beside the little drummer boy.

I ask, "Can I sit here?"

She nods.

"Is that your son?" I nod toward Little Drummer Boy, who has spiky blond hair with lots of product in it.

Her lips pull back to reveal teeth that are billboard perfect, "Yes."

"He's really good."

She does't seem talkative, so I sit quietly.

I hear muted electric guitars, faint drum playing, and a bass guitar from the back of the building.

Lessons are in progress.

There's no receptionist, but I'm sure someone will come out into the waiting room eventually. If they don't I'll knock on the door leading to the rest of the building when it gets close to my interview time.

The waiting room walls have posters of rock bands from The Beatles all the way up to the Black Veil Brides. There's framed gold records of classic albums like Led Zeppelin IV, AC/DC's Back In Black, and Iron Maiden's Powerslave, which I assume are fake. And there's a few different framed electric guitars. One is a replica of Eddie Van Halen's famous red Frankenstein guitar with the black and white criss-crossed stripes.

A few minutes later, the door in the back of the waiting room opens and a twelve year old rockabilly-styled girl walks out. She has ponytails, black plastic hipster glasses, and wears a red and white gingham square dance dress with puffy shoulders and a flouncy skirt. She hauls a big Gretsch case with both hands. The case is so big compared to her, she rocks awkwardly from side to side but she's determined to do it herself. I imagine her peers give her crap for dressing like she does. I admire her courage.

For some reason, she seems familiar. I don't know why.

One of the moms sitting in the waiting room stands up. She's dressed in a stylish navy business suit. She says to Gingham Girl, "Ready, Chloe?"

Chloe nods, "Uh huh."

The mom says, "How was your lesson?"

"Awesome!"

The two of them walk outside.

It's getting close to the time for my interview.

The door opening on the hallway to the back of the building is still open. Maybe I should go look for someone? I half expect one of the kids to stand up and go in for a lesson, so I wait for a minute. When no one does, I stand and walk over to the hallway door.

I lean through the door frame and almost break my nose on someone's rock hard chest. The logo on the black t-shirt says Rock & Roll High School. My eyes climb up into the burning brown eyed gaze of Kellan.

"Victory?" he asks, surprised. "What are you doing here?" He doesn't sound very happy to see me. Oh well, that's his problem.

I say sarcastically, "Uh, what are *you* doing here?"

"I work here," he frowns.

"You do?" I ask, surprised.

He sneers, "Yeah. So, why are *you* here?"

"I have a job interview," I say firmly. I'm not backing down just because he sounds all pouty.

He shakes his head, "Don't tell me you're my eleven o'clock?"

I nod and sneer, "Yep."

Then I remember how mad I am at Kellan for the way he called me a stupid waste of time to whoever he was talking to on the phone the night I moved my stuff out of his place. I also told him I needed space, which was the truth. Ironically, that was two days after I met him and kissed him. Wow, I think that's the shortest relationship I've ever had. Ms. Sensible laughs merrily and admonishes me that two days does not a relationship make. Damn right. There's nothing between me and Kellan.

He shakes his head and rolls his eyes, "Rich told me someone was coming in for an interview. He didn't say it was going to be you."

"Surprise," I wrinkle my nose and grimace.

I don't know if I want to do this. Looking up at Kellan's beautifully brooding brown eyes, his handsome face, and that manly manliness he's always projecting, I can feel my chest fluttering against my will. I'm suddenly way too hot.

It's very hard to stay mad at him when he's so crazily cute.

The pressing question is, is it a bad idea for me to work with Kellan?

Duh.

Maybe I should leave and spare us both.

But I need a job, it pays well, and maybe I won't be working directly with Kellan. I mean, I'm teaching kids guitar, not Kellan. Maybe our schedules won't coincide and I won't see him.

I can hope.

He sighs, "Can you wait out here for another few minutes? I have to do something first."

"Sure," I say flatly.

Maybe he's hoping I'll leave. Maybe I should. Or maybe he'll run out the back door and never return. That would be fine by me. Then I can work here without any hassles.

I take a seat in the waiting room and wait. While I wait, I look repeatedly at the front door and fight it out inside my head.

Ms. Impetuous: I should go.

Ms. Sensible: I need a job.

Ms. Impetuous: The door is that way.

Ms. Sensible: I owe Johnny and Karen six grand.

Ms. Impetuous: Kellan is an ass, and I can reach the front door knob from where I'm sitting.

Ms. Sensible: I really need money to buy my own guitar to replace my stolen Fender and I'd rather not wait tables or answer phones someplace.

For once, Ms. Sensible makes good sense.

Ms. Impetuous doesn't care.

The two of them go back and forth.

I stand up and nearly bolt out the door.

Ms. Sensible: $6,000!!

Ms. Impetuous: Fuck!

I sit back down.

What am I getting myself into?

Chapter 63

KELLAN

"We gotta problem," I say to my boss Rich Aymes as I close his office door behind me.

"What?" Rich looks up from his computer, his face worried.

Rich wears a stylish sport coat over a threadbare Y&T white Mean Streak t-shirt he bought new at the concert during Y&T's tour in 1983. There's a photo of Rich on the wall behind him posing with Dave Meniketti, frontman of Y&T, taken that same year. In the photo, eighteen year old Rich has the same scraggly mustache and feathered hair parted down the middle he has now, as well as the very same Mean Streak t-shirt.

I say, "The new hire interview at eleven o'clock."

"You mean Victory Payne?" Rich asks in his gruff baritone voice.

"Yeah. We can't hire her."

"Why not?" Rich glances at the clock on the wood paneled wall. The clock is made from a picture disk record of the British Steel album by Judas Priest. The hour and minute hands mounted in the center of the record are metal daggers. "It isn't even eleven. Have you interviewed her already?"

"No. She's in the waiting room. But I know her…"

"You *know* her? Let me guess…" Rich leans back in his creaky office chair, laces his fingers casually behind his head, and cracks a good-natured grin over teeth that have seen better days, "…you banged her."

I chuckle, "No."

Rich knows me too well.

He says, "Then what's the problem, man? Can't she play?"

"Oh, she can play. She's one of the most amazing shredders I've seen in a long time."

"Is she Paul Gilbert good?" he asks.

"Pretty damn close," I say seriously.

"So hire her already," Rich chuckles.

"Dude, I can't work with her."

Rich surveys my face for a moment. He nods slowly, "Oh, I get it. You *want* to bang her."

I frown, "No," I growl a bit too forcefully.

Rich nods, eyes narrowed, "You wanna bang her. I can tell."

"No, man! I totally don't!"

Rich leans over to the closed circuit monitor next to his desk that shows the waiting room. "She's the one with long hair, sitting by the front door, right?" Rich turns the monitor so I can see it.

"Yeah, that's her."

Rich nods, "Uh huh. You want to bang her."

"I don't, man. I swear."

He looks at the monitor shrewdly, "Hell, Kellan, *I* want to bang her.

Don't tell me you don't." Rich is all bluster when it comes to the ladies. I don't think I've ever seen him go on a date, he's so busy running the school.

"I'm tellin' you, Rich, it's not that."

"Yeah, uh huh. I know you, man. You ain't foolin' me."

I roll my eyes, "Whatever, man."

Rich leans forward in his chair, resting his elbows on his paper strewn desk. "Then what's the problem?"

"It's just…fuck, I don't know. I just don't want to work with her."

"Come on, man. You know Steve is leaving soon. He's gonna be on tour for six months. There's no way you and I can pick up all his guitar students for that long. We need a third guitar teacher to replace him ASAP."

I've always appreciated Rich's level-headed, no bullshit approach to running his business. He's the best boss I've ever worked for. I think it's because he loves running Rock & Roll High School. And I love working here alongside him. But there's no way I can work alongside Victory. Not after…

I blurt, "I can pick up the slack. You know me, Rich. I'm a work horse."

"Yeah, but you can't teach two one-on-one lessons at the same time."

"It's summer," I argue, "we can shuffle their schedules around."

"Easier said than done. I know the students love you, man, but people like regularity. Especially kids. They need structure. And so do their parents. We don't want to change up times on them unless we have a good reason. So far, you haven't given me one."

"Yeah," I sigh. He's right. The last thing I want to do is make things harder on the kids because I can't suck it up and deal with Victory.

"Look," Rich says, "it's not like you're going to be working side by side with her. You guys'll be in different rooms. So what if you bump into each other in the hallways?"

"You're right," I hiss. "I've just gotta man up."

"You shouldn't have any problem with that," Rich chuckles. "Didn't you tell me you wrote I'm A Man for Bo Diddley back in the day?" he jokes.

I didn't but I chuckle, "Yeah. M. A. N."

Rich smiles, "Show Victory how much of a man you are by being one. Now go interview her and hire her if she's right for the job." He looks around, like he's checking if anyone's listening, and says in a low voice, "If she's not right for the job, get her number so I can ask her out."

I growl, "No way, man!"

Rich erupts with laughter, "You want to bang her!"

"Dude, I don't!"

Rich continues to laugh. It's slightly infectious.

I chuckle, "Dude, you need to get laid."

"When do I have time, man? I'm too busy running the school and babysitting your ass. Now go do the interview. If it's really a problem, tell me and we'll find somebody you *aren't* attracted to. I hear some of those old circus monkeys that smoke cigarettes can also play a mean guitar. If I have to, I'll hire one and hope for the best." His face turns serious, "But it'll be on you if the bitter old monkey goes ape shit in the practice room with one of the kids." He winks at me.

It's funny because I know that Rich is the sweetest guy ever, and would never do anything remotely like that. He loves the school and the students way too much. He's really just giving me shit.

I smile, "All right, all right. I'll suck it up."

"Good. Now get out of here," he grins, "I have work to do."

Chapter 64

VICTORY

"So, Ms. Payne," Kellan says sarcastically while reading from a paper on a clipboard, "it says on your job application that you've been playing guitar for a long time. Can you specify an exact number of years?"

We sit in one of the lesson rooms. There are two practice amps on the floor, a computer and speakers in the corner, swiveling office chairs, sound baffles on the walls, and various rock and roll posters. Overhead, a fluorescent rectangle lights the room. Even in this crappy lighting, Kellan is incredibly gorgeous.

I frown and roll my eyes, "Does it matter? You've seen me play."

He chuckles, "I need to know how many years. There's a box for it right here on the interview paperwork."

"I don't know. Forever?" I grumble. "Is that long enough?"

He jots something down on the clipboard, saying it out loud as he writes it, "For-ev-er. Good. Thank you, Ms. Payne."

"Quit calling me Ms. Payne," I groan.

"That's your name, isn't it?" he asks seriously.

"Yeah." Despite my irritation, the corner of my mouth lifts with mild amusement. I can't help it. Kellan's snooty professor behavior is funny. "So is Victory."

"Can you spell that?" he quips.

"Isn't it on the paperwork right in front of you?"

"The paper is smudged. I need you to spell it." He gives me a serious look.

I stand up so I can see what's on his clipboard, but he flattens it against his chest, hiding the paper.

He says, "No fair peeking."

I plop back down in the chair. "Fine," Rapid fire, I say, "V-I-C-T-O-R-Y."

He frowns, sticking his tongue out the corner of his mouth, and in slow motion says, "Vee. Eye. Cee—wait. Can you repeat that?"

I shake my head, smiling slightly against my will, and groan, "You know how to spell it."

He looks up and levels a serious look at me, "If you can't be patient with me, how can you possibly expect me to believe you'll be patient with the students?" He arches his brows confrontationally.

"Ahhh!" I huff. "V. I. C. You still with me?"

"Yes, Ms. Payne. Please continue."

"T. O."

"I'm sorry," he holds up a stop sign hand, "Where does the T go? After the C or before it?"

I fold my arms across my chest, but I can't help smiling, "You know!"

"Indulge me, Ms. Payne," he says seriously.

"The T goes after the C. You ready for the next letter? This one goes after the T."

"Are you getting flip with me, Ms. Payne?"

"Stop calling me that!" I giggle.

"What comes after the T again?"

"O, R, Y! O, R, Y!" I'm laughing completely against my will.

"Are, Why. Got it." He looks up at me like he's accomplished something significant. "Oh, wait. Whoops. I think I put in one to many Ohs." He turns over his ball point pen and tries erasing with the cap. "Hmm, that doesn't work."

"It's a pen! It doesn't erase!" I'm laughing freely now.

"Ms. Payne, if you can't demonstrate a professional attitude during the interview, I really don't think you can be expected to deal with the children."

"Kill me now!" I laugh.

He chuckles, finally breaking character.

I chuckle too, "Hey, what's your last name, anyway?"

Kellan frowns, "Didn't I tell you?"

"No."

"It's Burns."

"Really?"

He nods.

"Kellan Burns?" I ask doubtfully.

"That's me," he smiles.

"It fits," I say.

"Oh? How?"

Oops. Why did I have to say that? I'm not going to tell him that I've seen his brown eyes burn like embers on more than one occasion, during one of which he had his hand between my legs…

I repress a pleasant shiver.

He smiles, "Are you cold?"

Oops again. "Uh, the A/C must be getting to me." I rub my arms like I'm trying to warm myself.

He gives me this knowing look that I can't hold because he's probably thinking about the exact same thing I am. I'm sure he remembers.

He asks, "Want me to turn it down?"

I almost say, "What, the heat, or the A/C?" But that would be a dead giveaway. Instead, I say, "I'm fine."

"You sure?"

I nod.

"Okay, let's get serious."

My eyes goggle, but he's looking at the clipboard and doesn't notice. I hope he doesn't mean *relationship* serious. No, he can't mean that.

"Now," he says, "I know you can play and perform. But I need to know how good your music theory knowledge is, and if you can teach."

"Sure," I say.

"What are the seven modes?"

"Ionian, Dorian, Phrygian, Lydian, Mixolydian, Aeolian…"

"And?"

I lean toward him like I'm a spy sharing secret information, "And Locrian. The devil's mode."

He snorts, "Ha! You know about the devil's mode?"

"I play metal. What did you expect?"

He grins. "Nice."

For the next ten minutes he asks me a series of questions about music theory, all of which I answer easily and quickly. Now maybe he'll apologize for calling me stupid to whoever he talked to on the phone that night.

"Wow," he says, "you really know your music theory cold."

You can apologize any time.

He doesn't.

He needs reminding. With great superiority I say, "I guess I'm not as stupid as you thought."

"What? I never thought you were stupid."

"Did too!" I sound five years old. "You told your friend or whoever on the phone the night I moved out!" Wow, I sound like I'm having a relationship argument.

...two days does not a relationship make.

Thank you, Ms. Sensible.

Kellan frowns thoughtfully. "I don't...oh! I remember. I wasn't talking about you."

"Yeah, right," I sneer.

He shakes his head, but he's smiling and relaxed. "I was talking about Savannah."

"Who?"

He arches an eyebrow, "Femme Flakes?"

"Femme Flakes?"

He looks at me expectantly, "The female corn flake?"

Then it clicks. "Oh! Femme Flakes! The girl you told you had the squirts!"

He points a finger gun at me and fires it, "That's her. Savannah."

"So you were talking about Savannah? *She's* the stupid one?"

He nods, "Couldn't you tell?"

"I thought—" then I stop myself. "You *really* weren't talking about me?"

He shakes his head, "No. I think you're the opposite of stupid."

I crinkle my nose, "Why does that not sound like a compliment?"

"Are you fishing now?"

"For what?" I grin.

"Compliments?"

"No!"

"Uh huh. So we don't have to go over this again..." he places a hand on my knee and levels a serious gaze at me.

His hand is very large, firm, warm, and making me very very hot. His burning brown eyes add fuel to my fire.

He continues, "...you're probably the smartest woman I've ever met." He leans back, releasing his hand from my knee. "Got it?"

Don't let go of my knee! I like your hand! But I don't say anything. Instead I nod dumbly. Yes, dumbly. Because I feel stupid for doubting him, and because I seem to lose my brain when he looks at me with those beautiful super novas smoldering beneath his handsome brow. I think his eyes are about to set my skin on fire. They've already incinerated my brain, which is probably dribbling out my ears at the moment.

"So, back to the interview," he says seriously. "We know you know your music theory and how to shred the shit out of your guitar, but how are you with kids? Most of our students are young. It's not like teaching adults."

I'm taken aback by his question.

Here I am, sitting across from an admittedly hot but still slutty motorcycle riding manwhore who I thought would be the last person on the planet to ask *me* if *I* was good with kids. What does *he* know about kids? Oh yeah, he teaches them guitar every day. Probably a fair amount.

I say, "I don't know. But I'm sure I'll be fine." At that moment, I notice the paper on Kellan's clipboard is blank, except for the word Forever and VICTORY. "Hey!" I say, "Your paper is blank!"

"It's not blank," he snickers, "It says Forever. It also says Victory, see?" he points at the words.

I frown, "So?! I thought it would be some sort of official employment form! What was all that b.s. about?! Asking me to spell my name like you didn't know!"

"Just b.s.," he laughs, "I couldn't help myself."

"Jerk," I kick his shin with the ball of my booted foot, but not hard.

"I hope you don't plan on kicking your students," he chuckles.

"No," I sneer.

"Anyway," he smiles, "we were talking about you and teaching kids. My next class is at noon. Why don't you sit in with us and I'll have you teach part of the lesson."

"Okay," I smile.

"Hey, I've gotta use the restroom before class starts. You wanna wait here?"

"Sure."

He stands and opens the door.

"Oh, uh," I say, "do you have a guitar I can warm up on? I haven't played in a few days, so I'm probably kind of rusty."

"You rusty? I doubt that," he chuckles.

"I am! I don't have a guitar right now."

He gives me a compassionate look, "You still haven't found one?"

I shake my head, slightly embarrassed, "No."

"Sorry. Anyway, use my Ibanez for now. Go crazy."

"Thanks. Oh, hey, I have to ask. What was Paul Gilbert doing here?"

Kellan smiles, "Did you meet him?"

"Yeah, when he was leaving. He doesn't teach here, does he?"

"No. But Paul knows Rich, the owner. They're talking about having Paul do a clinic for the kids this summer."

"That would be awesome!" I smile. "Can I go?"

He snorts, "What could Paul possibly show *you*?"

I'm totally flattered by the epic compliment, but it's a bit of an exaggeration. I toss my hair and blush, "I still want to go…"

"Don't worry. If you're a teacher here you can go for free. If not, I'll make sure you get in either way."

"Nice," I grin.

Kellan closes the door when he leaves.

I do my best to catch a glimpse of his butt in his tight jeans while his back is turned, but I only get a snippet before he's gone.

Wait, Ms. Sensible barks, don't go rushing into things, young lady! Ignore that ass!

As if.

I guess I'm not mad at Kellan anymore?

I shake my head, smiling at myself as I grab his RG550 off the guitar stand. It's the same one I played at his house. Is it just me, or does it feel hot to the touch? Either way, picking it up reminds of the night I played it…

…and everything that followed.

Is my working here *really* a good idea?

Or should I leave now before I make a big mistake?

I shrug my shoulders and fish a yellow Tortex guitar pick out of my pocket.

Ms. Mischievous says, Mistakes can be fun.

Ms. Sensible shakes her head, I warned you.

Ms. Mischievous and most of my internal committee stick out tongues and shrug shoulders at Ms. Sensible.

Chapter 65

KELLAN

Man, I'm confused.

I lock the bathroom door behind me and turn on the light in the one person restroom that contains a toilet, sink, mirror, and trash can. Various band stickers and band names pepper the walls.

I should be mad at Victory, but I'm not. I'm actually in a good mood after busting her chops back there in the practice room.

She looks fucking hot as hell today. Maybe that's all it is. Guess I should've banged Red the other night and gotten it out of my system.

No worries. I can fix that tonight. Me and Dubs can go hit up some clubs after rehearsal. I'm sure I'll find some girl to pass the time. Or I could dip into my phone list.

But I hate reruns.

Whatever. I'll figure something out.

I rinse my hands in the bathroom sink and dry them with a paper towel. There's a Metallica sticker on the corner of the mirror which I put there myself. In the mirror, I notice all the hand written messages on the wall behind me that pay tribute to various bands:

.1# si dlofneveS degnevA !!SKCOR maJ lraeP .srethgiF ooF !kcus syoB teertskcaB .seluR ttaR .nekkoD htiw 'nikcoR

The kids are allowed to write anything music related on the bathroom walls as long as they don't cover up anyone else's scribbles. It adds a bit of that adult music venue vibe to the school that makes the kids feel more like rock & roll rebels.

It's all a front.

The kids who can afford to go here are lucky. We don't even charge that much compared to some schools. That was Rich's idea. He doesn't drive a ten year old Toyota because he thinks it's ironic or hip. It's all he can afford.

Even with our cheap rates, I know a lot of kids all over L.A. can't afford to take our classes, or even buy a musical instrument.

Man, if I had more money, I'd open a free music school.

Someday.

I check my hair in the mirror. It looks great. I look great.

Why do I care about my hair all of a sudden?

It can't be because of Victory.

She's not into me. She made that clear already.

And I'm not into her.

I really need to give Dubs a call about going out tonight to look for fresh tail.

Chapter 66

VICTORY

Kellan knocks on the practice room door and leans his head in, "You ready?"

"Yeah," I answer, looking up from the Ibanez I've been playing for the last ten minutes. I really love this guitar. It has nothing to do with the fact

Kellan owns it.

"Come on," he motions, "we'll be in the main room for the lesson."

"Okay. Do I bring the guitar?"

"Nope. Follow me."

I set the guitar in a stand and we walk down the hall.

"I hope you're ready…" Kellan warns.

"For what?"

"This isn't any old guitar lesson…"

"And?"

He stops and turns in the hallway and I almost bump into his chest. I stop myself short and stare up into his blazing brown eyes.

We stand in a right-angle turn in the hallway, there's a closed door a few feet behind Kellan, and there's no fluorescent light bank overhead, so it's much dimmer here than the rest of the hallway. You could even call it romantic…

"…And," Kellan whispers, "*anything* could happen…"

He looks down at me, his lips only inches from mine. I watch the tip of his tongue slide lusciously over his teeth. I catch a good whiff of his clean, alluring man scent, which includes a subtle note of guitar hardware, making Kellan twice as scentalicious. I pretend not to be affected by it.

Despite my pretense, I fall back against the wall, bumping my head clumsily against the sheetrock with a thud.

"An—any, *anything*?" I stutter and pause to clear my throat.

No, my close proximity to Kellan is not bothering me at all. Nope. Uh-uh.

He nods, his brown eyes searching mine.

Is he leaning closer?

Yes, he's leaning closer.

I try to clear my throat, but the only sound that comes out of me is a church mouse's high pitched sneeze: *peep!*

Kellan is now uncomfortably close, very large, über muscular, and hellaciously hot in every way possible.

This close, his eyes really do have a smoldering, burning ember quality. Something about seeing them in the half light of the dark corner makes them glow and makes all my muscles melt like a well used candle.

He suddenly leans toward me and I'm certain he's going to kiss me right here, right now, and I want it. I need it. I want this handsome, musical, magical man to take me on a magic carpet ride…

Oh, Kellan…my carpet is ready for you…

I can almost feel his warm lips brushing against mine, I can imagine his big hand covering the small of my back as he pulls me into him. Or pushes me back against the wall with his strong, tattooed arms, trapping me in this dark corner so he can tear my clothes off, bite my neck, force his tongue down my throat, squeeze my ass, and do nasty things to me and my magic carpet.

My heart flies into overdrive, tittering to a wicked tempo past 200 beats a minute like an overworked metronome…

My knees quiver…

My thigh muscles spasm rapidly…

He leans closer… closer…

Do it!

Kiss me!

Kellan suddenly twists the doorknob behind him and opens the door into the room.

A blast of bright light hits my eyes.

Cacophonous noise erupts from inside and shatters our moment into pathetic pieces.

Chapter 67

VICTORY

"Kellan!" a little girl in a vibrant fuchsia knee length summer dress with a giant pile of curly blonde hair throws her arms around Kellan's waist and squeezes her cheek into his stomach. She looks like she's about seven or eight.

I'm standing in the practice room behind Kellan, this little girl, and three other boys. One boy has a guitar, over his shoulder, another a bass guitar, and the third sits behind a drum kit. They all look really young and tiny compared to their instruments.

I can tell from the way they're all grinning at Kellan, they really like him.

Kellan laughs and pats the girl on the back affectionately, returning the hug. He chuckles, "Hey, Hayley. I haven't seen you in a long time."

"I missed you so much!" she squeals.

"I missed you too," he smiles, but he's looking at me and grinning from ear to ear and blushing. Kellan Burns is blushing. I never thought I'd see it.

I smile at Kellan. I can't help it.

When Hayley releases her hug, Kellan goes around to the three boys and fist bumps each one. They're obviously in awe of him. It's spelled out in their shining smiles.

"Hey, guys," Kellan says, "I want you all to meet my friend Victory."

They all smile and say, "Hi, Victory."

I wave at them and smile, "Hey, guys."

"Victory," Kellan says, "This is Matthew, Ethan, and Nick."

I go around and shake all their hands.

Matthew has short spiky black hair and wears a Powell Peralta BONES t-shirt with the evil skeleton ripping out of the front, skater shorts, and black Adidas. He seems shy and plays guitar.

Ethan has a bass guitar over his shoulder that is probably taller than he is, and wears a Jethro Tull "Broadsword" concert shirt that is way too big and nearly covers his brown shorts.

I say, "I love your shirt."

He says, "My grandpa gave it to me." He's obviously proud of it. "You're pretty," he grins. And not shy.

Nick has shaggy shoulder length blond hair and sits behind the drums wearing a yellow tank top and surfer shorts. "Hey." I think Nick is the oldest of the kids and he's too cool for school, but he keeps peeking at me through the scrub of long hair hiding his eyes.

Kellan says to me, "Welcome to performance class."

"What about me?!" Hayley jumps up and down beside Kellan, pulling on his arm, "You forgot me!"

Kellan smiles at her, "I'm sorry, I'll never forget you, Hayley. Hayley, this is Victory."

I lean down and shake her little hand.

She grins apple cheeks at me, "Hi!"

"Hey. Nice to meet you, Hayley!" She's incredibly cute.

I'm not sure what to do next, but these junior rockers look ready to roll.

"So," Kellan says, "Hayley, Matthew, Ethan, and Nick have been working on a song. As a band."

"Really?" I grin. That's not how music school was taught when I was girl. It was sitting in a tiny room with a music teacher who said nothing and waited for you to mess up so they could frown at you and say nothing helpful. I'm so lucky I had my dad take over my lessons almost from the start.

"Yup," Kellan nods.

"What song?" I ask.

"Shoot 'Em Down!" Ethan shouts.

"By Twisted Sister," Hayley adds proudly. "Dee Snider sings it."

Kellan says, "Are you guys ready to show Victory how to play it?"

"Yeah!" they all chorus.

Kellan nods at Nick.

Nick counts off, "One, two, three, four!"

The four of them bang out the beginning chords.

I grin big. I know the song well. It's easy to play, but it totally rocks and brings back a flood of memories. Shoot 'Em Down is one of the first ones my dad taught me. It also brings back memories of working in Dad's shop. We always had music going. In fact, I helped him rebuild the engine on a '63 Impala when I was fourteen while listening almost entirely to Twisted Sister albums. Wow, I really need to call my dad. I haven't talked to him in months.

The kids do an awesome job with the song. It's a little rough, but they know it, and they're pretty tight for young kids. Hayley is easily the star of the show in her fuchsia dress and blond curls. She almost looks like a miniature Dee Snider. She continuously jumps up and down to the beat, singing into the mic with gleeful abandon.

Ethan harmonizes during the chorus and his voice blends nicely with Hayley's.

This is the most awesome music school ever!

I have to work here!!!!

I glance over at Kellan, and he's grinning, his teeth shining, nodding his head in time with the music. He silently mouths the lyrics along with Hayley. She glances at him several times and he winks at her or gives her a thumbs up. He obviously loves working with these kids. I can't blame him.

I'm having so much fun, I start pumping my fist and the next thing I know, I'm singing the chorus along with the kids. The second I realize I'm singing, my chest tightens up and I stop.

"Yeah!" Kellan says, egging me on, "Keep going!"

I don't.

(*never ever sing*)

I shake my head no.

(*singsingsing*)

I cough a few times, and smile thinly.

Kellan smiles sympathetically and shrugs his shoulders, then joins in singing the chorus himself. Even without a mic, his voice is loud and powerful. He sings like he means it, totally into the music.

Matthew starts the guitar solo. Considering his age, he's pretty damn good.

Kellan cheers him on, "Yeah! Matt! Whoo, boy! Play it!"

Matthew grins from ear to ear and does his best to fire off the rest of the solo.

I'm blown away and having fun again and I totally forget about my singing

(*never ever ever sing*)

and coughing.

Ethan shifts from foot to foot while playing his bass.

After Hayley sings the final vocal line, she bends over in a full length bow.

Nick hammers every drum in his kit like machine gun fire. Matthew and Ethan strum their guitars wildly. Ethan shakes his hips like maracas. I laugh.

Nick's drumming slows, then he, Matthew, and Ethan hit their final note. BOOM!

I immediately clap rapidly and shout, "Yay! Woo-hoo! You guys rock!"

Kellan shouts, "YEAH! Awesome! Incredible!"

Oh my god, I need this job!

Chapter 68

VICTORY

Kellan turns to me, "So, Victory, was there anything you can think of for the kids to work on?"

"Oh, gosh," I smile, looking at the kids, "You guys were all so awesome! I don't know what to say!" I giggle and grin.

The kids all smile back at me.

"I'm really impressed," I sigh.

"Me too," Kellan smiles, "but if you wanted to make things better, what would you do?"

I realize he's testing me. This is where spectating ends and teaching begins. I need to actually come up with something constructive. They all knew the song well, so what do I say?

"Remember," Kellan says, "this is performance class. The focus here is on band dynamics and stage presence."

Oh, that's easy. I know all about both. And I know exactly how to help. I say, "Who likes to play make believe?"

"I do!" Ethan cheers, "I want to be a Tyrannosaurus Rex!" I think he's probably the youngest.

"Me too!" Hayley says, "Me too!"

I glance at Matthew.

He shrugs and smiles shyly.

Good enough. The three of them are on board.

But Nick grimaces like the idea is stupid. He says, "Make believe is for kids."

I give him a long look while I think what to do. Here goes nothing, "Nick, do you know what air guitar is?"

"Uh huh," he nods.

"Do you know what air drums are?"

"I guess?" he answers.

"What is it?" I ask.

"It's when someone pretends to play guitar, or pretends to play drums."

"Do you know how to play air drums?"

"But I already have a drum set."

And an answer for everything. I roll my eyes, "Have you ever seen an air guitar competition?"

"Yeah," he chuckles, "on YouTube. It's when guys dance around like crazy and pretend to play guitar like big rockstars."

"You said the magic word."

"What?" he frowns.

"Pretend."

"But I'm really playing," he protests, "not pretending."

I need to try a different approach. "Nick, I'm not asking you to pretend to play the drums. I'm asking you to pretend you're playing in front of a crowd of people. A really big crowd. And *you* are the really big rockstar."

I notice Kellan watching my exchange with Nick carefully. I imagine I'm being graded right now. *Work with me, Nick.* If you don't get this, I don't get this job.

Nick says thoughtfully, "You mean like Ozzy?"

I'm not sure what he means, but I blurt, "Yes!"

Nick says, "Like the Blizzard of Ozz tour? My dad showed me the video online. That concert was rad. Tommy Aldridge is awesome on drums."

"Yes! Pretend you're on stage with Ozzy! In front of a huge crowd!" I'm just rolling with it as I watch Nick mentally connecting the dots.

Nick frowns, "You want me to pretend I'm Tommy Aldridge? On stage?"

"Yes!" I wait in dread for him to tell me that Tommy Aldridge doesn't play drums for Twisted Sister.

Nick smiles, "I can do that."

Phew. I say, "When you guys play the song, go crazy for Ozzy's audience."

Nick nods, a light in his eyes, "Yeah!"

I turn to the other kids, "Can you all pretend you're on stage at a big concert?"

"Can I be a Tyrannosaurus Rex too?" Ethan asks.

"Sure," I smile, because who *doesn't* want to see a giant dinosaur on a rock stage? And I don't know what else to tell him.

"What do I do?" Hayley asks.

"Um..." I stall for time.

My personal belief is there's three things important to stage presence: high energy, which Hayley has, a sense that you and you're bandmates are best friends who love rocking out on stage together, and the group of you are having more fun than anyone else on the planet.

How am I supposed to convey that to a kid?

I suddenly remember Steph, the woman who was kind enough to give me a shower and a meal the morning after Scott kicked me out of Skin Trade. I remember how confident she was with her kids Tyler and Aubrey. I do my very best to channel Steph's motherly talents.

What would Steph do?

All I can think to say is, "Hayley, you remember how to play Duck, Duck, Goose?"

"Yeah! I love that game!"

"Remember how you go around to every person in the circle, tagging them?"

"Uh huh!" she beams.

"This is sort of like that. When you sing, I want you to go around to Matthew, Nick and Ethan, and say hi to them a bunch of times during the song. Like they're your best friends." Man, I hope this works.

"Okay," she smiles.

"Ethan?" I ask.

"Yeah?"

"You do your dinosaur thing. Stomp around big, but be careful you don't hit anybody with your bass guitar."

"Okay!"

I suddenly picture accidental black eyes, a lawsuit, and me never getting this job.

I grab a spare instrument cable I see lying on a shelf in the corner and make a circle with it on the floor around Ethan.

"Ethan," I say, "Don't step outside this circle."

"But I'm a Tyrannosaurus Rex! I can step over anything!"

"Well, pretend it's an invisible wall as high as the sky and you can't!"

"Okay!" he smiles.

I hope he remembers it.

I turn to Matthew. I sense he needs something simple. "Matt, can you walk back and forth?"

He looks at me, lost.

"Hokey Pokey style? Left foot in, left foot out?"

He takes a tentative step forward, then pulls his leg back.

"Again," I smile encouragingly.

He continues.

"That's it!" I cheer. I turn to Hayley, "Remember, Hayley, watch out for the guitars. Don't bump into them because they're poison!"

"Poison!" she gasps.

"Yeah! You don't want to get hit."

She nods gravely, her eyes bigs.

I hope nobody gets killed.

I look at Kellan.

"Nice work," he nods at me approvingly. "Okay, kids. You guys ready to play the song again?"

"Yeah!" they chorus.

Kellan smiles at them, "Remember what Victory said. Watch out for each other's instruments, and watch out you don't hit anybody. Nick? Count it in."

Nick hollers, "One, two, three, four!"

And they're off, playing Shoot 'Em Down grade school style.

At first, the kids are concentrating on moving so much, their playing falls to pieces.

Nick gives Kellan a frustrated "I'm above this" look from behind his drums.

Kellan shouts, "Keep going!"

Nick does.

I shout, "Tommy Aldridge, Nick!"

He starts banging his head.

I cheer and clap at him. Then I dance over to Kellan and bump his hip with mine, "Come on, Kellan! Cheer! We're supposed to be ten thousand people!"

Kellan smiles and cups his hands around his mouth and shouts over the amplifiers and drums, "Play it, Nick!"

Nick grins at both of us as we cheer and shout.

Hayley runs around the front of Matthew, watching his guitar carefully, her eyes wide, and slaps him on the side of his shoulder, shouting, "Duck!" before running away. Good enough. She circles back around between Matthew and Ethan.

"Don't forget to sing," I holler.

"Oh yeah!" she shouts into the mic and picks up the lyrics on the next bar.

Ethan is stomping dramatically inside the circle of the instrument cable on the floor. He roars several times into his microphone for no particular reason other than he's a T-Rex.

Matthew is standing shyly in place.

I shout, "Hokey Pokey, Matt!"

He tentatively lifts his left foot back and forth a few times.

Works for me.

During the guitar solo, I holler at Hayley, "Turn and wave to Nick!"

She does.

"Now wave at Ethan!"

She does.

When they finish the song, I cheer because nobody was impaled on a guitar neck and no bones were broken.

Thank you, Steph! I felt her by my side the whole time.

Chapter 69

VICTORY

Kellan mutters in my ear, "Nice work, Gigi."

I smile to myself. Guitar Goddess. He remembered. I feel warm all over. And not because I was running around the room for four minutes making sure no one got hurt.

Kellan claps loudly, "Nice work, you guys! Nick, great work, buddy."

"Thanks, Kellan," Nick grins at him like he wishes Kellan was his older brother or best friend.

Kellan pats Ethan on the shoulder, "That was the best T-Rex I've ever seen, man."

Ethan smiles from ear to ear and shouts "ROAR!"

Kellan chuckles. "Hayley, good job, girl. Dee Snider would be proud. Matthew, good job, man."

"Thanks," he says shyly, but he steals glances at Kellan.

"That was incredible you guys," Kellan says. "Wanna do it again?"

No, please no.

"YEAH!!" they chorus.

For the next thirty minutes, I work with the kids. By the end, I've got them doing a reasonable job of stage performing. I manage to transition them from dinosaurs, Hokey Pokey, and Duck, Duck, Goose to more traditional rock & roll stage antics.

I'm sweating my ass off and totally need a break. I don't know how moms and childcare pros do it.

Kellan hasn't even broken a sweat, and he's been as busy as me coaching and corralling the kids the entire time.

We make a great team.

I mean, as co-workers.

Nothing more.

"Time's up, you guys!" Kellan says.

"Awww!!" they all moan.

"Did you guys like working with Victory?" Kellan asks.

"YEAH!!" they chorus.

"Would you like to have her teach class next time?"

"YEAH!!!!"

Hayley jumps up and down, clapping, "Please, please, please!"

Ethan says, "Please be our teacher!"

Kellan arches an eyebrow at me. "Sounds like they like you."

"I guess so," I gasp.

Kellan leads the kids out of the practice room.

"Should I wait here?" I ask.

"Yeah, I'll be right back."

He turns and marshals the kids out of the room.

Is it just me, or were his eyes just smoldering at me? I remember my moment with Kellan in the hallway before we entered the practice room an hour ago. Was he feeling it too?

Or was I imagining all of it?

I don't know for sure.

Now I'm worried I'm going to have a problem working with Kellan for the opposite reason I had when I came in here.

Am I the one who's into Kellan and not the other way around?

Of course you are, Ms. Sensible grumbles, But remember, young lady, you need a paycheck, not a plaything.

I like to play with things, Ms. Mischievous says suggestively.

Ms. Sensible rolls her eyes.

I tune out my internal committee.

The truth is, I really want to work here. And not screw it up by getting involved with my co-worker.

A very *hot* co-worker, Ms. Mischievous reminds.

I ignore her.

I remind myself I probably won't be teaching classes with Kellan most of the time. It'll just be me and the students.

I'll be fine.

Ms. Sensible shakes her head, curling her lips in a thin grimace, You're fooling yourself, young lady!

Ms. Mischievous barks, Hush, you!

Kellan walks into the practice room a second later, "Were you talking to yourself just now?"

"No!" I bark.

He cinches his brows, "I could've sworn I heard you talking before I turned the corner…"

I shake my head violently, "Nope. Not me. Must've been the wind."

He nods thoughtfully. "Anyway, the kids loved you. And…"

You love me, Ms. Mischievous blurts telepathically so Kellan can't hear her.

"…you did amazing," he finishes. "The Hokey Pokey was genius."

"Thanks," I grin.

"Anyway," Kellan sighs, "I have to run everything by the boss."

Why does Kellan suddenly sound like he's not into the idea of me working here anymore? That's weird. Or maybe it's just me?

Am I imagining everything I thought was happening between me and Kellan? I can't really tell. But I do know that starting with the night I slept in his apartment, he hasn't put a single move on me.

What happened to all his hot passion the night we met at The Cobra?

Is he *not* into me anymore?

I sigh internally.

Kellan is totally inscrutable at the moment.

"Sure," I say confidently, despite my sudden doubts, "I totally understand."

"Assuming Rich says yes to hiring you—"

My Ms. Salesgirl telepathically blurts, *Which he will, duh, because I rock.*

"—do I tell him you want the job?"

Does Kellan have mixed feelings about me working here? I don't care. I need the job, and Ms. Salesgirl is in control at the moment. She doesn't think about long term consequences. She's a closer.

I confidently say to Kellan Burns, "I do."

Chapter 70

VICTORY

My phone rings in my purse which lies on the passenger seat of my Altima. I'm halfway back to Hollywood. I grab the phone but I don't recognize the number.

I answer anyway. "Hello?"

"Hey, Victory," a strange voice says.

I blurt, "Kellan?"

"It's me."

Wow, I totally didn't recognize his voice. Why does he sound so strange? I pull the phone away from my ear and look at the number, "What number are you calling from?"

"I'm calling from the school phone. Anyway, you got the job. When you have a chance, you need to call Rich Aymes so he can go over some stuff with you. He's the owner, but he had to run out for awhile. You need to fill out the employee paperwork and tax stuff."

"Okay. When do I start?"

"For now, it'll be a few days. You're replacing Steve, one of our regular teachers. He has to finish out his lessons, but you'll be taking over his students. Probably next week or something."

Wow, Kellan sounds really apathetic about all this. Does he hate me all of a sudden? That doesn't make any sense. We had a ton of fun working with those kids.

But he's all reserved and distant.

What happened?

I don't know.

I sigh.

Maybe his disinterest and distance is for the best.

I say to him, "That's cool. Do I need to do any prep work for the lessons? I've never really taught seriously before."

"You'll figure it out," he sighs.

Geez, thanks for the help.

Whatever. I suddenly feel defensive because he's being so cold. I don't need his help anyway. I ask impatiently, "Anything else?"

He says, "You should probably get your own guitar."

"I'll take care of it."

A heavy silence lingers between us. But he isn't hanging up or saying goodbye.

I sigh again, "I should probably go. I'm driving. Need to focus on the road."

"Okay."

"Bye."

I end the call and toss my phone into my purse.

What was that?

What happened to fun Kellan when we were both working with Hayley, Ethan, Matthew and Nick?

Whatever.

With any luck, I'll be teaching on my own and not stuck in a room with uncomfortable Kellan.

But more importantly, Yay!

I've got a job!

Chapter 71

VICTORY

Time for me to get a guitar.

When I arrive in Hollywood, I drive up to guitar alley on Sunset Boulevard and park on a side street near Guitar Central.

I feel a pinch of guilt when I approach the Guitar Central building, like I should buy my guitar from Johnny and Karen's shop, which I can see down the block. But there's no way I can afford a vintage guitar. I need something bare bones. A cheap new guitar, or a cheap used one. Not a classic work of art.

I skulk toward the doors of the gigantic Guitar Central building. They have huge ten foot tall posters of guitar icons mounted on the front of the building: Eric Clapton, B.B. King, Jimi Hendrix, Randy Rhoads, Zakk Wylde, Joe Satriani, George Lynch, and Stevie Ray Vaughn.

I open one of the double doors and I'm assaulted by a cacophony of ten people playing ten different styles of guitar and bass all at the same time. Someone is testing out a drum kit in the drum department, beating out a rhythm that is not in time with any of the people playing guitar. It sounds like a sawmill and it brings a smile to my face.

I love guitar stores.

"Welcome to Guitar Central," says the girl stationed at the counter inside the doors. She has black emo hair, black eye makeup, a lip ring, and leggings ringed in purple and black.

"Hey," I smile as I walk past her.

I take a moment to survey the scene.

Guitar Central contains literally thousands of guitars, amplifiers, bass guitars, drum sets, keyboards, microphones, and every other possible piece of gear related to playing rock or popular music.

All the usual suspects are in attendance.

The Beginner. He nervously strums a cheap Chinese Strat copy four or five times before stopping because he's afraid everyone is listening to how bad he sucks. The truth is, *no one* is listening. They're too busy playing with all the toys in the store, meaning the expensive guitars and amps they can't yet afford but dream of buying one day.

The Showoff. He's on the opposite end of the spectrum. He's the kind of guy who has been playing for years but isn't in a band. So he comes down to Guitar Central to show off his chops to whoever will listen to him noodle for hours. The showoffs never buy anything.

The Snooty Blues Purist. He wears a Stevie Ray Vaughn style hat and constantly snarks about how all non-Blues guitar players suck, except maybe Jimi Hendrix, and blues is the only true form of music from which all styles of rock music were born. These guys forget that the lute came along before the guitar, and minstrels were writing lute music long before anything other than alligators lived on the Mississippi Delta.

The Jazz Devotee. He only plays hollow body guitars, Roland Jazz Chorus amps, and knows literally every chord ever invented, all of which he manages to play quietly without anybody noticing or caring.

The Terrible Metalhead. He wears a Wild Child concert shirt and plays louder than anyone in the store. It's all about the noise. They're my favorite. They have no shame and make no apologies. If the sales people would let them, they would turn the amps up to eleven. Metal, metal, metal!

Lastly, the rare and elusive Girl Guitarist. She looks out of place in a predominantly man's world. She's either in the acoustic guitar room, which is soundproofed, and she's letting her inner singer-songwriter shine, or she's a tough as nails badass like me.

Oh, I almost forgot. The Bored Girlfriend. She isn't a musician but is forced to accompany her man while he drools over the next guitar or amp he wants to buy. These women are the equivalent of the men you see dragged along on shoe shopping expeditions to parts unknown by inconsiderate wives or girlfriends. Personally, I would never make a man go shoe shopping with me. Ladies, you know why. No matter how old the men are, they always sound like insistent infants who incessantly whine, "Are we done yet? Are we done yet? I need to pee. I'm tired. I'm hungry. Can we go home now?"

A Guitar Central salesman walks up to me. His name tag says Felix. He doesn't look like a Felix, but he's pretty cute. He asks, "Can I help you find anything?"

I smile politely, "I'm gonna look around first."

"Okay, let me know if you need anything."

I nod and he walks away.

I scan the wall of hanging guitars. There's at least two or three hundred of them, if not more. The ones closest to the front door are the super expensive American Made guitars. Les Pauls. Fender Strats and

Telecasters. Paul Reed Smith. Jacksons and Deans. Music Man. Next to those are the expensive Ibanezes and ESPs from Japan. I can't afford any of them.

As I move down the wall, the guitars get cheaper, and they're made in other countries like Mexico and China. I know from experience the cheap guitars are junk. They don't stay in tune, they don't sound good, and they don't play well.

I need to find something used that isn't crap.

The used guitars are hidden way at the back. I recognize a bunch of 70s and 80s guitars nobody wants anymore. A bright pink Kramer. I take it down and play it. It feels solid and plays nice. But do I want a pink guitar? It looks like fingernail polish.

Is it me?

Nope. I wear black nail polish.

I hang the Kramer back on the wall.

That's when I notice it.

It.

Some guy is playing a white Fender Strat.

My Fender Strat.

I recognize it from a mile away.

The guy playing it is plugging into an amp, playing random distorted guitar chords. He's middle aged, dressed in a fancy button down shirt and designer jeans, and has thick shoulder length curly black hair and glasses. He's focused on playing and doesn't notice me.

I edge closer and closer until he finally notices me.

He looks up and says, "Hey."

"Hi," I say nervously, "Um, this is going to sound weird, but that's my guitar."

He takes a good look at me and smiles.

I'm going to use every bit of my girl power to woo him over into giving me my guitar. I say, "What's your name?"

He slides his guitar pick between the strings on the neck, which holds the pick in place. It's a trick many guitar players use so they don't lose their pick. He extends his hand, "I'm Frank."

I shake his hand. "Hi, Frank," I try to sound super friendly, like I've known Frank for twenty years, "I know it's weird, but that's really my guitar."

He says, "What do you mean it's your guitar? I was kind of thinking about buying it. I really like it. It's a really nice guitar," he chuckles enthusiastically, holding the guitar in both hands at arm's length, admiring it.

"I know," I say ironically. "I've been playing it every day for fifteen years. Until it was stolen last week."

He says skeptically, "Did *you* want to buy it?"

The first thought that crosses my mind is, *Buy?! I shouldn't have to BUY back my stolen guitar!* He's still not getting it, but I understand. He doesn't know me from nobody. That's okay. I'm walking out of here with my Fender even if I have to pry it from his cold dead fingers. My rainbow rape knife is in my purse and ready for action, if need be. Not that murder is my preference, but I'm not above drastic measures when it comes to my Fender.

It's my baby, after all.

I'll try pity first. It's gentler than murder, and often works better.

I say, "The guitar in your hands was stolen from my car a week ago. If you check the back of the headstock, you'll see the name Shawn Payne stamped into the wood. Shawn is my dad. He bought that guitar new in 1987 and gave it to me for Christmas when I was seven."

It sounds like a sob story, but it's totally true.

Frank checks the headstock. A pained look passes across his face. He chuckles despondently, "But I really like this guitar…"

I sense he's believing me. But he's not giving up my Fender just yet. Hoping to grease the wheels of his good will, I pull out my driver's license and show him. "See? My name is Victory Payne. Just like on the headstock."

Frank leans over and reads my license. He sits back and sighs heavily. He thinks for several moments then finally nods. "I have a daughter too. I've seen the look on your face right now on *her* face many times. I believe you." He holds out my guitar, motioning for me to take it.

"Really?" I squeal.

He nods, "Yes."

"Oh my god! Thank you!" I take the guitar and give him a spontaneous one-armed hug and kiss him on the cheek. "Thank you so much, Frank, you have no idea how much I appreciate this."

He chuckles, "I think you just showed me."

I look down at my Fender. I almost can't believe it's back! I thought maybe I'd never see it again. Holding it in my hands feels *so* good. So natural. "Wow, thank you, Frank. You have no idea how happy I am right now."

"I think I do," he smiles. "Now I just need to find a guitar that makes *me* that happy!"

I laugh. "Maybe I can help you find one?"

At that moment, Felix the salesman walks up. "You guys need any help?"

"Yeah, actually," I smile. "My friend Frank needs a guitar."

"Oh?" Felix asks. "What kind?"

Frank nods toward my Fender, "Whatever you have as good as that Strat."

"I've got just the thing," Felix smiles. "Do you like Les Pauls?"

"Sure," Frank says.

"Follow me," Felix gestures, "I've got the perfect purple Paul for you over here. I hang it up high on the wall so nobody plays it. I've been saving it to sell to someone who can appreciate an awesome guitar."

"Let's see it," Frank says as the two of them wander down the wall of guitars.

I'm happy dancing in my head like jumping beans on a trampoline. I actually do several little hops. I got my Fender back!

Now I just need to find my case for it and I'm outta here with a free guitar!

My guitar!

Score!

There's no way they'll make me pay for *my* guitar once I explain everything.

I look around for a salesman.

Chapter 72

VICTORY

"Miss, why didn't you file a police report when your guitar was stolen?" the surly store manager of Guitar Central asks me ten minutes later.

We're standing around the counter in the guitar department with two other salesman watching us. I feel like I'm trying to convince a bunch of Flat Earthers from the 12th century that the world is round.

"Because," I say slowly, since I'm talking to idiots, "I didn't have time. It was just stolen and I have to work." I don't bother to mention that every spare moment I've had in the past several days has been monopolized by a couple of hotties named Kellan Burns and Julian Whittaker.

The store manager, who's name tag says Rob, sighs heavily, leaning against the countertop with stiff arms. "We bought this guitar in good faith from a customer. We check the serial number of every instrument we buy against the police database. This guitar was not in the police database. I don't know what to tell you." He gives me a resolute look that says he's not budging. His rigid body language backs it up.

"But my name's stamped on the back of the headstock!" I grouse. "Payne! Look!"

Rob the Knob checks it, but isn't impressed.

I whip out my driver's license, which he reluctantly reads.

He frowns, "How do I know you're the same Payne? Or, maybe you sold the guitar last week or last year to the guy who brought it in here. Either way, you can't have the guitar for free. But we'll gladly sell it to you."

I have no doubt he would. But I'm not giving up. "I'm telling you, *Rob*," I sneer, "it's mine. I've had it forever!"

Rob the Knob sighs and glances at the headstock again. He covers the front of the headstock with his hand then scowls, "If it's your guitar, what's the serial number?"

"I have no idea! Who memorizes their guitar serial numbers?"

"I do," Rob chuckles.

"Of all these guitars?" I motion my arm at the wall of hanging guitars.

"No," he says indulgently, "my personal collection at home. I know all the serial numbers off the top of my head. Would you like to hear them?" he asks with superior satisfaction.

"No," I spit. I fold my arms across my chest and plant my feet. I'm not going anywhere until I get my guitar back.

"Look, miss, without a serial number, or some other form of proof, I can't let this guitar go out the door without you paying for it."

Inspiration strikes! I reach into my purse for my cell phone. The first thing I feel is my rainbow rape knife. I briefly consider using it to slash Rob the Knob's throat before running out the door with my Fender. I grab my phone instead. I speed dial.

I hold my phone to my ear while it rings. Please answer. If it goes to voicemail, I'm screwed.

"Vicky! How are you!" my dad answers.

"Dad! Thank god!"

"Is something wrong?" he asks in his gravelly baritone.

"Yes, I mean no, nothing life threatening."

"What is it, plum?"

Dad always calls me plum or any of a million other nicknames.

I take a deep breath and let it out. "Someone stole my Fender—"

"What!" he shouts.

"—but I found it. I'm at Guitar Central in Hollywood. It was hanging from the wall and I found it! But they want me to buy it back. Do you have the paper work for the guitar? Like the serial number or whatever?"

"Yeah. I have it in the file cabinet here in my office at the shop. Hold on a sec."

I can hear an air wrench firing in the background as someone works on a car in the garage. The sound evokes the smell of grease and engine oil and I can totally picture my dad with his work boots up on his old steel office desk and the Mopar calendars hanging from the walls and the cheesecake Snap-on posters with the girls in bikinis caressing socket wrenches. Ah, memories.

"Found it," Dad says. "Who are you talking to at the store over there? Put 'em on and I'll read the number off to them."

"The store manager is named Rob." I say to Rob the Knob, "My dad has the serial number. He'll read it to you." I put my phone on speaker. "You're on speaker, Dad."

Dad asks, "Who am I talking to?"

"This is Rob Pickford. Store manager at Guitar Central. Who is this?"

"This is Shawn Payne. My name is stamped onto the back of that guitar you've got."

Yay, Dad!

Rob the Knob glances at the Fender decal on the front of the head stock again and nods. He leans toward my phone, which I hold out to him, and says, "Good afternoon, Mr. Payne."

"Afternoon, Rob. I got the serial number handy. You ready for it?"

"Sure," Rob the Knob says. He keeps his hand over the numbered decal, like maybe I'll try and read it and shout it to my dad, or maybe Dad will see it over the stupid phone.

My dad says, "E407777. Lucky sevens."

"Well," Rob the Knob says, "it matches. But that doesn't prove your daughter didn't sell the guitar to the third party who brought it into our store this past week."

"Look, Rob," my Dad growls, "Do I need to hop on my Harley and make time down to Hollywood? If my daughter says that guitar was stolen, it was stolen."

"I appreciate that you trust your daughter's word," Rob Pickford the Dickford sneers, "but that doesn't help my situation any. Guitar Central paid for this guitar fair and square."

"Rob," Dad says in his booming voice, which is intimidating even on a cell phone speaker, "you don't want to piss me off. I'm up in Bakersfield but I can be in Hollywood in an hour. If that happens, you and I will not be friends. Do you understand what I'm saying?"

An amused grin spreads across Rob's face. In a voice that is half laughing, half disbelieving, he says, "Are you threatening me, Mr. Payne?"

"Yes."

Silence hangs in the air, its feet dangling as it sways side to side at the end of a hangman's noose.

My dad rocks.

The two junior salesmen have surprised looks on their faces. They look at Rob, their leader, waiting to see what happens.

Rob the Knob says confidently, "Please come down, Mr. Payne. I'd love to meet you. And I'm sure you'll be happy to explain yourself to the police."

My dad chuckles, "They're not going to hang around at your store waiting for me. You're not the President of the United States, my friend."

"Be that as it may, I assure you, Mr. Payne, if you come down here looking for trouble, I will call the police."

"That's it," Dad says, "I'm getting on my hog right now. I hope your health insurance is paid up, buddy."

"Dad," I say soothingly, "Don't."

There's a long pause and I hear my dad sigh. "What do you want me to do, princess?"

I smile nervously at Rob and say, "Just a sec." I take the phone off speaker and hold it to my ear. "Hey, Dad. I'm off speaker."

"I'm sorry, plum. I shouldn't have lost my temper like that."

"It's okay, Dad." My dad has been in jail for fighting more than once. He knows better, but I guess he doesn't think when it comes to me. He gets protective. I'm grateful but also wish he wouldn't be so quick on the trigger. If he was here, he probably would've decked Rob the Knob instead of saying anything. Luckily he wasn't here.

Dad says, "Do you want me to pay for the guitar, plum? How much is it? I'll cover it."

I haven't even looked at the price tag. But I know my dad doesn't have money to spare any more than I do. "No, Dad. I've got money. I can pay for the guitar."

"You sure?"

"Yes, I'm sure," I smile. My dad would give me his last dollar if I asked for it. He's the best.

"Then I guess you don't need anything from me? I'll come down if you do."

"No, Dad. Thanks. I'll handle it."

"You sure?"

"Yes, Dad!" I laugh.

"Okay, plum. Call me if you need anything. Or call just to chat. I haven't talked to you in a long time. You need to tell me what's going on in your life. And when're you gonna visit me in Bakersfield? I haven't seen you in ages and the guys in the shop miss you."

"Oh, Dad, I have so much to tell you. Maybe I'll call you tonight?"

"I would like that."

"I gotta go."

"I love you, Vicky."

"I love you too, Dad. Bye."

I end the call.

Rob the Knob smirks at me and arches his eyebrows, "I hope you don't think I'm letting you buy this guitar after that performance."

"What!"

He shakes his head, sneering, and sets the guitar on the counter. He plants his hands defiantly on his hips.

"But I'll buy it!"

"No you won't." He turns to his salesman. "Don't sell this guitar to this girl. In fact, don't sell any guitars to her. What was your name again, miss?"

"I'm not telling you!"

"Oh, I remember. Victory. And your last name is on the back of the guitar. Payne. That is your last name, isn't it?" he says sarcastically.

"You're a prick, Rob!" I blurt.

"Yeah," he sneers smarmily, "I am. My last name isn't Pickford for nothing."

"Do you want me to call my Dad?!" I say suddenly desperate. "I will!"

"Go right ahead," Rob the Knob says.

He called my bluff.

There's no way I'm calling my dad now. He'd kill Rob if he knew what just happened.

Rob looks at the two salesman beside him, "Gentlemen, please escort the young lady onto the street. Politely." He gives me another shitty sneer. "Have a nice day."

Fuck.

What do I do now?

Chapter 73

VICTORY

"Don't touch me!" I bark at the two salesmen as one tries to guide my elbow. "I'm going, douchebag!"

The next thing I know, I'm out on the street.

I turn around and stare at the giant Guitar Central building and its twenty foot cement walls. Right now, it resembles a mammoth castle. The framed ten foot photos of guitar icons remind me of the royalty on playing cards: Kings, Queens, and Jacks. Above it all, they look down at me with marked disinterest.

"Damn it!" I shout, clench my fists, and stamp my foot. "Fuck you, Rob the Knob!" I indulge in my tantrum momentarily, feeling like a little peasant pounding on the gates and demanding to see the king to no avail.

A minute later, I'm done.

People on the sidewalk are staring at me.

One is a bald guy walking by in a disheveled white dress shirt and ill fitting gray slacks. He holds a Jack In The Box sack and sips on a soda while eyeballing me furtively.

"WHAT!" I challenge.

He hunches his shoulders, sucks extra hard on his empty drink which bubbles a barking protest, and walks past quickly like I'm a bomb about to go off.

I sort of am.

I need to deal with this.

I need to find an Ace to win this game.

Before Guitar Central sells my guitar to someone else.

I pace up and down the sidewalk in front of the store, thinking through my options. I could run in and steal my Fender. Rip it right from Rob the Knob's cold dick-like fingers.

I picture three guys tackling me on my way out the door. My Fender pops out of my hands as I hit the ground. It then pogo sticks across the sidewalk on its headstock, snapping the neck from the body. The mangled mess then leans against a parking meter. Bad idea.

Next.

Maybe I could send someone inside to buy it for me.

That's it!

But who?

It has to be someone I can trust with my money, or someone who trusts me that I'll pay them back. Kellan? No, he's probably still at work, way over on the west side.

Liv!

I dial her number but it goes to voicemail. I need someone now.

Julian! He lives close by! He'll totally do it! Heck, he'll probably offer to buy it for me!

I dial his number.

A second later, the phone answers. Yay!

"Hello?" a female voice says.

"Is, is this Colette?"

"Speaking?" It's her.

"Colette, this is Victory Payne. Is Julian there?"

"I'm afraid not. He's in Stockholm for another week at least," Colette says in her gentle European accent.

"Where?"

"Stockholm, Sweden."

Geez, Julian sure gets around. No way he's jumping on a rocket to bail me out of this mess. "Okay, thanks."

"Would you like me to relay a message to him?"

"Uh, not really," I say, disappointed. "Hey! Is Max in the studio?" I ask hopefully.

"No, Max is in Stockholm with Julian."

"Oh. Okay. Thanks."

"Is there anything I can help you with, Victory?" Colette asks. "You sound agitated."

"No, I'm fine. Thanks for asking, Colette."

"My pleasure. Anything else."

I sigh, "No, thanks."

"*Ciao,*" Colette says and ends the call.

Crap.

I eye Big Momma's down the street. Johnny and Karen are probably both there. I shake my head to myself. I can't ask them to buy the guitar for me. I already owe them way too much, including the $6,000 for the Contrares.

I sigh. Fuck. What do I do?

The front door of Guitar Central opens and Frank walks out with a Les Paul guitar case by his side. He turns and walks up the sidewalk.

I stare at his back for a long time, then suddenly shout, "Frank!" and run after him.

Frank is my Ace.

He will be my winning hand.

He doesn't hear me. It's a long block, and there's a lot of traffic noise from all the cars on Sunset Boulevard.

I shout again, more desperately, as Frank turns the corner at the end of the block. "FRANK!!" I round the Guitar Central building at a dead run. "FRANK!!!!" He probably thinks I'm a mugger.

I turn the corner and nearly run him over. "FRANK!!!!"

He looks surprised. Well, shocked and about to have a heart attack is more like it. He chuckles, "Victory? Are you okay?"

I'm breathing hard from the sprint. I must look half insane. I certainly feel 90% bonkers. "I need your help!"

"Is something wrong?" he chuckles. I'm sure he's totally confused by my behavior.

I nod breathlessly, "I'm fine. But I need you to buy that Fender."

"What?" he laughs. "I thought you were going to buy it."

"I was, but—" how do I explain my dad pissed off Rob the Knob "—well, it's complicated. They won't sell it to me."

"What? Why not?"

I'm gonna have to tell him. "I got my dad on the phone, he had the guitar serial number and paperwork and everything, but when the manager wouldn't give me the guitar for free, my dad sort of… threatened him?" Yeah, it sounds bad.

"He *what*?" Frank laughs.

"He, uh…threatened the manager?" I squint and my face screws into a knot. This is really embarrassing.

Frank shakes his head and chuckles, "Your dad must really love you."

I nod, "He does."

"I can relate. What do you need me to do?"

Surprised, I say, "I just need you to go in and buy it for me. But I'll totally pay for it. I have cash and everything. Right here in my purse."

Frank glances at my purse while I'm digging through it. For a second, I feel like he's going to purse snatch my money.

Instead, he looks me in the eyes and says, "Okay. I'll do it."

Now I'm suddenly nervous. I have to hand a huge amount of money to a relative stranger. Can I trust this guy? I give Frank a visual once over then check my gut. Ms. Gut tells me that Frank has an honest vibe. And he has a daughter, which means he can't be all bad.

"Um," I ask, "Do you remember how much the guitar was?"

"The tag said $699."

"I bet you could talk them down to $500."

"You think so?"

"Sure. I work in a guitar store. We always bargain. So does Guitar Central."

"Okay, give me $500 and I'll go do it."

I pull the money out of my purse, counting out the bills, which are hundreds. I hold it out to Frank. Moment of truth. Do I really trust him?

Ms. Gut says yes.

Ms. Sensible says, *Gosh, I don't know…*

Shut up, Ms. Sensible! I need to get my Fender back!

Frank takes the money, folds it, and pushes it into his pocket. He looks at me shrewdly. "You're nervous about the money, aren't you?"

"How did you know?"

"I can tell," he smiles. He pulls the money out of his pocket and holds it out to me. "I'm not taking your money—"

"What, aren't you gonna buy it for me?!" Ms. Gut goes cold. She didn't read Frank as well as I thought.

"No..." he proffers the money, "...I'll put the guitar on my credit card. When I come out, you can give me the cash. Okay?"

Phew! Relief! "Totally."

"Be right back," he says and walks away.

"I'll wait right here. Oh!"

He turns, "What?"

"Don't forget to ask for the case that came with it! It says Payne on it in spray painted silver letters above the Fender logo!"

"Got it." Frank walks away, still holding his Les Paul case at his side.

I skulk down to the corner of the Guitar Central building and watch Frank walk toward the front doors. I'm suddenly nervous one of the Guitar Central salesmen will see me, and make a connection between me and Frank. Then I'm screwed. I pull back and wait nervously around the corner, out of sight. But I check repeatedly, glancing carefully with one eye around the edge of the building.

It takes forever.

Which isn't a surprise. You can't walk in and buy a guitar like you can a candy bar at a convenience store. Especially if the salesmen are busy. This could easily take an hour.

My nerves mount as the time ticks by. I stop checking how many minutes have passed after fifteen because it's driving me nuts.

I catch myself biting a fingernail and make myself stop. I pace in circles, wearing a groove in the cement sidewalk. Come on! How long is this going to take!

Some woman in fancy jogging clothes walks by with an Irish Setter on a leash. She takes one look at my harried face and gives me a wide berth.

What is taking so long?!

Did Frank give up and go home?

No, he doesn't seem like the type.

Ms. Sensible reminds me, You don't really know him.

Ms. Gut says, SHUT IT!!

I pace and pace. The circular groove I've worn into the cement is now a foot deep.

Do I go inside and check for Frank?

No, Ms. Sensible warns, if you do that, Rob the Knob will figure it out.

She's right.

I wait and wait.

Fuck, I can't deal with this!!

"Hey," Frank says as he walks around the corner, holding two guitar cases. "Sorry it took so long."

I recognize my Fender case instantly. "You did it!"

He smiles, "Yes I did! And I got Felix to throw in the case for five hundred out the door."

"Yay!" I throw my arms around him. "Thank you so much Frank!" I pull the money out of my purse and hand it to him.

He sets my Fender at my feet and puts the wad of bills in his wallet without counting it.

I squat down and lay the guitar case flat and pop it open. There it is! My Fender! I pick it up and cradle it like a newborn child or long lost love. "You did it, Frank!"

He smiles. "You look like my daughter when I bought her a cello last Christmas."

"Your daughter plays the cello?"

"She does. She's pretty good, too. She takes lessons."

"That's awesome! You're a musical family! That is so cool!" I gush with gratitude and excitement.

"Victory, it was a pleasure," Frank holds out his hand.

I grab it with both of mine and shake it energetically.

"If you ever need anything," he says, "give me a ring. Here's my card." He hands me a business card. "That's my cell phone and office number."

"Okay, I will!"

"I've got to run. See you around."

He walks off into the sunset on Sunset Boulevard like a hero from days gone by.

I glance at his business card. It has the familiar blue, red, yellow and green letters that reads:

"Google. Frank Giacomo."

Hmmm. That could come in handy.

But more importantly, I got my Fender back!

I literally jump for joy, both fists in the air.

Chapter 74

VICTORY

When I walk past the front doors of Guitar Central, my Fender case in hand, I flip off the storefront, grimacing, and mutter, "Fuck you, Guitar Central!"

At that exact moment, one of the front doors opens and a salesman walks out.

Oh shit! They want my guitar back!

I make a mad run for my car.

"Wait!" the salesman at my back shouts.

No way in hell I'm waiting! I run as fast as I can, which is hard with a clunky guitar case in hand. I wrap both arms around it, hugging it against my side while I run. "Shit! Shit! Shit!"

I hear feet slapping the sidewalk as I turn the corner and run up the side street to my car.

"Hold on!" the guy shouts.

The only thing I'm holding onto is my guitar. My purse bounces against my side as I run for dear life. My car is only half a block away.

"Hey! Wait!" my pursuer shouts.

Nope, not me.

I reach my car and squeeze between my back bumper and the station wagon parked behind me. I set the guitar down and hastily fish through my purse. The guy is right behind me. Found it!

I whip my rainbow rape knife out of my purse and flick the blade out. "Back the fuck off!" I growl into the face of the salesman.

He instantly has his hands up, open palmed. He backs up a step, his eyes glued to my rainbow blade, "Whoa! Wait a second! Put that away…"

"Back off!" I jab the knife toward him, but he's several feet away, dancing nervously in the middle of the street.

"Easy," he says calmly. "I just wanted to—"

"No!" I shout as I dig through my purse with my free hand, trying to find my keys. "You can't have my guitar! So fuck off!"

He drops his hands, and stops dancing suddenly, "What? Your guitar? I don't want your guitar…"

I find my keys and yank them out of my purse, but the look on his face causes pause. "Wait, you're not here to take my Fender back?"

"What?" He's totally confused.

"I thought your manager sent you to take back my Fender."

"Huh?"

I can tell by the look on his face, that's not why he's here. I also remember that he wasn't one of the salesmen standing around the guitar counter when I called my dad and Rob the Knob got all uppity with me. He was busy helping Frank. I remember they were sitting in front of a Line 6 amplifier trying out guitars. Then I remember his name, "You're Felix."

He grins, "Yeah."

"You sold a Les Paul to Frank."

"Uh huh."

"The purple one?"

Felix smiles, "That's the one. And some used Fender Strat we just got."

He's talking about my guitar. I say defensively, "You sure you're not here for my Fender?"

He shakes his head, "Nope.

Cool, clean relief washes over me. I drop my knife to my side. "Then what *are* you here for?"

"Uh..." he nervously runs his fingers through his hair, "I kinda wanted to ask for your number? Maybe I could take you out for a drink sometime?"

Muggy discomfort soils my mood. I hate it when guys ask me out and I'm not in the mood. I sigh, "I'm really sorry, Felix, I'm not dating anyone right now." I smile as politely as I can. I hate the disappointment on a guy's face when you have to brush them off.

Just then, a black whale-tail Porsche 911 rolls past and honks. Frank sits at the wheel. The Gibson case sits in the passenger seat next to him. He waves at me, "Good luck, Victory!" He cocks his chin at Felix and they exchange a smile.

"Later, man!" Felix waves as Frank drives away, then turns back to face me.

I can see the wheels turning in his head. What is he suddenly thinking? I realize I've unconsciously tightened my grip on the rainbow rape knife still dangling at my side. You never know when some guy might get the wrong idea.

"Hey," he says, his eyes narrowed.

I tense my knife arm.

He says, "Is your name Victory?"

"Yeah," I say suspiciously, "why?"

"You're in that video."

Confused, I say, "What video?"

"The one on YouTube."

That's the second time today someone has asked me about a YouTube video. The first time was when Paul Gilbert asked me outside Rock & Roll High School. I say, "You're not talking about a Skin Trade video, are you?" Maybe someone posted cell phone video of our show at The Cobra Lounge. I never bothered to check, because I don't care about anything having to do with Skin Trade at this point.

"I'm not sure," Felix shakes his head. "It's the one with that guy?"

What guy? I open my mouth then close it. I have no idea. Is there some sex tape video circulating the internet I don't know about? Did Scott secretly film us having sex at some point and post it online after the breakup? I wouldn't put it past him. Fucking Scott. "You sure it's not a Skin Trade video? I used to be in the band."

"I don't think so. Did you guys have a second guitar player?"

"No." I'm lost. "Are you talking about Rex? The bass player?"

He looks up thoughtfully, "I don't really know..."

"Well, I have no idea what you're talking about."

"That's cool. Hey, anyway, you sure you don't want to go out sometime?"

I smile, appreciating his persistence. He seems like a nice enough guy, and he's cute, but I've got too many cute guys meddling in my life already. "Thanks, Felix. That's really sweet of you. I just can't."

"Okay," he shrugs. "If you ever need any deals on guitars or whatever," he reaches into his pocket, "here's my card."

I take it. "Thanks."

"Nice meeting you, Victory," he lingers.

"You too."

"I've got to go get some lunch before my break runs out. You sure you don't want to join me?"

His persistence is charming. "Sorry," I sigh.

"All right. Well, later." He walks back to Sunset Boulevard.

He does have a cute butt. But no! No more men! I have too much to do with my new job and getting my chops up for the L.A. Gunslingers competition. If I win that $5,000, that will seriously ease my financial woes.

I glance at his business card.

It reads:

"Guitar Central. Felix 'The Business' Hudson. Sales Associate."

What a strange name.

Then it hits me. The L.A. Gunslingers competition is hosted by Guitar Central! Will they even let me enter after today? I'm sure Rob the Knob won't be too happy about the idea of giving me a shot at the prize money. I may be barred from entry entirely.

Crap, maybe I should've joined Felix for lunch and flirted with him for thirty minutes?

But he's already turned the corner at the end of the block.

Whatever.

I'll deal with it later.

I can always use a stage name and wear a disguise like Buckethead.

KFC, anyone?

Chapter 75

VICTORY

I dive bomb the whammy bar on my Fender before pulling up on it and make my guitar squeal.

"Wow!" Aleksandra says, her eyes popping out of her head in astonishment. "How did you do that?!" Aleksandra is thirteen, has long silk straight beach blonde hair and golden brown skin. She wears an Ocean Pacific tank tee, bright orange shorts, and flip flops that don't match because it's too hot to bother with mismatching shoes and socks. She grins gleefully, "I totally want to learn how to do that! Show me, show me!"

"For sure," I giggle, "It's pretty easy. You do it like this…"

Needless to say, teaching at Rock & Roll High School for the past two weeks has been the bomb. I had four students today and they've all been the coolest kids. They're all so different and want to learn different musical styles on guitar. Blues, punk, funk, rock, you name it. It's a challenge figuring out what teaching approach works best for each student, but it keeps it interesting. And the appreciation from the kids makes it totally rewarding. They all want to be here.

It makes all the difference that they're learning songs they want to play, not boring music school standards. Seriously, who thinks it's cool to be able to play nursery rhyme melodies except for grandmas?

When I finish Aleksandra's lesson, I walk her into the waiting room out front.

Her mom stands up from a chair. She smiles at me and asks, "How did Aleksandra do? Was she well behaved?"

"Mom!" Aleksandra frowns and tosses her hair like an agitated pony.

"She was incredible," I giggle. "She's a really fast learner. Isn't that right, Aleksandra?"

Aleksandra rolls her eyes, but she's smiling.

"And," I smile, "I only had to give her one time-out during the lesson."

"Nuh uh!" Aleksandra protests.

"I'm kidding," I grin. "She was great."

"I'm glad," her mom says. "Thank you so much, Victory." She extends her hand, which I shake.

"Any time." As they walk out the front door, I say, "Don't forget to practice!"

"I won't!" Aleksandra grins and waves.

I already know she will. She's as into guitar as I was at her age.

Before the front door latches behind Aleksandra and her mom, a very attractive young woman who looks slightly older than me with long neon pink hair walks inside. She looks like a punk rocker, complete with Doc Marten lace up boots. Is she my next student? No, she seems a bit too old. All of my students have been teenagers or kids. But maybe we teach adults here too?

Pink Hair looks around uncertainly.

"Can I help you?" I ask.

"Yeah. Is Kellan here?" she asks.

"Are you here for a lesson?"

"No. I'm picking him up. Is he done with teaching for today?"

I try not to frown, "I'll go check."

"Awesome."

I walk through the door to the back of the building. I find Kellan in the kitchen leaning one hand on the open refrigerator door, sorting through the various bottles and cans on the top shelf.

"There you are," he says to the refrigerator and pulls out an unlabeled bottle of dark green juice. He twists off the cap and guzzles half of it. "Oh, hey, Victory. What up?"

I grimace, "How do you drink that stuff? It looks rotten."

"What, this?" he holds up the bottle. "I get it at the health food store. They make it fresh. Kale, spinach, pineapple, honey dew, a bunch of other fruit, and lots of ginger. It's great. You should try it." He holds the bottle out to me.

I wince, "Uh, no thanks."

He smiles and takes a swallow of his rotten looking juice before saying, "I noticed you got your Fender back."

"Yeah," I say casually.

"I bet that makes you happy," he smiles.

I nod, "Totally." I don't know what else to say.

He doesn't say anything else either, just swallows more juice.

Crickets chirp.

I consider not telling him about Pink Hair in the waiting room, but that would be lame. Although Kellan has been distant since I started working here, he hasn't been the tiniest bit rude. He's always polite. I owe him the same amount of respect.

I'd thought maybe we were past whatever weirdness there was between us after I spent the night at his apartment and we could officially be friends, but I guess not.

Men make no sense.

Whatevs.

I say, "Some woman with pink hair is waiting for you in the waiting room. She said she's here to pick you up?"

Kellan nods and grins, "Switchblade."

"What?"

"Switchblade. She's here to pick me up," Kellan says before swallowing the last of his sewage juice. He tosses the empty bottle in the trash can in the corner of the room. "See ya," he smiles and walks out of the kitchen.

Now I'm a hundred kinds of curious about this Switchblade girl of his. I mean, I know Kellan's a manwhore, but after two weeks teaching at the school, this is the first time a woman has come by for him. I got the sense the school was a special place and he didn't bring women here. So, what's so different about Pink Hair?

I'm not in control of my feet when they guide me down the hallway after Kellan. They also tiptoe of their own accord. Seriously, I'm just along for the ride.

The door between the hallway and the waiting room is on a spring and it's already shushing closed when I reach it.

I hear Kellan drawl, "Hey, Switchblade…"

My foot, which is still doing its own thing, stops the door a half inch before it closes. I can just see Kellan with pink haired Switchblade. I frown to myself. What kind of name is *Switchblade*? She's probably lame. Not that I care. Because I totally don't.

It's hard to see both Kellan and Switchblade at the same time because the gap in the doorframe is so narrow. But I clearly see Switchblade gazing up into Kellan's eyes with a big grin on her face. She places her fingers on Kellan's forearm. She seems very familiar with him. And her eyes are twinkling. A lot.

Ms. Sensible harrumphs in my head and folds her arms across her chest. She isn't a heartless bitch. She's just very protective of our heart.

Not that I care what Kellan does.

"I wrote a new song last night," Switchblade says.

"Nice," Kellan says. I can't see his face, but he sounds happy to hear it.

"I think you're really going to like it," Switchblade finishes.

"Sweet. We can try it out at practice tonight with the guys. But I need to get some food first. You hungry?"

Practice? With the guys? Are these two in a band?

Pink haired Switchblade nods, "Sure. Oh, I made up a list of band names. I came up with a whole bunch."

"I've got some too," Kellan says. "We'll see what the guys came up with and vote tonight. The quicker we pick a name, the sooner we can start promoting ourselves. I'm itching to get back onstage."

They *are* in a band. They suck. I haven't had time to call up Olivia to work on song writing. All I've had time to do was get my lesson plans together for teaching my students. Turns out this job is more time consuming than I'd anticpated. Maybe that's why Kellan is so standoffish? Too many lesson plans to prepare?

"Me too," Switchblade grins at Kellan. "I haven't played guitar in front of an audience since I moved to L.A."

She plays guitar? She probably sucks.

Kellan chuckles, "When people in town hear you play, they're gonna go nuts."

He can't be serious. How good can she be? She has a *nose* ring! And pink hair! Everyone knows that people with nose rings and pink hair aren't any good at guitar! I learned that in high school! I think it's even a question on the PSATs!

42. Women with ___, ___ at playing guitar.

(A) pink hair ... suck

(B) nose rings ... blow

(C) pink hair and nose rings ... epic fail

(D) All of the above

In response to Kellan's compliment, Switchblade giggles. She *giggles*. Lame. Ms. Sensible rolls her eyes. In fact, everyone on my internal committee rolls their eyes.

Switchblade asks Kellan, "You think we'll be ready for L.A. Gunslingers in a few weeks?"

"Hells yeah," Kellan smiles. "We've got a bunch of solid songs already. Plus, a buddy of mine runs The Dive Bomb's open mic night every week. I bet we can get the band rehearsed and try out our set there before we play Gunslingers."

They're planning on playing L.A. Gunslingers? Wow, I'm jealous. And I feel like a slacker. I haven't done shit to find a band.

"Yup," Switchblade nods and grins at Kellan. "It's cool as hell when everyone in a band can pull their own weight and there's no drama. I can't believe we've made so much progress in only a couple weeks."

"I know," Kellan chuckles, "we're on our way to the top. Ready for some food?"

"Let's do it," Switchblade smiles.

Rich Aymes' gruff voice startles me from behind, "Mind if I squeeze by?"

I whip around, "Oh! Sorry!" I step aside so he can pass.

Rich opens the door and I peer around him. Kellan and Switchblade are already gone. Rich walks up to a mom sitting with her son and the three of them chat amiably.

I spin on my rocker boot heel and march back to my practice room where I teach. I pull the door closed so I can have some privacy. I lean against the door, my arms folded across my chest, and frown.

Why am I so irritable all of a sudden?

Is it because of Switchblade? Attractive and apparently amazing on guitar Switchblade? That shouldn't matter to me, should it? Kellan can do whatever he wants with his life. I don't really care.

Someone in my internal committee arches a doubtful eyebrow.

I don't care!

Another committee member raises her eyebrows as well, and politely covers a giggle with the side of her hand.

I'm serious! I don't!

Now the whole committee is tittering in my head.

Fuck you guys!

I know how to fix this.

I grab my purse from where it's stashed behind a practice amp and pull out my cell phone. I dial a number.

This situation is going to be rectified right now.

The band thing and the man thing.

Chapter 76

VICTORY

"Are they cute?" Olivia asks.

I say, "I can't believe I've never introduced you to Lucas and Logan Summer."

"If they're cute, neither can I," Olivia jokes.

We're setting up our gear inside Quadrophenia, a rehearsal studio in Silver Lake. We picked it because it's close to Liv's apartment and not too far from Hollywood.

Like the name would suggest, Quadrophenia has four rehearsal rooms that bands rent by the hour. The converted building on Hyperion Avenue looks like it was built in 1952. The scalloped pointy awning outside resembles abstract twinkling stars. It has a very spacey vibe that I love.

Inside, the floor of our rehearsal room is carpeted in a sumptuous burnt orange pile. Furry mustard colored shag carpeting lines the walls up to waist height. From the top of the mustard shag to the ceiling, the walls are covered with old school acoustic tiling from the 1960s. A couple of dusty Sunn amps from the 1970s are in the corners for musicians to use as needed. Mic stands are scattered around the room.

This place reminds me of the kind of studio The Who or Iron Butterfly recorded their albums back in the day.

Olivia's modern keyboard setup, which is hooked up to her laptop and Roland KC-550 keyboard amp, contrasts starkly with the throwback vibe of the room. But not her outfit, which is a fitted carnation pink and white 1960s shirtwaist dress encircled by a white belt. Olivia stands tall on carnation platform sandals and I notice her toenails match the carnation pink of the dress, which has wide lapels and short sleeves that are rolled up past her elbows. The outfit goes perfectly with her black Bettie Page bangs and waves. I don't know how she manages to look so damn stylish all the time.

I ask, "Do you have a dresser or your own stylist, or what?"

Liv grins, "No. I just do a lot of shoplifting," she winks.

I laugh, "Really?"

"No," she smiles, "but I do have several credit cards. But if I ever max them out, I will stoop to stealing." She pretends to check the wristwatch she doesn't have and says, "That should be in about two weeks. I need my fashion fix."

"Oh, Liv. You're such a junkie," I snicker.

"And proud of it. Hey, do you think your friends are stuck in traffic?"

I check the time on my cell phone. "Between here and San Diego? Probably."

When I called Lucas and Logan about jamming with me and Olivia to write some new material, they said yes without hesitation. The only downside to working with them is the two hour drive between San Diego and L.A. And that's without traffic. It can easily be three or more hours if you hit rush hour.

Olivia says, "Let's jam until they get here." She clicks around on her laptop and a sample drum beat starts playing from her keyboard amp.

I plug my Fender into the Bogner Spider Valve combo Rich Aymes let me borrow from the school. It turns out Rich is totally cool and super generous.

Olivia sets her keyboard to a groovy gritty hammond organ sound reminiscent of Deep Purple's Hush. Her fingers tap dance on the keys as she hammers out a bouncy riff.

"Hey," I say, "that sounds rad. What key is that?"

"C major," she says.

I start playing a funky rock riff on top of her keyboards. I totally have Hush in my head, but it doesn't take long for me to steer it in a different, heavier direction.

Olivia starts humming into a mic in harmony with our playing.

"Yeah!" I cheer as we both really get into it. "LIV! ARE WE RECORDING THIS?!" I shout while playing.

She reaches over to her laptop with one hand, still hitting chords on the keyboard with her right, and clicks on the laptop several times. "ROLLING!" she shouts.

We keep playing for a long time, fleshing out the basic rhythms and riffs into a more complete song. At a natural stopping point, we both make a lot of noise with the keyboard and guitar, then Liv reaches over and stops the drum beat. Not quite the same as having a drummer, but close enough.

The door to the rehearsal room opens and Lucas Summer cheers, "Hells yeah!" He holds his bass guitar case in hand. "That was awesome!"

His brother Logan stands beside him, smiling and holding a big bass drum in both arms.

"Hello," Olivia blurts, eyeing Lucas and Logan hungrily. She's *so* obvious, but she doesn't care.

I can't blame her.

Lucas and Logan are a couple of hotties who both exude San Diego beach casualness. Tall, muscular and deeply bronzed from living under the sun. Their summer blond hair has a natural curl that touches their shoulders. They could almost be twins, but they're not. Lucas is a year older than me at 23, and Logan is a year younger at 21. The only obvious difference between them is Lucas' blue eyes and Logan's green.

Both wear surf t-shirts, shorts, and flip flops.

"You guys are late!" I say, "I was worried you weren't gonna make it."

"Blame him," Lucas chuckles, elbowing Logan.

Logan rolls his eyes, "You were driving, dude."

"What took you so long?" I ask.

"Oh, dude, traffic was insane," Lucas says. He turns to his brother, "But we would've been here sooner if Logan hadn't stayed in the water all morning."

Logan shrugs shyly and mumbles. "The waves were off the hook. I didn't see you quitin' early, bro."

A guilty smile spreads across Lucas' wide, perfect mouth.

"You guys surf?" Olivia asks, her hip now cocked flirtatiously.

"Daily," Lucas grins.

"I've always wanted to learn how to surf," Olivia says suggestively. Olivia works quickly when she's attracted to a guy. She may as well have a sign flashing over her head that says AVAILABLE.

Lucas says, "Let me know when you want lessons." He checks out Olivia with admiring eyes.

I need to stop them before they drive to the beach for adult playtime in the waves at Venice Beach. I say, "You guys need help with your gear?"

"Sure," Lucas says.

We all walk outside. Liv makes sure to "accidentally" bump into Lucas about twenty times on the way out. I'm just waiting for her to pretend to drop something and do a breathy Legally Blonde "bend and snap" for him.

When we get to the sidewalk outside, Lucas asks, "What were you guys playing when we walked in?"

"Just jamming," I say.

"Sounded awesome," Logan mumbles. He's always so shy. It's so cute on him. Heck, everything is cute on Logan.

Lucas and Logan's immaculate 1977 white-roofed orange-bodied VW bus is parked next to the curb in front of Quadrophenia. They love the bus because it's perfect for surfboards or band equipment. It's pretty reliable, but I've helped them work on the engine more than once. Had to show them I knew my way around a dual port carburetor. They were impressed. My dad taught me a lot.

"Hey," Lucas says to me, "We heard about what happened with Skin Trade. Sorry about that."

I roll my eyes and groan, "Don't remind me."

Logan says, "Scott was a prick."

I chuckle, "I wish you'd told me sooner."

Logan shrugs and smiles.

Lucas laughs, "That's what I'm always telling him. He's not as dumb as he acts."

Logan rolls his eyes at his brother.

Changing the subject, I ask, "How's Jake doing? I haven't seen him since we played the Belly Up."

Lucas smiles, "He's in Hawaii with his girlfriend Madison, cutting up waves on the North Shore."

I grin, "I'm surprised you guys haven't joined them."

Logan grins, "We would if the airlines let me bring my drum set."

Lucas chuckles, "I tried to stuff his kick drum in the overhead before, but it wouldn't fit."

I joke, "Logan, you should take up bongos."

Logan grins, "Thinking about it."

It takes the four of us a few trips to haul all their gear inside the building. The boys get the heaviest stuff like Lucas' amp and Logan's hardware bag for his drum stands. Olivia cheerleads and flirts while carrying the snare drum, which is the lightest thing she can find.

Lucas plugs in his bass and warms up while Logan sets up his drum kit.

Lucas asks, "Can you guys play what you were playing when we showed up?"

"Do you want to hear the recording," Olivia says, "or we can just play it?" She glances at me.

"I remember it," I say. "Let's just play it. We're in C major," I say to Lucas.

He nods.

The three of us play while Logan bolts all his drums together.

It doesn't take long for Lucas to work up a nice bumping bass line. When Logan is all set up, he sits behind his kit and adjusts the positioning of his drums until he's happy. Without warming up, he joins the beat, keeping tight time with Lucas.

It's an incredible experience working with skilled musicians. The music comes together effortlessly. While we jam through the impromptu tune, we get tighter each time we play it through.

We stop after the third time, Liv asks, "Who's gonna sing?"

"I can," Lucas says.

Having played with Lucas and Logan many times, I know Lucas has an amazing voice, and Logan sings amazing harmony. And of course, Liv sings like a pop diva.

I feel a pinch of jealousy because I don't sing.

(*singsingsing*)

I push it out of my mind.

I play guitar.

And I'm fine with that.

(*singsingsingsingsingsing*)

Olivia asks, "Lucas, do you have any lyrics in mind?"

"Not yet," he says. "Do you?"

I notice a distinct chemistry and tension between them. I hope I don't have to remind them of the only rule in rock & roll. If things pan out between the four of us, I'd hate to see some drama between them blow it all up. Maybe it won't matter. We'll see.

"I have a few ideas," Olivia grins at Lucas.

He smirks, aware of her flirtatiousness, "Yeah, what?"

"Something about a boy?"

I chuckle "You always sing about boys, Liv."

"What can I say?" she smiles, "I happen to like them. A lot." Her eyes are all over Lucas.

I'm going to have to corral her or she and Lucas are going to go at it like wild horses before the sun goes down.

An hour later, after we've jammed hard, we're all sweating in the hot rehearsal room, which has no A/C.

"That rocked!" I cheer. "What did you guys think?"

"Sounding good," Lucas says.

"I like it," Olivia smiles.

Logan nods and grins.

I'm hopeful that between the four of us we can come up with some good music in time for L.A. Gunslingers. The show date is breathing down our necks, but with the skills the four of us have, we just might pull it off.

I say, "You guys wanna take a quick break?"

Lucas sets his bass in a guitar stand.

Logan pulls his shirt over his head. His chiseled abs accordion exquisitely. Even I can't help but stare.

Olivia is openly gawking and waving her hands in her face, "I need oxygen," she moans. "It's really hot in here."

Lucas chuckles, watching Olivia drool, taking it all in stride. I've seen groupies throw themselves at Lucas and Logan hundreds of times. The brothers are used to it.

Logan still hasn't noticed Olivia and he wipes his face with his t-shirt before dropping it on the top of his floor tom. That's when he realizes we're all staring at him.

"What?" Logan asks.

"Woo, I'm going to faint," Olivia sighs and looks at me while fanning her face agitatedly, "I can't decide who's hotter, them or me." She glances between the brothers, "One of you two brown skinned babes needs to catch me in your arms because I'm seriously about to faint."

I roll my eyes, "She's fine."

"No, seriously," Olivia says breathlessly, still waving her hands in her face, "I'm gonna pass out. I'm seeing stars. Oh wait, that's just Lucas and Logan," she giggles. "Someone catch me?"

Neither Lucas nor Logan makes any sudden moves.

Lucas says, "Logan, you want me to do it?"

"Be my guest," he says.

Olivia says, "I think I need both of you. Not because I'm heavy, because we all know I'm nearly weightless, but because I have slender bones. Quick, you two," she glances between the brothers, "I don't want to break anything when I collapse. I'm very delicate," she sighs.

I laugh, "She's not delicate. She's just an attention whore."

"I'm ignoring that," Olivia announces.

Lucas strolls toward Olivia behind her keyboard stand.

Olivia sighs, "Your brother too."

Logan laughs and stands up.

When both of them stand on either side of Olivia, she says, "Mmmm, Summer Sandwich. My favorite."

I shake my head, "You're such a ho, Liv."

She whispers loud enough for everyone to hear, "Don't tell them that."

I chuckle, "I think they can figure that out on their own."

Olivia giggles and says to the brothers, "When Victory says ho, she means the high class kind. You'll never catch me standing under a lamppost soliciting drive by Johnsons."

"Good to know," Lucas chuckles.

I giggle, "It's Johns, Liv."

She says dismissively, "Johns, Johnsons, Dicks, I don't care what their names are. I'm nobody's street corner whore."

"Anybody want food?" Logan asks. "I'm starving."

"I could use a bite," I say.

Olivia glances between the brothers and says, "I could use a bite too. Which one of you is sweeter?"

"Liv!" I bark.

"It doesn't matter," Olivia says, ignoring me. "With a little whipped cream and sugar, I bet you're both as sweet as pie."

I say, "Liv doesn't get out much." I glare at her, "Can we go now?"

Olivia asks the brothers, "Which one of you wants to carry me? I feel ready to swoon."

Lucas and Logan laugh.

I walk behind Liv and push her back with both my hands, "Go, girl! Food is that way!"

Olivia stumbles forward, spinning her legs to keep from tripping. "Victory," she laughs, "watch it!"

The edge of the sun slides behind the Silver Lake hillsides when we reach the sidewalk outside.

Olivia hooks her arms through the brothers' elbows.

"We ready?" she asks.

"Be nice," I warn. "They're brothers. And Logan is sensitive."

"Ooh," Olivia coos, "I like the sensitive quiet types the *best*," she crinkles her nose, "they're *so* tender on the inside."

I blurt, "You make him sound like squishy candy or something."

Olivia looks up at Logan and smiles, "I would say more of a hard candy shell that melts in your mouth…"

Exasperated, I roll my eyes and say, "You need to get laid, Liv!"

"I'm working on it," she purrs. "Let's go, boys. I'm starving…" she says seductively.

Lucas and Logan both laugh heartily as the three of them walk down the sidewalk together, arm in arm.

I really hope Liv isn't serious about arranging a three way with Lucas and Logan.

That'll really screw up my plans for a band.

I sigh, but I can't blame her. The Summer brothers are incredibly sexy. Oh well. I follow behind them, admiring the brothers' butts in their clingy surf shorts.

Maybe we'll have a four way and the band will never go anywhere.

Not!

Chapter 77

VICTORY

Late morning sun bleaches all the buildings on Wilshire Boulevard blinding white. I walk from my parked car to the front entrance of Rock & Roll High School, my Fender case in hand. I'm so glad I have my guitar back.

It's a hot day so I'm wearing my sleeveless Whitesnake 'Slide It In' shirt. Lucky for me, Johnny and Karen's apartment building has a big laundry room so I have clean clothes without having to use the Lucy's laundromat down the street.

When I near Rock & Roll High School, I notice Kellan leaning against the doorframe.

When he sees me, he folds his muscled, inked-up arms across his chest. The muscles contract and pop dramatically, but I'm pretty sure he's not doing it on purpose. He just has big muscles and very little body fat.

I say, "Hey."

"Rich is late," Kellan grunts, "he called and said he'd be here soon."

Kellan clearly isn't in a talkative mood.

"Okay," I say and lean against the front wall on the other side of the door, leaving space between us. I realize that the locked door between me and Kellan is vaguely symbolic. It's a portal between the two of us that leads to a wonderful world of guitar and kids and smiles and endless laughter and happiness, but the door is locked, and neither Kellan nor me has the key, apparently.

Whatever.

I steal a quick glance at Kellan.

He stares into the distance, looking a lot like one of those cigarette ad cowboys. I really wish Kellan was super ugly. Then I wouldn't feel compelled to drink in his beauty with my thirsty eyes.

Neither of us says anything.

We watch cars drive slowly by on Wilshire Boulevard.

Ms. Instigator takes control of my mouth and I say, "How's your band with Switchblade coming along?"

He frowns, still staring into the distance thoughtfully, then swivels his head around, "I didn't tell you I was in a band."

"Yeah you did," I blurt.

He shakes his head resolutely, "No I didn't."

"Well, uh," I say nervously, "I think Rich mentioned it."

"No he didn't. I haven't told him yet."

"You must have," I say with false confidence. "How else would I know about Switchblade?"

"I didn't tell Rich about Switchblade either."

"Uhh..."

Kellan smirks, "Have you been stalking me, Victory?"

"No," I scoff. "Why would I want to?" I say it like his personal life is as appealing to me as discussions about sewage treatment plants.

"Okay," he says dismissively. "Whatever you say." He totally doesn't believe me. He goes back to staring into the distance. His brows are knit together, deep in thought. Damn it, he really is hunky from every angle. His jaw muscles dance in his cheeks.

What is he thinking about? Is he mad I asked about Switchblade? I want to know more, but I don't want to ask. Maybe I don't even care.

A voice in my internal committee pipes up, Yeah, right!

"Hey, guys," Rich Aymes says as he walks up, a big key ring in one hand, a Guitar Central plastic bag in the other. He unlocks the front door, "Sorry I'm late. I had to stop at Guitar Central and buy a few boxes of high E strings. I swear, one of the kids breaks one during their lessons just about every day," he chuckles.

Kellan gives Rich a friendly smile.

Kellan didn't give me a friendly smile. But I seriously don't care.

Kellan says to Rich, "Good call. Chloe broke an E yesterday. But I didn't have any elevens handy. Can you believe that girl plays elevens on the E?"

Rich asks, "She doesn't bend them, does she?"

"Yeah," Kellan chuckles.

"Kid has strong hands," Rich smiles. "I bought nines, tens, elevens, and twelves. We should be covered for awhile." When he twists the keys in the door lock, he smiles at me, "Morning, Victory. How you doing?"

Kellan shoulders inside before I respond. He doesn't care what I have to say. Whatever.

"Hey, Rich," I smile. At least Rich is happy to see me. "I'm good."

"Love the Whitesnake shirt," Rich chuckles, "I've got one just like it."

He holds the door open for me, "After you."

I walk inside and head toward the hallway door at the back of the waiting area. It's already open and I hear Kellan closing a door in the back. Wow, he really doesn't want to see my face.

What's up his ass?

As I'm stepping through the hallway door, Rich says, "Oh, hey, I've got some news I want to share with you and Kellan. Can you grab him and bring him to my office so I don't have to tell it twice?"

"Sure," I smile, but my smile is slightly forced. I don't want to go round up brooding Kellan.

But I do it anyway because Rich asked and I like Rich.

Chapter 78

KELLAN

Victory is wearing the same Whitesnake shirt today that she wore the night she slept in my apartment. The night we had pizza at N.Y. & C.'s. The night we recorded that video I uploaded to YouTube.

I did my best to forget about that night and the next day when she took all her stuff and bailed out of my apartment.

It still pisses me off thinking about it, so I try not to. But when she wears the same damn shirt, it's hard to block it all out of my mind.

I shake my head and sigh.

When she walked up to the school a half hour ago, her guitar case in hand, her long hair fluttering in the light breeze, tight jeans, Whitesnake shirt, and her aviator sunglasses on her face, she looked incredible. Like something out of an old Mötley Crüe video.

Looking at her all hot like that physically hurt.

I've never seen a woman do justice to the rocker chick look the way Victory does. I don't know why, but she rocks it better than anybody. It's not just that she's hot. Hot women are a dime a dozen in this town. But Victory represents the look. It's not a pose for her. She *is* a rocker. The best I've ever seen.

That's hot as hell in my book.

I don't want to think about it right now.

Shit, I don't want to think about it ever again.

I'm done with Victory.

I don't need her.

I sigh as I set my Ibanez case on the floor of the practice room and unlatch it. When I pull my RG550 out, someone knocks on the door.

"Hold on a second," I say while I rest the guitar in a stand. I open the practice room door and see Victory standing in front of me. "What?" I grunt, staring over the top of her head so I don't have to look at her eyes.

She says, "Rich wants to talk to us in his office."

"What about?"

"I don't know," she practically snarls. "He didn't say." She spins on her heel and walks down the hallway.

I suddenly wonder if Rich is going to sit us down and tell us to get over our cold shoulder act toward each other because it's affecting the students. I don't know why it would. I do my best not to be rude to Victory when I'm at work. Maybe I'm not very friendly, but what law says you have to be buddies with your co-workers?

You never know.

Maybe some perceptive parent noticed and said something to Rich.

Victory is already standing in Rich's office when I walk in. I don't acknowledge her. She ignores me.

Good.

"Hey, guys," Rich says. "Have a seat." He sounds serious. Maybe I was right about him noticing me and Victory's cold shoulder routine.

I pull out a chair for myself. Victory can get her own.

"What's up?" I ask Rich.

Rich sighs, "I know I'm shooting myself in the foot telling you two this, but I heard from a buddy of mine last night that Wild Child is holding auditions this weekend here in town."

This is not at all what I was expecting Rich to tell us.

"Wild Child?" I blurt. Wild Child is my favorite band. I've been a huge fan of them since their first album came out years ago. Amazingly, they're one of the few bands that has all the same members they started with in high school. "Why are they holding auditions? Did one of them die?" It's the only explanation I can think of.

"Close," Rich snorts. "My buddy, who's a roadie for them, told me one of their guitar players broke his hand in a skydiving accident yesterday."

"Danny Daggers or Chainsaw?" I ask in utter disbelief.

"Danny," Rich says.

Daggers is the lead guitar player. I know all of his solos note for note. "No way..." I groan.

Rich nods, "Yup."

"I can't believe it," I say, nearly awestruck. "And they're holding auditions?"

"Yup. They need a replacement right away. They're in the middle of a

200 city U.S. tour and they can't cancel eight weeks worth of shows while Daggers recovers. They need someone now."

"No shit!" I blurt.

I've dreamed of playing with Wild Child since I was a kid. I used to play along to their albums in my bedroom when I was in high school, pretending I was on stage with the band. I used to dream of something like this happening, but never thought it would. I mean, I feel bad Danny Daggers broke his hand, but if they need a replacement, I'm not gonna say no. I still know all of Daggers' solos. I don't even have to prepare for the audition. I could do it right now and own it. I'm speechless.

"Why are you telling us?" Victory asks.

Rich sighs, "My mission with this school has always been to help kids find their way into the music business any way I can because I never really made it myself. So I like to give back to the kids, and that includes you guys, my teachers. Even if it means one of you might land this Wild Child gig and leave me searching for another qualified guitar teacher two weeks after Steve left on *his* tour."

At the exact same moment, me and Victory both blurt, "When are the auditions?"

I glance at her, but she isn't paying attention to me. Her eyes are glued on Rich.

"This weekend," Rich answers. "Somewhere in Hollywood. I'm waiting to find out the details. But I'll let both you guys know as soon as I hear back from my buddy."

I stand up to leave, "Thanks, man."

"No problem," Rich smiles and sips from a cup of fresh coffee on his desk.

"Yeah," Victory says, also standing. "Thank you, Rich."

"My pleasure," Rich smiles. "Just make sure one of you two gets the gig. I'd hate to see it going to anybody else. My buddy says the pay is good and all expenses are covered. You could easily make ten or twenty grand for two months on tour with a headliner band like those guys."

Victory mutters, "Twenty *thousand*?"

"Yup," Rich nods and sips his coffee. He turns to his computer and says absently, "Did either of you notice if there's any leftover doughnuts in the kitchen? I didn't eat breakfast..." He's already sorting through email on his computer.

I turn to walk out of the room. All I can think is, Doughnuts? Who can think about food at a time like this? Wild Child needs a guitar player!

Victory and I hit the door frame at the same time. It's not wide enough for both of us and my beefy shoulder literally thuds into the wood when I shift right to avoid smashing Victory into the beam on the left. My impact literally shakes the room.

"Easy, guys," Rich chuckles without looking up from his computer screen, "the auditions aren't this minute."

I'm still blocking Victory's way out of the room.

She glares up at me and grunts, "Watch it!" She squeezes past me and tears down the hallway to her practice room.

I frown at her back as she disappears and slams the door behind her. I can't help but chuckle at her behavior.

A few seconds later I hear Cold Stoned coming from the computer speakers through Victory's door. It's the first track from Wild Child's first album, and one of my favorites. I wonder how well Victory knows their music? Probably not as good as I do based on how agitated she acted a minute ago, and the fact she's starting with their first song.

Rich asks, "Hey, Kellan?"

I'm still lingering in his doorway. "Yeah?"

"Can you check on those doughnuts for me, brother?"

"Sure, man." I stroll into the kitchen and find a pink box on the counter. I lift the lid and it's got three doughnuts left. Doughnut crumbs, rainbow sprinkles, and grease stains litter the rest of the box. I walk the box back to Rich's office. "Here ya go, bro." I set the box on his desk.

"Thanks, Kellan." Rich says without looking up from his computer. He takes a doughnut out of the box without examining it and takes a big bite. His cheeks puff and deflate as he munches hungrily.

I stroll past Victory's practice room and hear her rewind the guitar solo for Cold Stoned through the door. Yeah, she doesn't know it.

But I do.

I know all of their solos

I shake my head to myself and grin from ear to ear.

Wild Child.

Fucking Wild Child!

When I go into my own practice room, I still hear Victory playing along with the recording of Cold Stoned. She's already got the rhythm guitar part figured out and most of the solo. I have to hand it to her, she learns music quick. But Wild Child has a deep catalog, and I doubt she'll learn everything in two days.

Not my problem.

I pause for a second, thinking about Victory's financial situation. I know she needs money, but it's not like she's living on the street. She told me she's crashing at her friends' and I know she has a job. If she was desperate, that would be one thing. But she's not. She has options. She'll manage.

So I'm not cutting her any slack on this Wild Child gig. I plan to take it to the bank and spend two months touring with my idols.

Screw Victory.

She's on her own.

I chuckle to myself.

She never wanted my help anyway.

Chapter 79

VICTORY

My last student of the day finishes at six o'clock that evening. It's been tough keeping my mind on my students because that Wild Child audition has been pounding in the back of my head all day.

$20,000.

I could pay back Johnny and Karen the $6,000 I owe them for the Contrares. And have plenty of money to move out and leave them to their nightly tantric sex sessions, which by the way, are getting old. I can't decide if hearing them having sex every night is making me hate sex, or jealous that I'm having none. Either way, I need to move out of their apartment.

But the move can wait until after the Wild Child audition.

So I'm staying late at the school tonight, working my way through the Wild Child albums, learning all the guitar parts and solos. It's a lot to take in, but I'm up for the task. My stomach growls around 7:00pm. I don't want to stop for dinner, but I haven't eaten since breakfast, which was a yogurt. I'm starving and I can tell I'll run out of gas if I don't fill my tank.

I put my guitar down and walk into the school's kitchen. The vending machine is full of the usual junk: chocolate in every form imaginable: bars, pieces, bits, bites, cookies, and chocolate covered pretzels. The machine also has all kinds of potato chips, imitation cheese and sawdust crackers, microwave popcorn kernels encased in blocks of dehydrated motor oil, and Lifesavers in every flavor.

Is any of this healthy? I've been eating Johnny and Karen's vegetarian dinners so much lately, the contents of the vending machine turn my stomach.

The least awful alternative is the Lay's plain potato chips. With nothing but potatoes, oil, and salt, they seem vaguely nutritious, but not exactly a wholesome meal.

I feed change into the machine and buy a bag.

On a whim, I check the refrigerator.

Not that any of the contents inside are mine. I see Rich's tupperware container full of what looks like spaghetti and meatballs. Can't touch the boss' dinner. There's cans of sodas, which I don't want. Then I notice one of Kellan's rotten brown juice sitting on the shelf. He left earlier, so maybe he forgot to drink it today?

Ms. Mischievous wrings her crafty hands and suggests I steal his drink because he won't miss it.

Ms. Sensible reminds me that if it looks rotten, it probably *is* rotten.

Ms. Desperate eyes the bag of salty chips in my hands and reminds me it won't be enough to get me through my evening of music study.

I reach into the fridge and take Kellan's bottle. Then I lean my head out into the hallway to see if anyone is coming. Nope. All clear. I twist the cap off the bottle and smell the juice daintily. Doesn't smell bad. With my tongue I touch the bottle's rim, collecting a stray droplet of rot. I smack my lips, testing the taste.

It seems drinkable.

I take a swallow from the bottle.

It's an explosion of flavors and it's actually not bad. I'm surprised. At first, I taste fruits and vegetables. It's kind of like salad and fruit juice, but I can handle it. A moment later, this green grass aftertaste kicks in and I'm smacking my tongue on the roof of my mouth and grimacing. It tastes like freshly mowed lawn. How the hell does Kellan drink this stuff?

But I remind myself Kellan has lots of muscles and beautiful skin. Maybe he's on to something. I drink another swallow and wince in anticipation of the aftertaste.

It's not quite as bad this time.

I can get used to it.

Ms. Sensible reminds me I'm stealing Kellan's juice.

Ms. Rationalizer reminds me if Kellan wanted it, he would've drunk it already.

Ms. Lewdness reminds me Kellan's lips were on this bottle top and it's almost like I'm kissing him by drinking from his bottle.

Ms. Logical reminds me that the bottle was unopened, therefore, my lips are not in contact with Kellan's in any way, shape, or form.

I take another swallow, reminding myself how healthy it is.

"Are you drinking Kellan's moldy used bath water?" Rich Aymes asks out of nowhere, suddenly standing behind me in the kitchen doorframe.

Half the swallow goes down my windpipe and I start hacking out lung tissue. That's when the other half sprays out of my mouth in a green brown mist.

Rich leans back, a concerned look on his face, "You okay?"

I'm still coughing.

He asks thoughtfully, "Do you need the Heimlich?"

I cough, "No—" *HACK!* "—all—" *HACK!* "—good!" *HACK!*

"You sure?"

I shake my head, "I'm—" *HACK!* "—fine."

"I know if you're coughing your windpipe isn't blocked," Rich says, "but if we need to take you to the Emergency Room to drain your lungs, let me know. I'll be in my office," he jokes.

I open my mouth to say, *HACK!* "Thanks." Cough.

Rich smiles, "None of the candy in the machine is moldy. The vending machine guy fills it up every week. I suggest you stick with that." Rich grins and walks away while I recover.

It wasn't the taste of the juice that made me cough. Rich just surprised me.

I hold up the bottle of moldy brown bath water to the light. Not even sunlight could penetrate this brown cloud.

Maybe it was slightly the taste of the juice.

Ms. Sensible reminds me that we reap what we sow.

I tell her to fuck off before I pour the rest of the juice down my throat.

Chastised, she says nothing. Apparently, she doesn't like the juice either.

I empty the bottle down the kitchen sink. Then I plug quarters into the vending machine and punch the buttons for a bag of chocolate chip cookies. I should've gone with them in the first place. I rip the package open and take a bite. They even taste fresh.

I walk into my practice room and close the door.

I've got work to do for the Wild Child audition. Chocolate Chips and Lay's potato chips will fuel me through it.

$20,000, here I come!

Chapter 80

KELLAN

"Remember," I say to Switchblade as she drives the two of us to the Wild Child audition in Hollywood two days later, "The second we walk in the door, it's every man for himself."

"You wish you were a man, you fucking pussy," she barks. Switchblade drives a banged up 1997 Chevy Camaro. It's not exactly classic American Muscle, but it runs pretty good for a seventeen year old car and Switchblade looks great behind the wheel. The car is white with twin orange stripes running the length of the car.

It's Saturday afternoon and weekend traffic is sluggish. The Camaro's A/C is busted, so the windows are rolled down. Hot air blows inside the car as we cruise along the 10 freeway.

Switchblade smashes her fist against the wheel. "What's with all the fucking traffic? Is everybody going to this audition?"

"Probably," I chuckle.

"Tell them to turn around, because I'm getting the gig," she laughs.

"It's probably people coming back from the beach. Today was perfect weather for it. I wish I'd gone myself, but we've got more important things."

Switchblade nods.

Our guitars cases are jammed in the cramped backseat.

Switchblade asks, "Do you think we should've brought better amps? All I've got is my old Crate 1x12."

I chuckle, "It's not like your trunk had room for extra. Besides, we don't need good amps."

"Why not?" she asks skeptically.

"Have you ever seen that video on YouTube of Jason Becker covering Yngwie Malmsteen's song Black Star?"

"Which one?"

"The one when Jason is in high school playing the talent show?"

She grins, remembering, "Oh, yeah. Becker shreds. I love the part when the principal walks onstage and tells him to turn his amp down, but Jason only pretends like he's turning it down." Switchblade beams a smile, which looks really good on her. "Total rebel."

"Yeah, that's hilarious," I grin. "Anyway, the point is, Becker is playing some shitty 80s Peavey combo amp and his tone is amazing. It's all in the hands. Your Crate will be more than good enough for Wild Child."

She nods thoughtfully, "I hope you're right."

"I'm right," I say confidently. "You're going to kick ass during your audition."

She glances over at me and smiles, "How'd you get to be so cool, Kellan Burns?"

I chuckle and smile back at her, "I've always been this cool."

Out of nowhere, she gives me this soft look, which is new on her.

If I didn't know she was gay, I'd swear she's into me. Maybe she's bi? I can't tell. Or maybe she pretends she's gay so guys like me don't hit on her. Sometimes crazy shit like that happens. You never know.

Switchblade's eyes go nervous and she swings them back to the freeway ahead.

We drive in silence for a moment.

I ask, "You nervous about the audition?"

She blurts with her usual bravado, "Aren't you?"

"No." I mean it.

"We need some tunes," Switchblade turns on the CD player and cranks up the volume. Wild Child pumps out of the car stereo. Switchblade rattles her fingers against the wheel in time with the beat.

Is she covering something up?

Cuz she's acting way weird on me.

Chapter 81

VICTORY

A really tall guy wearing a comically tall black top hat and black top coat over tight black-and-white diamond-checked jester pants walks out of the back of the recording studio and into the reception area where I sit.

Top Hat's knee-high platform goth boots go *clomp, clomp, clomp*. He resembles a ghoulish evil freakshow version of The Cat In The Hat. I think this guy would be better suited auditioning for Rob Zombie than for a hard drinking, fast cars and fast women hard rock band like Wild Child.

An assistant with a clipboard who is handling the auditions for Wild Child follows The Ghoul In The Hat out of the back.

I've been sitting here waiting patiently for my chance to audition for several hours. If I land this gig, I'm going to make $20,000 in two months. I can't let anyone or anything stand in the way of me getting this gig.

I need this gig.

I will kill for this gig.

Starting with Ghoul In The Hat.

I'm going to follow him outside into the nearest alley and slit his throat with my rainbow rape knife. So, even if Wild Child picks him, they're not likely to hire his corpse. Then they'll be forced to hire me. Unless Ghoul In The Hat is actually a ghoul, in which case the ghoul surgeons will be able to stitch his head back on and he'll still be able to play for Wild Child.

Okay, I need a plan B.

I know! I'll burn Ghoul In The Hat's body!

Then he'll be totally out of commission.

I've got matches in my purse somewhere…

Ghoul In The Hat turns to the assistant guy and asks, "When do we find out if we get the job?"

The assistant, who has answered this same question repeatedly from a dozen other guitar players in the last two hours, says robotically, "We'll call you." I think it's a polite way of saying, "You don't have a chance, so get out of here."

Ghoul In The Hat walks out the front door onto the sunny street outside, letting the baking heat into the air conditioned reception room of the rented recording studio.

Instead of digging through my purse for those matches, I sink back in my waiting room seat and sigh.

At the moment, I'm fried because I've been up way too late the last two nights cramming Wild Child songs into my head and hands.

Apparently, tiredness leads to insanity.

My body burning plans are proof.

I swear, I would never *actually* hurt a ghoul. Not on purpose.

I snicker to myself.

Better to trust that my guitar playing skills and my hot black leather stage costume will be enough to win the job for me. My outfit is the same rocker chick ninja one I wore when Skin Trade played The Cobra Lounge. Skin tight low ride lace up leather pants, golden studded leather bra and jacket, bare midriff, hooker heels. When I walked from my car to the recording studio this morning, three different guys whistled at me.

Wild Child is going to love me.

The assistant checks his clipboard, lifting the sheet of paper. He reads off the next name, "Mark Kutler?"

Mark is busy thumb-typing on his iPhone. He smiles at the assistant, stands casually, and carries his guitar case toward the assistant.

I'm actually concerned about Mark Kutler. He's a big session musician in L.A. and he's really good. I've watched tons of his instructional videos online. He also has the right look for Wild Child. Handsome, shaggy hair, trim goatee, worn jeans, motorcycle boots, a faded Misfits shirt, and tattoo sleeves on both arms. He's a perfect fit for the band.

Mark and the assistant walk into the back together.

Unlike Ghoul In The Hat, Mark could easily land this gig. I need to do something about him. Luckily for me, Mark glanced at me at least twenty times while he sat on the other side of the waiting room for the past twenty minutes.

I think if I use my feminine wiles to lure Mark into a dark alley and distract him momentarily, I can conk him over the head with my guitar case. Then I'll tie him up, lock him in my trunk, and not tell anyone where he is until I'm already on the road touring with Wild Child.

That'll work.

I just need to buy some water bottles and a big bag of M&M's to leave in the trunk with Mark, and make sure I park my Altima under a shady tree so he doesn't die from the heat.

Problem solved.

The only thing left for me to do is wait patiently until they call my name.

Despite the fact I was the first person to put my name on the assistant's list this morning, they're giving preference to bigger name guitar players who showed up long after I did, like Mark Kutler.

Nobodies like me have to wait and hope for the best.

Ms. Hopeful reminds me that if I stay all day, they're bound to give me a shot eventually, right?

I cross my fingers.

Ms. Bitter decides that when I lock Mark in my trunk, he won't get water and M&M's. He'll get a gallon of Kellan's brown sewage juice and he'll like it.

Kellan's foul juice may be healthier, but if I was locked in a trunk, I'd rather have the M&M's.

I fold my arms across my chest.

Mark gets sewage juice.

I shake my head and grin.

All I can do is wait.

There's only a couple of other guitar players in the room who've been waiting and waiting with me.

I don't recognize either of them, so I *should* get called before they do.

One has been practicing Wild Child tunes on his Jackson Randy Rhoads V for the last hour. He wears headphones and is plugged into a Line 6 Pocket Pod. His unamplified guitar strings buzz tinnily. His playing is okay, but he's not as good as me.

The other guy sits in the corner. He's been chewing on his fingernails since he got here. I think he's down to the quick, and looks intent on working his way down to the bone. He's totally nervous and I bet his fingers will be bleeding before he gets called, so he won't be able to play. And I'm starting to wonder if he's actually here to audition, or if he just wandered in from the street to beat the heat.

Either way, I plan on clinching this audition the second I walk into the back and meet the band.

Chapter 82

VICTORY

The recording studio's front door opens and I hear hearty baritone laughter. I recognize it immediately.

"After you," Kellan says.

"Ladies first," a female voice says from outside.

All I can see is Kellan's hand holding the door open for someone.

"Age before beauty," Kellan says.

"Who you calling old, bitch?" the female answers gruffly.

"Your ass," Kellan laughs.

"You *like* my ass," the woman snickers. "I've seen the way you stare at it at band practice."

"Can you blame me?" Kellan laughs.

"No," the floozy says coyly. "I work hard on my ass."

The whole time they're talking, they're still standing outside, and I can't see who the floozy is, although her voice is vaguely familiar. Is it that pink haired girl named Switchblade who picked Kellan up at Rock & Roll High School the other day?

Not that I care.

Kellan chuckles, "I'll work hard on your ass if you don't squeeze it through the front door. Now move!"

The pink haired girl stumbles through the door, guitar case in hand. Yup, it's Switchblade. Kellan follows her inside. They both have guitars in hand and Kellan carries a practice amp as well.

He wears a tight t-shirt (when doesn't he) that reveals his tattooed arms, tight jeans (the crotch looks a bit snug on him, not that I pay it any attention), and motorcycle boots. Sunglasses rest on his nose. His plump lips are stretched across his pristine white teeth that beam from his tanned features.

Spectacular.

I'm *so* glad Kellan's here. Yeah, right.

I can only hope that I'll get called in first for my audition so I don't have to listen to him yammer on and on about I don't give a shit what with Switchblade, who I notice has a low cut top that reveals plenty of cleavage.

Is she here to audition too? She brought a guitar, so I'm guessing yes. Damn. I thought I was the only sexy chick guitar player. That was going to be my edge. Well, that and my playing. I wonder if Switchblade is any good? There's no way to know.

Kellan notices me at last. He chuckles, "Look who's here."

"Who?" Switchblade warbles, smiling innocently, still caught up in the good time vibe she shares with Kellan.

I'm not jealous. Why would I be? I'm here to audition.

"Victory," Kellan grins. "How are you, girl?"

Wow, he sounds lame for some reason. Probably because he's been yucking it up with Switchblade all day. Is she his girlfriend? I can't really tell. She's certainly his type: stunning and plays guitar.

Not that I care.

Kellan walks over and sets the practice amp and his guitar case on the floor next to mine. He tilts his sunglasses up on top of his head, pushing his thick hair back with them.

Damn, he has nice eyes.

I wonder if he'll say anything about my stage costume. I look super sexy in it. He's seen me in it before and liked it then.

He drops into the chair one seat away from mine, "How long you been waiting?"

"Oh, a half hour?" I lie. I glance at the two other guys, wondering if they'll say anything to correct me. They don't. Headphones is busy playing and Nails is down to his last pinky nail. Poor guy.

"That's not bad," Kellan says. "I guess there's not much of a wait?"

"I guess not," I lie. I'm not telling him I've been here six hours. And I don't think he's going to mention my stage costume. Not that it matters. I know I look good in it.

Switchblade, who looks like a punk rock stripper, wrinkles her petite nose and smiles at me, "Didn't I meet you at Kellan's work?"

Kellan's work? I work there too. "Yeah," I say absently, trying not to be overly disinterested or rude. I suddenly understand why Nails bites his fingernails because I totally feel like doing it right now myself.

"I'm Switchblade," she says, "What's your name? Victory?"

I nod, then notice she's holding out her hand to shake. I reluctantly shake it and drop it as soon as it's polite enough to let go.

She asks, "You play guitar?"

I glance at my guitar case, "Yeah?" Duh.

"Me too," she grins.

Wow, she seems dumb.

"I don't know about you," Switchblade sighs and rolls her eyes, "but I've spent the last few days immersed in Wild Child albums."

I'm not telling her I did the same. I nod absently.

She continues, "Ever since Kellan told me about the audition, I've been analyzing their music really closely. When you get deep into their song structures, it's amazing to see how widely they pull from the history of rock and blues, and even further back than that. There's a lot of classical influence in their first two albums. Kellan said it's got to be Bach and Beethoven, but I think it's more Franz Joseph Haydn and Stravinsky. Who knows," she giggles. "But I guess we can ask the band when we audition, right?"

Okay, she's not dumb.

I smile vapidly, "Yeah."

Man, it would be really awesome if Mark Kutler would finish up his audition and the assistant would walk out and call my name.

A minute later, my prayers are answered.

Mark walks out of the back, guitar case in hand.

Perfect timing. Because I keep noticing Switchblade's knee bumping against Kellan's, like she's going, "Flirt, flirt, flirt," every two seconds.

I really don't like her.

Not because she's a dumb bitch or anything, because she's not.

Just because.

Chapter 83

VICTORY

"Thanks a lot, man," Mark Kutler says to the assistant.

"Anytime, Mark," the assistant says. "I'll shoot you an email this evening."

"Solid," Mark says and bumps fists with the assistant. "Take it easy, man."

I can't tell if the assistant is being cool to Mark because it's Mark and not the Ghoul In The Hat, or because Mark's audition went well.

Hmmm.

Mark lowers the mirrored sunglasses on top of his head over his eyes and walks outside.

Do I need to follow Mark and stick him in my trunk with a gallon of Kellan's sewage juice like I planned? It's a tough call. If I do that, I might miss my chance to audition. Better to wait and hope I can impress Wild Child with my playing.

Okay, the only people in the room are me, Kellan, Switchblade, Headphones, and Nails. I'm the only one who's been here all day.

It's my turn.

The assistant peels his clipboard paper back and scans it, "Kellan

Burns?"

Fuck!

Are you kidding!

I fold my arms across my chest and hide my irritation.

Kellan cocks a smile in my direction, "That's me." He stands, grabs his guitar, and turns to Switchblade, "See you in a few."

"You want the amp?" Switchblade asks.

"No one else has one," he answers, "so I think I'm good."

She winks at him, "You sure you don't want the Jason Becker magic?"

"I'm good," Kellan says and walks into the back.

I know who Jason Becker is, but I have no idea what that reference meant. I guess it's buddy-buddy code between Kellan and his pink haired sweetheart, who I'm now stuck with.

I hope she doesn't want to chit chat.

"So," Switchblade asks, "Have you known Kellan a long time?"

I spoke too soon. I sigh, "No."

"Me neither. But he's a great guy."

"Sure." My plan is for one word answers to convey my disinterest without me having to spell it out. Switchblade is smart, so it shouldn't take long.

"So, you guys work together?"

"Yup." I pop the P for emphasis.

Switchblade smiles, "It must be fun teaching kids at the school. Kellan says he loves teaching kids. I think that's totally sweet. Don't you?"

I arch an eyebrow in response. She needs to take the hint and drop it. I really don't want to listen to her gush about how awesome Kellan is.

She says, "I've always thought it would be fun to teach, but I think I'm more impatient than the kids are," she twinkles.

I think I'm impatient for her to shut the fuck up. I'm going to reach into my purse and use my rainbow rape knife to slice her tongue out if she doesn't give it a rest soon.

Switchblade looks around the room at Nails and Headphones. I hope she's done talking.

She stretches her arms over head, displaying her boobs and cleavage to the room. Wow, she's such a slut.

I catch Nails stealing a good long look at the Switchblade Titty Show.

I frown at him.

He looks away briefly, but continues sneakily shoplifting as much of Switchblade's rack as his eyes can get away with.

Then I notice Headphones, who is still playing his Jackson, bend his high E string while gawking at Switchblade's tits. He bends the string higher and higher until it snaps. *Ping!* He looks at the broken string and whines, "Aw, man!"

I snicker.

Serves him right.

Switchblade doesn't notice the guys drooling over her. I can't tell if she's oblivious or if she does it all the time for attention. With her rack, I'm voting for attention. She knows.

Switchblade drops her arms innocently and smiles at me, "Kellan said you're a pretty good guitar player."

I blurt, "He did?"

"Yeah. And he says you're a natural with the students at the school. I totally respect that."

"Really?" Now I'm all ears.

She nods, but says no more.

Now she chooses to be tight lipped.

I sigh.

She stands up and walks to the cupboard in the corner that has a coffee brewer and columns of styrofoam cups on top. She pours herself a cup. She really does have a nice butt. I can see why Kellan was so complimentary about it earlier. Yet another reason to disdain her.

She sips her coffee and turns to me, "You want some? It tastes pretty good for waiting room coffee."

"No thanks," I smile flatly.

Wow, I get the distinct feeling my dislike for her is completely misplaced.

So why do I absolutely hate her?

Who knows.

Twenty minutes later, Kellan walks out of the back with his guitar, smiling big.

The assistant guy walks with him and says, "Tell Rich Aymes thanks from the band for sending you out." He shakes Kellan's hand firmly.

Holy shit! Did Kellan get the gig?

"Will do," Kellan grins cockily and bumps fists with the assistant.

I hate him!

The assistant slides his pen behind his ear, "You'll hear something one way or the other by next week. Thanks so much for jumping on the audition, man."

I guess he didn't get the gig?

"Any time," Kellan grins and walks over to me and Switchblade.

Switchblade blurts, "How'd it go?" She's smiling excitedly.

"Nailed it!" Kellan says confidently.

"I'm so happy for you, Kellan," she says, and jumps up to hug him, her arms around his neck. She presses her ample breasts against his chest and he hooks an arm around her narrow waist.

Kellan chuckles, "Thanks." He sets her down.

The assistant walks up behind Kellan and says, "Your friend can come in next."

Me? I'm Kellan's friend!

Switchblade stands up.

Oh. Her.

She twinkles, "See you in a minute, Kellan!"

"Good luck," Kellan says before slumping into the seat one over from me like he did earlier. Probably because he's dating Switchblade and doesn't want to sit too close to me. I can respect that.

He has boundaries.

His muscular tattooed arms are stretched over the seat backs to either side. Kellan is really a big young man who takes up a lot of space, in a hot bodied dominant male "I own the place" sort of way.

He turns his head and gives me a huge, ice-cream eating grin.

I roll my eyes, "I guess it went well?"

"You could say that," he smiles.

"Good for you." That came out a bit harsh. I try again, "I mean, great. Good job. I'm happy for you. Really." It's still coming out wrong, so I stop talking because I don't mean any of it. I want the damn gig.

"You nervous?"

"No," I say confidently.

"I heard you working over the songs back at the school the past few nights. You put in a lot of time learning Wild Child's music."

"I had to. I didn't really know the songs that well."

He nods, "I could tell."

For a second, I think he's being superior about it, but he's not. His compassion is obvious.

He continues, "I've been in your shoes before. Trying to prep for an audition you're not ready for, or isn't the right fit, or you find out about it last minute like we did, but you're determined to make it work no matter what. It sucks when that happens. No matter how hard you prepare, it's a stress fest. I guess it's just fate that I lucked out this time and knew Wild Child's music. If it had been any other band, I wouldn't have been so prepared. Me and you would've been wood shedding late nights at the school together." He pauses, looks off into space, and grins thoughtfully. After a moment, he shakes his head, "Anyway, knowing you, you'll do fine. You really know your shit, Victory."

"Thanks," I say sincerely. Wow, he's being really nice for some reason. I say spontaneously, "I drank your sewage juice."

"What?" he chuckles.

"The other night, when I stayed late working on Wild Child songs, I didn't have any food. So I bought some chips from the vending machine and took the juice you left in the fridge." I feel vaguely guilty, but Kellan's niceness drew it out of me. I can't bear to tell him I poured most of it down the sink.

He smiles, "So that's where it went." He shakes his head, "I knew there was no way Rich would steal it. He doesn't eat vegetables."

I grimace, "What was that foul taste in it?"

"Wheat grass."

"I knew it! It tasted like the bottom of a lawnmower!"

He smirks, "How would you know what a lawnmower tastes like?"

"I don't," I grin. "But my dad made me mow growing up, and your juice reminded me of the smell of a used lawnmower."

"You make it sound like that's a bad thing," he chuckles.

"I tasted your juice," I wince. "Trust me. It is."

"Does this mean I don't have to worry about you stealing more of my juice?"

"What? No!" I giggle. "I can pay you back, if you want. When I get the Wild Child gig, I'll have plenty of spare cash."

"When *you* get it?" he arches an eyebrow and chuckles, "You wish."

I slap his ribs, "I'm going to blow you out of the skies, *Smellan*. Once they hear me play, they're gonna forget your name!"

Why did I slap his ribs?

Oh well. He didn't seem to mind.

He snickers, "I'll be sure to tell the band that when I'm on the road in a cush tour bus with them."

"Don't start measuring your bus bunk bed just yet, bub! They haven't heard me play."

He jokes, "Why don't you spare them the trouble and go home before you mess up your audition?"

I can't tell he's bullshitting with me or if he's saying it in a mean way.

It doesn't matter because, for the next half hour, we chat casually about the students at Rock & Roll High School, trading teaching stories. This is the first civil conversation I've had with him in weeks. It seems so easy and comfortable.

"So I told Rich," Kellan says, finishing up another story, "either that kid starts practicing, or I swear I'm gonna—" he stops himself suddenly short.

Switchblade walks out of the back, smiling from ear to ear. She shakes her head, making her long pink hair shimmer and wave. She cheers, "Yay!"

Kellan smiles at her directly, like he completely forgot he and I were talking like good friends only a second ago.

He asks Switchblade, "You did good?"

She nods, "I knocked it out of the park like Barry Fucking Bonds!"

"Nice," Kellan grins, standing to give her a hug.

Switchblade jumps into his arms. and squeals, "Let's go celebrate!"

Boy, she really likes Kellan.

Sigh.

I mean, I don't give a shit.

Chapter 84

VICTORY

Switchblade drags Kellan out the front door while screaming about getting drinks at a bar in Los Feliz.

Headphones finally puts away his guitar. I think he tired himself out. And broke all his strings. I hope he brought spares.

Nails eyes his shoes like he wants to pull them off and go to work on his toes because his fingers are a shredded mess.

And I wait.

I really hope I get called in for the audition.

But at this point, I'm starting not to care.

I huff out a sigh.

Nails stands up and walks over to me. I hope he's not in the mood to talk.

He asks, "Do you know how long we have to wait?"

I shake my head.

His nibbled fingers are throbbing red. Poor guy. He scratches his head and says, "You know, I think I know you."

He must be mistaken. I don't associate with known nail biters.

He points at me and smiles, "Yeah! You're the girl in that video!"

What video! Everyone keeps telling me I'm in some video!

I say blandly, "The one on YouTube, right?"

"Yeah!" He hops once for emphasis.

"With the guy?"

"That's the one!" He hops again and punches down at the air.

I shake my head, "I have no idea what you're talking about."

"Oh," he says softly, disappointed. After a moment, he asks, "So, uh, are you ready to audition?"

"I'm past ready," I roll my eyes.

He holds up his battered fingers and looks at them, "I know what you mean. I'm ready to chew off my guitar calluses on my fingertips."

I wince, "Please don't?"

He drops his hands to his sides, "You're probably right." He looks around absently. "I'm really just here to meet the guys in the band. I don't stand a chance of getting the gig."

"Don't talk like that," I encourage, "you can't give up before you try."

"You're right," he nods absently. "Do you think I'll piss them off if I ask for their autographs?"

I frown, "Don't do that. Then they'll know you're an amateur."

"But it's Wild Child, man!" His eyes shine with starry wonder.

"So? If you think about it, this is just a job interview. They're not the masters of the universe of whatever."

"Are you kidding?" Nails asks in utter disbelief. "Wild Child is the biggest metal band of all time, man!"

I scoff, "Haven't you heard of Iron Maiden or Metallica or Deep Purple?"

He shakes his head, "Those guys are *classic* rock. Wild Child is cutting edge, man."

I wish he'd stop calling me man. "No they're not," I say dismissively. "They used to be, but they've been around for years."

"Maybe you're right," he nods thoughtfully. "Hey, uh, do you have a boyfriend?"

I squinch my nose, "Yeah, sorry," I lie.

Ms. Mischievous whispers in my ear, *He walked out the door with the pink haired punk rocker ten minutes ago. You never should've moved your stuff out of his apartment! What more invitation did you need!?!*

Shut up, you.

"That's cool," Nails sighs dejectedly, "Had to ask, man." He lingers, obviously looking for something else to talk about. "Your outfit is hot, man."

I fold my arms across my chest, pulling the leather jacket closed over my studded leather bra and exposed stomach.

Nails watches me do this very closely.

He's harmless. Pathetic, but harmless.

The assistant walks out a second later, "Victory Payne?"

"That's me!" I jump up from my seat, grab my guitar, and hustle past Nails.

I follow the assistant into the back of the building.

The spiky haired assistant leads me around corners in the hallway, which has framed records hanging on the wall. I'm moving so fast, I don't notice the names.

Despite my nonchalance talking to Nails, this IS a big deal. It's the first time I'm meeting huge rockstars like the guys in Wild Child, but I'm so ready for this. I'm not their number one fan, but I've heard their music for years, and I did my homework. I learned the songs. I read up about the band, learned their real names in case I need to know them, anything I could think of. I'm dressed to impress. Despite my tiredness, I will be casual but respectful. I will do my best to act like I belong in their band, like I'm the perfect fit for their particular band chemistry.

The assistant stops at the open door to the recording room and says, "After you."

I'm all smiles when I walk inside.

Chapter 85

VICTORY

I'm a little disappointed.

I was kind of expecting the entire band to be in here, instruments in hand, ready to jam, and surrounded by an entourage of their attendees like rock & roll royalty.

But it's just two people sitting behind a boring old table with a camera mounted on a tripod next to them. The room's not even that big, and it's brown walled and boring. Where's the glamour?

Oh, he's sitting behind the table.

I instantly recognize Danny Daggers of Wild Child. He has a cast on his left hand that covers his fingers and goes past his elbow. I guess the break was worse than I'd pictured.

The guy sitting next to him is clean cut and wears a sport coat over a Wild Child t-shirt, and slacks.

I take a better look at Danny because he's probably the one I need to impress most, since I'll be filling his shoes for two months.

See how I'm thinking positive? Like it's a done deal?

That $20,000 is mine.

Danny's wayward black hair is held up by a black headband. Heavy black eyeliner surrounds his eyes. Tattoos start on the backs of his fingers and climb all the way up to the sleeves of his old school RUSH t-shirt, which has the logo from RUSH's first album.

I smile at Danny and nod toward his shirt, "Working Man is my favorite track on that album."

Danny glances down at his shirt, "Oh, yeah," he chuckles, "I've always thought Alex Lifeson is one of the most underrated hard rock guitar players of all time."

"You too?!" I grin genuinely.

Okay, I already like this guy. I reach over the table to shake Danny's hand. "I'm Victory Payne." I let my leather jacket fall open. No reason not to let my bare midriff and cleavage help get me the job. But I don't over do it.

Danny stands up halfway and shakes my hand. He's a pretty big guy and has a gravelly rockstar voice. "Nice to meet you, Victory. I'm Danny."

I don't mention that I knew that already because I'm playing it cool. "Nice to meet you, Danny." I turn to the clean cut guy, extending my hand, "And you are?"

He glances up, "I'm Tom Hines. Assistant manager of the band."

"Nice to meet you, Tom."

He smiles at me, rakes his eyes up and down my body quickly, then turns to Danny, "Do you want anything to eat? I'm starving."

"Yeah," Danny says, "Can you get me a burger or a sandwich? Something with beef in it?"

It's so weird hearing Danny Daggers ask a normal human question about his lunch order. I'm slightly giddy and fan-girling inside like crazy, but I don't let it show.

Ms. Fan Girl screams, Danny eats beef! Can you believe it!! Beef!!!

Tom asks him, "You want chips or fries or something?"

"Either," Danny nods.

Ms. Fan Girl screams, Danny likes chips AND french fries!!! OMG!!!!!

Luckily, no one can hear Ms. Fan Girl except me.

Tom pats his sport coat then asks Danny, "You got any smokes? I left mine in the hotel."

Danny leans over and reaches into a backpack on the floor. He pulls out a pack of Marlboros and a lighter and hands both to Tom.

Ms. Fan Girl screams, Danny smokes!

Ms. Sensible grumbles, That's a good thing?

Tom walks out of the room, "Be right back."

"Can you shut the door so we can start?" Danny asks me.

"Sure," I smile and do so.

"You ready to shred?" Danny asks.

I nod confidently, "Totally." I set my Fender case on the floor and pull out my guitar. There's a MESA/Boogie Dual Rectifier half stack in the corner and an instrument cable plugged in. I plug the free end of the cable into my Fender and flip the Standby switch to On.

Ms. Fan Girl gushes, I'm using Danny's amp!!

A pair of powered speakers on the floor are attached to a laptop on the table next to Danny. He says, "Do you want to play along with a Wild Child track, or just wing it?"

"I can wing," I grin, "or play with the band. Do you have the album tracks, or is it live stuff?"

"It's live," Danny says, scrolling around on the laptop. "We play everything faster live. How about we start with Four On The Floor."

"I love that song. Fast cars and fast women, right?" I'm referring to the lyrics of the song.

"Yeah," he smiles. "You like fast cars?"

"Totally. My dad fixes cars for a living and taught me how to work on them," I grin.

"Cool," he nods. "How about fast women?" he arches an eyebrow and gives me a penetrating look.

What is he asking me?

Duh. He's a rockstar. He fucks groupies. He's used to a certain type of behavior from women who like his music. I can deal. It was always like this with Scott, Rex and Bobby. I'm sure Wild Child is just as much of a hard core boys club.

The only difference was that I was dating Scott, so Rex and Bobby knew to keep their hands off. This is a different dynamic.

$20,000.

I'll deal.

I throw him a curve ball, "The faster the better," I say, intending it to sound like I'm more into women than men.

"Are you fast?" he grins.

"Why don't you play the song, and I'll show you." It's a fine balance between flirtatious and professional.

Danny presses play and Four On The Floor pumps out of the speakers, starting with a rolling drum and bass riff that sounds a lot like a dragster engine. Overall, this is a fast tempo song with a machine gun guitar riff. It's a challenge to play even at the CD speed. But this is a live recording, and yes, it's even faster.

Not a problem. I have a fast right hand. I start playing at the exact same moment as the guitars on the recording and hang with them like I've played the song for years.

The lyrics to Four On The Floor are about, surprise, fast cars and doggy style sex.

"Grip my shifter
Stick it quicker
Feel your gears grind

I come from behind

Gimme four on the floor, baby
Hear my engine roar
Gimme four on the floor, baby
You know I want more"

Etc.

You get the idea.

When it gets to Danny's guitar solo, I blaze through it just fine and hit all the pinch harmonics in the right pitch and wangle my whammy bar flawlessly.

Danny nods approvingly, a big smile on his face.

When the song finishes, he claps enthusiastically. "Nice work. What did you say your name was?"

"Victory." I can't believe he already forgot. At least now he's taking me seriously.

"Wow, Victory, you're on fire, girl. Where'd you learn to play like that?"

"My dad," I smile bashfully. Have I mentioned my dad rocks? He really does.

Danny cocks his head, "How about you do another track? This time I'll film you. The boys in the band are going to be impressed. Chainsaw isn't going to believe how good you are." He turns to the camera and starts it recording. A red LED blinks on the front.

I feel better knowing the camera's running, like Danny will behave himself if we're being recorded. I don't know why I'm worried about it. I just am.

Danny chuckles, "Once they see what a piece of ass you are, they'll probably kick me out of the band!"

That's why.

So much for Danny behaving.

He slides his finger around on his laptop trackpad. "This time, play… let's see, how about… Sacrificial Princess?" He grins at me suggestively. "You know that one?"

"Yup," I say, tight lipped now.

"This time," he says, "can you move around, show me some stage presence?"

"Sure."

"And can you give me a twirl for the camera?"

"A twirl?" I ask skeptically. I know exactly what he means.

"Yeah, so we can see your… outfit."

Yeah, he totally wants to see my "outfit."

I don't twirl.

"Come on, girl, twirl for me."

"Does that really have anything to do with my playing?"

"No, but it has everything to do with you getting the gig," he says forcefully.

"Really." I say rhetorically.

He leans back in his chair and plants a booted foot on edge of the table. He is spreading his legs, which are covered in jeans, but he's displaying his royal package. "Think about it. Seventy, maybe eighty percent of our fans are men. How do you think they'll react when they see a shredder guitar girl on our stage, playing my licks like a pro? You think they're gonna boo?" He chuckles, "Hardly."

I snort, "I think you were right. They're gonna see my ass and when they hear me play, you'll be out of a job."

A sneery grin spreads across his mouth. "I like a girl with attitude."

I arch a defiant eyebrow, "Are you gonna press play so I can play Sacrificial Princess or not?"

He gives me a long, lizardy look, "I think you already are."

"Are what?" I challenge. I know where he's going.

"A sacrificial pri—"

"Play the song," I bark.

He chuckles slowly and leans forward, clicking the track pad.

The song plays through and I kill it.

This time, I unleash my full guitar goddess fury like I'm in front of 100,000 screaming fans. If they don't hire me, they're idiots.

I'm sweating by the time I finish the song.

Danny claps slowly.

I hate slow clappers. "Nice work."

I realize his face has gone red aggressive. Is he high? Mad? I can't tell. But his blood is up.

He stands and walks around the table. "You did great, except for one part on the guitar solo." He walks toward me. "Let me show you…" he reaches toward me and I don't like the look in his eyes.

"Back off, man!" I growl.

He stops and leans back, opening his arms wide, like he's showing he's not holding any weapons or wasn't about to pounce. His brows are heavy and his eyes feral. He grunts with lusty amusement, much like you would expect from a caveman who doesn't have the words to explain to the future mother of his pups that he's going to club her over the head and drag her back to his cave to start the baby making.

Who does this guy think he is?

He slurs, "I thought you wanted the gig?"

"I do."

"Then show me how bad you want it..."

I've never heard of a heavy metal casting couch, but obviously there is one.

My inner Ms. Fan Girl wilts pathetically, her heart broken.

Danny leans toward me.

I grab the neck of my guitar with my left hand to stabilize it, ball my right hand into a fist, and cold cock him in the fucking eye.

"Ow!" He staggers backward, covering his injured eye with his good hand. His arm with the cast wiggles in the air like a limp snake or a limp dick, whichever fits. "What the fuck was that?" he whines.

I smirk, "What? Don't you speak caveman?" I smile sarcastically, "That was 'NO!' in caveman."

"Fuck, woman, why did you do that?!"

"My name is Victory, not woman. And I could ask you the same thing. Man."

That's pretty much the point at which my audition for Wild Child went into the toilet.

I literally picture someone dumping a stack of hundred dollar bills into a toilet bowl and flushing away $20,000. One of those high horsepower public bathroom toilets.

WHOOSH!

That $20,000 leaves the building so quick, I don't even have a chance to wave goodbye.

My collective internal committee weeps crocodile tears at the lost money while consoling Ms. Fan Girl with loving pats and tender "There, theres."

Not one of them sheds a tear for Danny Daggers' eye, which is going to be purple and yellow by tomorrow morning.

He should've listened when I told him my name was Victory Payne.

I guess he thought I said Shrinking Violet.

His bad.

Chapter 86

VICTORY

My botched audition makes me hungry for beef.

I feel kind of cavewomanish at the moment. I'm not worried about counting calories tonight.

Blame Danny Daggers.

I end up driving to Zankou Chicken in the heart of Little Armenia, which is basically East Hollywood. I call Olivia on the way because she lives close by. She's home and drives over to meet me.

I order Lule Kebab plates for both of us from the yellow shirted cashier. Everyone behind the counter wears matching yellow Zankou Chicken shirts which match the yellow formica bench tables

I sit down to wait for the food.

Liv walks in through the glass front door a few minutes later. An aqua blue silk scarf covers her hair and matches her 1950s aqua dress. She wears vintage movie star sunglasses that have dark green lenses and tortoise shell frames.

"Darling!" she squeaks when she sees me. "There you are!" Her white pumps click when she walks across the brown tiled floor. She holds both hands high, elbows down, like a pretend rich-bitch socialite. Her white handbag is hooked around one elbow.

She removes her sunglasses, leans down, and air kisses my cheek with her candy apple red lips.

"Did you drive over in a convertible?" I ask.

"No, why?"

"Your scarf."

"Oh, this old thing? I just felt like wearing it."

"You really need to get a convertible to go with that outfit," I grin.

She drops into the bench seat across from me. "Do you think the yellow formica goes with my dress?" she asks askance.

"Picture perfect," I smile.

She still has her hands high, elbows low. "I'm picturing myself in a 1950 mint green Buick Super convertible."

"I don't have a clear picture of it."

She pulls out her phone and finds a picture on Wikipedia. "Here," she holds out her phone. "What do you think?"

I look at it appreciatively, "How did you come up with that one?"

"Watching old movies, I guess."

"The only thing you need is a long scarf to trail behind you and flutter in the breeze when you drive to pick up Rock Hudson or Cary Grant."

"I was thinking both of them. I know Rock would be into the three way, but I'm not so sure about Cary. Anyway, one or both of them would be dynamite."

I blurt laughter, "You need your own reality show, Liv!"

"Good idea! It might help me get my stalling recording career off the ground! Speaking of, when are we going to rehearse again with Lucas and Logan? Now there's a three way I'm dying to try!" she laughs melodiously.

"What," I grin, "You haven't been there, done that, already?"

"Oh, I wish! I'd move to Utah if I could marry both of them!"

I laugh heartily. "Wow, Liv, you are in heat! Do I need to have you spayed?"

"I doubt it would help," she rolls her eyes. "Where's the food? I'm starving. All this talk about three-ways and heat is making me hungry," she pants. "If I don't eat soon, I'm going to bite somebody."

"Then we'd better get you rabies shots first," I joke.

"I can't wait that long," she barks.

"Hold your horses, Liv. They're making ours right now."

We both glance at the open kitchen, which is covered floor to ceiling in stainless steel kitchen equipment. The yellow-shirted Zankou staff tend to the cones of meat rotating in front of orange heat coils and the sizzling kebabs on the grill.

Olivia hops up and walks to the counter. She is a ball of energy. She grabs utensils and napkins while she waits. As soon as the cashier sets the orange plastic tray on the counter, Olivia pounces on it and clacks back to our table.

Our Lule Kebab plates each contain two strips of ground steak, seasoned rice, a pile of hummus with a puddle of olive oil in the center, spiced onions, tomatoes, and pickled pink vegetables. It comes with pita bread and this creamy garlic sauce which is 100% bad for you and tastes 100% the bomb.

Me and Liv chow down.

Olivia eats delicately but ravenously. She rolls her eyes dramatically, "I *love* eating meat." She moans and groans and chews.

"What kind of meat?" I titter.

"The male kind. This is bull meat, right?" She looks around for confirmation.

I quip, "I think it's cow."

"It doesn't matter. Girl meat is just as good."

I laugh. "Liv, you are such a nut."

"Mmmm, nuts would be good." She winces, "But shaved, please. I hate hairy nuts."

I spit laugh rice out of my mouth but manage to catch it in my hand. "Liv!" I suck down a sip from my water cup, trying not to choke. I wipe my hand on a paper napkin.

"Speaking of nuts," she grins, "when was the last time you cracked any?"

"Uh..." I chuckle, "I assume you mean the kind that don't require a nutcracker?"

She gestures with her fork, which has a hunk of meat on the end, "Oh, the flesh kind need cracking now and then too. Keeps the men at heel."

"What, like dogs?" I laugh.

"Sure. I bet if you'd cracked Scott's nuts more often, he wouldn't have done what he did."

An image pops into my head of Liv chasing a naked Scott through the streets, holding a wooden soldier nutcracker in hand and clacking the jaw piece repeatedly while yelling, "You better run! If I catch you, I'm making nut butter!" I snicker to myself.

"What?" Liv grins.

"Nothing," I smile. I don't want to give her any ideas. Liv has follow through like you wouldn't believe. I say, "Anyway, I think I came out ahead when it comes to Scott. I'm not missing him at all."

"You have your eye on someone else?"

"Uh...not really."

She scrutinizes my face and blots her lips with a napkin. "You took a long time to answer, sister. And your tone suggests otherwise."

I sigh and spear a bite of meat kebab with my fork, "I guess."

"Guess what? That some hot stud wants to bang your bones?"

"Liv!?!"

"Does Mr. Stud have a name?"

Do I want to open this can of worms? Liz might eat every single one. "No," I joke. "He's just some hot guy I saw in a fashion magazine."

"You're lusting over a photo?" she asks skeptically. "This is L.A.! Call the magazine, find out who the photographer or model is, and call him up! A bottle of hot sauce like you won't have any troubles turning on a fashion magazine man."

Fine, I'll tell her. "I know him."

She sips her straw. "You do! Do tell!"

"Actually, I work with him."

"What! Has he sexually harassed you yet?"

"No," I giggle.

Olivia frowns, "Why not? Are you playing hard to get?"

"No."

"Then corner him in the broom closet or whatever and hike up your skirt! It's not rocket science."

I roll my eyes. Liv can be very tiring, but I love her. I laugh, "I think he's seeing someone."

"No problem. We'll follow her home, bash her over the head with a frying pan, and bury her in the desert outside of Vegas. Problem solved.

We can do it tonight and be back by morning."

I grin. Yeah, I love Liv. I don't know why I stopped hanging out with her. Oh yeah. Scott. He was such a monopolizer. In fact, now that I think about it, it wasn't me who pushed away my friends. It was Scott being overly controlling. Why did I let him?

Olivia asks seriously, "Do you have a frying pan in your car? We can get one from my apartment if you don't."

"No," I laugh. "Anyway, I don't know if I want to get into anything right now."

She gives me a serious look, "All you're getting into is some guy's pants. You don't have to marry him." She tears off a triangle of pita and dabs it in the little plastic cup of creamy garlic sauce.

"I'm not like that, Liv. I don't just 'bang' guys."

"Neither do I. I make mad passionate love to each one. Sometimes I call them back."

I chuckle, "I can't do that. My feelings always get in the way."

"Feelings are for 20th century women. This is the space age, Victory."

"I thought the space age was in the 60s or whatever?"

"Same diff. Anyway, you don't have to love a guy to sleep with him." She pauses thoughtfully, "Like is usually good enough, but a rousing hate fuck is always fun."

I slump in my seat. Olivia has exhausted me. I joke, "Okay, I'll sleep with the first guy I see."

The side door of Zankou chicken opens up at that moment and a homeless guy in tattered rags with tape around his battered mismatched tennis shoes bends down in front of the square trash bins beside the door, pushes the little swinging rectangle lid up with a squeak, and peaks inside the bin, looking for leftovers.

Olivia blurts laughter, "Go get him!"

"Um…no?" I giggle.

"You said you would!" she jeers.

I wince, "You first?"

"Okay!" she titters. "But you have to shave him! Remember, I said no hair!"

I mutter so the bum won't hear. "He has lizard skin, and I'm pretty sure lizards don't have hairy balls. So he's ready for you, Liv. Go get him!"

Olivia sinks down in the yellow bench seat and cackles heartily, her hands resting on her spasming belly.

Chapter 87

VICTORY

Me and Olivia end up in Los Feliz after we finish our food at Zankou.

We bar hop randomly, trying to find a fun vibe. Not because I'm unconsciously looking for Kellan. Seriously. Because I didn't tell Liv that Switchblade took Kellan to Los Feliz.

Los Feliz was Liv's idea.

She must have ESPed it out of me.

The last bar we hit is The Dresden Lounge on Vermont Avenue in the heart of downtown Los Feliz. The Dresden is the bar featured in the movie Swingers, and it still looks the same. I absolutely love the dark sultry ambiance. It's a time warp back to 1950s lounge culture. Wood paneling mixed with stone, vinyl booths and hanging globes of light.

The place is packed with hipsters and random Angelenos.

Liv pushes through the crowd like an insistent mongoose until we make it up to the bar.

Marty and Elayne, the husband and wife jazz duo featured in Swingers playing Stayin' Alive by the Bee Gees, are busy working their music magic. Marty is on drums, Elayne is on keyboard and they're both improvising vocals over various romantic jazz standards. These two have been playing here for over thirty years and totally love each other. They kind of remind me of Johnny and Karen. I don't know why Johnny and Karen opened a guitar shop when they could be playing music every night like Marty and Elayne.

Who knows.

Liv orders vodka cranberries and hands me a glass.

She says, "This place is packed with men. You should be able to find someone in here who isn't homeless."

"Just because they're dressed nice doesn't mean they aren't living in a van or an RV."

"True," Liv says thoughtfully, "L.A. does have a thriving caravan culture. I know a guy who lives in an RV and moves it around to different neighborhoods. He says it's cheaper than having an apartment. I couldn't do it. I need a hot shower on a daily basis."

"I think you need a cold shower on a daily basis," I grin.

She winks, "I've got toys for that at my apartment. Which reminds me, I need to buy more batteries. I'm all out."

I roll my eyes and sip my vodka cranberry. Luckily, I have a belly full of fatty Zankou yumminess, so I'm not worried about being too drunk to drive on one drink. But Liv has a high metabolism and will get tipsy quickly, leaving me as the designated driver.

"So, pick a guy already," she flaps her fingers at the crowded room, "There's at least five eligible candidates in here tonight."

I glance around skeptically, "Where?"

"That guy at the end of the bar. The guy sitting in front of Marty and Elayne with the knit beanie. The guy standing by the front door—"

"How do you do it, Liv? You've got this whole place mapped out."

"What? I simply take note as I pass by each one. Like that guy over their, the Man Bomb standing talking to the girl with pink hair."

I turn my head. Oh no! It's Kellan and Switchblade! If I say anything to Liv, she will berate me into talking to him until I do, or if I resist, wheel me over strapped to a hand truck and move my mouth for me like I'm a talking puppet.

I sip my drink, trying to cover my nerves.

Olivia eyes me suspiciously, "Do you know him?"

I maintain a poker face.

Liv's eyes light up, "Your poker face means yes!"

Shit.

"You know that Man Bomb! Is that the guy you work with?"

I roll my eyes.

"Let's go talk to him!" She yanks me through the crowd by the wrist before I can resist, nearly giving me whiplash.

I shake my head, smiling. Liv is bordering on being a frienemy tonight. Not really. She's too much fun for that.

"What's his name?" Liv barks, stopping far enough away that Kellan hasn't seen us yet.

"Bill," I lie.

"His name isn't *Bill*," she admonishes. "A guy that hot is not named Bill!"

I sigh and roll my eyes, "Aiden."

She scrutinizes my face and says reluctantly, "Okay, I believe you. That better be his name," she threatens.

"It is!" I lie. She deserves it.

Liv runs up to Kellan, screaming, "Aiden! So good to see you!" She throws her arms around Kellan's neck.

He looks surprised. But he also looks like he's used to this sort of behavior from strange women.

I'm close enough I can hear what they say next, but Kellan can't see me where I stand behind a couple of tall guys watching Marty and Elayne play.

"Hey," Kellan says casually, rolling with Liv's bizarre behavior. "Do I know you?"

"Of course you do, Aiden!" Liv squeals. "Don't you remember?"

Kellan cocks a grin, "Refresh my memory."

"Vegas? New Year's Eve 2013?"

"Oh yeah," Kellan says.

I can't believe him! Does he just assume he hooked up with her even if he doesn't remember?

Switchblade snickers at Kellan, "Does this always happen to you?"

"Yeah," he chuckles. "Usually."

Oh my gawd. He's so full of himself.

Switchblade laughs and asks Liv, "What's your name, honey?"

Liv grins, "My name is Lisa." She slaps Kellan coquettishly on the chest, "You remember that, don't you, Aiden? You said you were going to have it tattooed on your wrist. Did you?" Liv's arms shoot out like a chameleon's sticky tongue and she grabs his left hand aggressively. She turns his arm wrist up. "It must be the other one." She drops it and grabs his right arm. "It's not here! You promised, Aiden! You said you would!" She whines and stamps her foot. And I think her eyes swivel in two different directions at once, just like a chameleon.

Liv is doing an amazing job of mimicking a psycho crazy ex-hookup. But it's only partially an act in her case. I think her plan is to scare off Switchblade. So far, it isn't working.

Switchblade seems amused by it all.

Wow, she must be a really understanding girlfriend.

No wonder Kellan likes her so much.

"Aiden," Liv laughs throatily, "Since you didn't get a tattoo like you *promised*, let's go get one right now!" She pulls at his arm.

Switchblade asks, "Why does she keep calling you Aiden?"

Kellan shrugs.

He doesn't care. Male slut!

I decide it's time to call off the attack dogs. In Liv's case, it's more of a purse dog thing, but still dangerous because of the rabies.

I walk out of the crowd.

"Victory?" Kellan says, amused.

"Hey, Kellan," I sigh.

"Hey, Victory," Switchblade smiles genuinely. She really is nice. The consummate catch.

"Kellan?" Liv asks. "Who's Kellan?"

"Me," he nods.

Liv frowns at me, "I thought you said his name was Aiden!"

"I did," I grin and sip my drink.

"Traitor!" she shouts. "You could be beheaded for that in some countries!"

I giggle.

Liv recovers, "It doesn't matter. Let's take Aiden to that tattoo parlor," she says archly.

Kellan chuckles, "Do I look like I need more ink?"

He doesn't.

"Yes!" Liv barks like a high-pitched purse dog, "Let's go!" She pulls his arm.

Switchblade laughs at all of this. Is she not his girlfriend? I can't really tell. But she's way up in his personal space like she is, standing one inch away from him the whole time. Maybe that's cuz the bar is crowded? I don't know.

Switchblade asks me, 'Does your friend have rabies?"

She read my mind.

Liv growls, "Yes! So watch out! I bite!"

"I bite too," Switchblade chuckles.

What does that mean? Maybe she likes to fight. With her punk rock look, I can picture it.

"Let's go, Liv," I pull on her arm. I don't want her getting snapped in half by Switchblade.

Switchblade says to Liv, "I thought you said your name was Lisa?"

"I did! And his name is Aiden, and we need to go!" She pulls on Kellan's arm and grunts ineffectually.

Kellan laughs, "Easy, Lisa, or Liv, or Loca, or whatever your name is. You're going to break the merchandise."

Liv scowl-smiles, "You look like you could break a bull in half, I'm not worried about hurting you. Let's go." Liv yanks like she's pulling on a building.

"Relax," Kellan says casually, "I don't want you to pull a muscle."

Liv relents, "Fine." She drops her hands to her sides. "I tried."

"Tried what? " Kellan asks.

Liv opens her mouth to speak but I slap my hand over it.

Time for damage control.

"We should go," I giggle nervously and pull Liv into the crowd.

Liv twinkles her nose and waves goodbye, "We'll always have New Year's Eve 2013, Aiden!"

Liv is definitely loca.

Chapter 88

VICTORY

I drop Liv off at her apartment and put her to bed. We left her car parked in Los Feliz because she was way too loaded to drive by the end of the night.

I wanted to stay and chat with Kellan and Switchblade and tell them about my botched audition with Wild Child, but Liv had an attack plan and she wasn't veering from it. I wonder if Danny Daggers put the moves on Switchblade too?

I'll have to ask her some other time.

When Liv is dozing sleepily in her bed, I drive back to Johnny and Karen's apartment to crash.

I unlock the door and set my Fender case on the floor.

I listen for the telltale moans and gasps of sexual pleasure.

Silence.

Thank the goddesses.

For once, Johnny and Karen aren't having noisy sex in their bedroom. The bedroom door is open, which means they're out for the evening.

I grab sweats and walk into the bathroom to shower. I turn on the water to warm it up and peel off my stage outfit, which is sticky at this point. I got a lot of looks wearing it out tonight. But none from anyone I wanted to go home with.

Liv sure tried to hook me up with every cute guy she could find, but I wasn't feeling it.

I step into the hot shower and soak in the soothing water. After I finish and towel off, I slide into my sweats and climb under the covers on the couch and close my eyes. Today was way longer than necessary and I was tired going in.

Sleep should be easy, but visions of Kellan sneak into my mental theater.

He's too good looking. I mean, he should be outlawed. Those muscles and tattoos and burning eyes.

I'm not going to sleep thinking about him.

So I imagine one of those long vaudeville hooks pulling Kellan off the stage of my mental theater. He's replaced by three identical Livs who tap dance onto the stage doing synchronized soft shoe, twirling regular sized canes in their hands in time with some Al Jolson song or something.

I giggle sleepily as I picture the image.

Liv would've been great on a real vaudeville stage alongside Charlie

Chaplin or Lucille Ball or whoever.

I slowly drift to sleep…

…until a knock at the door wakes me.

Is it Johnny and Karen?

They have their own keys.

Who could it be?

I peel back my covers in slow motion and float to the front door.

I don't even think to check the peephole for prowlers. I just open it.

"Kellan?" I gasp. "How did you know where I lived?"

He wears nothing but black leather pants and is surrounded by a glowing purple mist and back lit by purple light that pulses through a range of violet hues. It doesn't seem weird. I just go with it.

He strides purposefully into the apartment. His brow is heavy and dark. His eyes burn, like, literally. They have little flames in them. He looks dangerous. A lone lock of hair dangles in front of one burning eye.

He grabs my hair in his fist and yanks my head back forcefully. He bites my neck without asking.

I don't think to tell him how impolite that is. But I do believe he's going to fuck, I mean suck, my blood.

I never pictured Kellan as a vampire. But he certainly could play one in a big screen movie.

He lifts me up and I wrap my legs around his waist. He holds me low, my core against his crotch, and carries me deep into the apartment until my back presses against a wall. I wrap my legs tighter and he presses harder into me.

The purple mist surrounds us like impossibly thick glowing fog.

"Oh, Kellan," I moan.

"Victory," he purrs, his lips caressing my neck. "I need you…"

I feel heat in my veins. Is it because he's a vampire and I'm infected with vampirus virus? Has his immortal blood hunger become mine, and we'll live like creatures of the night until eternity ends?

I can hang with that.

His lips are so full, so warm, so comforting, I lose myself in them. Heat, pressure, need, hunger. His tongue invades me, diving into me with desperate passion. Strong hands clench my ass, digging into the muscles, sending bolts of pleasure into my pelvis.

My electric breasts hum with need.

Kellan responds by licking, squeezing, pressing, releasing.

I am hot, I am wet, and I need more of this vampire man.

He grabs the collar of my t-shirt and tears the shirt wide open, exposing my heavy breasts. He gazes down at them with desire, his eyes aflame.

"Yes…" he hisses, "yes…"

His mouth dives at my breast and he consumes it, sinking his teeth into my nipple. I feel my lifeblood flow into him, his into mine, as we commingle our heated need. I am infected with his strange animal desire, and I know that my eyes now burn with the same fire I see in Kellan's.

"Kellan…" I whisper.

He thrusts his pelvis up into me, pressing against my now wet flesh. He grunts with pent up desire, a caged animal in need of release. He pounds his leather clad crotch into me, "I…" *pound,* "need…" *pound,* "you…"

Each thrust sends pure lust up my spine.

I unhook my legs and slide down his chiseled abs, my mouth nearing his hot manhood. I can see it glowing red beneath his black leather pants. I rip them open and he's a red hot raging rod of fire, like a sword pulled from a blacksmith's forge, glowing orange and hot and ready.

I stand, and we both gaze down at his fiery weapon in awe.

In a seething, deep, manly voice, he says, "Quench my fire, woman."

In the moment, there is nothing remotely comical. I nod seriously.

He lays me down on a bed of clouds and I open myself to him.

He plunges his hot red cock into me.

There is a loud hiss and puff of steam as my wetness cools his need.

But it only takes seconds before I feel his heat reignite inside me.

He begins thrusting.

I need you…

The pleasure I feel is indescribable.

I need YOU…

I've never felt a man as deeply as I feel Kellan.

She's asleep…

He stokes my fires like the god of fire.

Take me, lover…

My hair ignites, and I am a woman of flame.

Take me now…

I am lost in the fire of Kellan Burns. He is inside me, thrusting deeply into my core, into my heart, taking me out of this world into another, better one. I rise on his heat as he fills me with flames.

I am intimately aware of his thrusting fire, his insatiable need, and my pleasure. My hot, wet, slippery pleasure.

I want more.

He takes me as he gives, fills me as I swallow him.

Oh…

The beginning of an orgasm twines around my legs like a serpent of flame.

Yes...

I feel Kellan's burning breath against my ear as he moans with his own pleasure.

Aaahhh!!!

The serpent of flame coils around my thighs, forcing them apart as it slides inside me, into my volcanic center.

Ooohhh!!!

Fire explodes in my pelvis, filling me with ecstasy.

I'm coming.

Oh, god, I'm coming!

The fire snake fills my chest, rushes up my throat, and pours out my mouth in an exploding geyser of magma.

I scream my ecstasy...

JOHNNY!!!

...What?!?!

I open my eyes and Kellan isn't on top of me.

No one is on top of me.

I'm in Johnny and Karen's dark apartment.

No purple glow.

No Kellan.

But my fingers are pinned between my thighs doing who knows what. I swear, I didn't put them there!

"Yes! Johnny, Yes!" Karen shouts from the bedroom.

"Oooaaaggghhh!" Johnny groans.

I yank my slick fingers out of my crotch.

Johnny and Karen's headboard bangs against the bedroom wall repeatedly.

Karen shouts, "YES, YES, YES, YES!!"

I drape my forearm over my eyes and laugh-cry fake tears. I think the Northridge fault line decided now was a good time to shake the apartment once again. This time, the earthquake scientists are all pointing at me and laughing.

I really, really, really need to get my own place.

"OOOOH!" Karen moans.

Tonight.

I grab my pillow from behind my head and jam it in my face.

Can you suffocate yourself with a pillow?

I think I'll try right now.

"KAREN!!" Johnny shouts.

"JOHNNY!!" Karen wails.

Kill me now.

Because the pillow isn't working.

"WEEEEEEE!!" Karen squeals.

Chapter 89

KELLAN

I'm fucking Victory plain old missionary style and it's the greatest sex I've ever had in my entire life. We're in a circular room and the walls are made of Marshall speaker cabinets stacked upward into eternity like we're in some rock & roll nirvana having religious sex like the gods intended. It's sex, it's love, it's rock & roll, it's passionate, and it's connected.

It's incredible.

Until I wake up and realize I'm dry fucking my sheets.

My arms are wrapped around my pillow like it's a cotton girl.

Not much of a turn on.

She doesn't have arms, legs or a head. I know that's what some guys prefer, but not me. I like a whole person.

I flop onto my back and rip off the top sheet and throw it in the corner in a wad. The heat of the day is still stuck in the billion tons of cement that make L.A., which includes my oven of an apartment. I twist the knob on the A/C mounted in the window above my headboard, seeking relief.

That's not gonna help anytime in the next five minutes.

I get out of bed and walk to my bathroom. My dick is a raging red sword and leads the way like Russell Crowe in the beginning of Gladiator when he charges into battle on horseback, waving his own raging sword in the air.

Hold the Fucking LINE!!!

Or whatever.

I step into the shower and crank the water onto full cold. It comes out hot at first then cools to slightly less than tepid. L.A. pipe water is never actually cold in the middle of summer. That said, the point of the cold water is to cool my body temperature, not reduce my sex drive.

That cold shower shit is a myth.

I rub one out with my eyes closed, pretending I'm banging Switchblade's awesome ass from behind. Not that I've ever seen it pantsless. And I still haven't figured out if she's really gay or not. But in my imagination, she's sick for the dick and we fuck like rabbits and live in a rock & roll beach mansion in Cancún or Bora Bora or wherever the water is ice blue and the beaches are silver and gold.

And it's totally not working. I'm not turned on at all.

Then an image of Victory in her hot ass heavy metal hooker costume, the one she wore on stage with Skin Trade the night I met her, and again today at the Wild Child audition, stomps all over my Switchblade fantasy.

Get out!

I squeeze my eyes shut hard, doing my best to picture Switchblade and our tropical beach mansion.

Dammit.

It's not working.

I scroll through my extensive mental Pinterest list of the finest hotties I've hooked up with and I populate my fantasy beach mansion with all of them. I can see Switchblade on some red velvet bed surrounded by two dozen tight bodied hotties in a sex bedroom.

It's like the fucking Playboy Mansion in my head.

But it isn't helping my rager. I'm never going to sleep tonight until my boiler blows.

Sorry, Switchblade, honey. You're just not doing it for me tonight.

I roll mental video of all the supernatural sex sessions I've had in the past, trying to find a particularly intense one. There's quite a few to chose from. I snicker to myself.

I've had some mind blowing orgasms.

It's a fact that men can have multiple orgasms.

You just need to learn how to relax your dick muscles and not shoot your load when you get the orgasm rush. You can have as many as you want, believe me. It's best when you've got a girl who gives amazing head or wants to keep fucking after she has an orgasm. The kind of girl who absolutely loves incredible sex…

(*Giselle*)

I can't deal with that right now.

I tilt my head back under the shower head and let water cleanse my face.

I go back in my mind through all the incredible and meaningless sex I've had with countless pinup hotties. There's gotta be something in my back catalog that will get me off so I can go back to sleep.

Sadly, it's like surfing internet porn. There's too much to choose from.

Fuck it.

I don't have a choice tonight.

I'm going with the obvious.

I picture Victory in that studded leather bra, her flat stomach, her perfect waist and legs, her long hair, and her incredible face. And those eyes, those spirited, rambunctious, fun-loving eyes…

Victory…

I hear her guitar playing in my head.

I hear the two of us playing together the night she slept right here in my apartment and recorded that video with me. And I remember how she

(*Giselle*)

showered in this very shower.

I didn't get to see Victory naked, but I was totally tempted to tear the shower curtain off when I brought her all that shampoo just so I could get a good look, but I didn't. I'm respectful like that. But damn, I wanted to and I can totally picture her naked from head to toe, right inside the shower with me, her hands caressing me, sliding up and down my shaft, cupping my balls, teasing the head, her tongue hot, wet, ravenous…

That's when hot butter fills me from the ankles up, heat rising up my legs in mellow waves. Tickling pleasure in my dick trips me over the edge and my whole body rushes out the end of my cock in a geyser of heat release.

My back arches and I hiss out a grunty, "Fuck!"

I realize I'm breathing hard and that was a really fucking good orgasm.

Jerking off doesn't usually feel this good.

Damn.

That was a first.

I glance down and watch my load circle down the drain.

I feel a distinct sense of emptiness.

That was lame.

I never feel empty after an orgasm. I always feel satisfied.

What the fuck is this emptiness shit?

And why didn't I bang Red when she took me home from The Canal Club?

(*Victory*)

Red was way hot and ready.

What's my fucking

(*Victory*)

problem?

I lean my head back under the spray and let the cold water soak my hair and wash down my face for a long time.

Eventually, my skin is no longer broiling to the touch. The shower water feels like cold needles because it has finally lowered my body temperature to the point that I'm almost shivering.

I twist off the squeaky shower knobs and don't bother to towel off before trudging back to bed. It's so freakin' hot in my apartment, all the water will dry in an hour, and I'll be broiling once again.

I need to get a better A/C, and goddammit, I need to get laid. It's been something like a month since the last time I had sex. That's gotta be some kind of a record for me. I'm practically a born again virgin at this point.

All because of fucking Victory.

Or should I say, not fucking Victory.

Man, that chick rattles my nuts.

In a bad way.

Chapter 90

VICTORY

The morning is muggy.

The sun is already up, preheating the day to 350, which is the right temperature to bake brains. I know, because I'm trudging along like a zombie through the Hollywood neighborhood near Johnny and Karen's apartment. Palm trees line both sides of the street. It's all small apartment buildings in this part of town. No houses.

I did manage to sleep some last night.

After Johnny and Karen wore themselves out.

I don't know how they do it so much. They're worse than teenagers.

I left the apartment early to seek out some coffee and some peace and quiet before I head into the guitar shop. I also need some space from the two lovebirds before I spend the rest of the day glaring at them behind their backs for ruining my Kellan fantasy.

That was only slightly embarrassing.

My phone rings while I'm walking down the sidewalk.

I pull it out of my pocket and answer, "Julian Whittaker," I chuckle. "I didn't expect to hear from you."

"Victory…" I can hear him smiling "I've missed you."

"You have?" I grin.

"You have no idea," he chuckles.

"Where were you?"

"I was in Sweden."

"I know, Colette told me. What were you doing there?"

"I was stuck in a recording studio."

"That's a bad thing?" I ask skeptically.

"This time it most certainly was," he laughs.

This is the first time I've spoken to Julian since the night he took me to Trois Mec for dinner. And threw me against the side of his Ferrari back at his house and snuck his fingers between my legs.

I repress a sudden shiver as I remember the night.

And…

"Hey!" I blurt. "You were supposed to call me to come by the studio to listen to whatever top secret project you and Max were working on!"

Julian chuckles guiltily, "My sincerest apologizes. Things got a little carried away. When you're dealing with a prima donna, it's bound to happen."

"Prima donna? Who, me?" I'm offended.

"No," he laughs, "Layce."

"Wait, did you just say Layce?"

"I did," he chuckles. "You most definitely are not a prima donna, my dear Victory."

I don't even register his last words because my head is still bouncing, "You mean *the* Layce? Number one selling pop mega star LAYCE Layce?"

"Yes," Julian says, "the very same."

"Was she the reason you bailed on me after our dinner date that night?" And left me hot and bothered and never called? Julian is pretty typical for a guy. Should I even be talking to him?

"Sadly, yes. It wasn't my choice, believe me…" his voice trails off suggestively. "I would much rather have spent that evening with you, Victory."

I shiver pleasantly, thankful for the fact we're on the phone and not face to face.

"So," I ask, "What did you and Max have to do that night? And in Sweden?"

"How about I tell you over breakfast? Are you hungry?"

"I could eat some food," I grin. I want to say no, but I'm way too curious to hear about Julian working with Layce. That is a big deal. He's rubbing elbows with one of the most successful pop stars on the planet. I can only imagine what part he plays in the whole process. I guess I didn't realize how big a deal Julian actually is.

He asks, "Where are you? I'll come get you right now."

"Oh, I need a few minutes to get cleaned up. Can you pick me up at 9:30?"

"Certainly. Just give me the address."

I do.

He says, "I'll see you at 9:30, sharp."

Chapter 91

VICTORY

Julian takes me to THE Blvd in Beverly Hills for breakfast. It's on the corner of Wilshire Boulevard and Rodeo Drive, the epicenter of swanky upscale L.A., on the ground floor of the Beverly Wilshire Hotel.

Everything about THE Blvd is upscale. You know it before you walk in the doors. A flaming orange Lamborghini Diablo and an angry carbon black Hennessey Venom GT are parked in the white loading zone in front of the hotel.

Julian valets his Ferrari 458 Spider, which seems inferior compared to the super cars parked on Wilshire.

We walk inside the plush art deco restaurant.

Every table inside is full. People mill around the entrance, obviously trying to look important while they wait.

Based on the crowd, I get the impression that Julian and I won't sit down to eat for at least two hours. If we wait, I'll be late for work.

Maybe Julian will give up and we can go someplace less crowded. And less intimidating.

Julian glances at me, "Wait right here." He strolls over to the maitre d'.

The maitre d' smiles immediately and they chat briefly.

I hear the maitre d' say, "Yes, sir. Right away, sir." He strides purposefully toward the back of the restaurant.

Julian turns and grins at me. He's wearing a misty blue double breasted summer suit that is a striking contrast to his always tan skin and goldenblond hair. He must've gotten a lot of sun in Sweden. Do they even get sun up there, or does he tan regularly? Either way, it looks good on him.

He walks up to me and leans toward my ear and mutters, "We'll be seated shortly."

He's obviously proud of his ability to make things happen in a ritzy place like this.

True to his word, we're seated right away and handed leather menus.

The waiter walks up shortly after and clasps his hands together, "Would the lady like a mimosa for starters?"

I wrinkle my nose and whisper at Julian across the table, "What's a mimosa? It sounds like a flower."

Julian grins.

The waiter obviously overhears and is about to say something but defers to Julian and says, "Would you care to explain, sir?"

"Certainly," Julian smiles at me. "A mimosa is champagne and chilled citrus. Either orange or grapefruit."

The waiter looks at me, "We serve only the finest fresh squeezed Valencia oranges with Veuve Clicquot BRUT."

I know what orange juice is, and I know they grow them in Valencia up north, but the other part, I have no idea. I giggle stupidly. I can't help it. I don't speak rich.

"You'll like it," Julian encourages.

"Okay?" I wince.

The waiter arches his eyebrows, still clasping his hands together, "A glass for the lady?"

"Sure," I nod.

Julian smiles casually, "I'll have one as well."

"Very good, sir," the waiter says before walking off.

I look around at the people sitting at the tables. Everyone is dressed in expensive yet casual clothes. I don't know how, but it's obvious no one here shops at Target or the mall. Except me. I'm wearing the same cutoff denim shorts I wore on my first date with Julian. But at least it's a different t-shirt.

"Oh my god," I whisper, "is that Kim and Kanye?"

Julian turns to look.

"Don't look!" I hiss, "It's rude!"

"What do I care?" he chuckles. "Do *you* care?"

"Yes! I can't be seen with *them*!" I say sarcastically.

Julian chuckles, "You're a gem, Victory. Do you know that?"

I shrug and grin.

When the mimosas arrive, I sip mine enthusiastically. "That's yummy."

Julian raises his for a toast, "To yummy alcoholic beverages for breakfast."

I smile, "I can drink to that."

We clink and I sip again. I wonder if drinking on an empty stomach before breakfast after I slept poorly is a good idea?

Who cares.

It's not like I'm going to do anything stupid.

A tall handsome guy strolls past our table with a beautiful woman at his side.

I lean over the table and hiss at Julian, "That's Wolverine!" Normally I'm not so blatant about celebrity sightings, but today, I blame the champagne.

He grins, "You mean Hugh Jackman?"

I whisper, "Do you think he'll show us his adamantium claws if we ask politely?"

Julian chuckles, "Go ahead and ask."

I roll my eyes, "I'm not that starstruck."

"It's okay if you are. I enjoy your uninhibited enthusiasm. It's a pleasant change from the pressure cooker I've been in the last several weeks."

"Oh?"

He leans back in his leather chair, and folds one leg over the other. He sips his mimosa then lets the glass dangle casually from his hand. He looks so at ease in this environment, like he belongs here. "I don't want to talk about it here. Too many ears. But let me just say, you, my dear Victory, are sweet sunshine and a breath of fresh air."

I grin, "Thank you, Julian."

The waiter returns, "Is the lady ready to order?"

"Oh," I say, "Uh, I haven't looked at my menu." I flip it open. "How about the Lazy Duvet?" It's crepes, caramelized apple, and ricotta. I'm pretty sure crepes are like pancakes, and I love caramel apples. Oh, geez. It's nineteen bucks! For pancakes?

"Very good," the waiter smiles. "And for you, sir?"

"I'll have the Truffle Brothers," Julian says.

A $34.00 omelette? Wow, this place ain't cheap! Duh.

The waiter takes our menus and wafts away.

Julian asks me, "And what have you been up to? I imagine you're taking the session musician world by storm?"

How do I explain that Julian is the only person I really know who works in that world, other than Olivia? And she's just an underling. She can't hire me. "Oh, not really. But I found a really cool job teaching guitar."

He sips his mimosa, "Do you enjoy teaching?"

"I do," I smile. "The kids are great. I've never really taught lessons before, but it's a lot of fun."

"I need to bring you back to my studio. There's a lot I could do with you…" he says suggestively through narrowed eyes.

Hello! I know what he's talking about. I'm still wound up from my sex dream last night and I blurt, "Do you think the paint job on your Ferrari can take it?"

"What?" he chuckles.

That sounded weird. "Uh, I mean, when you, you know… My shorts have rivets? On the back pockets? I was, uh, thinking about your… paint job? I know how, ah… guys with nice cars can get wound up, about their, um, cars?" Yeah, I'm not thinking about cars or paint jobs. I'm thinking about Julian's… you know. His tongue. Totally thinking about his plunging… tongue.

His beast beneath…

Yeah, that.

Julian nods and grins while I stumble over my words.

He knows exactly what I'm talking about.

The gleam in his green eyes says it all.

At the moment, his chair is pulled right up to the table and I'm waiting for his side of the table to start levitating. Not by magic, but because I can picture the hot rod in his pants jacking up the table top.

"I'm suddenly ravenous," Julian mutters for my ears only, his eyes glinting with obvious desire. "And I'm not talking about the food..."

Gosh, what did I do?

Tee hee.

I totally blame my mimosa and that stupid sex dream I had last night, which was all Johnny and Karen's fault. What do you expect when I sleep one room over from those two hippy nymphos? It's catching, I tell ya!

"Your Lazy Duvet," the waiter says, setting the plate of crepes in front of me. "And your Truffle Brothers." He sets Julian's plate in front of him.

How do waiters always know when to interrupt things so perfectly?

Chapter 92

VICTORY

Me and Julian stand politely side by side waiting for the valet on the curb outside THE Blvd.

I feel Julian boiling in his mist blue suit. Not because it's too hot. We're standing in the shade. But *he's* too hot. Yes, he's gorgeous, but that's not the kind of hot I mean. It's coming off him in waves.

I bask in his desire.

The desire *coming* off him.

Coming.

The valet drives up a moment later in Julian's black Ferrari and hops out. He dashes around the car and opens the passenger door for me. I slide inside and Julian tips the guy before easing into the driver's seat.

We drive down Wilshire at a casual pace. The engine inside the Ferrari is capable of going far faster than the speed limit. I think Julian is too. Both he and the pent up car are ready to accelerate into the red line.

"So," he purrs, "What now?"

I sigh, "I have to get to work." Not my first choice. But I have bills to pay.

"Of course," he nods and wrings his white knuckled fists around the steering wheel like he wants to snap it off with his bare hands.

Sexy.

Julian chuckles, "Why don't you call in sick and spend the day with me?"

My eyes pop open.

Tempting.

But I remember that Julian is used to getting his way. Do I want to encourage that? On the other hand, it's not like Johnny and Karen can't handle the shop without me. But I don't like giving in to someone else's whim. Especially when that someone says he'll call me in two days and doesn't call for weeks.

Yeah, Julian is a bit too "all over the globe" for me. Literally.

Time to change the subject. "Hey, Julian, how'd you end up working with Layce, anyway?"

"I worked on her last two albums. She asked me to produce the next one."

"Is that what you and Max did in Sweden?"

"Yes."

It doesn't sound like he wants to talk about Layce right now. I don't think he wants to *talk* about anything. I don't care. I'm curious.

I ask, "You were recording tracks for her next album?"

He nods.

This is super exciting. I'm an arm's length away from someone who is super successful in the music business. He's sitting where I dream of being, both career-wise, and behind the wheel of his own Ferrari.

And he really wants to have sex with me.

It kind of weirds me out.

I could obviously play this to my advantage.

An image of Danny Daggers flashes in my mind. He wanted me to play things to my advantage too.

I didn't then, and not because I wasn't attracted to Danny Daggers. He was handsome in his own way. Until he turned into a caveman, that is.

But I don't want to sleep my way to success.

I actually want to make music that people want to listen to with my own two hands.

"So," Julian asks, "Where am I driving?"

"Back to the apartment? I really have to get to work."

He nods and we drive to Hollywood in silence.

Julian pulls up to the curb beside Johnny and Karen's building. "It was good seeing you again, Victory."

I smile at him.

Shouldn't have done that.

His emerald eyes mesmerize me. They are jeweled green and sparkle in the morning sunlight. His smile widens across his perfect teeth.

Then I remember my Kellan dream.

I groan and roll my eyes internally.

I don't want to think about Kellan right now.

Someone on my internal committee reminds me that Kellan is with Switchblade.

So what am I worrying about?

A giant chalk board with the word KELLAN printed in 20 foot pink letters is suddenly furiously erased by a team of elves hired by my internal committee for just such occasions. When the board is cleaned, the elves hastily replace it with JULIAN.

A little kiss goodbye is okay, right?

Ms. Sensible pipes up, But only a little kiss. And that's it. Then you have to get to work.

Julian's eyes regain their hold over me and I'm giddy and close to delirious. His face is excruciatingly handsome and manly. The phrase "Jesus wept" pops into my head. I feel you, Jesus. You probably oversaw the angels when they molded Julian's face out of clay and shot him down to earth. Jesus probably wept because

(*Kellan*)

Julian was his finest work.

Second finest.

Anyway.

Jesus wept twice.

You get the picture.

I gaze back at Julian and giggle, "What?"

Julian leans toward me...

I bite my lower lip.

His mouth is an inch from mine.

Oh, he smells so, so...wow.

Oh, I need this.

His lips ease into mine. He tastes so good.

We're kissing and it's super intense and I want more, and he responds with passion, pulling me into him, pushing his tongue into me. His hand cups my cheek. His thumb runs along my jaw, his manicured nail skating across my skin.

My whole body quivers with desire.

He sighs and slides a hand between my naked thighs. His fingers tease between the skin, begging to be let in.

I relax my legs and his hand slips through the opening in my denim shorts. Wow, he doesn't waste any time. I feel his finger peel back my thong and brush along my wetness.

A long sigh rolls out of my mouth and I moan in my throat.

I've completely forgotten that we're parked in the middle of the street in broad daylight. The top of Julian's Ferrari is not on at the moment. Anyone could be watching from the windows in the surrounding apartments. I'm sure people on the second floor and above are getting a great view.

I don't care.

Julian kisses me again and his finger slides inside me.

I am so wet.

And his car is way too small for sex.

We can't go into the apartment. Johnny and Karen are probably eating breakfast. Yeah, I'm sure if I explained to them I needed to have sex, they'd kindly offer up their bedroom and say, "Have fun, kids!" But that would spoil the mood. And I have no place else to go. If we go to Julian's, I'm afraid I'll never leave.

His house is too far of a drive anyways, because Julian's penetrating finger is thrusting in and out of me.

It feels *so* good…

In…

Out…

So wet…

Slowly in…

Dragging lazily out…

I haven't had sex in forever.

I miss it.

Oh, I *so* miss it.

Without thinking, I grab the crotch of Julian's slacks and fumble around for his cock. It's rock hard and heat pours through the slacks' fabric. Julian grunts as I grip him and his hips lift from the seat.

We kiss hard, our tongues fighting for control.

His finger jams into me up to the knuckle, bumping against my clitoris. Jolts fire up into my belly.

I want more.

People are totally watching like silent birds or staring cats from the surrounding balconies, gaping at the young man and young woman in the Ferrari pawing each other like desperate animals.

I don't even notice.

I tug at Julian's fly. He reaches down and unfastens it. My fingers crawl through fabric until I find his rigid velvet skin. I touch the tip of his cock with my thumb and feel a wet drop of pre come dribbling out. I smear it around his head and he shivers in my hand.

His finger presses into me, straining to go deeper, his knuckle repeatedly bumping my clit.

Our tongues are tied together, knotted with need. Our hands squeeze and release, slide and glide, back and forth, in and out.

Julian's cock starts to shake in my hand. He pulls his tongue out of my mouth and leans his forehead against mine, hissing through clenched teeth. "Fuh..." he sputters as his cock strains in my hand, swelling, the head bulging. "Fuck!" he whispers, even though we're outside.

In plain sight.

Hot cum shoots from his cock, the first bullet going who knows where. More pours over my hand, warming my skin under the California sun.

But Julian isn't done.

His hand works inside me hungrily, forcefully, and I feel my own pleasant tension tighten in my hips.

"Oh, oh," I whisper moan, "Juh—Julian. Don't stop. Don't... Don't, don't, don't..."

I come hard, my orgasm squeezing his finger. I imagine his cock is inside me. I imagine all the hot cum on my hand is filling me up instead of wasted on the wet folds of Julian's dampened slacks.

Eventually, our hands slowly withdraw from each other and we lean back in the seats of the Ferrari, breathless and panting.

I don't know if this was a good idea.

That was Ms. Sensible.

She can suck it.

The rest of my internal committee heaves a healthy sigh of relief.

Aaaaahhhhh. MUCH better.

Now maybe I can sleep tonight.

After I go to work and spend the day thinking about Julian's finger.

I mean cock.

I guess Goldenblond is back in town.

Chapter 93

KELLAN

The music booms around us inside Dubs' garage at the end of our afternoon rehearsal. Joaquin beats his drums like he's cracking skulls. Dubs points his guitar neck at the ceiling like a missile and rattles the strings. Me and Switchblade are facing each other, strumming our guitars violently, grinning at each other like lunatics.

We make a rock & roll racket that is loud, lewd and fucking awesome. Joaquin pounds his toms like bombs and his double bass drums are kicking like machine guns. Dubs' bass is a 10.0 earthquake that shakes the garage. Me and Switchblade's guitars are Gatling guns going off.

I scream into the P.A. mic, *"HELL YEAH!!!"*

We hit the final ending note as a band.

BOOM!!

"Fuck yeah!" Switchblade shouts.

Dubs is laughing, he's having so much fun.

"Órale!" Joaquin yells.

I give fist bumps to everybody, "We are going to blow them away at L.A. Gunslingers!"

Joaquin and Dubs nod.

"Fuck yeah, we are," Switchblade grins.

"I hate to kick y'all out," Dubs says, "But I'm trainin' a client at the beach in a half hour."

We all start packing up our instruments and amps.

"Is your client hot?" Switchblade asks. Dubs told her about his personal training business awhile back.

"You know they all hot," Dubs grins at her. "I don't train no dogs, yo."

"Need any help whipping them into shape?" Switchblade asks.

"You bringin' the whips?" Dubs smiles.

Joaquin chuckles, "What kind of fucked up shit you do with your clients, Ése?"

Dubs says cockily, "The kind they be like, 'Give it to me harder, Dubs! Ooh! Ooh!'" he moans in a raspy falsetto like an orgasmic woman and mimes fucking the air doggy style while spanking the air's ass. With his deep baritone voice and masculine features, his grunting air fuck is hilariously horrifying.

Switchblade curls her lips in mock disgust, "Dude, that's disturbing."

I snicker, "Go easy on the guy, Switchblade. That right there is the best pussy Dubs has had in months."

She frowns, "You mean air pussy?"

I quip, "Like I said, it's all Dubs can get."

Dubs flips me off.

Switchblade laughs.

Joaquin asks Dubs jokingly, "That the face you make when you hittin' the hynas, homes?"

Sensing them ganging up on him, Dubs protests, "I ain't hittin' no hyenas, dawg!"

Joaquin and I bust into laughter.

Dubs looks around, "What?"

I chuckle, "Joa said hynas, bro. Not hyenas."

"There a difference?" Dubs asks dubiously.

Joaquin snickers, "Dubs can't tell between hyna panocha and hyena panocha, homes!"

Dubs shakes his head and grins, "Get the fuck out my house, y'all. My hyena is waitin' for me."

We all laugh and carry our gear outside and bump fists out on the driveway.

"When we rehearsing next?" Dubs asks.

I say, "Tomorrow night?"

"I'm there," Switchblade says

Joa nods.

"You know it," Dubs agrees.

"Laters," I say to him and Joaquin as Switchblade and I carry our guitars to her white with orange racing stripes Camaro. She drives me back to my apartment.

When we roll to a stop in front of my building, I say to her, "Great rehearsal this morning. I can't believe how solid the music is after only a few days."

She nods, "What do you expect from awesome musicians like the four of us?"

"No less," I grin.

Her cell phone rings suddenly. "Hold on a second," she says and checks the phone. She answers, "Yeah?"

I watch her face explode into a smile a mile wide.

She turns to me and screams, *"I got the gig! I got the Wild Child gig!"* She squeals at the top of her lungs.

I literally plug my ears with my fingers. Inside the confines of her Camaro, she's louder than a Motörhead concert.

To the phone, Switchblade says, "Okay. Yeah. Yes, I can do that. Yes. Definitely." When she hangs up, she turns to me, "I fly out on a plane next week! I'm joining Wild Child in Detroit! I'm going on tour!"

I've never seen another human being this happy or this excited. Her joy is catching. But at the same time, it means she's leaving our band.

Damn.

Switchblade starts spinning around in her seat, looking at me, looking ahead, looking at me, looking ahead. The only thing in front of us is my street, but she's ready to go forward at a million miles an hour. I'm waiting for her head to explode or just spin right off the top of her neck.

Then she freezes. Slowly, she turns to me, "I'm so sorry Kellan. I won't be able to make L.A. Gunslingers."

I nod my head heavily, "It's cool. I totally get it. If they called me, I'd be telling you the same thing."

She leans over and practically strangles me while she hugs me. She kisses my cheek, "I'm going to miss you! We were just getting started."

I sigh, "I know. But go. Seriously. You have to do this gig."

She smiles at me. Her eyes dart around my face.

Out of nowhere, she kisses me smack on the mouth.

We just hold lips.

Neither of us feels anything.

I guess I misread her weird behavior on the way to the Wild Child audition.

She slides back into her seat and says, "Sorry about that. I just, I don't know. You're awesome Kellan."

"You are too, Switchblade."

"I wish you were a girl," she says sincerely.

"Yeah," I laugh. "I wish you were too," I quip.

"I have a pussy! You wanna see it?!" She sounds serious. She arches her back and starts frantically unbuckling her bullet belt like she's gonna push her pants down and show me.

Maybe I didn't misread her?

Maybe she doesn't even know herself.

Either way, I know I'm not into her, no matter how awesome she is, and no matter how hot

(*Victory*)

she is. I pretty much knew in my shower when my Switchblade fantasy wasn't doing it for me that nothing was going to happen between us.

But she's unzipping her pants and says, "I'll prove it to you! I have a pussy!"

I joke, "Yeah, but you secretly wish you had a dick." I'm treating this situation like she's good for her word, and she's really a lesbian. At this point, it doesn't matter if she is or not. I just don't want to send the wrong signals. "We're born the way we're born."

She stops unbuckling, drops her butt into the seat, and looks vaguely disappointed. A moment later, she leans over again and hugs me hard. "You're the coolest, Kellan." She sounds like she's crying.

I pat her on the back affectionately and mumble, "You are too."

I'm going to miss her bad because she *is* awesome, gay or straight.

Eventually she releases the hug and I see tears on her cheeks. I wipe away one with my thumb.

"Those aren't mine," she sniffs, "They're yours, you pussy." She punches my arm and starts crying quietly, but she's smiling too.

I say softly, "You should probably go home. I bet you have a ton of shit to do before you go."

"You're right." She slaps the steering wheel a bunch of times, excited again. "I'm playing guitar for Wild Child! I'm going on tour!"

"Yes you are," I say sadly.

She starts spinning around again in her seat, "I need to pack! I need to tell my apartment manager I'm moving! I have a million things to do!"

"You're gonna blow the world away, Switchblade. They're gonna love you. You're gonna impress the shit out of everyone who watches you play at the shows. They'll never forget you."

And neither will I.

In a good way.

I heave a sigh and climb out of her Camaro. I stop myself before I close the door and lean back inside, "You gonna be able to play the open mic at The Dive Bomb before you fly out?"

"What night is it?"

"Tuesday."

"I fly out Wednesday morning," she winces, "Early."

"It's up to you," I say casually.

She gives me a long look, "I wouldn't have heard about the Wild Child audition if it wasn't for you, Kellan..."

I crack a grin, "We have to get video of you and me on stage at a gig at least once, right?"

"Fuck yeah," she smiles. "I'll be there. And it's not like you're never going to see me again once I fly out."

"I hope you're right," I smile and close the door.

I slap the roof of her Camaro and stand in the middle of the street as she drives away.

Chapter 94

KELLAN

I trudge up the driveway of my building and to my apartment. It's pretty hot inside, so I open some windows and leave the front door open with the screen door closed to let in a draft. The flies will have to buzz around outside. I stick my head in the fridge, enjoying the cool air as it slides out. I grab a beer from the bottom shelf and pop the top.

I drop down on my couch and stare at my recording equipment. It reminds me of

(*Victory*)

how bummed I am that Switchblade is leaving. Finding a musician as good as

(*Victory*)

Switchblade is hard enough. Finding one as cool as her who's easy to get along with is twice as hard. Finding one who is talented, cool, and sticks around, is apparently impossible.

(*Giselle*)

I heave a sigh and sip my beer.

I think back over all the bands I've been in over the years. My high school buddies I thought I'd be touring the world with. They're gone. They got jobs or had kids or joined other bands that went nowhere. Every time that happened, a little piece of my heart died.

I notice the copy of Guitar World magazine sitting on top of my computer table with Eddie and Alex Van Halen on the cover. Those two guys have been playing together since the crib. Their dad was a musician and bought them instruments when they were barely out of diapers. Eddie and Alex have played together their entire lives. I know about zero musicians personally who can make that claim.

If you want to form a successful band, you need more than musical chemistry. You need

(*Victory*)

human chemistry.

And a total commitment to making it as a band. Without that, the band will always fall apart.

Always.

I guess I'll have to keep searching for that kind of bond with someone

(*Victory*)

as dedicated as I am.

I take another sip of beer and gaze around my lonely living room.

There's only one thing that can cure the sickness in my heart right now. I pull my Martin acoustic out of its hardshell case in the bedroom closet and sit back down on the living room couch with a pad of paper and a pencil.

I start strumming some chords. Like every other singer, my voice works good in some keys, but not in others. Considering my mood tonight, I go with C and noodle around until I find the bittersweet

(*Victory*)

vibe I'm looking for. I settle for a chord progression of C major, F minor 7, E flat major 7, C major. I play it fingerstyle until I like what I hear. It's got that sad ballad slow vibe which is perfect for heartbreak songs that everybody loves.

Now all I need is a chord progression for the chorus. Something mournful. That's easy.

A flat major, B flat major, back to C.

It's interesting how the major chords, when you stack them like that, create the minor key. The power in the darkness is how I always describe those chords to my guitar students.

It suits my mood.

While I work all the chords into my muscles, I start to hum a melody on top of everything. I jot down phrases and words on my pad of paper as they come to me. I already have a clear idea what the song is about.

It's about wanting.

I'm not talking some passing thing, like a spoiled kid who wants some new toy really, really bad, and he begs and begs for it until his mom is going nuts and finally she gives in and buys the stupid thing, and when the kid finally gets the magic toy out of the box, the toy he needed more than his next breath or life itself, he's done with it two hours later and tosses it on the floor with the rest of his shit, to be quickly forgotten.

No, I'm not talking about that.

I'm talking about a once in a lifetime treasure.

(*Victory*)

The kind you never forget.

(*Giselle*)

The kind you know is meant for you the moment you meet them.

(*Victory*)

The deepest bone yearning a human being can possibly have.

(*Victory*)

The kind of wanting I'm feeling right now.

The desire to find true love. The kind that doesn't walk away. The kind of love most people only find one time in their entire life, if they're lucky. The luckiest people of all find it when they're young. Others don't find it until late in life after going through one failed relationship after another. The unlucky ones never find it at all. But for the ones who do, they know they need to hold onto it with everything they've got, because it's not gonna come back around if they let it go. They protect that love, do anything to keep that love, because it truly is the ultimate treasure life has to offer.

I thought I'd found that connection with Giselle.

Boy, was I fucking wrong about her.

It was good with her for awhile. Incredible. I can still picture her beautiful smile.

Too bad that smile was a lie.

Too bad it hid a different person underneath. How did I fall for it? I grab my beer off the coaster beside the couch and pull a swallow. Giselle was a master of disguises, that's why. I sometimes think she had nothing beneath her disguises except maybe a logic computer or whatever. But not a heart or anything remotely human. The strange thing is, she wasn't so heartless in the beginning. At least I thought she wasn't. Either way, she changed.

Fucking Giselle.

But I'm an optimist.

Giselle is way behind me now.

I'm looking forward.

Love is still out there. And I'm gonna keep looking for that one special person

(*Victory*)

until I find her.

That's when I realize the song I'm writing right now is about Victory. It's about *not* having her but wanting her so bad it's driving me crazy.

And it's about Giselle.

It's about thinking Giselle was it, that she was THE one, but finding out the hard way she wasn't.

I scowl to myself.

Giselle wasn't *shit*.

But I'm over her.

The next thing I work out for my song is the verse lyrics. I play around with various vocal approaches to the melody while strumming the chords:

"Whispered kisses
on my lips
from the ghost of you
We've never met
yet it's true
your the one I seek"

I know some people will think it's a song about a lost love who died because of the word ghost, and that's okay. The secret to good lyrics is leaving them open ended enough that every listener can find a way into the song.

For me, it feels like Victory drifted out of my life as quick as she came into it. And yeah, I've already met her, but I know that everyone on the planet can relate to the feeling that your true love is out there waiting for you to find them, but you're still looking and looking and looking.

Some people give up looking after awhile. They settle for the best person they can find and call it good enough. I guess I'm not like that. Not because I'm picky, but because I've never felt any sort of real connection with any of the women I've seriously dated. Not that there've been many I dated longer than a few months. In fact, there was only one.

Giselle.

We had an amazing connection. Too bad she had nothing going on in the commitment department.

When she tore my heart apart, I think she took any sense of commitment I might have had and shredded it to pieces.

That's why I've been wasting time with soulless women like Savannah or Red, or any of a thousand other nameless faces I barely remember. I didn't want to go through the same shit Giselle put me through.

But some corner of my heart is still looking for true love anyway. Like a dopey dumb dog, loyal to the last, too stupid to know any better, a corner of my heart still wants that special connection with a woman who gets me on every level. Not just one who thinks I'm hot. I'm over that. It doesn't mean anything.

I want someone who I can get wound up about even if we're both wearing blindfolds.

Victory.

Yeah, her.

From word one, talking to her was like talking to an old friend. That was something I never thought I'd find with a woman in my whole life.

My eyes pop open and excitement rushes through me. That's it.

The title for this song.

My Whole Life.

I jot it at the top of the page and underline it several times.

The words for a pre-chorus and the chorus come quick. I carve them into the pad of paper as fast as I can.

Then I start singing them over the chords.

Before I know it, I'm singing the entire song with all my heart. Victory is forefront in my mind the entire time. She's the girl I've been looking for since forever.

I set up my computer and a mic to record the song. Once it's running, I replay the beginning verse over sad gentle fingerstyle guitar work. It's totally soft and haunting. Then I transition into the pre-chorus, which is plaintive but picking up speed:

"My whole life
I searched for you
my need like a disease
I can't live

without your love
you bring me to my knees

I'm thinking about Victory.

As my heart pours out of me, all I'm thinking about is Victory.

Then I kick in the chorus, which is wailing, driving and powerful. It's a song about a man who is never giving up until he gets what he's always wanted:

"My
Whole
Life
(I've searched)
For
A love
Like you
(I've searched)

The past tense refrain, "I've searched," reflects the feeling we've all had that we've looked and looked and looked, but we can't find our true love.

I found Victory, but she isn't anywhere close to being mine. I have to go after her and make her mine. Somehow. Otherwise, I'll never find what I've been looking for since day one.

I alter the repeat of the chorus to a present tense refrain, "I search," to reflect the fiery idea of *never* giving up. Of searching until you crumble to dust, you want your true love so bad.

No way am I giving up on Victory.

"My
Whole
Life
(I'll search)
For
A love
That's true
(I search)"

The lyrics totally capture the feeling I'm going for. We all know it. It hums beneath the surface of every human being who has a beating heart.

In my case, my heart beats for Victory.

I'm never giving up on her.

She's the one.

I've known it since I saw her playing at The Cobra.

I knew it instantly.

I sing over the hard, melancholic chords, my voice sliding between desperate and determined. From choked with emotion to smooth and clear, then gravelly and passionate:

"I still search
For a love
That's you

On and on
I crawl
I still search

For You"

I slowly pluck out the final notes of the last chord, my heart spilled all over my apartment.

A female voice drifts through the screen door, "Kellan?"

Because it's dark outside and I've got the lights on in my apartment, I can't see who it is.

But I recognize the voice.

I know it well.

Chapter 95

KELLAN

"What up, Em," I say as I open the screen door.

"Hey, Kellan," she smiles. "I heard you singing."

I sigh, "Sorry if I distracted you."

"Oh, no worries. I needed a study break. And I brought Chunky Chips-Ahoy." She holds up the bag.

I arch an eyebrow, "You wanna come inside?"

She smiles, "Sure."

Emily Needham, who I call Em, lives upstairs. She's a med student at UCLA, which is about two miles east of our building, just past the 405 freeway.

She's always wearing a UCLA t-shirt or sweats or whatever, whether she's studying or jogging or going to the grocery store. She has glasses, which look totally cute on her, and her long auburn hair is always in a ponytail. She also has a tight body from all the running she does. If she ever let her hair down and took her glasses off, she'd be hot.

I honestly believe she doesn't realize this. She's been my neighbor long enough that I know her brainy vibe isn't an act. But she's cool.

We hang out randomly like this pretty often, but we've never hooked up. I think she's too straight laced for my tastes. And she's ultra focused on med school, which means her life revolves around studying. I know she has friends, but they rarely visit. And I'm pretty sure I've never seen her date anybody. Maybe she's pining for me. Who knows. I never asked. I just like kickin' it with her when she needs a study break. And she always brings Chips Ahoy.

She walks inside and I ask, "You want anything to drink?"

"For sure."

"What can I getcha?"

She sees my bottle of suds and asks, "Do you have any more beer?"

I arch an eyebrow, "Does beer go with Chips Ahoy?"

"I don't know," she grins as she sits down on my couch next to my acoustic guitar.

I smile-frown, "I don't remember you ever drinking."

Emily rolls her eyes, "My neuroscience reading is giving me a bad headache."

I snicker, "That's funny."

"What is?" she asks, confused.

I wait a second to see if she connects the dots. When she doesn't I say, "Isn't neuroscience studying the brain?"

"Yeah?"

"And it's giving you a headache?"

She nods, lost. Emily is smart enough to get good grades in medical school, but she's way too literal.

I say, "Studying the brain is making your head hurt?"

"Oh," she smiles, "I get it."

But she doesn't really laugh. Now you see why Em and I haven't hooked up. I say, "How about some milk for those cookies?"

"Sounds perfect," Emily smiles.

I walk into the kitchen, set my empty beer bottle on the counter, and pour two glasses of milk from the jug in the fridge.

"Anyway," she calls out from the living room, "I couldn't help but listen to your song."

I walk to the couch with the glasses of milk and tease her a little, "You stalking me?"

"Oh," she says defensively, "I didn't mean to eaves drop, but you were singing pretty loud."

I smile and hand her a milk, "It's okay. I guess I forgot the doors and windows were open."

"Is it a love song or something? I really liked it." She already has the bag of cookies open and nibbles on one.

"Sort of," I say. There's not room to sit on the couch with Emily and all my notes from the song and my guitar, so I stand.

"Is your song about anyone I know?" she asks, sounding slightly hopeful.

Another reason I've never tried anything with Em is I think she's the kind of woman who's going to have sex with maybe two guys in her entire life, and marry the second one. I don't want to play around with someone like her. From the way she talks, I think she's probably still a virgin at 23. She's way too innocent and deserves to stay that way. I mean, she's drinking milk and eating chocolate chip cookies to blow off steam. She doesn't need a guy like me.

"No," I answer, "It's about…someone I met recently."

"Have you played it for her?"

"No," I chuckle, "I just wrote it tonight."

"Oh," she smiles and takes a dainty sip of milk. "Can I hear it? Again, I mean?"

"Sure," I smile. This isn't the first time I've sung and played in front of someone or even some crowd. I'm used to it. I sit on the edge of the easy chair facing my couch, put the Martin over my knee, and run through the tune again. I don't really pay attention to Emily while I'm playing because I'm still working out the timing of playing and singing at the same time.

When I finish, I hike my eyebrows. "Whaddya think?"

She sits on the edge of the couch, slightly slouched, elbows resting on her knees. Her head hangs over the half eaten Chips Ahoy cookie cradled in her hands, "You should really play that for the girl you wrote it about," she mutters. "Any girl would melt if she heard you singing like that about her." She sounds bummed or maybe slightly depressed.

I know she likes me. There's nothing I can do about it. "Thanks," I say.

A moment later, she straightens her back and plucks a Chips Ahoy out of the bag. "Want a cookie?" she grins. Like I said, Em is a determined girl with a lot of focus.

"Sure," I smile, leaning over from my easy chair to grab the cookie from her. I eat it in the chair.

Em sits on the couch.

I don't want any chance of mixed signals.

We chat about random shit for the next twenty minutes.

When Em leaves to go back to her studying, I call Victory.

She doesn't answer.

No problem. I'll see her at the school soon enough.

Chapter 96

VICTORY

"Cameras are rolling," someone yells in the darkness.

I think it's the cinematographer of the music video, or the cameraman. I'm not sure who. There are so many people on the big soundstage, I can't keep them all straight.

The day after our exhibitionist Ferrari fingering session, Julian called to tell me he had arranged another surprise. Getting to watch the video shoot for Layce's upcoming single 'I Rise' is way beyond anything I imagined.

It's like being on the set of a full-blown Hollywood movie production.

The 'I Rise' music video is set in a huge dark gothic castle surrounded by gray skies crowded with storm clouds. A palatial stone staircase leads up to the arched entrance where a handsome prince awaits.

The model playing the prince reminds me of a renaissance manga vampire. He's dressed in a princely black riding coat with tails. The coat has white satin appointments that circle the cuffs and collar. Tight white pants and black thigh high riding boots complete the outfit. Pale makeup contrasts strikingly against his painted blood red lips. I have no doubt the girls of the world will swoon over his leading man good looks when they see the video online.

"Cue music," someone else yells from the shadows.

The music for 'I Rise' plays through the P.A. speakers positioned throughout the darkened soundstage.

Julian told me this song is the first single from Layce's next album, and the reason why he and Max flew to Sweden to rework it at the last minute. I've never heard the song before today, but since I arrived on set this morning, I've heard it at least twenty times.

Julian and Max's work must have paid off, because the tune is instantly catchy and I absolutely love it. I've always enjoyed all styles of music, especially pop. I can appreciate a good hook and a good chorus, and 'I Rise' has both. This song is going to be big. Based on the amount of money going into the video production, I think Layce's record company thinks so too.

There's an energy on set because everyone working the soundstage is excited about the song and the production of the video. They all believe in it and are working hard to make everything perfect. Between takes, I've heard people chattering about how many views it will have on YouTube. Some are saying it will be bigger than Katy Perry's Roar. I believe them.

"Action!" someone yells in the darkness.

Super bright strobe lights flash on and off several times, simulating lightning.

A crystalline carriage drawn by four white horses pulls up to the base of the staircase. White mist a foot deep swirls around their hooves and the wheels of the carriage. The white horses are real and they're huge and their hooves are loud compared to the music pumping out of the P.A. speakers, sounding like pistol shots that echo around the soundstage.

Earlier, I was lucky enough to see the horses up close between takes. Their trainer was friendly but cautioned me to stay out of the way because the horses were getting spooked by the fake strobe light lightning.

When the crystalline carriage stops, a princess in an elegant white gown steps carefully out of the carriage. It's Layce in costume as a gothic manga princess, dressed in white lace, just like her name. She's a beautiful young woman.

I looked Layce up on my phone earlier and found out she's 26. Four years older than me, but a million times more successful in the music business than I am. I've heard her music, seen her in cosmetics commercials on TV, seen her videos online, but didn't know much about her before today.

According to her Wikipedia page, three singles from her last album "Penny Princess: Rags to Riches" hit number one on Billboard's Hot 100. One of the singles, Young In Love, held at number one for eight weeks. Penny Princess spent a total of 44 weeks on the Billboard 200 album chart and received a Grammy nomination for Album of the Year in 2012. And, Layce's net worth is estimated at almost a hundred million dollars. The buzz is that Layce's next album is going to be even bigger than Penny Princess, and 2014 is the year that Layce is going to own the pop starlet crown.

Based on hearing 'I Rise' on set all day, and this lavish video production, I think the buzz is right.

Layce is the next big thing.

Am I jealous?

Yes and no. I never wanted to be a pop star. But when I listen to the lyrics for 'I Rise,' a lump forms in my throat that threatens to suffocate me. I wish *I'd* written this song myself. I wish *I* was the one singing it. It's so damn cool and catchy.

But I *don't* sing.

I'll *never* sing.

The idea of me singing is so painful, it threatens to collapse my chest into the black hole where my heart is supposed to be.

I *wish*...I *want*...

But I can't.

I can't *ever* sing.

I *promised*...

I shake my head, trying to clear it. I don't want to think about it right now. I focus on the beautiful story unfolding before me in the music video.

I feel so lucky to be here, and I owe it all to Julian's generosity. I need to think of a good way to thank him for this opportunity. But I have no idea what I could possibly do for him that can compare to what he's done for me.

As Layce walks up the bleak stone steps of the gothic castle, she is the only bright being in the Prince's gloomy gray world. A camera man with a steadicam rig strapped to his shoulders climbs backward up the steps in front of Layce, his camera tracking her in close up as she lip syncs to the words of the first verse:

"Your smile disarming
Your eyes alarming
You were my very own Prince Charming"

Another camera is close on the handsome prince, capturing his devilishly delectable features. I stand behind the director's area which is near the back wall of the sound stage. The director, the cinematographer, and ten other assistants with numerous official titles huddle around several playback monitors which show what all the different cameras are capturing. The lyrical description of the Prince is accurate. The model they hired to play the Prince is beautiful, but has a hint of brooding danger trapped behind his thin grin.

Layce continues to mouth the rest of the first verse:

"I should've known
You'd take it all
The day I slipped into your fall"

Layce, as the Princess, reaches the top of the stairs, and the Prince takes her hand to kiss it delicately. She lip syncs the pre-chorus:

"I tried so hard

It's over now
Won't sink into your meltdown"

The camera reveals a look of tearful sorrow haunting Layce's eyes as she reluctantly accepts the Prince's kiss as he holds her wrist.

"I've had enough
I gave my all
I will not live within your fall"

At that moment, the Prince motions toward the entrance of the gothic castle, which is a gaping black maw. The pointed spikes of the fake iron portcullis overhead form the teeth in the castle's mouth. There is a wicked gleam in the eyes of the handsome Prince as he leads the Princess inside. The castle is obviously symbolic and represents the dark personality of the broken Prince.

'I Rise' is clearly a song about a girl who falls for a damaged boy she thought she could fix, but couldn't. I can relate. Can I get a Scott Walker, anyone? Scott was so broken, he ruined everything we built. The relationship *and* the band. So much for Skin Trade. I should've known better. Oh well. What's done is done. I've forgotten all about Scott.

Sort of.

I still don't have a band of my own.

The thing with Olivia, Lucas, and Logan has potential, but everyone is so busy it's stalling. It frustrates me like you can't imagine. Watching Layce's video production where everyone is giving 110% to make her a success stabs my heart. I'm the only person in my life giving my music career 110%.

I want to make music that moves people like 'I Rise' moves me.

But I can't do it alone.

I refuse to think about it right now.

I shove it out of my head and watch the majesty of the video shoot.

Surrounding the Prince and Princess on the sound stage at the entrance to the castle are a crowd of the Prince's loyal subjects, all dressed in black. They have garish white and black facial makeup that makes them appear almost skeletal. Their clothing is all black, twisted, and wicked like something out of a Tim Burton movie. They all have slightly insane looks on their faces, and all of them glare and sneer at the Princess. They grab at her as she walks through the gates of the castle, but she ignores them, and sings the chorus to the song:

"The beat of my heart,

my angel wings, and finally,
I rise
Soaring above it all
I fly
My heart beat, dreams and desires
Finally, I rise
I fly
Soaring above it all
Aa-ah-ah-ah-ah-ah-all
All
Soaring above it all
Aa-ah-ah-ah-ah-ah-all
Aa-ah-ah-ah-ah-ah-all
All, all
Soaring above it all"

The power pop glam rock music is so powerful as it pumps out of the sound stage P.A., it sends shivers into my heart. I want to

(sing)

cry, I'm so jealous. This song is really, really good. It may be teenage girl pop music, but it's honest. I wish I wrote it. I wish I was the one

(singing)

in costume, playing the part of the Princess. This surprises me, because I never really thought of doing anything other than playing lead guitar in a hard rock band. I imagined that would be enough for me. But now that I don't have Skin Trade, and now that I'm seeing a video like this shot first hand and hearing the amazing song that goes with it, I want to

(singsingsing)

be a part of something like this.

On the plus side, now that I'm out of Skin Trade, maybe some day I can. Scott would never have done a video like this. For one, we could never have afforded it. I can only wonder how much of Layce's personal fortune is being spent on this huge production.

Also, Scott would never do something this fantastic. I can imagine him saying, "This isn't rock and roll. This is bullshit. This is corporate crack for teenage twits too stupid to think for themselves." Before our break up, I probably would've agreed with him.

Now, I'm swept away. It's awesome.

Scott was a douche. A repressive, suffocating douche bag.

I wish I knew how to build a career like Layce's for myself. I feel lucky just witnessing a piece of it unfolding.

Chapter 97

VICTORY

I don't know who Layce is behind her pop star persona, but I do know she's the luckiest girl I've ever stood twenty feet away from.

Throughout the day, Layce has come down to the director's area with all the playback monitors to talk with the director and his assistants between takes. During those moments, Layce has been so close, I could've called her name and she would've heard me. But I didn't because several of the production assistants have been kind enough to warn me not to bother the star if I want to stay on set. Apparently, it's literally in their contracts that they are not allowed to look Layce in the eyes or talk to her. That includes me.

"Cut!" the director shouts at the end of yet another take. "Love it!" He turns to the assistant director and says in a low voice, "If Layce doesn't like this take, tell her she can hire George Lucas to finish the shoot."

The assistant director grins and nods, "If George is busy, I'll put in a call to Spielberg. I'm sure he'll be happy to do it."

The two of them exchange a long smile before shaking their heads and chuckling quietly together.

The assistant director says, "She really is a pain in the ass, isn't she?"

The director rolls his eyes, "You said it, not me!"

"I didn't say anything," the assistant director lies, clearly amused.

The director sighs, "We can bitch about it later. Right now, we have scenes to shoot before we run out of budget. I think we can move everyone around to the ballroom set and shoot that after lunch."

"Good call," the assistant director nods. He grabs a bullhorn from the table in front of the monitors and walks to the base of the gothic staircase. He starts calling out instructions to everyone. Bright work lights flicker on, illuminating the set, cutting through the gloom. Tall stage doors are opened, letting in sunlight.

The horses are unharnessed from the crystalline carriage and led outside for water and fresh air. One of the horses dumps a huge basketful of horse apples on set, and one of the animal trainer's assistants rushes over with a shovel and a wheelbarrow to clean up. A union guy with a mop scrubs the area until it's spic and span.

Outside the studio, a food truck is parked next to the building. A white tent covers a row of picnic tables. Some of the crew is lined up to get food, but most of the crew is inside preparing the next shot.

I wait in line and get a burger. I haven't eaten anything all day, and I'm happily surprised I don't have to pay for it. None of the crew do.

Before I know it, the crew are being summoned inside. I hastily finish the rest of my burger and toss my trash in a waste can at the end of the picnic tables.

As I near the stage doors, Layce is walking toward me and the doors from the opposite direction in her white lace wedding gown. She is surrounded by an entourage of people in non-costume trendy business casual.

I stop near the stage entrance to watch. I hope they don't notice me.

One of the women with Layce has a short black bob with bangs and wears a kimono crop top with a white pencil skirt and strappy heels. She says to Layce, "...and they've designed three new scents exclusively for your fragrance line." She holds an iPad in one arm and cradles several perfume bottles in the other.

Layce frowns, "I hope they gave me something good to work with. The last batch smelled heinous."

Kimono Top says, "They really need you to make a decision on which scent you like and choose a bottle design so they can begin production on the bottles now. It takes weeks for them to ship overseas from China."

"I thought they made the perfume in New Jersey?"

"They do. But the bottles are manufactured in China."

Layce stops beside one of the tall doors to the soundstage and says, "Have we picked a name yet?"

Kimono Top shakes her head, "No. We're waiting for focus group results on Uplift, Flight, and Wings."

"What?" Layce growls, "what happened to my picks for the name?"

Kimono Top shrugs, "That's what the suits at the record label wanted."

Layce scowls, "Are you serious? Uplift makes me think of a forklift or a hoist, and Flight makes me think of being trapped on Southwest Airlines next to a fat guy who farts all the way from Kansas to Kalamazoo. What about my suggestions: Soar or Rise? It's the name of the damn single!"

Kimono Top is merely the messenger, but she winces unconsciously away from Layce's intensity. After she recovers, she says, "Do you want to smell them?"

"Now?" Layce whines.

"We've pushed back two weeks already," Kimono Top says sheepishly.

"Fine," Layce barks and holds out her wrist. "Hit me."

Kimono top juggles her iPad and the bottles until she has one in hand. She spritzes Layce's outstretched wrist.

Layce sniffs it and grimaces, "That's awful. Next."

Kimono Top readies another bottle. "Where do you want it? Next to this one?"

Layce rolls her eyes like Kimono Top is the stupid one and shoves her other wrist out. Kimono sprays, and Layce sniffs. This time her brows furrow thoughtfully, "It's okay, I guess. But nothing I haven't smelled a hundred times. Wasn't anybody listening when I said I wanted something new, something that says 'Layce', not something that says Kmart?"

Kimono Top shrugs her shoulders and readies the third bottle. She holds it out to spray.

"I need another wrist," Layce says. "You," she commands the woman standing next to her with a clipboard in hand and a headset mic on her head, "Gimme your wrist."

When Clipboard Lady doesn't respond, Layce grabs the woman's arm. She appears old enough to be Layce's mom, but I don't think she is, and she's totally surprised by how Layce is manhandling her, but she doesn't resist. Layce holds the woman's wrist out in front of Kimono Top.

"Spray," Layce orders.

Kimono Top looks reluctant, eyes darting back and forth between Clipboard Lady and Layce.

"What are you waiting for?" Layce barks.

Clipboard Lady offers a creaky smile to Kimono top and says, "It's okay."

Kimono Top spritzes Clipboard Lady's wrist and Layce sniffs.

"Not bad," Layce says thoughtfully.

"Do I tell them you picked this one?" Kimono Top asks reluctantly.

Layce frowns, still holding Clipboard Lady's arm, and sniffs again. She shakes her head, "No. It still needs work. Tell them I want three more versions of this one. It needs to smell youthful. Sweeter. This smells too much like old ladies."

Clipboard Lady purses her lips. She can't be more than forty something.

Kimono Top lifts her eyebrows apologetically toward her.

Clipboard Lady rolls her eyes for Kimono Top's benefit.

Layce notices their exchange and frowns at Clipboard Lady, "I didn't mean you. I meant the scent." Layce releases the woman's arm distastefully and stares up at the sky while shaking her head, as if speaking to the gods, "Doesn't anyone realize my fans are young? They're not going to buy their mom's perfume. When my fragrance doesn't sell, everyone is going to blame me." She looks to Clipboard Lady for sympathy, "You know what I mean?"

Clipboard Lady shrugs.

"What about the outfits?" Layce asks Kimono Top.

Kimono Top hands her the iPad and says, "Here are the new designs for your Fall Collection."

Layce starts skimming through the iPad with her index finger, presumably looking at design sketches. "These are okay." She hands the iPad back to Kimono Top. "Who is going to carry the line?"

"We're still talking to buyers at H&M, Forever 21, and Wet Seal. So far, nobody likes the price point. It's too high."

"How cheap do they want it? If we go any lower, all the dresses will be made out of grocery bags."

"Copy that," Clipboard Lady says into her mic. To Layce, she says, "The director wants you inside for the next shot, Miss Layce."

Layce looks suddenly frazzled. She glances at her upheld wrists, which had been dusted in pale white makeup like her face and neck, but are now dripping from the spritzes of perfume, revealing her tan skin beneath. "Damn it! I'm running!"

"Your nose is smudged, too," Kimono Top says, reaching a careful hand toward Layce.

Layce twists her face away like a baby after breakfast when Mommy pulls out the baby wipes. She growls, "Stop! You'll make it worse!"

Kimono Top shrinks back.

I can't decide if Layce is a total entitled bitch, or if she's stressing out having to deal with everything getting thrown at her. I can't imagine being in her shoes. It would be hella stressful. Maybe pop stardom is more than it's cracked up to be?

And suddenly I realize Layce is staring right at me.

She growls, "What are you looking at?"

I remember the stage hands warning me I wasn't supposed to look her in the eyes, which is exactly what I'm doing right now. My first instinct is to shout, "Fuck you, you entitled bitch!" My last instinct is to look away. So I go with my middle instinct and say, "Uh…"

"Are you on the crew?" Layce barks.

"No?" I wince.

"Who let you in here?" she growls.

Okay, that's enough. I don't care if I'm not supposed to talk to the star. As far as I'm concerned, she's just a bitch. I scowl, "What is wrong with you?!"

"*Me*?" She strides toward me and shouts in my face, "*ME!!* This is *my* soundstage! I *paid* for it! I'm paying everyone here! Which doesn't include you! So get out of here!" She looks around agitatedly, "Someone call security and get rid of this—" she glares at me, "This *whatever* she is."

That's it. I growl, "I guess since you're rich and famous, nobody tells you how much of a bitch you are anymore…"

Layce's brows crunch into a hard frown and the corner of her upper lip starts to twitch.

Kimono Top and Clipboard Lady openly goggle at my bravado.

Undeterred, I growl at Layce, "...So, in case you forgot, let me remind you. You're a total—"

"Julian!" Layce's face suddenly lights up with a huge smile.

Chapter 98

VICTORY

Surprised, I spin around.

Julian stands behind me, as dashing and distinctly debonair as ever. He wears yet another fancy double breasted suit and fine silk tie. This suit is light grey and the shirt and tie are shades of lavender. It goes nicely with his bronze skin.

He grins at me for a second before addressing Layce directly, "Hello, Layce. I see you've met my friend Victory Payne."

Layce grimaces, "You let her in?"

Julian puts a friendly and protective hand on my shoulders and smiles pleasantly at Layce while saying soothingly, "Yes I did. I thought she might enjoy seeing how a world famous pop star such as yourself behaves when the paparazzi aren't around to document your every move."

I stifle a giggle because Julian is obviously giving her shit in the politest way possible.

I expect Layce to explode and shout at Julian. Instead, she gets ahold of herself and forces out a smile. But her face still glows angry red under her makeup. In a sex kittenish voice she says, "You always live up to your name, don't you? *Lord* Julian." She chuckles throatily and flirtatiously.

Julian merely arches an eyebrow at Layce in response.

Lord Julian? What is Layce talking about?

A moment of heated tension passes between Julian and Layce. It's palpable. They had to have been an item at some point. Layce spontaneously lifts her arms and steps forward to embrace Julian.

With her bulky lace wedding dress, it's a careful ordeal, but she manages to elbow me out of the way while tiptoeing up to kiss Julian hello.

Bitch.

She doesn't give Julian an air kiss or a cheek kiss. No, she stakes her territory and kisses him right on the mouth. It's a relatively short kiss, but she lingers in it before pulling away. When she takes a step back, she flashes me a self-satisfied look.

Like I said, Bitch.

Now looking only at Julian, Layce purrs, "I've missed you. We had so much fun in Stockholm." She's practically pouting as she pretends to fix the lapel of his suit. "Remember that night at The White Room in Ostermalm?"

Yeah, she and Julian have a history.

"*Östermalm*?" Julian corrects, pronouncing the word in a fluidly accented voice. He really does have a musical way of speaking.

"Oh, Julian," Layce sighs but smiles, "always the perfectionist."

Julian cocks a smile at her, "When has that ever been a problem for you, my dear? Who called me at the last minute and begged me to fly to Sweden to remix 'I Rise' for the *fourth* time?"

Layce giggles and says seductively, "Didn't you realize it was just an excuse to spend time with you, Lord Julian? Locked away on the other side of the world in a remote and intimate studio with no distractions?"

Layce is pretending to ignore me, but it's obvious every word out of her mouth is aimed at me like bows and arrows.

Standing this close to her, I can truly appreciate the handiwork on her intricate lace wedding gown. It's highly detailed and layered and probably cost ten thousand bucks. Her makeup is stylized, ghostly, and dotted with dusky rhinestone jewels around her smokey eyes. It's as beautiful as Layce. She's as flawless up close in person as she appears in all those glossy magazine photos I've seen. Between her looks and her voice, no wonder she's so famous and successful.

Too bad she isn't as grateful as she is successful.

Layce plays with Julian's lapel again, "Well, maybe *one* distraction..." She's obviously saying that she had sex with Julian as recently as a week ago.

I really don't care.

She's a self-centered manipulative bitch, and whatever did or didn't happen between her and Julian doesn't matter to me. She can stake out her territory however she wants. I don't care.

Well, maybe a little. But it's hard to take her seriously.

Clipboard Lady steps toward Layce and in a gentle voice says, "Ms. Layce, it's the director again. He's asking for you."

"Not now," Layce hisses at her.

Clipboard Lady steps back abruptly, chastened.

Julian says to Layce, "How is the shoot going?"

"Fabulous," Layce smiles. "The designers have really brought your concept to life better than I imagined possible. This video and this single are going to be huge, Julian. We make a perfect team, you and I," she purrs.

His concept? I'll have to ask him about that later. And, wow, she's trying really hard to make me feel like I mean nothing to her. Which means that I'm making her nervous. I'm a tiny bit proud of myself. I never imagined I'd have this kind of effect on one of the world's biggest pop stars.

Who knew?

"I'm glad to hear it," Julian says to Layce.

"Have you seen the set?" she asks excitedly.

"I toured it yesterday. It looks spectacular."

"But have you seen the dancers?"

"I have not," Julian smiles.

"Oh, you *have* to see the dancers. Today they're in costume and they look unbelievable. You *have* to see them in action. The choreographer did such an amazing job. Can you stay and watch?" She pleads.

"I would like to," Julian smiles politely, "But I have a meeting at Sony in thirty minutes."

"Tell them they can wait," Layce pouts.

Julian chuckles, "Do you tell Sony they can wait?"

Layce rolls her eyes. "Stay, Julian."

I'm somewhat blown away by the fact that Layce has gone from being a commanding bitch to a gushing girl in the span of five minutes while talking to Julian. She must really like him. I can only wonder what sort of hold he has on her. And what sort of relationship they've had.

Clipboard Lady says, "I'm very sorry, Ms. Layce, but the director *really* needs you on set so the stunt coordinator can attach your wire harness."

Layce ignores her but looks at Julian, "Duty calls."

"Don't want to keep everyone waiting," Julian smiles.

Layce gives Julian a girlish wave and walks toward the stage doors.

Kimono Top says, "Your wrists?"

"What?" Layce barks, back to being a bitch.

"Your makeup ran? The perfume samples?"

Layce examines the smudged makeup, rolls her eyes, and growls, "Why didn't you say something sooner?"

Kimono Top winces, "I did?"

Layce growls at her then shouts, "Back to makeup!"

Clipboard Lady says, "What should I tell the director?"

"Tell him he can wait!" Layce spins on her heel and marches back to the makeup trailer.

Chapter 99

VICTORY

When Layce is gone, I joke, "She's nice."

Julian snickers, "That's one word. But I can think of several that are more appropriate."

"I bet you love working with her," I quip, "half way around the world in intimate recording studios."

Julian chuckles, "You're not jealous, are you?"

I grin, "Who, me? Why would I be jealous of you, *Lord* Julian?"

"I meant her. You're jealous of Layce."

I scoff, "Are you kidding? Why would I ever be jealous of someone as entitled as her? Who wants to be rich and famous if it turns you into an ass?"

"Money and power doesn't ruin everyone," he arches an eyebrow.

I pause. "You mean you?"

He winks.

I wink back, "I barely know you. We'll see what you're like six months from now."

"Is that an offer? Because if it is, I will gladly accept."

Julian and I haven't talked about what's going on between us since the fingering in the Ferrari. Maybe we should? I think he's getting ideas. I don't know how I feel about that.

Now is probably not a good time to go into it. I change the subject, "You look great today. As always. I love this suit. Are you all dressed up for your meeting?"

"Yes," he nods. "And you look singularly marvelous yourself."

I'm dressed in my regular rocker chick clothes. I thought it would fit in with the stage hands, which it does. I'm glad Julian likes it.

"Who's your meeting with?" I ask.

"The A&R people at Sony and some up and comer female vocalist. I'm supposed to sit down with her and see if we can work together in the studio like I did with Layce."

"Would that include nights at The White Room and Oster-whatever?" I quip. Yes, I'm fishing for information.

"*Östermalm,* " Julian chuckles. "I am now thoroughly convinced that you are in no way jealous of Layce."

"Here, let me fix your perfect lapel," I joke, mocking Layce's earlier attentions.

Julian grins at me, "Are you finished?"

"Wait, missed a piece of lint!" I pretend to pluck one from his collar.

Julian rolls his eyes, but he's enjoying it.

"So, what's with *Lord* Julian?"

"Oh, that's my producing nick name."

"Lord Julian?" I frown.

"Don't you like it? I thought it rather appropriate."

"I bet," I snicker. "So, what was it like being all locked away in Sweden with Layce?"

"It wasn't just her and I. My brother Max was there too."

I ask in disbelief, "Wait, you mean studio Max? He's your brother?"

"He is." Julian cocks his head, "Didn't I tell you that already?"

"No!"

He shrugs, "Now you know."

I remember noticing a physical resemblance between Julian and Max, but they seem so different personality-wise. Julian has the uptight preppy thing going while Max is totally punk and laid back.

I say, "Wow, that's so cool that you and your brother work together."

He nods, "On just about everything. We make a great team."

That's when it clicks. "You guys are Lord Julian and Mad Max! The producing team!"

"We are indeed," he smiles.

I've never followed pop music nearly as closely as I follow hard rock and metal, but I have heard of Lord Julian and Mad Max before. They write songs for all the big pop stars, and produce a lot of them as well. This is kind of a big deal. No, this is a *really* big deal. Because I *know* them. And I didn't even know it!

I do my best to restrain my excitement as I ask, "Okay, I have to know. How much of her own music does Layce write?"

In the world of rock and metal, the whole point is to write your own songs, not pay someone to do it for you. Many rock bands don't even use producers. They do all the recording themselves and maybe have an engineer in the booth handling the recording equipment. The smaller bands often don't even do that.

Julian looks around for a moment. We are on a movie studio lot, between big numbered sound stage buildings. No one is outside but us and the food truck. "Can we talk about this later? I'm not comfortable going into it here."

Julian is so mysterious, which piques my curiosity. And he's obviously humble about it, which excites me even more. I lean into him and grab his arm. I giggle, "Just whisper it." I feel like a teenager secretly texting my girlfriends the answers during a history test.

Julian grins and leans toward me, "Make no mistake, Layce's voice is the magic ingredient that pulls everything together. Without her, I'm just a songwriter and a recording engineer."

"Don't be modest," I grin. "Tell me the truth." This is so exciting, it's like I'm asking the Vice President of the United States if Barack Obama actually does anything beyond reading the speeches written for him by speech writers and posing for photos.

Julian puts an arm around my shoulder and whispers into my ear, "If you must know, Max and I do a tremendous amount of work. We build the chord structure of the songs, the beat, and the harmony. Max is very smart when it comes to creating samples and he is a master with Pro Tools. But I do contribute to the arrangement of the overall composition."

"Who writes the lyrics?"

"Layce, primarily."

I'm very aware that I'm snuggled up against Julian on a Hollywood studio lot, and he's dishing dirt about a mega star that no one else is ever going to know. It's delicious!

I ask, "Does she write *all* of them? Like, every last word and phrase?"

"That would be a bit of an overstatement," Julian says carefully.

"Do *you* write them?"

"Well, not exactly. Layce creates her own vocal melodies over the music Max and I deliver, but I do help her shape her ideas into actual words. And Max always has input. He has a talent for an artful turn of phrase."

I scoff, "It sounds to me like you hand Layce a script when she walks into the studio and she just sings your words over your music."

Julian shakes his head, "No, she's there from the beginning. She throws out ideas which Max and I organize and shape into a poetic form."

"Poetic? What, does she blurt random thoughts and you and Max turn it into poetic lyrics?"

"No, it's not like that," Julian says seriously. He seems so defensive, I bet he does way more than he's letting on.

"But who *writes* the lyrics? You know, the finished poetry?"

An uncomfortable grin stretches across his mouth.

"It's you!" I gasp. "You write those amazing lyrics! Did you write the lyrics for 'I Rise'? The lyrics I've been listening to on the soundstage all morning?"

Julian looks at me but says nothing.

"You did!"

He doesn't deny it.

"And you wrote the music too, didn't you?"

Now he nods reluctantly, "Well, yes. I suppose. With a lot of help from

Max."

I blurt, "Layce really doesn't do anything, does she?!"

Julian's brows furrow, "You have to understand, Layce is the person who ties everything together. Without her voice and her face, Max and I would be nothing more than a couple of brothers writing music for teenage girls and looking for a vocalist to deliver it to them in a relatable format." He grins, "Can you imagine if Max or I tried to sing 'I Rise'?" He laughs. "How well would that go over?"

"Max I can imagine," I quip.

Julian rolls his eyes.

Although I've never heard either of them sing, I can't imagine Julian as a pop idol like Justin Timberlake. He's too uptight. The idea of Julian singing to teenage girls about their broken boyfriends and female empowerment is nearly comical.

Despite all that, this revelation from Julian is incredible. *Julian* is the mastermind behind the moving music of the song 'I Rise'. I know Max helped, but I doubt Layce did much. She seems too kooky and bitchy. I just can't picture her having the creative depth to deliver *any* of what I've heard today. It's Julian. I know it.

I'm stunned.

I knew Julian was hot, and smart, but he's a creative genius too?

Holy shit.

I didn't think it was possible to underestimate him, but I did.

This is incredible.

Just like his fucking finger.

Yeah, the one that gave me a orgasm the other day.

I blurt, "I bet the music video was your idea too! It goes so perfectly with the lyrics!"

Julian shakes his head, "I may have suggested the concept of the Princess of Light and the Prince of Shadows to Layce, but I assure you, all that work you see inside is the product of thousands of man hours and a collaboration between many talented creative people. I just planted a few seeds."

"But they're your ideas!"

Julian checks his wristwatch, which is big and gold and expensive. Probably a Rolex, but I wouldn't know a Rolex from a Timex. "I should go," he says, "or I'll be late for my meeting."

"What?! You have to stay! Watch it with me! Don't you want to see your ideas come to life?"

Julian laughs, "I wish I could. But Sony has been after me for a year to groom their next pop star, whoever it may turn out to be..." He arches an evocative eyebrow.

"I get it," I grin, "And thank you again for getting me in here to watch. This is mind blowing. I've never been on a real studio set before. The closest thing I've seen is the low budget videos my friends have filmed. But this is amazing. It's like a big budget movie or something."

"I'm glad you're enjoying yourself," he smiles. "And now, I must be off."

"If you must," I quip.

"I must," he grins and spontaneously leans over and kisses me on the mouth.

I blush but I kiss back.

It's quick, but soft, inviting, and I want it to last longer than it does.

He smiles, "You know..." he grins suggestively.

He's going to say something about sex, I know it, and I'm grinning against my will. I'm entirely entranced by Julian after everything I've seen and heard today. He's some kind of modern day Leonardo da Vinci as far as I'm concerned.

Julian's emerald eyes sparkle in the bright sunlight, "...when it turns out the girl Sony is showing me today isn't right for the job, maybe I should have you sing for them. Show them what a *real* musician can do..."

BLAM!

(*don't sing*)

I think I just had a stroke or a heart attack or someone shot me through the head. In a bad way.

(*don't sing*)

I can't deal. I'm going to crack into a billion pieces.

(*never ever sing*)

Between everything that happened to me

(*never ever ever sing*)

back then, and all the amazing excitement I've seen surrounding Layce and her video and Julian's musical genius, I'm on overload.

I can't deal.

(*never ever never ever sing*)

I'm torn in half.

(*Vict—*)

Concern darkens Julian's brow, "I'm sorry. I forgot. We went through this before. On our dinner date, after we left Trois Mec." His face hardens, and he hisses, "I should've remembered. Damn it, Victory, I'm sorry." He impulsively reaches out and hugs me.

I fall into his arms and he holds me close, enveloping me.

He strokes the top of my head, smoothing my long hair.

I want to punch him and run away, but I can't.

(*Victor—*)

My strength is gone.

(*Victory!!!*)

I'm crumbling in Julian's arms.

I'm starting to hyperventilate.

(*singsingsingsingsingsing*)

"Shh, shh, shh," Julian whispers, kissing the top of my head.

His comforting warmth washes over me, but I need to do this myself. I hitch once, but hold everything in, closing the doors of my heart. I'm not ready to cry about it in front of Julian.

"Victory, I'm so very sorry. I should've thought before I spoke."

I barely hear his words, because it takes all my concentration to bury my emotional misery underneath layers of denial.

I stand in Julian's arms for I don't know how long.

When I finally regain control, I say in a small voice, "You should go to your meeting."

I can't bring myself to look him in the eyes.

Not right now.

Maybe a month from now.

"I can cancel," he says.

"No, don't do that."

"It's not that important." He gently lifts my chin and gazes into my eyes. "But you are."

Okay, for the first time in my life, I'm about to just up and run away like a baby. But my broken heart is suddenly melting, which is way too confusing.

This is too much.

I dig deep and say, "I'm okay. Really."

I wipe tears from my cheeks.

When Julian sees my tears, he kisses them.

I'm going to start blubbering.

He needs to stop.

I push myself gently away from him, "I'll be okay, Julian."

Julian drops his hands to his sides. "I understand," he says calmly. "But if you need me, call me." He reaches into his pocket, pulls out his phone, and dials a number.

My phone rings in my pocket.

"It's me," he says.

I pull my phone out and look at it like it's some strange alien technology. I'm still not completely back to earth yet and my heart and mind are scattered across the galaxy like broken stars.

"This is my direct number," he says. "It doesn't route through Colette. You can reach me any time of day or night on this number and I will always answer it. I don't know why I didn't give it to you before."

"Okay," I say absently.

"Call me if you need me. I will drop everything, including this pointless Sony meeting, and come for you."

I'm shocked.

He asks, "Are you going to be okay?"

"Yeah," I sigh, "I can deal."

"Very well. I'm off." He walks four steps, stops, and turns. "Call me if you need *anything*. Agreed?"

That sounds so weird, I chuckle, "Agreed. Yes, sir." I give him a military salute and click my heels together.

He grins and shakes his head, "You are strange indeed, Victory Payne."

"Takes one to know one, sir," I quip.

He turns and walks away with a smile on his face.

Chapter 100

VICTORY

After Julian leaves, it only takes me a few minutes to recover and piece myself back together before walking inside the soundstage.

While the stagehands inside wait for Layce to return from her makeup trailer, the stunt crew wires up a number of the dancers who all wear the bleak black costumes of the Prince's loyal subjects. When they're strapped in, they practice wire lifts with the help of the stunt team behind the scenes, simulating flight.

The costumed dancers are all experienced aerial performers and watching them rehearse their routine is like watching a Cirque du Soleil show. The dancers on the ground are equally gymnastic and practice their tumbling maneuvers on the stage floor. The stunt coordinator is constantly offering comments and reminding everyone to keep their eyes open and keep safety first.

Twenty minutes later Layce returns through the main doors like a Queen entering her castle.

I make a beeline for the director's area, which is out of the way. I don't want Layce to notice me and have security boot me out. Who knows if she'll remember me, but I want to watch the rest of the shoot.

The tall stage doors close slowly behind Layce, cutting out the bright sunlight. It takes awhile for my eyes to adjust to the darkness.

Layce walks to the ballroom set, which sits on the back side of the castle exterior set.

The ballroom is also gothic and black, filled with towering jagged spires and serrated archways, almost like the interior of a razored black cathedral. The Prince's domain is bleaker on the inside than it was on the outside.

I wonder how much of this was Julian's idea? It's breathtakingly beautiful.

I watch while the stunt crew attaches wires to Layce's harness and her white lace wedding gown.

When Layce is fully strapped in, the director walks into the middle of the set. Wearing a red print Hawaiian shirt, cargo shorts, and sandals, he looks totally out of place in the fantastical black and white ballroom. He addresses everyone in a loud voice, "All right, everybody. We're shooting the final sequence next. You all know your places and your cues, and I trust that everyone's head is in the game. No one is going to get hurt, right?"

There are general nods from all the dancers, all of whom look very focused.

The director continues, "I just want to take a minute to remind you of the context of the scene. Layce, the Princess of Light, has spent the evening being courted and wooed by the Prince of Shadows. She has fallen for his charms, seduced by his beauty and the promise of true love. But when he reveals his true nature, when the Princess sees him for what he is, she refuses to be pulled into his darkness. Her inner spirit, her inner light, is what lifts her out of darkness. You, my amazing dancers," the directors smiles around at all of them, "are the darkness. Remember, when the wind fans start to blow, that signals the Princess' transformation into an angel. We'll be adding the wings as a CG element in post, but you should react as if you are seeing an actual angel before your eyes." He looks around at the dancers.

Many of the dancers nod understanding. There must be more than fifty of them. I hear some of them murmuring to each other, echoing some of the director's words.

The director says, "I know you've rehearsed the moves, and what I've seen is amazing, but just take a moment to remind yourself of the emotional story. You are darkness. You want to steal all light from the Princess. You are greedy for what she has. You're *starving* for her lightness. You are willing to *eat her alive* to take what she has, to fill the gaping hole in your own hearts with what she has. Does that make sense?"

I wonder how much of the director's speech was Julian's idea? It sounds so tragically romantic.

"All right!" The director claps his hands together and says cheerfully, "Let's make it happen!" He strolls off the set to where I stand near all the camera monitors and his awaiting assistants.

The dancers take their positions.

The work lights fade to blackness, and the gloomy mood lights come on, transforming the ballroom set back into an eerily believable pit of darkness.

I hear the familiar music for 'I Rise' play over the P.A.

The dancers start to move, writhing in the darkness, and the lights start to flash.

Layce walks regally into the ballroom. The dark prince stands in the center of the room, holding out his hand to her. He looks vulnerable and commanding at the same time.

Layce's character, the Princess of Light, can't resist his tragic appeal. She walks toward the Prince of Shadows, but the lyrics she lip syncs from the recording pumping out of the P.A. tell a different story:

"Dragged down by you
I pulled us up
My last stand for a broken man"

The dancers and gymnasts, who until now have been hidden in the shadows on the outskirts of the ballroom set, creep evilly into the light, skulking and circling and swirling around Layce. It's like the dancers symbolize the damage inside the poor Prince of Shadows.

Layce, the Princess of Light, acts as if she doesn't notice them. She sings with all her broken heart,

"I should've known
It wouldn't last
There's no way I could fix your broken past"

A column of light beams down on the dark Prince and strobes on and off like lightning, illuminating the boiling black mass of costumed dancers.

Now the Princess takes notice of the dancing demons.

The Steadicam operators are on the floor, shooting close ups of the Princess of Light and the Prince of Shadows. I can see their tortured faces on the director's monitors.

Layce does a great job of looking lost in love for the Prince of Shadows. The Prince aches with sadness and his eyes cry out for the Princess's love. She is uncertain whether to go to her sad Prince, or defend herself from his inner demons which circle around her dangerously.

Layce lip syncs the pre-chorus:

"I tried so hard
It's over now
Won't sink into your meltdown

I've had enough
I gave my all
I will not live within your fall"

Layce stands regally, resolutely, holding her ground. She will not go to the Prince. He must come to her. But he doesn't.

His minions do.

The dancers swirl around Layce, getting closer, making threatening gestures, snarling, growling, flashing their claws, licking their chops. They're going to tear Layce apart. Her eyes glare at them. She's ready to fight back.

The Princess of Light casts a final pleading glance at the Prince of Shadows.

The faintest sneer curls his lips. He's not going to budge from his throne of darkness.

The dancers pounce, converging on Layce, burying her in blackness. She's gone, her white dress completely hidden in boiling shadows.

The song's chorus starts:

"The beat of my heart,
my angel wings, and finally,
I rise
Soaring above it all
I fly"

Layce begins to emerge from the writhing mass, rising on the stunt wires, escaping the clutches of the Prince's inner demons.

But his minions rise with her, pulling her back down.

She sings with strength and power:

"My heart beat, dreams and desires
Finally, I rise
I fly"

Layce is lifted toward the light that now shines down on her as she chants the stuttering melody:

"Soaring above it all
Aa-aa-aa-aa-aa-aa-all
All"

The dark demons spin around her like an inverted vortex of jagged anger, a cone of shadows from which she'll never escape. The Prince doesn't want her to leave his darkly gothic abode.

But she does.

The Princess of Light floats higher and higher.

I hear the roar of the wind fans power up and Layce's wedding dress flutters up around her, signaling the beating of her immense white wings.

The demons of darkness shrink back in terror.

Strobe lights intensify and flicker. I hear air guns blowing puffs of smokey debris into the wind, swirling foggy wisps around Layce in her harness. She must be thirty feet above the stage. Many of the dancers hung from wires fly around Layce, circling her like demonic predators.

The chorus repeats as Layce is lifted to the heavens:

"Soaring above it all
Aa-aa-aa-aa-aa-aa-all
Aa-aa-aa-aa-aa-aa-all
All, all
Soaring above it all"

To my total surprise, pieces of the gothic ballroom set begin to crumble and fall to the floor. Many of them are attached to wires controlled by stage hands. Others bounce into the corners, obviously made of foam rubber or whatever.

The Prince's kingdom is collapsing as the Princess leaves him forever. His darkness was not enough to cage her light.

I'm so moved by the music and the visuals, I'm literally weeping. It's too beautiful for words. I half consider running off set to cry my eyes out in private, but the cameras are still rolling. And I'm literally rapt with fascination as the Princess of Light floats into eternity.

This is the most amazing musical spectacle I've ever seen. Even if Layce is a huge rich bitch.

I would do anything to

(*singsingsing*)

be a part of something like this.

And to my utter delight and amazement, Julian had a huge hand in all of it.

I wonder what other secrets he keeps?

"Cut!" the director shouts. "That was unbelievable!"

Everyone around him in the monitor area claps and cheers.

"Cut, everybody!" The assistant director calls out into a bullhorn.

The dancers on wires are lowered to the stage floor, followed by Layce. The gymnasts on the ground are applauding and congratulating each other with words and gestures. High fives, fist bumps, ass pats, shoulder nudges. They're having a blast.

So am I.

(*SINGSINGSINGSINGSINGSING!!!!*)

Chapter 101

VICTORY

I drive home that night in dire silence behind the wheel of my Altima.

The Layce video shoot literally blew my mind.

I was swept away by the fantasy and beauty and fame of it all.

Layce's music career is something most musicians, even successful ones, will never know. Heck, just making a living doing music to the point you don't have to work a second job is more success than most bands ever have.

But Layce has something incredible going for her career.

I drive past Johnny and Karen's apartment and keep going.

I want to be alone right now so I can process what I'm thinking and feeling.

Jealousy. Amazement. Envy. Awe.

(*sing*)

Jealousy.

Maybe I'm going about this music career thing all wrong. Maybe I need to be a singer instead of a guitar player.

(*singsingsing*)

No. That's insane. I'm never going to be a singer.

(*singsingsingsingsingsing*)

But maybe my music career needs some assistance.

My phone rings and I pull it out of my purse.

Julian.

"Hello?"

I'm glad he called.

"I'm so sorry, Victory."

"Why?"

"Oh," he groans, "Sony took forever. That new girl they had me meet was terrible. I didn't get out of the building until just now."

"That's okay," I chuckle.

"Yes, but are *you* okay?" he asks, concerned.

"I'm fine," I sigh. A little melancholy about my music career, but I'm holding it together. But I don't tell him that.

"Would you like to get dinner? I haven't eaten since lunch. There's an amazing new place on La Cienega called Il Susso. I've been dying to try it."

I remember what happened between me and Julian in his Ferrari after we had breakfast at THE Blvd. Our hot and heavy outdoor rendezvous. As much as I'd love to talk about the music business with Julian tonight over dinner, I'm afraid if I go out with him, I'll end up in bed with him.

After the emotional roller coaster of being on set for Layce's video shoot, I don't know if I can do it.

"It's sweet of you to offer," I sigh. "But I think I'm gonna go home to bed."

"Do you need company?"

I was right.

I mean, I don't think Julian would try to seduce me or whatever. He's been a perfect gentleman every step of the way. A slightly dirty, aggressive around the edges gentleman, but in the very best way.

I remember his finger deep inside me…

It's *so* tempting.

My phone beeps as a text comes in.

"Hold on a sec," I say.

I glance at the text.

It's from Liv:

I'm free to rehearse tonight. Wanna come over? We can write new music too. Got some fresh ideas.

That sounds like exactly what I need right now. Liv and I haven't had much time to work on the music we plan to play at L.A. Gunslingers. If we don't get stuff finished, we're never gonna be ready in time. And that means no chance of winning that $5,000 prize, which I could seriously use.

I say to Julian, "I'm really sorry, Julian. Tonight just isn't a good night. Can we do dinner another night?"

"Is everything okay?" he asks.

"Yeah, it's fine." I may as well tell him. I explain about Liv and finding time to write for Gunslingers, and finish by saying, "I really need to go over to Liv's place so we can get to work."

"What is L.A. Gunslingers?" he asks with distinct curiosity.

"Oh, it's this battle of the bands thing Guitar Central hosts every year. I put together a band with Liv and a couple friends so we could play it."

"Sounds interesting. Mind if I come?"

"What, to Gunslingers?"

"Yes. I think it might be fun to watch you perform on stage. I've only seen you in the studio, but I'm fascinated to know what you might be like in front of a crowd. I imagine you're a spectacular performer."

"Thanks," I smile. "If you want to come, that would be cool. But if I don't finish writing the music with Liv, we won't have a demo tape to submit, which means we won't play. I'm kind of worried we've missed the cutoff already."

"Ahhh. I see. I wouldn't want to stand in the way of your writing process," he says compassionately.

"You don't mind if we do dinner another time?"

"Not at all," Julian says genuinely. "Whenever you're ready, call me and I'll take you someplace extravagant and incredible."

I smile, "I know you will. It sounds wonderful. I'll call you."

"I look forward to it. And if you make the cutoff for this Gunslingers thing, let me know and I"ll come out to watch."

"I will. Wish me luck writing tonight!"

"Luck," he jokes.

"Bye, Julian."

"Good night, Victory."

I end the call and drive to Liv's so we can do some much needed song writing.

I'm all inspired to work on my own music after what I saw on Layce's sound stage. Her song 'I Rise' and the video gave me an idea for a song I've really been wanting to write myself.

Chapter 102

VICTORY

The Dive Bomb bar in Silver Lake rumbles as me and Olivia wheel our amps around back to the dingy graffiti-tagged back door. Behind the building, a chain link fence topped with coils of razor wire surrounds the back lot of an auto body shop filled with cars in various states of disrepair.

My kind of venue.

Olivia says, "I'm so glad we got all that writing done the other night. I think we've made a ton of progress."

"Me too," I smile. "At the rate we're going, we might even have four or five songs finished before L.A. Gunslingers. That's more than enough."

We stop at the back door of The Dive Bomb.

"Totally," Liv agrees. "I just hope we have time to rehearse them."

"At the rate you pick up stuff," I say, "We'll be fine."

"Thanks, Vee! You are *so* nice!" She smiles broadly, her painted red lips peeling back over her white teeth.

When we reach the back door, she says, "Let me get the door for you." She tries to open it, but it's locked. She yanks on the handle several times with both hands, grunting and squeaking like a squeezable baby toy. "I think we're locked out. Unless you brought the key?"

"I don't have a key," I grin, "Why would I have a key?"

"I don't know, but you should," she smiles.

"It's not like I own the bar, Liv."

"You should work on that," she smirks.

"Try knocking?"

She does. "I don't think anyone can hear me over the music."

"Try kicking," I suggest.

"I'm not kicking a dirty door with these boots!" Olivia wears shiny fuchsia Go-Go boots that match the vinyl belt cinched around her Go-Go dancer dress. The flared sleeve dress is an explosion of psychedelic colors that barely drops below her ass. "These boots cost me a hundred bucks used! You do it, combat boots," she sneers.

"These aren't combat boots," I point my toe and rotate my boot on the cracked cement. "They don't have steel toes."

She rolls her eyes, "Do I have to do everything?"

The door suddenly opens and Kellan walks out. He stops short, "What are you guys doing here?"

I quip, "It's open mic night, isn't it?"

He grins, "That it is."

"Why are you here?" I demand.

"To play."

"Us too," I smirk.

"Hey, Aiden," Olivia says to him.

Kellan flashes me a quick look that says, "Does your friend have brain damage?"

I ignore him.

Switchblade walks out at that moment, looking like hot punker girl as always, and says, "Kellan, I'll get the guitars from the car."

"Awesome," he says. To me, "So, Victory, you came to rock the house?"

"Yup."

"It's gonna be rubble after we finish. Hope you don't mind an empty house."

I shake my head, "You mean because you guys are going to suck so loud and hard, everyone leaves?"

"The only sucking will be after we play," Kellan says provocatively.

I'm sure he's referring to Switchblade and whatever he plans to do with her punk rock body when they go home together.

"Ew," Liv grimaces. "Victory, can you tell Chester the Molester here to move so we can wheel our amps inside?"

I flash Kellan a grin, "What she said."

He asks, "You guys need any help?"

Liv snaps, "Not the kind of help you mean." She tugs her keyboard amp up the step and drags it inside.

I push my Bogner combo up to the step.

Kellan picks it up, "I've got it."

I say, "I can do it."

But he's already lifted it and set it down inside the door.

He walks away, smiling, "Have fun tonight."

When I get inside, Liv is already flirting with the guy who organizes the bands playing the open mic. It's first come first serve, but a little flirtation always helps. The guy is handsome, has long flowing brown hair and wears a leather vest that reveals tanned, muscled arms. He looks like he's used to flirtation.

Liv literally runs her fingers through his hair and says, "I love your hair! So silky. And these arms! Wow." She giggles. "What's your name, hot stuff?"

"Yes," he quips.

"It's not Hot Stuff!" She swats his muscled arm.

Muscles chuckles, "It's Tracy."

They shake hands.

"Tracy, I'm Olivia. And this is my friend Victory."

Tracy nods, "Hey. What's your band called?"

Liv turns to me, "What are we called, Victory?"

"Ninth Street Nymphos?" I suggest.

"Good enough," Liv nods once and says to Tracy, "Ninth Street Nymphos."

He snickers and jots it down.

"When do we play?" Liv asks him.

"Hard to tell. We'll play it by ear."

"If I play with your ear," Liv reaches up and caresses her fingers across his ear and down his cheek, then his chest, where she parks it, "will that help our positioning any?"

"It might," Tracy grins. "But you're gonna have to play with it a lot more than that."

Liv rolls her eyes, "Don't spoil your luck, *Dick* Tracy."

He smiles, "I'll see what I can do. But I'm not promising anything."

"Fine," Liv relents. She grabs my hand and pulls me toward the stage.

Tracy stops us, "You can't go that way. You have to go around front."

Liv demands, "Do we get *any* royal treatment tonight?"

"You get what you give," Tracy jests.

"I don't give freebies," Liv laughs.

"Neither do I," Tracy smiles.

"Let's go, Liv," I say, "before Tracy puts us on the bottom of the list."

We walk around to the front of the bar.

A row of motorcycles are parked along the sidewalk. A bunch of leather jacketed or denim vested biker types mill around bullshitting with each other.

Liv waves at them, "Hi, boys!"

They all eye her appreciatively. Several lean over slightly, hoping to catch a glimpse up Liv's hazardly hemmed dress.

I lean into her, as we walk through the front door of The Dive Bomb and mumble, "I don't know why you even bothered wearing the dress, Liv, it's so short."

"It's the tease that pleases. If you show them everything, they get bored. But if you leave just enough to the imagination, and there's the distinct possibility that a slight breeze will give them a show, they never get bored. And, if Tracy decides there's not enough time for us to play tonight, I'm sure the Hell's Angels outside will be happy to encourage him to let the girl in the too short dress play before the night is over."

"Good thinking," I grin.

We buy drinks at the crowded bar and stand in a corner, waiting for the music to start.

The clientele is rockers and bikers and a few random citizens. Mostly young people. But the rockers are all ages.

There's even a silver haired guy with an older woman who wears what I think is a curly burgundy wig and a leather police hat. He and his woman both wear studded leather from head to toe and clearly belong together.

"I wish Lucas and Logan could've made it," Liv says as she sips on a Cosmo.

"Me too," I say and sip from my bottle of Sam Adams.

"What was the problem again?"

"They had a paying gig at The Casbah down in San Diego in Little

Italy."

"Considering we're getting zero dollars for open mic," Liv shrugs, "I can hardly blame them. At least we have backing tracks on my laptop. We'll manage."

"Do you think we need to find guys who live in L.A.?"

"Replace Lucas and Logan?" Liv gapes. "Not until I've hooked up with at least both of them!"

"Did you say *both* of them?"

She grins and nods.

"You're such a slut, Liv," I grin.

She nods proudly, "Yup!"

I shake my head, pausing my Sam Adams bottle an inch from my lips, "Remember how well that worked out for me and Scott?"

"I"m not going to move in with them! Just sleep with them."

I scoff, "And that's *not* going to create band drama?"

Liv winks at me, "Who said anything about avoiding band drama?"

I groan and roll my eyes.

A few minutes later, Tracy introduces the first band. They're so totally forgettable, I don't remember their name or their music. They play a couple of songs, and no one in the bar seems to be paying much attention.

Liv says, "These guys probably sucked Tracy's dick to play tonight."

I giggle.

When the forgettable band finishes, they haul their gear off the stage and the second band goes to work. Their music is reminiscent of old Scorpions, but with a female singer, who is actually pretty good. The crowd really gets into it.

"These guys are great!" Liv hollers. "We should have you be our front woman!"

My eyes bulge, "Uh, no?"

(*never ever sing*)

"Why not?" she demands.

I shrug my shoulders. "I'll leave the front womaning to you, Liv."

I can't get over how many people have been encouraging me to sing lately. It's becoming something of a joke and it almost doesn't bother me anymore.

I'm not nearly as traumatized by Liv's suggestion as I was when I watched Layce perform 'I Rise' at the soundstage and Julian asked me pretty much the same thing. It helps that the band on stage right now is just a Scorpions knockoff playing in a dive bar. They're not particularly original beyond the fact they have a female singer.

I'm much more excited about the original music I'll be playing with Liv when we take to the stage tonight.

Chapter 103

VICTORY

"All right everybody!" Tracy screams into the mic between bands. *"Are you ready to be blown away?!"*

The Dive Bomb crowd cheers.

"You all know Kellan Burns," Tracy shouts.

The crowd erupts with excitement and applause. I hear women screaming "KELLAN!!!" like he's The Beatles.

Liv shouts at me, "ARE THEY TALKING ABOUT YOUR KELLAN?"

"HE'S NOT MY KELLAN!"

"IF YOU SAY SO!" Liv grins.

"Everybody welcome Kellan and his new band Suffer The Gun to the stage!"

The colored stage lights flash and the whole band makes a shitload of noise. There's a shirtless tattooed Mexican guy behind the drums. A handsome black guy who looks like he belongs in a Reggae band plays bass. Switchblade holds a George Lynch Kamikaze ESP. My respect for her goes up. Anyone who plays that guitar is cool in my book. I don't know if she can play or not, but I'll find out soon enough.

Kellan strolls onstage with his skyburst blue Les Paul hanging from his shoulder. He's shirtless now and I notice he has on leather pants and boots.

The girls scream.

They're so shrill, I think my ears are going to bleed.

But I can't blame them.

Kellan stirs me up just as much. I just don't let it show. Too bad he's with Switchblade.

Kellan leans into the center stage mic, *"What up, Dive Bomb! How are you guys tonight?"*

The crowd roars.

You'd think Kellan's band was the headliner based on how packed the place is. He must be a regular here.

He growls, *"You guys ready to rock?!"*

More roaring cheers from the crowd.

"Hell yeah! Let's live it uuuppp!!!"

The band explodes into a driving riff that reminds me of We Die Young by Alice In Chains, but dirtier and sexier. Every member of the band is rocking out on stage, banging their heads, even their Reggae bass player. They're incredibly tight.

When Kellan sings, I'm blown away.

"King of today
Forever I pray
Hero of sorrow
Zero tomorrow"

His rock voice is gritty, manly, dangerous, and powerful. I'm not surprised. It sums up everything I know about him. Amazing.

He pours his heart into the mic as he plays the heavy riff on his guitar:

"All of this will pass
Youth won't last
Terror fills my head
Choices made in dread."

The riff changes for the pre-chorus. The drummer does an amazing fill. He's incredible.

Kellan sings:

"Addiction to gain
Birth of our pain
Then one day
We give it away
Oblivion
A cold dark grave awaits"

I'm struck by the maturity of Kellan's lyrics. They're not stupid "party all night and chase girls 24/7" hard rock fluff. I'm not surprised. Kellan never struck me as shallow.

When he sings the chorus, the whole band harmonizes with him and they sound amazing:

"Live it Uuuupppp!
Yeah!
Death ain't catching me!
Live it Uuuupppp!
Laughing while I'm free!"

After the chorus, Switchblade breaks into a guitar solo. Damn, she's really good. I'm impressed, and that's saying a lot.

While she plays, Kellan leans his back against hers. A huge grin lights his face. Switchblade leans against him like they've been playing together for thirty years. They're the perfect hard rock guitar duo.

The whole time Switchblade solos, Kellan plays the aggressive rhythm riff that gives context to the intricate melody spinning out of Switchblade's guitar.

It sounds really amazing.

Kellan watches Switchblade's solo over her shoulder and smiles appreciatively. No wonder he started ignoring me.

He found my replacement.

And she even sings harmony with him.

(*never ever ever sing*)

I remember back to that lone night I spent at Kellan's apartment. He told me enthusiastically about his musical vision, one that included my guitar skills and the possibility of me singing harmony vocals with him. The vision he described sounded exactly like what I'm seeing and hearing onstage right now.

Was I stupid to say no to Kellan?

His band is incredible.

I remind myself I've only heard one song.

But they play two more, and both songs are just as good as the first. I wish I wrote them. I'm totally jealous. That's why I know Kellan's band is really good. Because it hurts to hear him and his band sound so damn amazing.

Without me.

Liv nudges me, "YOUR FRIEND ROCKS!"

Yes he does.

And he sings.

(*singsingsing!!!*)

I have to go get some air.

This is too much.

Chapter 104

VICTORY

I lean against the front of The Dive Bomb while I listen to the muffled sounds of Kellan and his awesome band rocking the house.

"Where'd you go?" Liv asks as she walks out the front door.

"I needed some air," I say hoarsely.

"Are you okay?"

"I'm fine," I lie.

"Do you want to go? We don't have to wait around for our turn."

"It's up to you. My brain is scrambled right now."

"What's wrong, Victory?" Liv asks sympathetically.

I sigh, "I don't want to go into it. Let's go bug Tracy and see if we can get on stage tonight. Although, after Kellan's band, I don't know that anyone will care." I sigh again.

She says sarcastically, "That's the spirit."

I giggle.

"Don't worry about it, Vee. We'll show them. I'm dying to sing Sunset Farewell. I promise, every one of those bikers is going to shed tears in their beers after they hear you and me play it."

"Okay. But maybe we should go have a three way with Tracy so we can make sure we get on stage," I snicker.

"He's cute enough," Liv smiles, "but I get to sit on his face. No one's gone down on me in forever."

I laugh.

"Well, well, well," Scott Walker, my Ex, says as he walks up to the front door of The Dive Bomb with a big-titted rocker bimbo on his arm. He sneers, "If it isn't Victory Payne."

Splendid.

Scott is wearing sunglasses, even though the last hint of daylight is a thin orange line on the horizon, and a fur coat, even though it's way too hot for fur. The coat is open and reveals a too short silver shirt that shows off his flat stomach and black-and-white striped pants. His low-profile dress shoes are glittery silver. He's such a decadent rockstar.

"If it isn't Smellton John," Liv groans.

Scott frowns at her.

Liv rephrases, "I mean, Scott Cocker."

"Nice," Scott scowls. He taps his lips with his index finger and quips thoughtfully, "I can't remember. What was your name again? Something like Olivia... *Cunt*. Right? Or was it Dunce? I can't recall. It's been so long since I forgot your name the last time."

Liv shakes her head.

Big Tits titters and nuzzles against Scott while she stares down at me and Liv. Scott probably has his hand up her back like a ventriloquist dummy and decides when she does or doesn't speak.

"In case you forgot," Liv growls, "It's Olivia 'You Better Run Before I Put My Go-Go Boot Up Your Butt' Blunt."

I chuckle at Scott, "I see you didn't waste any time finding my replacement."

Scott chuffs dismissively, "It wasn't hard."

Big Tits goes, "Snicker, snicker."

I sneer, "Yeah, because you were probably hooking up with her long before we broke up."

He doesn't deny it. Instead, he says doubtfully,"We? I broke up with *you*."

Big Tits goes, "Cackle, cackle."

I guess since Scott doesn't know how to throw his voice like a real ventriloquist, he can only make Big Tits mumble and snort.

I take the high road, "And for that, Scott, I thank you. Breaking up with me was the nicest thing you ever did. Now I know for sure how worthless you are."

"Go, Victory!" Liv cheers.

Scott opens the door of The Dive Bomb and pulls his big titted dummy in after him. She walks stiffly on her too-tall heels. Like a mannequin.

Liv pinches her nose like something smells bad and drawls,"Scott is laaaaame."

I grin, "Do you smell farts or something?"

Liv winces, "Just Scott's breath."

"Same thing" I giggle.

Liv laughs, "I'm so glad you're done with Turd Breath. I missed you, Vee. You know that?" She smiles earnestly.

"I missed you too. Now let's go show Scott how we rock the house."

Liv raises her hand for a high five, "You go, girlfriend! Remember, I get to sit on Tracy's face! He has the nicest lips!"

"So do you, Liv."

"Which ones?" she giggles.

"I guess I'll find out in five minutes," I laugh as we walk around back.

"Are you going to let me sit on your face too?" She gasps gleefully.

"If you're nice," I joke.

"I'm always nice!" she shrieks.

We both laugh and walk around the back of the bar, arms around each other's shoulders.

Liv reaches down suddenly and pinches my butt.

"Hey!" I shout.

"Just getting you in the mood!" she giggles.

Chapter 105

VICTORY

Liv hisses in my ear, "You should've let me suck Tracy's dick earlier, Vee! The crowd is thinning out and the place is going to be empty before we hit the stage!"

I hiss in her ear, "Tracy is gay! Weren't you listening when he told us?"

Liv scoffs, "Show me a gay guy who doesn't like a good blowjob. For that matter, show me anything with a penis that doesn't like a good blowjob. Mice, goats, tarantulas…"

I frown, "Do tarantulas even have penises?"

Liv nods emphatically, "I'm pretty sure tarantulas have two penises!"

"Two?" I ask skeptically. "Where'd you get that number?"

"Duh! They have twice as many limbs as a person, so they must have twice as many penises!"

I chuckle and roll my eyes, "Don't ever ask me to have a three way with you and a tarantula."

She snorts, "I've got a hand, I can work both spiny appendages at once."

An image of Liv and a human sized tarantula in a seedy hotel having insectophelia sex attempts to enter my mental theater, but I drop the curtains before it fully forms. My mental audience whooshes a sigh of relief.

Liv definitely makes waiting less boring. Fortunately for us, the bar is still two-thirds full when Tracy motions for us to take to the brightly lit stage.

Tracy shouts over the microphone, *"Everybody, please welcome Ninth Street Nymphos to The Dive Bomb stage!"*

The applause is moderate. Nothing like the reception Kellan got from all the girl tarantulas in the audience. I snicker to myself. Liv sure put me in a wacky mood.

"You suck!" someone shouts.

It sounds like Scott. Wow, he's so magnanimous. And definitely a male tarantula.

I lean into one of the stage mics and say sarcastically, "Not you, I don't."

I hear one person laugh, or maybe that's my imagination.

This is a far cry from the reception I got as part of Skin Trade. The band I helped build.

Fucking Scott.

Why did he have to come here tonight?

Liv is at the front of the stage beside me, since it's just the two of us. She leans toward me and asks, "You ready?"

I nod.

We only have two songs, because that's all we've had time to write.

The first one is called Rave To The Grave. Liv wrote most of it, including the lyrics. Liv starts the backing track drums on her laptop, which is mounted to the top of her keyboard stand. It's not the same as Logan on drums, but it's good enough. Liv joins in with her keyboards, and a measure later, I add guitar. Liv wrote the lyrics and sings them. I think they're a bit too Party Pop for this crowd. The chorus doesn't sound nearly as good without Lucas and Logan harmonizing along with her.

But we get some token applause when we finish.

"Get off the stage!" Scott yells.

But we do get that.

"Shut the fuck up, man!" someone responds. Was that Kellan? I can't tell for sure. The lights are shining in my face, so I can't see the audience, just outlines. But it sounded like Kellan.

"Fuck you!" Scott grumbles absently.

Liv says on mic, "I think we have some admirers, Victory."

"Uh...yeah. We'll be signing autographs after the show," I joke into my mic.

A few laughs from the crowd.

"This next song," I say, "is called Sunset Farewell."

Liv cues up the backing tracks and the soft drums start with a slow tom fill. It's a power ballad. I wrote it about Scott.

"Get a drummer!" Scott shouts.

I can't wait to hear what he thinks.

Liv shoves her arm out in the general direction of Scott and flips him off.

Chuckles from the crowd.

"Tell it," a woman cheers. I think it might have been Switchblade, but I can't say for sure.

I play clean, shimmery chords as accompaniment for Liv's keyboards, which are set to an echoey grand piano sound. The chords are haunting, and so is Liv's voice. She does total justice to my lyrics.

She sings:

"You left me behind
Your journey into night
I asked you to return
The treasure of our light

You needed it for guidance
So keep it for a time
The only chance to find it
Your pathway into light"

The room is now silent, save our music and Liv's amazing singing.
I hope Scott is listening. He really needs to hear this.
Liv and I change keys as we move into the plaintive pre chorus:

"My soul has been unwell
Since your heart set sail
I never said goodbye
Still seek our holy grail
Memory fades with passing days
Forgotten how you fell"

We've played the song enough times, and the guitar part is really easy, so I'm able to concentrate on

(*Vic—*)

Liv's amazing singing and memories of

(*Vict—*)

my relationship with Scott climb into my awareness. He wasn't always an ass. But he was always troubled. I had high hopes in the beginning. I worked really hard to accept his bleak moods and his nasty temper. Even now, after his total rudeness since I saw him outside, I can feel the sadness of a lost relationship and all that

(*Victor—*)

wasted effort.

Liv sings the chorus over swelling ambient keyboards on the backing track that bolster her voice with added textural harmony:

"Trapped in your sunset spell
Eternal carousel
Believing my own lies
Trapped in our sunset spell
The prison where I dwell
Holding onto life
Trapped in your sunset spell

Eternal carousel"

We change to the bridge chords, and it takes everything I have to hold it together and not start weeping onstage. The song is powerful. Liv's voice is haunting and it seems to be peeling back the layers of my armor. I still haven't finished grieving about what I lost when Scott trashed everything.

Liv sings the second verse:

"You got lost in darkness
You said there's room for two
I begged for you come back to me
Together we'll renew

Your heart and eyes said yes
Your hurtful words said no
Your soul confessed it was distressed
And didn't want to go"

I realize I wrote this song as a way to grieve the loss of what I had with

(*Stop!!!*)

Scott.

I'm a bit jealous Liv gets to

(*singsingsing*)

sing it. But at least

(*Victory!!!*)

someone is singing it. Even if it isn't me. I can grieve through Liv's amazing performance just like I've done with songs played by other bands that I've loved and listened to hundreds of times because those songs speak to something deep within me. Just like most people who aren't musicians do with their favorite music, processing their pain with the help of music they love.

In this moment, I'm totally grateful for Liv's amazing voice:

"My soul has been unwell
Since your heart set sail
I never said goodbye
Still seek our holy grail
Memory fades with passing days
Forgotten how you fell"

When Liv finishes, I break into a wailing guitar solo. I pour my heart into it, and my sadness flows from my fingers, into my Fender and out of my amplifier, filling The Dive Bomb with my pain. I'm weeping by the end as my tears drip onto my guitar.

It feels so good to let Scott

(*Stop, Dad!!!*)

go.

Liv repeats the chorus a final time:

"Trapped in your sunset spell
Eternal carousel
Believing my own lies
Trapped in our sunset spell
The prison where I dwell
Holding onto life
Trapped in your sunset spell

Time to say farewell
Time to break your spell
Time to say farewell
Time to break your spell"

The song fades away softly on Liv's last word.

I hang my head over my guitar. My shoulders shake as I weep silently onstage in front of the entire room.

So much pain.

The Dive Bomb is dead silent.

Five seconds later, the crowd explodes and the whole room cheers. People are whistling, clapping, shouting.

I can't believe it.

I giggle through my sobs and look over at Liv.

She looks surprised, her eyes big, her lips pursed oddly. For once, she is speechless.

I smile at her, and I feel so much better

"That was shit!' Scott shouts.

Yeah, whatever, Scott.

I'm done with you.

But my pain remains…

(*Victor!!!!!!*)

Chapter 106

VICTORY

The caster wheels on our amps clatter across the cracked sidewalk as me and Liv push our amps back to my car, past the front of The Dive Bomb.

The crowd of bikers smoking cigarettes outside start clapping forcefully as we pass.

"Yeah!" one of them shouts. "You guys rocked!"

Another biker walks over and says, "You need help with those amps?"

Liv giggles and mutters to me, "We have fans!"

"Sure," I smile at the guy.

The two bikers pick up our amps and walk us to our car. We stash everything in my trunk. "Well," I say, "we're going inside to get some drinks."

The taller biker, who wears a Motörhead shirt under his thin leather vest says, "Can I buy you guys a round?"

"Make it two," Liv quips, "And you have a deal."

Tall Biker grins, "You got it."

They walk us back inside.

Although they buy drinks for me and Liv, so many other people want to talk to us about our performance and congratulate us, it's impossible to talk to just our two biker buddies. Luckily, they're cool, and roll with it.

I thought Kellan was going to be the big star tonight, but who knew this biker crowd loved a good broken hearted ballad? I guess it helps that Liv's Go-Go outfit is barely legal and I don't look half bad myself. I'm just wearing a skin tight Avenged Sevenfold shirt that is sized for a twelve year old and spandex jeans, but the jeans highlight my hips and legs as much as they cover them.

At one point, I notice with amusement that Liv is the only color in a sea of black leather and dark denim. I'd bet my paycheck she planned it this way.

But I'm getting my own fair share of male attention.

Kellan squeezes into the crowd surrounding me and Liv holding a beer bottle. He says, "I knew you were going to be incredible."

"Thanks," I grin. "Did you want to show your appreciation by buying me a drink?"

"Glad to," he chuckles. "What are you drinking?"

"Oh, I'm kidding. I've already had a hundred people offer me drinks already. I have to drive home."

"You want water?"

"No, thanks," I smile. "You guys were pretty amazing yourselves."

Kellan nods, "Thanks."

He's wearing a shirt right now, but still has on the rocker leather pants and boots.

"Your bass player and your drummer were incredible." I glance around the bar, "Are they here? I'd love to meet them."

"Dubs and Joa took off," Kellan says.

"How come?"

"Would you believe Dubs had another gig tonight?"

"Which one was he?"

"The bass player. He has a Reggae band called The Revelers."

I smile, "That's awesome. I love that he does both hard rock and Reggae."

"I do too," Kellan grins.

"Did you write those songs since you guys formed the band? Or were they old tunes you had in your back pocket?"

"Some of it was old riffs or lyrics, but a lot of it was new. Something about writing with Switchblade and the boys was incredibly easy."

I feel a pinch of jealousy. Sure, Liv and I did great, but Sunset Farewell was the only thing that got a response from the crowd, and it was mostly her singing that did it. A power ballad is always about the vocalist.

Kellan smiles, "Your solo on that ballad was incredible. You did some really gutsy playing. My jaw was dropped the whole time." He's totally sincere.

Why does Kellan have to be so damn nice? And handsome? Where is that Switchblade? I remember Liv mentioning conking her over the head and burying her body in the desert outside Vegas.

"Speaking of guitar solos," I say, "how come you didn't play any?"

"Ahh, I was too busy working on the songs. I let Switchblade handle them."

Switchblade again. I may as well accept it. And she really is a great guitarist. If I don't hold her relationship with Kellan against her, I could easily learn a thing or ten from her.

"So," I sigh, "Where is Switchblade? I wanted to ask her how her audition with Wild Child went."

"Didn't I tell you?"

"Nuh uh."

Kellan grins, "Switchblade got the gig!"

"What!" I'm shocked.

"Yeah," Kellan laughs, "she blew them away. That's why she went home already. She has to jump on a plane first thing tomorrow morning to catch up with the band in Detroit."

Wait a second. Do I tell Kellan what happened between me and Danny Daggers? Is Switchblade walking into a viper's den without realizing it? I have to say something, "Um, I hope it's not too late, but does Switchblade know that Danny Daggers is basically an amateur rapist?"

Kellan is taken aback, "What?"

"He came on to me during my audition."

"He what?"

I nod.

Liv tugs at my arm, "Do you want another drink?"

"No. I'm good," I smile. "Are you doing okay?"

"I have three marriage proposals. Two from cute guys, one from a woman who owns a Harley. Do I say yes?"

"To the woman with the Harley?" I ask.

"No, silly! All three!"

I giggle, "Go with the tarantula."

She wrinkles her nose and sinks back into her crowd of biker admirers.

I say to Kellan, "What was I saying?"

He prompts, "About Danny Daggers? The rapist?"

"Oh yeah. During my audition, he totally tried to grope me so I decked him."

Kellan laughs, "You did not deck him!"

"Yes, I did," I say defensively.

"Like, you punched him in the face and he fell down on his ass?"

"Not exactly fell. But he stumbled, and I know I gave him a shiner," I grin proudly.

"How would you know if you gave someone a shiner?" Kellan gawks.

"Want me to show you?" I hold up a fist.

He shakes his head, "I'll take your word for it. But you actually punched him in the face?"

I nod confidently.

"That deserves a bump," he holds up his fist and I punch it casually.

"So," I say, "do you need to warn Switchblade? I'd hate to see her get sexually harassed by a bunch of rich asshole rockstars."

"I don't think you need to worry." He tips back his bottle of beer and swallows.

"Why not?"

"Switchblade told me Daggers came on to her too."

"What a prick. What did she do?"

"She said she'd fuck him, but he'd have to pay her an extra $50,000. If he wanted to fuck her twice, it was going to be an extra $100,000. She also warned him that he couldn't afford to fuck her three times, but after fucking her twice, he would want to, and she hated the idea of bankrupting him, but she'd totally do it to get the gig."

I chuckle, "Wow, and she still got the job?"

"Of course she did," Kellan grins and swallows more beer.

"I like her style," I say thoughtfully. "Does that mean she fucked Danny Daggers?"

Kellan laughs, "Not even."

I ask coyly, "So, are you going to miss Switchblade while she's gone?"

"I guess so. Why?"

"Aren't you guys going out?"

Kellan frowns, "Where'd you get that idea?"

"I see you guys together all the time. She's really into you. It's obvious."

Kellan shakes his head, "Switchblade is gay."

"No way!"

Kellan nods.

"You're not going out with her?"

He shakes his head, "You seem surprised."

"I am. I just thought, I mean, you guys seem to really like each other."

"No doubt. Switchblade is a really cool chick. I'm totally gonna miss having her in the band and as a friend. But what can I do?"

I can think of a few things Kellan can do about it...

He finishes, "Anyway, people come and people go. I can't hold onto someone who wants to go." He gazes down at me with his burning brown eyes.

Is he talking about me or Switchblade?

I smile up at him and he gives me an unintentionally sexy look which is undeniably heart stopping. I say unintentional because Kellan never has to try and he's simply damn sexy. Although he's wearing a t-shirt now, I remember how hot he was onstage earlier when all his muscles were flexing as he strummed his guitar. His dancing abs were a show unto themselves.

And now that I know Kellan isn't dating Switchblade, and never was, maybe I need to re-evaluate my position on me and Kellan.

His eyes search mine.

Mine search his.

My chest warms with a pleasant peacefulness as the crowded and raucous surroundings of The Dive Bomb fade into a fuzzy background blur.

The only thing that exists in this moment is me and Kellan.

Kellan brushes his fingertips down my forearm.

Chills tickle my skin where he touched me, but the rest of my body blossoms with warmth and yearning.

He leans toward me.

Is he going to kiss me?

He smiles softly.

I think he is.

I want him to.

His fingers lace with mine and we are holding hands.

It feels so right, so intimate, and so incredibly perfect…

Why did I ever push him away?

His lips are inches from mine…

"There you are," Scott stumbles out of the crowd and into my face, wearing his Elton John shades and fur coat. He's drunk. Not falling-down plastered, but lit for sure.

Fucking Scott.

He always ruins everything, even when he's not involved. I scowl at him. How did I ever think he was handsome?

Scott looks at Kellan and points at him with the brown beer bottle in his hand, "I remember you."

Kellan nods dismissively, "And you're the guy who was heckling Victory when she was onstage. So get the fuck out of here."

"Fuck you, man," Scott spits. "She's my girlfriend."

I laugh in Scott's face, "Are you kidding? What happened to your date? Did you forget her already?" I don't add that she was entirely forgettable, except for her tits and vacant stare. Cackle, cackle, cackle. Maybe she went home with a hot biker and left Scott high and dry.

Scott sneers at me.

I ask, "What do you want, Scott?"

"You."

I laugh again and shake my head. "Don't you remember how you kicked me out of the band?"

His brows knit, "You want back in?"

My eyes goggle, "No?"

"I can't find a decent guitar player."

I growl, "I thought you said they were a dime a dozen in L.A."

"Not good ones," he sniffs.

"Oh," I bluster, "*now* you need me? You are a fucking prick, Scott."

"I have a fucking prick," he grins stupidly.

I grimace, "Get out of here, Scott. You had your chance not to be a worthless asshole, but you weren't up for the challenge because you're the least valuable asshole on the entire planet."

Kellan chuckles at my wordplay.

"Fuck you," Scott snarls at Kellan.

Kellan asks me, "Why did you ever date this douche, Gigi?"

I like that he called me G.G. Guitar Goddess. Kellan is the best. I chuckle, "I can't answer that without sounding like an idiot."

"Come on, Vic," Scott whines. "Come back to our apartment. I haven't changed the place."

"Don't call me Vic, you prick. And I'm not going back to your shithole."

Scott gestures with his beer bottle, "You know you miss it. You miss us."

I laugh.

Scott grabs my elbow, "Let's go, honey."

Kellan drops a heavy hand on Scott's shoulder, "Back off, Scott. She's not interested."

Scott twists out from under Kellan's hand and slams his beer bottle against the closest bar table. Glass tinkles to the floor. He waves the remnants of the jagged bottle in Kellan's face menacingly.

The crowd opens, forming a wide circle around the arc of Scott's waving arm. Conversation stops. The only sound in the bar is the music on the house P.A.

Everyone stares at Scott.

I can see that he is acutely aware of his audience. He is a consummate showman. But he's not a fighter.

Kellan chuckles, "Dude, do you look like you can kick my ass? I don't think so. Put the bottle down before you make a fool of yourself."

Scott is suddenly seething mad. His eyes are wild and his mouth quivers like crazy. He's winding himself up. I know the look. He's going to explode in a second. It's his only fighting strategy. Right now, that's probably a bad idea.

I've never seen Kellan fight, but he looks like he knows how. And he's much bigger and more muscular than Scott.

I don't want Scott to get hurt or accidentally cut me or an innocent bystander. Well, I wouldn't mind seeing Scott get hurt. But the broken bottle in his hand is a problem. Without realizing it, I slip into my well-worn "placate Scott" tone of voice. I say softly, "Scott, don't."

Scott pauses, his eyes blinking, and looks at me with sadness on his face. His features soften and he's the handsome man I remember. Almost angelic. I loved him for two years. I probably fell in love with him long before that, before we started Skin Trade and officially started dating. Right now, he's pathetic. I can't help feeling bad for him.

But it only takes a second to remember him for what he truly is: troubled, irritable, short tempered, and a deceitful liar. More than anything, I want to turn my back on him and walk away.

But he's still waving that sharded bottle around dangerously.

Kellan says, "Put the bottle down, Scott."

Scott's face twists in agony. He growls at me then turns on Kellan.

Kellan asks, "Have you stopped to ask yourself how stupid it is starting a bar fight wearing a fur coat and sunglasses? How well can you move or even see?"

Scott grunts and lunges at Kellan, leading with the bottle.

Kellan does this spinning move, pivoting his torso out of the bottle's trajectory and gripping the back of Scott's straightened elbow with one hand, yanking Scott forward and off balance while hammering Scott's head with the bottom of his fist like a falling hammer.

It all happens in half a second.

Scott drops like a bag of butter, knocking over a barstool that clatters to the floor while the jagged bottle top spins across the room into a corner.

Scott is out cold.

"Holy shit!" I blurt.

The crowd in the bar cheers.

Someone shouts, "You da man, Kellan!"

Kellan rolls his eyes. "We should go in case someone calls the cops. I don't want to be here if they do."

"Who's gonna call the cops?" I ask. "You're a hero!"

"You never know," he says, leading me by the hand out the front door.

I go willingly.

Chapter 107

VICTORY

"Where's Liv?!" I say to Kellan as we stumble onto the sidewalk outside The Dive Bomb.

His eyes flash, "I'll go get her."

I fold my arms and wait.

Seemingly seconds later, Kellan walks out the bar with Liv tossed over his shoulder. Her bare Go-Go booted legs dangle in front of him. Her psychedelic dress is so short I can see her fuchsia thong, which matches her boots.

The current group of bikers smoking outside stare appreciatively at Liv's basically naked ass. I try to pull her dress down to cover it, but it's too short.

"Shall we go?" Kellan asks me.

"Are you kidnapping me, Aiden?" Liv asks.

Kellan grins and shakes his head.

"No, Liv," I say, "you're not being kidnapped."

Disappointed, Liv whines, "Oh!"

I say to Kellan, "Maybe you should put her down?"

Liv lifts her head, hair dangling in her face, "I'm fine right here."

Kellan snickers, "I think she might be drunk."

"You think?" I say sarcastically.

"Which way?" Kellan asks, turning right and left uncertainly.

Liv's fuchsia Go-Go booted legs swing back and forth each time Kellan rotates. She squeals whimsically, "Weeeee!!!"

I roll my eyes and point, "I'm parked that way."

We walk toward my Altima.

"Vee!" Liv hisses. "Vee!"

"What?"

She props herself up against Kellan's back on an elbow so her head's not upside down while he bounces her along. Her hair drapes in her face in strings.

I push aside a random strand.

"Vee!" she hisses again, "Aiden is kidnapping me!" Her face is one big happy drunk smile.

I snicker, "Should I call the cops?"

"No!" she gasps.

While Kellan and I walk, Liv rambles, "…if you plan on tying me up, Aiden, use soft rope. I have tender skin. But you can do whatever you want to me after that. I promise I won't tell." Her head bounces while Kellan walks. "Can I keep him, Vee? Aiden is really hot." She makes a big O face when she says the word hot.

Kellan chuckles.

We stop in front of my Altima. I open the passenger door and Kellan pours Liv into the seat.

Liv reaches out to him with a noodley arm and pleads, "Don't go, Aiden!"

Kellan grins at me.

I glance at his smiling eyes, "I should probably take her home."

Liv slurs, "Don't cock block me, Vee! Aiden is taking me home!" She leans out of the car and nearly falls face first on the sidewalk, but Kellan swoops beneath her and catches her. He smoothes her back in the seat and buckles the shoulder belt around her.

Liv giggles, "Tying me up already?"

Kellan chuckles as he stands up.

"Don't go, Aiden!" Liv cries.

Kellan asks me, "Are you going to need any help getting her out of the car?"

"I can manage."

Liv barks, "No she can't! Aiden has to come with us!"

I consider it, but my backseat is full of amps. "There's not really room, Liv."

Kellan says, "I can follow in my car and help if you need it."

One look at his friendly and heartbreakingly handsome face and all I can say is, "Okay."

Kellan looks around, "Ah, my car is like four blocks that way."

Four minutes later, I'm behind the wheel of my Altima and Kellan sits in the passenger seat with Liv in his lap curled around him.

Liv's arms are draped around Kellan's muscular tanned neck. She coos, "He's even more handsome up close, Vee. His skin looks like caramel. I wonder if it tastes like caramel…" She licks Kellan's cheek.

Kellan winces comically and leans away.

"Don't be shy, Aiden," Liv mutters, "Momma won't hurt you…"

Kellan chuckles and I snicker with him.

Liv leans her cheek against Kellan's chest and sighs like a contented kitten, "I love you, Aiden."

I blurt laughter.

"Turn left here," Kellan says.

Two blocks past The Dive Bomb I turn up a hilly Silver Lake side street into a residential neighborhood. Old houses and 1940s bungalows line both sides of the street.

My Altima's headlights glide over the cars parked on both sides of the road. One in particular catches my attention. A blue Dodge Charger. I say admiringly, "Check out that Charger parked over there."

Kellan says, "You like muscle cars?"

"I *love* muscle cars." I slow my Altima to get a long look. "Looks like a 1972 with the pop up headlights. But it's got an air grabber hood scoop. They discontinued those in '71. Someone decided to customize it."

"I did," Kellan grins.

I stop my car and spin in my seat to face him, "That's *your* car?"

He nods, "Can't haul my guitar and amps on my bike."

I put my Altima into park in the middle of the quiet street and jump out to look at Kellan's awesome street rod.

Kellan climbs out of my Altima. Liv clings to him like a baby monkey holding onto mama, her legs wrapped around his waist. She's dozing.

I circle the Charger and gape, "This is *yours*?"

Kellan grins.

I don't think he realizes it, but he's swaying Liv side to side like an over-sized sleeping baby. It's oddly charming.

I look back at his car. "You've got the aluminum American Racing

Vector rims! Just like the General Lee from Dukes of Hazzard!" Kellan has good taste in cars.

He asks, "How do you know so much about cars?"

"My dad," I shrug. "What's under the hood? 440 Magnum V8?"

"Nope. 440 six pack. I pulled it out of the same '71 I got the hood from."

I nod, "Nice."

Kellan is unconsciously rubbing Liv's back. She rests her head on his shoulder, her cheek squished against him, her lips slack.

"I think the baby is drooling," I giggle and nod toward Liv.

Kellan glances down at her and quips, "Better get her home and put her down for the evening." He sets Liv in the passenger seat of my Altima and buckles her in.

When he closes the door, he says, "I'll follow you."

I grin sheepishly, "Wanna trade cars? You drive my Altima and I drive your Charger?"

Kellan snorts comically.

Yeah, I know. It's like I'm asking Kellan if I can sleep with his girlfriend or whatever, just to try her out. Not that I'm into girls. You know what I mean.

Kellan reaches into his pocket and tosses me his keys, which I catch. He grins, "Don't get a ticket and don't wreck it. My Les Paul is in the back."

"Same goes for my Altima," I quip.

"Yeah," he chuckles.

Chapter 108

VICTORY

I'd love to open up Kellan's Charger, wind the engine into the redline and see how fast it can go. But he's following in my Altima, and it's all neighborhoods between The Dive Bomb and Liv's apartment anyway. Not exactly the best place to put the car through its paces.

I'll have to get him to let me take it out on the five freeway late some night. Then I can chew up the asphalt without worrying about stop signs and reds.

A few minutes later, we park on the street outside Liv's apartment and Kellan carries Liv upstairs.

"We're home, Aiden!" Liv coos as I open her front door with her keys.

Liv's studio apartment is tiny. Her queen sized futon is cramped into the single room with her recording gear. The futon is opened into a bed and Kellan sets her down on top. All the windows are closed, and it's stuffy, so I go around and open all two of them to let in a cross draft.

Liv throws her forearm over her head, "Take me now, Aiden..." she sighs, eyes closed.

I unzip her Go-Go boots and pull them off.

"Is that you, Aiden?" Liv moans.

I say, "It's me, Liv."

"Victory? Are we going to have a three way with Aiden?" she asks sleepily.

"You're going to have a one way with your pillow."

Liv smiles, her eyes still closed, "I hear pillows give good head..." she giggles at her own joke.

I unbuckle her belt and drape it over the back of a chair beside the bed.

"That should be good enough," I say to Kellan.

Liv wiggles her feet, "Socks?"

I pull off her ankle socks and toss them into an overflowing laundry basket. "Anything else, your highness?"

"Rub my toes?"

I frown, "I'm not rubbing your toes, Liv."

Her eyes are still closed, "Have Aiden do it."

"There's no one here named Aiden, Liv."

Kellan chuckles.

"Okaaaay," Liv grouses sleepily.

I grab Kellan's wrist and lead him to the balcony outside Liv's front door. I leave the door open so I can keep tabs on her, but I lean against the hand railing and stare off at the twinkling lights of L.A. The night air is warm and pleasant.

Kellan leans on the railing beside me.

Liv's apartment is on the back of the building, and the balcony hangs over a hillside of dried grass that slopes down to a curving street far below. Although the view is spectacular, it feels isolated, like the chaotic sprawl of L.A. is merely a distant mirage, a place where dreams come true but you can never quite get there.

I say softly, "I love L.A. at night. Artificial starlight in every direction."

He chuckles, "Next best thing to actual stars, right?"

"The movie kind or the space kind?"

"Either one," he grins.

"You were really good tonight," I say. "On stage, I mean. And with Liv."

"Thanks."

"And punching out Scott."

"My pleasure," Kellan chuckles.

I'm intimately aware of his masculine energy. Kellan is a very big man. Heat radiates off him standing this close. I find myself thinking about purple fog, flaming swords, and sex vampires. I know I'm blushing, but it's dark so Kellan won't notice.

"I've been dreaming about you," Kellan says casually.

What?!

I blurt, "Purple fog?"

"Huh?" he turns to look at me, confused.

"Nothing," I say nervously.

"I keep having these dreams about you and me onstage—"

Having sex?

"—playing in a band."

"Oh?" I ask curiously.

"Now that Switchblade is leaving the band, I need another lead guitar player."

"Why don't you play lead? You're more than good enough," I say sincerely.

"Thanks. But like I said," he runs his hand through his hair, "It's too much to do with all the singing."

I'd like to run my hands through his hair...

He looks at me and his brown eyes burn beneath his brow.

Do I detect a hint of uncertainty in cocky Kellan's killer eyes?

"You interested?" he asks.

In having sex right now with the hot stud who punched out my shitty ex-boyfriend? I cough and cover my mouth before I stutter out, "You mean playing in your band?"

He nods.

Ooh. Sounds complicated. This is how Scott and I started out. Mutual attraction. Mutual musical tastes. Kellan even sings and wants me to play guitar, just like Scott. The only difference is that Kellan plays rhythm guitar, but he writes great songs and it feels too eerily familiar for comfort.

"I don't know, Kellan. Now isn't a good time. Liv and I are working on songs together."

His eyes flicker and the flames go out, "I understand." He looks away, gazing at the night lights twinkling in the distance.

A lone car drives quietly by on the street below. Red taillights disappear around a bend in the road. Then the street is empty. Despairingly empty.

If Kellan was any other man, I probably wouldn't say anything else. I'd let it drop. I'm a busy girl. I have a cool new job. Liv and I are working on good music. Julian is on the verge of opening up doors for me in the music business that I never knew existed. Of course, Julian is also a very busy guy himself. But still. My life is full of opportunity.

And yet.

And yet, I feel like opening up to Kellan. Because he'll understand where I'm coming from, one guitar player to another.

"It's just," I bite my lip uncertainly, "I want to—"

(*sing*)

"—write my own music. Scott wrote everything except my guitar solos. Me and Liv are writing songs together. I like that freedom. I want to see what I can do as a—"

(*sing*)

"—songwriter. I don't want to play guitar solos all my life. I want more. And I don't want anyone standing in my way."

Kellan says softly, "I know what you mean."

"You do?" I scoff, "I can't imagine you've ever let anyone stand in your way."

"Do you see me touring the world, supporting an album?"

"No."

"Putting a band together is harder than finding a long term girlfriend. It's all about chemistry. You know that."

I nod, "I played with Rex and Bobby for three years before we started Skin Trade with Scott. As much as I hate those guys now, I miss what we had. Those guys were the best rhythm section I've ever played with."

"And look what happened," Kellan sighs.

"Yeah," I shake my head and say sarcastically, "They fucked me over."

"Yup," Kellan sighs. "I think about bands like the Rolling Stones or RUSH who are still together forty years later with the same group of guys. It's like the mythical high school sweethearts. That shit is so rare, it's almost a myth. But it's real. If you're lucky. I've had so many half-start bands that never go anywhere. Not because of me. I give every ounce of energy I have to everything I do."

I chuckle, "I get that impression. You're an intense guy."

He turns to me, a big smile on his beautiful face, "You noticed?"

"Yeah! What was with all that Mr. Brooding Bullshit after you hired me at the school?"

He snickers. "You really wanna know?"

"Yeah," I smile, turning to face him.

His eyes are burning again but he's grinning, "Working with you is torture."

"Torture!" I blurt. "You're not exactly Mr. Fun Time!"

He shakes his head, "You're missing my point. I can't stop thinking about you. I think about you every day, whether I see you or not. I think about how fucking hot you looked in your stage costume the night I met you. I think about you naked in my shower—"

My tummy tingles when he says that. I remember fantasizing about him and me in a steamy jungle and a bed of rose petals…

He continues, "—I think about how you shred on guitar. I think about seeing you play that Contrares on the Promenade. But more than anything else, I think about the music we wrote the night you spent at my apartment. I've been looking for you my whole life, Victory."

I say doubtfully, "I thought you said writing with Switchblade was easy. How was I any different?"

"You and I wrote that piece together. Switchblade was more like a sponge. She played whatever I told her. But it wasn't a co-writing thing. It was mainly me. That's fine, but I really want someone I can bounce ideas around with and play off them. Anyway, look what happened to Switchblade. Now she's touring with Wild Child."

"Oh," I say softly.

"You and I have something, Gigi."

I smile shyly because he keeps calling me that.

He arches an eyebrow, "We have chemistry, Gigi."

Yeah we do. Woo! I'm getting really hot right now.

"Victory, I want to form a band with you. And write music. With you." He takes my hand in both of his and squeezes it.

His hands are so seductively warm.

He searches my eyes and says, "Me and you have potential to do something big together. Something long term. Something I can't do on my own. I need you, Gigi."

I'm thinking about purple fog and flaming swords and sex vampires. Oh, wait. Kellan isn't talking about that.

Kellan is offering me what I've always wanted.

(*Vic—*)

A musical partnership that will last a life time.

(*Vict—*)

But Kellan said it himself. Such connections are extremely rare. Most bands fall apart long before they go anywhere.

(*Victor—*)

I blink rapidly and break Kellan's gaze. I pull my hand from his and turn to the balcony railing. I lean into it and squeeze both hands around the painted metal tightly, feeling it digging into my skin. My knuckles turn white and my nails cut into my palms. I'm struggling to hold everything in. I'm going to shatter if it all comes out right now.

I look at the empty street below.

A sense of desperation pulls my heart in seven directions. My heart races as I remember…

(*Stop, Dad!!!*)

That day…

(*Victory!!!*)

No!

(*Let go, Victory. You have to let go…*)

I can't think about it right now.

NOOO!!!!!!

—don'tthink don'tthink don'tthink don'tthink don't—

I squeeze every muscle in my body as hard as I can, trying to hold myself together because it feels like my bones are about to fly apart.

I lose track of time as the storm inside me slowly passes.

I'm still staring down at the street below.

It seems like hours have passed, but I think it's only been seconds.

Not a single car has driven by since the last lone car disappeared around the bend seemingly hours ago. Another car might not come along for who knows how long. Maybe never.

I look up at Kellan, my eyes dance from his twin burning flames to his lips to the twin flames to his hot lips to the flames…

I want to jump in his fire.

I want his passion to burn me alive.

I want him to kiss me.

Right now.

My breath suddenly catches in my throat.

But I also want to join his band.

And write music with him. Together.

I tried both with Scott. It didn't work. I think I can only have one or the other.

Kellan's fire or the band.

The truth is, like Kellan, I *really* want to forge a musical relationship with *someone* that will last forever.

(*Let go, Victory…*)

But nobody gets forever.

(*You have to let go of your brother…*)

I have to choose.

One or the other.

Fuck it.

Nobody lives forever.

Victor didn't.

Kellan is right here.

Right now.

(*Victory!!! Wake up!!!*)

I choose now.

Chapter 109

VICTORY

"Take me home," I whisper desperately.

Kellan's brows draw together, "Is everything okay?"

"Take me home. Right now," I plead softly.

"What about Liv?"

I walk into Liv's apartment and check on her. She's breathing evenly. I walk out, lock the doorknob, and pull it closed behind me. "She'll be fine. Take me home."

"What about your car? Isn't your Fender in your trunk?"

Shit. He's right. There are way too many logistical issues trying to spoil the mood. I don't want to deal with any of them. But I can't leave my Fender in my car. Not after it was stolen once already. And I don't want to take Kellan and my stuff back to Johnny and Karen's. I'm sure they're busy having 'dark side of the moon' sex or something. Not the atmosphere I'm looking for right now.

I look at Kellan, "Let's go to your place."

He's taken aback. "Uh…is that a good idea?"

I nod.

"You're sure? It didn't go so smoothly last time."

"I don't care," I say flatly. "Let's go. I'll drive my car."

I'm all business now.

"Okay," he sighs uncertainly.

"Come on," I pull his hand and lead him down the balcony, down the stairs, and to our cars.

We drive to the west side. This late at night, there's not much traffic, but it still takes forever to cross town southward on surface streets to the 10 freeway and get to West L.A. I keep my mind blank the whole way. If I think about anything, I'm going to break.

I park my Altima in front of Kellan's driveway.

He parks behind me and steps out of his Charger. He asks, "Are you okay, Victory? Your eyes look haunted."

I can't answer that, or I will break.

I walk around to my trunk and start pulling out amps. "Let's put the gear inside."

Kellan doesn't move. He just looks at me for a long time. Finally, he steps toward my car and pulls out Liv's keyboard amp without saying a word.

We unload both our cars in a matter of minutes and carry everything inside his apartment.

"Let's park the cars," I say.

Kellan nods and follows me outside. It takes only a few more minutes to find a space. It's too small for his Charger so I park my Altima.

When I climb in his car, I grab his right hand with both of mine and say, "Let's park your car."

He turns and looks at me again. His eyes are worried.

"Park," I say.

He drives up the street and turns down an alley while I hold his right hand for dear life in both of mine.

I realize he has a parking space behind his building. He parks the Charger and turns off the engine. "Is everything all right, Victory? You're acting way strange right now."

I climb across the center console and dive for his mouth with mine. I pivot my butt and drop it into his lap. I snake my arms around his neck and kiss him hard.

He's into it instantly, kissing back with hot passion. Our lips melt together. His tongue finds mine and I feel his fire.

Kellan and I haven't kissed since the night we met.

Why did I wait so long to do it again?

His fire heals me. It burns away all my anger, all my tension, all my pain, all my sadness, all my doubt.

Or so I think.

His lips relax.

His mind is now elsewhere.

I lift my head, breaking our kiss, and look him in the eyes, "Something wrong?"

"Not with me," he says quietly. "But you're flipping out right now."

"No I'm not," I deny.

"Let's go inside," he sighs.

"What?" I grin, "Don't you want to have sex in the back seat of a Dodge Charger? I know I always have."

He smiles and shakes his head, "Me too."

"Oh, come on," I scoff, "You've probably had sex a hundred times in the back of this car."

"Are you kidding? And stain the upholstery?" he quips.

"Hah!" I blurt.

He grins.

I wrap my fists in his shirt, "Let's stain the upholstery."

"As much as I like the sound of that, you're not you right now. You're on some kind of a mission. I can feel it. You're running away from something."

I laugh, "Are you my therapist all of a sudden?" I lean back against the steering wheel, giving myself some distance. This huge car is suddenly way too small for the two of us.

"You don't need to be a therapist to see how whack you're acting."

I frown, "Whack? I'm not whack."

He arches an eyebrow, "You sure?"

I glare at him.

He arches his eyebrows higher.

I roll my eyes and climb back into the passenger seat. I fold my arms across my chest. "I was going to have sex with you tonight. Now you're out of luck."

Kellan shakes his head and snickers, "I think I'll get by."

"I was going to give you a blowjob too, because you've been so nice."

"While I appreciate the offer…" he smiles.

I cut him off, "The offer is off the table."

"I'll deal," he winks.

I glare at him and say snootily, "You had your chance."

"Is that a threat?" he smiles and his eyes twinkle.

It's impossible to be mad at him.

"Let's go inside," he suggests, "kick off our shoes and relax."

"Fine, but I'm not talking about my feelings, Mr. Therapist. Or blowing you."

He laughs and climbs out of the car.

Chapter 110

VICTORY

I climb out of the Charger and we both close our doors. I circle around to Kellan.

He offers me his hand, "Come on."

I scowl, "I'm not holding your hand. You had your chance." I fold my arms together, hiding my hands in my armpits.

Kellan grins and motions expectantly.

I sigh like a pouty teenager and grab his hand.

He pulls me along the walkway that runs between his building and the one next door. It's dark, but as always, the city lights reflect off the ocean mist overhead and there's plenty of light to see by. The walkway leads to the quiet courtyard outside his front door and we go inside.

Kellan automatically grabs bedding out of the linen closet in his L-shaped hallway and walks toward the couch..

"You don't need to do that," I say.

"You just wanna sleep on the cushions?" he asks, holding the stack of folded sheets in one hand.

"No. I'm sleeping with you."

He huffs a laugh and puts the sheets back in the closet. "Okay. But no blowjobs"

"Right," I grin, "no blowjobs."

He turns around and walks into his bedroom, flipping the light on.

I follow him.

I haven't been in his bedroom before. I carefully avoided it the last time I was here. "Hey! You have my Jimi Hendrix poster!"

"Same one," Kellan grins, 'Bought it in high school."

"I knew you were awesome!" I laugh.

"Me too," he smirks.

I drop onto his bed and bounce more than necessary, "This is comfy."

He smiles and strips his shirt over his head. He looks like he did on stage at The Dive Bomb. Leather pants and boots and nothing but muscles for miles. I want to jump him right now and lick every inch.

I ask, "Have you ever considered modeling?"

"No. I'm too busy with music. Maybe when I'm a megastar I'll have my own clothing line at Target or some shit, but until then, I could care less." He slides open his mirrored closet door and tosses his shirt in a hamper.

He lifts up one booted foot and slides the boot off while balancing on one leg. He repeats the process with the other.

"How do you do that?" I marvel. "I always fall over."

"Practice?"

He puts his boots away like a good boy. Kellan really is a clean and organized guy. Not anal, just not slobby.

He unbuttons his leather pants and arches a questioning eyebrow.

I'm leaning back on my elbows on his bed with my legs crossed, staring at his crotch, "Continue."

He unzips his leather pants and pushes them down, revealing black boxer briefs. He does the one leg trick and pulls off his leather pants, which he hangs in the closet. I can't help but notice his black boxer briefs have a very nice, uh, profile.

He smiles, "I'll be right back." He strolls into the bathroom and shuts the door.

I haven't moved an inch since I sat down on the bed. Now I jump to my feet, tear my too tight Avenged Sevenfold shirt off my head, throw it in a corner, unzip my spandex jeans, push them down as fast as I can, and nearly trip face first into the bedroom doorknob because I haven't taken my boots off. I sit down on the carpet, my jeans around my ankles, and yank my boots off. It's not very ladylike, but my focus is on speed. I peel my jeans off and throw them on top of my wadded shirt.

"You okay out there?" Kellan hollers from the bathroom.

"Yeah!" I shout.

I unhook my black bra, toss it aside, and push my black thong down and kick it off my ankles, aiming generally for the corner with the rest of my clothes. Then I sit back down on the bed in the same position I was in earlier, but completely naked.

I wait.

I hope Kellan isn't doing number two.

Hurry up!

Chapter 111

KELLAN

I flush the toilet after taking a whiz and wash my hands. I run my hand through my hair out of habit before shutting off the light and opening the bathroom door.

I turn to face my room and Victory is lying on my bed in the exact same position as when I walked out, but totally naked.

I burst into loud laughter.

I don't know what I was expecting when I heard her banging around in the bedroom a minute ago, but it wasn't this.

A shocked look bounces across her face and she flings her arms over her breasts protectively. She sits up and turns her body sideways, hiding her crotch. Not that it was hanging out before.

"What are you doing?" I chuckle.

"Covering up, asshole!" She glares at me like I was trying to steal a look when I wasn't supposed to.

"Then why are you naked?" I'm smiling from ear to ear.

"I thought I'd surprise you! I wasn't expecting you to laugh at me!" She's mad.

"I wasn't laughing at your body or anything."

"I'm confident of my body!" she growls.

"Are you?"

"Yes!"

Ahhh, women. "Then why are you covering up?"

"Because you laughed!"

"Awww," I say cutely. "I totally wasn't laughing at your body. And from what I can still see, you're easily ten times hotter under your clothes than I thought."

She relaxes, "You're not bullshitting, are you?"

"Nope. I was laughing because I didn't expect you to be naked when I walked out of my bathroom."

She frowns skeptically, "Really?"

"Yes, really. If you want, go back to lying the way you were, I'll just stand here for awhile and admire you. It'll be better than a blowjob."

"Yeah, right," she smirks and says cockily, "You haven't had one of my blowjobs."

"That's true. If you give head like you play guitar, I'm keeping you to myself."

"I told you," she tosses her hair, "you lost your chance out in the car."

"I don't get a do-over?" I chuckle.

"Well, maybe this once," she says seductively.

"Okay. I'll go back into the bathroom and come out again. This time, I won't laugh. I'll do something else."

"I don't know if I like the sound of that…"

"Trust me."

"Okay…"

I turn and walk into the bathroom and close the door. I grab something from under the sink and go to work. A minute later, I holler through the door, "You ready?"

"Yes."

I open the door and walk out.

Chapter 112

VICTORY

I'm back to my original position on the bed and still completely naked when Kellan opens the bathroom door a second time. I throw my head back and blurt my own hearty laughter.

Kellan has a Santa Claus beard of shaving cream all over his face. He grins, "Looks good, doesn't it?"

Then I notice Kellan's boxer briefs are gone. My eyes pop as I stare at his huge erection.

He says, "I told you I thought you were hot."

I don't know what to do with the shaving cream all over his face, so I say doubtfully, "I've always wanted to have sex with Santa?" I begin giggling uncontrollably.

"Do you think Mrs. Claus had a beard too?"

"Do you want me to put one on?" I ask uncertainly.

"No," he chuckles.

"Good," I giggle.

He walks into the bathroom and a moment later he walks out, wiping the shaving cream off with a big bath towel. "Better?"

I nod.

He tosses the towel into the bathroom. I hear it land on the floor.

See, he's not anal. He knows when to be spontaneous.

He walks up to the edge of the bed and plants his fists on his hips. His cock is pointing at my face, but I'm reclining on the bed, so it's several feet away.

"How about that blow job?" he grins.

"Ha!" I laugh.

"I'm kidding." He turns off the bedroom lights and eases onto the bed.

I turn over and crawl up beside him. I lie my head on the pillow facing him and gaze into his eyes. Moonlight drizzles through the window above the headboard. Kellan grins at me.

I can't resist. I grab his cock and squeeze it gently.

He smiles, "That's not a toy. I hope you've read the instruction manual and all the safety warnings. You wouldn't want it to go off in your hand."

I arch my eyebrow in the moonlight and say suggestively, "You think I should shoot it off some place else?"

He chuckles, "Just point it where no one gets hurt."

"Does that mean you want to have sex tonight?"

"I always want to have sex," he scoffs.

"I mean with me. Right now." I stroke his heavy cock in my hand. It's hot and throbs between my fingers.

"It's up to you. I'm fine either way."

"You sure?" I continue stroking.

"Yup."

I establish a rhythm with my hand, pumping up and down. "I guess my body doesn't turn you on?"

"Gee," he says sarcastically, "it's pretty hard to tell."

"It's pretty hard all right," I murmur.

We start to kiss. Our tongues touch tips, our lips press closed then open, tongues sliding in and out, lips pressing and releasing. The slicker our lips get, the more they slip and glide. His hand touches my cheek softly, his thumb circling my ear, brushing my hair back. His fingers trail down my neck and tickle my skin. The tickle echoes inside my body, streaming down into my chest and pouring down my belly between my legs.

His hand pushes between my thighs, stiff fingers probing for my folds. I lift my knee and his fingers plunge into my wetness, bathing in my lazy heat. He finds my clit and goes to work with slippery strokes. Tingles tease me and flicker deep.

I work the shaft of his cock as we kiss passionately for a long time. I'm shivering with pleasure, barely aware of what I'm doing with my hand but intimately and pleasurably aware of what he's doing with his. It's intense, overwhelming, and wonderful.

I want more.

I whisper, "I want you, Kellan. I want you now."

"Let me grab a condom." He stands up from the bed.

"Where are you going?"

"To get a condom."

"Don't you have a box by your bed like most guys?"

He shakes his head, "I never have sex in here."

I chuckle, "Where do you have sex then?"

"Usually someplace else."

"Really? But you keep your place so nice."

He shrugs, "What can I say? It's my recording studio. It's my sanctuary. I don't like bringing chicks here. So I keep the condoms in the bathroom under the sink."

"So go get one already!" I grin.

He walks into the bathroom. A moment later I hear him grunt, "Fuck!"

"What?" I holler.

He calls, "I'm out of condoms!"

I drop my head into the pillow and laugh, "How can you be out of condoms? Doesn't Trojan sponsor you or something? I can picture a big Trojan delivery truck backing up to your front door, 'Beep! Beep! Beep!' and dumping box after box on your porch."

He walks into the bedroom chuckling, "Funny. But no. Do you want me to go get some? There's a Rite-Aid around the corner."

I sit up on the bed, "That depends. I'm still on the pill from when I was with Scott. Do you always use condoms when you have sex?"

"Exclusively. And I get tested all the time. I'm clean."

I smile, "Then we don't need condoms." I hold out my arms to him.

"Do you trust Scott?"

SCREECH!

That was the sound of my Funmobile screeching to a stop on the road of love.

I wasn't expecting that question from Kellan of all people. But one thing I know about Scott, he absolutely hates using condoms. I remember his big-titted mannequin at The Dive Bomb tonight.

I sigh and say, "You mean, did Scott cheat on me and not tell me?"

"Yeah."

Wow. I hadn't considered it until now. But Kellan makes a great point. Shit. I drop back into the pillows and stare at the ceiling. "I thought I trusted him. But look what happened to the band."

"Want me to go buy condoms?"

"Fucking Scott!" I growl. I slap the bed in anger. "Time to go wait all day at the free clinic."

"I'm sure you're fine," Kellan encourages. "But you should get tested, just for peace of mind. I'll go with you, if you want."

I sigh heavily, "Maybe this is the universe's way of telling me that you and I are supposed to be in a band instead of having sex."

"Huh? I don't get it."

I sit up on the bed again.

Kellan leans against the door frame, completely naked. Even in the dim light, he looks incredible with his muscles and tattoos. I really want to have sex with him right now. But all signs point to no.

I pull my knees up to my chest and wrap my arms around them. I rest my chin on my knees forlornly.

Kellan sits down on the edge of the bed next to me.

Staring at the sheets, I say, "I guess I didn't think this evening through. But, after Scott, I pretty much promised myself I was never sleeping with anyone in any band I was in from here on out."

"Makes sense." Kellan nods with a vaguely surprised look on his face, "So, if we had sex tonight, you wouldn't want to be in a band with me? Ever?"

"Not if we're sleeping together." I look at him and wince, "Is that lame?"

"Not after what you've been through with Scott. I totally get it."

"Still want to go to Rite Aid and get those condoms?" I laugh nervously.

Kellan cracks a huge smile, "Hell no! I'd rather have you in my band!"

I can't decide if that's the dumbest thing I've ever heard, or the sweetest thing any man has ever said to me in my entire life.

Kellan rests a hand on my knee. "Victory, Gigi, you're easily the hottest woman I've ever laid eyes on."

"Bullshit," I chuckle.

"I'm serious."

"Don't give me that. There's someone with bigger tits or a nicer ass or a prettier face out there. Heck, from what I've seen of the women you hang with, I bet you've already had sex with most of them."

He shakes his head, "It's the balance of everything. You're the perfect mix of the perfect parts. For me. I can't explain it, but I knew it the second I laid eyes on you at The Cobra. The fact you shredded on your Fender was the crown jewel of your total royal rocker chick perfection," he chuckles.

I roll my eyes, but his compliments make me grin and blush.

"Anyway," he says resting a friendly hand on my foot, "I meant what I said at Liv's place. Building a band that has career potential is harder than finding a wife. Mick and Keith have been together longer than any of their female relationships. Alex Lifeson and Geddy Lee of RUSH have been playing together since they were kids."

While Kellan speaks, I start to weep silently.

He says, "Shit, Eddie and Alex Van Halen started playing together even younger than that."

My stomach clamps down and threatens to shoot out of my mouth, taking all my guts with it.

Unaware, Kellan continues, "I want that kind of bond with another musician. I've been looking for it my whole life. I think you and I have that."

When he finishes, I start bawling uncontrollably.

He wraps an arm gently around my shoulders and I fall into his chest. I sob like crazy.

"Did I say something wrong?" he asks nervously.

It takes a few minutes before I can speak between sobs, but I finally squeeze out in a weak voice, "I had that."

"Had what? I'm confused."

I sniffle and look into his eyes, "I had what you're talking about. Mick and Keith. Alex and Geddy. Eddie and Alex. I *had* that."

"With Scott?" Kellan asks doubtfully.

"No!' I cry laugh. "Not even close. I had it with my brother Victor."

"You have a brother?"

"Had," I sigh. I smear tears from my cheeks and rest my forehead against my knees for a long time.

Kellan asks softly, "Do you want to talk about it?"

(*Let go, Victory. You have to let go of your brother*)

I gaze into Kellan's welcoming eyes. Comfort washes over me. "Not really," I frown smile.

"That's okay," he murmurs. "Whatever you're comfortable with."

"But I need to tell you," I say desperately and grab his forearm. "I've never told this story to anybody. I mean, nobody outside my family. I didn't even tell Scott. But I need to tell you, Kellan. I don't know why."

Tears pour down my face.

Chapter 113

VICTORY

I sit up and cross my legs beneath me and drop my hands in my lap.

Kellan positions himself so he's facing me.

He wears the sincerest expression I've ever seen in my life. He's totally making it easier to talk about this. The last time I really talked about Victor to anyone was my therapist when I was a teenager.

I stare at my hands and say to Kellan, "Victor was killed when I was twelve. In a car accident. He's my fraternal twin. *Was* my fraternal twin. Gosh, it still breaks my heart to use the word 'was'." I shake my head and sigh. "This is so hard, Kellan," I plead.

My tears start again.

Kellan takes my hands from my lap and squeezes them in his affectionately. "Are you sure you want to go into it? It looks like it's breaking your heart."

"Thank you. But I'm going to. You really need to hear it."

"I do?"

"Yes. So you can understand why I ran away from you.

He smiles softly, "That doesn't matter. I don't care."

"Let me explain. When I was young, my dad had guitars around the house. He started playing when he was a teenager. So I grew up with them. It didn't take long for me and Victor to start playing too. We did everything together," I laugh thoughtfully. "My dad gave me my Fender Strat for Christmas when I was seven. He gave Victor a blond Les Paul."

Kellan's eyes widen, "Oh...I play a Les Paul."

I nod. He understands the significance of the fact that he and my brother played the same model guitar. Different color, but close enough.

"Me and Victor played guitar together all the time. We were both into all the 1980s shredder guitar players our dad turned us on to. Just like you and me, Kellan."

His eyes are big and he nods solemnly.

"And not long after that, Victor and I started singing together."

(*singsingsing*)

"Kellan," I say, but my breath hitches several times before I get out the words, "you asked me to sing and play guitar with you."

"Oh, Victory," he says softly, "I had no idea…"

"It's okay," I lean forward and kiss his cheek once gently.

I continue, "Anyway, my dad was so excited when he heard me and Victor singing together the first time. I think the first song we sang for him was Sergeant Peppers by the Beatles. We'd practice every day after school when he was still at work. My grandma would babysit us and she loved it. Victor would put the Sergeant Peppers CD on my dad's big stereo all the time, and we'd march around the living room, pretending we were in a big brass marching band. When we did it for my dad the first time one night, Victor pretended to laugh silently when the crowd laughs during the song. I remember. My dad laughed and I laughed too. Then Victor pretended to play the trumpets." I shake my head, smiling. "Anyway, the first time we did it in front of my dad, he was speechless. His eyes were all big like he'd discovered gold or something.

"Dad was never much of a singer. Just the lead guitar man in all his bands. But he still plays amazing," I smile fondly. "So, Dad had me and Victor perform for his singer friends, and they started teaching us whatever they could about singing. My mom and dad didn't have money to pay them, so Dad traded them by working on their cars whenever they needed it.

"Eventually, Victor and I started playing guitar while we sang. We did only covers in the beginning. All the classic rock and metal my dad grew up on. At some point, we started writing our own music. When that happened, my dad went nuts. He wanted us to have the music career he never did. Any time he heard about a local gig we could play, he would take us. Churches, talent shows, birthday parties, it didn't matter. He wanted people to see what we could do. Me and Victor had so much fun…"

I smile and look at Kellan.

"I bet you did," he grins.

"Anyway, we got really good, you know? We won our junior high school talent show in seventh grade. We played Enter Sandman and Helter Skelter with some other kids we knew who played drums and bass. Victor and I sang it together. The school kids loved it. Then we played More Than Words by Extreme. Just me and Victor on acoustic guitar. I think a hundred girls at the school wanted to be my brother's girlfriend after that." I pause and laugh, "Victor lied and told all the girls we wrote More Than Words. The girls didn't know, and that song was so old anyway."

I take a deep breath before I continue.

Kellan asks, "Do you want some water or anything?"

"I'm fine," I smile. "This is the hard part of the story. The summer after seventh grade, there was some battle of the bands up in Fresno at some outdoor summer street festival that me and Victor found online. It was all ages, which was awesome since we were both twelve. We begged our dad to take us. I remember he'd had a hard week at work leading up to the festival, and he was really tired the morning of the show. But my dad never let that stop him. Especially not when it came to Victor and me playing somewhere.

"The show was Saturday night, so Dad slept in Saturday morning, and drank a bunch of coffee for lunch before we drove up to Fresno. The drive was like two hours and I could tell he was tired and yawning a lot on the way up. It was after dinner when Victor and I finally got on stage. But we played our hearts out and had a blast. We even took second place and won two hundred and fifty bucks. Since we had to hang around for the prizes, I don't think we drove home until eleven o'clock that night.

"On the drive home, my dad was really tired. I was sitting in the back seat and Victor was in the front next to Dad. Victor and I were so excited, we kept talking and talking even though it was so late. I think it helped keep my dad awake the whole way home. When we ran out of things to say, we started singing our songs. Dad loved to listen to us sing. It kept him going all the way home.

"Not that it mattered.

"A half mile from home, we stopped at a stop sign. It was late. My dad didn't look carefully both ways. Funny how important that is."

(*Stop!!!*)

"Maybe my dad would've seen the car if he hadn't been so tired, or heard it if me and Victor hadn't been singing so loud. I don't know. It didn't matter. The lights of the car that hit us were off anyway. I guess the driver forgot to turn them on. So Dad didn't see the car. I didn't see it either. But Victor did. I remember Victor shouting

(*Stop, Dad!!!*)

at the top his lungs when my dad pulled into the intersection.

"The police said the drunk driver who T-boned our car never touched his brakes. He was going forty miles an hour when he rammed into our car. The doctors said Victor died instantly because he was in the front seat.

I was pinned in the back seat. I remember my dad shouting my name, trying to wake me up."

(*Victory!!! Wake up!!!*)

"He thought I was dead too. My scalp was cut and there was blood all over my face. I had to get fifty stitches. See?"

I pull my hair back from my scar and lift Kellan's fingers to my scalp so he can feel it.

He nods silently.

"After that night, I never sang again. At Victor's funeral, I promised him in my head that I would never sing or play guitar again. Not without him. And, I sort of believe all the singing me and Victor were doing when the drunk driver hit us was why Dad never heard the car coming. For years, my therapist told me not to blame myself, but I couldn't help it. I never sang again after the accident.

"For a long time, I barely even talked. I was completely numb and checked out most of the time. It's not like I had anything to say anyway. I mean, I couldn't talk without remembering Victor and falling apart into tears. So I tended not to say anything to anybody unless I had to.

"But it wasn't long after the accident that my mom and dad started trying to get me to sing and play guitar. They told me they missed it and it kept the memory of my brother alive. But I couldn't do it. It hurt too much. And it didn't seem fair to Victor. If he couldn't sing and play, I wasn't going to."

Kellan asks, "So, how did you end up playing guitar again?"

"My dad. If it wasn't for him, I don't think I *ever* would've played again. My dad is so awesome."

I start sobbing and Kellan holds me tight.

Several minutes pass before I can talk again.

I say, "One night, maybe a year and a half after Victor died, my dad put on a recording of me and Victor playing this haunting heavy metal instrumental we wrote called Andromeda. It was kind of like Orion by Metallica from Master of Puppets."

"That's an awesome song," Kellan says.

I grin, "We sort of ripped it off, but our own way. Anyway, my dad put on the recording of me and Victor in his office. I was in my room doing homework. I knew the recording, but it didn't sound right. It sounded like someone was playing along with it. Maybe Victor's ghost, I don't know. So I got up from my school books and walked into dad's office where he had his own amps and guitars, so I could see what was going on."

I take a deep breath, "When I saw Dad playing along to the track with Victor's blond Les Paul, I freaked out. Victor had brought that guitar with us to the summer festival in Fresno the night he died. The guitar was in the trunk with my Fender when our car got hit. It was the only piece of Victor that survived the accident, as far as I was concerned. For whatever reason, watching my dad play the guitar freaked me out, like he might break it or something, and then Victor would be gone forever.

"I remember screaming at my dad that he couldn't play Victor's guitar. I mean, *screaming*. I hit him and slapped him all over the back, screaming at him over and over, '*You can't play Victor's guitar! You can't play Victor's guitar!*' I probably talked more in those five minutes than I had the whole year leading up to that night.

"But my dad just turned up his amp and wailed on that Les Paul, playing Victor's guitar part in Andromeda. Dad knows how to play most of our original songs. He loved jamming with us at home. When I realized Dad wasn't going to stop playing Victor's Les Paul along with Andromeda, I sat down in front of him on the floor and cried into my hands. When he finished the song, he started over. He just kept playing it and playing it. At some point, I was out of tears. I picked up my Fender and plugged into another amp in Dad's office and joined in with him. And the recording of Victor. When my dad realized I was playing, he muted my recorded track in the mix. So it was literally me and my dad playing along with my brother's guitar track and the bass and drums. The three of us played that duet over and over for two hours. Just me and Dad." I sigh, "And Victor."

I pause, crying softly. I look up into Kellan's compassionate eyes and say, "I think we were trying to say goodbye to Victor."

Kellan nods and looks at me with open understanding. In silence, he comforts me.

"After that night," I say, "I knew I had to keep playing guitar. For Victor. But I couldn't sing without him. Something about hearing my voice without his was too much. I tried a couple of times, but it always felt wrong. Oddly, when I played the old songs with Dad, and Dad played Victor's Les Paul through Victor's amp, he could phrase his notes just like Victor and you'd swear it was Victor playing. But when it came to actual singing, I just couldn't do it without my brother. No one could replace his actual voice.

"I've always kept my promise to Victor that I would never ever *ever* sing again without him. Not without my brother."

(*never ever ever sing*)

I sigh heavily, "Sometimes, I feel like I'm dying inside because I don't sing. Sometimes, I can't stand the idea of *not* singing. When I hear an amazing singer, like you," I stop and look at Kellan sincerely, "putting it all out there with your voice, I get so jealous I want to die. But Victor *is* dead. He *can't* sing. Out of respect for him, I just don't."

I gaze into Kellan's eyes. He projects this amazingly understanding soothing softness.

I'm crying again.

He looks at me for a long time and says, "Maybe your brother wants you to sing. Because he can't."

(*singsingsing*)

My heart stops.

Kellan mutters, "Maybe your brother wants you to sing for both of you..."

(*singsingsingsingsingsing*)

Have I been betraying the spirit of my brother for ten long years?

(*SINGSINGSINGSINGSINGSING*)

I slap my hand over my mouth and start wailing. My whole body spasms as ten years of sadness comes pouring out.

Chapter 114

VICTORY

I wake to the smell of warm bagels. Blue sky drifts through the open window at the head of the bed.

Kellan's bed.

I hear him moving around quietly in his kitchen.

I slide my feet onto the floor and grab my panties and t-shirt from the pile in the corner and pull them on. I tiptoe toward the bathroom, hoping to get there before Kellan sees me.

He turns the corner of the short L-shaped hallway holding two plates with bagels and cream cheese, "You look beautiful."

After all the crying I did last night, he has to be lying.

I shoulder past him, "I have to use the bathroom."

When I close the door behind me, I hear him call through the door, "Nice ass, Gigi."

I smile to myself while I take care of business.

When I walk out of the bathroom, Kellan is on the couch, bagels untouched, "Ready for some food?"

"Sure," I say and sit next to him, curling my legs beneath me.

He hands me a plate.

"Sorry about last night," I say.

He's about to bite into his bagel, "Sorry? For what?"

"All that heaviness I laid on you."

"I don't mind," he bites his bagel and chews heartily on a big chunk.

"You don't care we didn't have sex last night?" I ask cautiously.

He shakes his head and chews.

I laugh, "I so don't believe you."

When he finishes chewing, he wipes his lips with a paper napkin, "Yes, I'd love to have crazy heavy metal sex with you, Gigi. But not if it means we can't be in a band."

I still have a hard time believing Kellan would forego sex for a band.

He says, "You don't believe me, do you?"

I arch an eyebrow, "It's a bit hard to swallow."

"That's what she said," Kellan says lightning quick.

"Lame!" I giggle.

"Look, I'll prove it to you. Join my band. I mean, let's form a band. We can play with my buddies Dubs and Joaquin, or whoever we agree on. It'll be *our* band. You and me. Equal partners. We can write all new material or whatever you want. But I want the band." He holds out his hand for me to shake.

I stare at his hand suspiciously. This is really hard. I don't think I'm ready to jump into it. I giggle tentatively, "Are you sure you don't want to just have sex? I'll even throw in a blowjob if it'll sweeten the deal."

He gives me the arching eyebrow that says, "Are you serious?"

Then he shakes his head.

"Gigi, I want the band."

Chapter 115

VICTORY

The line of ticket holders for the L.A. Gunslingers show runs around the outside of The Cobra Lounge and way up the side street toward the Hollywood Hills. The doors don't open for another two hours, but I've already been bringing gear inside for the last hour and stashing it in the back of the building with all the other equipment from competing bands.

The afternoon is hot and the crowd wears concert t-shirts and shorts or tight skirts and revealing tops. Rocker chicks love to put their boobs front and center. I distinctly smell pot coming from three different groups of people huddled in line as I walk past.

I'm in my studded tight leather stage costume. Heavy metal assassin and deadly sexy. My long hair flows behind me as I walk up the street. My All Access badge dangles from a red lanyard around my neck.

Guys stare and whistle and leer. I notice a few of the ladies throwing dagger eyes at me.

The daggers bounce off my assassin costume. I grin to myself.

Some random guy wearing a Megadeth shirt says, "That's her!"

Someone else mutters, "That's the girl on YouTube!"

I still haven't figured out what the hell video I'm supposed to be in. Not that I've looked very hard. I've been way too busy with Rock & Roll High School, my band, and everything else. I'm starting to think someone caught me on camera in a changing room at a lingerie store and sold the video to Girls Gone Wild or something equally stupid.

I'm heading to my car to get an instrument cable. I parked here way early to get a decent space. There's no parking for blocks now that the fans of the bands have started lining up.

I'm still passing people waiting in line when I spot Kellan strolling across the street from his parked Dodge Charger. The car sparkles blue in the daylight. It reminds me of his skyburst blue Les Paul, which is in the case he holds at his side. He wears a Testament t-shirt, leather pants, and boots. He doesn't have to get very dressed up to be hot.

He waves, "Hey, Victory! Good to see you here!"

"Hey, Kellan," I smile. "Representing Testament, I see."

He glances down at his shirt and grins, "Yeah. I was in an Alex Skolnick mood today."

He falls into step with me as I stroll toward my car.

I couldn't accept Kellan's offer to form a band with him. I already had the thing going with Olivia, Lucas and Logan. It didn't feel right to toss that in the garbage. It would've been too much like what Scott did to me with Skin Trade.

Kellan grins, "Your band ready to rock the house tonight?"

"We're taking first place," I smile confidently.

Kellan scoffs, "In your dreams. We're gonna shut you guys down!"

"Not without Switchblade, you aren't," I chide. "Who's gonna play your guitar solos?"

"What, you think I can't shred the shit out of the solos to my own songs?"

"I thought you said singing and soloing was too much extra work," I mock snidely.

Kellan shakes his head, "You think a little extra work is going to stop me? Hell no! After tonight, people are going to start calling Kellan Burns the new King of Shred Guitar."

I cackle, "You wish. I'm gonna be the one wearing the crown after tonight."

He smiles and nods. "A king has to have a queen, right? Maybe we can both wear it."

I sigh and smile at him. Ever since the night I slept at Kellan's (but didn't have sex with him) and told him about Victor, he's been bugging me about starting a band. He's never blatant about it. But he drops hints all the time when I see him at Rock & Roll High School. His perseverance is cute, but I just can't do it.

Also, I've been somewhat surprised that Kellan hasn't put any moves on me since I made it clear a band with him is a no go. Although he's super flirty, he never pushes it further. I kind of figured when he realized I was serious about not doing the band with him, he'd opt for sex instead. Nope. He meant what he said. He wants a band with me, not sex. I don't know if he's dating anyone to meet his physical needs or not. I never ask. Knowing him, he *has* to be. I don't think a guy like him could go more than a day without getting laid.

I say, "England doesn't have a king. I'm taking the crown. You can be my palace guard or something."

He grins, "No, no, no. You'll be *my* guard. Or a lady in waiting."

I frown, "I'm not waiting for nobody."

He chuckles.

We now stand at my car and I dig my spare instrument cable out of the trunk. "Found it," I smile and slam the trunk.

"You could've used one of mine," Kellan says. "I brought five."

Despite our competitive banter, I can tell Kellan has my best interests in mind.

We walk back down the line of people toward The Cobra.

As we pass, some chubby guy in line wearing a Savatage t-shirt says, "That's her! From the video!"

I turn to Kellan as we walk and mutter, "People keep telling me I'm in some video on the internet. I have no idea what they're talking about. I thought it was some Skin Trade bootleg, but I never found anything. Do you know anything about it?"

Kellan shrugs, "Naw."

A rocker girl popping out of her low cut and torn up Mercyful Fate shirt says, "That's him! That's the guy from the video! And that's her!"

I hiss at Kellan, "What the hell are they talking about!"

Kellan shrugs, "Uh, I don't know."

"Are you sure?" I say accusingly.

He shrugs again. "So, is your band here yet?"

"They're driving over."

"What about yours?"

"Joaquin and Dubs went to Guitar Central to get drum sticks for Joa. He forgot them at home. They'll be back in no time."

I don't tell Kellan that Lucas and Logan are still driving up from San Diego. I wish they'd left earlier, but they said they were having a problem with their VW bus. I hope they get it fixed in time. If not, they better rent a van or a truck and get their asses up here. Olivia is at work in Santa Monica, doing some recording thing, but she told me she finishes at five, which means she'll be here any minute.

If worse comes to worse, Liv and I can play over backing tracks like we did at The Dive Bomb open mic. It's not ideal, but it's better than me being up on the stage all by myself.

That would suck.

Chapter 116

VICTORY

Kellan says, "I need to get my badge so I can get inside. Wanna come with?"

"Sure," I smile.

We walk to the front entrance of The Cobra.

"What up, Tony!" Kellan says to his burly bouncer buddy.

Tony laughs uproariously, "Kellan! I haven't seen your ugly mug in weeks! Where you been, boy?"

They hug like macho men.

I remember Tony from the night I played here with Skin Trade. He wears the same black t-shirt with the blood red Cobra Lounge logo stretched across his brawny chest.

Kellan says, "I've been pretty busy teaching the kids."

Tony looks thoughtful, "Where was it you work again?" He starts snapping his fingers, "Rock School? School of Hard Rock? Something like that?"

"Rock & Roll High School," Kellan smiles.

"That's right!" Tony points at him enthusiastically. "How's that going?"

"Great," Kellan says, "Now that we've got another awesome teacher." He nods at me.

Tony recognizes me, "I remember you! You were here that night with that band?" Tony starts snapping his fingers again. "Help me out. What was the name? Skin Brave? Shin Cave?"

Kellan gives me a knowing smile.

Tony chuckles, red faced, "Come on, you guys! You're making me look bad. What was the name of the band?"

I say sarcastically, "I don't remember either."

"Whaddya mean?" Tony asks.

I frown, "I'm not in that band anymore."

Tony looks surprised, "You're not? But you guys had so many fans!"

I shake my head, "Long story. We had a little bit of a falling out."

Kellan says, "In other words, the guys in her band were pricks."

Tony nods, "Pricks are always the problem." He winks at Kellan, "Right?"

Kellan bumps Tony's fist and says, "Mine always is."

"That's what she said!" Tony laughs heartily, until he's red in the face again.

Kellan chuckles with him.

When Tony calms, he says, "Kellan, you need your badge, right?"

Kellan says, "Yeah."

"G'wan inside," Tony smiles and slaps Kellan on the arm heavily.

Kellan is so big, he barely budges. He asks Tony, "You gonna watch the show tonight? We're both playing."

"You and her?" Tony asks dubiously. "Together? That I'd like to see!" He grins.

I say, "We're in separate bands."

"Well," Tony says thoughtfully, "Good luck to both of ya." He grabs Kellan's arm and winks at me, "But a little more luck to Kellan. He's gonna need it."

Kellan scoffs, "You selling me up the river, Tony?"

Tony shakes his head dismissively, "Never. Good luck to ya, kid. Now go get your badges."

Kellan and I take a few steps inside.

Tony suddenly shouts behind us, "Shit Stain!"

Kellan and I whip around.

Tony is cracking a grin, "That was the name of your old band, right? Shit Stain!"

Kellan and I both laugh.

I tap the tip of my nose several times then point at Tony, "You hit it on the nose, Tony."

He chuckles and waves as Kellan and me go inside.

We stop at the table where they're handing out badges to participating bands. Two girls in Guitar Central t-shirts sit behind the table with boxes full of manilla folders.

Kellan walks up to the girl on the left with big boobs and platinum curls. Of course he does. Not that I care.

Cannonballs, as I'm calling her, looks like a stripper they hired from one of the nearby Hollywood strip joints to be a door girl here at the show tonight. She wasn't here when I arrived earlier. I guess they bring in the A talent closer to show time. Or she's on stripper time, which means she just woke up.

When Cannonballs looks up at Kellan, her eyes light up, "Hey," she purrs at him.

I'm waiting for her to do a cat crawl over the table top and pull Kellan's zipper down with her teeth.

"Hey," Kellan smiles at her.

"What's your name?" she says breathlessly.

Geez, she's obvious.

"Kellan Burns," he says casually.

"Ooh," she giggles suggestively, "I like your name. Sounds like you're on fire."

Kellan nods cockily, "I will be when I hit the stage tonight."

Of course he said that.

Cannonballs chews on her inflated lower lip, "How about after? Will you still be on fire then?"

"I'm always on fire," Kellan chuckles.

Cannonballs is leaning over the table, her eyes mesmerized by Kellan's. She's totally forgotten she's here to do a job. She's shooting sexual energy out of her eyes, and probably other bodily orifices, trying to snare Kellan so she can take him back to her lair.

Not that I have anything against that. I certainly can't blame her for trying. I know I did. But I didn't have any luck. Who would've guessed Kellan would turn out to be such a Boy Scout under all that bad boy beauty?

No one on my internal committee has an answer for that. They're all stumped.

Cannonballs picks up a Sharpie pen from the table and says to Kellan, "Can I see your hand?"

He asks sincerely, "Do you need to stamp it?"

"Mmmm-hmmm," she purrs.

He holds out his hand.

She writes a phone number on it, "Call me when you finish tonight."

Kellan grins at her, "Sure."

I guess you need big artillery like Cannonballs if you want Kellan in your bed.

Cannonballs stares at Kellan, obviously imagining what they're going to do later this evening.

Again, not that I care.

"So, uh," Kellans says, "Do I get a badge?"

"Oh!" Cannonballs says peppily, the spell finally broken. "What's your band called?"

"Suffer The Gun."

"Ooh," she coos, "Sounds dangerous."

"That's me," Kellan smiles cockily.

"I bet *your* gun *is* dangerous…" she sighs.

Give it a rest already!

I can't tell if Kellan is enjoying this or not.

Cannonballs finally finds the envelope with Kellan's badges and hands it to him.

"Thanks," he smiles.

She says, "Badges and lanyards are in the envelope." She winks, "Let me know if you need helping putting yours on…"

"I think I'll manage," Kellan chuckles.

"Then I'll help you take *it* off later," she murmurs.

"Sure," Kellan smiles.

I'm tired of watching their mating ritual, so I start looking around for the nearest distraction and my eyes land right on Rob the Knob.

Shit!

Rob the Knob, as in Rob Pickford, the Guitar Central store manager! The guy who wouldn't give me back my Fender! And banned me from the store!

Rob stands to the side of Cannonballs' table talking to a couple of guys in Guitar Central t-shirts. But he already recognized me. His eyes pop, "You! I remember you!"

I duck my head and try to flee outside but I bump into Kellan who is a flesh brick wall.

Rob the Knob strides right up to me, "What do you think you're doing here?"

"Uh…" I stammer.

Rob glances at the All Access badge on my chest and says, "Uh uh. No way. You are not playing here tonight."

Damn it! I was worried about this! I even had Olivia put all the registration info in her name just in case! My plans are crumbling around my ears! I should've worn that KFC bucket disguise!

Rob grabs the badge around my neck and pulls on it like he's trying to rip it off my neck.

"Hey!" I shout, slapping away his hand. "Watch it!"

Kellan barks, "What're you doing, dude?"

Rob the Knob looks up at Kellan's burning eyes while still holding onto my badge. Kellan is way bigger than Rob. But Rob isn't exactly small, and he clearly has a pugnacious attitude. Plus, he's the Guitar Central store manager. I imagine he's in charge of this whole affair.

"Who are you?" Rob barks back at Kellan.

"I'm playing with one of the bands tonight."

Rob looks between me and Kellan and says to him, "Not her band, I hope."

Kellan shakes his head, "No."

Rob the Knob nods, "Then this shouldn't concern you. Right?"

Kellan arches an eyebrow, "If you stop manhandling her, it won't concern me. But I think you should probably let go of her badge."

"Oh yeah?" Rob the Knob says confrontationally. "Why?"

Shit. I appreciate Kellan's standing up for me, but I don't want him getting kicked out tonight too. Through gritted teeth I grunt, "Because, Rob, I'm going to kick you in the balls if you don't let go of my badge right now."

Rob snorts, "I'd like to see that."

Kellan chuckles, "Don't tempt her."

Rob the Knob shows the whites of his eyes and growls, "I like danger." And he still holds my badge.

"You can let go any time," I threaten.

Rob reaches up and unclips the badge from my lanyard, which falls to my chest. With badge in hand, he chides, "Problem solved. Now get out."

"What!" I shriek.

"I said," he says calmly but with restrained anger, "Get out. You're not playing here tonight. Understand?" Rob looks around and motions to the two guys in Guitar Central t-shirts to come over. They do. Rob says to them, "Escort this woman outside. Do not let her back in under any circumstances."

The Guitar Central goons nod at Rob. The tall one looks at me expectantly.

"My gear is inside!" I protest.

"What?" Rob asks.

"My amps and my guitar!"

Rob grinds his teeth and his lips knot around them. To the goons, he seethes, "Take her into the back to get her stuff. Then she's gone. Understand?"

The goons nod again.

"And," Rob the Knob says archly, "Once she leaves, I want one of you on the front door, and one of you on the back door all night. She's not sneaking in here. Got it?"

The goons nod again.

Five minutes later, I'm strutting up the sidewalk with my Fender while Kellan carries the Line 6 Bogner combo I've been borrowing from Rich Aymes.

"I'm fucked!" I shout at the sky.

No way I'm winning that $5,000 prize money now.

I scream at the heavens.

"FUUUUCCCCKKKK!"

Chapter 117

VICTORY

"What are you gonna do?" Kellan asks as we walk up the sidewalk.

I scream in his face, *"I DON'T KNOW WHAT I'M GONNA DO!!"*

Kellan looks stunned.

I shake my head, "I'm sorry. It's not your fault. I'm just so fucking pissed right now!"

"Maybe your band can sneak you in when they get here?"

I slow my stride, "You're right! That might work! But what about those Guitar Central Goons guarding the doors?"

"Maybe we can distract them?" Kellan suggests. "But how?"

My eyes gleam suddenly, "Cannonballs!!"

Kellan scoffs, "What?"

"That girl at the desk when you got your badge!"

Kellan snickers, "You mean the stripper with the tits?"

"Yes! Get her to help! I bet you could talk her into flirting with the Goons!"

Kellan nods appreciatively, "Could work. But I'll probably have to fuck her as payback. I wasn't really planning on it," he sighs.

I chuckle, "Gimme a break. You were totally planning on doing her tonight after the show."

"Not really," Kellan says sincerely.

I actually believe him.

Kellan really is in a class by himself. He's like a one of a kind million dollar super car. Beautiful, powerful, high class, and only the luckiest people in the world get to drive him. I wasn't one of them.

Whatevs.

I have other problems right now.

I smile at him, "You know, I was considering getting a KFC bucket and doing the Buckethead thing in case this happened."

Buckethead literally wears a KFC bucket on his head and a mask when he performs live. It's his trademark stage costume. It works because he's an incredible guitar shredder and because he looks creepy and ridiculous at the same time.

Kellan laughs, "That's an awesome idea, Gigi! You should totally do it. The crowd will love it, especially if you take the mask off at the end. All the guitar players will freak when they see a hot girl underneath!"

"I know, right!" I grin. "I'm sure there's a KFC near here! They'll give me a new bucket, even if I have to pay for it. But I need a Michael Myers mask like Buckethead uses. Where the hell do I get a Michael Myers mask last minute?"

He frowns in thought, then his face crackles with delight, "Hollywood Costumes & Collectibles! They're just east of Highland!"

I jump up, throw my arms around him, and kiss his cheek, "I love you, Kellan!"

Whoops, I didn't mean to say that.

I slide down his muscled chest until my toes touch cement. "I mean…" I trail off.

He nods, "I know what you meant." But his eyes hint at disappointment. "Anyway, we've got shopping to do!"

"Which car do we take?"

"Mine's faster," Kellan grins.

"Yeah, but we're not driving very far. What we need is smaller for better maneuverability and easier parking."

"Good point. But we have to move quick. Want me to drive?" he asks.

"Hell no! I can handle it!"

We jump into my Altima and speed toward Sunset.

Kellan points left when we get to Sunset, "That way!"

When the light turns green, I punch it. "I sure hope the costume shop is still open."

Kellan pulls his smart phone out of his pocket and surfs around. "They close at seven. We've got…thirty minutes. That should be enough if we don't hit too much traffic."

"How far is it?"

"Three and a half miles. But that's L.A. miles. It could take thirty minutes if we hit too many reds."

"We'll make it."

I weave my Altima in and out of the sluggish cars on Sunset Boulevard, dodging around buses, running yellows, whatever it takes. I'm getting that damn mask. I just hope I don't get pulled over for speeding.

Lucky for me, there's never a cop in L.A. when you need one or don't need one.

A lumbering red double decker Hollywood Tours bus suddenly turns onto Sunset, pulling out in front of me. It's going one mile an hour.

"Move!" I shout at my windshield. There's no way the driver is gonna hear me. I don't even bother with the horn. But I use the one in my head, "Mooooovvvvveee!!!"

Kellan snickers.

"What?" I growl at him.

He shakes his smiling head, "Nothing. Keep driving."

I glance in my side mirror. The second there's an opening between passing cars, I dart out from behind the bus and floor it. My Altima screams. It's not used to this kind of abuse.

I hope I don't blow a head gasket. I mean, in the engine. I've already blown the one in my head.

It's amazing how slow traffic in Hollywood actually moves because of all the lights. Even with my hazardous no holds driving, I watch the clock on my dash ticking down to zero. I mean, 7:00pm.

6:47pm.

It's gonna be close.

SCREEEECH!!!

I slam on the brakes, laying down rubber as my Altima slides to a stop at a light that was not even yellow, orange, or pink. It was flat out red. I don't want to hit anybody and cause an accident.

Smoke from my tires literally puffs out of the wheel wells.

Kellan snickers, "There went two thousand miles of tire tread."

I shake my head. "Fuck!" I pat my steering wheel tenderly and say, "I'm sorry, girl. I didn't mean to do that."

"You talk to your car too?" Kellan grins.

"Only when I abuse her."

"Keeps 'em loyal," Kellan quips.

The light turns green and I don't quite floor it. For my Altima's sake.

A couple blocks later, a three-wheeled Parking Enforcement wagon is blocking my lane, stopping traffic. I can't get over in time, and I'm boxed in by cars passing on the left.

Kellan says, "I'd tell you to push the Parking Enforcement go cart off the road, but I won't out of respect for your car. If we had a huge truck with a big ass bullbar on the front, I'd say otherwise."

"Totally," I laugh, picturing me in a huge diesel truck plowing the Parking Enforcement wagon off the road and laughing as it tumbles end over end. I smile.

Then I glance at the clock.

I frown.

6:54pm.

This is way too close.

The second there's an opening on my left, I bolt around the Parking Enforcement wagon and floor it.

Sorry, Altima!

Two blocks later, we pass Highland Avenue where it crosses Hollywood Boulevard.

"There it is!" I shout as we near Hollywood Costumes & Collectibles.

6:58pm.

"Shit!" I blurt. "Where do we park?"

Because the shop is near the heart of Hollywood & Highland, the touristy section of Hollywood, there is never any parking this time of day on a Saturday. Not only is the famous Hollywood and Highland mall a tourist draw, so is The Walk of Fame with all the stars on the sidewalk, Grauman's Chinese Theater with the movie star handprints in cement, The Egyptian Theater, Ripley's Believe It Or Not, and all that other junk.

Tons of tourists and NO parking.

Anywhere!

"There's no place to park!" I shout.

I roll to a stop at the red light at the end of the block where the costume store is.

Kellan says, "Turn right here and pull over. I'll stay with the car while you go inside for the mask. If I have to move cuz of Parking Enforcement, I've got my phone. You've got my number, right?"

"Yeah."

When the light turns, I go right and stop the car twenty feet from the corner. I yank the parking break, leave the engine running, and jump out of the car.

6:59pm.

Kellan runs around to the driver's seat and hops in like a well oiled machine. A very attractive, well oiled machine. I wouldn't mind seeing him well oiled sometime, come to think of it.

What am I doing daydreaming! I need to buy a mask!

"Be right back," I turn and run.

He shouts, "Do you have cash?"

"Shit! It's in my purse! In the car!" I sprint back to my Altima. I'm not nearly as well oiled as Kellan.

He holds my purse out the window. "Go!" he shouts.

I grab it and run around the corner to the costume shop at top speed.

When I reach the double glass front doors, some guy is locking the door.

"No!" I scream. "I need to buy a mask!"

"Sorry," his voice is muted by the glass, "We're closed."

"I need to buy a mask! Please!" I cry desperately.

His eyes bulge at me like I'm insane. He backs away from the door.

I can't decide if my studded black leather heavy metal assassin costume is helping my case or hurting it. Not that I have much choice.

"Please don't go!" I pound on the glass of the front door, "I swear I'm not crazy! I just need a serial killer mask!"

He backs up cautiously.

Maybe that was the wrong thing to say. "I mean, I need to buy a mask! A Michael Myers mask! Please! I swear, that's all I need!" I reach into my purse and pull out cash. "I have money!"

"I'm sorry, ma'am, we're closed."

"No!" I plead desperately. I do my best to turn up the tears. "I just need the one mask, that's it, and I'll be out of your hair!"

That's when I notice he's bald.

He frowns. He has no hair to be out of.

Whoops.

"I'm sorry, sir," I put my face up to the glass. "I just need to buy a Michael Myers mask. For tonight. It's really important. I can't tell you *how* important. Please..." Now I really do start to weep.

"What kind of mask?" he frowns thoughtfully.

"A Michael Myers mask! From the movie Halloween! Do you have one?"

He nods, "Yeah, I stock those. That's all you need?"

"I promise!"

He fishes his keys out of his pocket and unlocks the door carefully. "You don't have a gun, do you?"

"No," I laugh. "Just a kn—" I stop myself short.

He frowns sternly, "What?"

I almost mentioned my rainbow rape knife in my purse. Probably not what he needs to hear. "No. All I have is cash for a mask," I smile and pull out some bills from my wallet and wave them at him.

He opens the door. After I'm inside, he locks it behind me and stashes the keys in his pocket.

"The mask is this way," he leads me back into the store.

It turns out Hollywood Costumes & Collectibles is gigantic. They have *everything* you could possibly want for Halloween. Year round.

We walk up to a glass counter in front of a wall covered floor to ceiling with rubber monster masks. He walks behind the counter and pulls out a box from beneath it and sets it on the glass top. "Here you go."

"How much?"

"Two fifty," he says casually.

"Two *hundred*?"

"And fifty," he nods.

Fuck. I don't *have* $250. "Uhh..."

"What," he says, offended, "it's collectible. They're hand molded and hand painted. You pay a premium for it."

"Do you have a non collectible version," I wince.

He smirks gruffly, "Did you want the mask or not? I need to get home to my wife."

"I do. But I only have..." I count through my money, "Eighty five and change?"

He shakes his head, "Sorry. Can't do it. That's below cost."

I start to shake. I'm going to crumble to pieces if I don't get this mask. I consider grabbing it and dashing out the front door. But I remember he locked it behind me when I came inside. That's not gonna work.

"Please..." I beg. "I need a mask for tonight. For my show. I can't play if I don't have the mask. Please, sir. Your wife would understand." I'm reaching, but I can't think of anything else.

He chuckles, "You don't know my wife. Why you think I need to get home on time?"

"Sorry?" I grimace.

He stitches his lips together and nods dramatically, thinking. "You said you don't need a collectible mask?"

I nod, "Just something white and nondescript?" That's pretty much what Buckethead uses anyway.

His eyes narrow, "You mean like a blank?"

"What's a blank?"

"A blank mask. It's all white. So the kids can paint anything they want on it."

"How much are those?"

"Ten ninety-nine."

"I have $10.99!"

He walks out from behind the counter and leads me to another aisle. He pulls a box kit off a hook. The colorful box says "Paint Your Own Halloween Mask!" It has a clear window over a blank white plastic face mask.

"It's perfect" I squeal.

He hands me the box and I hug it to my chest.

"Where do we pay?" I ask.

"Just give me thirteen bucks to cover sales tax. I'll ring it in tomorrow."

I count out a ten and three ones. "Here you go, thirteen dollars."

"My lucky number," he grins.

"Thirteen is your lucky number?"

"Hey," he motions, "Look around."

I'm surrounded by masks and costumes of demons, werewolves, sea monsters, evil clowns, Brides of Frankensteins, Freddy Kruegers, Pinheads, Jason hockey masks, every horror movie villain you can think of.

I smile, "I need to come back here and do some more shopping…"

He smirks, "Try to do it at least an hour before we close, Okay?"

I nod, "Yeah, totally. Thank you so much!"

He walks me to the front door and lets me out.

I run around the corner to where I left my car with Kellan.

My car is gone.

Where the hell is Kellan?!?!

Chapter 118

VICTORY

I frantically dial Kellan on my phone.

It rings.

And rings.

And rings.

And rings.

And goes to voicemail.

Please tell me he didn't leave.

I hope he isn't planning on ditching me here so he can make sure I don't play at L.A. Gunslingers tonight.

He wouldn't do that, would he?

I mean, he's not *mad* because I won't be in a band with him.

Right?

Everyone on my internal committee looks nervous, eyes dancing around, examining fingernails, whistling incriminatingly.

I call his phone again.

Voicemail

Damn it.

I text him.

where r u!!!!!

No text response.

Fuck, fuck, fuck!!

I look up and down the street. My Altima is nowhere in sight.

I run back to Hollywood Boulevard.

I don't see him there either.

"God damn it, Kellan!" I scream at the top of my lungs.

Twenty people turn and look at me like I'm a lunatic. Right now, I pretty much am. They part around me as I start running west on Hollywood toward The Cobra Lounge.

It's only 3.5 miles. That can't take more than, what, a half hour to run?

Except I'm in heels.

But there's gotta be a shoe store between here and The Cobra. In fact, I'm pretty sure I can buy running shoes at the DSW store just west of Madame Tussauds Wax Museum!

In the mean time, I peel off my heels and run barefoot along the Hollywood Walk of Fame.

I hate you, Kellan Burns!

I keep my eyes open for used condoms and cigarette butts. Fortunately, I see none, but my feet will be completely black within five blocks from all the sidewalk grime.

I have to stop at the light for Highland. There's way too many cars passing through the intersection to run for it. A big crowd of tourists hordes around me. Everyone stares at me in my Heavy Metal assassin costume while I hold my heels in my hands.

I'm sure I look like a hooker who just got off the clock.

Some slimy tourist guy with a bad sunburn and a Duck Dynasty beard over his Budweiser t-shirt eyes me hungrily and asks, "How much, baby?"

I glare at him, "To kick you in the nuts? I'll do it free."

He scowls.

I don't care. I clutch the mask box and my purse strap with one hand while I dig out my rainbow rape knife. I hold the knife at my side, unopened. But my thumb is ready to pop the blade at a moment's notice. I'll slice that guy's beard off and feed it to him if he tries anything.

He doesn't.

The light turns green and I sprint across the street.

Ow! Ow! Ow! The asphalt in the street is sharp compared to the polished Walk of Fame sidewalk. I hope I didn't cut my foot just then!

I gingerly tap dance across to the far street corner.

That's when my phone rings in my purse.

I yank it out of the bag.

Kellan.

I answer, "Where the fuck did you go?!"

"I had to drive around the block because of a cop."

I roll my eyes. "Stay right there."

I put my heels back on to protect my feet from further abuse and wait for the Highland light to change to green again.

When it does, I dash back to where Kellan is indeed waiting.

I yank the passenger door open and slide into the seat. I heave a harsh sigh, "Why did you leave?"

"I told you," he says defensively, "A cop told me to move. So I did."

"Why didn't you tell him…" I don't know what to say, I'm just mad.

"Tell him what? That I was waiting for some crazy nut job hottie with a knife in her hand to buy a Halloween mask?"

I throw my head back and laugh now that the stress is off.

Kellan chuckles with me, "Did you get the mask?"

I hold up the box.

"Nice," he grins. "Now we need KFC. I already looked up the nearest one."

"Where is it?"

"Three miles south. By the La Brea Tar Pits."

"Damn, that's out of the way."

"We'll be fine. The show doesn't start until eight. You want me to drive?"

"Would you?" I ask hopefully. "At this point, I'm liable to drive through crowded crosswalks and take out everything from pedestrians to poodles if they get in my way."

"No problem," he chuckles.

I hope he's right about problems.

I don't need any more this evening.

Chapter 119

VICTORY

Luckily, there's little traffic on the way to KFC. They're even happy to give me a clean, empty KFC bucket for free. I ask for two, just in case. You never know what else might go wrong.

Kellan drives northwest toward The Cobra, taking side streets, and we make good time.

Half way there, my phone rings.

It's Logan.

I answer, "Hey Logan!"

"Victory?"

I hear traffic sounds in the background. "Where are you guys?"

"Mission Viejo," Logan says.

"How far is that?"

"It would be an hour, except our bus broke down."

No! The stupid VW bus of theirs! "What do you mean broken down? Do you have a flat or something?"

"Naw. I think the transmission is done. I can't get out of second and the engine is over heating like crazy. We had to pull off the freeway for it to cool down."

Oh no.

"Something wrong?" Kellan asks.

I'm sure my eyes are popping out of my head. "Logan, who do you know with a truck or something who can come pick you up?"

"Right now? Everyone's still at the beach in the water. No one is answering their phones."

Stupid surfers!

I groan, "Can you get a cab to drive you up to Hollywood?"

"We'd need a minivan for Logan's drums and my bass amp."

Shit. This is getting too complicated. I don't have a choice, "Okay, you start calling cab companies in Mission Viejo or wherever, and I'll see if I can find any."

"All right. Sorry, Victory. This totally blows."

"Don't worry, Logan. We'll figure it out. Talk to you soon."

"Okay, bye."

I hang up. "Shit."

"What?" Kellan asks.

"My drummer and bassist are broken down in Mission Viejo."

"Oh," he grimaces. "That's over an hour away. Without traffic. And it's Saturday, which means beach traffic."

I lean my head against the seat cushion, "I know. Do you know anyone who owns a helicopter?"

He chuckles, "Sorry, I don't."

"Why isn't this working out for me tonight?"

Kellan shrugs his tattooed arm, which rests on the steering wheel of my Altima.

We head back to The Cobra Lounge.

If worse comes to worst, I'll still have Olivia with the backing tracks on her computer.

It worked once.

I hope her car doesn't break down too.

No, that's ridiculous.

What are the chances of that happening?

Chapter 120

VICTORY

We make it back to The Cobra at 7:40pm.

Time to spare.

It takes fifteen minutes to find parking. But that's okay, neither of our bands goes on stage at eight.

Kellan parallel parks my Altima then shuts the engine off. He says, "What's the game plan?"

I'm already thinking ten steps ahead, "You need to find Cannonballs and grease her wheels."

He chuckles lasciviously, "I bet she's totally greasy."

"Greasy with STDs," I smirk.

"I told you I wear condoms."

"You need a Hazmat suit for someone like her. Unless you hose her down with a power washer first." I scowl, "Do you even know her name?"

He snickers, "I never know their names, Gigi."

I'm tickled as always when he call me Guitar Goddess.

He asks, "What are you going to do?"

"I think I need to wait in my car until Liv gets here."

"What if that Guitar Central guy puts two and two together and realizes the badge he took from you is the same band your friend Liv is in? He could've torn up all your badges."

"Shit!" I gasp. "You're right!"

"Maybe you should come in with my band. I still have Switchblade's badge. If you wear the disguise, they might let you in."

"What about my stage costume?" I look down at it. "This is a one of a kind deal. It stands out."

Kellan gazes at my body appreciatively, "The way you wear it, that's for damn sure."

I grin, "I know you want to have sex with me Kellan. All you have to do is say the magic word, and I'm yours…" I start giggling.

"Is the magic word, 'We'll form a band AND have sex?'"

I laugh softly, "No. Just the sex."

"Sorry, Gigi. I'd rather have the band."

"You're sure stubborn," I smile. "How do you ever manage to get laid?"

He snorts, "Are you kidding? I've got Cannonballs waiting for me. I have pussy-a-plenty any time I need it."

I wince, "You would screw her?"

"I will if I have to," he laughs.

"It's your funeral," I say dismissively. "Anyway, do you think I should change?"

"Do you have extra clothes?"

"No."

"What if you take off your jacket and put my Testament shirt over your bra top? Then it'll just be your pants."

"That could work!" I shoulder my jacket off. "Gimme your shirt."

Kellan pulls the black t-shirt over his head, revealing his naked muscled arms, chest, and abs. And all those sharp inky tattoos of his.

I'm in a studded leather bra top with skin tight studded leather pants, sitting across from a gorgeous guy, who wears nothing but sexy leather pants. We're sitting in my car on a random neighborhood street in the Hollywood Hills with no people around.

He stares at my cleavage and sighs, "You are so fucking hot, Gigi. I can't stand it."

"Hotter than Cannonballs?"

He snorts, "Of course. Don't you know that every night, after her clockwork motor winds down, Cannonballs has to go back to the Wax Museum where they store her and wait until they wind her up again the next morning?"

I grin gleefully, "I was thinking the exact same thing!"

He frowns, "You were?"

"Totally!"

He laughs suddenly, "Do you think her clockwork pussy has a kung fu grip?"

"A *what*?" I giggle.

"It's an action figure thing."

I gave him the "you're crazy" look.

"G.I. Joe?"

I shake my head.

"I had one when I was a kid."

I chortle, "I think you need to see a doctor about that."

We both laugh for a moment.

And then we're both silent.

We stare at each other's near nakedness.

I lock eyes with Kellan. His are on fire like always.

He's going to kiss me.

I can feel it. I feel it from my toes to the tip of my nose and every destination in between. I'm tingling and ready for whatever he does next.

He clamps his eyes shut and grits his teeth and sighs. He leans his head back against his headrest and hisses, "I can't, Gigi. I won't. I want a band with you."

Maybe I need to rethink my position on no sex with band members. Perhaps Kellan is the exception to the rule.

My phone rings and I jump out of my seat.

I blurt, "That must be Lucas calling about a cab!"

I answer, "Hello!"

"Vee!" Olivia cries desperately.

"What is it, Liv?"

"I'm still in Santa Monica!"

"What?! What happened?"

Liv cries, "My producer decided to go in a new direction at the last minute. We have a bunch of gospel singers coming in tonight to record backing vocals. I have to oversee vocal production."

"Can you get out of it?"

"No! Not if I want to keep working for this guy. I'm his go-to girl, but if I bail on him, I become his no-go girl."

I squeeze my face with my fingers. Shit. "Can you get your computer over here so I can use the backing tracks?"

"No, but I could email you the mp3 files!" she says hopefully. "If someone has a smart phone they can probably plug it into the mixing console."

"That's great! Will your keyboards be on the tracks?"

"Uh, no. Just the drums and bass and the harmony swells."

I say, "And there's no way you can get here with your keyboards?"

"I really doubt it. I'm so sorry, Vee. There's nothing I can do."

I sigh, "It's okay, Liv. Just email me the backing tracks and I'll take care of it."

"Where do you want me to email them?"

"Ahh... Hold on a second." I say to Kellan, "Can you get email on your phone?"

"Yeah."

"Can I have Liv email you my backing tracks?"

"Sure."

I say to Liv, "Email them to Kellan. I'll text you his address when I get off the phone."

"You mean Aiden?" she says with hopeful amusement.

"Yes," I grin. "Just make sure you text me once you send the files to him, okay?"

"Okay. And I'm really sorry I can't make it, Vee," she says meekly.

I hear a man's voice yelling in the background behind Liv, "Why aren't you setting up those mics, Olivia? The singers are on their way over! Get on it already! Or do I have to find someone else to do your job for you?" The angry voice fades as the person walks out of the room.

There's a long pause before Liv hisses quietly, "Sorry, Vee. I have to go. I'll email you the files as soon as I can. Sorry," she says nervously.

I sigh, "Bye, Liv."

I end the call. Kellan tells me his email address and I text it off to Liv.

I turn to Kellan.

Shirtless Kellan.

His hot body is the last thing I can think about right now.

He says, "She can't make it?"

I shake my head no.

"But you've got the backing tracks?"

"If she has time to send them."

Chapter 121

VICTORY

Kellan's bass player buddy Dubs and his drummer Joaquin rap on the window of my Altima twenty minutes later. He called them and told them where we were. Kellan already put his shirt back on, and I have my jacket back over my bra top.

Me and Kellan both step out of the car.

"Qué pasa, homes!" Joaquin smiles at Kellan.

I briefly met Joaquin and Dubs in the back of The Dive Bomb during open mic night. But we didn't talk for more than two minutes before they loaded out their gear.

Joaquin looks me up and down in my stage costume and drawls appreciatively, "Hola, chica!"

Dubs bites his lower lip while he stares at me brazenly. He snaps a pimp hand gesture and jeers, "Woo, you fine, girl!"

I watch Kellan closely, wondering if he'll say something jealous.

He smiles proudly at Dubs, "Right?"

Dubs asks Kellan, "She your lady now?"

Kellan shakes his head, "Nope."

Dubs grins, "Get on that shit, dawg! Girl like her ain't stayin' single for long!"

Joaquin says to Kellan, "What's wrong with you, ése?" He flicks a glance at me, "You should be hittin' that shit ten times a day, homes!"

I can't help grinning.

I agree with Joaquin and Dubs.

Kellan winks at me but says to Joaquin, "I'm working on it, bro. But I got a ways to go before I wear her down all the way."

I guess he's talking about the band thing? Because the sex thing with Kellan is a go. I really can't figure him out.

Kellan changes the subject and says to Joaquin, "I see you bought some sticks?"

Joaquin holds up a Guitar Central bag with drum sticks poking out the top.

Dubs asks Kellan, "So, what up with all this shady ninja shit, yo?"

Kellan says, "Victory needs our help. You guys up for it?"

Dubs and Joaquin nod.

Kellan explains everything to them in detail then hands them their All Access badges.

Kellan asks, "You guys got it?"

"Solid," Dubs nods.

"No hay pedo," Joaquin says.

Dubs turns to him and frowns, "What the fuck that even mean, Joa?"

"What?" Joaquin asks. "No hay pedo?"

"Yeah," Dubs nods. "Ain't pedo mean fart? You sayin' you ain't fartin'?"

Joaquin laughs, "Yeah. But it's slang for 'no problem.'"

Dubs grins, "Farts are always a problem, dawg. Especially yours."

"Chinga tu madre," Joaquin drawls.

Dubs glares at him, "You talkin shit about my momma?"

Dubs is taller and more muscular than Joaquin by a lot.

Joaquin doesn't care. He says confidently, "Yeah, homes. I tear her shit up every night, ése."

"No you didn't," Dubs growls comically.

Kellan chuckles, "Shut the fuck up, both of you. We got work to do."

I pull my Fender case and my Line 6 amp out of my trunk and hand them to Dubs and Joaquin to carry.

Kellan says to the guys, "Tell the Guitar Central guys guarding the back door that this is our gear. They shouldn't give you a problem."

"Got it," Dubs says.

"Vamonos," Joaquin says and the two of them walk toward The Cobra holding my guitar and amp.

Kellan says to me, "I'm gonna go find Cannonballs and work my magic. When everything is ready, I'll text you. You should probably put your mask and the KFC bucket on before you get too close to The Cobra. And maybe put your hair up so no one recognizes it.

"Okay."

Kellan pulls off his Testament t-shirt once again and hands it to me.

As much as I'd like to jump him, we really don't have time for a quickie. Not that it would do any good with Choir Boy Kellan Burns.

I take off my jacket and drop it in my trunk.

Kellan holds up an All Access badge, "This is Switchblade's badge. Her name is on it. I'm sure no one will ask, but if they do, you're Switchblade. Got it?"

I nod.

"See you in a few," he says as he walks down the street toward The Cobra.

"Don't you need a shirt?" I call after him.

He stops and turns, "Naw. I'm good."

Yes he is. I admire the beautifully sculpted muscles of his back as he strides down the street.

Maybe my 'no sex with band members' policy is becoming outdated. I'll have to convene a meeting with my internal committee after the show tonight and see if we can't reach a treaty of some sort.

When Kellan is gone, I go to work putting up my hair under the KFC bucket.

Chapter 122

VICTORY

The crowded line of ticket holders beside The Cobra is now slowly walking toward the front doors as I walk past them. I'm sure security is busily checking everyone for guns, knives, booze, and drugs down at the main doors.

The KFC bucket is on my head covering my bunned up hair, and the white plastic mask is covering my face. I wear Kellan's Testament t-shirt over my bra top. The shirt smells like him and makes it hard to concentrate on the plan at hand, but I manage. I still have my skin tight low-ride lace-up black leather pants and black stripper heels covered in silver spikes.

I don't have a mirror, but I have no doubt I'm reasonably sexy from the neck down and completely ridiculous from the neck up. It's not like I have much of a choice.

As I pass by a guy in an Anthrax shirt, he points at me and says, "Dude! That's Buckethead!"

The guy next to him wearing a Joe Satriani shirt says, "Naw, man, Buckethead is really tall. And that's a girl. See her ass?"

"Shit yeah, I do!"

I'm already past them, but I hear the other guy say, "You think she's a butter face under the mask?"

"Probably," his friend blurts. "Why else would she be wearing a mask?"

Not my problem.

I stop a half block up from the back entrance to The Cobra.

A few minutes later, I receive a text from Kellan,

Ready at the back door

I walk toward it, my heart accelerating. If this doesn't work, I probably won't get to play.

The long line of people waiting to get in the main doors blocks the alley leading to the back door, so I have to squeeze through the crowd.

Several other people call out, "That's Buckethead!"

Once I pass through, I pause.

Cannonballs is pulling on the hand of the Guitar Central goon who was watching the back door. He looks generally dorky, and having Cannonballs hold his hand is blowing his mind. She leads him toward the line of people I just squeezed through.

The men waiting in line part like the Red Sea for Cannonballs, undressing her with their eyes. She ignores them, totally focused on smiling at the dorky Guitar Central goon like he's Prince Charming.

I wait for them to pass.

Cannonballs says breathily to Dorky Goon, "Rob needs you up front."

The goon says, "I thought I was supposed to cover the back door."

"Change of plans." Cannonballs gives him a flirty look, "I'm just doing what Rob told me."

The goon gushes, "Okay."

She leads him toward Sunset and I walk toward the back door. Before I knock, it cracks open and Kellan leans out.

"Come on," he mutters and I slip inside The Cobra Lounge.

Kellan leads me down the crowded hallway, which is bristling with anxious musicians. I have no idea how many bands are playing tonight, but it's at least a dozen or more. We probably have a long wait.

Dubs and Joaquin are standing at the end of a dark hallway with their gear. I feel relief when I see my Fender case and amp.

"Buckethead!" Joa chuckles.

"Shhh," Kellan whispers.

"You look funny in that mask, girl" Dubs says.

I frown, "You look funny without a mask, dog."

Joaquin and Kellan jeer at Dubs.

Dubs shakes his head, grinning.

I want to lift up my mask because it's hot, but with the bucket, it's a pain in the ass. Good thing I wiped off all my makeup before I put it on. Otherwise I'd be a drippy raccoon by now.

I ask, "What do we do now?"

"Now we wait," Kellan says quietly.

I check my phone to see if Liv has sent the backing track files. Nothing yet. Shit. I won't have anything to play if I don't get those tracks! I'm afraid to call her because I don't want to get her fired, so I send her a quick text asking for the tracks.

Then I cross my fingers.

Not long after, someone on the P.A. says to the entire house, *"Welcome to Guitar Central's annual L.A. Gunslingers battle of the bands competition!"*

The crowd cheers and whistles from the main room. They're loud even backstage where I sit with the guys.

"We've got a lot of great bands tonight!"

More cheering.

"But only one of them will win the $5,000 grand prize!"

More applause from the audience.

Is that Rob the Knob making the announcements? I can't tell for sure because of the subtle distortions of the vocal mic over the P.A., but if Rob's the master of ceremonies, he's never going to let me play.

Joaquin asks me, "You playin' with us tonight, ésa?"

I shake my head, "I don't know your guys' music."

"Too bad," he says. "I saw your shit on video. You shred, ésa."

"What video!" I hiss and shoot Kellan a look.

He shrugs, but I get the distinct impression he's holding something back.

The announcer says, *"Will you please welcome our first band of the night to the stage! Poisoned Princes!"*

At the end of the hallway, I see four guys in black walk past, heading toward the stage with guitars in hand.

The crowd cheers and the band plays. They sound like any other random seven string growler metal band. I tune them out.

I ask Kellan, "Do you know the order of the bands tonight?"

"Yeah, I got the list from Cannonballs."

"Who?" Dubs frowns.

Kellan smirks, "Nobody."

I ask, "Can I see it?"

He hands it to me. I scan the list. I see a bunch of names, including Suffer The Gun, Kellan's band.

But I don't see Ninth Street Nymphos, the name Olivia submitted because we haven't had time to come up with a better one. "I'm not on here!"

"What?" Kellan asks.

"My band isn't on here!"

"Let me see," Kellan takes the list. "What are you guys called?"

"Ninth Street Nymphos."

Dubs and Joa chuckle.

Kellan searches the list, "You're right."

I groan, "What am I gonna do?"

Kellan arches an eyebrow, "You wanna play with us?"

"I don't know your songs!" I say desperately. Now I'm sort of wishing I'd teamed up with Kellan from the beginning. Tonight is going to be a bust. I sigh to myself.

Kellan asks, "Didn't you hear us play at The Dive Bomb?"

"Uh...I sort of spent most of your set outside," I say sheepishly.

"You did?" he asks doubtfully. "Why?"

I roll my eyes, not wanting to answer.

"Yeah, ésa," Joaquin says, "Why you diss us like that?"

I wince. I don't want them to think I'm a bitch or whatever. Usually, the truth works, so I go with that. I say, "I was jealous of Switchblade."

Dubs says thoughtfully, "Yeah, she real good. Too bad she gone."

Joaquin asks, "Why were you jealous of Switchblade, ésa? You play way better than her."

I'm flattered, but I can't answer without explaining how I was mostly jealous of the amazing stage chemistry Kellan had with Switchblade, not her playing. Watching the two of them play together reminded me of what I used to have with Victor. And it broke my heart that Kellan had replaced me, even though I told him I didn't want to be in his band. It doesn't make any sense, so I don't bother to mention it.

So I say, "I don't know. I just was."

"No worries," Kellan nods.

I check my phone to see if Liv has sent the files out.

Still nothing.

Waiting sucks ass.

Chapter 123

JULIAN

I'm not a tremendous fan of hard rock and heavy metal, but I can appreciate it. Especially when the performer I'm going to see is Victory Payne.

Since there won't be a valet at a club like The Cobra Lounge, I took the black Range Rover instead of the Ferrari.

I drive the Rover down my driveway and past my front gate onto the road outside my home.

I've been very curious to see Victory perform live in front of an audience since the day we first met. She has a distinct quality of self-assuredness combined with emotional honesty and a sense of humor that I rarely see in an individual performer. Couple that with her technical mastery of the guitar and she has the makings of a super star.

I had hoped Victory would get back to me regarding her performance at the L.A. Gunslingers competition, but she did not. Not a problem. I had previously asked Colette to put the date of the Gunslingers competition on my calendar so there would be no chance that I would miss it.

The timing of the Gunslingers show is perfect. I've spent the day in the studio with Layce and I desperately need to clear my head. A raucous rock club should knock out the cobwebs. It will also expose me to a music scene I rarely see. I welcome the variety.

I hope Layce has a similarly open mind because she insisted on accompanying me to tonight's show.

Layce reclines in the leather passenger seat beside me. She sighs, "How long do we have to stay?"

In the entire time I've known her, which has been a period of many years, Layce has never once been patient. Living in the moment is a concept she cannot fathom.

"Relax," I smile without looking at her. My eyes focus on the serpentine road leading down from my home in the Hollywood Hills. "This should be fun. I thought you might enjoy a break from the studio tonight."

Layce drums her fingernails on the arm rest nervously, "I suppose you're right." She sighs, "But I really want to finish mastering 'I Rise' tonight. That rough master I had to listen to at the video shoot was making my ears bleed. Way too much treble."

I stop at the bottom of the hill and wait for the red light, "I have no doubt it was the sound stage P.A. You heard the mix in my studio. The high end was delicately balanced to emphasize your voice over all."

"I guess," she sighs. "But I want to listen to it one more time tonight when we get back. With fresh ears."

Layce is the consummate perfectionist. I thought I was troublesome. She is far worse. But she's been very successful in the music business and taught me a few things along the way. In fact, she tends to be an inspiration despite her public persona as a diva. Yes, she is a diva. But she has earned it.

The light turns green and I turn onto Sunset Boulevard.

Traffic is moderate for a Saturday evening. The last faint light of the setting sun stains the western horizon as we glide toward it.

Layce asks, "Do you think anyone will recognize me?"

I glance over at her. She wears a plain wig of dark hair that looks believable. I told her that we were going to a rock club tonight, so she arrived at the studio this afternoon wearing a stylish head to toe black leather outfit that looks torn from the pages of Vogue magazine rather than a Sunset Strip rock club. I don't know that anyone will recognize her, but she will certainly stand out from the crowd, a conscious decision on her part.

Layce is addicted to attention.

"Put on the dark glasses," I suggest.

She slides large dark aviator sunglasses onto her exquisitely beautiful face.

I smile, "No one will recognize you except me."

"Good," she smiles. "I wouldn't want to think you've forgotten about me, Julian..."

She slides her fingertips down my shoulder.

"How could I ever forget you, my dear Layce?"

She smiles, her full lips easing across her wide mouth. Even in her dark glasses, she is beautiful in the extreme.

Layce and I have had our fun in the past. She's as passionate in private as she is in public. But we're both extremely busy creatives in a cutthroat business. Neither of us has ever spoken of the long term.

When we near The Cobra Lounge, I ask, "Would you prefer I drop you off at the front and park, or shall I escort you from wherever I park to the front door?"

Layce chuckles seductively, "You can be my escort."

"Excellent," I grin.

I park the Range Rover in a residential neighborhood then walk around to get Layce's door. I open it like I'm the valet and take her hand.

"You are such a gentleman, Julian," Layce purrs.

"Nothing less for you, my dear," I smile.

We walk toward The Cobra Lounge, her arm draped over my elbow.

When we reach the front doors, the crowd is mostly inside, but a few stragglers remain in line, waiting for entry. The men in line gawk at Layce like prairie dogs. Yes, she is that beautiful.

I lead Layce directly to the doorman in front.

He is a wide, muscular man who seems a bit crude for my tastes. He says, "You gotta wait in line like everybody else, buddy."

"We have V.I.P. tickets," I say confidently.

The doorman frowns, "Nobody told me anything about V.I.P. tickets."

I pull my wallet out of my suit jacket and hand him four crisp one hundred dollar bills.

The doorman looks at the money, then runs his eyes over my features, "Yeah, okay. But I still have to pat you down." He folds the bills into his pocket.

I raise my arms while he checks me for firearms or whatever illegal paraphernalia he thinks I might be hiding. Then he checks Layce's handbag, which is the size of a coin purse.

"Okay," the doorman cocks his thumb toward the entrance, "You guys are good. Have fun."

I joke, "Do we get bottle service with the V.I.P. tickets?"

The doorman grins, "That's extra."

I chuckle and lead Layce inside The Cobra Lounge. We squeeze our way through the crowd.

All male eyes are on Layce.

I can tell she is thoroughly enjoying herself.

We work our way into the main room where the audience is facing the stage, jumping and flailing enthusiastically. It's very crowded and Layce and I are pressed together.

She leans into me and murmurs into my ear in an affected high society accent, "All these filthy men are staring at me, Julian. You know what happens to me when men stare at…"

Layce uses the accent when she wants to feel superior in public settings such as these. Without paparazzi flashing cameras at her as proof of her superiority over the unwashed masses, her insecurities tend to get the best of her. She never hid behind the accent when I first met her years ago. She was much more down to earth then, more honest, direct, and sincere. But her success has turned her into the Stellar Princess she always wanted to be.

Oh, how she has changed.

Her innocence is gone.

Forever, I think.

I suspect she's forgotten what a turn on innocence can be.

Layce continues breathily, "All these filthy men and their filthy stares are making me horny, Julian. But none of them are good enough for me."

"Isn't that always the case with you, my dear?"

"Mmmm..." she purrs. "When we get back to your place, I want you to fuck me hard and make me feel dirty, Julian. You're the only man who knows how to make me feel dirty just the way I like it."

Layce believes that a man's ego is at all times defenseless to feminine attack.

She still doesn't know me nearly as well as she likes to believe.

I nod ambiguously at her.

She coils around to face me, maintaining body contact at all times, her pelvis pressing against mine. She tips her aviator sunglasses down with delicate fingers and shines sultry eyes over the frames.

In the dark night club, no one can see when she reaches down and guides my fingers between her leather covered legs.

She emits intense heat.

She is definitely turned on.

I know her games well.

As tantalizing as her beauty and passion always are, I didn't come here for her.

I came here for Victory.

Chapter 124

VICTORY

Two hours later, Kellan is shirtless and has his skyburst blue Les Paul over his shoulder. Dubs is also shirtless and leans his bass against his hip. It's hard to decide which one of them has a better body. It's damn close.

Joa is also shirtless, sporting tattoos on every inch of skin, and has been drumming on the thighs of his skater shorts for the last twenty minutes, warming up his hands. Kellan has been playing random riffs on his guitar. Dubs stands patiently. Bass players never seem to warm up.

I've been wearing the KFC bucket and blank white Halloween mask the entire time. It's damp and miserable, but a small price to pay to play on stage tonight.

After another band finishes and gear gets moved around, the announcer voice finally says on the P.A., *"Everybody welcome Suffer The Gun to the stage!"*

"Time to rock," Kellan says to the boys. Dubs and Joa follow him to the stage.

"*All right!*" Kellan screams into the microphone a minute later.

I hear the shrill screams of every woman in the house.

Man, he sure has a way with the ladies.

"*Let's Live It Up!!!!*" he screams.

The band kicks into their first song, which I recognize from The Dive Bomb.

I remain huddled at the end of the dark hallway. I check my phone for the hundredth time.

Aiden should have files.

Oh my god! The files! Liv sent them! I can't believe it! I have my backing tracks! She came through!

Kellan left his phone with me and showed he how to unlock it and check his email. It only takes me a few moments to find Liv's email. The mp3s from Liv are attached! Now I'm in business.

I just need to get them to the sound board guy or they won't do me any good.

Time for me to emerge from hiding. I skulk toward the main hallway that leads to the stage. The waiting musicians all look at me.

Yet another person makes a Buckethead comment which I ignore.

When the coast is clear of Guitar Central staff, I walk toward the stage where the soundboard guy stands behind the mixing console, monitoring the sound and making minor adjustments throughout Kellan's performance.

I have to give Kellan's phone to the soundboard guy so he can run Liv's mp3 tracks through the P.A. and the monitors. Then I'll be able to play my own music with at least a basic accompaniment. I wish Liv was here with her keyboard, and Lucas and Logan with their bass and drums, but the mp3 tracks will be better than nothing.

When I get to the stairs that lead to the stage, I pause.

I went up this exact staircase with Scott, Rex, and Bobby less than two months ago. My, how time has flown and times have changed. I was welcomed here that night. Tonight, I'm an interloper and a criminal wearing a KFC bucket and a face mask.

And I have no band.

Fuck it.

No sense crying over spilt milk.

I march up the stairs toward the sound booth.

And see Rob the Knob standing right in front of it, arms folded across his chest, watching Kellan's band.

I can't get to the sound booth without going past Rob the Knob. I have my mask on, but he's right in front of the booth. Will he recognize me? Will the sound board guy be able to hear me with my mask on, or will I have to take it off, right in front of Rob?

Shit, if only Rob the Knob was gone.

I need to think about this before I dive in. I turn and walk toward the dark hallway where I was hiding and bump right into a Guitar Central goon.

"Oof!" he says.

My eyes pop, but they're hidden behind my mask. Masks sure come in handy when you don't want people seeing your guilty looks. "Excuse me," I say in the manliest voice I can muster. I don't even remotely sound masculine.

"Oh, sorry," the goon says. Then he looks at my face, or should I say mask. "Hey, you're not Buckethead, are you?" he asks doubtfully. "Nobody told me Buckethead was supposed to be here."

If I say more, will I incriminate myself? I nod my masked head noncommittally.

"Yeah," the goon says thoughtfully, "I would've heard." He pulls a sheet of paper out of his pocket. It's the band list for tonight. He starts reading it over.

If I had a hammer, I'd knock him over the head and run for it. But I don't. Then recognition hits. In my normal voice, I blurt, "Felix!" It's the guy who asked me out at Guitar Central they day I got my Fender back.

He looks at me, confused, "Do I know you?"

I grab him by the hand and lead him to the dark hallway where my Fender is with Kellan and Dubs' guitar cases.

"Felix," I hiss, "It's me! Victory!"

"Who?"

I lift up my mask, "Victory! You asked me out that day at Guitar Central? You followed me to my car!"

He smiles, "Yeah! The girl from the video! What are you doing here?"

"I'm playing tonight."

"Sweet," he nods. "What's your band?" He looks down at the paper still in his hand.

"I'm not on the list! There was a mix up."

"But you're playing?" he asks doubtfully.

"Yeah. But I need your help."

He smiles, "Anything for you, Victory."

"Felix?" Rob the Knob yells at the far end of the dark hallway.

I spin around, hiding my face in shadows. My heart accelerates like a top fuel dragster exploding off the starting line.

Felix turns to Rob, "Yeah?"

"You're supposed to be in the sound booth, buddy. Come on, get moving!"

"I'll be right there," Felix hollers.

"Hurry it up!" Rob says and walks away.

Felix turns back to me and scowls, "That guy is such a knob."

I blurt laughter.

"What?" Felix smiles.

I shake my head, "Nothing."

"So, what do you need me to do?"

I hand him Kellan's phone. "There's backing tracks on here. I'm going to play along to them, but I need them hooked up to the P.A."

He takes the phone, "I can totally do that. When are you going on?"

"At the end of Suffer The Gun's set. They're letting me onstage to play one song."

He nods, "Got it."

"I'll be wearing my mask, so you'll know it's me."

"Okay. No problem. I better get to the booth." He turns and takes a step, then stops. "So, ah, can I maybe buy you a drink later? After the show?"

"Maybe?" I feel like a jerk.

He smiles, "Cool." Then he walks to the end of the hall and turns toward the stairs and the sound booth.

I put my mask back on and pull my Fender out of my case and start warming up.

As long as Rob the Knob doesn't notice my guitar and make a connection, I'm good to go.

Chapter 125

VICTORY

The crowd roars as Kellan and the boys finish their third song.

"All right!!!" Kellan screams into the mic.

I stop at the base of the stairs to the stage with my guitar over my shoulder, my KFC bucket on my head, and my mask in place.

The crowd cheers, the women squealing like teenagers at a Beatles concert.

"You guys fucking rock!!!" Kellan screams.

"Excuse me," someone says at my shoulder.

I turn and it's Rob the Knob, heading toward the sound booth.

Oh no!

He stops and looks at me, "If you're with the next band, you need to wait in back until your band is called."

No!

"Come on," Rob the Knob says, "Move it."

In my lame man voice, I say, "Uhh…"

Kellan suddenly says over the P.A., *"All right, everybody. Thank you so much. We've got a special guest tonight for our last song."*

"That's me," I say in my man voice to Rob.

Rob the Knob frowns, "Who?"

"I'm the special guest," I grunt, trying to sound more mannish, "For Suffer The Gun."

Kellan continues, *"A very good friend of mine…"*

Rob looks toward the stage, then back at me. Then he looks at my white Fender Strat. "Why do I know that guitar?"

Kellan continues, *"You may have heard her play before…"*

"All Fenders look alike," I say lamely.

I watch Rob the Knob mentally connecting the dots. He says, "No, I remember this guitar. It was…we bought it used and resold it too—" The light bulb goes off over Rob's head.

Kellan continues, *"Her video now has over a million views on YouTube…"*

"Hey!" Felix trundles down the stairs and grabs my hand, "You're on! Right now!" He yanks me up the stairs

"Get back here!" Rob the Knob shouts at my back. His arm shoots out, trying to grab me.

Kellan continues, *"You all know her as Victory! Victory Payne, everybody! Give her a big hand!"*

I dodge Rob's grasp and stumble up the stairs onto the stage.

I can't believe what happens next.

Chapter 126

VICTORY

The stage lights blare in my face. To my amusement, the face mask cuts down on the glare and I can see the crowd better than I normally can.

They are going crazy as I stumble onto the stage.

I vaguely hear Rob the Knob behind me shouting, 'Get her off my stage!"

I twist and see Felix intercept him and bodily restrain him. I'm really going to owe Felix after this.

Kellan is standing at the mic center stage, clapping enthusiastically, *"Victory Payne, everybody!"*

I wave at the crowd while I walk up to Kellan and shout in his ear, "What the hell is going on?"

Kellan looks over my shoulder at Rob the Knob who is still shouting, "Get her off my stage!"

Felix is struggling to hold Rob back.

Kellan frowns, "You tell me what the hell is going on."

"Rob recognized my guitar!"

Kellan's eyes bulge. A second later, he says, "Take your mask off. Right now."

Since Rob the Knob recognized me, it doesn't really matter. I take the KFC bucket off my head and pull the face mask off.

"Let your hair down," he commands.

I shake it out and let it flow.

Kellan unplugs his instrument cable from his guitar and jacks it into my Fender. "Now shred," he orders. "I'll take care of that guy," Kellan motions at Rob the Knob. Then Kellan takes off his Les Paul and hands it to Dubs to hold. He rushes over to Rob and Felix.

I'm half stunned.

Kellan turns back to me, "Shred!"

I can do that.

I crank the volume on my Fender and distortion rolls out of the amps behind me, the monitors at my feet, and the P.A.

The sound of my guitar shakes the house.

There's is nothing more awesome than wielding an amped up electric guitar that shakes the entire building. I feel like Zeus throwing thunderbolts down from the heavens.

It's incredible every time.

I start jamming out random show stopper guitar solo riffs and the crowd goes wild. I throw in every cool lick I can think of, including two handed tapping runs. I can tell the crowd is loving it. They cheer like crazy.

I periodically glance over at Kellan, who is busy talking to Rob the Knob and Felix, gesturing wildly with his muscled arms.

I keep playing, working the crowd, and they love it. Nobody loves a guitar solo better than a heavy metal crowd.

I'm in my element.

After a couple more minutes, I see that Rob the Knob has calmed, and is nodding at whatever Kellan is saying. I bet the insane noise of approval, cheers, and applause made by the crowd during my extended guitar solo is helping Kellan convince Rob the Knob to let me continue playing.

When I get to a natural stopping point, I strum my guitar rapidly and bring it all to a close.

The crowd erupts and people start screaming my name.

"Victory!!! Woooo!!! You rock! Shred it!!! Victory!!!"

It's totally awesome.

No one is yelling Skin Trade or Scott's name.

They're yelling my name.

Victory Payne.

It feels incredible.

What I can't get over is, how did everyone know my name?

In my experience, when you're a nobody, nobody gives a shit when you play, no matter how good you are.

Kellan strides over and grabs the mic center stage, *"Wasn't that fucking incredible?!?!"*

The crowd goes crazy. I laugh. I can't help it. This is too awesome.

"Victory Payne, everybody!!!" Kellan points at me and the crowd explodes again.

When the applause finally dies down, I hear some guy in the crowd shout, "Play the video! Play the video!"

Kellan looks at me expectantly.

I walk over to him and shout in his ear, "What are they talking about? What fucking video?"

He grins and hollers, "You don't know, do you?"

"Know what?" I demand. I really have zero clue.

"About our video?"

I growl, "Our video?!?!" I shake my head, "I have *no* idea what the hell you're talking about!!!"

Kellan's face softens into an amused grin. He leans over, cups my cheek and mutters into my ear, "Remember that first night you spent at my apartment?"

I nod, "Yeah?"

"And I made us record that video of the two of us playing?"

"You mean the one you forced me to record?" I joke.

"Yeah, that one."

"What about it?"

"I uploaded it on YouTube awhile back. Now it has something like one point two million views."

"What?"

He grins and nods, "You're famous, Victory. Probably every guitar shredder on the planet has seen your video by now."

"What?" I'm stunned. I can't believe what he's saying. It seems impossible and doesn't make any sense.

Kellan looks over at the sound booth and makes a cranking motion with his hand. The guy behind the booth nods.

"Look," Kellan points behind me.

There's a huge projector screen on the wall behind and above the drum kit. It shows a computer desktop. The mouse pointer moves around and clicks on Firefox. When the browser window pops open, the guy behind the sound board enters in some words in the search window:

"Hot girl guitar shredder Ms. Yngwie Malmsteen."

A second later, a YouTube page loads. I notice that it has 1,275,296 views. The mouse pointer clicks on the full screen button, then the play button.

The video shows Kellan sitting down on his living room couch next to me with his blue Skyburst Les Paul. I'm holding his Ibanez RG550.

A second later, the two of us on the video are playing that riff we wrote. The sound pumps out loudly from the club's P.A. speakers. The recording of me and Kellan sounds really good. I forgot how good it actually is. We're amazing together. Super tight, super melodic, super fast guitar playing, and powerful emotive music above all else.

My heart hammers in my chest as I remember everything from that night. The intense connection I felt with Kellan when we played guitar together, almost like I was playing with Victor again. Seeing Kellan's incredible nearly naked body before bed. Tossing and turning all night thinking about going into his room but not. Fantasizing about him in the shower the next morning, breakfast afterward. Him asking me to start a band. And him asking me to sing.

I remember every last second of it.

I realize the audience is dead silent. I can see them clearly because the stage lights are dimmed to allow everyone to see the video. The light of the projection screen bounces off their awed faces.

I'm going to cry.

I can't believe Kellan did this for me.

He posted the video without telling me.

He has gone out of his way to help me out at every turn.

Why couldn't I see it before?

What was my problem?

He's the incredible one here tonight.

The most incredible man I've ever met.

Chapter 127

VICTORY

When the video finishes, the crowd explodes with cheers of approval.

They love it.

I'm ready to die, I feel so overwhelmed.

"Play it!" the crowd shouts. *"Play the song!"*

Kellan walks up to me, "I think they want us to play the riff from the video. Do you remember it?"

I wipe a tear from my cheek, "Yeah. Do you?"

He scoffs, "I've watched that video of us a thousand times. I know it by heart."

I almost start blubbering.

Kellan grabs the mic, *"You guys want to see us do that shit live?"*

The crowd goes crazy.

Kellan takes his Les Paul from Dubs, who now stands at the far side of the stage. Then Kellan plugs into a different amp. He plays a couple chords to make sure it works, then walks over to me. "Ready?" he asks.

I nod.

Kellan looks at the sound board guy and makes a "cut" motion with his finger across his neck.

The projector turns off and a lone spotlight shines on me and Kellan. We are front and center, the stars of the moment.

Me and Kellan Badboy Burns.

He counts, "One, two, three, four."

Then we play the riff together like that first night.

We're perfectly in synch. It sounds beautiful, harmonious, and hard as hell to play. We're a perfect pair of virtuoso guitarists. Half way through, Kellan leans his back against mine, just like he did with Switchblade at The Dive Bomb when I got jealous of her.

But now, Kellan is playing with me.

Me.

We're onstage together and the crowd loves it. They're so loud I can barely hear our guitars over them.

Kellan and I finish with a flourish and I do a big dive bomb on my Fender. The strings rattle against the pickups and the deep bass sound shakes the entire Cobra Lounge.

The crowd is twice as loud with their applause.

Kellan grabs my waist and kisses my cheek and into my ear he mutters, "You did that."

He releases me and points at me. He leans into the mic, *"Victory Payne, everybody!!!"*

The crowd cheers.

I grab the mic from Kellan and shout, *"Kellan Burns, everybody!!!"*

I tiptoe up and kiss him passionately on the mouth.

His tongue meets mine immediately and we kiss like we invented french kissing.

The crowd loves it. They cheer and jeer their approval.

I don't know how long I kiss Kellan, but it feels far too short and eternal at the same time. My whole body is infected with his fire. I'm tempted to have sex with Kellan right on this stage in front of everyone, but that would be too much.

After I reluctantly break our kiss, I lean into him again and shout over the crowd so he can hear me,

"WE did that."

Chapter 128

VICTORY

"Calm down everybody," Kellan laughs over the mic, "Calm down." When the crowd quiets, he says, "There's one more special surprise for you guys tonight! You guys want some more?"

The crowd cheers.

When they settle, Kellan says, "None of you know this, but not only is Victory an amazing guitar player, she's also an amazing singer."

My throat locks, but I do my best to relax it.

He's never heard me sing before. He just took my word for it.

My stomach knots, but I inhale slowly and try to let out my tension.

Kellan and I went over this several times backstage, so I know what's coming next.

Kellan shouts over the mic, *"Who wants to hear Victory Payne sing?"*

The crowd begs for it like natives demanding a human sacrifice or peasants at a beheading. And I'm the one about to have their heart cut out or their head chopped off. That's how it feels, anyway.

Still on the mic, Kellan says, *"I've also got a special surprise for you, Victory."*

He walks over to me and leans his head against mine.

I say in his ear, "You got my backing tracks ready?"

"Better. We're your backing tracks."

"Who is? I'm confused."

"My buddy who runs open mic at The Dive Bomb records the shows. I asked him for the tape of the show the night Suffer The Gun played. It also had tape of you and your friend Liv. I learned all the songs you guys played."

I frown, "Why?"

He rolls his eyes, "Because, I want you and me to make a band. That's why," he smiles.

I'm ready to cry all over again. "You know Sunset Farewell?"

"By heart," he says earnestly.

"What about Dubs and Joaquin?"

"They've seen the video of you and Liv ten times. They've heard your song. They can follow along."

"Are you sure?"

Kellan shakes his head, "Joa can learn a tune front to back after hearing it once. Especially a basic ballad like Sunset Farewell. Dubs can cover it as long as he knows what key we're in, and the basic chords. Trust me, they're good to go."

I can't believe this. It's the next best thing to having Olivia, Lucas, and Logan here with me.

"Who's singing harmony?" I ask.

Kellan levels an intense look at me, "Who do you think?"

My heart goes crazy in my chest.

He arches his eyebrows, "Me."

Victor.

I haven't sung with anyone since Victor.

And now I'm going to sing with Kellan.

I don't know if I can do this.

I *have* to do this.

I nod at Kellan, "Let's do this."

I walk to the mic center stage and people cheer.

"Hey everybody!" I laugh into the mic, overwhelmed by the wonderful reception I'm getting.

More cheers.

I glance over and notice Kellan is huddling up with Dubs and Joaquin, who both nod at whatever Kellan is telling them.

A moment later, Kellan walks over to me and says, "Whenever you're ready."

I nod and say into the mic, *"This song is called Sunset Farewell. I thought I wrote it about my ex boyfriend. But I realized I really wrote it about my brother Victor...*" I look up toward the heavens, and I see the blinding white lights over the stage that shine down from eternity.

I take a deep breath and say, "*Wherever you are, brother, this song is for you. I miss you so much. I love you, Victor Payne...*"

I step back from the mic and play the shimmering opening chords by myself.

On the second measure, the band joins in flawlessly. Joaquin and Dubs do an amazing job. Kellan is in perfect rhythm with me and them. He doubles my guitar part while I sing:

"You left me behind
Your journey into night
I asked you to return
The treasure of our light

You needed it for guidance
So keep it for a time
The only chance to find it
Your pathway into light"

Memories of Victor flash through my mind as I
(*singsingsing*)
sing. I can't believe I didn't realize I was writing this song to him all along. I miss Victor so badly, and it all comes out in my singing.

When I sing the pre-chorus, Kellan harmonizes with me:

"My soul has been unwell
Since your heart set sail
I never said goodbye
Still seek our holy grail
Memory fades with passing days
Forgotten how you fell"

Kellan's deep adult voice is nothing like Victor's twelve year old voice, but the sound of Kellan and me singing together is impossibly beautiful. I haven't heard him sing a mellow ballad until right now, just ballsy hard rock and metal style.

But his voice is perfectly suited for something soft and heart-felt like this.

The sound of the two of us makes me shiver from head to toe.

Dubs adds a third voice during the chorus, singing bass beneath

Kellan's baritone and my mezzo soprano. Dubs doesn't sing the lyrics, he just goes, "Aaaaaah, aaaaah, aaaaaah." But our three part harmony is beautiful and haunting.

My shivers intensify and goose bumps tickle my skin while we sing:

"Trapped in your sunset spell
Eternal carousel
Believing my own lies
Trapped in our sunset spell
The prison where I dwell
Holding onto life
Trapped in your sunset spell

Eternal carousel"

When I start the next verse, I'm weeping, and doing my best not to break my voice. But it's hard. The emotion is overpowering as I conjure more memories of

(*singsingsingsingsingsing*)

Victor.

It's like he's here with me right now, singing with me for the first time in ten years:

"You got lost in darkness
You said there's room for two
I begged for you come back to me
Together we'll renew

Your heart and eyes said yes
Your hurtful words said no
Your soul confessed it was distressed
And didn't want to go"

After we repeat the pre chorus and chorus, I break into my wailing guitar solo. To my surprise, Kellan knows it note for note and harmonizes with me through the whole thing, but he plays a support role, adding chords here and there for a fuller tone, and letting me play all the flourishes.

It sounds perfect.

After we repeat the chorus a final time, and the music calms, I softly sing the last lines to the awestruck crowd:

"Time to say farewell
Time to break your spell
Time to say farewell
Time to break your spell"

I'm weeping freely, my face wet, as the band comes to a rest and all goes silent.

I whisper into the mic:

"Goodbye, Victor."

The house lights fade to black.

Chapter 129

VICTORY

I walk off stage while the crowd cheers and shakes the building.

I need to be alone. I can't deal with the overwhelming feelings of sadness I'm feeling right now thinking about Victor.

It's rude, I know, but I'm going to fall apart.

Kellan shouts on mic, *"Victory Payne, everybody! Woo!!!"*

I walk down the stairs and Felix catches up with me, "That was phenomenal, Victory!"

"Th—Thanks," I mutter and keep walking. I can't talk to him right now.

"We've got that on video!" he says enthusiastically. "If Rob doesn't let me post it on the Guitar Central YouTube channel, I'll post it myself. That was a once in a lifetime performance!" He's so excited his eyes are practically jumping out of his head when I turn to him.

I say, "Yes, it was."

I don't know if I'll ever be able to sing again after that.

"You guys wanna hear one more?" Kellan asks the crowd.

I walk to the dark hallway where my Fender case is. I need to put my guitar away and get out of here.

"I wrote this song about a special girl," Kellan says on mic. *"She means more to me than I ever thought any woman could."*

I hear the strumming of acoustic guitar as I lift my Fender over my head and set it in the case.

Kellan strums chords and I'm immediately pulled in by his delicate fingerstyle playing. I can't help it, I stop to listen.

As Kellan strums the guitar, he starts to sing:

"Whispered kisses
on my lips
from the ghost of you
We've never met
yet it's true
your the one I seek"

His singing is so tender, so heartfelt. I'm rapt. I can't walk away now. And when he talks about a ghost, I can't help but think about Victor.

(*singsingsingsingsingsing*)

The chords change, growing darker and the rhythm picks up speed. Kellan's voice becomes plaintive but driven:

"My whole life
I searched for you
my need like a disease
I can't live
without your love
you bring me to my knees"

Is he singing about me?

"My
Whole
Life
(I've searched)
For
A love
Like you
(Victory)"

Yeah, he's singing about me.

"My
Whole
Life
(I'll search)
For
A love
That's true

(Victory)"

The sound of Kellan's gravelly singing and the acoustic guitar reminds me of a lost lonesome cowboy crawling across the desert, dying for a drink of water, one last drink of water before he dies a slow painful death. And that drink of water is me. I'm the only thing keeping him going. I'm the only thing that gives him purpose and strength and hope.

Oh my god. My heart is melting into sugary goo. I smile and laugh and cry at the same time. It crosses my mind that Scott never wrote a song about me. Not a single one.

Kellan continues to wail, his strumming becoming more frantic and demanding, but powerful and determined:

"I still search
For a love
That's you
(Victory)
On and on
I crawl
I still search

For You"

There's a confidence in Kellan's voice, like he will never ever give up looking for that drink of water until he can quench his thirst.

He'll never give up until he finds me.

Me.

I'm an idiot.

Chapter 130

KELLAN

I sing the last line of My Whole Life to the crowd at The Cobra Lounge, sitting on the bar stool I brought on stage, my boot hooked over one of the rungs, my Martin on my knee.

My body is tingling with adrenalin. I pour my guts into my performance, thinking about Victory, my eyes closed as I sing out the lyrics.

All I can think about is Victory.

I need her.

I'm dying for her.

I don't know if she's even here.

She walked off stage before I started this song.

Maybe she's still in the building and she can hear it.

Maybe she's gone.

It doesn't matter.

I'll keep searching.

I'm never giving up.

I'm so into the song, I repeat the final lyrics and strum my acoustic with everything I have, altering the vocal melody so it harmonizes differently with the chords, giving it an even more powerful demanding sound:

"I still search
For a love
That's you
(Victory)
On and on
I crawl
I still search

For You"

I practically fall over my guitar when I finish, nearly passing out from pushing so much air out of my lungs on the final lines.

I inhale deeply and the black out thing fades.

I've never sung so hard in my entire life.

And the room is dead silent.

No one knows what to do.

I don't either.

I hope Victory heard that.

"Kellan!" she calls out as she runs across the stage and nearly knocks me off the bar stool.

I stand up, my guitar in one hand, and wrap my other arm around her. She kisses me desperately, passionately, like I've never been kissed before.

I don't even hear the crowd go wild.

All I'm aware of is Victory in my arms.

At last.

Chapter 131

VICTORY

"When we find out who wins, yo?" Dubs asks.

"Not till all the bands finish," Kellan says.

I wait backstage with Kellan, Joaquin, and Dubs while the other bands from tonight's lineup play their sets. We put our guitars away already and we're just chatting while we wait for the show to be over.

None of the other bands tonight receive anything close to the kind of applause we did. So we're hopeful that we'll win.

We hear the last band finish playing.

Someone yells over the P.A., *"That was Hangman's Noose! Everybody give them a hand!"*

It's not long before the moderate cheers from the audience die down.

"Don't forget to text your vote to the numbers you see up on the projection screen. Or you can vote at the Guitar Central website where we've simulcast tonight's entire show!"

"So, Gigi," Kellan says to me bashfully, "I know I've asked you this a thousand times, but do you want to join the band?"

I glance at Dubs and Joaquin, "What do you guys think?"

Joaquin purses his lips into an impressed smile, "Fuck yeah, ésa."

Dubs grins, "I'm down."

"Yes!" I throw my arms around Kellan's neck and kiss him repeatedly, smacking my lips all over his. Although I'm now in two bands, it's not the first time I've been in more than one at the same time. I sense that unless Lucas and Logan move to L.A., it's always going to be difficult to get together with them to write and rehearse. As for Liv, she really is moving in much more of a pop direction than I am. But I'll keep working with her just because we have so much fun. And who knows, maybe things with Kellan and the boys won't last either. That's how it is with bands. But for now, I'm open to whatever happens.

But I'm going to give everything I can to working with Kellan, Dubs, and Joaquin.

"Cast your votes, people! Voting closes in ten minutes!"

"Can anyone check the website?" I ask. "And see what the votes are?"

"I'll do it," Kellan says and pulls out his phone, which he got back from Felix after we left the stage. It takes awhile, but eventually, a smile spreads across Kellan's face.

"What?" I ask, excited.

He holds up his smart phone so I can see it.

Suffer The Gun is way out in front of everybody with 25,344 votes.

But ahead of Suffer The Gun is Victory Payne with 57,966.

"Oh my god!" I blurt. "I thought I wasn't on the list!"

Kellan grins, "Guess you are now."

"Did you do that?"

He shakes his head, "Nope."

I frown, "Is this like the thing where you didn't know about my YouTube video?"

He chuckles, "I swear, I didn't do it."

I leer, "You're *sure* sure?"

"I'm serious!" he laughs.

A few minutes later, the P.A. voice says, *"The results are in!"* I think it's Rob the Knob. *"You guys wanna know who won?"*

The crowd cheers, "YEAH!!"

"The winner is..." He clears his throat, and pulls the mic away, but you can still hear him mutter to someone off mic, *"Is this right? I thought I told you to take her off the list?"*

"What?" Kellan frowns.

I hiss, "Wait, shh!"

There's more mumbling on the mic but I can't make it out.

Random people in the crowd start shouting, "IT'S VICTORY PAYNE!!"

"THE WEBSITE SAYS VICTORY PAYNE!!"

"VICTORY WON!!"

"Okay!" Rob says on mic, *"Okay! And the winner of the $5,000 first prize for Guitar Central's annual L.A. Gunslingers battle of the bands competition is Victory Payne!"*

The crowd goes crazy.

"Victory Payne, where are you? Come up on stage and claim your prize!"

"Go!" Kellan says.

I run down the hallway toward the stage stairs and rush up them.

Felix stands by the side of the sound booth, clapping, watching me.

I give him a shrewd look, "Did you do this?"

He's grinning ear to ear, but he shrugs like he doesn't know.

Yeah, right.

I owe him that drink for sure.

He smiles, "Go claim your prize, Victory!"

Rob the Knob stands center stage, bathed in the spotlight, holding a trophy that is a golden electric guitar shoved neck first into a golden holster mounted on a crystal block.

I walk up to him.

The grimaced smile on Rob the Knob's face can be described as completely devoid of real enthusiasm. His lips are strained to the point of constipation. But he's going to play along.

"*Victory Payne, everybody,*" Rob the Knob says into the mic. He hands me the trophy and I take it. Then, to my surprise, he claps enthusiastically. I notice he has a rectangle of paper in his hand.

The crowds cheers and claps too.

Rob says into the mic, "*And we also have a check for $5,000, payable to you.*"

He hands me the check. I read it and notice it's hand written in ink on a Guitar Central check. Made out to me, Victory Payne, for $5,000. Signed by Rob Pickford.

"Thanks, Rob," I say to him genuinely.

He leans over to me and says, "Do me a favor. Try to spend it all at Guitar Central."

I smile at him like I mean it, but all I can think is how I'm going to give it all to Johnny and Karen. With this $5,000 and the remaining money Julian paid me for my work on the dick hardener commercial, I have just enough to cover every cent of the $6,000 I owe Johnny and Karen for the busted Contrares.

Sure, I'll be back to broke, but I won't owe Johnny and Karen! Yay!

I lean toward the mic and say to the crowd, "*Thank you guys, so much! You rock!*"

They applaud and cheer somewhat sedately. I think everyone here tonight is as exhausted as I am right now.

I laugh into the mic, "*Thank you, seriously. You guys are the best!*"

I hold the trophy up and shake it Victoriously.

My name is Victory Payne.

Chapter 132

VICTORY

Kellan walks out the back door of The Cobra holding up a Marshall speaker cabinet in front of him.

I follow him with my guitar case in one hand and his case in the other.

The crowd outside behind The Cobra is pretty thin.

Most of the other bands have already loaded up their cars and driven off.

Joaquin emerges from The Cobra holding a stack of toms and sets them next to his bass drum and hardware bag near the rest of our gear.

Dubs says, "I'll go get the van, yo." He jogs up the street.

Joaquin walks back inside to get more gear.

"I think that's the last of it," Kellan says to me, leaning his elbow on top of Dubs' big bass speaker cabinet.

We watch people walk past the alley, heading toward their cars.

I say to Kellan, "What an incredible evening."

"You and me both," he grins.

I smile. I think this might be a good time to finally kiss Kellan again in relative private.

He smiles down at me.

I gaze into his burning brown eyes…

"There you are!" Cannonballs singsongs as she turns into the alley. "I thought you were gone, Kellan!"

"Still here," Kellan says dryly.

Cannonballs hasn't noticed me yet because I stand behind Kellan and Dubs' big bass amp speaker cabinet.

I wonder if Cannonballs saw Kellan and me kiss onstage? Or maybe she wasn't inside the main room watching the bands. Or maybe she's a self-centered bitch who doesn't care about anything but what she wants, which is Kellan.

Kellan steps aside so I am in full view of Cannonballs.

"Oh," she says abruptly, "Hello. What was your name again?"

I smirk, "I'm Victory Payne."

"Oh! You won tonight, didn't you?"

"I did," I smile proudly and hold up my trophy.

"Congratulations!" she says fakely.

"Thanks," I grimace.

She turns to Kellan, "How about a drink?"

Kellan runs his hand through his hair, "I'm pretty busy tonight. Sorry."

Cannonballs glances between me and Kellan, "With her?"

I frown, "Yeah, with me!"

Cannonballs grimaces, "Why?"

Kellan says to Cannonballs, "You're not that hot."

Cannonballs eyes pop and her face turns brick red. She flips Kellan off and growls, "Neither are you!" She storms off.

Kellan chuckles at her back dismissively then smiles at me.

"What a bitch!" I blurt as Cannonballs clicks around the corner on her stripper heels. I turn back to Kellan, once again ready to kiss him.

Joaquin walks out with more drum hardware and nearly drops everything when the back door springs shut on him. He barks, "Pinche puerta pendeja!"

Kellan says, "Dude, let me help you with that." He rushes over to the door and takes drum hardware from Joaquin before it spills all over the ground.

"Gracias, ése" Joaquin smiles while juggling the heavy hardware.

"Victory Payne," someone calls out behind me.

I whip my head around.

Julian Whittaker rounds the corner of the building with a gorgeous woman on his arm.

So much for kissing Kellan.

The woman with Julian wears dark aviator sunglasses and is dressed in an expensive leather outfit that looks like it cost more than my $5,000 prize winnings. She looks vaguely familiar to me, but I can't place her.

"Hey, Julian!" I say nervously. "What are you doing here?!"

"I came to watch you perform," he smiles.

I totally forgot to tell him I was playing, but I guess he remembered, "Did you see me play?"

"I did," he smiles, "and I heard you sing. You were wonderful. Your voice is incredible. One of the finest I've ever heard."

"Wow," I smile, "Thanks, Julian!"

I suddenly wonder, did Julian see me kiss Kellan? He must have if he watched me perform. Unless he left after I walked off stage? I don't know. Either way, this is really uncomfortable since Kellan is ten feet away helping Joaquin.

I notice the woman with Julian leans against him like she's his date.

Maybe I shouldn't be worried about Kellan or Julian.

Maybe Julian found himself a girlfriend? It's not like me and him talk every day or even every week.

Kellan sets his armload of drum hardware in the pile with the rest of our gear and walks up beside me.

When the woman on Julian's arm sees Kellan, she chuckles, "As I live and breathe..." She releases Julian's arm, cocks her hip, and slides her sunglasses off. Her lips ease into a sultry smile, "Hello, Kellan. It's been a long time."

What?! Does Kellan know this woman?

Kellan grits his teeth, "Hello, Giselle."

I guess he does.

And why do I think I recognize her? She is now close enough for me to inspect her face carefully. Then it hits me. This Giselle woman is Layce. Pop super star Layce. I think she's wearing a wig. But she is definitely video shoot entitled bitch Layce.

I know Layce and Julian know each other. They work together. But she knows Kellan too?

Holy shit.

This is news.

Giselle a.k.a. Layce asks Kellan, "Have you missed me?"

Kellan slowly shakes his head and smiles angrily. He growls, "Not for a second." His jaw muscles dance in his cheek. He's fuming, I can tell. Heck, anybody could tell from the stormy look on his face. But he's holding it in.

Okay, you only talk like that to your ex-girlfriend that you hate, or someone who kidnapped your children, or stole a million dollars from you and framed you for murder. Which leads me to the conclusion that Kellan and Layce must have dated at some point.

Kellan and Layce?

My mind is boggling.

I blurt out a short laugh of disbelief.

At that exact moment, a plain white van turns into the alley and parks in front of the back door of The Cobra. Dubs climbs out of the driver's door and stops short, staring at the four of us. "Ah, hell naw," he says to Kellan, "What the fuck Giselle doing here, yo?"

Dubs knows Giselle too?

Kellan glances at Dubs briefly and they exchange a quick look that is long on historic drama. Then Kellan turns back to face Giselle a.k.a. Layce.

Dubs warns Layce-Giselle, "You brave showin' up here, yo." Dubs' guarded body language and tone of voice makes it clear he really doesn't like her.

Kellan stares at her and smirks.

Giselle ignores Dubs' critical comments. She says directly to Kellan, "You were ravishing tonight."

Kellan narrows his eyes like he's not believing it. He's totally pissed now. He rolls his eyes while shaking his head dismissively. In a quiet cold tone, he hisses, "Shut. *Up*. Giselle."

Wow. Kellan *hates* her.

Giselle smiles at Kellan, completely amused, and purrs, "You know your anger only makes you *more* ravishing. It always did…"

"You never quit," Kellan scoffs, "do you, Giselle?"

She arches an eyebrow over her smirk.

Kellan turns to Julian and says, "And what the fuck do you want, Julian?"

Julian smiles politely, "I came to talk to Victory." He turns to me and smiles as if Kellan suddenly ceased to exist, then says calmly, "Victory, I had hoped to catch you alone. Can we talk in private?"

I glance at Kellan. His face is hard and he stares at me. I don't know what to make of it. "Ahh," I say tentatively to Julian, "I guess so?"

He nods, "Can we step over there?" He motions toward the far side of the alley, twenty feet away.

"Sure."

Julian leads me into the shadows on the other side of the alley next to the cinder block wall that separates the back of The Cobra Lounge from the row of residential houses running behind it. Although it's not completely dark where we stand, the corner of The Cobra blocks the bright white light shining over the back door where Kellan stands with Dubs, Joaquin, and our pile of gear.

"What's up?" I ask Julian.

He smiles, "First off, I have to tell you again how incredible you were tonight."

(*sing*)

I smile, "Thank you, Julian."

"Your stage presence is powerful. Are you aware how natural you are in front of a mic?"

"I guess," I blush.

"I thought you didn't like to sing?"

I sigh, "It's a long story."

(*singsing*)

He smiles, "Some other time, right?"

I nod.

He says, "Let's talk about that song you sang."

"Sunset Farewell?" I ask.

(*singsingsing*)

"Yes. That was a show stopper," Julian grins.

"Thanks," I say quietly.

"I want to record it."

(*singsingsingsing*)

I frown, "What do you mean?"

"I want to produce Sunset Farewell. In my studio. And release it as a single. I'd also like to shoot a video to release with the single. Are you interested?"

(*singsingsingsingsingsing*)

I laugh in disbelief, "Are you serious?"

"Very." He grins at me knowingly.

"I would love to!"

He nods several times and slides his hands into his pockets. "There's only one thing," he says cryptically.

"What?"

"I only want you, Victory..." he glances briefly over at where Kellan stands with Dubs and Joaquin, "…not them."

(*Victory!!!*)

I frown uncertainly, "What?"

"You don't need them, Victory," Julian soothes. "You have true talent, my dear. If you'll allow it, I can build your career and make you a star far bigger than Layce could ever dream of becoming." Julian glances over at Kellan and the boys again with obvious distaste and says "Those three will only stand in your way."

I swallow hard.

Julian is asking me to do to Kellan the exact same thing Scott did to me and Skin Trade. Betray him and the band for the promise of success.

Julian says archly, "Haven't you always dreamed of having a successful music career, dear Victory?"

(*Victory!!! STOP!!!*)

Chapter 133

KELLAN

"How have you been, Kellan?" Giselle purrs and steps toward me tentatively.

I flash her a warning glare to stay back.

Giselle stops. Her eyes flash in response to mine, but not with warning. Hers flash with invitation. Her lips slide seductively over her teeth in a sexy smirk, "I swear, Kellan, you're better looking tonight than I've ever seen you."

I ignore her.

I don't care about Giselle.

I'm over her.

All I care about is Victory and the band.

Right now, Victory is talking to Julian on the other side of the shadowy alley behind The Cobra Lounge.

It takes everything I have not to walk right over and tear Julian's head off his neck, which I could easily do. I almost did once before. If Giselle hadn't stopped me, I would've finished the job. Now I'm wishing I had.

I can only imagine what kind of snake oil Julian is selling to Victory right now.

This is a fucking disaster.

Giselle was fine until Julian got to her and turned her into Layce.

Then she transformed into the freak standing in front of me right now. A mega rich superstar freak. But a total lunatic freak.

He's going to try to do the same fucking thing to Victory.

Fuck.

Short of killing him, I don't know if there's anything I can do to stop him.

I just have to hope Victory is strong enough to resist his bullshit.

I thought Giselle would be, but I was so wrong.

I hope I'm right about Victory.

I hope she's different.

All I can do is hope.

Hope.

Epilogue

KELLAN

"Dude," I hiss to Dubs, "I gotta get the fuck outta here. Right now." My entire body shakes with anger and adrenalin.

I'm two seconds away from killing Julian.

Dubs licks his lips, his brows tight. His eyes dart around, "What the fuck Julian be thinkin' showin' up with Giselle's ass, yo? You think he knew you was here?"

I shake my head and growl, "I doubt it. Look, bro, I need to go or I'm going to do something really stupid. Can you and Joa load up my gear in your van and hold onto it?"

"You got it, dawg."

"I'll call you later." I stride out of the alley and up the side street to my Charger without looking back. Every muscle in my body is firing like I should be hitting things. But I'm not going to.

Punching isn't going to fix anything.

The next reasonable alternative I can think of is running. I sprint up the steeply sloped street behind The Cobra as fast as I can, going right up the middle of the road.

It takes about three minutes before I'm breathing so hard I think I'm going to have a heart attack. I slow to a walk.

When I stop and look back the way I ran, the curving road and all the houses block out The Cobra and all the drama unfolding just outside its back doors. All I see is a boring old neighborhood and the distant city lights of L.A. at night.

I shake my head. I don't want to think about whatever the fuck is happening between Victory and Julian right now.

I just need to get out of here.

I jog back down the road until I find my Charger. I climb inside and rev the engine.

It growls angrily.

As always in L.A., my big car takes up plenty of room and I now notice I'm practically boxed in by the cars parked in front and back of me. I have to laugh, it's so ridiculous.

L.A.

Gotta love it.

I have enough room to get my car out, but I'm forced to forward-reverse six times to squeeze out of the parallel space. If I wasn't worried about my cherry chrome bumpers, I would've plowed the Kia in front of me out of the way. But I care too much about my Charger. I put a lot of love into it over the years, and I'm not going to mess it up over a girl.

It's been with me every step of the way.

Unlike many people in my life.

God damn Giselle.

I drive down the road and turn onto a residential side street long before I get down to The Cobra.

I want to forget about tonight as quickly as possible.

I drive home in silence.

Usually, I always have music going in my car.

Right now, I don't want anything to do with music.

Music is a pain in my ass.

Half an hour later, I park my Charger behind my apartment building and walk inside.

I drop into my couch and lean my head back against the couch cushions.

I can't believe what happened tonight.

Julian? Giselle? Victory?

If I hadn't lived it, I wouldn't believe it.

I'm just glad I walked away from the whole mess before shit went off.

The thing about stepping in shit is, if you keep your eyes open, you can avoid it.

I need to learn to keep my eyes open.

I shake my head and chuckle to myself.

What the fuck have I been doing the last two months?

Pining for Victory like a fucking bitch? Like I did with Giselle?

I'm a fucking idiot.

Look where it got me with Giselle.

I shoot up from the couch and clomp into my kitchen.

Good thing I stocked up my fridge with beer.

I grab two bottles and pop both tops. I throw the caps in the sink and guzzle down the first beer.

Then I guzzle the second.

Then I remember the bottle of Jack Daniels I keep in the cupboard over the fridge. I pull it out and walk into the living room.

I don't want to think about music tonight.

I need to push music and everything else out of my head.

I load up Netflix on my computer and scroll around until I find something new. I stumble across some show called The Inbetweeners and try that.

It's a British sitcom about high school dudes who can't get laid and it's fucking hilarious. The next thing I know, I'm drinking from my bottle of Jack like it's a two liter of Coke and I'm laughing my ass off at the show.

I'm good and drunk after four or five episodes.

I feel a million times better.

At one point, I blurt loud laughter and hazily realize my front door is wide open. I don't want to piss off my neighbors. They're not dicks, so I show the same respect.

I stand up to close my front door and hear a female voice outside shout, "Ow, fuck!"

I open my screen door.

Some chick has just fallen into the bushes across from my front door. All I can see is naked arms and legs poking out of the leaves and branches and wiggling like crazy. The shoes on the feet are four inch heels, and I can't for the life of me figure out who the hell this is based on the footwear and legs alone. Not one of my neighbors. Maybe a friend of a neighbor?

I call out, "You okay?"

"Help?" she squeaks.

She can't climb out of the bush.

I chuckle and walk toward her. My head spins nicely from the booze. I feel pretty damn fine right now. I grab one of the reaching hands and pull her out of the bushes.

The first thing I notice is the tight black dress. Whoever this is has a rockin' body. But her hair is a tangled mess of leaves and the tresses cover her face.

She stands up and stumbles into my chest.

Her head tilts up and she brushes hair away until I see her face. Emily Needham.

"Em?" I ask, surprised.

"Kellan!" she squeals. "How are you?" She wraps her arms around my waist and hugs me. Her cheek squeezes against my chest.

"Where are your glasses, Em?"

She looks up at me and smiles, "I'm wearing contacts."

She really is pretty without the glasses.

I say, "You never wear contacts."

She grins, "I am tonight!"

Whoa, she is super drunk and smells like a distillery. I can't believe it. She also has on a ton of makeup. I've never seen her wear makeup. She looks hot, and I know it's not beer goggles. I always knew she was hot, she just never did anything with herself because she's always too busy studying all her UCLA med school shit.

I ask, "Did you go out or something?"

She nods.

"Em, you *never* go out. What's the occasion?"

She shrugs, "My friends and I decided to take a real study break and go to a bunch of bars in Santa Monica for once."

"No way."

"Yes way," she grins. "I'm tired of being boring. I realized I have no life outside of studying. I decided to change that."

"You didn't quit school, did you?"

She shakes her head, "No, I just went out with my friends. And maybe drank more than I should have." She giggles and burps. "Oops!" Embarrassed, she covers her mouth and giggles more. Then her eyes light up excitedly. "Hey! Do you want some chocolate chip cookies? I have a bag upstairs!"

"Sure," I smile. "Why not?"

"Lemme go get them!" She stumbles upstairs and I hear keys jingling. "I can't find the door key!" she chuckles. "Oh, wait, here it is! Be right back" I hear her door open and thumping footsteps. A moment later, she walks carefully down the stairs in bare feet. "I can't walk in those shoes! I don't know how girls do it day after day. I have blisters!"

She stops at the base of the stairs and holds up a bag of Chunky Chips Ahoy. She grins, "Cookies!"

We walk into my apartment and sit down on the couch. I close the front door so our chatter doesn't wake anybody.

Em opens the bag of cookies and slides out the crinkly plastic tray. She pulls too hard and cookies fly everywhere. "Oh shit!' she laughs.

I bend over and pick up cookies, "I hope you don't mind carpet lint."

"It's just fiber, right?" she winks.

I pause and look at her funny.

I think that's the first joke Em has ever made. Around me, anyway. But

I'm surprised to discover she has a sense of humor beneath all her book smarts.

"Yeah," I quip, "nothing like a little roughage to clean you out."

She grimaces and cackles, "Your intestines are filled with *pooh*! Winnie the *Pooh*!!" She laughs like it's the funniest thing anyone ever said. "All those little yellow teddy bears with red shirts inside your guts!" She reaches over and plants both her palms on my stomach and pushes three times, "Pooh! Pooh! Pooh!" She falls back on the couch and wraps her arms around her belly and laugh and laughs.

Yeah, she's totally drunk.

I never thought Em had it in her.

I start chuckling at her ridiculous observations about pooh.

After her laughter dies down, she looks at me with a big grin, "Hey," she says coyly and leans over to press her finger against my chest. "Play that song for me."

"Which song?" I chuckle, still amused by her newly found sense of humor.

"That love song you wrote?"

"Love song?" I frown.

She nods slowly, "The one you sang me awhile back?"

"Oh, you mean My Whole Life?"

"Yeah," she grins.

"You remember it?"

Her delicate brows knit together kittenishly, "Of course I do. It was so beautiful, I never forgot it… Plus, you've been playing it a lot lately," she giggles.

"Yeah," I chuckle.

"Were you rehearsing it or something?"

"Yeah."

"Did you ever play it for that girl you wrote it for?"

I shake my head and huff out a single humorless laugh, "Yeah. Tonight"

Em arches her eyebrow and asks uncertainly, "Did she like it?"

"I thought she did," I scoff.

"So how come you're not with her right now?"

"It's way too fucking complicated," I laugh softly and drop my head back against the couch, which causes the entire room to tip up drunkenly around me. Man, I must've downed more of that Jack than I realized.

"Will you play it for me?" Em asks timidly.

I gaze into her eyes.

Then I notice she has a leaf in her hair. I reach out it pluck it out of the strands. "Leaf," I say casually.

She grabs it from my fingers and blurts, "Sorry."

I've never seen Em with her hair down. It's long and looks nice despite the disarray. The auburn locks frame her face beautifully. She really looks amazing without her glasses. I arch an eyebrow, "You really want to hear that song?"

She nods.

"Right now?"

"Yeah," she smiles widely.

"Okay," I say. My Martin is in Dubs' van, but I have a Taylor acoustic in the closet which is nearly as good. I grab it and sit back down next to Em on the couch.

Considering my fingers are now made of wiggling worms, I play through the song as best I can. My singing is fine, but I struggle not to laugh at my lyrics.

My Whole Life.

What the fuck was I thinking when I wrote this song?

It sounds so stupid to me right now.

I snicker but keep playing.

Em asks inquisitively, "What?"

"Nothing," I mutter while I play the bridge chords.

Maybe the lyrics of this song are bullshit. My Whole Life? Who waits forever for that perfect person to come along? Only an idiot.

Maybe all love songs are bullshit.

Maybe true love is bullshit, and I've been too stupid to figure that out.

Maybe you just need a decent person who wants to be with you. Not some mythical "The One."

Yeah, that's a load of fucking bullshit.

Ten trucks worth of bullshit.

I'm old enough I should know better.

I smile at Em while I play.

She smiles back at me bashfully.

Em is a good person with a good head on her shoulders. A pretty one, too.

She's not going to get sucked up into some big time record business insanity. She's going to get her medical degree, probably find a house and a husband somewhere and have a family.

Do you really need any more than that?

Man, I've been a fucking idiot, haven't I?

Overlooked the obvious that was right in front of my face.

I finish the final chords of the song and Em applauds rapidly.

"Yeah!" she cheers, "That was beautiful, Kellan!"

I'm not sure how good my playing and singing were just now. I'm drunk and my head was totally not in the right place to sing a heartfelt love song.

But Em doesn't seem to care. She beams, "You are so talented, Kellan!"

"Thanks," I grin and set the guitar on the carpet.

She holds up the tray of Chunkie Chips Ahoy, which are half gone, and asks, "Want another cookie?"

"Sure." I pluck one out and munch on it.

"So, your girl really didn't like your song?"

I chew on a cookie and mumble, "She's not my girl."

"She's an idiot," Em scoffs.

I chuckle and shake my head, "I think she's just confused."

"I'm not," Em says suddenly.

I look into her eyes. They sparkle with impish delight.

She says, "Some people are too stupid to realize a good thing right in front of them…"

I arch an eyebrow. Is she talking about me or Victory? Probably both of us.

I stand up from the couch, "You want some water? You probably need some after drinking all night. Otherwise your hangover tomorrow is going to be a hammer."

"I'm fine," she burps, "Excuse me." She breaks into more giggles.

I fill two glasses in the kitchen, just in case. I walk back to the couch and hand one to Em.

"You're so sweet, Kellan," she grins and takes the glass.

I sit down and sip my water.

She takes several swallows from her glass then looks around, "Why don't you have a coffee table?"

"There's not much room," I say. The table with my computer and recording gear is only a few feet from the couch, so I never bothered getting one.

Em half stands from the couch and leans toward the table. She sets the glass on the top, but she's so drunk, she doesn't realize she put it too close to the edge.

I jump up but it's too late.

The glass topples onto the carpet.

"Shit!" Em jumps forward, trying to catch it, but the water splashes everywhere.

We end up squatting by the glass at the same time.

Our faces are inches apart.

"I'm sorry," she croons, "That was dumb."

I smile, "No, you're just drunk."

Her eyes twinkle and she smiles like an angel.

She leans toward me, staring at my lips.

She's going to kiss me or wants me to kiss her.

She really is gorgeous…

She sighs breathily, "Kellan…"

I gently place my index finger on her lips and mutter, "Don't, Em."

She sits back on her butt. Her face twists with frustration.

I frown, "I'm really sorry, Em. We're both drunk."

Her face knots with sudden sadness. Silent tears drip down her face. She drops her hands in her lap and stares at the ceiling, "I really like you, Kellan."

I smile warmly, my own eyes dampening, "I know, Em."

"Why don't you like me?" she demands desperately.

"I do like you, Em. Just not like that."

She sobs and holds out her arms for a hug. I lean toward her and hug her hard.

I sigh, "I'm really sorry, Em."

She cries for awhile and I rub her back soothingly.

When she finally pulls away, she rubs her eyes and chuckles, "You must think I'm a stupid little girl."

"No, Em," I say softly, "You're a smart amazing young woman."

She laughs and cries, too confused to settle on one emotion.

After awhile, I say, "Hey, you want to watch a funny show?"

She frowns, "Huh?"

I stand up and offer her my hand, "Come on, it'll make you feel better."

I guide her to the couch and put on another episode of The Inbetweeners.

Em gets into it right away.

For the next hour, we sit on the couch with the tray of remaining Chunky Chips Ahoy between us and finish them off while watching three episodes of the British sitcom.

When the credits roll after the third episode, Em says, "I should go to bed. I have to study all day tomorrow. Blah!" She giggles sheepishly.

I chuckle, "Yeah, you should get some sleep."

I walk her upstairs to her apartment and say goodnight.

Back in my apartment, I grab a towel from the bathroom and blot up the water where Em spilled her glass. I throw out the Chips Ahoy wrapper and turn off my computer.

The only thing left to do is put away my Taylor.

I stare at it.

Fuck it.

I pick up the acoustic guitar and start playing My Whole Life.

This time, it isn't bullshit.

This time, I sing it like I mean it.
This time, I sing it for Victory:

"Whispered kisses
on my lips
from the ghost of you
We've never met
yet it's true
your the one I seek

My whole life
I searched for you
my need like a disease
I can't live
without your love
you bring me to my knees

My
Whole
Life
(I've searched)
For
A love
Like you
(Victory)

My
Whole
Life
(I'll search)
For
A love
That's true
(Victory)

I still search
For a love
That's you
(Victory)
On and on
I crawl
I still search

For You"

When I pluck out the final chord, the strings ring throughout my lonely apartment.

My head hangs heavily over my guitar.

There's a knock at my door.

I look up from my guitar.

It's probably Em asking me why I didn't sing it that way for her. The answer to that is simple. I don't feel that way about anybody except Victory.

I lean the Taylor against my couch and trudge to the door.

I pull it open softly and sigh, "What, Em?"

Victory stands on the other side of my screen door.

She wears her stage costume, the golden studded skin tight black leather one with the hot fucking lace up pants and the bra top and the jacket.

Her arms are wrapped around her chest like she's freezing.

But it's not cold outside.

I say, "What are you doing here, Victory? It's after four a.m."

She stares at me, the most beautiful woman I've ever seen in my whole life, and she says, "I've been driving around by myself for the last three hours trying to make sense of my life. The last two months have been insane. Scott dumped me. Rex and Bobby abandoned me. I met you. I met Julian. I even met Layce before tonight," she winks. "I bet you didn't know that."

I shake my head in disbelief. I don't know what to say. But my heart is literally shaking in my chest, tensing up with a combination of fear and hope I've never felt before.

She smiles, "Heck, Julian even arranged for me to see Layce's video shoot on a big Hollywood sound stage. It was the most amazing thing I've ever seen, and made me wonder if maybe I could be a big pop star like Layce someday."

I shake my head imperceptibly.

Julian knows exactly how to brainwash someone like Giselle or Victory. He tempts them with promises of fulfilling impossible dreams, then he actually delivers on it. It's an irresistible combination.

It's how he took Giselle from me.

Victory smiles, "Then I thought about everything you did for me tonight. And I thought about my brother Victor. And everything we shared while he was alive."

She swallows hard, "That's when I realized I'm crazy."

I arch an eyebrow, not sure where she's going with this.

She says, "I'm crazy for not trusting you, Kellan. I'm crazy for doubting you. I'm crazy for thinking you're like Scott. But you're not. You're the most amazing man I've ever met. You're always helping me, always trying to make my life better, make it easier, and help me find my own dreams. You never push me. And you offer up your heart like you mean it. You want me for *me*. And you offered me the forever I never had with Victor without ever asking for anything in return..." Her eyes are watering and her voice is desperate with fear and courage. "No one has ever done that for me, Kellan. No one but you..."

The screen door between me and Victory is flimsy, but at the moment, it's thicker than the walls of a castle. I would open it, but I can't even lift my arm. It weighs more than an oak tree.

Victory reaches up and opens the screen door like it's a feather.

I've been waiting for her to open this door protecting her heart since she walked out of my apartment the first time. Now she walks inside my apartment and stands on the threshold of my home.

She gazes up at me with naked eyes and an open heart.

The look is unmistakeable, yet I've never seen it before on anyone. I've waited for this moment for My Whole Life.

I lean down and kiss Victory passionately.

My search is over.

She's more than I ever dreamed possible.

She's beyond mere hope. She's not a ghost.

Victory is real and she breathes.

She's alive, and...

She's TRUE.

A NOTE FROM DEVON HARTFORD:

My dear readers:

I have plenty more story to tell about Kellan and Victory. Their band and their music careers are just getting started. Both of them have big dreams.

Would you like to live their rock and roll dreams with them? I know I would.

I have three more full-length Victory novels outlined and ready to write. Victory : TRUE, Victory : FREE, and Victory : TOUR.

Let me know if you'd like to read them.

If you guys do, I will write them.

Together, we can all make Victory and Kellan's dreams come TRUE.

Contact me at my Facebook, Twitter, or website and tell me what you want.

:-D

Thanks,
Devon

Want to get an email when Devon's next book is released and receive a FREE Bonus Story by email?

Sign up here: **http://eepurl.com/B7crf**

or go to **devonhartford.com**

and **click** the **blue SIGN UP button**

Personal thanks from Devon Hartford:

Thank you, dear reader, for taking the time to live with Victory and Kellan for a while! If you enjoyed *Victory RUN 1-2-3*, please leave a review wherever you purchased this ebook, on Goodreads, or any book blogs you frequent. Be sure to tell your friends about it!

Contact me and let me know if you want to read more about Victory and Kellan!!

Like me on Facebook

Friend me on Facebook

Follow me on Twitter @DevonHartford

Follow me on WordPress at devonhartford.com

ABOUT THE AUTHOR

Devon Hartford fell in love with heavy metal from the first moment he heard an electric guitar. He bought his first electric guitar in high school with money he earned working at McDonald's. He's been playing ever since. Devon lived in Los Angeles for many years and frequented many of the locations in this book. Hear Devon's metal on YouTube: Devon Hartford - My Evil

OTHER BOOKS BY DEVON HARTFORD:

Fearless (The Story of Samantha Smith #1)
Reckless (The Story of Samantha Smith #2)
Painless (The Story of Samantha Smith #3)
COVER MODEL
Stealing Chastity
Taking Back Beautiful
Stepbrother Obsessed
ONE YEAR LOVE - Collected Edition (Parts 1-4)

ACKNOWLEDGMENTS

A HUGE thanks to all my passionate and fantastic beta readers: Jenn Hedge (Beta Speed Queen), Sandye, Steffini Walker Texas Ranger, Rosanne Triegaardt, The REAL Julie England, Emaleth Morrigan (mermaid), Neicy Cassidy, Ashley Lorene Hall, Ange May, Eileen Fitzharris, Wendy Boyer, Stephanie Svajgl, Sandye, Sarah Welsh (a.k.a. Princess Frilly-Bottoms of the Land of Willow), Kimber, Natasha Slater, Mandy Jamerson, Tania Clark, Michele McKenzie, Kerrisha Budhu, Sarah Tree, Mandy Karsa, Renee Julian, Melanie Starr (My favorite Comma Bomber), Jordan Bault, Anna Lamonica, Maria Combee, Anne Berkeley, Mel Bushell, Jini Perez, Mylinda Abraham-Powell, Megan C Christmas, Nicki Hewitt-Hart, Tamara Clark, Muriel Garcia, and Shannon Margaret for invaluable feedback and encouragement! You guys rock the typo sauce!

Becs Glass and Sinfully Sexy Books for dedicated book pimping love!

Chrissy Zent Sharp for awesome book pimpery via The Book Whoreder's Delights. Be sure to check them out if you're a Romance reader.

Hayley Picknell for awesome reviews everywhere!

Everybody's ever luvin' cowbag, Lindsey Melia for ghetto ghood pimpin'.

And thanks to everybody else who has helped make this book a reality!

www.ingramcontent.com/pod-product-compliance
Lightning Source LLC
Chambersburg PA
CBHW030924020726
47498CB00001B/103
9780989769792